THE PRICE OF POWER

BOOK ONE

MICHAEL MICHEL

MORNINGSTAR BOOKS

CONTENTS

stretched within. Yellowed with time and smeared with the soot of battle, light bled through the gauntleted fist and broken chain stitched inside the icon.

She dropped to one knee, forehead touching the Slave Banner's haft. "As Duchess of Anjuhkar, I pledge myself, here, now, and always to the Crown of Namarr." Silence and dust swirled behind her as she returned to her place at her husband's side.

A quiet interval passed before Danath spoke. "When we win this war, you know I will not position myself as a tyrant. I stand before you now, a product of the cumulative wisdom and guidance of those gathered here today. Therefore, our new nation will have no king. It will be governed by the voices of its people." He stepped forward. "Through the blood you've willingly shed and the coin you've freely given, I find you all worthy of a seat at the Namorite Collective. However, I have selected the most trusted and capable among you to join myself and my wife, as well as the Monastic Orders, to serve the Collective, Namarr's new governing body!"

Danath cut their cheers short with a wave. Belara knew what came next. She and Danath had discussed it in detail with her father before they'd signed the Unification Treaty. Her eyes found a thin man with a round face and discerning disposition. Sessero Saud.

Danath's tone shifted to be more formal, imperious even. "Sessero, of the House of Saud, will you serve the people of Namarr as Duke of Peladonia?"

The diminutive man saluted Danath, then walked over to Solicerames to repeat the same pledge Belara had.

Once he rejoined the assembly, Danath turned to the man standing at his side. "Malzai D'Alzir, master merchant from the Corridor of Storms. First among my followers. First among my friends. Will you serve the people of Namarr as Duke of Lah-Tsarra?"

Malzai smiled. "It would please me to no end to—"

A Kurg grunted loudly, then parted from the rows of benches. He crossed the intervening space and spat at the feet of the richly dressed Lah-Tsarene merchant. A litany of jeers rained.

With steely calm, Danath stepped between Malzai and the bristling Kurg. Belara noted that, like the rest of his kind, he was shorter than most Namorites, broader than all, and with amber skin that was strange to behold.

"Easy, Tondarro." Danath placed a hand firmly against the Kurg's thick chest. "What troubles you?"

The Kurg's chiseled face swung toward Danath. "I mean no offense to you, my Prince." The common tongue flowed naturally from his lips. "But to *him*, I give all of it."

"Malzai D'Alzir is now a Duke of Namarr," said Danath. "He represents me and the Crown to which you swore yourself. Your actions *do* offend me. On the eve of my wedding, the eve of our victory, you spur chaos. We may have shed Scoth blood together, but I warn you, I'll brook no disruptions to our mission."

"My Prince, this man's reputation..." Tondarro looked to the dusty floor, massive chest heaving with rage, then snorted. "Long before he was your friend, the blood of a thousand Kurgs colored his hands. Could you choose no other?"

Danath gave a somber smile. "The past dies today, Tondarro. When we were a fractured nation, all of us here were foes. Those days are no longer. Tomorrow will be different. As will every tomorrow thereafter. Scothea faces its last sunset as rulers of our land." The leader of the Sons of the Ardent Heart raised his voice for all to hear. "Besides, you too will take a seat on the Namorite Collective."

The Kurg's head jerked up, his brow furrowed in disbelief.

Murmurs broke out among those gathered. Danath ignored them. "Lord Malzai himself suggested it."

Inwardly, Belara smiled. The move to seat a Kurg on the Namorite Collective was brilliant; it ensured peace beyond the numbered days of the revolution. Kurgs fought alongside the Sons of the Ardent Heart out of necessity, making their allegiance tentative at best and likely to last only so long as Scothean occupation did.

Danath clapped a hand on the chieftain's bare, blocky shoulder. "Tondarro of the Moon Clan, will you represent the Kurgish enclaves?"

Tondarro glowered at Malzai. Corded neck muscles twitched as he shook his head. "The River and Forest enclaves cannot have agreed to this."

A rush of sound and air pulled Belara's attention to the back of the pavilion where a dark figure materialized from a black cloud. He spoke with a deep, gravelly voice to match his imposing visage. "They will."

All eyes turned to the man wreathed in otherworldly shadow as darkness dilated into a blot behind him and then dissipated. Blood pounded in Belara's ears. She touched her throat a split second before a score of others gasped with her in unison. A word circulated the assembly—spoken low as if sacred.

Awakened.

The hulking man strode past the rows of seated rebel lords, black vapor leaking from his eyes. The rich and the dangerous alike made way. Benches dragged hastily backward, kicking up dust. He came to a stop, turned, blinking at the fear in his wake. The inky vapor dissipated, revealing flint-hard eyes.

The man was a Kurg, same as Tondarro, but that was where the similarities stopped.

From the nose up, the Awakened's face was tattooed black but for a circle of untouched golden flesh around one eye. The massive horns of an ebhor curled down and thrust outward around a ram's head helm. Most Kurgs wore little. This one dressed like a priest. Robes of dark maroon swathed him and slithered across the ground, a whisper heralding his coming.

"I could be matching lips with a goddess right now, so if anyone has something to cry about, it's me." His tone softens, soothes like warm honey. "Listen, sometimes it takes a hundred attempts at first. And that's okay. But I won't let you quit. So...imagine this is the first time. Imagine you've never tried before. Start from the beginning. Focus on your hands, not your thoughts. And remember, it only takes one spark."

How right you are, my boy.

Akyris leans in, makes sure his student meets his eyes. "If you do this, you'll be proud of yourself, right?"

The younger boy nods and sucks in a shaking breath.

Patiently, Akyris watches the younger boy fail a dozen times. After each, he repeats the words, "You're doing it."

I see what he's doing, why he's doing it. Pain is not the only pathway to learning but it is the fastest. Having failed the fast way—with harshness—my grandson has pivoted to a new tactic, and one I think more aligns with who he truly is. As much as I wanted to cuff him for his earlier cruelty, I'm pleased to find he's smart enough to alter course.

It pays off. The younger boy looks focused.

"You're doing it," Akyris says. "Only a matter of time."

As the sun spreads over the horizon like a pierced egg yolk, flame spits to life. A thin tendril of smoke winds its way toward sun-pinked clouds. Pride rises with it. The younger boy smiles, then looks to my grandson who claps him on the back.

Akryis gives him a single word of praise, though it comes out almost as a question. "See."

I do, Akyris. A desired result oft wipes away poor effort. Each boy was made of more than I assumed.

After Akyris shows the younger boy how to douse the flame with a clay pitcher, he runs off back to his cretin father. To my surprise, a tear speeds down my grandson's cheek as he watches his student go. Though we're at the edge of town, far from prying eyes, he brushes it away quickly as he searches for witnesses.

Just a boy brimming with ready embarrassment.

He starts home. A dozen steps in, he freezes as if sensing something. Lizard slow, his face turns to where I watch from the elm tree's shadow. He squints, chest rapidly expanding and contracting. "Hello?" His tongue flickers over dry lips. This is not the way I'll introduce myself. "Is—is someone there?"

I'll give him something to worry over. A spectacle he'll not soon forget. A seed planted for what comes later tonight. I turn my Locus inward, drawing forth my power with the skill of a master Awakened.

Vaporous gray light pours from my necklace. Dawning terror stretches his eyes wide as he sees it...

Somewhere in the distance, wind blows a wooden barrel slat to the ground with a bang. Akyris bolts, sprinting the rest of the way home. Best for him to become familiar with a quickened heartbeat. His agitation is essential for what I must do and training must go smoothly.

I take a seat on an upthrust root to enjoy the amber-soaked twilight. Toads sing me the worst of lullabies as I ease my ancient back against the bark to wait for Akyris to sleep. Time rushes past. Night bleeds across my awareness. Stars wink to life in the deep dark. My old lungs labor to breathe life into my decrepit vessel.

But my mind moves with power, unencumbered, wheeling across the infinite.

With a flash of smoky light, my Locus unites with the River. I enter its depths and find the boy asleep.

Akyris is having a nightmare about a stranger watching him from under a tree. I chuckle and strike it from his thoughts. Next, the face of a homely blond girl lying in a bed of straw manifests in his mind's eye. Sima I assume. Far from a goddess. If you ask me, she's plain as a canvas sack. This too I cast into nothingness. I must send him something dire to focus on. Something disturbing.

When I present myself to the boy, I wish for him to be on edge, not love-struck. Time has narrowed as I've aged, become more specific in its revealings of what I'm called to do. There's little room for error now. I must handle my grandson with precision.

If Akyris truly knew what pain awaited him...the speed by which I will force him to learn and grow beyond childish impulse, or the way in which I'll strip away all he's come to know and love and then challenge the naked illusions left at the end of it...

Sadness fills my stomach and churns it sour. A part of me still struggles against the inevitable cost. The fact of it kills a sacred part of me.

I sense my own death too. Decades ago, I saw it. But that only brings a minor pang of regret anymore. To deny inevitabilities such as death and destiny is to deny one's true Path. And to deny that is to live no life at all. Denial's web no longer holds me. I passed through it when I ascended Unturrus long ago to become Awakened. For those who journey up the Mountain of Power and forget themselves, those who fail to strike the web moving in concert with the entirety of their soul, annihilation awaits. The web simply shudders, unbroken, beckoning hungry spiders to feast.

If I am to succeed, I must act with my entire soul. That includes the ache of grief. If we are to have any hope of altering the world's course from doom, I must accept it...claim it even as I march to my own grave.

I *will* sacrifice Akyris.

The pain is unbearable, a winch of broken glass wrapped around my chest. Destiny demands I accept it. With a stilted gasp, I push the sensation down, burying it deep.

I watch Akyris through the jeweled eye of time...

With my consciousness, I reach out and direct his sleeping mind to where it needs to go and what it needs to see.

A vision of the past.

The one that started the end.

Akyris flew. The silvery pall of a dream veiling his eyes as he soared over miles of lush forest. He smiled, completely unaware of his grandmother's consciousness merged with his own.

Two minds inhabited that space. One knowingly steering every action, the other an ignorant puppet.

The feeling of absolute freedom rushed around Akyris's outstretched arms. Nine Lakes passed beneath him, spread out like the footprints of some ancient titan on Unturrus's west side. A thunderhead coalesced atop its hooked peak.

I'm in the Dawn Vale.

He scanned the horizon. The keep of Breckenbright squatted on the distant coastline, no more than a dark cube hemmed in by a handful of shorter ones. To his right, thick plumes of smoke rolled toward the heavens, the acrid smell mingling with another fouler scent. He wheeled away.

A glint of metal drew his eye to the forest below. He descended to investigate and caught more flashes in the fading rays of daylight. He crossed a river and then alighted on a branch overlooking a shallow stretch of coursing water.

Behind an upthrust curtain of rock, he found the source of glimmering metal.

Roughly four hundred men, armored head to toe in steel plate, cast wary glances around the gloaming forest. The gauntleted fist and broken chain on their honor plates marked them as knights of the Crown. Scorch marks and dark stains covered their emerald green surcoats. Huddled in wait behind the curtain of rock, they faced the rushing river, their warhorses snorting gouts of steam that suffused with the gathering mists in the canopy.

A hush fell over them as the faint jostle of steel sounded from the opposite bank. A distant shout in a broken tongue brought the knights of the Crown to a punctuated silence. Vibrations traveled through Akyris's feet where he perched. The knights of Alistar slid great helms overhead with practiced precision, and stroked their horses' necks, soothing them to quiet.

A young man with shorn dark hair and a hawkish nose kept his great helm tucked under one arm. He stared through the trees at the far bank, face set in a grim mask. A knight behind him carried a battle standard: twelve feet of ash with a banded circle atop it with pieces of stitched-together canvas stretched within.

Akyris recalled an image from one of his books and matched it to a story his mother told. *Not canvas—flesh.* A surge of anticipation constricted his chest. *The Slave Banner! Solicerames!* The symbol of Namorite unification and the Ironlight line. The sigils of the first hold lords and ladies to pledge allegiance to Danath were carved into the haft. A charging bison, a hawk, twin hammers wreathed in laurels, a bull horn crossing a maul, and many others.

Akyris swallowed hard, glancing furtively at the leader of the knights. The last time Solicerames was seen...

The man turned, revealing a youthful but hard-lined face.

This must be Barodane Ironlight. The Mad Prince.

Somewhere beneath an elm tree, Akyris's grandmother smiled through her sadness. *I'm sorry, little fly. You'll soon know more of history than you ever wished.* Akyris neither heard nor felt her.

Taking to the air, he flew to the other side of the river in search of those the Namorites awaited and then settled onto a tree branch. He heard them before he saw them. A clamoring, shimmering, wave of war. Scoths. Thousands of them.

They hurried through the forest looking frantic and exhausted. *If that's Barodane Ironlight, then this has to be the battle of King's Crossing.* If it was, it meant the Scothean king, Acramis the Twice-Burned was leading his forces in a tactical retreat to regroup with Raeklord Sahuhd.

A meeting that would never occur.

Darksteel armor glimmered milky white where the twilight found it through the trees. Crescent-bladed axes swayed like pendulums in leather-gloved hands. Plated warskirts hung a palm's width from the tops of their boots. Unlike the Namorite knights waiting for them, the Scoths only wore heavy plate across their shoulders and chests, leaving the protection of their midsections to a light fall of chain. Their gold and white surcoats depicted an antlered snake coiled around a sun.

Like beasts at the plow, Scoth troops labored into the swirling tributary. Spittle and steam heaved forth from the narrow slits of horned great helms. They swarmed across, a sea of bobbing heads. Boots threshed thigh-high waters. The feeling of so many enemies beneath Akyris unsettled him. He retreated back across the river to his place overlooking the Namorite knights where they waited, crypt silent, all eyes fixed on Barodane Ironlight.

From the shadows of the stone redoubt, the Mad Prince watched the enemy army with raptor focus.

A knot of soldiers standing a head or more above their Scoth brethren sent a dagger of dread into Akyris's breast as they splashed into the river. Oxen-thick necks strained beneath tightly clasped iron collars. Loops of chain were draped over

CHAPTER TWO

FATE OF THE FALLEN

- WESTERN NAMARR, YEAR 64 -

In a flurry of straw, Barodane scrambled to his knees and retched.

The strain forced tears to his eyes, pressure into his face. He gasped over the pile of vomit a moment. With the hem of his cloak, he wiped his mouth before rolling onto his backside with a groan.

In the neighboring stall, a horse whinnied. Barodane winced. "Too loud, damn it." His voice was a rasp, dried out from a night of heavy drinking at the Dregs.

Gray light poured through a broken brace along the stable door, warming his boot tips and setting his toes to itching. Then again, everything itched when he came down from a godsthorn high.

He tried to stand—pitched immediately to one side.

I need to level out.

Careful to avoid his own vomit, he churned through the straw until he was greeted with the crush of velvet underhand. He sighed relief as he unrolled the tied cloth. Three gold wheels worth of godsthorn sat in the lining. A paltry amount compared to the half-dozen barrels Meckin kept hidden for him at the Dregs. Plenty for his needs at present though.

He withdrew a long, slender thorn. It pinched where it entered his arm, but he was used to the pain now. A subtle rush melted his breath. His heartbeat thudded, drumbeat fast for a short span, before falling into a slow, sonorous rhythm.

One thorn brought relaxation and a slight sense of euphoria. Three or more meant certain death. Barodane preferred two. Two gave thorn addicts emotional waves, hallucinations, and a glance beyond the veil of reality. "Ascension" they called it, the experience of godhood. It was named after those unfortunate souls called to journey up Unturrus, seeking death or hoping to be Awakened. Only one in fifty lived. And half of those were driven insane.

What if I'm already mad? What would happen then?

He shrugged. Only fools chased power. Barodane preferred to avoid it.

He stared at a second thorn but thought better of it and tucked it back into the velvet cloth roll. Since he had a meeting with a buyer later that night at the Dregs, he'd keep it to one...for now. *I can't handle my business if my mind is wheeling through the cosmos.*

Following the Great Betrayal, Barodane's existence was a tapestry woven together by frayed threads. From stupor to painful remembering to stupor again, the pattern persisted. For a drug dealer it was a fitting life. And by his estimation, a well-deserved one.

For the grandson of Danath Ironlight it was an absolute disgrace.

Voices from the past pushed to the fore of his mind, doling out shame and damnation. *You've not suffered nearly long enough.* The host of the dead spoke to him in bitter tones. *Fourteen years is nothing weighed against what you stole from us. You owe us the rest of your miserable life!*

Scab whinnied again, so sharply and so close that it forced Barodane's palms to his ears. He glared. "Sometimes I wish you'd stayed dead." His warhorse flicked its black mane and snorted.

The rafters ceased their rotating and a wave of bliss rolled through his gut. The godsthorn's mollifying effects. He was centered now and feeling more normal. He gained his feet.

A half-open bag of coin lay on the ground outside the stall. He counted himself lucky the stable girl hadn't stolen it. It hung heavy where he tied it to his belt even though it was less a pair of silver wheels for reasons his blurred memory failed to recall.

Light reflected off his honor plate from where it dangled on a nail. His hand hovered over the gleaming pauldron. The narrow space between the honor plate and his fingertips yawned wide, swallowing whatever pride his name once carried.

No. That man died at King's Crossing.

Barodane brushed away a few clinging stalks as he took the steel plate into stiff hands. Fourteen years had passed since he'd hammered the fist and chain flat. Fourteen years since he'd paid a near-sighted old hermit to paint it black. For fourteen years, he'd been nothing more than a shadowguard, a retired soldier of the Crown.

He traced a thumb over the shiny patch of rent steel where King Acramis's ax had fallen short.

Why do you keep it? The voices said. *You love the pain of your own misdeeds, don't you? As it should be. Your worth can be measured no other way.*

Vomit rose at the back of his throat. He grit his teeth, choked back the bile. Scab reared. He slammed a fist against the stall slats. "Calm yourself! She'll be in to feed you shortly."

He strapped the honor plate onto his left shoulder then buckled a series of leather straps around bicep and torso. He drew the dagger sheathed in the chest strap, checked it, and then replaced it. He buckled a plain sword to his hip, worthless compared to the darksteel one he'd thrust into Acramis's sternum. But that sword was long buried. To be seen with a prince's blade would draw the type of attention Barodane sought to avoid.

Forever.

Barodane Ironlight is dead. I'm Kord now. Only Kord.

The voices hissed at the back of his mind in answer to his thoughts. *No royal blade, no title, no honor. No prince at all. Stripped of them, your true character is revealed. See what you are? You. Are. Nothing.*

Stepping out into the open air beneath the stable's eaves, he watched the sky spill itself. A favorite saying of Meckin brought a smile to Barodane's lips, "The gods love pissing on us most." Even rain fell with a lazy weakness both unique and reflective of the people of Digtown. Sunny days were rare. Completely dry days more so. Most of the time the weather ranged from sad drizzle to depressing downpour. For any traveler who lost their way or was morbid enough to pass through the destitute town, it would have been poetic outrage to do so without fully experiencing at least one night soaked to the bone.

Though most would say it was whores, godsbrew, and godsthorn that were Digtown's main commerce, it traded in misery most frequently and expertly. Anyone who walked its streets and looked into the forlorn eyes of its people would offer thanks for where they lived and who their neighbors were. If they didn't, then they were indeed a doomed soul and might as well take up residence. The people of Digtown welcomed outsiders, though more often as not, it was in the way of bandits inviting a traveler to share a campfire, or a rapist offering a woman safety on her walk home.

The stable girl came around a corner. No older than ten, she moved on bare, silent feet. Like a rat raised to instinctively avoid cats.

She paused, watching Barodane with a flat affect all too common to Digtown's youth. Hollow. Hopeless.

Her eyes are a reflection of your soul, Mad Prince. The voices wasted no opportunity to drive pain into any vulnerability. *Think of the children who were at Rainy Meadows. The ones whose eyes you closed forever.*

Barodane glanced behind himself, motioned her close. She complied. He crouched and met the stable girl at eye level. "Is your mother still sick?"

She nodded.

"And your father has yet to return from..." He waved a hand. "...wherever he went?"

A flicker of something other than hollowness passed over her expression. Anger perhaps. She nodded again.

Barodane whipped matted lank hair over his shoulder then drew up the hood of his cloak. He dug into the coin purse at his belt, withdrew a gold wheel, and then placed it in the girl's hands. She stared blankly at the boon a heartbeat then stuffed it into a hidden pocket of her grime-smeared shift.

Why try to be her hero? the voices said. *Giving her hope is only a pathway to suffering. She was born here, will languish here, will die and rot here. Just like the rest of us. Because of you!*

Barodane stepped into the muddy streets headed for the Dregs Inn. It was what a local might call the upscale establishment in town. Most outsiders simply called it a cesspool of the lowest order.

Drovers hacked spit and snapped their horse's reins, hurrying through town as quickly as possible. Whores from the Gem Loft chatted on its porch, neither calling out nor batting eyes to lure in customers; as the only other pastime available in Digtown besides ascending on godsthorn or getting black out drunk, not a day went by without ample work for any whore who wanted it. Even Madame Gratha, a one-eyed Kurg of advancing years, stayed busy enough to lounge around the brothel's landing when she pleased.

Barodane trudged through the mud. He owned a couple stables and a handful of horses, but he walked when he could rather than go through the trouble. Besides, he'd fallen off enough times to know it was never a good idea to ride while recovering from the night before.

Imralta, or the Baroness as her girls called her, watched him from the window of the Gem Loft's second story. She wore a lavish, high-collared gown fixed with a broach. She was the richest person in town besides Barodane and her estranged husband, Meckin. In greeting, he raised his chin at her. She nodded back with a wry smile.

When he'd first shambled into Digtown, Barodane was a regular with one of Imralta's girls, Tyne. Over a decade had come and gone since then. He'd not cared for another woman since. Not a day went by where he did not think of her. But she was gone now, moved to Alistar to make her fortune dancing for lords.

In an alley to his right, a pair of drunks fought, hissing and cursing and vying for advantage. For what reason, he couldn't say. Little did it matter. Men rarely needed a reason to fight. And a good one never stopped them. He sighed, not because he knew he'd likely pass more of the same on his short walk, but because it failed to rattle him or anyone else in the slightest.

This was what Digtown was: a mud-caked fight for survival.

The slums around Digtown were the most dire example of the sentiment. Sticks propping up patches of canvas and rain-soaked cloth provided meager cover for the bone-thin denizens who skulked beneath them. They ventured forth at night to stalk the streets for scraps of food. Begging was foolish, for none had much to give but the mercy of a dagger if pushed too far.

Barodane paused just outside the Dregs, eyes wandering to the barrow hills a half mile distant. It rose like the chest of a dying man frozen at the final intake of breath. On the other side of the barrow hills lay the ruins of Rainy Meadows, and from it came painful memories burned into the wild places of his mind where he could not control them. They arrived when they wished. Drove him like a marionette as they pleased. Punished him as they desired.

Barodane's fists clenched.

You are nothing, the voices laughed cruelly. *A pitiful waste of breath.*

His hands loosed, fell limp at his sides as familiar numbness crept in along his ears and shoulders.

Within the barrows rested the bones of hundreds. An entire city of half-Scoth men, women, and children, all slaughtered and buried. Each one knew the name of their enemy. The man who had come collecting lives in retribution for his own grief. The one dealing death to release himself from the burden of suffering. The torment of what Barodane had done passed through his heart like broken glass. To suffer enough was a dream undeserved for one with so much blood to his name, so he'd buried Barodane Ironlight alongside the people he'd murdered at the Rainy Meadows Massacre.

He swallowed hard, pushed through the bar door into candlelight and silence. A harpist sat in the corner, draped over his instrument in drunken surrender. *Stay asleep, bastard. I'll have another night without bleeding ears.*

"You look like shit, Kord," Meckin said from behind the bar. "Did my wife finally lure you into her cougar's den?"

"That she did." Barodane smiled. "You should have told me she likes to play with her food first."

His arrangement with the innkeeper was exceedingly useful. In exchange for a dry place to store his drug supply and meet with buyers, Barodane gave Meckin as much godsthorn as he needed for brewing. Beyond the necessary means of earning an income that the dynamic provided, it kept the former prince of Namarr drunk enough and high enough to forget the past with regularity.

Somewhere along the way, they'd become friends.

"Liar," Meckin said flatly. "If you'd fucked Imralta, you'd have crawled through the door. Got to be a man with iron in his loins to handle the Baroness."

"I saw her but kept a safe distance."

"Smart choice." Meckin's eyes narrowed. "But if you ever did take my wife to bed, I'd know it on your face as soon as you walked in. You'd have this look about you in which all the self-respect a man could have has been stripped from him, leaving only the gleam in his eye of one seeking the tight end of a noose." He grunted. "Yet here you are, alive and intact."

A hefty tankard plopped down onto the bar, sloshing godsbrew.

"Intact, I am. The alive part however..." Barodane took the tankard in hand as he sat at the bar. He drank deep, drained it by half. He lowered the brew, caught his breath, wiped his mouth. "I'm working hard to correct that. With your help, I may be dead soon enough."

Meckin gestured at Barodane's honor plate. "I know what it's like to run from the past. Death ain't a bad answer. Sure to get you where you want to go quickest. But it's only one answer and I daresay the least creative by far." He flicked a bar towel at a passing fly. "Word is you're not the only one who wants to end things."

"How's that?"

"News from the capital. The Namorite Collective finally convened their yearly session."

A tremor moved through Barodane's hand. The tankard hovered at his lips. News of a governmental nature was news he worked hard to ignore, but Meckin's amused tone told him the change he long desired had finally come.

They'd forgotten him.

They'd crowned a new prince.

"And?" Barodane threw back the tankard, finished it in three gulps.

Hope sighed through him. *It's finally over.*

"The crown remains vacant, as predicted," said Meckin. "Another year without a Crown Prince of Namarr. And another year spent waiting for Ishoa Ironlight to come of age. But hey, maybe it's better that..."

Barodane's attention drifted from the conversation.

So, they're unwilling to move on? To Barodane's surprise, there was something other than disappointment bubbling to the surface. He wanted nothing more than to be forgotten—for things to end as Meckin put it. But that might be bad for his niece, Ishoa, and he wished her the best despite their estrangement.

The image of an emerald-eyed babe drew him into memories long suffocated. Only once, before the Great Betrayal, had he held her, and that briefly. *Who has she become? Does she have the Ironlight fire? Or maybe—*

She must never know of you! the voices commanded. *You would only bring shame and ruin to her life.*

Meckin snapped his fingers in Barodane's face.

Barodane flinched. "I'm listening, damn it." He shoved the hand aside. "Now tell me what you said."

The frowning innkeeper relieved Barodane of the empty tankard. "Maybe we're better off without an Ironlight. That's all. Look no further than the Mad Prince. Yes, he killed King Acramis the Twice-Burned. For that he'll always be a war hero, but considering what he did before..." Meckin shrugged as he poured. "Who knows what kind of tyrant he might have become?"

Probably the worst kind. The drunk kind.

Using the sill of a window for support, Ishoa laughed uncontrollably. Only Rakeema and her uncle Wolst could bring her near to tears. She looked out the window.

Birch trees dotted the grounds, and winter blossoms lined a path from the Gate of the Tiger to the ramp leading up to the High Hall. Pink-hued flowers littered the white blanket of snowy earth. Horses whinnied in the distance to the ring of blacksmiths rendering arms for the Duchess's crownguard or shoes for their horses. Swords thudded against iron-banded shields amid grunts of exertion as knight-captains shouted directions to vying trainees in the yard.

Across the way, the Ice Maiden's Keep loomed. Soon, ladies and lords from all over Anjuhkar would fill its towers in preparation of the coming Trials. She sighed. A year stood between her and entry into the sacred ritual. She longed to do more than wait to be crowned. While success during the rituals brought with it a pivotal vote in Anjuhkar's court, it was her people's respect she looked forward to most.

When she found Rakeema already pawing at the door to the library, she gave thanks to her ancestors for receiving an intelligent anjuhtarg and not a dumb one.

A rangy man opened the door and ducked through. Her tutor, Othwii the seneschal. Torchlight reflected off a balding pate, sparse brown hair encircling the crown of his head. Protruding collar bones propped up a tan, ill-fitting tunic. His trousers too appeared made for a man twice his girth. A gold earring looped through one ear, and a hummingbird brooch pinned a fur-lined cloak to a shoulder beneath a jutting thrapple.

"Greetings, Highness." Othwii folded at the waist to gently stroke Rakeema's ears.

"You're her favorite."

Othwii smiled. A rare occurrence, but when it came it was sure to put anyone at ease. In fact, everything about Othwii incited relaxation. Except his numbers lessons, of course. Those gave Ishoa nightmares.

"I've always been comfortable with animals. Cats especially." Straightening, he ducked back inside and beckoned her to follow. "We seem to understand each other."

Books lay everywhere. She followed him along a wall of shelves full of them. They passed towers of tomes overlooking parchment and inkpot on a handful of neat and tidy tables. There was a feeling of crisp-angled rightness to the space. Everything had its place. Othwii took great measures to ensure the library remained well kept.

Motes of dust swirled inside a pane of light as he passed through it. Richly colored tapestries hung from the rafters between windows. These were more beautiful than those in the High Hall, but because they were peaceful depictions of nature and animals, displaying them anywhere but Othwii's library would be a projection of weakness. At least that was what Ishoa's great-grandmother Belara Frost had said.

As Duchess of Anjuhkar, she had overruled Ishoa's idea to have Othwii contract the next artist. "Best to keep the ugly, bloody ones. It deters the overly ambitious when you remind them of wars fought and won and of violence wrought."

Othwii's tone was flat. "I wasn't expecting you, Highness. What brings you?"

Before she could respond, a tapestry caught her eye. She slowed. Her grandfather, Danath Ironlight hoisted Solicerames into the air. Rays of golden sunlight burst in every direction from the circular icon.

"That," Ishoa stopped, pointed.

Othwii turned on his heels.

"I am to be crowned princess of Namarr in less than four years, so I think it would be a good idea to take a more active part in my training." Her promise to her parents, echoed through her mind. *I'll prove myself to you soon enough.*

This time when she said them there was a hollowness to the words, as if spoken inside a chamber, empty of any deeds worthy of note. When she turned fifteen in nine month's time, she'd be of an age to participate in the Trials.

The Crossing. The Summit. The Quelling. Each of the Trials presented its own danger and difficulty. *The only thing that could prove I'm worthy of the Ironlight mantle.*

"Ah." Othwii glanced at Danath's tapestry. "You worry you'll never live up to the legend?"

She nodded, hesitated, then said, "How can I be like him? Like grandmother?"

"Well," the seneschal's throat apple bobbed. "The future can be a troubling place to ruminate over. The past too can be catastrophic. So in order to truly learn and grow we must grasp understanding in all directions and from all sources."

"I wasn't asking for a lesson on unimism, Othwii."

"Unimist that I am, I cannot help but tell you lessons themselves *are* the very nature of unimism. Thus, I invite you to pay attention and listen." The towering seneschal waved a finger. "You said you wanted to take a more active part in your training. Let that start with patience."

"My favorite." Ishoa crossed her arms. "Fine, I'm listening."

"In the days before Scothea invaded the fractured Lands of the Endless Coast, the Trials consisted of young Anjuhks risking life and limb for something called *kotarg* and *kotarg* alone."

"The word sounds vaguely familiar," Ishoa said.

Othwii pulled a book from a shelf at shoulder level. If Ishoa had wanted the same book, she would have needed to jump to get it. "The word means honor." He flipped quickly through, thumped a finger down on a page.

Ishoa peered at it a fleeting second and then flinched. The author had drawn a gruesome picture of a wild-eyed Anjuhk stabbing a white wolverine, while simultaneously being disemboweled by a swipe of its claws.

"And now we get a vote at court if we complete them." A bitter taste filled Ishoa's mouth. "Seems like it's more worth the risk now than it used to be."

"That's where you're wrong." Othwii gave a complacent grin. "Whether it is a vote at court or simply honor, the influence one gains from the Trials remains equivalent. Look no further than Syphion Muul. The man is a zealot from lowborn means and has no vote at court, yet his voice harbors immense power. Without him, the call for Anjuhkar to break from Namarr and be a sovereign nation once more would falter. If he didn't possess the influence he does now, Revocation would not ride the lips of every hold lord and lady's mouth in anticipation of our next court. Only your great-grandmother, the duchess of Anjuhkar, has more sway at present."

The seneschal's last comment sent a tingle of worry into Ishoa's neck and shoulders. Rakeema swiped her body against Ishoa's leg, but she ignored the anjuhtarg. "I thought only the Scarborn follow Syphion Muul?"

"They do. But if you let a barn burn long enough, eventually all the rats are sure to emerge." Othwii snapped the book closed. "The downtrodden are but the first tool used by revolutionaries. Of all people, you should understand this. Your great-grandfather was a slave before he was a Namorite prince."

The idea of one day being Crown Princess herself made Ishoa's stomach clench. The eyes of her dead mother and father bore into the back of her mind.

Othwii seemed to notice her discomfort. He tossed the book onto a nearby table, voice taking on velvet-soft tones. "You worry about the impending vote on Revocation. And it's clear to me you blame yourself. Why?"

The tapestry of Danath Ironlight loomed. Her eyes fell to the floor, a band of tightness drawing around her chest. She gave a resolute nod. "If I were stronger, perhaps there would be more faith in me. But I'm untested. A young female, and half-Anjuhk besides."

Othwii raised his slender chin in the air. "Stacking evidence from insecurity is a sure way to blind yourself to all but what is most irrational and feared. Let us draw conclusions from places more concrete. Above all else, you are an Ironlight. No other can claim such."

The weakest Ironlight who ever lived.

A dark veil fell over her mind's eye. She wanted to retreat to her room and lie with Rakeema until sleep took her. Resolve stayed her feet from flight. Her jaw clenched. She took a breath as her uncle Wolst had taught her and stayed put.

"Just as the Namorite Collective meets every year, the court of Anjuhkar does the same. This year's vote for Revocation won't be the first, nor will it be the last. Around this time next year, you'll be completing the Trials yourself, Ishoa. Your image and influence will strengthen, loom large enough to cast Revocation into the shadows where it belongs."

Panic built in her chest as the seneschal spoke. "But it won't go away, will it? It will never go away." The weight of responsibility dropped across her shoulders like a felled tree. She spoke in a burst. "My birth was a curse. First it killed my mother. Shortly after it killed my father and grandfather. And then, mad or not, it took my uncle Barodane. All of them dead within a year of my being born. I'll be Namarr's death too."

"Highness." Othwii regarded her coolly. "Never say that again."

A long silence rang through the space as they stared at each other.

Finally, Ishoa uncrossed her arms and shook her head. "I'm sorry. I just wish I could be more. I want to prove I'm worthy of my name—the legacy of my family. I just..." Her great grandmother had always been too busy to dedicate time to Ishoa outside of matters of state. That left her upbringing and education to Othwii and her adoptive uncle, Wolst.

She sniffled. "Sometimes it's hard being the only one. It's...lonely."

"Is that why you've been corresponding with the Scarborn boy?"

Panic tore through Ishoa. Her eyes went wide. "How did you know?"

"It is my duty to know all that happens in Jarik, especially while the duchess is away at Alistar." He cocked his head to a vulture-like shoulder. "Let's see...you first spoke with Lodaris Warnock at your birthday in the passageway outside of the High Hall. Since then you've received ten messages and sent seven yourself. Though you've written far more."

Ishoa stammered.

On her fourteenth birthday, there had been a large celebration in the High Hall. Ladies and lords from holds both large and small had gathered to eat and drink, sing and laugh in honor of the last Ironlight. For Ishoa, it wasn't just her birthday, it was the anniversary of her mother's death. In secret, she'd stolen a moment to herself in a passage beyond the High Hall. Tears came to her eyes as she recalled a gentle hand finding her shoulder.

"A moment alone," Ishoa had said without turning, her tone severe. "Please."

The hand remained. "I know what it's like to be born with pain."

She'd whirled around and slapped the gentle but firm hand from her shoulder.

Under torchlight, with a chill wind rustling his fiery hair in the passageway, his gaze was comforting. Almost like he understood. There was no judgment in his eyes, no condemnation of weakness for displaying vulnerability or conduct unbecoming of a princess.

A serious young man, Lodaris Warnock smiled rarely. But when he'd talked to Ishoa, his face softened. "Sometimes pain makes us stronger."

If anyone could claim such a thing, it was Lodaris. Like Ishoa, he'd been an outcast since birth. Raked across the face by the steel claw of a Jurati during his first year of life, he'd been designated to the lower class of Anjuhk society for the disloyalty of his ancestors sixty-four years prior. Three thin white scars trailed diagonally from his left eye, over full lips, and disappeared into the cleft of his chin.

"It's brave of you to be here." Ishoa looked over Lodaris's shoulder, wary of prying eyes. A handful of crownguard stood at intervals along the length of the passageway out of earshot. "Even braver to lay hands on a princess."

"The future Crown Princess," Lodaris corrected. He shrugged. "You're still a person."

"Am I?" Stepping back, Ishoa drew a strand of hair from her face. "In light of my lineage, I think most forget that."

"It's a lot to live up to. Enough to crush a weaker person. But not you." Lodaris raised a fist to his shoulder as he bowed. "You are strong. Stronger than you know."

Torchlight danced in his eyes as they stared at one another.

He pivoted to go, but before he took a step, Ishoa grabbed him by the hand. "Wait." She squeezed harder than she'd meant. "Sorry."

She pulled him into a tearful embrace. After that they'd sat on the floor talking without a lull for so long the cold stone floor number Ishoa's backside. The hour grew late. Mirth and drumbeats reached them from the High Hall, mixed with the occasional yowl from those "too drunk to die" as her Uncle Wolst put it.

And it was Wolst who found them deep in conversation, disapproval forming deep grooves in his knitted brow. Lodaris Warnock—a Scarborn.

Her first friend. The very last one she should have.

Lips parted, Ishoa glared at Othwii. Heat poured from the collar of Ishoa's dress. Sweat dampened the back of her neck as the memories faded. "You're a spy."

The seneschal looked taken aback, almost offended. "Of course I am. It is a skill necessary for all rulers, and one which all their advisor's must be well versed in."

"Oh." She frowned. "No one has trained me."

"Subterfuge requires a certain degree of maturity. And in equal measure, it requires dedication to a cause greater than oneself." Othwii smiled, skin pulling taut around bony cheeks. "You said you wish you could be more—help more. You wish to prove yourself worthy of your family's name and legacy, correct? Well, here we are. The duchess of Anjuhkar and I have been trading messenger ravens during her return journey from the capital. She's set to arrive soon but after the Warnocks. It seems you and your grandmother think similarly, for she too has decided you are to take a more active part in your training. Specifically, subterfuge."

A tremor shook Ishoa's hand. She reached down, patted Rakeema to steady it.

"You have a duty to Namarr that must be fulfilled." Clasping hands behind his back, Othwii straightened and then turned toward the beams of daylight filtering through the windows. "You will not speak a word of your task to anyone. Most certainly not the Warnock boy."

"If you've known about the letters, why have I been allowed to keep in contact with Lodaris?" Ishoa shot Othwii a wary glance, horror dawning in the wake of understanding. "Why wasn't I stopped?"

Othwii ignored her question. "Ishoa Ironlight, do you accept your task?"

Rage lit like a brazier in Ishoa's chest. Othwii casually leaned forward onto a table and drummed spidery fingers. Silence dragged between them. A bird or rat scrabbled across the rafters, kicking down a slurry of dust. The tapestry of Danath wavered.

My father sacrificed his life for Namarr. I cannot balk.

She nodded.

Holding up a smooth-palm, Othwii stared behind him for a long time, then swept the room intently with his gaze. He stooped forward like a buzzard at a carcass until his face was mere inches from Ishoa's. "You will receive Lodaris Warnock and the rest of the Scarborn on behalf of the duchess of Anjuhkar. Once pleasantries are exchanged, you will deliver these decrees..." From seemingly out of nowhere, he produced a tightly rolled piece of parchment and handed it to her. "Memorize them. Deliver them. Then watch. Pay special attention to Syphion Muul."

Ishoa's eyes snapped up from the scroll in her hands. "He'll be with them?"

"Yes," Othwii said. "We're told Lodaris's parents, Lodecka and Ularis Warnock, have given Muul patronage. Your grandmother expects your report on their reactions to the decrees at the next counsel meeting. Do you think—"

"If you're going to ask if I think I can handle it, you don't know me as well as I thought," Ishoa snapped. "I may not like the task, but I'm still an Ironlight. I can watch people as well as anyone." Thinking better of her reaction, Ishoa let the agitation in her tone die. "I watch you, you know. You prefer the company of books to people. You don't think you belong with other Anjuhks, so you spend your time here—alone." She puffed her chest. "How's that?"

"Ah yes, clearly you see. The question is how deeply. For this task, you'll need to look deeper than surface-level reactions. You'll need to observe with all your senses." Othwii sighed. "And you're wrong about me, actually. I do *not* prefer the company of books. I have learned to love them over time. Long ago, Belara Frost gave me an important mission. A responsibility with dire consequences. I failed her. What you see before you is a shamed man. The post of seneschal is where I'm most needed, and so I suffer it gladly. I'm alone because I have no time for any love but the one of duty." His eyelids fluttered. "I will never fail your grandmother again."

"I'm sorry," Ishoa felt suddenly exposed. "I...I didn't know."

"But now you do. And as a ruler you must know the stories of those who serve you as well as those who oppose you. Information is the shield that protects nations. Knowing what motivates your enemies, the killing blade. Without understanding of your people, you are left naked. Weak."

He waved a hand in dismissal. "If you had a desire to do so, you could take what I've told you and bend me to your will. Do you understand?"

Ishoa swallowed a lump in her throat as Othwii's words echoed through her. "Yes."

"Then you know how important it is to observe Syphion Muul and the Warnock's reaction to your grandmother's decrees." His eyes narrowed. "I know you have feelings for the boy."

"My duty to Namarr comes first," Ishoa declared. The very thing she'd prayed to for that morning had come to pass: a chance to prove herself. She tucked the parchment into a pocket of her dress.

What harm is done by watching Lodaris's parents react to some tiny scroll?

A leaden ball of guilt had already begun to form in her stomach. *Perhaps it will harm me most.* The idea of lying to her friend, regardless of if he was Scarborn, didn't sit well.

As she turned to go, Othwii's long-fingered hand held her fast. "Be careful, Ishoa."

She shot the tapestry of Danath a withering glare, then left, Rakeema bounding at her side.

CHAPTER FOUR

GODSTHORN

A t night, the Dregs came alive. Dance, drink, and thorn made its way throughout the taproom in a current of hedonistic striving. A pair of drovers and their porters slammed tankards together, slopping godsbrew across the floor. Women from the Gem Loft slid through the door, leering at the business the night would bring them. Unsavory and disreputable sorts of folk trickled in and out as the night dragged into the late hours. Stark naked and toothless, a man from the slums wandered into the Dregs, hoping to cajole a drunk into giving him some food for coin no doubt. But Meckin shooed him away. A gnarled man and what seemed to be his grandson smoked pipes in one corner, here and there clapping for the harpist.

At the back of the taproom, Barodane drank and brooded alone. He barely felt the warmth from the hearth on his grimace.

Harp song slithered through the air alongside a thick pall of smoke hanging over the gathered patrons. The harpist himself had awoken when he wet himself. He rebounded well enough after a couple of tankards of godsbrew and the attention of a young couple who'd never heard a harp before. The pissant musician beamed, bragged, and slurred about his skill, and then he indulged them.

Fucking harps. If I were Crown Prince, they'd be outlawed.

Somehow the young couple seemed to like it and danced with a broad woman Meckin had hired to entertain for the night. Her heavy steps rattled the floorboards, adding a certain upbeat energy to the space.

Barodane watched Garlenna descend the stairs, each step measured and powerful as if she could, with any sudden added force, snap the boards underfoot in two. Her shoulders stayed level and open, regardless of whatever motion her body made. Proud, powerful, and polite, Garlenna was a higher breed of human. And an exceedingly dangerous one. The type of person so foreign to the people of Digtown that Barodane knew they all saw it.

After the battle of King's Crossing, the first thing Barodane had done was strip himself of anything making him appear of higher standing than a commoner. So he rounded his shoulders more, made eye contact less, spoke in gruff, plain language—or not at all—and buried his past at Rainy Meadows.

Why should you live when we are all dead? the dead host said. *You should have buried your corpse with ours. But we deserve no such dishonor. You deserve to die alone...Prince.*

Meckin greeted Garlenna warmly at the bar with a mug of mead. Then a second tankard. As she approached Barodane's table, he turned away from her to watch the harpist poorly regale the crowded inn with a song about Barodane's grandparents called *"The Eyes of Love."*

To consort with Garlenna was to draw unwanted suspicion. After meeting with his buyer, he would dedicate his time to getting rid of her. A difficult prospect to imagine.

Her back to the hearth, Garlenna's shadow stretched across his table. Memory flashed. He'd seen this before. Her, standing over him, flame and smoke and shame hovering like a shovel over a grave. Behind her, Meckin and some patrons were clearing a space for dancing at the center of the room. The fireplace crackled and spit an ember next to Garlenna's foot. She ground it out then put a tankard next to Barodane's arm.

Three long strides and she took a seat at a nearby table.

Barodane felt her watching him with her one good eye. How had she found him? What did she want? For fourteen years he'd eluded his past. He was where he belonged now. Where Kord belonged.

And nothing will change that.

It was close to midnight, which meant his buyer was late. He'd never wanted a deal over with more. He wanted to sleep, or ascend, or be alone to think. With Garlenna staying at the Dregs, he'd need to sleep at the Gem Loft. He didn't want her following him to either of his stables.

No—she would already know where he was staying. Most likely she'd been watching him for a while. Inwardly, he cursed.

With a resounding bang, the inn's door ricocheted off the interior wall. Three men stepped into the Dregs. The way each of them immediately searched the room marked them as his buyers. A young man with red hair and a stringy beard looked somewhat familiar to Barodane, but he couldn't place him. In the lead was a broad-shouldered man with a demanding air. His clothing was fine in the way of highborns. The third, a hollow-eyed companion, was dressed plainly and loomed at the group's rear. He was tall and thin with a neck that flanged out wider than his weak chin. All but the redhead wore neatly crafted swords at their hips.

The redhead spotted Barodane and whispered into the broad-shouldered man's ear. They approached and took seats without asking. Once, Barodane might have reprimanded them for their presumptuousness.

He did nothing but slurp from his tankard.

Barodane didn't have to see Garlenna to know she discreetly watched his interaction with the buyer and his muscle. She was a trained agent of the Sempyrean. A spy of the highest caliber.

"You're Kord." The broad man reached across the table and laid a slap on Barodane's honor plate. "No one said you were a shadowguard."

Barodane stared.

The bull-chested buyer also bore an honor plate but kept it covered with a finely woven cloak. Intuition told him it was the steel of a knight he hid rather than the bronze plate of a crownguard. Dealing with such a highly trained man was both a rare and risky affair.

"Great," the man said. He afforded a quick glance of affirmation at the redhead, the familiar face. "Jennim tells me you're the man for godsthorn around here."

It wasn't until that moment, when the redhead smiled a wide, gap-toothed grin, that Barodane realized who he was. This was Tyne's son. Tyne, who he'd foolishly let himself fall in love with.

Jennim...

He'd been a little boy when Barodane first wandered into Digtown, half-dead and blood-caked. The young man's face became a child's face in his memory, pale and expectant. His visits to the Gem Loft had been oft. "Isn't my boy the sweetest?" Tyne would say.

Time, however, had been anything but sweet for the boy. He looked maltreated, strung out, a few bad breaks away from living in the slums. Sorrow passed through Barodane like a sip of bitter drink.

"Hey," the broad man said, snapping his fingers in Barodane's face. People seemed to think that acceptable of late. Really, it just pissed him off. "I'm making you an offer."

"Offer?"

"I'm buying you out." The broad man smiled.

The lanky third man surveyed the room, dead eyes alighting everywhere but on Barodane. When his gaze settled on Garlenna, she too, looked elsewhere. The tall henchman watched her with unconcealed suspicion.

"Buying me out." Barodane grew serious. "Who are you?"

The man drew his cloak off one shoulder to reveal a burnished-steel honor plate. The sigil depicted two mason hammers crisscrossing, framed by a pair of laurels. "Hyram Olabran. My father is Roddic Olabran, the Magnate of Lah-Tsarra and a member of the Namorite Collective. I don't expect matters of state to appeal to every drug lord, but surely you've heard of the Hammer of Breckenbright?"

I've met the prick. When he was young, he vaguely recalled meeting a concrete man with a rigid quiet about him while attending his father at court in Alistar. During the Great Betrayal, Roddic Olabran and his masons had famously held Breckenbright against Scothean siege for the entirety of the war. The armies of Anjuhkar had finally arrived and crushed Raeklord Sahuhd's forces against Breckenbright's walls. The battle of the Forgotten Fields, they called it.

By that time, Barodane had already slain Acramis at King's Crossing and disappeared.

"I'm buying your business and willing to pay quite a lot for it. More than it's worth, if that helps. I know we told your man Danuuk we were just here to make a small purchase, but the truth is one of my men bought your stuff two months ago and claimed it to be some of the best this side of Unturrus." Hyram waved dismissively. "I'll own the operation and you get to go back to whatever life you desired before you became a drug dealer."

Barodane shook his head. "Not interested." He took a loud pull from his tankard. Jennim blanched.

Hyram remained smiling, though only in the way of smiles held long after mirth had come and gone. He chuckled. "I'm not familiar with the kind of humor you use in this shit-caked town. Digtown, is it? If it's anything like the weather, I'm sure it can be quite...dark." He paused. "You're joking. Of course you are. Thorn dealer, shadowguard, and humorist. A man of many talents."

Barodane's hands curled tighter around his tankard. "I'm far more boring than you imply. My answer is no."

With an expression of false concern, Hyram Olabran leaned forward. "So let me get this straight. I'm offering you a small fortune to live out your days drinking wherever and whenever you desire *without* needing to deal godsthorn...and you're saying no. Are you mad?"

The Mad Prince. Yes. Many call me that. "Quite."

At this, the hollow-eyed man turned his attention from Garlenna to Barodane and stared with deadly focus.

Rage filled Barodane. "Your man here thinks it wise to watch me with a rapist's gaze?"

Hyram frowned. His eyes wandered to the tankard in Barodane's hand, then to the full tankard at his elbow. "Expecting company?"

The rage. The tensions. The threats buttered with pleasantry. Barodane glanced at the harpist then took a quick swig of godsbrew. He sucked his teeth before falling into contented silence.

With a grunt, Hyram slapped Jennim on the shoulder. "Let's restart, shall we? I'll introduce my friends properly. This is Jennim here." He hiked a thumb at the tall man. "Eustus there. Eustus doesn't talk much. He may be a dullard, so I'm sorry if his gaze offended you."

The holdlord was in no way sorry.

"You travel long distances and do dark deals with a dullard?" Barodane scoffed.

"Oh, I don't think you should worry about that. Eustus may be slow of mind, but he is fast in the ways I need. Very fast, some uncompromising ghosts will tell you." Hyram's chin lifted. "Now, how much of your product are you willing to sell since you're refusing to let me buy you out entirely?"

"Twenty thorns."

Hyram laughed. Jennim went a shade paler. Twenty thorns would last a heavy addict less than a month.

"You don't understand, do you, Kord?" Hyram wagged a finger at Barodane. "You could be a very rich man. You have what, a handful of runners harvesting on Unturrus's slopes? Maybe two wains? If you share your spots with me as well as your processing techniques, I can supply the coin for a fleet of wains and dozens of men to man them. We could have the most lucrative godsthorn operation from Unturrus to Breckenbright. We could turn this shit heap into a proper city."

Lies. Don't let him take you from us. Digtown stays. The voices said. *You stay...*

He knew Hyram's promises rang false. He wanted Barodane to give away his secrets, to stumble into telling him how many men he employed. Important for some darker aims.

Barodane stared into his tankard. "Twenty thorns."

"The innkeeper has more than that on hand for fermenting drink. I can do nothing with that amount."

Barodane shrugged. "You could have a good time with it. Or sell it. Or stick it up each other's asses. I really don't care what you do with it. I imagine Eustus there may enjoy the latter option."

Hyram's brow knit with fury. "You have a harsh tongue, Kord."

"And you have an exhausting one. I sell twenty thorns at a time. That's all."

"It isn't." Hyram slapped a gloved hand on the table. "Jennim, you said this man was like a father to you. You said he was different. Wise. Why do I feel as though I've been lied to?"

"Please, Kord," Jennim said. "It's a good deal. Hyram—"

Jennim's head bounced off the wall as the highborn delivered a snapping backhand to the young man's mouth "Silence, ass. I've heard enough of your empty words." Hyram looked at the ceiling, took a breath. "Apologies, Kord. I'll be clearer. I'm willing to offer—"

"No. I'll be clearer. You imagine this is some kind of negotiation, a dance I'm doing to get the price of your purchase higher. I'll tell you one last time it is not. I won't sell my operation, not any part of it. You've wasted your time." Barodane hunkered deeper around his cup of brew. He scrunched his face into a mask of fake pleasantry. "Unless you want to buy twenty thorns."

Hyram drummed the wood with thick fingers as he looked around the room. "You have..." He leaned back in the chair, stretching. "Offended me." He shot

Jennim a withering glare then let it meander back to Barodane. "I am very offended. Now, I want your supply. I want your operation...the whole thing."

The young lord of Breckenbright chuckled. "Twenty thorns...up each other's asses? Unbelievable. Oh well, Kord. I hope you've enjoyed your life."

"Yeah," Barodane said.

"Eustus," Hyram said. "Teach him."

The reed-thin dullard's hand wrapped around the hilt of a dagger at his belt. Garlenna's chair scraped across the floor as she stood and faced their table. One hand folded back her cloak to reveal a flanged mace culminating in four points, one for each of the Sempyrean's gods of light. She stood still as a glacier. Her good eye roamed the crowd for other threats while confidently ignoring the two before her.

Silence hung over them like an executioner's ax.

Hyram frowned. When his eyes found Barodane's, there was a mix of admiration with the annoyance there. "Kord, you keep interesting company. I wonder how many are willing to face death at your side?"

He rose. "Eustus, we're leaving. For now."

From the corner of his eye, Barodane watched them go. Jennim slunk behind, searching for a way out of whatever awaited him once the trio were out of view of others.

Barodane settled back as Garlenna returned to her seat.

There was little doubt Hyram intended to return. Perhaps at the night's end they would be waiting for him. Taking a dagger in the ribs and being left to bleed out in a muddy alley without fanfare seemed a fitting end.

But have you suffered enough to deserve even that? the voices questioned. *There is more pain yet to feel.*

He shook his head and took account of his crew.

Danuuk, the half-Kurg nephew of Madame Gratha would do most deeds if paid enough, but anything beyond a knife in the dark with the advantage of surprise and the man was untrustworthy. The Redhand brothers were thrill-seekers to the bone. Whether it was attempting to ride a horse standing on the saddle, bed a highborn lady, or fight a group of men with three times their numbers, the brothers refused to be outdone by their counterpart. But they were also Barodane's runners and currently harvested Unturrus for godsthorn. They may not be back in time for whatever Hyram was planning. A few others came to mind, children who ran errands and messages or smaller dealers he took a cut from. Nothing a lord of Breckenbright couldn't squash.

Then there was Garlenna.

He ground his teeth. He hadn't asked her to step in, but if she hadn't would Eustus's knife be stuck in his heart? Would he be staring up at a frantic Meckin as his lifeblood drained through the floorboards? Despite Hyram Olabran's claim of

Eustus being a dullard, Barodane had searched the eyes of enough soldiers to know neither Hyram nor his man shied from violence.

The broad-hipped dancer had taken a break and was now sweating onto the bar as she spoke with Meckin. The innkeeper caught Barodane's eye, winked, and then slapped the dancing woman on the shoulder. Flipping back a snarl of graying blond hair, she gyrated her hips slowly and then moved to the center of the dance floor on languid feet. A clap began. Stomping followed. The harpist plucked a tune to go with the beat, although he was off. The dancer moved with it expertly, making up in skill what the harpist lacked in talent.

The room cheered.

These people's lives were hard. They deadened their emotions like he did with thorn and drink, or fighting and fucking. They sought to own their environment only to be owned by it. But on some occasions, they pushed back and took control by letting go. They exposed themselves. Chose happiness in the face of destitution. An endeavor of complete vulnerability.

Barodane fell inward. For a moment, he wished he could be like them. He wished his anger and sadness and pain could be harnessed in his feet and hands and throat and passed through him by dance or song.

He didn't clap nor stomp in mirth. He drew up his hood and bent over his drink. He stared at the dark reflective surface within.

As if his mood dictated reality, rain began hammering at the roof. Unlike most structures in Digtown, the Dregs had few leaks. "Driest place in town to quench one's thirst," Meckin often said when a new face wandered in.

Barodane pulled his cloak tight around his shoulders. His honor plate lay cold as a corpse on his shoulder. A reminder, though not the kind honor plates were created for. Fourteen years had passed since his own hung over his bed like a good little Namorite.

When his grandfather, Danath Ironlight, had made the armor pieces sacred, it had acted as a badge of service to the Sons of the Ardent Heart for fighting against Scothean tyranny and helping unite Namarr.

A legendary shadow I'll never be free of. A reminder of who I never was nor could ever be.

I'm Kord now.

To enjoy was to disrespect. To relieve pain was to dishonor. To love another was to savage the memory of those who no longer could. He would unite his suffering with those he'd unjustly slain in whatever way possible. Singing along with some miscreant harpist and moving in step with an aging bar maid was for those worthy of happiness.

Not him. Not Kord.

Garlenna stood at his elbow. "May I join you?"

"A gold wheel for twenty thorns. A silver wheel for one." Barodane sniffled. "For anything else, the answer is no."

She sighed. A silver wheel tumbled from her hand to the table. "Keep your filth. I'll pay to have a seat all the same."

She sat. The chair groaned. They faced the dance floor. "She sings well enough. Even here there's some beauty." Garlenna waved her mead cup at the crowd.

Like a child testing a mother's limits, Barodane pulled out his roll, plucked two thorns, and laid them on the table.

Garlenna glanced at them, then at Barodane, her chiseled face impassive. "I could arrest you. Drag you before the Crown's Justice. As you know, they do not treat godsthorn dealers kindly. Or users for that matter."

"Nor should they." Barodane inserted a thorn into a vein in his arm, letting its drug-coated tip soak into his bloodstream. "Unturrus wouldn't be profitable for them if they did."

"I'm sure our recently departed friend wouldn't mind seeing you in shackles." She spoke seriously, discomfited by his drug use. "He'll take matters into his own hands."

Flicking the first thorn to the ground, Barodane inserted another. He eyed his former prosort's clothing. "You're not here on behalf of the Collective or the Sempyrium, are you?"

She looked away, leaving the question unanswered. "Barodane—"

"Do not speak that name here," he growled. "That man is dead." The room spun. Panic came and went. Euphoria filled him...his vision dimmed. He removed the thorn from his arm.

Garlenna shook her head. "Kord then." She took a measured breath as she watched the dancing barmaid work her way around the room, pulling the young couple beside the harpist onto the dance floor, followed by a drover.

Barodane's body was light. Free. "Why are *you* here?"

"I've not given up on you. I will not. You are my friend."

"If you think that, then you don't know me, Garlenna Renwood." The ceiling undulated in a wave. He laughed. His breath was in his chest, a bundle of blankets. "I, Kord, have no friends. I deal godsthorn now. I'll do nothing else until my dying day."

When he looked at Garlenna, she seemed brighter than anything else in the room. Black lines framed her figure like a picture.

"You are wrong." Glaring with her single good eye, she leaned over. "Hating yourself will not change the past. We've all done wrong in the name of what we thought to be right. Do not forget, it was a war. I dipped my weapon in the same blood you did."

"I never forget!" Barodane's eyes narrowed as wrath took him. Godsthorn coursed through him. The euphoria of the single thorn dissipated. The veil of reality started to fall...

Power flooded his arms and legs. Hallucinations peeled back reality. Skin tingled against the fabric of his clothes. Clothes tingled against the eddies of cool and warm air.

He felt everything as one, a singular intensity.

"I have never once forgotten—even for a second. The Mad Prince, I've heard them say. That is the legacy of a man I do not wish to be. Yet it's one I'll never be rid of. Where I go, suffering follows." He gave a low hiss. "It can be no other way."

In his mind's eye, the past snaked forward. A sign hung before him like a dream, the tether smoking, ready to snap. It read, "The Crown's Justice."

Nearby, someone begged him.

Words of betrayal, of rightness and reason.

He spoke the traitor's words aloud in hollow tones, translating memory to present moment. "Abandon, Garlenna Renwood. Abandon...before it's too late."

He rose. "If you're looking for a place to hide your shame, just know, this burial mound is taken." He bent at the waist, stared directly into her eye. "Your prince is dead."

The barmaid approached, smiling in his periphery with hands extended, fingers coiling and coaxing him to dance. He turned, looked at her, and watched the smile fade as she hurried on to the next patron.

Power surrounded him, a crackling dark thing. Common for ascending. A bitter mood became a bitter storm. The drug had a way of bringing one's emotions to the fore and making it their god for a short time.

I deserve no pleasant ascension. The worst. That's what I've earned.

Garlenna took a drink. "I'll leave when my business is done here. No sooner."

"You'd...uh...you'd sleep better than I if you did..." Words fell into the abyss of feeling and sensation. Barodane lurched, nearly bulling over the aging bar maid on his way to the exit. Meckin waved, but Barodane ignored him.

Outside, rain pelted him in merciless sheets, soaking through hood and cloak in a matter of seconds. Instead of walking under the covered eaves of the rows of shop fronts, he walked the center of the muddy street.

Godsthorn crawled into his skull.

Hyram's face swam before him. Eustus's too, a knife in hand. Reaction slowed, became frozen surrender.

Hyram placed a crown upon his brow while the weak-chinned dullard cut him, belly to throat. Rather than blood, indigo moths burst forth and he coughed them out. Watched the images flutter into the rain. Then gone. His stables were somewhere not far. Comfort—he could not find it. Never could.

A bony person, or perhaps a skeleton, wandered toward him. For a flashing moment he thought Garlenna had brought some other friend long dead to his heart with her to entrap Barodane, but the face was a stranger's, hideous, sickly, and pocked. He shoved them into the mud. Curses fell like rain.

He sprinted down an alley. Alone.

Puddles and squelching mud slowed him as he made his way through a slum of thirty canvas shanties at the edge of Digtown. He climbed up the burial mounds, feeling a second wave of the godsthorn's effects mounting.

A fox's moonbeam eyes drifted over him then flickered back into the dark to hunt. Beyond the lights of town, the stars afforded a subtle overlay of luminescence along the shape of things. Rocks here and there sought to trip him, but the godsthorn coursing through his veins heightened his senses.

Climbing the barrows a half mile from town, his breath grew ragged, his limbs cold and rubbery. Soon he realized he was lying on the ground at the top of a mass grave. A throne. A cradle of mud. His chest heaved as godsthorn took hold...

He stared at the stars.

The world bucked and spun.

Sobs rose in his throat. He coughed—choked.

He turned onto his side and stared out over a town he'd always hated. And for that very reason, he loved it. Bursts of orange torchlight, hazy from the rainfall, lie across the landscape of shadowed structures like the eyes of some immense spider.

Its web snared him, held him for eternity. The spider whispered to him why its web felt so soft.

The voices of dead mothers and their children cried out: "Mad Prince! Murderer!" The words vibrated through him. The past breathed into him.

Panic beat his heart faster...

The hoofbeats of charging horses, going down, down, into a valley of fire and blood and ash. Down to Rainy Meadows.

The earth opened, stealing him from blissful clarity the moment before seeing it.

He fell in—down into the earth—dragged under.

The spider rotated overhead as the corpses of his victims sucked him into their graves in a sacred reckoning. Warmth suffused all. A comfort.

He let go...

Felt his mind drop from his mind into roiling earth and abyss, his body and soul caught in the spider's web to be forever feasted upon.

Awareness tumbled out of awareness, thoughts and shooting stars briefly known at speeds incomprehensible.

Slow and harsh—

Barodane or Kord or Barodane or Kord...one disintegrated into the other.

CHAPTER FIVE

SCARBORN

G usts of wind scattered winter blossom petals, pressing them up against the base of the barracks, stables, and a dozen other buildings throughout the snowy bailey grounds. A thick stone wall, twice as tall as a man, surrounded the Ice Maiden's Keep, separating it from the sprawling city of Jarik beyond.

The cold mixed with Ishoa's nerves, making her shiver. She drew her fur-lined cloak around her throat. This was no place to display weakness.

She turned to her escort, a pair of crownguard. "Which gate?"

"The Gate of the Tiger," one said.

Half a week had passed since her unsettling conversation with Othwii in the library. Now the Scarborn were set to arrive. Word of their approach traveled fast. A messenger had fetched her with only enough time to dress and give Rakeema a brief farewell.

Ishoa nodded to her crownguard then rode in the direction of the Gate of the Tiger. The other gate, the Gate of the Bear, circumvented Jarik's town proper. *Why go through the hassle of riding through a busy city when you could come up the southern slopes directly?* Most hold ladies and lords would never be caught dead bothering with navigating the streets of Jarik.

Just as she reached the Gate of the Tiger, a whistle spun her about.

Dressed for battle, Wolst was unmistakable as he thundered toward her, a handful of knights in tow. The breadth of the man dwarfed his stallion, and he wore a spiked-helmet wrought from the skull of a raek. Storm bear pelts pinned to the armored shoulders of the knights of Jarik snapped in the wind. Broad-bladed spears gripped in grizzled hands, jutted at an overcast sky. Thick puffs of steam rolled backward from their horse's nostrils and dissipated against the Frost sigil on their shields, a snow bison with its head tilted forward, preparing to charge.

On each of the knight's shoulders rode the steel honor plate of Namarr, a fist sundering chain. Ancient veterans and master storytellers claimed the emblem more than a mere metaphor of great potency. Those who worshiped Danath as more legend than man said his rebellion started when he broke his chains with his bare hands. Ishoa looked at her own. They could do no such thing. *Unless I go up Unturrus and recieve powers.*

Her shoulders sagged, heavy with resignation in the face of her fate. She was an Anjuhk and a princess, besides. *The chain Danath broke to free Namarr is the one that binds me forever.*

A huffing Wolst reined in his stallion, bringing the knights of Jarik behind him to a stop. "Isha!" It warmed Ishoa to have her uncle call her by the same nickname her mother had gone by. Then again, most everything he did warmed her. The hulking man removed his helm with hands that could strangle a bull. Hiking the helmet under one arm, his grin spread wide in a thicket of gray beard. He patted the neck of Ishoa's palfrey.

If anyone could break a chain with hands alone, it was the infamous Beast of Anjuhkar. As warmaster, Wolst had pledged the twin broadswords hanging from each hip to Belara Frost. While Othwii was an extension of Belara Frost's intellectual whims, Wolst executed those of a physical nature. To Ishoa, he was like a father.

"You should have chosen a destrier," he said.

"I'm not riding to war, uncle. I thought it best if they saw a ruling lady."

"Aye." Wolst spat in the snow, mirth suddenly gone. "Maybe you're right. If it were up to me, they'd be met with a charging vanguard of Jarik's best."

The clutch of knights grunted assent.

Ishoa rolled her eyes. "Whatever gets you back to the feasting table quickest, right?"

Wolst shot her a look of indignation as his knights broke into laughter. Ishoa smiled to herself as Wolst joined in, slapping a bare knee. "So a man likes to eat!" He shouted. Then he muttered, "Man my size requires ample sustenance."

Ishoa wore a coy smile. "It's a bit of a chicken or the egg kind of situation though, isn't it?"

"You've your grandmother's sharp tongue." Wolst pointed a root-thick finger toward the Gate of the Tiger. "Hope you've saved some for the Scarborn."

Crownguard on the battlements shouted. A flush crept up Ishoa's neck and into her cheeks. She took a shuddering breath. Whether it was in response to the apprehension of her impending task or the excitement of seeing her friend Lodaris again, she couldn't be sure. *At least I get to see him.*

"So, they have chosen to make a show of it, eh?" Wolst said. "Let's not entertain their posturing. A spectacle without spectators gives little satisfaction. Hestia!" Wolst's eldest child spurred her horse forward. She was a knight of Jarik, and while she seemed a fine soldier Ishoa had never been close with her due to their age gap. "Clear the bailey. Order all servants to cease errands until the Scarborn have been escorted to their camp."

With a salute, Hestia peeled away from the group.

"Is that really necessary?" Ishoa said.

Wolst leaned across his horse's withers to whisper in her ear. "Strike and counterstrike, that's the dance of blades, Isha. It goes the same way in politics as well. A blow landed, unchecked, builds confidence. We can't allow that. A parry is needed."

Panic fluttered through her belly as she considered the task given to her by Othwii. Watch. Listen. Report. "I understand." She drew herself up. "They want to demonstrate to the people of Jarik that they're strong with the hope of winning more to their cause."

"Aye, that's right." Wolst sat straighter in the saddle, an eyebrow raised. "It appears I attempt to teach a master."

As the only remaining Ironlight living in a land that was only half her own, making friends had always been difficult. Finding herself alone more often than not, she had a great deal of time to think about the way others interacted. Friendship, sadly, had been more of a strategy to her than a reality.

A crownguard signaled to his counterpart along the wall to open the gate. Pulleys whined and creaked, setting the Gate of the Tiger to groaning. Steel-banded wood rumbled upward, revealing the silhouette of the inside of the tiger's open mouth. Through it, Ishoa saw a waiting column of soldiers, three abreast. Behind them, a cold haze stretched over Jarik.

Many times over, Ishoa had stood where the Scarborn column now did. They faced a steel tiger with its lower jaw built into the earth such that only its fangs poked up from the ground. The upper jaw loomed over the heads of any who marched through its throat and into the keep.

"Scouts say two hundred," said one of Ishoa's crownguard.

"Nay." Though Wolst spoke calmly, Ishoa had known him long enough to recognize the purple hue creeping into his cheeks—the hyper focus in the set of his eyes. This was a man made for war. At the slightest scent of enemies, the faintest sound of steel scraping scabbard, he was prepared for impending violence. "A hundred and sixty by the sound of it. Have those scouts replaced."

The Scarborn passed under shadow through the tiger's mouth then emerged into daylight inside the walls. Each of the three columns was led by a Warnock. Ishoa found the match of Lodaris's parents...odd. His father, Ularis, was half a head shorter than his wife and had the pinched face and sharp stare of a hazel-eyed fox. A mane of crimson hair flowed like blood around thick mutton chops; it was no mystery which parent gave Lodaris his fiery visage. Scars across the bridge of Ularis's clean-shaven upper lip and chin told Ishoa that he didn't fear harassment for his lineage like so many other Scarborn. Presumably, he bore his scars with pride.

But it was Lodaris's mother who stirred greater mystery.

In the saddle, Lodecka Warnock sat as tall as any of the men behind her. A series of tight blond braids descended to chin length—a chin held perpetually high. She was broad in nearly every way except for lips so thin they could barely be named such. Only one side of her face had been scarred by the Jurati. But what made Lodecka uncommon—downright unnerving—were the other scars. Covering the other side of her face were dozens of self-inflicted wounds. If the whispers could be trusted, these were but the sprouts of an unseen root system Lodecka had carved into her entire body.

At her fourteenth birthday celebration, Ishoa had pressed Lodaris for the reason behind his mother's mutilation practices. "Because she says she's ten times the Scarborn," he had told her as he seemed to go somewhere else in his mind. His tone had become hollow and weak. "And so, she deserves ten times the respect of one." The way Lodaris seemed to disappear in that moment told Ishoa it was not a pleasant topic, so she had changed the subject.

At the fore of the third column, Lodaris's hazel eyes met Ishoa's. A smile rippled across his full lips. He glanced furtively at his mother, then shifted in the saddle.

Ishoa stifled her own excitement. *He's finally here.* For a long moment, she matched his gaze, eager for the distance between them to disappear. A wave of heat spread down her legs. What she wanted to do was sprint across the snow and leap onto his horse. But she was a princess. An Ironlight.

And he, a Scarborn.

Like both his parents, Lodaris wore plated warskirts, riding boots, and a black leather cuirass. Crimson enameled pauldrons were fixed to each shoulder, and he carried the Warnock standard. The sight of it made Ishoa nauseous, for it was soaked in a barbaric and shameful ritual. Three scarlet droplets of blood on a field of black symbolized the three scars given to babes by the Jurati. For Ishoa, it was a reminder that duty to Namarr came before her feelings for Lodaris. To say the banner rankled Ishoa's great-grandmother was an understatement. Officially, the hold at the Fringes belonged to the Keelers, a family of shipwrights. In function, however, the Warnocks had taken the hold as their own.

The column came to a halt.

Ishoa greeted them first. Wolst followed suit, offering a quick bow. Horse and soldier alike huffed steam into the frigid air as Ishoa waited longer than expected for return bows, each one deeper than her own.

"We are pleased to welcome you." Ishoa's eyes flitted toward a smiling Lodaris. "I am especially pleased to know your son, Lodaris, will be the first Scarborn Claimant to attempt the Trials."

"If only your great-grandmother shared such sentiment." Ularis squinted at the Ice Maiden's Keep. "Perhaps she would have greeted us herself. Or are we beneath such honors?"

"The duchess has not yet returned from Alistar." Wolst's tone was flat. "Busy ensuring the best for Anjuhkar and Namarr. Just as she's done since the Unity Wars." He emphasized the last. "She'll treat with you when she returns."

Gruff laughter came from somewhere behind Ularis Warnock. A man with a broad, flat face separated from the ranks and brought his steed alongside Lodecka's. The sight of the man summoned a bitter taste at the back of Ishoa's throat.

A charcoal beard reached wildly over a potbelly. Beady, piggish eyes regarded Wolst from under a boot-heel brow. "We need no grand reception, Warmaster. Pomp and ceremony is for those grown accustomed to parading their power," said the disheveled man. "Myself and the Scarborn are of a simpler nature."

He looks a pauper but bears himself like a lord.

"Syphion Muul. We are truly blessed to have a man of such..." Wolst smacked his lips. "...celebrity at the Trials this year."

So this is Syphion Muul. The zealot wore gray homespun robes covered in stains; how he could command the respect of anyone, or Belara Frost's concern for that matter, baffled Ishoa. *He looks more likely to pass out behind a tavern than to give a rousing speech.*

"If you haven't heard, I'm a supporter of the old ways. All of them." A smile twisted up one side of Syphion Muul's flat face. "So too are many others. As you'll see when the court votes on Revocation."

Leather creaked as Wolst strangled his horse's reins. Tension flooded the bailey. Ishoa's breath was trapped in her chest as silence dragged.

She could handle it no longer and blurted, "You've arrived earlier than expected. You—you're the first, actually."

Turning porcine eyes on Ishoa for the first time, Syphion's upper lip curled with disdain. "When you ride alongside those considered the lowest in honor, you must work all the harder to demand respect. Scarborn have not the privilege you possess, Highness. We cannot show up late to cause a stir of false importance. We cannot sweep into a room with a flourish to curry adoration for our unearned titles."

Ishoa's lips parted in shock, but she regained her composure and quickly closed them. Never had anyone spoken to her with such unbridled contempt.

"Syphion, you jest," said Ularis. "She's innocent."

"Indeed, an innocent! Aren't they all? Frosts, Quinns, Ironlights...exalted and righteous, every last one. We lowborn however are worthy only of their scratches and their scorn." He grabbed a Warnock mercenary by the collar of his cloak and pulled him forward. The man complied without hesitation, his demeanor placid as Syphion lifted a section of beard to reveal puckered purple scars tapering down the man's neck. "See, Highness? He was a baby when one of your Jurati bungled the scarring. Her claw nicked his artery and bled him pale. Just a babe...he nearly died." White slaver rimmed the corners of Syphion Muul's mouth. "Only by luck was he saved by a Sister of the Rose passing through town on her way to Jarik. Tell me, was he innocent?"

The man's feverish intensity prodded Ishoa's own ire. Fear and anger tumbled through her, vying for a response. Before she could manage one, Wolst stepped in. "A sad story, to be sure, Master Syphion. Life is full of such tragedies. I understand you've lost a daughter. My condolences to you. Clearly some ideologies can be harmful."

Syphion Muul bristled.

Ishoa had heard the gossip. The fanatic had refused to let his daughter eat any goods imported from Lah-Tsarra or Peladonia to prove his dedication to the cause of Revocation. As a result, she'd died of malnourishment.

Ishoa cleared her throat, affecting a diplomatic tone. "A child's life, whether Scarborn or other, should be left out of politics."

Bitterness crowded Syphion's words. "My daughter happily gave her life so that *real* Anjuhks could live theirs once more. Without vampiric overlords in distant lands bleeding the riches and resources from its hardworking people." He looked at Ishoa. "Do *you* think this just, Highness?"

Ishoa looked to Wolst. Her uncle's massive chest expanded and contracted with quickened breath. When she shifted her gaze back to Syphion and the Scarborn, she noticed Lodaris glaring at the Revocation fanatic.

"Maybe you should give it a rest for now, Syphion." Honeyed words from Ularis. "I'm sure the young lady is well versed in the idea of Revocation." A gust of wind stirred his mutton chops. "She's an Ironlight, after all. Who knows the desire for revolution better than Danath's own blood? She probably wishes for Anjuhkar to cede from Namarr as much as we do."

Silent until that moment, Lodecka Warnock spoke with quiet power and glanced at her son. "Not all who share blood are of the same mind." In apparent shame, the boy's eyes fell to the snow. Lodaris had alluded to having a distant and troubling relationship with his mother in their letters to one another.

Lodecka turned her attention to Wolst. "Has the Ice Maiden prepared for our soldiers? I assume you prefer a force as large and dangerous as ours camped *outside* your walls?"

A knight of Jarik chuckled. Wolst shot a withering look over a shoulder at the man, then locked eyes with Lodecka. "Aye. We have a space on the southern slopes. Though I assure you, we worry very little."

"In your place, I would have said the same." Lodecka thrust a fist in the air. "Scarborn!"

Like a rolling wave, the soldiers of the Fringes complied. Horsemen in the front third of the column and the foot soldiers behind snapped to attention. A long silence followed as they stood sentinel still, awaiting the next order.

"Captain Korpa," Lodecka said. "The Beast of Anjuhkar himself will show you to our camp. Take heed, Wolst is a warmaster. You may learn a great deal from him while you have his ear."

A stump of a man leading a horse limped from the ranks. Ishoa sucked in a breath at the sight of him.

Captain Korpa saluted Wolst. Nearly every inch of him was puckered with scars, a living canvas of opalescent and pinkish smears. Near unrecognizable as a human. A dark thought entered her mind as she considered that the damages might be self-inflicted.

Like Lodecka. Ishoa glanced at the woman and was met with a mirthless, thin-lipped smile.

With a voice like gravel, the stout Scarborn captain addressed Wolst. "Well met, Warmaster. I've been meaning to greet you since the Great Betrayal. I didn't see you do the deed, but I sure respect that you did it."

Wolst frowned. "What deed?"

The Scarborn captain's red-dotted tongue flicked out, wetting raw, puffy lips. "That helmet you're holding. I remember the bastard...Raeklord Sahuhd's war snake, Bloodhorn. I see the teeth have been removed. A good thing. I'm not sure what it might do to my mind were I to see those fangs again. I only wish I'd run behind you that day at the Forgotten Fields. The day you slew it. I was more impulsive then. Thought myself invincible." The Scarborn captain proffered his hands, surveying the papery flesh covering them. "I suppose maybe I am. Ain't many who get chewed up by a raek and live."

Wolst cleared his throat. "You may ride at my side, Captain." He lowered his voice so only Ishoa could hear. "When you're finished giving the Warnocks the new decrees, I'll meet you in your quarters."

The stout, scar-covered captain grunted as he mounted his horse with apparent discomfort. No man among the Scarborn seemed to think him unmanly or worthy of disrespect. All held attention. Once ahorse, spittle flew from sundered lips as the captain shouted at his mercenaries. "I won't tolerate another sloppy attention! You dogs embarrassed me in front of a war hero! The man who avenged my tattered hide! Any of you pathetic louts doesn't execute orders like a fucking god is getting ten lashes. Understand? Now show the Beast of Anjuhkar what a Scarborn soldier is!"

The crownguard were taken aback by the harshness of the captain. Even Wolst's brow knit when the man said his soldiers were sloppy. Ishoa had seen enough training to know the Scarborn were as poised and crisp as any warriors.

Wolst led the Scarborn to the Gate of the Bear and the southern slopes beyond, a handful of the knights of Jarik leaving with him.

Syphion Muul and the Warnocks, remained. Despite being surrounded by crownguard and a half dozen knights of Jarik, Ishoa felt suddenly exposed without Wolst there. Lodecka's icy gaze settled on Ishoa while Syphion and Ularis surveyed the walls ringing the grounds.

"You have more to say, Highness?" said Lodecka.

In Ishoa's mind's eye, her parents looked down on her. Waiting. Judging. She thought of the decrees given her by Othwii...by order of her great-grandmother, the duchess of Anjuhkar. A sharp, unyielding ache started in her belly. Thunder boomed in her chest.

I will prove myself.

She exhaled and rose in the saddle. "Master and Mistress Warnock, there have been some changes I need to make you aware of."

Ularis cupped an ear. "What's that, Highness? Please, speak up."

A knight of Jarik surged forward, spear leveled. "Do not mock—"

Ishoa whipped out a hand, cutting him off. "I can speak for myself, Sir."

"Power." Syphion Muul snorted derisively. "Power is a concept held only by those who *believe* they have it. You do well, girl."

Shame sent prickles across her skin. Anger followed. "You speak to Ishoa Ironlight. I'll be crown princess of Namarr in four years, Master Syphion. You'll address me as, Highness...pig."

The fanatic glared and whispered, "Highness."

It took a half minute for Ishoa's fire to cool. Lodaris's words sprang to the back of her mind. *You are strong. Stronger than you know.* She proceeded with a more restrained tone. "The Ice Maiden, Belara Frost, has decreed that the tithe for Scarborn to enter the Trials be doubled."

Lodecka sat stiffly, dead eyes boring into Ishoa. Ularis and Syphion fell to hushed conversation amongst themselves.

"Additionally, no Scarborn shall bear weapons in the High Hall." Ishoa forced herself to relax. *Watch. Listen. Report.*

Annoyance flickered in Syphion's eyes. The corner of Ularis's ever-present smile twisted sharply upward. *A nervous tick, perhaps?* Meanwhile, Lodecka bore a density of calm—like a glacier.

The second decree spurred no discussion. The Scarborn sat and waited in return. *They're angry but trying not to show it.* The decrees, she realized, were petty insults, meant to rile them. *And here I sit in silence, looking a fool. They know what I'm doing!*

Discomfort clamped around her every joint like an ice tiger's jaws. She locked eyes with Lodaris, stayed there one heartbeat too many. "That is all for now." She gave a shallow bow.

Lodecka indicated her son with a scoop of her chin. "Aren't you going to stay and speak with my boy, Highness? It's been a while. I know you're both eager to enjoy one another's company."

Lodaris blushed as he dismounted. Powdery snow flurried about his ankles. Shorter than Ishoa by a couple of inches, he was broad through the chest like his mother. "It is a week's ride from the Fringes, and I've been in the company of my parents and Syphion the entire way. It would be refreshing to share some time with you instead, Highness. Perhaps a stroll along the Blue River?"

As Lodaris gathered the reins of his destrier, his motions slowed as he seemed to notice Ishoa's lack of response. While she wanted nothing more than to be with him, the offer had come from Lodecka. And that gave her pause.

The young Scarborn's voice lost its joyous overtones. "Unless it would displease you to do so."

"No—well..." Ishoa stammered, her throat suddenly thick. "Perhaps."

"Come now, Highness," Ularis patronized. "You're to be ruler of Namarr one day. Surely you can decide whether or not to go on a walk."

Behind Ishoa, a crownguard spat.

Strike and counterstrike—that's the dance of blades, Isha. It goes the same in politics as well. She saw it more clearly than a frozen lake before her. The decrees were Ishoa's weapon in the absence of her great-grandmother. The duchess had known the Scarborn would work to goad Ishoa into upset.

She would give them no further satisfaction.

"Yes, of course. I only hesitate because I have important matters to attend this afternoon," she lied. "A stroll would be nice but it must be brief."

Strike and counterstrike... If politics are truly like the dance of blades, then uncle is wrong. One can allow a blow to go unchecked. A feint or false injury to lure the overconfident off balance.

She threw back her shoulders and gestured at Syphion. "When I am Crown Princess of Namarr, what if I forgave the Scarborn officially? What if I eliminated the Jurati?"

Behind her, a knight of Jarik whistled low. Syphion raised his singular line of thick eyebrow in surprise.

As soon as the words left her, Ishoa regretted the move. Although it was something she'd spent long hours considering after she'd first met Lodaris, to openly declare it could have lasting negative effects. She cursed herself.

"You ask me what I think?" Syphion watched her as a storm bear might watch a seal pup surface from a break in the ice. "I think there is no answer I can give to one who sees the Scarborn in need of forgiveness."

"She is a precious liar," said Ularis.

"Father," hissed Lodaris.

A sharp look from Lodecka summoned her son to her. Obedient but wary, like a beaten hound, Lodaris approached. Though the wind had stopped gusting, an icy feeling wound through Ishoa's cloak.

Lodecka leaned over in the saddle to whisper into her son's ear. A flush crept up the boy's neck, flares of red to match his hair.

Without another word, Lodecka bowed low to Ishoa, then nudged her horse to a walk in the direction of the Gate of the Bear. Ularis followed. The former ignored Ishoa while the latter stared down his thin nose at her like a fox honing in on a cornered rabbit.

"Precious indeed," said Syphion as he too pushed his horse past. "And woefully naive."

The bailey was all but empty. Only Ishoa and Lodaris and the pair of crownguard remained.

Finally, Ishoa was with her friend, a moment she'd desired every single day in the months they'd spent apart. When she had dreamed of their reunion, she had imagined laughter. Joy and fullness. Precious hours spent in the presence of someone who understood her.

But that was only a dream.

Lodaris stood nearby, dejected by whatever his mother had said. Icy winds returned, burrowing into Ishoa's bones. Stripped of the warmth of dreams, she felt completely and totally alone.

CHAPTER SIX

LITTLE FLY

A sunbeam peeks through a warped board in the wall just short of Akyris's face. He lays on the bed, dead asleep. An inarticulate moan accompanies a twitch. I take no credit for the unease. Whatever his nightmare, he conjured it himself.

I study my grandson. It's best to take the measure of children while they sleep. When their innocence is clearest.

A strong brow and high cheekbones highlight vibrant green eyes. A firm jawline tapers into a square chin. Dark hair, olive skin. He looks so much like my daughter. A good sign, for she's the strongest woman I know. She will bear the grief of his fate as I have.

I look at him through the jeweled eye of time...

All at once, every pane of light becomes a pathway into truth, reflecting a future and past inextricably woven into the ever-flowing braid of reality. Images of outcomes, of triumph and apocalypse, rush toward me. To disentangle a braid takes great effort but when there are no other choices, ease bleeds through effort. Each step, one deeper into the dark waters of surrender. I shudder at what must come to pass, shudder more at the images materializing of Akyris's future.

But before that day, if I am successful in training him, he will see as I see now. He will wield the power of the jeweled eye, and with it, he'll pierce the Veil of Illusions. Unhindered by tethers of the flesh, he will stand in the currents of creation, where energy ebbs and flows as a malleable force beneath one's Locus.

Akyris *will* master the River of conscious reality, and once he does, his Locus will be unrivaled in its power.

But first, the boy must wake up.

In one corner of his room, something props up a bolt of cloth cut from a grain sack against the wall. I lift it with my gnarled staff, revealing a few short book stacks. Unless he collects them out of a childish penchant to possess things, it's a good sign. A tome on top of the stack is open, a corner of a page folded—he reads them.

Minutes slip by. The sunbeam creeps up to the boy's face. With a frustrated sigh, Akyris draws a drab blanket overhead and turns onto his side. Escape from discomfort. Escape from the many burns life leaves.

Escape, a child's concept.

All think they are capable of it, yet no one ever seems to accomplish it. The truth is coarse—raw. Once a person's Path is set, there is no return.

A glimmer passes across the jeweled eye...

A sword slides into the boy's chest. The hand of a prince grips it. Akyris stares down—

I thrust the image from my mind, shift my weight to my bad hip, and wince. A floorboard creaks.

Akyris stirs. His breathing becomes rabbit-quick. He knows I am here but fears me an intruder, so he acts asleep.

Intuitive. Like me.

There's a rusted knife under his straw-stuffed pillow. He probes under the blanket for it, careful to conceal his movements. I have malicious intentions, he thinks. Of course, he fools me not at all. I see it happening. I see everything. Perhaps the dream of the past I forced him to observe has put him a little *too* on edge.

I clear my throat. "You're awake."

Akyris bolts upright, the knife shaking in his fist. He blinks, cocks his head. He's baffled to come face to face with a stunted old woman standing over his bed, a rich woman's shawl with tassels of gilded wire wrapped around her torso and held there with one hand. His eyes comb over me and narrow at the sight of the knotted walking staff grasped in my liver-spotted hand.

Something between a laugh and a grunt escapes me. My lower lip curls back as I smile. A prominent gum line pushes forward. I've been told since I was born I had more gums than teeth. My tongue wets my lower lip.

He blinks dumbly. I slam the butt of my staff against the floorboards. "You're in my room, boy."

Now he's truly awake. "What?" Wild-eyed, he stares at me, breathing like a cornered possum.

With effort, I bend forward, lean onto my staff so my face is only a couple feet from his. "Let me be utterly clear. You are sleeping on *my* bed."

"But this is my—" is all Akyris manages to say before I snap my fingers an inch from his nose.

"You're not gettin' it, kid. Get out of the bed, get dressed, change my sleeping mat's linens you're currently soiling, and then don't come back into this room until I tell you. Understand?"

He doesn't.

I straighten up, at least as straight as I ever get. There's always a slant to my body caused by a weak hip. "I've traveled a long way to be here. I'm tired and have much work to do."

"Who...who are you?" he says, breathless. Impulsively he adds, "Besides a rude old hag."

Even he's taken aback by his insult. Instead of apologizing, his lips bunch around his mouth in mannerless repose. He thrusts his chin up at me like he's leveling a weapon at an opponent in a duel. Defiance to be broken.

My tongue fills a cheek. I shake my head.

Righteous, confident, and impulsive. The last is foolish. It must die. Like so much of Akyris, I'll strip it away for good and all. To enter the River untethered, the soul needs to be naked—free of its reactive nature.

"I'm your grandmother."

Akyris blinks, frowns.

"You're a bit thick, aren't you?" I sigh. "How old are you now?"

"Twelve."

Not even in his teen years.

Through the jeweled eye of time, I watch a sword slide into his chest, a prince's hand wrapped around the hilt. An image from long ago—nothing more.

"Akyris, you're two times too old to be half so thick. Now go." I reach forth with the head of my staff and prod his ribs. My bitter tones leech away, become like that of a mother cooing a baby to sleep as the boy rises from his pallet on the floor. "That's right...there you go."

He retrieves his sandals. The scowl says it all. He hates me fiercely. My grandson, the first time I've really met him, wants me gone as soon as I've arrived.

Exactly what is needed.

"Don't forget your toy," I say. I flip his sleeping pallet over in a swirl of musty blankets and twine bundled straw. His knife clatters to the floor. Pinning it with the butt of my staff like a speared fish, I whisk it past him, send it skittering out the door.

With a growl, he scoops it up.

"Wait," I call as he leaves. "You forgot to change the linens."

But he's already gone.

That's when Magomedes arrives, her essence burbling from the River and into my ears across incomprehensible distances. "The future hangs in the balance." She isn't angry, but her tone betrays that she's as close as she's ever been. "And you choose to use a hornet's sting rather than honey with our only chance?"

"You may feel the future, Mags, but I see it. Think! Why is it we are more likely to remember each time we are stung, but not each time we eat honey? The more painful an experience, the greater the power it holds over us. I need him associating me with such power, or I'll have no control of him when it's needed. Now stop your pestering."

I withdraw from the River. Magomedes's consciousness recedes from my mind. If she wanted, she could hunt the energetic pulse of my Locus, but such violations are reserved for emergencies only.

Her previous warning conveys a growing unrest that I frankly cannot stand. Mags is led by her feelings. By frantic worry. If I had her Awakened powers rather than my own, I might do the same. But that's not how I operate. I need my focus on the task at hand, fully, completely, and without fail. Not on doomsday theories stoking fear that isn't yet here.

The sleeping pallet isn't so soft as it looks. The floor beneath is hard and unyielding. I ease myself down and cross my legs.

I access my Locus—let power flow through me.

I watch Akyris through the jeweled eye...

He searches for his mother. Stumbling through the dirt, indignation wears him like a tattered shirt. He struggles to shake the fog of one so freshly and rudely awakened.

Multiple times he circles the cottage and casts looks of outrage at his room where I now sit, unaware that I watch him through supernatural means. The last place he fails to find his mother is the chicken coup. He curses aloud.

I leave my power behind and make my way bodily to the porch to give him a boost.

When he comes around the corner, his head is down and he's muttering. "How can it be my grandmother...she's my grandmother?"

"Exactly," I say.

Startled, he stumbles then pitches onto hands and knees in the dirt. He rolls onto his backside, chest heaving with animalistic fear. When he sees it's just me, he curses. For the second time in an hour, I come to stand over him.

"If you insist on delaying the preparation of my room in order for you to get a handle on reality, further wasting both of our time, I'll help you." I gesture in the direction of the town square. "Your mother is that way, buying fruit from a trader. Hurry now." I grimace, wave a hand before my nose. "Your bed smells."

I pull my shawl tight across my chest and hobble back inside, leaning heavily into my oak staff. I'm content with my lie. Unpredictability forces a mind to greater focus. I must keep him guessing to hold his attention on me and the work we must do.

I watch him through the jeweled eye...

He seeks his mother in the town square, jaw clenched with determination, a much-needed quality for what's coming. A caravan train forms a crescent at the center of town. One wain is from Anjuhkar, guarded by a pair of scar-faced men. Its driver bears the crest of a cattleman: a bull horn crossing with a maul on a brown and white checkered field. The rest of the wains are from Peladonia, stamped with the sigil of the Golden Silos: a pair of sickles with the blades turned outward.

Fruitlessly, the boy searches the market square until he finds trouble. Or more accurately, trouble finds him. The homely blond girl from his dreams catches him by a sleeve. He's whirled around to face her. "Sima?"

She's no goddess as Akyris claimed. I suppose for young men, the girl who gets you to overcome your fear of them enough to match lips must hold the power of some kind of god. When I consider my daughter's own beauty, how the world's history and its future is shaped in secret by women with ready lips and a willingness to use them dangerously, I know the enchantment Akyris has fallen under.

As much as a man's devotion to women is a curse, it is all that keeps the world from destruction.

Sima's hand flies, staggers the boy with a slap across the cheek. He never saw it coming.

But I did. It's the very reason I sent him to the square. He'll never forget to meet her at the barn again, but not for a lack of desire.

I knew if the girl saw Akyris soon enough after their missed date, she would hurt him. More important than the physical pain was the emotional finality. It was an echo of possibilities forever closed. Akyris has too much pride to seek her forgiveness. I knew if she slapped him he would be just as done with her as she was with him.

No outside attachment.

No pressure impeding our future trainings.

No worries about having something better to do. Our work is all that matters. Sima's life would be saved, but only if she felt rage when she found Akyris in the town square.

Only if she struck him.

And so another piece falls into place.

Recovered, Akyris watches Sima flee the crowd, tears trailing. He's hurting now. I need that pain coursing through him. I need him to *need* me gone. If he hates me enough, he'll overcome the internal barriers necessary to Awaken.

To defeat the Arrow of Light.

He looks at his hand for some sense of the familiar, an experience I know all too well from my time atop Unturrus. He's hoping he still has five fingers, a palm, and a crescent-shaped burn from the time he tripped into a cook-pot as a toddler.

Red finger imprints mark his cheek. The muscles in his jaw jump. Everything in order as it should be. He makes a fist, curses. "Wretched hag!" he shouts. He draw the stares of many nearby who know him well. They wonder at how he could speak with a vitriol typically reserved for a drunk six tankards deep. His mother, a light against darkness, a polished diamond among coal, would never tolerate such disrespect—they know this.

A pair of young women twist into one another's ears, whispering and laughing. A Scarborn caravan guard offers him some free advice, which Akyris takes but only because he's too enraged to do anything but listen. "Sometimes they cry. Stay strong, boy. She'll be back. It's when they leave you without tears that you need to worry."

Akyris approaches the town's constable, who leans against a wain eating an apple and watching the crowd. His gut peeks over a belt from which hangs a rusted mace. The corroded black honor plate of a shadowguard tells of glory days come and gone.

"Have you seen my mother?" Akyris asks.

The constable, who would be a criminal if he wasn't a lawman, sniffles then spits in the dirt. "Was here. Saw her heading in the direction of the orchard some time ago." A comely woman saunters by. The constable tosses his apple core in the dirt and then pats Akyris's shoulder before following her.

Sometime later, Akryis stops running and comes to a rest under a shadow-dappled canopy. Between heaving breaths, he shouts for my daughter. Light beats through the branches, obscuring pickers' faces and making his search more difficult.

He'll not be deterred. He finds her and latches onto her shoulders.

Brow creased, she turns...

My daughter is as beautiful as ever. The lines of age work with her looks more than detract from them. She's still a few decades from the crash of pride that comes with the loss of feminine allure.

"You have to come back to the cottage!" Akyris pleads. "A woman claiming to be your mother is there. I think she's a swindler who came in with the caravan's—she could be robbing us right now!"

I chuckle. He's convinced himself of anything but the truth to be rid of me. That's how I know he's where I want him. As much as it pains me.

To my daughter's credit, she does as I've instructed. Exactly what is needed. That's the true horror of my Path. Using her like this. We both know what it is and yet understand there can be no other way.

She has always known when. Has always known why.

"Calm down, Aky." She lays a gentle hand on Akyris's chest. "She's no swindler. She is my mother. Your grandmother."

The air seems to leave him. Shoulders deflate.

"She didn't treat you kindly, did she?" My daughter's chin dips. "I'm sorry."

Mouth agape, a frantic expression emerges on Akyris's face. His mother sniffs sharply and then turns her back on him to fill another basket with apples. In the void of expectations unmet, of hurt unconsoled, he's crippled by shock.

"Unfortunately, that's nothing new about my mother. I dare to say I believe this will be good for you. She is difficult at first, but she can teach you a great deal."

My daughter pauses, seeming to consider something. Sunlight spins off the red and yellow blotched fruit in her hand. "If you're willing to learn, that is."

Akyris watches his mother as if she's a rabid animal. Worry laces his tone. "How long will she be with us?"

My daughter says nothing.

"I see." Hands limp at his sides, concern bunching his brow, he makes to leave.

"Akyris." My daughter's tone is grave as she adds one last dagger of advice. "Do as she says. Do it without question."

The Path continues to be laid, one step at a time.

Caked in dust and defeat, Akyris returns to the cottage. I await him on the porch. He drags himself down the lane as if fate itself carries him by the scruff.

In reality, it is my hand holding his neck.

"You look like the dog of a strict and unforgiving master." I offer a wanton grin. "Life got you down, little fly?"

He glares. Our eyes lock.

With a hand blocking the sun, I look past him, back toward town square and the orchard beyond. "You didn't get what you wanted in the market square. And you certainly didn't hear the news you wished for in the orchard." I adopt a mocking frown. "Bad day?"

A voice from the River flows through my mind. "If you destroy the boy's spirit, you destroy us all."

I'm busy and so respond unkindly. "Sometimes, Mags, I wonder if you're nothing more than a glorified wind chime. I don't need you to tell me its raining when I'm already soaked."

"Without me, you would not know what comes. You would be blind to the Path. Susceptible to—"

I ignore her. Akyris stands before me. Disdain overcoming incredulity, he makes to speak. His fists shake with hate. He opens his mouth to confirm as much. I wave a hand dismissively, silencing him. "Save it for someone who cares, little fly. Just make sure my bed is satisfactory when I seek it, which will be shortly. You're not the only one with heavy thoughts on the mind."

My consciousness flows alongside Magomedes's. "Learn to take a joke, Mags."

Magomedes is silent a moment. "I find little mirth anymore. I feel it all, feel it so strongly. The pain...like a drink of water that will not stop flowing...it chokes me, forces its way down my throat to fill me when all I want is a breath of air. Each month that passes, I sense the future dimming. Can you imagine seeing the lights of the night sky winking out of existence by the second? It happens. The darkness comes. The Arrow of Light comes." Awe edges her tone. "Unstoppable."

I grit my teeth. "Talk to me when you have something new to say."

As Akyris walks past, he punches the frame of the front door. I feel his frustration, though it is for different people and different reasons. To the sound of curses and the rustle of linens being changed, I reflect on our first day's work.

The seed of fear Magomedes has planted fuels me to be harsher with Akyris than I intended. But I've learned to trust. Such things occur as they are meant to, regardless of my preference or tampering. For what Magomedes in all her wisdom and power has yet to discover is almighty trust.

As much as the future is fickle, the past is solid and certain. What it tells me is things continue forward. The future persists even when bleak.

I fight fear with wisdom.

I whisper into the River. "Trust, Mags. Trust."

CHAPTER SEVEN

MOONLIGHT AND MENACE

E ven Digtown's rain had a violating touch. It found every angle left unprotected by Garlenna's cloak and soaked through any stretch of fabric she'd failed to treat with beeswax. In the alley adjacent the Dregs Inn, it was dark beyond the lantern light. It was there, she waited.

In the distance, Barodane wandered down the main road in a stupor, his every thought and action dictated by the godsthorn coursing through his system. High as he was, her pleas would fall on deaf ears. Nevertheless, she needed to keep an eye on him.

She pulled her cloak tight at the throat as rain swept over the high collar of her leather vest, scoring her cheeks. *Of all your decisions, Barodane, living here is most worthy of question.*

Her prince had withered some, losing both fat, muscle, and a once-healthy tint to his caramel skin. To see him in such a state was difficult. The worst of it had hit her the moment they'd locked eyes. It was as though someone else had taken over the reins of the man she once knew. Gone was the passionate leader. Gone was the prince born of hero's blood. The mirthful humor she loved him for had been replaced by bitter cynicism. Of the friend she once knew, only darkness and disdain remained.

She hoped she was wrong, that some part of Barodane Ironlight was still there. She prayed to the Sempyrean:

Payon, may he be centered by your hand.

Ozoi, may the fire of his soul burn for what is just and true.

Maletha, may his path flow unimpeded.

Srah, may all your good surround him and all evil drift away like smoke.

She considered sending one last prayer to the fifth god, Nacronus, the Taker of Light, Scion of the Abyssal Sea, Lord of the Maw Eternal, but thought better of it. *He's danced with the dark god long enough, I think.*

She stepped into the muddy thoroughfare to follow her prince, keeping close to the shadows of quiet storefronts. *Of course, it couldn't be so simple as a conversation. I have to break him free of his self-indulgent nightmare.*

Rain crept into her small clothes, further evidence to her idea that it made prey of what could be no more destitute. Yet there were those who sought to match the rain's unrelenting predation.

A man stood between buildings across the street. He beckoned her to join him for a drink in the shadows. He was shirtless and shaky. Wraith-like. "Your size is no problem for me." He spoke in soothing tones. "I like a wench who don't break easy."

She ignored him.

"Come now. I'm cold. You don't want me to shiver to death, do ya?"

I wouldn't mind if you did.

All it took was a glance toward her harasser to lose the prince. Barodane was gone. She sighed inwardly; it could be a long, wet night of cat and mouse with someone dedicated to losing her.

I'm fooling no one but myself skulking about like this.

Forgoing cover, she stepped from the shadows and hurried toward the town well where she'd last seen Barodane. She slowed, searching muddy tracks barely visible in the cloud-thick night. Digtown was a small settlement. Nowhere near so busy as most towns of a similar size, but the day's thoroughfare had combined with the unceasing rain to drown out any discernible tracks. Her hopes of finding which direction Barodane had gone were dimming.

She drew back the hood of her cloak to listen. Rain pounded against rooftops. Distant laughter and music drowned out the rest.

She exhaled. A puff of steam sacrificed to the night sky. Water dripped from her nose and soaked her leather eye-patch, setting it to itching. It was not in her to give in, but falling ill her first week in Digtown would not serve her mission. Given Barodane's initial response, it seemed clear he'd make this difficult for her. Time and patience were required. *Barodane, stubborn as you are, you'll soon remember I am more so.*

She drew her hood overhead, then made her way back to her room at the Dregs.

"Sweet wench," called the shirtless man with the soothing tones. "Thank the Sempyrean! The gods have sent you back to me. Thought I might not be enough man for ya, so I got us a friend."

A brutish companion stood at the sweet talker's side. They were no longer under the cover of shadow and instead watched her from a tavern front lit by torches. The sign over the entrance showed a man pissing into a cup. *Thank you, Barodane, for choosing the Dregs.* She thought perhaps Meckin's blustery brag about having the best inn in town was not false after all.

The brutish man said, "The three of us are sure to keep warm together." More promise than threat.

Garlenna watched them from the periphery of her good eye as she went. The rain stopped suddenly and a break in the clouds admitted a glaring moon.

"You mean to be a cold bitch?" The brute's eyes shone with menace. When they tromped through the mud toward her, she turned to face them.

"Oh, she's big indeed! I seen her before in the Dregs. Damn fine hair. Clean. Bet it smells sweet." The shirtless man swooned with excitement. "Come now, I know why you walked back this way. A giant woman like you is sure to be lonely."

Fearless, the brute moved forward. "You get her legs."

Garlenna pulled back her cloak at the hip to reveal an arm-length flanged mace. Four corners for the four gods of light each capable of stoving in a fool's skull. A heavy ball-counter on the bottom made of black iron denoted the fifth god, Nacronus. It gleamed in the moonlight. The brute stopped in his tracks. He looked her up and down. Blinked. Confused.

"What's wrong?" said the sweet talker. "Ya 'fraid of a woman, Hack?"

"Ain't afraid, damn it! Just thinkin' is all."

"Why ain't she runnin'?" said the sweet talker.

I don't run. Steel whispered through the leather thong as she drew her mace. She stepped in their direction.

"Well...I ain't fuckin' with her." The sweet talker threw up his hands. "Apologies wench, we'll entertain ourselves now."

The big man, Hack, backpedaled two measured steps, tongue darting nervously over his lips. "You're uh...you're free to go on your way." Panic cracked his voice.

Garlenna replaced her mace. "I always was."

The rest of the way to the Dregs, only mud dogged her boot heels. *No wonder everyone avoids this place. Its reputation is not falsely earned.*

It was both surprising and not surprising that her prince had lived among Namarr's worst for as many years as he had. No self-respecting hold lord would come anywhere near the place, ensuring Barodane's identity would remain safe. Having never seen the Mad Prince, common folk would be unlikely to assume their local godsthorn dealer was anything more than what he claimed to be. Especially with hair worn long in the way of the Lah-Tsarene rather than the short-cropped style of his Kanian lineage. The short beard and honor plate of one retired to the shadow-guard helped too.

The real question was what would make him leave.

To know that answer, Garlenna needed to know what forced him to stay.

Where I go, suffering follows, he had said.

He hates himself. I need to help him see it differently.

Her boots thudded up the boarded steps of the landing outside the Dregs Inn. Before she entered, a muffled cry drew attention to the corner of the landing. Torchlight revealed the leg of a man sitting propped against the side of the building. Another man's naked foot and grimy arm worked busily over the first in a flurry of motion. Shadows swallowed the rest.

Garlenna's first thought was about lovers doing what lovers do—paid or otherwise. But then she heard a man's strained cries, "Bastard...stop."

Does it ever stop?

Garlenna leapt into the mud, torchlight rippling along her mace. "What happens here?"

Her eye had yet to adjust to the dark again, but it made no matter. The bare-footed assailant fled down the alley to the safety of deeper shadows.

She approached the victim. "Are you hurt?"

A pained grunt. By the sound of his breathing, he was alive and would continue to be. She'd heard death rattles before. This was no such thing.

She crouched beside him and watched his features resolve. In a matter of moments, she saw it was the young man who'd accompanied Hyram Olabran. "Jennim, right?"

He nodded. Through ragged breaths he said, "Bastard was robbing me."

"You've been beaten. Badly."

"I think I knew that." He tried sitting straighter and winced. "Not the first time. Wait—I know you. You were with Kord."

"Did Hyram do this to you, Jennim?"

He winced, nodded. "He ain't happy with Kord."

Leaning in, Garlenna lowered her voice. "And the message?"

"Message?"

"The one he intended to send by beating you."

Jennim shook his head.

"I figured as much. Hyram gets what he wants, doesn't he?"

A swell of heat rose off the young man moments before he sobbed. Spittle slung outward from his mouth onto his chest. "Sempyrean protect me! He's gonna kill me. I know it. He told me he would if I didn't make good on my promise. I thought Kord would go along with the fuckin' deal. Why wouldn't he want to get away from here? Go somewhere nice...get a lady like my momma again."

Garlenna's eye narrowed. "Your momma?"

"Yeah. He was with her a lot the first couple of years he came to Digtown. Then we left for Breckinbright." A spasm of pain made Jennim clutch his ribs. He grunted. "She gave me up to a Sempyrean orphanage hoping I'd have a better life. Clearly that didn't work out. I didn't stay long."

Garlenna glanced either direction down the alley. He could be bait for an ambush. She lowered her voice even more. "How did you come into the company of Hyram?"

"Wish I never had. They say a man has regrets at the end of his life. Since I'm destined for the Eternal Maw soon, I can say meeting Hyram is mine." Jennim's chin sank to his chest, a sad calm fell over him. "I watched him kill 'em. A group of priests in West Headwaters who didn't want to sell their stake—"

"Priests?" Garlenna's tone slapped the air. Jennim shrank back. Wide eyes told the story of a hard life where beatings were commonplace.

"I'm sorry, Jennim. It's just that I was raised by priests for a time. Like you." It was only half a lie. "It surprised me to hear you say they were involved in the dealing of godsthorn." She'd met enough priests to know they were capable of any atrocity. Priests, farmers, mothers, princes, criminals, they were all just people, which meant some were well-intentioned while others were quite the opposite.

However, West Headwaters was where she'd been when she'd received the message from her father, Gyr Renwood telling her Prince Barodane lived. It also told her the harrowing discovery that necessitated his return to power.

Namarr is fracturing. Scothea, rising.

"They weren't all bad," Jennim said. "The priests said they needed the money to start a soup kitchen."

Doubtful.

"I take it Hyram wasn't interested in their reasons?"

Jennim shook his head. "Hyram don't care about money, he's a full-blood Olabran. He's got plenty. He wants territory. He wants people to know he's in charge, and he doesn't want to share power with anyone. It's easier and cheaper to buy dealers out rather than hire men to kill 'em. But he'll do that too, like he did those priests." Sadness washed over Jennim's face. "That dumb bastard Eustus held a dagger to my throat and made me watch as they lined 'em up. Hyram forced 'em to kneel and pray. He—he had their hands tied up and stretched out flat across the floor. One mason, shorter than the rest but mean enough to account for it, hammered their fingers to pulp. The mangled piles..." Jennim's eyes were distant. "The priest's screams...I couldn't keep my dinner down. The worst part was Hyram toying with them. After each one, Hyram asked 'em, 'will you sell now?' Even if they said yes. He didn't listen, he was just taking out his agitations. Once their hands were ruins, he said, 'What good are priests who can't pray?' then had the mean mason with fancy armor cave their heads in."

"The small, mean mason," Garlenna said. "Was he ugly like a pig?"

Jennim nodded. "Name was Alder or Alger...something like that."

The War Pig?

Sir Alber Gwinn was Roddic Olabran's knight-captain. A notoriously hate-fueled man famous for covering himself in pig blood before battle. He was intractable and unpredictable. The War Pig's involvement in Hyram's drug endeavors meant the young lord likely acted with his father's permission.

Tears raced down Jennim's reddened cheeks. "They had a wine cask they were going to stuff me in. You ever felt what it's like to stare at your own reflection in a barrel of wine meant to drown you? I ain't had a drink since. They knew I could bring in other dealers. I could set up a meeting or take my last drink." Jennim's head slammed back against the building in despair. "Gods, they're gonna kill me."

"How many masons does Hyram have"

Jennim's shoulders shook as his crying intensified. "I don't wanna die."

Garlenna stood, towering over him. "How many masons does Hyram have with him?"

For the first time, Jennim seemed to register how imposing Garlenna was. He sniffled and calmed some. "He doesn't usually call on more than half a dozen, but he can get more."

"And Kord?" she asked.

"What about him?"

"What's his muster?"

"You mean, who works for him?"

She nodded.

"Madame Gratha's nephew, Danuuk. Not much of a fighter, but he might stand by him. The Redhand brothers are always up for violence. Hyram knows about Danuuk."

"You told him?"

Jennim winced. "Kord isn't the mustering type is what I told him. If things ain't changed since I was young, he hasn't needed it. I could count on one hand the amount of times he had to deal with issues in an unkindly way when I was little. He was always more likely to get one of Imralta's girls to do things in a sneaky fashion or handle it himself. One look in Kord's eyes was usually enough to keep people from starting trouble."

"Imralta's girls? Say more."

"The Gem Loft." A wistful smile emerged through the tears. "Where my mom used to live. Where I grew up."

"Ah," Garlenna said. Imralta would undoubtedly be the madame there. "Thank you, Jennim."

She helped him to his feet. "Fuck me!" Jennim took in a sharp breath. "Gentle now, I think they got a rib."

Once standing, Garlenna lay hands along both his sides. "Hold still." She pressed softly and told him to breathe. He whined as she repeated the process a handful of times. "They just angered it. I doubt it's broken. With rest, you'll be fine."

"Don't know about that," he whispered. "I've got to convince Kord. I've got to. If he doesn't sell to Hyram, I'm dead."

The young man had sealed his fate. Hyram didn't seem the type to break such promises. Sadness weighed down on her at the prospect. *Jennim seems a decent man.*

The deal he'd attempted to broker was harmless. One could even say it was altruistically motivated on Barodane's behalf. Garlenna suspected that Jennim saw Barodane as a father figure. *Perhaps I can use him as leverage to get Barodane to sell. Let Hyram have his territory. Barodane can deal with him once he has the crown back.*

Garlenna was a realist. Life was worthless here; no one thought that more than those living in it. Jennim knew it. Hyram, too. But Garlenna wasn't heartless. She hoped Barodane wasn't either. Jennim could be used for a greater purpose.

"I don't know why I'm telling you all this, lady."

"Call me, Gyra," she said. "Maybe because you know I can help you."

This drew a suspect look from Jennim. "How so?"

"Well, Kord has at least one person who'll fight for him," she said. "Though I'd prefer to see him sell to Hyram as much as you would. What's your plan?"

"Recover. Track down Kord. Beg my ass off and hope my life is worth enough to change his mind."

"Here," Garlenna helped him onto the raised landing of the Dregs, then pressed a silver wheel into his palm. "Find bonethistle. It'll help you recover faster and numb the pain a bit. That way you can start begging Kord sooner."

Jennim unlimbered his arm from around her shoulders and stood under his own power. His wiry, red beard looked almost manly in the torchlight. "Why?" He studied the silver wheel in his hand. "Why help me? Why help Kord?" He shook his head. "I've not lived so long as yourself but still long enough to know if you get a silver wheel from a stranger it means they want something you shouldn't give 'em."

"Kord used to be my friend." Garlenna's voice was somber. "I would see him live."

"Kord had a friend?" Jennim huffed, cradled his side. "I'll be damned."

Garlenna turned to leave. The days ahead would require her full energy, and for that she needed sleep. The door to the Dregs thudded open. As she made her way up the stairs to her room, Meckin offered her a drink. She declined.

Outside her room, she listened, cautious of any traps Hyram or the lovely citizens of Digtown might have for her. A man and woman in a nearby room panted, moaned in ecstasy, fell silent. Nothing else. Out of habit, she paused in the doorway before stepping through, one hand on the dagger's hilt strapped across her chest. Given how the day had gone so far, she imagined being attacked on her way to bed a fitting way to top it off.

Once she deemed the space clear of danger, she set to hanging wet clothing on hooks. Then she went to her rucksack and emptied it.

Polish and a rag for her mace. Cook supplies for the open road. A change of undergarments. Sewn into the bottom of the bag, the letter from her father. She worked a knife along the bottom, popping threads holding back secret folds, then drew the letter forth:

Dearest Daughter,

I know I've put duty above all else since I entered the life of a prosort. That meant sacrifice. Other things for which I care about greatly have faltered. As you know, a servant to Crown and Sempyrium is consumed by duty.

I feared, given my age and profession, I would wait too long to tell you these words in person. I'll wait no longer.

I should have cared for you in equal measure to my duty. You deserve so much more than what I gave you. As a father, I am sorry. As a fellow prosort, I could not be more proud. Truly, you are the greatest the Sempyrium has ever seen.

You may wonder why the long admission of shame-laced truth. Why, after so many years, have I finally reached out? The gods of the Sempyrean, it seems, push us when we fail to push ourselves to do and say what is right.

There is impetus.

Both myself and Duke Malus are most direly concerned for the future of our nation. Our spies report of a threat rising yet again in Scothea. A young messiah seizes power in the east. We imagine it only a matter of time before Scothea invades again.

What is more concerning still is the most recent vote of the Collective. We believe there is a traitor at the highest level who actively orchestrates Namarr's downfall. We have found evidence of spies in Brighthaven. On our very own doorstep!

At least one of our own has turned against us.

We are a sundered nation once more. Dark clouds of Revocation hang over Belara Frost's seat of power in Anjuhkar, threatening Ishoa Ironlight's crowning. The Collective in Alistar feuds. We suspect one among their number desires the crown for themselves.

We cannot allow this.

Namarr needs to be unified. Otherwise it faces destruction. As my daughter and as a prosort of the Sempyrium, I task you, Garlenna Renwood, with finding Prince Barodane Ironlight.

I know this may come as a shock to you, but we've been given word from Locastrii herself to seek him out in Digtown. Get Solicerames into his hands. Raise the name of Ironlight across the land. Once you find him, go to Nserthes the Sophophant on Martyr's Isle for further instruction.

We cannot allow Barodane to fall into the enemy's hands—whoever they may be.

As for you and I, it's no secret time has been lost to us.

When your mission is complete and the United Lands of Namarr rest easy once more, it would warm my heart to see you. The years have been too many, our conversations too few. I would make amends.

I beg you to forgive the lateness of my admissions. May the Sempyrean watch over you always,

Gyr Renwood

Tears threatened. She cleared her throat, choking down the emotion there. She folded the letter and then sewed it back into place at the bottom of the rucksack.

Worry slipped into her dreams, blurring the lines between sleep and wakefulness. Once, she woke to find herself rubbing her forehead, elbow raised in the air.

Is the Barodane I knew gone?

Despite the day's disappointments and difficulties, there was a sense of aliveness she'd long missed, a purpose in serving her prince again that made her heartbeat quicken.

He cannot be gone. I will not allow it.

After Barodane had disappeared fourteen years earlier, she'd spent countless nights covering the tracks of her sins and hunting the guilt and pain down to the root. Some mornings she rose clutching her mace, tears streaming from her eyes. *No matter what I do, it shall remain a dark, indomitable ballast in my soul until my dying breath.*

Until that day came, there was one other thing she would hold to with abject certainty. A hill not built upon the bones of the innocent, but upon a purpose greater than herself.

She would restore Prince Barodane to the Crown. She would watch him raise the Slave Banner, Solicerames.

Only death can stop me.

CHAPTER EIGHT

WARNING

Excitement rushed through Ishoa. When she returned to her chambers in the Sister Keep, she set to chewing her nails as she paced, waiting for Wolst.

Her time with Lodaris had been a blur. Together they'd strolled the bailey under the watchful eye of crownguard. As promised, she'd kept the interaction brief, a thing made easier by Lodaris's sour mood. Lodecka's whispers stained their interaction, dampening the joy Ishoa expected.

Letters were one thing. Being at her best friend's side was another. The indelible feeling of belonging he sparked radiated through her heart and pulsed in her hands.

Energy surging, Ishoa sought an outlet.

She crept past a sleeping Rakeema to her wardrobe. The hooks holding her formal garb gave a hiss as she swept them aside. The sight of her leather training vest and studded, fur-lined skirt made her smile. Anxious fury pumped through her veins, and training was the only way to quell it.

There was a proper order to battle dress, she'd learned. Boots and warskirt came first, followed by a fur-lined leather training vest. Then it was onto steel half-helm and gauntlets before strapping a short sword and rounded shield on last. The shield was always a little tricky to affix with one hand, but Ishoa was working diligently to master the skill.

In a reversal of roles, she padded to the bed where her young ice tiger slept and cleared her throat. Nothing. Frowning, she performed a series of movements meant to loosen her muscles that Wolst had taught her, hoping the creak of leather armor would wake Rakeema. Usually it did—not this time. Rakeema was growing, and sleep was vital for her to be a healthy war cat. Plus, she had just fallen asleep under a swath of sunlight. Ishoa's anjuhtarg was the most precious thing in her life, and never more so than in that moment of sleeping innocence. Part of her felt guilty about waking the anjuhtarg. But Ishoa was fourteen, so impatience overcame motherly instinct.

She drew her short sword then brought it against the steel cap on her shield with a resounding clang.

Rakeema leapt into a low stance. Jade eyes froze on Ishoa, instinct assessing threat. Ishoa bulled forward, pushing Rakeema over with the shield and exposing the cat's white-furred belly. She tossed the sword onto the bed and mercilessly scratched the pinned anjuhtarg.

Rakeema clutched the shield between her paws then bit the rim. Ishoa laughed. The cat's back legs kicked upward, scraping against the steel rim.

"Wretched, love! You dare unsheathe claws at me?" Ishoa said with mock incredulity. In a year's time, the anjuhtarg would be three times this size, twice that of any hound in the High Hall. In two years, she'd be a battle-ready war cat capable of bearing armor.

Rakeema twisted awkwardly to her feet, bounded backward, hindquarters high, tail lashing the air. Her jaws were parted, relaxed. Unmoving, she watched Ishoa as if she were a rat scrabbling across the floor. Rakeema's mouth closed, eyes hyper-focused.

Her forelegs tensed.

"Oh, really?"

When Wolst had given her the anjhutarg, he'd told her to train it every day or else the war cat could grow up unruly and dangerous, even to Ishoa. So she did. Rakeema needed to know who her master was. Taking a defensive stance, Ishoa whirled away and shouted, "Sajac!"

Rakeema bounded after, sliding into position beneath her shield arm and facing the door. Ishoa imagined C'Dathun trolls filling its frame, crude weapons in their clawed hands.

The trolls didn't realize they faced an Ironlight and her war cat. No meager foes.

The ice tiger growled, a low crackle like that of a glacial chunk the moment it crumbled. Ishoa moved one direction, then the other. Rakeema mirrored the movements. Sloppy. A slight lag kept her from staying directly under Ishoa's shield arm. At four months old, Ishoa thought it decent progress.

"Heeti!" she barked in Fjordsong, the tongue of ancient Anjuhkar, then slashed forward.

Rakeema leapt sideways to divide their imagined enemy's focus, then leapt again to put herself in the blind flank of any right-handed attacker. If it were a live drill, Rakeema would have taken the assailant's leather-protected arm in her young but powerful jaws and bore them to the ground, then gripped their padded neck with a second bite. Once properly trained, Rakeema would be the white and gray doom of any foe.

"Sajac." Rakeema broke off her attack and sped to her master's side. They repeated the maneuver twice more. On a third attempt, Rakeema flopped onto her back and kicked playfully at Ishoa with hind paws. This time her claws remained sheathed.

"Up, lazy puss! Up!"

Rakeema stared instead, her brilliant green eyes a reflection of Ishoa's own.

When Wolst had presented the cub to her on her fourteenth birthday, he'd told her, "I chose the beast because it has fire. Like you. Willful and intractable."

Ishoa sighed. She had to agree with her uncle. Often the anjuhtarg did this when she'd hit the limit of her attention, putting a halt to their daily training.

"No." Ishoa sheathed her sword. "No play." She stepped to avoid the cat's out-stretched paws.

In the winding stairwell outside her room, heavy bootsteps echoed. Rakeema lifted her head, ears twitching.

Spanning the width of the door's frame, Wolst maneuvered his bulk to slide into the room at a slight angle. Fur, leather, and steel covered every part of him. His gray beard descended to the navel. Wolf fur hung from the belt of his warskirt. Bison heads were wrought into the pommels of his broadswords at each hip. Under one arm, he cradled his legendary raek helm. Steel plate lined the giant serpent's black-boned jaws and crown. Where the raek's horn had once been, a spike now rested.

"Hello, Uncle."

"Training your kitty, eh?" He looked as if his mind were being pulled to tasks out of sight.

"At your suggestion, I work with her daily. You wanted to speak with me?"

He surveyed her room, finger tapping against the raek skull under arm.

"While you're debating whatever it is on your mind, why don't you come all the way in and have a seat? I'll never understand why you're always choosing to block doorways."

Wolst puffed his chest, a proud smile tugging at the corner of his mouth. Ishoa knew he loved her like a daughter. It both riled and humbled him to have her treat him playfully when no other would.

He appreciates not being feared for once.

Warmaster Wolst, the Beast of Anjuhkar. Hero of the Great Betrayal. Not only had he slain Raeklord Sahuhd in single combat, but he'd killed the infamous, Bloodhorn, as well. As far as legends were concerned, few claimed killing a raek. There was not a man in all of Namarr—perhaps the world—who didn't feel a little fear in the Beast of Anjuhkar's titanic shadow.

Ishoa, on the other hand, feared him about as much as she feared the storm bear doll Othwii had sewn and stuffed for her when she was eight. That was to say not at all.

"I'll block as many doorways as I please. What's the point of being built so broad if I'm not allowed to impose it on others here and there, eh?"

Ishoa frowned. "Try blocking the wall instead. Maybe you'll have something to aspire to when you attend your next feast. They'll rename you The Barn of Anjuhkar."

Wolst laughed. "Gah! Mercy, my lady. I'll come in if you promise to save your barbs. You show flashes of your grandmother, yet. Besides..." He eyed Rakeema. "I know I make your kitten nervous. She should learn friend from foe." He stepped forward. Rakeema's ears jumped and her eyes went wide. When he finally squeezed into a chair near the foot of the bed, the anjuhtarg relaxed somewhat.

Ishoa grit her teeth and rubbed Rakeema's belly. "You're not a kitten, are you? You're a scary ice tiger!" The anjuhtarg obliged, rolling over so the scratches would land along the ridge of slender belly and breast.

Wolst placed his raek helm onto his lap. Brick-like fingers traced the steel rivets driven into the black bone. He lifted his gaze to the painting of her parents on the far wall. "I see them sometimes, Isha. Every time I look at this thing," he hoisted the helm and sighed. "I see them."

Numbness crept from Ishoa's hands up into her arms. It suddenly felt as though her mind separated from her body and became a thing out of reach.

She plopped onto the bed beside Rakeema. *If only they'd lived.* She wanted to avoid the pain brought on by talking about them. But that was only a want, weak by comparison to a primal drive in her to know them better. A longing to make them proud, even if they were nothing but ash, wind, and snow.

You are strong. Stronger than you know.

"Why does the skull remind you of them?" The words trickled forth on shaky foundations. "I thought you weren't at the Bloody Beach with my father. You fought in the north."

Wolst lifted the helmet. "Aye. So it is. And I pray you never have to learn that it's all the same. One battle becomes all the battles. One death becomes all deaths. Like the body, the mind can also be wounded in a way that healing cannot help. The memories bleed through...through the years, staining everything you look at, everything you touch." With a snort, he laid the skull down on the ground beside the chair and settled back. His eyes met hers. "Everything you love."

"Well, I hope never to be a part of any bloodshed, but if I'm to be Crown Princess when I'm eighteen..." She set her jaw. "I'm not a little girl anymore. I know what the responsibility of ruling brings."

A meek smile trembled on the warmaster's cheek. "Aye. You're not a little girl, are you?" It was more a realization than a question to be answered. For a span of heartbeats, he regarded her. "The Ice Maiden returns. Tomorrow."

Ishoa sensed he had more to say. When he remained quiet, she asked, "I assume we're having counsel then?"

"Aye, and she's given me leave to prepare you for it." Wolst screwed up his face. "There's nothing to fear."

No one says there's nothing to fear when there's nothing to fear.

Wolst went to the door and shut it with a single swat of a powerful hand then returned to his chair. Mirroring him, she leaned forward until their foreheads nearly touched. He smelled of warm earth and sweat. Anticipation rose hot on the back of her neck.

Wolst spoke as if delivering news of a loved one's death. "For reasons she wishes to explain herself, Belara Frost wants you to enter this year's Trials."

Disbelief creased her brow. "But I'm not yet fifteen. It's not custom."

"It is now. The Ice Maiden has made it so. No others will get the news in time to capitalize. None but you, of course."

Ishoa sat back. "Why would—"

Wolst waved her to silence. "It is your grandmother's place to explain, not mine. We thought it best you be prepared for the news."

"But I've not been training for it." She pulled at a strand of hair. "I'll be far less ready than the others. Far younger too."

"Whether or not you're ready, this will happen," Wolst said. "You're an Ironlight. You have to grow up fast."

Thoughts ricocheted through Ishoa's mind as she stared at the floor. It didn't take long for her to see a possible motivation for the custom's change. If she completed the Trials, she would have a vote at court after the ceremony's conclusion.

A vote against Revocation.

What she'd asked for less than a week ago, to prove herself as a worthy Ironlight, was being thrust upon her at a rapid, overwhelming pace. The duchess had given her a first task, now a second. Something deep inside of her cried out against the cold realization that the momentum of her future would not slow, even if she begged it to. From that moment, to her dying day, politics would consume every bit of Ishoa's life.

For better or worse, she was in it now.

I'll be a Claimant alongside Lodaris, at least. That too weighed heavy on her. A star swallowed by darkness, only to be admired from a distance.

A light snow began. Errant flakes drifted onto the stone floor just inside the window. She glanced at the portrait of her parents. "If they were still alive, what do you think..." She hesitated, then spoke in a rush. "What would they think of me?"

Wolst rested elbows on broad knees. "Your father would say, 'You have the same eyes as Danath, all green and full of fury.' Your mother, well, she was a Quinn. As you know, they're not ones for excessive words."

Her older cousin, Arick Quinn, was a cold, unknowable man. He would return from Alistar with Ishoa's great-grandmother a freshly trained knight. Their relationship had always felt overly formal, which only served to further Ishoa's feelings of isolation from her kin.

Wolst continued. "Likely your mother would have just shown you how much she loved you in simple ways. Being around you more. Listening to you talk. Maybe playing a song for you on the flute. She was quite skilled. Shy about it though. But you knew you were special if she let you hear her play. Both would be proud to see you now, Isha. Dressed like a true Anjuhk. Training your ice tiger. Entering the Trials." He looked away, grunted around what seemed a swell of emotions. "Scares the piss out of me."

"Really?" Ishoa stifled laughter. "The Beast of Anjuhkar...afraid?"

A scowl swept over Wolst like a storm cloud. "There's nothing funny about the Trials, Isha. They're dangerous. Even if you're a princess."

While Claimants rarely died, it did happen. The Trials took place every few years when there were enough highborn and rich merchants' children to pay the tithe. A decade did not pass without at least one death.

"You could be maimed," Wolst said. "Or worse."

She thought of Lodaris Warnock and the three cuts rendered along his left cheek and over one eye; it was a blessing the Jurati hadn't blinded him. Having just spent time with the young Scarborn, rage ushered to the fore. Her tone was harsh. "A little maiming never made you bat an eye before."

Since meeting Lodaris, her mind was wide open. The practice of men pulling a babe from their mother's arms, of a father watching idly, unable to react as a father should while a strange woman with a claw slashed their child for doing nothing wrong but being born.

Barbarous. Something Scoths would do. Not Namorites.

The shame made her sick to her stomach.

The look on Wolst's face was one of disappointment. "I do not make the laws of Anjuhkar." Wolst wasn't a fervent supporter of the scarring ritual, but he defended it all the same, as if justifying it could make him feel less dirty about it. "And just because you know one good Scarborn does not mean they're all good."

Grim determination bristled within. "And one bad one doesn't make them all bad. The blade cuts both ways in this, Uncle."

Silence descended. Wolst drummed root-thick fingers on the arm of his chair. "I know you think you're right, Isha. And when you're Crown Princess, you may choose to do what you like. But for now, I implore you to be more cautious in your thinking. The Scarborn are not to be trusted. That includes Lodaris."

"When I rule, things will be different." She crossed her arms. "That I promise."

"Aye, and you're welcome to it." Wolst stood. "In a month's time, you'll complete the Trials. In less than two, you'll be voting in the court of Anjuhkar. Four years from now, you'll be swept off into the wolverine's den to be the leader of the United

Lands of Namarr. But every day between here and there, I'll do my damn best to ensure you're ready for it. That means protecting you in every way I can—even from yourself. I'm on your side, Isha, and I always will be, even when we disagree."

A slap may have hurt less. Her chin dipped.

Wolst scooped up his raek helm from the floor. "You cannot let your emotions dictate your decisions. As a ruler, you'll have to do things you don't agree with. We all have to do things we don't agree with." He nodded curtly. "Because that is what duty calls for."

She squared her shoulders. Affected a calm tone. "I understand what you are saying. Grandmother has said as much before. A ruler can never please everyone. There will always be enemies." She inhaled slowly. "But I don't think Lodaris is one of them. In this, I ask you to have a little faith in *me*. I can manage my relationship with him just fine."

"Aye." Wolst smiled, sadness rimming his eyes. "Careful what you wish for, Isha."

Ishoa tensed. His words conveyed an unpleasant promise yet to come.

A warning.

Rakeema watched Ishoa, seeming to sense her unease. She stroked the ice tiger's head, but not even the feel of Rakeema's fur underhand brought comfort.

After Wolst left, Ishoa drifted into dark foreboding. She stared at the storm bear fur covering the stone floor until night settled. Fears of the unknown fogged her thoughts. *What did Uncle mean?*

She squinted in an attempt to shut out the worries, but they clung to her like mold to old bread. She tried repeating Lodaris's words to herself. *You are strong. Stronger than you know.*

That too failed.

In light of her uncle's warning, whatever courage she possessed had slithered away to shadowed crevices of her mind.

Cold and sharp, fear slid into her.

CHAPTER NINE

THE BEAUTIFUL DEAD

- NEAR UNTURRUS, YEAR 64 -

Nothing good had ever come from living.

Abuse. Shame. Pity. All of them, all the time, a slurried paste no amount of bathing could wash clean.

For Thephos, death was the last resort. The only one.

Dirt passed under his feet. Feet caked in dust. Feet cracked from dehydration. They'd carried him a hundred miles or more from Carthane. Great men had traveled the Prince's Highway, called to great deeds for causes greater still.

Nothing like Thephos.

I am too cowardly even to kill myself, so I'll have Unturrus do it for me.

A quiet voice inside, less than the stirring of a blade of grass, called to him. With each bone-bruising step toward the Mountain of Power, Thephos answered it.

The caravan train shook and creaked up ahead, the lead drover snapping a whip over the flanks of his oxen and spurring the bellowing team up a rolling hill. The rest of the caravan trundled behind. A wheel groaned as it bounced over a stone. The lead drover leaned out—spat. "Bloody damn, Carthane! Shoddy damn wheel-wrights!"

Forced to journey on foot, Thephos lagged behind. A seat in the wain was an extra fee, one the eldest son of a dead pig farmer couldn't afford.

A priest of the Sempyrean lumbered to his feet the rear wagon, and threw back a tankard of godsbrew with willful abandon.

"From the plentiful plains of Peladonia, they come! Hurled from the Ardent Heart, they journey! Summoned from Lah-Tsarra, they answer. From all across Namarr!"

The priest flicked his head, casting drooping bangs from his face. He gestured with his tankard at those surrounding the caravan. "I beseech you, faithful wan-derers, to Unturrus! A place where fools go to die, but from which gods return, Awakened! You are the chosen, called to your own path, your own destiny, your own making, or perhaps your—" With a thunderous belch he raised his arms from his sides like a bird spreading its wings, or a toddler seeking to be picked up, and nearly fell from the wain. "Your own death. One in fifty brave souls return alive from the Mountain of Power. Of that one in fifty, only half come back Awakened. The other ninety-nine, well..." The heavyset priest clasped his godsbrew in fat-fingered hands covered in rings and downed it. "Driven right straight into the arms of Nacronus. May they swim easy in the Abyssal Sea. May the Eternal Maw treat them—"

"We need no history lesson, priest," sneered a wheat stalk of a man wearing a fox mask. Thephos hadn't spoken with him much, but then again he hadn't really spoken with anyone but himself for most of the journey. "Twould be a kindness to us all if you threw yourself head first onto a rock."

"History lesson! I'll give you a history lesson, you Maw-begotten pissant." The slovenly priest wiped brew from heavy lips. "After King Jathos Wrathhand seized Unturrus during the first Scothean invasion, he sent a thousand pea-hearted soldiers, not unlike yourself, up the damn mountain and—" He made to take a hasty drink but had already started to talk, so he lowered the tankard. "And not a one of them lived. Not a one. But Namorites? Chosen by the Sempyrean gods themselves. A calling, ya Maw begotten pissant!"

"What would you know of a calling, priest? Do you intend to ascend the Mountain of Power at my side or did your courage disappear with your sobriety?" The masked man cackled. "Perhaps cowardice grows in tandem with one's waistline."

The priest smiled, a sloppy, glistening thing, then patted his belly. "Right you are. I love my life as it is and have little ambition for power. And I don't much fancy the cold nor heights." Forgetting the godsbrew in his hand, the priest motioned abruptly and sent an orange-brown wave sloshing onto the wagon bed. He side-eyed the mess indifferently. "I go to Unturrus to oversee a new section of wall the Sempyrium's taken over from a hold lord. I'm to manage a brew operation. In the name of the four gods of light, no less."

"Lies," said the masked man. "What lord would sell their stake of Unturrus."

"I neither care," said the priest, "nor am I saddened by it. While your scurvy arse is running from the Ever-Grasping Worm, I'll be getting rich in the name of the gods. Drunk, too, of course."

"I've no doubt you'll do your best to drink and whore your profits away."

The priest smiled. "I mean to!" The tankard in his fist tipped back. His thick throat tensed around each successive swallow. And with each, Thephos saw the past.

He stared at the priest's fat hands as they slowly changed into those of a familiar devil.

My father...

Darkness snared his mind and dragged him helplessly away.

The old devil had staggered into their meager farmhouse on the windswept plains of Peladonia. Thephos has been a boy on the cusp of manhood. A manhood that never truly came.

"Theffy." His father slathered the air with his name. To Thephos, it was like the screech of a rusty hinge. "Do you hate me?"

Thephos had been trembling. Even now at eighteen he shook as he remembered. A fall of muddy blond hair had covered his face, his best attempt to go unseen.

It had never been enough to hide him. Thephos used to wish his hair would grow faster and thicker. Armor against attention.

"Well, you should," his father said. "I hate you."

Thephos had glanced at his siblings as they silently cleaned. They cast wary glances in return, but did their best to ignore the unfolding interaction. To be invisible in the house of the old devil was a gift. Thephos envied his siblings. As the oldest, he was the closest thing the evil man had to a confidant.

Thephos's father staggered close, each boot heel stamp a peal of doom. He dragged out a chair beside Thephos and eased himself down. Age and a bad hip caused him to rely on copious amounts of godsbrew and godsthorn, which in turned sucked the fat and muscle from his frame and made him look ever more like a hideous wraith.

Inwardly, Thephos recoiled. He'd been taught the cruel way to never move a muscle when the old devil was near.

"You see, Theffy." His father's voice was matter-of-fact. "You *should* hate me."

Silence commanded attention—expanded it.

"But you have no fire. If you did, I'd be dead. You'd have killed me long ago, buried me with your brother beneath the willow tree." He grabbed Thephos's arm. A wealth of cruel experiences had taught him to never pull away, so he let grimy nails do their digging. "Old bastards like me always take too long to die. Young cowards like you though, with nary a spark in 'em, you die every day you live. You're a pathetic worm of a boy. It bothers me little because I know it's your mother's doing, but you should know if you ever try to kill me, you better succeed because I've got a fire in me that burns like forge irons. You listening, Theffy!" he shouted. "I'd kill the fuck out of ya!"

He spit at the floor, hit one of Thephos's brothers instead, then went to his room to sleep. The thought of killing his father had never crossed Thephos's mind. Not even in his dreams did he allow himself to consider hurting the man. The old devil was right. Thephos was already dead and had been for as long as he could remember. But he was wrong about being a coward. A coward had something they feared losing. Thephos had no such thing. Whatever feelings he had were left at the edge of his younger brother's grave.

I do not deserve to feel.

When the old devil had finally succumbed to the poison of drink, Thephos buried him under the willow tree alongside the brother the old man had beaten to death. Thephos had cried. Not from grief. From hatred. He didn't know hate had tears.

Later that night, while his siblings slept, he dug the devil's body back up so he could beat at his bloated chest.

He should have died by my hand.

Regret and rage roared through his mind like a storm. "You should have been the one to end him!" Clods of dirt flew in every direction. "You!" After that, he stuffed his emotions down into a numb abyss.

The little whisper started a day later. "Unturrus," it called. "Death," it begged.

At month's end, he gave the farm into the trust of the Sisterhood of the Rose and joined a caravan train heading west.

As the distance between Thephos and the pig farm grew, so did the guilt of leaving his brothers behind. *An irrevocable act of cowardice, abandoning them like that. The old devil was right. I'm a pathetic worm.* Yet not killing his father was a far worse injustice. It left a hollow ache—the only thing he felt.

It clung to him like an itchy blanket, covered his soul in a stink like hog shit, sucked at him like hungry mud. He looked at his hands, trembling and weak, capable of burying brothers but too weak to kill fathers.

Shouts of excitement rose from the head of the caravan as they crested a knoll, breaking Thephos from his reverie. He lifted his gaze just as the lead driver brought his team to a halt at the top.

"There she is!" bawled the priest.

Thephos's breath caught.

Unturrus.

A jagged claw rose from the sea of clouds packed around its bosom. Swaths of snow and forest covered it from base to peak. A ghostly daytime crescent moon hung over its shoulder. Those who'd seen Unturrus before pointed out differences for those who hadn't.

"See that? The peak leans left now."

"Shorter than last winter. Stouter, too."

"I've come by the last three years, and every year that patch of trees on the eastern slope has changed shape."

Thephos felt a gentle tug at the core of his being, drawing him toward Unturrus. Hope kindled weakly in his narrow chest. A death that called to him shone on the horizon, and with it, he might finally have relief.

A chance to feel free in a way life had never given.

Passing his fellow travelers, he approached the lead wain. "I have to get something," he said in low tones.

The lead driver nodded then spat onto the Prince's Highway. *He despises me.* Thephos had been around his father long enough to know the signs. *Why wouldn't he? I'm pathetic. I belong underground with the other worms.*

His travel sack contained four things: a half loaf of molding bread, a book by a woman whose name he couldn't read that showed drawings of Unturrus, and two copper wheels. If he'd planned it right, he'd be up the mountain before he starved. Growing up a pig farmer, he'd never been forced to beg but assumed he'd be bad at it.

While he'd never learned to read, his father forced him to know his numbers for when he went to market for pig-feed. He counted off days on his fingers as he assessed the number of clean bites of bread left. A twisting sensation in his guts had been with him for the entirety of the journey, so the idea of going a few more days on meager rations failed to stir new worries.

He squinted at Unturrus, judged it less than a day to the settlement at Eastshadow. He pulled forth the book with the drawings as the wains started off again.

Over the course of the journey, his bare feet had become numb planks. Late in the day, they would cause him to slow, lagging further from the group until he was alone. At night, he would catch up as the group was settling into sleep. No one cared enough about him to wait.

The day waned. Time slipped by.

The wains bounced and shook and groaned, drifting further from sight. Then hearing. The caravan train became a speck on a far-off hill, a banner of dust...and then nothing at all.

A gentle breeze bent the grass around him in a wave and set the flowers to bobbing. There was peace in decisions made, no matter how dire. For the first time in as long as he could remember, Thephos's stride felt lighter.

Not strong—never that—but neither was it weak.

He studied the renderings of Unturrus in his book. The Sister of the Rose he'd left his brothers with had given it to him in parting, sorrow lining her face. "May you find peace," she'd said.

I intend to. Even now the book seemed like a promise in his hands. Heavy and warm.

The cold nipped at the exposed skin of his ankles, brushed icily against the nape of his neck. The loose cuffs of his tattered tunic gathered its share of the discomfort too. His battered feet remained immune and unfeeling.

The crescent moon hanging over Unturrus like a sickle brightened as the sun set.

"Hey there."

Thephos turned to the sound. A low shout, as if the person wished to share a secret from a distance. To his right, only rolling knolls. To his left, a series of boulders jutted from the earth. Behind those, a pond surrounded by trees.

A man's head and shoulders rose from behind a boulder. "Come here." His tone was kind.

Unnervingly so.

Thephos stumbled up the road as fast as he could, numb feet scuffing through the dirt.

"Get back here." A second voice. Not kindly at all like the first. Thephos knew what actions followed such tones. Had known them his whole life. He wanted nothing more than to escape such tones and words and images burned into the fore of his mind.

He glanced sidelong over a shoulder, found two men and a Kurg rushing toward him. One carried a rock, the other two rusted blades.

Miles separated him from the caravan by now. *I can't outrun them.*

He stopped and lifted his hands meekly in surrender. The book flapped to the ground. Licking dry lips, he shot one final look at Unturrus, the pang of regret leaden in his gut.

So much for that.

The bandits slowed, cautious as wolves circling a stag as they looked him over. The one holding a rock smiled, showing off rotten brown teeth. He looked in either direction down the Prince's Highway. "No dust. No saviors. No one to hear you shout."

"What you have?" The Kurg spoke the common tongue with a thick Unti accent.

"Naught but wicker and wind," said Rotten Teeth. "Look at him...collarbones are holding up his tunic like a tent's poles."

Thephos made to show them his bag. The Kurg lunged forth and slapped his face with the side of a rusty sword. Thephos cried out. A puff of rust stung his eyes even more than the welt left along his cheek. He blinked watering eyes, lifted shaking hands. "I'm sorry," he trembled. "I have nothing. I have nothing."

Rotten Teeth ripped the travel bag from around Thephos's torso. "Let's see...moldy bread...two copper wheels."

"A book," said the third bandit.

It had been his favorite possession. *My only one.* He supposed it was fitting to lose it now at the end, a final grim offering to a life poorly lived.

"Written by Locastrii, the Mistress of Time," read the third bandit. "Headed to Unturrus?"

Thephos nodded.

Rotten Teeth laughed. "You're to be Awakened, eh? Walk the Hall of Heroes and all that?"

Thephos nodded.

"Oh boy, we ain't even need to kill this one. He's already dead!" Sulfur-tinged breath billowed across Thephos's face as the man stepped in close, rock poised overhead for a crushing blow. He sucked cadaverous teeth. "Guess we could have a bit of fun with him before he goes. Hate to waste a bit of ass, skinny as it may be. In the right light, with that shaggy brown hair, you could look a proper woman."

Rough fingers clamped around Thephos's elbow and propelled him toward the boulders. "Come on then. Fight back and I'll crush your skull."

Having subsisted for days on only nibbles of molding bread and apple cores cast away by others in the wagon train, Thephos had little strength left to resist. A pathetic sadness rose in him when he considered that even if he'd had the strength, he might still have lacked the spine. They had weapons, threats, cruelty—things he'd been trained to submit to. Dignity was an idea for the privileged, for those not born under the old devil's roof. He couldn't fight for it. Wouldn't.

Luckily, he didn't have to. "No." The Kurg moved to block their path.

Rotten Teeth was short and stood face to face with his companion, but the Kurg outweighed him by nearly double.

"What's your problem? You liked the last one fine." Rotten Teeth's jaw clenched as he turned to the third bandit beseechingly. "What's his problem?"

"Not this one." The Kurg pointed at Thephos. "He goes to Unturrus. It is calling. We not interfere." The Kurg gave Thephos a solemn nod. "It is sacred."

"Fuck all. You're a bandit! Robbing and raping and murdering all along the Prince's fucking Highway." Rotten Teeth sputtered. "And *you're* talking about what's sacred."

The Kurg's heavy brow formed a menacing knot. "Maybe I do those things to you."

Rotten Teeth gulped and released his grip on Thephos's arm. The man spun, cursed, then stomped his way back to their hideout among the boulders. The third bandit shrugged, took a few steps in pursuit of Rotten Teeth but turned back to wait for the Kurg when he realized he hadn't moved.

It was clear who the group's leader was.

"We keep the copper wheels and book but give back the bread." The Kurg tossed the bag into Thephos's arms. Bringing fingertips together, the golden-skinned Kurg performed the unimistic blessing, first touching thumbs to his heart followed by pointer-fingers to the center of his forehead.

Thephos stared blankly. The Kurg and the other bandit strode off, carrying his last possessions with them. If he'd been a spiritual man, Thephos might have given thanks or prayed to the gods for sparing his life and dignity. But his father had never tolerated any of that, so Thephos shrugged at the deeper question of chance versus fate and then made to catch up with the wains as quickly as possible.

A coil of smoke a short way from the main road alerted Thephos to the caravan. The wains formed a ring in a caldera under the stars. None cared enough to leave him signs or have others lag back to guide him. If he wandered off or died, it was his own fault. They had places to be, after all.

A sheen of sweat dampened his filthy clothing, chilling him. He shambled into the center of the circled wains and collapsed beside the fire. One other traveler remained awake. The man in the fox-mask stared intently at the smoking embers of the dying fire.

Thephos breathed heavily into the grass as he lied on his side. A beetle clung to a swaying weed at eye level. The cool earth eased the burning sensation on his cheek left by the Kurg's strike.

In the background of his focus, a blur of movement passed in front of the fire, blocking its light momentarily while Thephos studied the beetle.

The bug seemed to watch him...

Are you waiting for something?

Its antennae twitched.

A shadow fell over Thephos. A lordly shoe in a state of abject disrepair crushed the beetle. Another foot, this one bare with gnarled toenails, locked into place beside the first.

Thephos kept his eyes fixed on the spot where the bug died. *Was that all?* Suddenly, he thought he understood the beetle's existence a little better.

"Would you like to hear a poem?" said the shadowy figure.

Thephos pushed the earth, rose to a seated position, then looked up into the face of a fox; or more accurately, the mask of one.

"Are you certain?" whined the masked man. "My poems carry great power. It may help you to survive Unturrus. Possibly even become Awakened as I will be."

Thephos remained silent.

The man lifted the fox mask. Around a partially bald skull, the man's hair stood out as a wild mushroom cap of gray. A jutting, blade-like nose eclipsed thin lips stretched into a grin.

"You think you are one of those who simply goes to die, don't you? Maybe my words will inspire you to do differently." He inhaled sharply, flourished a hand. "A somewhat renowned merchant of Alistar once told me that I saved his life. How many poets can claim that, hmmm?"

"I don't know any poets. I can't even read."

"What?" To the masked man, Thephos's lack of literacy seemed to be the punchline of some joke. "I've seen you carrying a book around." A cackle shook him, frail hands forming into claws at his chest.

Suddenly, he twisted toward the fire. "Puzzling indeed."

"Are you a famous poet?" Thephos asked.

He stared into the flames and nodded. Fire danced in the man's black eyes. His smile faded and his forehead fell slack as the poet seemed to gaze into some distant place.

Just when Thephos thought the man had forgotten him, he spoke. "I'm the Wordfox. Surprised you've never heard of me. Very surprised actually. I once performed in the House of Saud for Lord Onai and his family."

Thephos *was* surprised. "The Duke of Peladonia?" Thephos's pig farm in Carthane fell under the man's rule.

The Wordfox nodded.

"Why go to Unturrus then? It sounds like you're successful. Like you have a lot to live for." *More than I do, at least.*

The Wordfox jolted as if slapped. His face contorted into an expression of unbridled disgust. "An artist's craft is never mastered. But I, the Wordfox, am most dedicated. I would become an Awakened with the power to compel the world through my words."

The Wordfox's smile broadened, a lustful thing riding cracked lips. "My words! Mine!"

A tingle climbed the nape of Thephos's neck. He changed the subject. "Did you grow up poor?"

"Of course I did! I see you wish to know more of me. I do not blame you. You sit at the feet of a great man. Let me explain my story as only the Wordfox can."

He cleared his throat. His voice took on a lyrical, lilting tone.

"A child sits among the thorns, waiting to be safe, all the while saving himself.

"To step beyond the thorn bush's ring is a crime against his nature, for he knows what lies beyond.

"A mother, brain broken, pieces of her madness like shattered glass, cutting the child's feet if they wander too near.

"A father, hands like anvils, breaking the brains of mothers, but never could he break the child's dreams.

"Moonlight dancing along stolen books stacked high, the child's armor against doom.

"Words and wonder, like weapons, cunning, the banner born unto his most famous of dreams.

"Of a life no longer lived among nameless bushes and painful thorns, rather he, a rose blossoming above them."

Thephos was so fixated on the part about a father with hands like anvils that he couldn't make sense of most of the rest. The old devil had always used something he called a "pigswitch." If he'd used anvils, Thephos would have buried more than just the one brother. He looked at his hands...still felt the bite of splinters from the spade... Dirt splashed over his brother's slack and pale face.

I deserve death.

"I—I'm sorry you had to go through that as a child," Thephos said, eager to escape his own thoughts. "If you're the child in the story, I mean."

The Wordfox had closed his eyes at the conclusion of his poem, skeletal thumb and forefinger pinching the bridge of his crescent nose.

At Thephos's words, the older man's eyes snapped open. "It's a poem, not a story. And yes, I am the child. But I reject your pity."

Thephos stammered. "I didn't mean to—"

"I regret sharing my art with you if pity is all you gained from it. Worry not, I don't take it personally, for I understand the horrors in one's own mind are oft reflected upon others unduly. A projection, if you will. A shadow we give to others." His angular chin jerked upward. "My intention was to inspire you, not masticate further upon your own insecurities."

Thephos attempted to speak, but the Wordfox stabbed a shaking finger at him. "Why would any feel sorry for *me*? I am the rose, rising above the thorns. I am to be admired. It is for *you* that I feel sorry."

The poet yanked the fox mask down over his face then strode beyond the wains into shadows. It sounded as though the Wordfox cursed the name of Onai Saud as he went.

Wind rifled through the valley, pressing the fire low. A couple of bodies huddled closer together as a second, stronger gust rocked the wagon they slept beneath.

The fire dwindled to embers. Embers to dark coals. Sleep eluded Thephos.

Every so often, he heard the Wordfox wander close by, muttering. He imagined the masked-man pacing back and forth in the dark, working mismatched grooves into the earth, deeper on one side from his rich man's shoe.

At least he sees himself as a rose among thorns. I've only ever been a beetle, waiting to be crushed.

Being anything different seemed about as possible as becoming a prince, learning to read, or becoming an Awakened.

In the distance, Unturrus waited, wreathed in a silver glow.

What appeared to be stars twinkled up and down the Mountain of Power's sloping heights. The truth of what these shining lights were struck fear into the hearts of most onlookers.

Ascendants.

Specifically, Ascendants who'd fallen prey to Vaniton's Gasp, a flowing river of liquid mirror. One of the many demons that haunted Unturrus.

Thephos could almost see them in his mind: men and women caught while sprinting for their lives, now destined for all time to be warning beacons for those who dared to summit the Mountain of Power. Women frozen in fear, now frozen. Mirrored statues.

For Thephos, the thought of dying in this way had the opposite effect of fear. When his eyes fell on the glinting statues of the dead, hope thudded dully in his breast.

To be a beautiful thing, like a flower among thorns. To be seen as anything other than a worthless pig farmer. It was almost too much good fortune to wish for.

Vaniton's Gasp, he decided. That was the way he wanted Unturrus to kill him.

CHAPTER TEN

THE WAY OF THINGS

Barodane slipped and shouted, "Fuck!" as he fell onto his backside. Pain flared in his hip where he struck a rock. His neck jerked back at an awkward angle. He groaned.

Cold, stone-riddled grass, scraped across his palms as he dragged himself to an upright position. Every sensation—every movement—recoiled against a budding illness within. He flipped onto hands and knees, then forced himself upright.

A mistake.

Blood rushed to his head, pounded between his ears. For a moment, he feared his skull might burst. He inhaled, sharp and stilted. The exhale was worse; it deteriorated into a violent coughing fit that crackled somewhere deep in his chest. Morning dew had accumulated from a night spent sleeping outside. Now it jumped from hood and cloak.

A gull wheeled overhead and screamed.

"Bastard." *Even birds mock me now?* "I hope a hawk gets you."

From between swollen clouds, sunlight spilled over the barrow hills. He picked his way down, each movement a reminder to go gingerly. Steam rose from the earth in slow-moving veils like the ghosts of the dead, whose restless bones were buried deep in the soil.

In the distance, Digtown clamored, cursed, and got good and drunk as the day's business began. A comforting sound. Barodane had his own tasks to see to.

Conversations with both Hyram and Garlenna from the night before weighed heavy. Out of habit, he sought the thorn roll at his belt—stopped short. *If I'm to be rid of them, I must act quickly and clearly. I'm already sick from my foolish impulse.*

A chill rifled through him, settled as a tightness in his chest. His bones ached. His throat was tender as if burned. The sensation reminded him of the time he'd visited the imperial family in Malzacor at the ignorant age of sixteen. The Light Adetys had insisted he try carp simmered in tserra venom. *Arrogant bastard.* Sweat dripping, he had spit out the spicy food to a chorus of laughter from the others of the Fourty-Four Imperial Lights. For his bowel's sake, he vowed never to return to Malzacor.

Mud jerked a boot from under him. Feet slipping backward, he pitched forward onto hands and knees. "Oof!" He stared at the earth. A worm writhed up from a hole in the ground inches from his nose.

This is my life now.

Teeth clenched, he stood. His heart beat at a pace more befitting a day in the weapons yard or an afternoon romp than a trek downhill.

You do not live, Mad Prince. The voices rolled through him like thunder. *You merely die slowly.*

Given the illness ransacking every part of him, he found no argument with the dead.

Taking folds of his cloak in either hand, he wrapped himself in a soggy cocoon. He knew he should plan ways to deal with Hyram but could not shake Garlenna from his mind. Were there others with her? Her father, Gyr Renwood? Or Barodane's old friend, Malus D'Alzir the Duke of Lah-Tsarra?

No. They would be returning from the most recent session of the Collective at Alistar. They'd leave it to Garlenna to retrieve me.

He considered others who might be involved with his former prosort's mission. Nserthes the Sophophant. A rebellious man possessing a sense of purpose capable of leading him to any end he saw worthy of his attention. No. Nserthes is likely still under scrutiny from the Sempyrium. He could never leave Martyr's Isle unnoticed. Nor would he.

That left Kaitos Barabi. As defiant as Nserthes but only for the sake of delighting in the simplicity of dangerous affairs.

Never Kaitos. He made it clear at Rainy Meadows, he has forsaken me. The words of Barodane's former friend coiled around his heart like a snake clutching a bird's egg. *Abandon...before it's too late.*

A dagger of guilt sank into Barodane. It had been years since he'd thought of his friends. Kaitos, with his flashing smile and velvet voice. Malus D'Alzir, always curious, always igniting meaningful conversation with well-wrought questions.

Would any of them rejoice to know I live? Certainly not Kaitos. But Omari D'Alzir might.

Barodane had not heard news about his betrothed since he'd disappeared. It seemed an impossible hope for her to have remained unwed, and so, he was resigned to the gut wrenching truth. She loved another now.

Damn you, Garlenna. Damn you for dragging it all back. He shook his head, winced, his neck stiffer than darksteel. *Maybe what Omari and I had was only a product of the moment. Nothing timeless. Maybe we were never meant to be.* The love they had shared was buried at Rainy Meadows along with the rest of his past.

He slipped a third time, landing hard enough for circles of dark and light to creep into the corners of his vision. The gull screamed but didn't stick around to see Barodane rise and glare at the sky.

As he neared the base of the barrow hills, another possibility took seed. If he failed to convince Garlenna to leave Digtown, she might resort to other means. In a fight, he stood no chance against her. As a young prince of nineteen, with vigor and youth on his side, he could stand his ground against men-become-monsters like Mastius Manalore and the Whiteflame, Pyr Syat. But the last time he'd fought for his life was when he'd slain Acramis. *Even if I were fully trained and battle ready, Garlenna is Garlenna. She'll take me by force if she wishes.*

He'd have to act first.

At the base of the barrows, he paused. Rain threaded between his shoulder blades. He shivered.

"I know words can't erase what my hands have done." Sobs rumbled through his chest like tumbling stone, but no tears came. He clenched a numb fist. "I'm sorry. That's all."

Then he staggered into town, heading for the Gem Loft.

The streets were busy but not overly crowded. Eager citizens hurried to complete their daily tasks before the rain's inevitable return. He kept his hood up to avoid being seen.

A coughing fit seized him, causing him to lurch toward a cart hitched to an ox. Blood surged between his ears. His head felt ready to erupt. Blurry points of light lurked at his peripheries. He grabbed the lip of the cab for balance. "Gods man, you need a healer?" A drover stood up from behind the cart, brow furrowed.

"Maybe..." Barodane said. "...maybe a priest."

The drover laughed then came around the cart to slap Barodane repeatedly on the back. "Here, this helping?"

It was not. The coughing intensified. Fire seared his lungs. He nodded emphatically and ducked out from under the drover's thunderous blows. He shot the man a thumb's up as he fled.

A pair of naked children, caked to the ankle in slurry, leapt into the fountain at the center of the town's main road. A haggard baker woman shouted at them for muddying the drinking water. A slavering mouth stitched into the hag's apron marked her as a baker of Prav. When the children ignored her, she snorted and then tossed moldy bread into an alley. They scurried after it.

Reeking of filth, a vacant-eyed addict bumped into Barodane and stared at him before smiling skyward. *One of Danuuk's regulars.* The Kurg managed godsthorn distribution in the slums for a cut of the profits, while Barodane focused on bigger but less frequent sales to free up time for his own highs.

Ahead, the Gem Loft towered twice as high as the building on either side. The shadow of the whore house fell over Barodane just as a chill forced him to pull his cloak tighter about himself. His boots banged against the landing's steps as he ascended.

He seized a whore by the elbow as she attempted to sweep past. "I need Madame Gratha."

At a stranger in a hood, the whore glared, but once she realized who it was underneath, the anger melted away. "Sure thing, Kord. Follow me."

A pair of whores folded linens in the parlor's corner. Madame Gratha lounged nearby, smoke rolling from her mouth and meandering around the pipe she held. When the elderly Kurg saw Barodane, she waved it at him with her pipe.

"Madame," he coughed.

One enormous breast lay freely on her belly. Out of reflex, she covered it. Though not because she cared if he saw her naked. It was an old tactic ingrained into a well-trained whore meant to spark a man's interest. Tyne had once told him, "For what they're allowed to have, men pay silver. But for what they're denied, they'll gladly pay gold."

Where robes failed to cover, the Kurg's golden skin sat in wrinkled folds riddled with age spots. Between Madame Gratha's melted figure and her one naked eye socket, it was a wonder how drunk or lonely a man might need to be in order to sleep with her. But then Barodane remembered what men were like. *Especially those of Digtown.* Still, he surmised, few enjoyed Madame Gratha sexually anymore. Nowadays, she was valued for skills beyond her lady parts.

Madame Gratha smacked her gob loudly, single eye roaming Barodane up and down. "You are wet."

"Yes," he said. "I am."

"Sleeping outside gets you sick. And getting sick gets you dead." She took a pull from her pipe. Smoke crawled through the air. "So why do this?"

Barodane smiled. For whatever reason, Madame Gratha was one of the few people in town who could improve his mood. Whenever he spoke to her, he couldn't help but feel the burdens of his past lessen. Being raised beneath a crown, he wondered if he had a natural distrust for those who would play the fake for his favor. The old Kurg had no capacity to be anything but herself regardless of who she spoke to.

"You know why, Madame. A troubled man does troubling things. You yourself have said as much."

"I say many things." Smoke pooled in her mouth. "Most of them true."

One of the whores sighed. "That she does."

"But why last night, Kord?" Madame Gratha said.

"Can't say at the moment." *Because I carry the weight of a thousand lost souls in my heart. Or because I am a drug-addled fool. Or perhaps to escape the shame dragged before me by a long-lost friend. Most likely...all of it.* "Could you fetch Danuuk here?" he said instead. "I'm not feeling well or I'd get him myself."

The ancient Kurg stared a long while at him before nodding. "Qippa, fetch my nephew." She snapped fingers at the whores folding linens.

Although the Baroness, Imralta, owned and ran the Gem Loft as its true madame, the other girls revered old Gratha. Without her, bastard children would cluster about at the knees in alarming numbers, and the girls would certainly contract far more unsavory ailments than they did. So, all turned to Gratha as defacto mother, healer, and honorary madame. Even Imralta approved.

Barodane watched Qippa go. "Is Lyansorca here?"

Madame Gratha nodded. "Free, too. It's been slow this week. Speaking of," she spit into a bucket on the floor. "You've not come around much—the last decade, really. It didn't fall off, did it?"

"No. Still there."

"That's good," she said. "A man who drinks and ascends on godsthorn as much as you do should make time for life's other pleasures."

"I stay busy enough."

"Who is this man who sells himself such silly ideas? No time for love!" Madame Gratha gestured a stubby-fingered hand at Barodane, the skin surrounding her good eye nearly swallowed in the folds of a frown. "Silly like a little boy. Don't you know love keeps the demons away?"

How right you are. He shrugged. "I—I haven't had an urge since Tyne left. But you speak wisely, as always."

Turning slowly, he made his way to the stairs. Madame Gratha's velvet voice called after him, "Sex is an act of life, Kord. Try not to give up on either one. Lyansorca will be happy to get you back in the right *rut*, if you desire."

At the top of the stairs, Barodane knocked on Lyansorca's door. A pair of women, one older and heavier and another who was slender and young, stepped into the hall. Both beckoned to him, attempting to steal their sister-whore's customer.

"Lyansorca wouldn't know what to do with you if the Triune God guided her cunt for her. Come to me, powerful man, I won't bite." The younger leaned against the frame of her door. "Too hard."

The older and heavier croaked out a laugh. "Ain't no God for you and me but those of the Sempyrium. But for Kord, I got his God right here." She lifted her dress, flashing a thick mound.

From the other side of Lyansorca's door, a husky voice said, "Who is it?"

"Kord."

At this, the heavier woman dropped her dress and returned to her room with a chuckle. The younger lingered in her doorway. Blushing. Biting her lower lip. "When you're done, maybe. I'd wait for a man who can go a couple rounds."

Lyansorca's door swung open, revealing a mad-eyed woman with a rangy frame and bouncing brown curls. "Kord! Come in, my sexy man."

Once inside, he slapped a wooden latch down into place.

Lyansorca leapt onto a bed, then spun around, tongue tracing her upper lip. "A cheap one for you?"

He shook his head. "Business only."

"Well, if you're in the right line of work. Pleasure and business need no borders."

"All the same." He took a seat on a stool near the foot of the bed. A bowl of water for cleaning up after each client sat near his feet. A stack of clean bed linens and a pile of crumpled ones lay in opposite corners. Given Digtown's standards for almost everything else, the Gem Loft was out of place for its quality. It was the most profitable business in the area—more so even than Meckin's Dregs Inn. "As generous as your offer is, Lyansorca, I know you're all business. I'd end up paying for it...one way or another."

She sat back on her heels on the bed. "I would have enjoyed it a little though. What *do* you want?" Her playful tone faded, replaced by disappointment. "Something more exciting than a tumble, I hope."

"Indeed. I have a task for you. A dangerous one."

At the word "danger," her eyes lit up. "How much?" Barodane drew out a gold wheel. She snatched it from him and told him to wait outside. When she'd finished hiding it, she called him back in. "Can't be too careful with these other bitches around. They'd slit their sister's cunt for a gold wheel."

Pretty as she was, Barodane found Lyansorca's intensity overwhelming. If not for business, he'd steer far clear of her. She had a hold lord's thirst for gold and a demon's hunger for excitement, both of which made her ideal for his needs. Besides, she'd never said no before. In fact, he'd never heard of her saying no to anyone about anything when the right color and count of coin filled her hand.

"What would you have me do?"

He explained Garlenna's presence, omitting how he knew her. He told her to watch his former prosort and figure out if she was alone. If there were others, she was to report with a detailed description of them.

Lyansorca blew a raspberry then rolled her eyes, clearly disappointed. "You want me to spy on some woman? What's dangerous about that? Sounds like a fucking bore."

A cough sent pain lancing through Barodane's head. He closed his eyes, breathing slowly until it passed. *I'm exhausted. I need to rest.* "She is not some woman." His tone betrayed frustration. "You misunderstand. If this woman, Gyra, deems you a threat, she'll not hesitate to kill you."

"Well then." Lyansorca raised an eyebrow, a smile hinting at the corner of her mouth. "Sounds like I'll need my knife."

"No. Don't do that. It would only give her more reason to kill you. If caught, you're best off pleading for your life and telling her I hired you." He waved a hand. "But that won't matter because you won't be caught, will you?"

Lyansorca lied back on the bed and stretched like a cat. The cut of her gown separated, revealing a flat stomach and pert breasts. "If I get caught, will you punish me? We can ascend on godsthorn first. You like that, don't you? We'll ascend together. Like you and Tyne used to—"

"Be silent," he snapped. "Do not speak of Tyne."

Lyansorca's brow knit as she stared at him, hard-eyed. Something inside her switched and her affect became suddenly placid.

Barodane rose, wobbled. *Rest. I need rest.* "I have to go."

"Wait. If this woman is as dangerous as you say." Lyansorca's expression was as impassive as ice. "I want two gold wheels."

Hand hovering at the latch, Barodane turned around.

"If this woman is as dangerous as you say, I want double." Lyansorca folded her arms. "Or I won't do it."

This was the way of things. He reminded himself that those who willingly lived in a place like this had few motivations beyond the next up to avoid the last down. Places like Digtown were made for people like Lyansorca.

I should know, for I am no different.

The face of the little girl at the stables flashed across his mind's eye. He chided himself for discounting the young and innocent born beneath these ever-spitting skies.

You're the selfish wretch who chooses this place, the voices said. *How heartless you are to think it a choice for others. Not everyone has the freedom and good fortune of a prince.*

A second gold wheel left his hand, hit the floor, and rolled. Lyansorca sprang, a starving dog after a carcass.

"When you're done, find me." He thought of Hyram Olabran and the towering dullard with the blade. "I may have more work for you."

He left.

When he reached the bottom of the stairs, a wave of nausea struck. To keep from toppling head over heels down the steps, he threw a hand against a wall—worked to catch his breath. His vision swam. A whore asked if he was okay.

"I'm fine," he said. "Where's Danuuk?"

"Here, Kord," came the gravelly voice of his man.

Although the Kurg was well over forty years of age, no gray had touched Danuuk's long mane of jet hair, which he kept in a fat ponytail. For a Kurg, he had a gentle chin but still possessed the kite-shield cheek bones common among his race.

Danuuk climbed the stairs, gripped Barodane's forearm with a thick hand and helped him upright. "You look of shit."

Barodane nodded. "Which is why what I need you to do is so important."

"I listen." Raised in an outclan on the cusp of Kurgish society, Dannuk had never quite grasped the common tongue of Namarr nor its Val roots. With his aunt, Gratha, he spoke only Unti.

"Have a couple of your runner-boys take a message to the Redhand brothers." Barodane wheezed. "Tell them to get back here as fast as they can. There's a fight coming, and we're going to need them."

Danuuk nodded, his face a knotted mask of heavy bone. "Fight bring them here fast. Fast as fortune would."

"That's the idea." Barodane coughed. "They should be at Unturrus. The southern edge of Eastshadow. Your boys know where?"

"They know route. My runners, smart boys." He tapped his forehead with a meaty finger.

"Good."

Danuuk hovered a moment. "Gratha want you."

She was right where Barodane left her. He paused in the parlor's entrance.

"No, no, I will come to you." She shuffled across the floor toward him, a vial clutched in her hands, silk robes cascading behind. "Take five drops of this under your tongue every day until you are better. It will clear the cough, but the fever will need to pass on its own."

His hand shook as he took the vial and packed it away. "My thanks—"

"Is enough," Madame Gratha intercepted his hand on its way to the purse at his belt. "For now. You can think about repayment when you are well."

The elderly woman kissed his forehead. "Now, don't be a fool. Sleep somewhere dry tonight. I won't have my talents wasted on those too stupid to do what is good for them."

He sighed, his lungs feeling a little lighter now that he'd set in motion all he'd needed to. Lyansorca would help him discover Garlenna's intent. Danuuk would summon the Redhand brothers here within the week. The idea of sleep seemed somewhat more reasonable.

It wasn't much later when he entered the stables on trembling legs. It took longer to get there than he wished, but he'd taken several turns and back streets to ensure no one followed.

He intended to sleep for a long while without interruption.

He pressed a silver into the stable-girl's palm. "If a big woman comes, get her to go away. Tell her I went to the Rainy Meadows ruins. She might believe that. If men come looking for me, tell them I'm at the Gem Loft. If they say they were just there, tell them I'm at the Dregs. If they don't go away, wake me fast as you can. If Danuuk comes—you know him, yes? Good. Have him wait out of sight until I wake. Got all that?"

She nodded.

Nausea hit him again, nearly bringing him to his knees. "Is it getting dark already?"

The stable door slid open. Barodane shivered despite the fire inside slicking him with sweat. At the edge of awareness, he sensed his legs failing...light suddenly dimming.

Unyielding force struck his face and shoulder. A flat plane of straw-covered earth rotated slowly away. Consciousness became slippery.

Then he slid into darkness.

CHAPTER ELEVEN

SAY THE WORDS

The High Hall of the Ice Maiden's Keep teemed. Servants hung tapestries in honor of the holds set to arrive. Othwii walked beside Ishoa, stooped like a chicken hunting for insects.

Despite the Trials being an ancient coming-of-age ritual, it had changed during the thirty-five years of Scothean occupation. Now only those with enough wealth bought their way in, making the Trials exclusive to highborn.

This year was different. For the first time in history, a Scarborn would take part. Lodaris Warnock.

If successful, he would receive more than the old honor—*kotarg* as it was called in Fjordsong—he would be the first Scarborn to vote at Anjuhkar's court.

They passed the tapestries of the most prestigious holds. The furriers of Ghastiin: a wolf dancing over a trap, wrought in gray and purple thread. The seal hunters of Twilight Cape: three black spears thrust through a crescent moon. A gust wormed through the High Hall, rustling the tapestry of Shadowheart: mirrored halves of oak trees, one alive and green, the other dead and leafless. Beside it, the seal of the smiths of Summerforge, embers encircling an anvil, lifted slightly with the wind. Last in the line of tapestries were the cattlemen of Baen's Handle: a bull's horn crossing a maul on a brown and white checkered field.

Ishoa frowned. "I see grandmother has decided to omit the Warnocks."

Othwii presented a rigid smile. "They have no official sigil and no official hold. The Keelers are the true governors of the Fringes. But you'll not see them here. Torst Keeler is elderly and oft sick. Easily manipulated by the Warnocks."

The northernmost stronghold in all of Namarr was the Fringes. It bordered C'Dath, a lawless land of nomadic troll people. It had seen its share of bloody conflict. Most Anjuhks referred to it as the "Frigids" due to its inhospitable cold caused by merciless winds blowing through the nearby Straits of C'Dath.

"How did the Keelers let their hold be stolen?" Ishoa cocked her head. "Couldn't Grandmother take it back?"

"Your confusion is warranted. The answer to your second question is simple. Belara Frost wishes to avoid war. Armed conflict has taken all her family but you. If she takes back the Fringes, there will be a revolt. She hopes to defeat Syphion Muul and the Scarborn diplomatically."

"Your first question, I'll answer with a story." Othwii cleared his throat. "Three years ago, C'Dath had its worst freeze in hundreds of years. Even trolls are victim to winter's deadly touch. The Fringes was not prepared for what came next. They'd grown accustomed to small raiding parties coming over the mountains. Ten to thirty trolls at most, picking off livestock or the occasional caravan. If Torst Keeler had predicted what would transpire, it's possible he could have dealt with it."

Othwii paused beside a row of tables where servants slid benches into place beneath them. The seneschal leaned forward, his tone low. "Nearly five hundred C'Dathun trolls came down from the Ice King. Goat-legged, bearded, carrying crude axe's and swords of bronze. They overran the walls. To the man, the Keeler's holdguard were cut down or fled. The trolls managed to steal entire herds of livestock and grain stores before an appropriate defense was mustered. If not for Lodecka Warnock and her Scarborn, the C'Dathuns might have taken the city."

A shiver crawled up Ishoa's spine. Of the three Trials she'd soon face, she feared the Ice King's summit most. There were years in which Claimants went missing during the arduous journey. Dragged off by C'Dathun warbands, witnesses said. On rare occasions, Claimants rallied together to fight them off on the mountain's slopes.

Although Ishoa's skill at arms had increased with more frequent practice in recent years, she sorely doubted her ability to kill a C'Dathun, much less an entire warband. *At least I'll have Lodaris at my side.* A sliver of comfort as Othwii continued.

"Before the attack, Lodecka and Ularis Warnock had made a name for themselves training Scarborn as caravan guards. Their ruthless methods coupled with their pauper's rates made them the most sought-after private guards in all of Namarr. Where other businesses were forced to pay their caravan guards decent wages to risk their necks, the Scarborn needed no such compensation. It was far more than a job to them. They became...fanatical. A cult, you could say. Before long, wealthy merchants realized it was cheaper to hire Scarborn from halfway across Namarr than pay mercenaries in their own city. Contracts through the Winding Way and the north fork and south fork of the Prince's Highway landed in the Warnocks' lap with increasing regularity.

"Every wheel of profit went into hiring more guards, more trainers, more Scarborn. Two became twenty, twenty became fifty, fifty became a hundred. When the Keelers' holdguard fell before the troll's onslaught, it was those Scarborn who took the streets of the Fringes, and with Lodecka Warnock at their command gave not one foot of earth to the C'Dathuns beyond the livestock pens."

"Othwii, you know as well as I, some stories are more myth than fact. Is Lodecka Warnock truly that..." Ishoa squinted, unable to find the word.

Othwii raised an eyebrow. "Dangerous? Yes. And not only in combat. She is a master strategist. It's no coincidence that Syphion Muul sought her out to serve as the muscle to his Revocation dogma. Martial prowess alone must only be feared in limited conditions. Enemies with mental prowess however are of limitless concern. Lodecka understood the C'Dathun's motivations."

Ishoa muttered, "Knowing what motivates your enemies, the killing blade."

Othwii regarded her proudly. "You listen well, Isha. If Lodecka had tried to stop the trolls *before* they took the livestock, they would have remained desperate and maintained their assault to the very last. Faced with the slow death of starvation or the quick end of a blade, it was easier for the C'Dathuns to ignore their dying brethren at their side. There are few urges as powerful as the need to eat or feed one's offspring. By first allowing the C'Dathuns a small sense of victory, and then meeting them with harsh resistance, Lodecka knew they would lack the motivation to continue. They would flee. That, more than anything, is reason to both respect and fear Lodecka Warnock."

Ishoa gulped as she recalled the woman's blond braids pulled back around a scarred face, a challenge to any who dared meet her gaze.

"And in waiting, she let all the Keelers holdguard die, leaving Torst vulnerable."

Othwii's cheek twisted with seeming amusement. "I'd not thought of that, but yes. The timing of her action was cunning on many levels."

"Then what?" Ishoa shrugged. "Torst Keeler gave the Fringes to them?"

"At first the Warnocks only lent their strength. With the loss of their livestock and half their fighting force, Lord Keeler faced a serious dilemma. If he couldn't feed his people, he couldn't build ships. And without soldiers to protect the city, the likelihood of the Ice Maiden replacing the Keelers with another family of shipwrights drastically increased. So the Warnocks lent the Keelers soldiers at a cheap rate. It wasn't long before every holdguard in the Fringes was a Scarborn and Lodecka and Ularis were advising Torst Keeler. When the old man fell into ill health, none of his offspring dared step forward to claim leadership."

A trio of servants hustled past with a ladder and a heavy bolt of cloth.

Othwii glanced at them. "Scarborn from all over Anjuhkar have been flocking to the Fringes like a beacon fire ever since. And they are angry, Isha. The standard flying over the Fringes is not the wave and sail of the Keelers, it is three bloody droplets on a field of black hate. The Warnocks, in everything but an official title, are lady and lord of the Fringes. In the coldest, most dangerous city in all of Namarr, the Scarborn have found a place to call home."

Over Othwii's shoulder, a black tapestry rolled down the stone wall, embroidered with three crimson droplets. When the seneschal noticed Ishoa staring at it, he turned to regard it with her.

"Ah yes. Like I said, Isha, you must allow a small of sense of victory before you meet an enemy with harsh resistance."

By the standard of any Anjuhk, the counsel room beyond the High Hall was lavish. Rich blue tapestries filled the corners, the charging snow bison of the Frosts etched in shimmering silver thread. A garland of flowers hung on each wall, the azure sentry rose at their center, white and pink winter blossoms surrounding. On a table shaped like a horn, gold platters bore an odd assortment of goods, most but not all of which were food.

The handful of other counsel members present appeared equally confused by the spread. Every face was familiar, though there was one she'd not seen in many years.

She bowed to Arick Quinn. "Congratulations, cousin. You've returned to Jarik a fully trained knight of the Crown." Braids of white hair hung to his waist. Quinns, like Frosts, were known to have white hair, but Danath had snuffed the trait from the Frost line, leaving Ishoa with a dark-brown mane.

She'd never been close with Arick. His five years in Alistar training to be a knight didn't help. Seven years separated them in age, but it was a difference in personality that forced distance between them.

In truth, he unnerved her. There was no scrap of fat to him, no wasted motion in how he sat or moved, and wherever he turned his attention it seemed eerily purposeful. He was like an ice tiger on the hunt, his focus dire as if survival depended on it. Yet there was a gracefulness to him as well. Light as wind, hard as steel, and with a demeanor matching both. Startling blue eyes locked with hers. He folded forward with precision. "Thank you, Highness. You have grown as well. The Trials don't stand a chance."

A flutter filled her. The Trials were fast approaching.

"Aye." Wolst clapped a hand on Arick's shoulder and reached past him to tear a hunk of greasy meat from a platter of salted seal ribs. "She's ready as she's going to be. Enough fire in her to boil the Blue river, singe the white wolverine's backside, and stay the Ice King's chill."

"She'll need more than passion." Arick Quinn stared through her. "Calmer heads prevail." When Arick had been a Claimant, he'd been the first to complete every trial.

But do I have what it takes?

Othwii took a seat and championed her where she failed to champion herself. "Soon we'll see there is more to our princess than we thought."

At the back of the room, a door shuddered to a close. Belara Frost had entered, Hast in tow. The knight-captain of Jarik was not so large as his father, but then again no one was. Hast's red-braided beard and hair cascaded down the front of a blue tabard, covering chain armor. He carried a spear and wore a storm bear pelt around his shoulders. His plated warskirt jostled throughout the room as he led the Ice Maiden to the horn-shaped table.

"Greetings, Anjuhks." From ear to ear, Belara Frost's gummy smile stretched out her wrinkles. A small tuft of elegant white curls covered the back half of her head, and she wore a silver dress lined in wolf fur. *She's over eighty now. How can she stand so straight and smile so broadly?*

For Ishoa, her grandmother had always been an enigma. Strength conveyed through a diplomat's confidence. Danger issued with a tone of motherly love. One of Namarr's oldest and most prestigious heroes embodied in the frail form of an aged woman.

The wife of Danath Ironlight. The Ice Maiden. Duchess of Anjuhkar.

"I would have loved for different circumstances to surround this meeting, but alas." Belara shrugged. "Life moves forward regardless of our little preferences, doesn't it? Let us begin."

Wolst, Othwii, Arick, and Ishoa ringed the table, while Hast remained at attention beside Belara Frost as she addressed the small counsel.

"Look around you." She gestured at the contents of each gold platter. "Go on."

Wolst inspected a pile of furs. "A dancing wolf...branded into the skin."

Belara made her way slowly around the table. "Precisely. You have in your hand the work of the furriers of Ghastiin." She pointed to a platter of smoked meats and cheeses. "Snow bison yield from the cattlemen of Baen's Handle. Wool from the shepherds of White Plains. Salted seal ribs from Twilight Cape. The very table you sit around, a gift from Megalor Bog's father a decade past. I'm told they cut it from the oldest oak in all of Shadowheart."

Coming to stand behind Wolst, Belara hooked a finger under the honor plate on his shoulder. "Every piece of plate and weapon we bear...worked by the smiths of Summerforge."

Ishoa dragged a thumb along the button of her sword's pommel, felt a bumpy surface. She glanced down. A tiny anvil surrounded by embers: the sigil of Summerforge.

Belara's voice rose. "But what is it the Warnocks and their Scarborn bring to the table? No meat, no cloth, no lumber. Not even the ships and sails the Fringes were once known for. Barnacles and blood cover the work Torst Keeler and his family once did for Anjuhkar." Her eyebrows jumped, tone demurring. "Now the Warnocks bring an ideologue to the table."

Belara's smile faded. "The fraction of goods you see before you are but a reflection of the resources we have. There is a misconception among many Namorites that Anjuhkar is a cold and desolate land, dependent upon the fruits of Peladonia and Lah-Tsarra. That is only partially true. Cold, yes. Rugged, yes. But where they're wrong is that we need to rely on our sister duchies.

"Before the missionaries from Valat settled the plains of Peladonia, we Anjuks were here. Before the explorers of Malzacor set up trade routes in the mountains of Lah-Tsarra to mine gold, we Anjuhks were here. After Scothea invaded and subjugated both territories, we Anjuhks remained—unconquered. When the smoke cleared, the blood dried, and the dead were laid to rest from my husband's rebellion, *we* Anjuhks were here. We are now, and always have been, completely self-sufficient."

A bony fist wrapped in branching veins rose at Belara's side. Her smile returned as she addressed Ishoa. "Tell me, did Scothea conquer us during their invasion?"

Ishoa had been paying such close attention, the question caught her off guard. "No, Duchess."

The Ice Maiden swept the back of a hand across her brow in mock relief. "If she'd not known that answer, I'd have had your head, seneschal." She wandered behind Othwii. Seated, his eyes were nearly parallel with hers.

Othwii's protruding throat apple bobbed with a chuckle. Belara kissed his sparsely haired pate. "I jest. It's a good head. We should keep it."

Wolst leaned onto his elbows and pulled another seal rib off the rack. "If it had come to armed conflict, we'd have bled the Scoths more than they liked, Duchess." He studied the rib meat in his hands. "But in the end, they'd have threshed us like wheat if we hadn't made peace."

Belara straightened. "Peace is what happens when enemies fear each other enough to avoid the uncertain results of attempted conquest."

Wolst chewed, grumbling around the meat in his mouth. "That's optimistic."

"So it is. Yet even with the mightiest army the world had seen, Scothea did *not* invade Anjuhkar. Perhaps they thought victory less assured than you make it out." She turned to Arick Quinn. "Young Arick, perhaps you can answer my next question. Have we Anjuhks ever defeated Scothea?"

He gave a series of deep nods, three long, white, braids flopping onto his honor plate. "Yes, Duchess."

"Correct. Anjuhkar, as part of Namarr, defeated Scothea. Without our participation, my husband's slave rebellion would have failed. The moment I married Danath Ironlight, Scothea was vanquished."

She met the eyes of each counsel member in turn. A baffled silence hung over them. Wolst's chewing slowed. His brow knit together. Othwii inspected the table as if answers lied among the goods there.

Understanding struck Ishoa like an arrow. She sat upright but held her tongue. She didn't want to be wrong.

Her grandmother seemed to notice her urge to speak. "Isha, you're to do the Trials soon. Using your voice is no different than undertaking the Trial of Crossing. There is but one way to do it. That is to throw oneself in fully. Come now, we're well past the moment of toe-dipping. What do you see?"

Ishoa licked dry lips. "You—you're making Syphion Muul's case for Revocation. You're trying to convince us that Anjuhkar should break away from the United Lands of Namarr and be its own sovereign nation again...like it was before Scothea invaded."

For a few thundering heartbeats, the counsel room drifted into quiet reflection.

"She's clever." Belara Frost raised an eyebrow at Othwii. "Consider your head safe."

Pride eddied through Ishoa's chest. Wolst issued her a reverent tilt of the head.

"I must say, Duchess," Othwii blinked at Belara. "You laid it out in an almost convincing manner."

"Almost? It is *very* convincing," she said. "After the Trials comes the annual court of Anjuhkar. Revocation will be put to a vote. We must do everything in our power to see it crushed."

Arick Quinn's even tone pierced the air. "Why stop it? Why not support Revocation? You would be Queen of Anjuhkar."

Wolst scowled, shoulders hunching like a storm bear preparing to charge. "What's that now, boy?"

"Apologies, Uncle," Arick said impassively. "Like the Ice Maiden, I make the case of our enemies so we might better understand how to counter them."

Wolst relaxed and trailed off into agitated muttering.

"The answer lies in the last part of what I've just mentioned, Arick," said Belara. "United as a nation behind Danath and working with a singular purpose, we won the Unity Wars. The disparate pieces of Namarr were able to stand against the Scothean war juggernaut. However, that peace came at a price. Even with Anjuhkar's might married to that of the Kurgs, the Dominarri, Peladonia and Lah-Tsarra, I lost my son and both grandchildren."

Belara referred to Ishoa's father, Malath. A flush of sadness compelled Ishoa to draw inward.

"If Syphion Muul and the Scarborn rally enough hearts and minds to their cause, rest assured the vote for Revocation will pass. And that means, Scothea will be back." Belara Frost stopped before a garland of flowers, inhaled the fragrance of a sentry rose. She sighed. "We must *never* let that happen."

"Thus, I've altered custom," the duchess said. "Ishoa will enter the Trials ahead of her fifteenth birthday."

"Why?" Ishoa lifted her chin. Under the table, she picked viciously at her nail beds. "I understand you wish to crush Revocation, but would my single vote truly make the difference?"

"It doesn't seem worth the risk," said Arick. "Ishoa is the last Ironlight. By my count, Revocation doesn't stand a chance. Why subject her to the Trials before she's ready if all we gain from it is a meaningless vote?"

"Because." Belara motioned for Hast. The knight-captain offered his elbow, which the duchess used to ease herself down into a seat. "The Collective of Namarr has begun to turn."

The temperature in the counsel chamber increased. Sweat broke across Ishoa's neck and forehead. Wild eyes darted from face to face, as if seeking to confirm with one another that the duchess's words were rightly heard.

Numb fingers wrapped around Ishoa's insides and squeezed.

Belara summoned attention with a hand upheld. "The Collective grows weary of voting in a shadowcrown. Every year, they look at one another wondering who will be the new Crown Prince. I see their hearts clear enough though. Ambitious men cannot contain such things."

The duchess locked eyes with Ishoa. "You must play the game now, darling. You must gain your vote. If Revocation is overwhelmingly shot down, it may never recover. But more important still. You must prove your strength, Ishoa. At fifteen, it would have been normal. But if you complete the Trials now, you'll be the youngest to have done so."

"Overshadowing the first Scarborn," Wolst nodded emphatically. "A clever counter-stroke, Duchess."

"It sends a message to the rest of the Namorite Collective." Othwii stooped forward onto elbows, sleeves piling around slender arms. "It says the last Ironlight is more like her predecessors than they thought."

"It gives us time," Belara said. "Hopefully, four years worth. If not, I fear the future will be most challenging."

"What if she doesn't complete them?" Arick's face swiveled toward Ishoa's with the smoothness of an eagle spotting a hare. "What if she fails?"

"Damn it boy!" Wolst slapped the table with a bludgeoning palm. "Have some faith."

"I'm ready." Despite her words, doubt dripped persistent at the back of Ishoa's mind.

"What about Lodaris Warnock?" Arick's gleaming azure eyes did not waver. "She's friends with the boy. During the Trial of Summit, she'll be out of our sight. Unprotected."

Ishoa rose halfway from her seat. "Lodaris would never hurt me."

"Another then," Arick said. "Who knows what allies they've secured."

"I've made arrangements for her safety," said the duchess tersely. "While they're not foolproof, we must take risks. There is more at stake here than Ishoa's life. The fate of all of Namarr is at hand. If she fails to complete the Trials—or dies in the attempt—I fear tens of thousands will be buried alongside her."

The room spun. Darkness pressed in at the edges of Ishoa's vision. Bile filled the back of her throat. Faces flashed past...

Ularis Warnock looked down his thin nose at her. His condescending smirk became his wife's flat affect. A network of scars. Full of icy hatred, Lodecka watched Ishoa.

*Woefully naive...*Syphion Muul's words.

Ishoa sputtered, coughed, inhaled...

Light returned to the world. She took another deep breath, and made a fist where only a limp hand had been moments before.

When Ishoa looked up from her lap, she found Wolst watching her, concern etched into the creases around his eyes. She mouthed the words, "I'm fine."

Belara Frost meanwhile had continued, "...sanction a rabid dog, would you? Or a charging bison? Maybe throw sanctions at an ice tiger as it sinks its teeth into your nape? If only something so simple worked." The duchess's voice climbed as it swept the room. "No. We must approach the Scarborn with balance, my dears. To go too far in either direction appears as weakness. It destabilizes my seat of power and affords them an opportunity to garner influence.

"So, we keep them guessing. *Delay* their momentum. Gather information. Wait. We offer inconsequential ground while standing resolute with what is most important. They've been given the honor of a hold in my High Hall and I've allowed the first Scarborn child ever to take part in the Trials. If Scarborn see the scraps of progress toward equality that we give them, their motivation to join the Warnocks at the Fringes may be hamstrung. I've also writ into law two decrees. The first...Scarborn offspring shall require double the tithe for admittance into the Trials. There's a debt to pay, and by our ancestors, they shall pay it. The second...no Scarborn shall be allowed to bear steel in the High Hall."

Wolst cleared his throat. "Syphion Muul is no Scarborn."

"Nor is he a soldier," said Belara. "The man's weapon of choice is his tongue. That, unfortunately, I cannot bar. Now, Ishoa, how did they respond to the decrees?"

Ishoa recounted their reactions.

A brooding silence followed. Othwii sighed then steepled spidery fingers together and pressed them to his lips.

A flicker of acknowledgment passed between Belara Frost and Wolst.

"Ishoa..." Her grandmother leaned to one side in her chair. She rubbed her thumb and index finger together as she mused. The hair at the back of Ishoa's neck stood straight, her arms too. Words she didn't wish to hear were coming.

Careful what you wish for, Isha.

"Lodaris could be an asset in the fight against Revocation. And you, my dear, are our greatest leverage." Belara tone flattened, became emotionless, as if she ordered an execution. "I want you to gain his trust."

Wolst's chair shot back as he stood. "I don't like this. Duchess, please, it's too dangerous. The Warnocks already suspect her."

"Let them suspect." The duchess rolled her eyes. "Ishoa is to be Crown Princess of Namarr. She'll need to make far more dangerous choices than this. The duty to rule demands she set aside self-interest. From here on, everything she does or *doesn't* do carries momentous consequences."

If I'm to rule Namarr, I must answer duty's call.

"Well, Ishoa. Your interactions with Lodaris Warnock could reveal vital information." Belara Frost rested her chin on a cadaverous fist propped up the arm of the chair. "What say you?"

Ishoa wanted to flee. Instead, she bore down, flexing the muscles of her torso to stymie the swirling chaos there. "I can manage him." Blood squeezed forth from the inside of her cheek where she chewed. "I already have his trust."

Wolst pounded the table. A goblet jumped and clattered to its side, maroon contents splashing. "The Warnocks must believe their boy in a similar position. They wouldn't let Isha close if they didn't!"

A lump formed in Ishoa's throat. *Could Lodaris be using me? Do his parents force him to gain my favor?*

The duchess stood, hip joints popping. The force of her voice dashed any question regarding her strength. "If she cannot handle one Scarborn child, then Namarr is doomed."

Ishoa's body tightened with frustration. "Uncle," she hissed, "I can do this." She stood, the pit of her stomach lurching.

I've waited my entire life to feel like a true Ironlight. To be worthy of Namarr's crown.

"I understand the situation. I will take precautions." Ishoa's mouth formed a hard line. She crossed a threshold from which there was no turning back. "I will spy on the Warnocks. Lodaris trusts me. I can use that...for the good of Namarr."

"Indeed." Belara smiled, though Ishoa noted a wet sheen in one eye. "Indeed." The duchess blinked then sniffled. "Othwii, have you made sure we have a way to listen in on the rooms?"

"Our holds have done nothing to suspect them of siding with Scarborn?" said Arick.

Belara Frost's response was mocking. "My dear boy, until they've voted down Revocation, we spy on them. You must understand the ambition of the holds. Without a tax from the Crown on their goods, most of them would see ample financial gain from Revocation. Words are one thing. Actions, another. Wave enough gold in a lord's face and they'll sell you their mother." She turned to her seneschal. "Alter the rooms. Immediately."

"Yes, Duchess," said Othwii. "A man from the masonry of Breckenbright is in the town prop—"

"No," Belara said, "I want an Anjuhk. Preferably a veteran of the Great Betrayal. Not some outsider. Too easily corrupted. Especially a gold-fingered mason from Breckenbright."

Othwii nodded.

The duchess indicated the counsel meeting was over.

All rose to recite Danath's words. The same ones Namarr was founded upon.

As one, their voices echoed throughout the chamber:

"Shackles only hold those who allow it.

"One who does not seek to break their chain is already broken by it.

"Here and now.

"Free your swords! Free your souls!

"My Sons and Daughters of Namarr, you cannot die but once. Let us live, boldly and without fear!"

But Ishoa could not shake her fear. She'd finally been given a chance to prove herself worthy of her family's name.

However, the cost was high. She would betray the only one who made her feel like she already belonged.

CHAPTER TWELVE

WAGERING OBLIVION

Akyris makes for a poor slave.

Weeks pass. He heeds my daughter's words. Suffers my every command. If I see a speck, I snap my fingers for it to be swept away. If I feel a lump in my bedding, I summon him to beat it with a stick until gone. If my feet ache, a basin is to be filled with hot water and laid before me. Chores are done. Done again. Then done more to my liking, even when they're already perfect. Inane tasks, for which there is no purpose but for me to forget their intention, he completes without question.

Akyris gives only a look. Contempt holds his chin high. Hate rims the eyes. Cool rage rides his brow.

I wish the resenting grooves of his face to deepen, so I set him to backbreaking labor that would have a grown man cursing my name.

A name he has yet to ask in his selfish woe.

Normally, the diligence with which Akyris obeys, the vigor with which he tackles every duty, would be ideal for a slave. But after all of it, the look is still there.

He refuses to buckle.

I tell him to dig a line of thirty-three holes from the cottage to the elm tree, exactly three feet deep and three feet apart. He does it without a word. Malice bends him to his work, drives every shovel full day and night until the task is done. Good slaves would either beg and bow subserviently to let their master know who is in control or smile and do the work with an air of joy.

Akyris does neither. He refuses to break. A futile attempt to prove I am his lesser. Admirable.

I don't break either. I have my own mission and it far outweighs his pride. If he learns nothing else by the time we're through, he'll learn where the stubbornness in his bones comes from.

Another week passes, pushing his limits, testing his spirit in earnest. "Make me a seat for sitting under the elm tree. A stump will do," I say. "And make one for yourself while you're at it, little fly. I may want company."

From sunrise to sundown, I hear him hacking. *Thack. Thack. Thack.* The next day, I hear him complaining. A bad sign. The herald of despair. Taking a break to catch his breath, with sweat and wood chips coating his shoulders, Akyris wanders to the cottage for a drink of water. His eyes tell the story of one nearing his edge.

I fear failure for all of us.

Mags is quick to point out the same concern. Nothing regarding the future goes by without her feeling it first, much to my chagrin.

"He's close to the breaking point," she says. "You push him too far."

"What does it matter how close he is?" I snap. "Criticize me *if* we fail."

Magomedes emits a ripple of unrest. "If we fail, there won't be a 'you' or an 'I.' No success. No failure."

"In that case, tell me something that helps. Encourage me, perhaps. Tell me I'm pretty or special, like you want me to do for the boy."

Pensive silence surrounds Magomedes for a few heartbeats. "I've been trying to help you, but the buzz of your own pride is all you seem to hear. Akyris needs something."

Finished with the stump-seats, he comes to me, sun scorched and streaked with dirt. A patch of sap covered in wood chips blotches his elbow and dots the backs of his hands. I nod then give him tomorrow's task.

Tomorrow could never come and he'd be okay with it, I suspect.

At dusk on the second day, he stares at me, exhausted. Tears stream down his cheeks. A few dozen bloody scratches streak the skin on his arms and legs. It took him the better part of two days to clear out the wall of blackberry bushes encroaching on either side of the lane leading to the cottage. Armed with only his rusty dagger and an ax, Akyris sawed and slashed the brambles, barely coming out victorious.

"Why?" his voice cracks. "Why are you doing this?"

"They were in my way," I say. "If you haven't noticed, I hobble. What if I tripped on a bramble during my morning walk? You want your grandmother to be safe, don't you?"

He pouts. "I mean, why are you doing this to me? Do you enjoy seeing me suffer?"

I don't. I want to tell him so, but I don't. That has to be something he learns in time. Magomedes chimes in, convinces me to give him something.

"Take a break for a couple of days," I say. "Then come to me. I have an idea you'll like for once."

"Doubtful." His chin drops to his chest. He mutters about an additional torment he doesn't deserve.

Despair inches ever closer.

I wait on the porch as he approaches. The scrapes have healed into half a hundred crisscrossing, thin scabs. Since I told him to rest, he's avoided me like the plague, fearing I would break my promise and deliver on his worries about some new torment. He doesn't know me, doesn't know I don't break my word out of hand. I want him to feel some sense of control. As much as he despises me, there is a chance he trusts me.

To him, I'm a nightmare. By now, I hope, I'm a predictable one.

"Akyris, how long have I been here?"

"Too long," he says.

I laugh, wait for a true response.

"Over a month," he says. "Enough to last a lifetime. I'll be okay if you leave for another twelve years after this."

"Oh, really?" My tongue darts over my lower lip. He cringes at the sight. The little bastard does nothing to withhold his contempt. "But I've come to enjoy my life here. Thanks in particular to your sterling service. I dub thee best grandson I've ever had." Waving a hand through the air, I mockingly trace the four arrows of the gods of light and a fifth for the dark god.

He shuffles, staring at his feet. Green eyes rise to meet my own, a starving dog honing in on a scrap of meat. "Is this how you treated my mother?"

The hate there begins to plot dark futures. The boy has a dangerous side when it comes to protecting my daughter. For that, I love him.

I dispel his vengeful thinking with a chuckle. "Of course not. I treated your mother like the princess she is. But don't blame her for the differences here. You're a good kid, Akyris."

Rapid blinking and a creased forehead. The only response he musters.

"That's right. You are a good kid. You respect your mother a great deal, and I've squeezed every last drop of that respect out of you for my own endeavors." I make my voice stern. Steel. A guarantee. "I promise you this though. It won't stop, not unless you do one last thing for me."

"Anything." He means it. I could ask him to shave the head of the town constable while he sleeps and he'd do it.

"You're certain? You may not like—"

"Damn it, yes!" Thinking better of his outburst, he affects more subdued tones. "I'll do anything. It can't be worse than what I've been doing."

He's exactly where I want him. Where I've needed him. Self-satisfied, I struggle to keep from smiling. "It's actually quite simple. But as you've seen, a simple task does not necessarily equate to an easy one."

Rapt attention. He nods.

"You must sit in silence, unthinking, for three hours a day for thirty days."

One green eye narrows as he seems to realize something. "Three and thirty...like the holes you made me dig."

I nod. "Three hours a day for thirty days. If you do that, I leave."

"Why do this? It makes no sense. You're picking random numbers, random tasks—"

"If not," I hold up a finger. "I stay until my death. I assure you, I may look old and feeble and crippled, but I have the heartbeat of a lioness." I pound my chest. "I could out dance you any day of the week, little fly."

Akyris growls at the nickname. "That's a lot of hours and a lot of days."

"To the young, time is often a headwind. For the motivated, quite the opposite. You either want me gone or you don't." I shrug. "This is my only offer."

If we're to be successful, Akyris must understand that hard decisions require one to sacrifice hedonistic impulse. There is no other way to clear space for the Path that must be and the benefits that may come.

As the Anjuhks say, "A hungry belly in spring makes for a full larder in winter." More cynical Anjuhks might say, "You eat a whole steak, you eat the last steak."

To his credit, Akyris chooses the larder. "When can we start?"

"Now."

"So you'll leave in thirty days?"

I nod. "Care to know where I'll be going?"

The boy shrugs. A smile splits his face as if the deed is already done. His first smile in weeks. "Not really."

I turn away, tongue darting over lower lip as I inspect a hangnail. I speak in playful tones. "What if you decide to go with me when I leave? You'd want to know where then, wouldn't you?"

A look of abject disgust springs across Akyris's face, his upper lip curling. "Why would I ever want to go anywhere with you? You're a mean old hag who only cares about herself."

I chuckle, noting the hypocrisy in his judgment about what is selfish. "Know anything about crows?"

He gives an imperceptible shake of his head.

"Crows are wonderful birds, but what most people don't know is they are exceedingly smart. You know nothing about me, little fly, and I'd like to keep it that way—for now. But one thing I will tell you is I've spent a great deal of time observing birds. What *you* might find interesting..." I chew the hangnail. "...is that a crow is so smart, it can predict the future actions of other crows based on its own prior behaviors. Because a crow steals from other animals, including its peers, it knows it should hide its hoard in order to avoid being stolen from. Because of its past, so does it shape its future. In a sense, you could say its survival depends on such self-reflection."

Akyris frowns, searches the ground for an answer. After a while, his head jerks upward. He stares at me with narrowed eyes. "Are you trying to say I need to be more self-reflective or are you saying I called you selfish because *I'm* selfish."

He's even more clever than I thought. Not even thirteen.

"Both," I say. Pride tugs at the corners of my mouth. "You are a smart one, aren't you? Smart as a crow, one might say."

He can't tell whether to take what I've said as a compliment or dig. Miraculously, it's the former. "Thanks," he mumbles.

"So, do we have a deal?"

Akyris thrusts out an arm. "Deal."

Our hands wrap around forearms, silence filling the space between us. Wind kicks a dead vine from the blackberry bushes lining the lane, sending it tumbling through the dust.

Our hands fall to our sides. Our dooms are sealed.

"Well then, why don't you endeavor to be rid of me and start your silence now."

He walks hurriedly toward the stump under the elm tree, tosses the word, "Gladly," over a shoulder.

I hobble after.

My hand aches from the morning walk, which is often the case when one must rely so heavily upon a staff. My hip weakens by the months rather than the years.

The sun pierces through a bank of layered clouds, white wisps over dense gray. It's that tentative time when things could go any which way with the weather. A chill wind that brings storm showers or a powerful gust to push it all away and leave naught but blue skies. Such is the transition into autumn.

Either way, I hold a hand over my eyes to block the brightness.

Akyris perches on the stump like a brooding vulture, thin shoulders propping up a drab shirt. He scrapes at the dirt with a stick as I arrive.

He wears a suspicious frown. "What are you doing?"

"I've come to observe."

Akyris raises an eyebrow. "You mean you'll be watching me when I do this? All thirty days?"

"Indeed. How else am I supposed to know you're doing what we agreed?" I take a seat on a stump within arm's reach of the Akyris. "What a lovely seat." My body aches more and more in my old age. If it were safe, I'd spend all my time in the River and exist solely as untethered energy rather than rely on this decaying vessel.

Akyris rotates on the stump to face away from me. "Whatever it takes."

Whatever it takes...

On that, at least, we agree. On the matter of silence however...

The stick in his hand scratches the dirt. I reach forth with my twisted staff and nudge him in the ribs, just sharp enough to piss him off. He sits bolt upright. Face framed in dark, wind-tousled hair. His glare is menacing despite his boyishness. A brooding look, some might say.

His tone is breathy accusation. "What. Are. You. Doing?"

"I'd say the same to you. Do you know what silence means?"

He looks down at the stick in his hand, then pulls up his knees and crosses his arms around them protectively before tossing it away. I sit still, unmoving despite the discomfort in my body. I close my eyes...breathe slowly...deliberately. Moments and images and waves of sensation shift around me. Through me.

A ballast in the River.

I watch him through the jeweled eye...

See his puzzled expression. The way his eyes dart back and forth as if reading his own thoughts. Judgments, curiosities, worries—all of it a deafening roar.

Without opening my eyes, I say, "You are too loud."

Akyris sneers. "I'm not making a sound you crazy old—"

"Your thoughts scream," I say.

"How do you—"

I cut him off. He's not ready for the how. Not yet. "Your eyes dance. Your fingers tap. Your body shifts and worms around. You are not silent. Silence is silence. Complete and utter. If you want me gone, drop your feet to the earth. Close your eyes. Sit straight and be still in all ways."

"This deal gets worse by the second. How can my mother have been birthed from someone so..." Akyris groans the word, "...intolerable."

"It's the truth you can't tolerate." My eyes remain closed. The jeweled eye is all I need. "Here's the reality. I can stay with you and your mother for years or I can stay with you for thirty more days. If I am to leave, I will do so on my own terms. You can meet them or you can shrink from them. Whichever you choose, choose it now, for I am not one to waste time with cowards."

Emotional hooks are the best hooks when manipulating someone. I'm the first not to approve of my methods but time forces my hand to be less thoughtful of feelings.

He scoffs. "You don't like to waste time but you have me sitting on a stump in silence and—" A strangled cry of frustration fills his throat. "Whatever it takes."

His arms and knees drop. He straightens. Eyelids flutter closed.

Good choice, little fly.

I watch him the whole time, and the whole time, he does what is required. He sits in silence, brow alternating between bunching and relaxing as is expected for one managing the ebb and flow between thoughts and being.

I've learned time favors decisions both clear and bold. For those working against the River's current, commitment is a necessity. More precious than gold, or weapons, or magic powers, none of which are earned without commitment. In this, Akyris proves capable. But this is only the start of his training.

I held more tension than I thought. It melts away as I watch my grandson hone his Locus on the stump. I'm relieved. No longer must I chop at him like a sinewy oak. I am free to love the boy, to shape him with care, to call forth his innate power rather than stoke its embers through malicious methods.

This is the first day of our last days.

There is no going back now. Then again, there never was. Only onward. Ever onward. Toward doom and destruction, or if we're lucky a future that falls slightly short of it.

We will arrive there from here. This place of silence.

Beginnings are but mirrors for the end. A first step becomes a last step. So we sit, the first day of training, the last day of being swept away in the current of sleep. A day mirroring future mastery of the River's powers.

That is the hope upon which all life hangs.

Silence, the place from which all action emerges.

Space, the place from which one's Locus becomes.

We begin and end here.

Tears gather, plummet down my weathered cheeks, tremble on my chin like a dewdrop in a spider's web.

Wheels groan into motion.

CHAPTER THIRTEEN

YOUR FATE IS YOUR OWN

T he moment Barodane realized he was going to die, he crawled from the stall. The air was thick with the scent of mildew and horse shit. Even with a stoppered nose, he tasted the bitter stench. After heavy rains, the stable's scent was always worse than usual for a few days, and on those days, Barodane made it a priority to sleep at the Dregs.

He winced as he strapped the shadowguard honor plate to his shoulder from a seated position.

Damn you, Garlenna. He cursed his prosort for forcing him to suffer his recovery in such conditions. By his best estimate, the better part of three days had come and gone in a state of fevered delirium. After the first night in the stables, he'd stuck a couple of thorns into his arm to stay his misery. He learned the hard way that ascending while sick was a poor idea. Demons had stretched in the shadows. A thousand lusting eyes, a hundred fanged mouths, a hundred bellies roaring for a taste of his soul. They tore at his body, worried at it like a brood of vultures at a carcass. He thrashed so much and displaced so much straw that he eventually rested on cold earth. *Maybe this will be my grave,* he had thought.

His pleas for mercy from the demons had set the horses to screaming and kicking in their stalls. Once it appeared the stable girl sat beside him, pressing a damp cloth against his forehead. A wishful hallucination or a sliver of reality? He wasn't sure.

He'd returned to conscious reality feeling far worse. A true descent. The next day and a half passed in abject misery. *A torment well deserved*, the dead had said. He wondered if it was them who'd come to him as demons. After a moment's consideration, he was certain it was them; it wouldn't be the first time such specters had visited during ascension.

He recalled a quote from a book he'd once read by Locastrii, the Mistress of Time, one of the most famous Awakened. "Godsthorn gives what it needs to give and takes what it needs to take. What's left is the truth, no matter if you wish to hear it or not." Barodane shook his head. Pain shot through his neck and iron-stiff shoulders.

Life is pain. That's the truth. His nose felt as though someone had pumped it full of wine, and his chest crackled with phlegm when he breathed.

If I stay here another day, I'll die in this stable. I need help.

It wasn't ideal to go to the Dregs. Garlenna was there, and it was where Hyram would look for him. The alternative: stay and die. The voices of his past were not ready for him to join them. *You'll die when you've suffered enough for a thousand lifetimes.*

Breathless, he stood, every joint feeling like it was clamped in a steel vice. His low back was tender to the touch—even his clothing was uncomfortable lying against it. Pulling the tiny vial Madame Gratha had given him, he slammed it back, hoping it was near enough the right amount. *Maybe a little more will work faster?*

He doubted it. But patience was never his strong suit.

A patient man wouldn't have our blood on his hands.

The barn door slid open.

"Kord! Kord, thank the Sempyrean! I gotta talk with you."

"Jennim?"

The young man blocked the entrance. "Please."

Barodane shouldered past, pushing Jennim out of the stable and then sliding the door closed behind him. The sun's light stabbed his eyes as he took in his surroundings. "Where's the girl?"

"I sent her off to get you more medicine from Madame Gratha," Jennim said, "and fresh water. See? I wanna help you."

Barodane kicked himself for not giving the girl instructions about Jennim. When he turned back to the young man, he noticed bursts of purple and green covering lumps on one side of his face.

"Looks like you've got your own problems." Barodane made to hobble past. "Now leave me alone."

"Please, Kord." Jennim brought his hands into a position of prayer and closed his eyes. "If you don't give Hyram what he wants, he'll kill me. I remember, when I was little, I remember you owned this stable. Kept it for your own horse and a couple other folk. My momma too. You didn't want anyone to know where it was and I didn't tell Hyram 'bout it either. If I did, we'd both be dead. I know you loved my momma. Otherwise, why buy her a horse?"

Jennim grabbed Barodane's cloak. The cloth bunched, slipped off the shadow-guard honor plate underneath. "Why smile at me when I was a kid? Why bring me wooden swords to play with?"

Instead of love and wistful remembrance, anger swelled within Barodane. Memories of Tyne, of happiness lost, brought pain and guilt. "What a cretin you've become." He slapped the young man's hand from his shoulder. Bunched cloak unfurled to cover the false honor plate once more. "Why should I bend to your will? Because I treated you kindly? You're no child. Accept your fate like a man and stop dragging your mother into this. It's despicable, attempting to use my feelings for Tyne against me."

Barodane hesitated. Then he lied. "I assure you, there are no such feelings left. She was merely a whore. A passing comfort. My kindness to you was nothing more than collateral to keep her under thumb." He felt colder and harder than the stones of a crypt. "You hear me, Jennim? You were nothing to me then." He turned away. "And you're even less to me now."

Mustering all the strength left in him, Barodane shoved the boy he'd once played with. Jennim backpedaled, landed hard in the mud.

"Follow me again and it will not be Hyram who kills you," Barodane said.

Motion beside a building in the distance caught Barodane's attention. A shadowed figure. *Eustus?* He tried blinking his vision to greater clarity, but they'd already ducked out of sight. *If anyone was truly even there.* A harsh godsthorn journey sometimes had residual effects. It wouldn't have been the first time. If it truly was Hyram's dullard, the stable was no longer an option for sleep. Besides, Jennim had already spoiled it.

Regret cut at Barodane. He glanced at the young man now rubbing a hand on his back in the mud. He imagined Eustus running a sword through Jennim's neck, red blood mingling with sparse, red beard. The boy *was* kind.

Tyne's boy.

Barodane had loved her. Having Jennim around was a pleasant piece of the relationship he hadn't expected. He'd never had a child of his own. This man, caked in mud and groaning, was as close as he'd ever come.

I would have had one with Omari if I'd not forsaken my crown for misery and godsthorn.

A life alongside Omari and a pair of mythical children was ringed in light as it flashed before his mind's eye.

Then the shadows crept in to steal the fantasy.

Reality was far grimmer.

Green eyes with brown flecks stared at Barodane from the past. Life drained from them...

You deserve no child! the voices screamed.

He pushed away the thoughts. *Jennim is not my burden to bear.*

The doom chorus rose. *You were his hero. A terrible choice had he known who you truly are. Prince of death! Don't you see? Only suffering awaits those who seek to love you.*

His chin fell to his chest. Drained of an already scarce emotional well, the push had stolen every drop of the physical one. Daggers danced across his lungs with every wheeze and cough. He left Jennim groaning in the mud and made his way toward the Dregs Inn.

Barodane pounded a fist against the back door. The brief journey from stable to inn had been arduous and left his clothing soaked through with sweat. The sun burned at a thin layer of gray-white cloud without poking through. Barodane's eyes responded poorly to the light, so he went back to staring at the ground. He hammered at the door again, swayed on his feet and nearly fell. That inspired him to slump against the wall to wait.

The door flung open a moment later. Meckin stepped out, glaring and searching for someone to shout at for the racket. Barodane waved a hand for assistance.

"Great Triune God, Kord! You okay?"

Barodane huddled deeper into his cloak.

Meckin snorted. "Get your ass in here. I'll get a bed ready for—"

Before they could get through the door, Jennim's voice turned them around. "Kord, they're coming for you!"

"What's this now?" said Meckin.

Barodane didn't have the energy to respond.

"I've seen what they do to competitors, Kord." Jennim barely took a breath between words. "First, they'll crush your hands with hammers, then they'll cave your skull in if you're lucky. If you ain't, they'll stuff you in a wine barrel." He pointed to the hills and forest ringing Digtown. "Hyram's got a half-dozen men in the woods. Waiting on some masons from Breckenbright to join him. And when they do, they'll come down on you, Kord." Jennim pointed a shaking finger at Meckin. "And—and you too, innkeeper. They know you're his friend. If they can't find him, they'll find you. You can be sure about that."

Meckin stepped down into the mud, hands planted on hips. "Who boy?"

"Hyram." Jennim's tongue darted over dry lips. "He's coming. Gods save me, he's coming." The last was a near whisper.

"Calm down, kid." Meckin's eyes narrowed. "Now, you said this Hyram's got masons working for him?"

Jennim nodded.

"Hmmm. I had a couple of masons in here this morning asking where to get some godsthorn. I said that's Kord's department but I ain't seen him. Then that big woman, Gyra, joined them at the bar. Started asking all kinds of questions. That seemed to make the masons uncomfortable, and they took off."

Barodane's voice came out in a wheeze. "What questions?"

"Damn, I almost forgot about you," Meckin bent and slipped a shoulder under Barodane's armpit. "Where they were camped. If they were alone or had more friends. What business they had in town. If the Hammer sent them."

That, Barodane knew, had sealed Garlenna's fate with his own. With that single question, Hyram would never let her live. *Even if he kills me, he'll need to kill her now too.*

Jennim's face paled to a milky hue. He rubbed his hands nervously through wiry red beard. "Damn...damn. They're here." He clawed at Barodane's cloak. "We're fucked, Kord. You hear me? We're dead! Why couldn't you just take the fucking deal?"

"Leave off," said Meckin gruffly.

But Jennim continued to yank at Barodane's clothing. This time Barodane had no fight in him to shove the young man. Even standing had become a near insurmountable chore. He stumbled from Meckin's shoulder and onto his knees in the mud.

Meckin spun to face Jennim. "Can't you see the man's sick? Back off with you!"

Jennim continued grabbing at Barodane. "Sell, fool! Sell!"

Meckin swung a sturdy fist into the younger man's side, doubling him over. Jennim wrapped arms around his ribs, gasping for air, and as he did Meckin brought another fist over the top of the first. Straight into his jaw with a crack.

Jennim's head jerked sideways. He dropped like a sack of meal, arms folding under chest, ass pointing skyward, face thudding into the mud. "Hnnnnuh." He tried to rise and speak at the same time but ended up doing neither. He toppled to one side to writhe and flounder in the muck.

Barodane hoped the knockout would give the young man a brief reprieve from his panic. Meckin was anything but pleased. Instead of gloating over his opponent, he shook a fist at the dumbstruck man. "Stupid son of a bitch. What'd you make me do that for? I told you to back off."

He scooped Barodane up onto his shoulder and helped him inside. "Stupid son of a bitch," he muttered.

The door banged closed behind them. They moved up the stairs, step by mincing step. "I want to avoid Garlenna," Barodane said.

"Garlenna?"

Barodane cursed himself. "Whoever that woman is. Gyra, was it?" He hoped the man was fooled. Knowing how sharp Meckin usually was, he sincerely doubted it.

"Have no worries there. She headed out a short time after the masons. Seemed to me like she meant to find out the answers to those questions herself. This one here," Meckin paused in front of a door. "Can you stand?"

Barodane nodded. Meckin gently leaned him against the wall as he fished out a key. "I don't know what you got yourself into, Kord, but it doesn't sound like it's something to take lightly. You rest up in here and I'll do what I can to keep you safe." The lock clicked. Together, they entered and then Meckin helped lower Barodane onto the bed. "But I ain't giving up my life or my inn for your stubborn ass. You put yourself in this position just like that idiot laying in the mud out back. You get yourself out of it."

A symphony of guilt reminded him. *You're a cancer to the ones you care about.*

Meckin let loose an exasperated breath. "Ain't had to knock a fool silly for some time, and I don't mean to make it a habit. I trust you. That's why I let you do business in my inn. Turns me a good profit too. But when the danger outweighs the gain, well, I'd prefer to keep it far from the Dregs."

"I hear you, Meckin. I promise, once I'm well, I'll take my supply and go."

Liar!

"Good." Meckin grunted. "I'm not holding for you if masons are going to be coming around giving me the ugly eye."

Barodane closed his eyes. The light in the room clawed into his brain. He rubbed his forehead. His voice was weak. "Nor should you have to."

The innkeeper turned to leave. "I'll send one of the kitchen girls up with some water and hot broth."

Before Meckin passed through the door, Barodane called to him. "It's my fault you had to hit him."

"It's been a while." Meckin stared at the floor, snorted a laugh. "Good to know I've still got some fight in me though. Rest easy, friend."

Almost as soon as Barodane lie down, the linens soaked through. *So this is it? A wet coffin to die alone in. And sober no less. What rotten fate.*

CHAPTER FOURTEEN

DISCORD AND DUTY

H oldguard lined the walls of the High Hall, spears and rounded shields held firmly at attention. Wolst stood beside Belara Frost on the dais overlooking the Scarborn retinue as it came to an abrupt stop. The horribly maimed captain and a dozen mercenaries strapped head to toe in black leather and crimson cloaks flanked the Warnock family.

Syphion Muul's boot-heel brow knit together in consternation.

In contrast, the duchess received them with an heir of relaxation. Legs crossed, she leaned back, hands resting lightly on the arms of her ducal throne.

Ishoa caught Lodaris staring. They smiled at each other, her joy quickly replaced with nausea at the memory of her own words. *I will spy on the Warnocks...for the good of Namarr.*

She looked away. *Lodaris trusts me. I can use that.*

Once pleasantries were exchanged, proceedings began and they were anything but pleasant. Syphion Muul bore a series of swords, axes, and daggers belted and sheathed across every inch of his person. Bowing obscenely low, they jostled. "As a show of respect and deference, the Scarborn observe the decrees of the Ice Maiden." The Warnocks stood naked of any weaponry.

"A hearty jest," said Belara, "though I'm sure it would be more humorous to watch you take a turn in the yard. Princess Ishoa is still training." The duchess glanced at Ishoa. "Perhaps it would be a decent contest."

Syphion Muul laughed. "I'm afraid scarring children is your business, Highness. Not mine."

Wolst shifted his weight, leather creaking.

"No." Belara cocked her head. "You merely starve them."

Ularis Warnock pulled the glowering fanatic back by the arm.

Ishoa had watched her grandmother bandy words with scores of hold ladies and lords who sought to crack her glacial calm. All failed. With swords, her uncle Wolst was the deadliest man in all of Namarr. But when the weapon of choice was words, Belara Frost had no equal.

Lodecka motioned the Scarborn captain forward. His stout legs bowed under the weight of the chest he carried. Patches of pinkish scars turned a purple hue as he huffed and grunted up to the dais.

"My son's tithe for the Trials," said Lodecka. "Twice the amount for twice the child."

The Scarborn captain caught his breath then sauntered back to the front of their retinue.

Belara ignored Lodecka's brag. "Congratulations, Lodaris. You are the first Scarborn to enter the Trials." With her most ingratiating smile she added, "I wish you the best of luck."

Lodecka gave a curt bow. "We need no luck."

With a voice sounding as if it could never be clear of phlegm, the stout Scarborn captain shouted, "You whore's sons! Show your betters a snappy step! About face and make haste back to camp!"

As one, a dozen mercenaries turned on their heels then marched out the door to the sound of their captain's degradations. "The duchess can't stomach your hideous faces a second longer. Every step your best now! Dishonorable Scarborn scum—the knights of Jarik are laughing at you! No motion wasted or it'll be more scars for ya!"

They chose this life? Ishoa recalled the words from Othwii's story about the Fringes. The words fanatic and cult slid into place with her own experience. *What must it be like to be Scarborn that this is the best they can hope for?*

Lodaris's eyes sought hers. Sought them again.

A subtle nod from Belara told Ishoa it was time to do her part. She found the steps leading down from the dais. If no one were looking, she'd have simply leapt off.

She followed the Scarborn.

Ularis and Syphion's heads were nearly touching. They spoke in low tones. Ahead of them, Lodaris walked beside the limping captain.

I'll spy on the Warnocks. The words she'd spoken still surprised her. Though not as much as her actions did now. Step by step, she eased her weight forward, rolling from heel to toe to eliminate the sound of a slapping boot sole.

The Scarborn captain barked at his men, gravelly voice helping to drown out the sound of Ishoa's approach. She drew closer, her senses heightening as she angled toward the conversation between Syphion and Ularis. A rush of blood throbbed in her ears. The back of her neck tingled. Rapid breaths swept through nasal passages, suddenly clear and dry.

Instead of rushing ahead to join Lodaris, she slowed, ears vibrating, straining to hear the conversation between Syphion and Ularis.

I need to listen without looking like I'm listening. Syphion thinks me naive, so I shall be.

She undid the clasp holding her cloak in place then began fiddling with it. *Just a naive girl fussing with her clothes as she seeks the favor of a boy.*

"...would have forced us to pay the tithe *after* the other holds arrived," said Ularis.

"Still," said Syphion, "we move too slow. With the duchess's coffers and influence, all she needs to do is wait us out. Time will douse the spark of our movement. Make us appear as toothless dogs capable only of endless barking. We need to capitalize on our momentum. Turn ember to blaze before it's too late."

Ularis scoffed. "You're impulsive, Syphion. You must watch your bark. It's dangerous to goad Belara Frost before we're ready. Have a little faith in Lodecka. The long game *is* ours. Do not—pardon, Highness?"

At less than a half-dozen paces behind the pair, Ishoa had allowed her boot's to hit flush as she sped past them.

"Yes?" She turned in a swirl, still working to fasten her cloak as they came to a stop.

"I..." Ularis shot a look at Syphion, inhaled and then relaxed. "Nothing. I didn't see you there is all...Highness."

Embarrassed that I startled you?

The clasp on her cloak clicked into place. Syphion Muul watched her with narrowed eyes.

"I was hoping to take Lodaris for a walk along the river." She said, all youthful enthusiasm. "We could exchange strategies for the Trial of Crossing."

With a grunt, Syphion moved past.

"An excellent plan." Lodaris appeared at her side. "Lead the way, Princess."

At the sight of her friend, warmth spread through Ishoa's chest.

But the sly smile Ularis gave his son stirred Ishoa's mind into a discordant tumbling.

Snow fell in sparse drifts as Ishoa and Lodaris made their way through the Gate of the Bear. Given that it was only used by visiting hold ladies and lords, it was more rusted than its counterpart, the Gate of the Tiger.

A hold knight and four holdguard trailed behind the young pair at a distance. A dirt road led down the hill from the keep walls then forked. The path to the left turned into a short bridge before disappearing into the distance. Tundra stretched all the way to White Plains and the Prince's Highway. The other path ran along the Blue River through the city proper of Jarik.

It also passed the Scarborn camp.

Looking out over dozens of tents and a handful of thin plumes of smoke from cook fires, the crimson and black banner of the Warnock's snapped in the wind.

Ishoa's guards drew closer as she and Lodaris took the right fork toward Jarik. She glanced back. The hold knight watched the Scarborn camp warily. She followed his gaze. Most of the mercenaries trained or silently attended to their duties. An unsettled feeling bled into the place between Ishoa's shoulder blades.

None played dice. None drank. None laughed.

The Scarborn camp may as well have been a graveyard.

As the Blue River's rushing grew louder, Ishoa turned her attention to Lodaris at her side. "Who is that captain...the one with the limp and the scars?"

"Captain Korpa?" Lodaris affected a deep, rasping voice, imitating the man. "Above all, fear cowardice. A raek, a voar, a charging knight—not a one compares. For no blade kills quicker than a timid heart."

Ishoa laughed. "He's not wrong, is he?"

With a sniffle and a shrug, Lodaris watched the Blue River wending beside them. "Not usually."

Hesitant, Ishoa said, "He sounds as awful as he looks."

Lodaris shook his head. "I respect him."

A few heartbeats of silence stretched between them. Despite sharing the fiery mane of his father, Lodaris had a streak of his mother's stiff demeanor and rigid pride. "He urged my mother to let me train with the grown men. If I was going to be seen as a highborn, he thought I still needed to be able to fight like a Scarborn. My mother is dubious of my progress."

Words leapt into Ishoa's mouth, spewed forth before she could think them through. "You feel the need to prove yourself, don't you?"

Lodaris stopped. Full lips pressed into a thin, hard line.

Ishoa turned to meet his impassive gaze. "I'm sorry." She released a loud exhale. "I know it's unlikely to change anything, as I've dealt with it my whole life, but in my eyes you have nothing to prove. I only wish I could steal away that pain in you. In both of us."

"I'm..." Upper lip twitching, Lodaris searched the muddy ground at his feet.

"Passionate?" Ishoa supplied, her voice firm. "Honorable? Strong? You're many things, Lodaris. Not all of them must be measured against your parents. Or other Scarborn for that matter."

Flushing red, Lodaris's chin hovered over a shoulder. Along cheek and jawline, the cold had turned his scars bone white. "Thank you."

Ahead, the city of Jarik loomed. He stared at it, eyes tense and hard.

Ishoa's throat tightened. She wanted to take his hands in hers, wanted to squeeze comfort and confidence back into him. But memories from the counsel meeting stayed the impulse. *Does he hate me as much as his parents and Syphion? Does he act the friend to gain my sympathy and trust like I've been tasked to do?*

Guilt grew in her stomach. *No, Lodaris is good. Better than me. I'm the only spy here.*

They walked in silence. Ishoa's guards followed a hundred feet behind. The sight of Lodaris so crestfallen made her skin crawl. *I want nothing more than to see him smile.*

"Look," she pointed at the surging waters. Towering cedars lined the stony banks. Junipers twisted out over the water. The Blue River was wide but not so wide that Ishoa couldn't throw a rock across to the other tumbledown bank. In other parts of Namarr, it widened such that even Wolst could not clear its breadth with two throws. "In less than a week's time, we'll be there."

"The Trial of Crossing." Reluctance etched Lodaris's face. At least he looked at her again. "Such short notice. Do you feel prepared? You said you wanted to talk strategy."

An excuse to walk with you.

"My cousin Arick says no Claimant is ever truly prepared for the Trials. All those eyes watching you...it does something. It makes some falter and others flourish. I won't be the strongest or the most skilled, but as an Ironlight I'll certainly experience the most pressure."

A hundred yards from the city proper, Lodaris squared his shoulders to Ishoa. He smiled, eyes dancing. "More pressure than the first Scarborn?" A gloved hand took her own.

Warmth suffused her breast. She bit her lip.

At the sound of rushing footsteps, she jerked her chin to find the knight and crownguard hurrying toward them. She stopped them with an outstretched palm. The knight of Jarik at their fore brought them to a halt. He hacked, spit, and then watched their exchange with a hand on the pommel of his sword.

To his credit, Lodaris ignored her guards. When she looked back, he was staring at her, a coy smile tugging at the corners of his mouth. Snow drifted lazily around them. Errant flakes stuck in his red mane. Melted on the collar of his leather cuirass.

If only you weren't Scarborn.

A stern voice—her own—cut deep, rattling her from blissful reverie. *Regardless the cost, I have a duty to Namarr.*

She forced a smile back at him, saw only kindness and acceptance there.

"All eyes will be on you." Lodaris whispered in velvet soft tones. "Because you are the most lovely Anjuhk who ever lived."

A swell of giddiness seized Ishoa.

Lodaris stepped close, so close the warmth of their breath mingled in a moment she hoped would never end. "You're different from the others," he said.

"Uh—other girls, you mean?" She fought a tremble in her hand—squeezed Lodaris's to make it stop.

"Other highborn. You don't let your title define you. Nor me for that matter." His smile broadened. "It hasn't swept you away, Ishoa. You're still in there. Not just an Ironlight—a person. The most beautiful one of all." He craned forward.

Stomach fluttering, Ishoa fought the urge to meet him. Lodaris seemed to sense her hesitation. He stepped back, then gently tugged at her hand. "Come."

Cold air rushed into the space he'd occupied, and with it guilt returned.

Lodaris trusts me. I can use that.

As he led her toward Jarik's city proper, his grip was firm, safe, certain.

Her own hand felt quite numb.

Chapter Fifteen

THE NUMBERS

A wide road broke off from the Prince's Highway, leading them toward a sprawling settlement nestled on the lowest slopes of Unturrus. The whisper in Thephos's head gave a contented sigh. Thephos felt his stomach relax, the knot of hunger loosening as he took in his destination.

Eastshadow.

Clusters of drab buildings. Plumes of smoke belched skyward. Thin tendrils of steam rising and dissipating. Lanes full of scrabbling forms with shadows stretching at their heels. The rumble of handcarts, the endless hollering of upstart merchants hawking wares.

All of it an overwhelming commotion surging up against a fifteen-foot curtain wall like a wave and then beaten back and dispersed along its length.

To the south were the Sisters. Mountains half the size of Unturrus thrust up from the earth like the canine teeth of some titanic hound. To the north was Sacred Hill, a squat blemish of earth—more wart than hill.

The road split.

The lead drover twisted in his seat, hand cupped to mouth. "All those bound to Northwild settlement, go that way!" He pointed northward. Then south. "And that way's the Darkside." A flash of spit arced from the gap in his teeth. He smiled. "Don't go there."

One wain departed from the main caravan, making for the Northwilds settlement.

Seated backward in the bed of the rear wain and swinging his feet merrily, the Sempyrean priest shrugged at Thephos. "Northwilds, pfah! Bandits, beggar holds, and a pathetic yield on godsbrew. Be glad you don't go there, young fella." He paused. "What was your name again?"

Me?

Thephos blinked twice. He checked back over a shoulder. Like usual he was the last of their party. "Thephos...of Carthane."

"You're a bit young for an Ascendant." The glossy-eyed priest looked him over with a smirk. "You sure you want to do this?"

Thephos's chin fell to his chest. He stared at the packed dirt road. Stones. Clumps of grass. A ladybug crawling in the recesses of a crack. More cracks. More ladybugs. Life and death, passing underfoot.

Nothing special. Nothing important.

Thephos nodded.

The priest set his tankard down on the wood planking at his side. He shifted his weight, arms stiff, pushing the wagon bed down. "If you're so desperate to die, why not go to the Darkside?"

The whisper coiled up from the hollow place. *Ascend Unturrus,* it said. He supposed that could mean the mountain's dark side, but the urging in his gut drew him toward Eastshadow.

Thephos opened his mouth, worked his jaw, shut it tight. He never did well with questioning. The old devil taught him the virtue of silence. He kept it now.

"I see," said the priest. "I'll grant ya your solitude. Do me one favor..."

I have nothing to give.

"Ask yourself why, Thephos. Why ascend?"

He thought of Vaniton's Gasp, of becoming a mirrored statue for all time. *I want to be something beautiful for once.*

The priest slurped his godsbrew. "There are easier ways for a man to die. Far easier."

With a sharp upturn, the road and the wains climbed. Hands to thighs, Thephos pumped his fatigued legs up the steady incline. They passed the outskirts of the settlement.

Drunks staggered about, eyes narrow and lazy, intermixed with hardworking men and women lathered in sweat who hustled to-and-fro across the lanes. Gold-skinned Kurgs, swarthy Lah-Tsarene, and Namorites of paler origins marked Eastshadow as a hub of diversity. Thephos had never seen its equal.

The icon denoting the Sempyrean gods sat within a banded circle on the door of a quiet chapel. On the other side of the road, a row of massive brewhouses bore the sigil of the Golden Silos under their eaves: a pair of sickles with the blades turned outward.

It didn't take long to discover most of the building were brewhouses belonging to different holds. Or inns. Or chapels. Sometimes all three in one.

The lanes opened into a broad circular plaza. A gleaming statue stood at its center. The ability to read the placard at the statue's base was unnecessary. The angular featured man staring at the eastern horizon with a broken chain dangling in one hand, and the upthrust Slave Banner in the other, could only be one person. Danath Ironlight. Son of the Ardent Heart.

Even if Vaniton's Gasp gets me, I won't come close to his magnificence. But that's okay. If anyone deserves to be immortalized, it's Danath.

The fat priest clambered down from the wain, then staggered toward Thephos and delivered a mighty clap on the back. "Cut from the very rock the Scoths forced Namorite slaves to build the wall with." He grimaced. "An artist from Valat constructed it on the very spot they say Danath broke the chain of his sleeping post."

Thephos balled fists at his sides, testing his strength. *I could barely break a stick.*

He thought back to stories the old devil had told him of The Great Betrayal. How he'd served Danath's son, Prince Kordin Ironlight.

"The Bloody Beach. Fucking massacre," Thephos's father had said. "Should have seen it coming. Can't unsee it now." Thephos could almost taste the pungent scent of godsbrew on his father's breath, strong and sour as a corpse wind. Any time the old devil had spoken of the second war with Scothea it meant two things.

One, that he'd been drinking heavily.

Two, that he'd soon exact the pain of his memories on a son.

Bleary, flint-hard eyes had stared at Thephos "You. You're the oldest of my whelps but aren't worth the shit off a Scoth shock trooper's boot." The old devil rocked back in his chair by the fire and threw back the horn of godsbrew in his fist. "You'd have fuckin' died like the rest of us. Lying there in the sand...next to our dead prince and his dead son and the rest of the dead fucks..."

Thephos spoke without thinking. "But you didn't die. You survived."

When the old man turned those buzzard's eyes on him, Thephos dropped chin to chest and deferentially added, "Father."

"You saying I should have died? Like it was the honorable thing to do? You calling me a coward, Theffy? You?" His face contorted into a mask of pleasure. The certainty of imminent revenge. He drawled, "That's what you're saying, ain't it?"

Thephos pulled back from the memories.

He noticed his hands trembled. He looked to the sky, a lush expanse of darkening blue, crowded on one side by Unturrus's bulk. A crow flapped down from its perch on the curtain wall, cawing and mocking. A single cloud dissipated slowly.

He envied clouds their ability to come and go unburdened by the meat of reality. Meat that could be beaten, burned, spit on. Left to rot.

Like brothers.

He swallowed hard, throat so parched it burned. The priest met Thephos's tired gaze, nudged him in the chest with the tankard. "Awe is warranted! You stand on the ground of revolution, my man. Don't forget it." The priest tripped as he stepped away, though he gave it no mind and winked at Thephos as he went. "And remember to ask why before you go up. Important question, that."

At a dozen feet, the brawny, godly man, bellowed. "Now where is a representative of the Sempyrium! Attend me, damn it!"

A handful of others were unloading their belongings from the caravan. The lead drover leapt from the rumble seat and set deftly to worrying at a cargo knot.

THE PRICE OF POWER   127

On tentative feet, Thephos moved to his side. "Um...where—"

Without looking, the drover said, "Find the Numbers. Find Syn." The knot sprang apart. The drover shouldered past.

Thephos decided he wouldn't miss the man much.

He watched the drover have the same conversation with the Wordfox. *I hope he knows where he's going.* The slender, masked poet turned in a circle, snorted, then set out.

Hundreds moved through the lanes of Eastshadow. Most bore the stitched sigil of a hold on their homespun clothing as they rolled barrels or drew handcarts laden with godsthorn bushes. Others wore the mark of the Sempyrium, four upthrust arrows for the gods of light, and one pointing downward for the dark god, Nacronus. *I wonder if I'll meet him soon.*

Eastshadow looked different from the picture's in his book. The author—Locastrii was it?—had written it decades prior. Tents had become small buildings. Wood buildings had become larger ones supplemented with stone. The stone wall ringing Unturrus had also changed. More guard towers had been added to its curtain wall, as had overarching poles from which hung black bells.

That was how crownguard alerted the settlement about the descent of a potential Awakened. Though half the time it was a Ruptured who returned, mad with power. Scorch marks along some sections of the wall told Thephos of the potentially deadly toll wrought by those the Dominarri had struggled to stop.

It was said that few Ruptured escaped the executions, but that still left some. A horrifying thought stiffened the hair on the backs of Thephos's arms and neck.

What if I become Ruptured?

What if I kill people?

He liked that idea almost as much as he liked the old devil, so he pushed it from his mind. *I ascend regardless.* He went solely to die. By Vaniton's Gasp if he was lucky. By Hemgowwa if he wasn't. The stories told of the Ever-Grasping Worm ripping Ascendants apart made his bowels clench.

I suppose it would only last a few moments. Compared to eighteen years of the old devil, how bad could it be?

The bandit leader on the Prince's Highway from the day before had been only the second Kurg Thephos had ever seen. Here they were as plentiful as any people in Namarr. Their skin color ranged from a dull flax to honeyed gold. Thephos stared openly, earning him more than a few baleful looks from under thick brows.

Shorter and stouter, Kurgs were far broader than other Namorites. Most assisted brewers, hefting barrels onto stocky shoulders or standing guard in the entryways of the largest brew houses. A normal affair, it seemed.

His father once told him that because of the Kurgish Accord, there was peace between the Kurgish enclaves and the rest of Namarr. So long as their shamans were allowed to shepherd Ascendants up the Mountain of Power, the accord was upheld.

"So many," Thephos muttered in shock.

A black Kurg was the last of their race Thephos dared look at. As rare as an albino, Thephos gawped at the man's seemingly pale flesh lying under a thin layer of mottled charcoal. The Kurg glowered, raised a marbled fist and slapped his palm violently against a concrete chin. Thephos didn't know the gesture's exact meaning, but he understood the intent well enough.

"I'm sorry," he said as he scuttled away.

The distraction nearly made him lose the Wordfox. After a moment, he found him or more accurately, found his gray mushroom cap of hair sticking out above the crowd.

With the sun setting over Unturrus's shoulder, the settlement was plunged into diffused shadow. The Wordfox stopped, stepped a half dozen paces from the lane.

Careful not to be caught skulking, Thephos trailed close behind and out of sight.

A circular pavilion striped black and white and covered in painted numbers, sat back a short distance from the thoroughfare. The structure screamed for attention, a child seeking to set itself apart from its sibling buildings. Whether it did so out of necessity or preference, Thephos couldn't be sure.

The poet gave the building a disdainful snort before continuing down the lane. A sign was hammered into the ground beside a pair of torches. But Thephos only needed to glance at the painted pavilion to know where he was.

The Numbers.

He entered.

Dazzling light and raucous laughter threatened to overwhelm him. He threw up his hands in warding. The Numbers was a massive dugout. Three carved earthen steps descended from the entrance. The blinding light concealed this fact from Thephos.

He tripped and sprawled, chin, palms, and knees striking the hard-packed floor. He winced as he clambered onto his elbows and knees. Sound swirled around him. He coughed dust from his lungs and stood, not bothering to swipe clean his clothes.

Maybe a hundred or more packed the Numbers.

There was a sweet stench. Of drink and sweat and something floral. A thin pall of smoke meandered along the pavilion's low ceiling, made a luminous white by...

Thephos gasped as he identified the source of light. Five orbs of unconfined energy were fixed at equal intervals around the circular den. The orbs floated, seemingly unattached, bobbing a head higher than the mingling patrons.

The activity of the Numbers washed over him as he gaped at the orbs. When he finally reined in his awe, he found the man responsible for the illumination.

A haze of scintillating light matching the orbs poured from his eyes.

Laughing, drinking, cajoling, the man moved casually about the room as if it were common for one to have light leaking from his face. Wherever he went, the five orbs followed.

"Yup! He's an Awakened alright!"

Thephos started. A bald man towered over him, queerly jovial and even more queerly dressed. Jewels pinned the entire length of both earlobes, and a gold ring pierced a nostril. He wore a velvet doublet, flap aside, his downy chest glistening with sweat. Baggy pants striped black and white and covered with numbers—seemingly cut from the same cloth as the pavilion—ballooned out of the tops of red leather boots.

He spoke with a nasally, punctuating voice. "Welcome to the Numbers! It isn't the best inn or gambling den in Namarr, but I'd say it's definitely the most fun. Where you from?"

"I...I—uh."

The eccentric man slapped him on the back. "It's all good. I know you were probably just seeing an Awakened for the first time. We call him Radiance for obvious reasons. I can introduce you if you want."

"No. That's...I'm okay."

Am I?

"I'm Syn. Syn Backlegarm." He swept his arms out wide. "This is my place."

"Syn?" Thephos blinked. "Backlegarm?"

"You are correct. You can say it 'back, leg, arm,' or 'backle—garm,' or maybe make up a new way of saying it that I haven't heard before. I'd like that. Anyway, you have to admit, it's a perfectly odd name for a perfectly odd place. I mean, go up a mountain, maybe get slaughtered by some demons, maybe get unbelievable powers." Bearded chin aimed at the ceiling, he gave a chuckle. "Maybe get the latter and become the former. Life's mysterious, right?"

"Yeah. I suppose you're right."

"Of course I'm right." Syn encircled Thephos's shoulders with a long, thick arm and then started to walk him around the Numbers. "So, new friend, tell me about yourself."

Why do you care to know? I'll be dead soon. "I'm Thephos. From Carthane. I'm—I'm a..." The title of "pig farmer" refused to come. *That was my father. I am nothing.* "That's really all there is about me."

"Ah! The Golden Silos of Peladonia. Pretty place during the harvest. Wheat and corn jumpin' right off the stalks. Views are kind of flat for my tastes. I prefer mountains, clearly."

To either side, men and women threw wheels at games of chance. They rolled dice in a box or watched rodents fight to the death in crates. At one table, a man and woman sat across from each. Stone still. Unblinking.

Life is mysterious indeed.

"So," Syn's voice went higher. "Why did you come to Unturrus?"

"You're kind, Syn, but..." Thephos frowned. "Do you always ask Ascendants these questions?"

Syn Backlegarm chuckled. Thephos wished he found anything half so funny as the Numbers owner seemed to find everything.

It was at the rear of the pavilion that Thephos saw the answer to his question. Hundreds of corks from godsbrew jugs and wine bottles had been fashioned together to make a board the size of a wagon bed, propped up by wooden planks so that it stood. Red targets were painted onto the board and scraps of parchment with names and numbers scribbled onto them were pinned at different points across it.

"We got an Ascendant here!" shouted Syn. "Thephos from Carthane!"

A couple dozen patrons flew at them, sizing up Thephos and then digging into their pockets for wheels of copper, silver, and the rare gold. Eyes aglow, the Awakened known as Radiance approached as well, holding a sheaf of paper slips. He dipped quill to ink on a nearby table and then wrote furiously to track shouted wagers.

"Gold. Death," was the most common bet, followed by, "Silver. Death," and then, "Copper. Death."

"Silver. Ruptured," said one particularly drunk woman. "It's always the softies who've got the evil in 'em." She winked at Thephos.

The Numbers's patrons didn't come close to the cruelty of his father, but Thephos couldn't help being disappointed as he watched so many place enthusiastic bets on him dying.

They hoped for it, he realized. Would profit from it.

"Hey now!" Syn said. "No one thinks he's got the makings of an Awakened? In a few weeks' time, Thephos could be walking the Hall of Heroes."

Terse laughter met the theory.

"They're right," Thephos said. "I'm going to die. That's why I came here, anyway."

Syn's smile faded. He raised an eyebrow. "Of course you will, Theffy. That's kind of the whole point."

At mention of the moniker the old devil had used, Thephos's skin tingled all over as if struck by lightning. "Don't call me that."

Thephos stood erect, but just as quickly his shoulders slumped back down. "Sorry. Just don't call me that."

"My apologies. Thephos it is." Syn grinned, a childish thing. "But like I was saying, death *is* the point. You've got to die in order to live sometimes. No one who goes up the Mountain of Power returns with their old self. That person is dead and gone."

Dying without dying? If who I am right now were to die...

Thephos shied from the vague sense of hope that accompanied the thought. *Death is what I seek.* "Aren't you going to bet?"

Syn nodded. "I always make my wager last. It's a strategy. Bets will come flooding in, so the payouts will change by the time the final Ascendant arrives. Could be weeks. Not sure if anyone has told you this, but you go up in batches of ten, and you, Thephos, are only number eight. Though I heard there's some weirdo in a fox mask gallivanting around somewhere. We get about ten every other month. So if you're doing the math, I get to see someone get very rich about once a year when there's an Awakened."

Weeks? But I'll starve by then.

"Is there a bet for...death before ascent?"

The gaudy dressed man laughed. "Oh, ho ho! There's a bet for everything, my friend. Something the book-writing types have figured out is that in the years before a war, the ratio of those becoming Awakened drops. Meaning, you'd want to bet on death more often then. But in the years after a war, you'd want to bet on Ascendants gaining powers slightly more often. My theory is that more suffering leads to more Awakened, but more fear leads to more death. Might help to remember that."

"I'm sorry...but I don't really care, Syn. I came here to die."

"Hey, minds change. You never know until you get up there, right?"

A short woman with close cropped hair slid into place beside Syn. A cape swept the floor behind her, and she gripped the hilt of a sword sheathed at her belt. Shrewd eyes flickered over Thephos, then back to the Numbers owner.

"Wife!" Syn roared. He flung a meaty arm around her shoulder. "Meet Thephos. Thephos meet Ash my—"

"He knows I'm your wife," she said in pithy tones. "You just said it."

Where Syn was open, Ash was standoffish. Where he smiled, she scowled. Where he towered, chest out, she was short and slouched, shoulders huddled around her breasts.

"Hello," Thephos said.

Ash Backlegarm locked Thephos in a harsh, dismissive stare and seemed to calculate something. Thephos cleared his throat, looked away. Many times he'd been intimidated in his life, even by women, but Ash was by far the smallest person to do so.

Her head turned before her eyes did, then she looked up at her husband. "Something needs your immediate attention."

Syn raised an eyebrow. "You sure you're not being paranoid?"

"Yes!" Ash hissed. "Come. Now."

"My wife is a bit of a cynic." Syn was dragged off by the hand, leaving Thephos alone with the Numbers betting board.

He sat in the dirt and studied it. An old drunk man came to stand over him. Thephos told him he couldn't read. The drunkard obliged, telling Thephos every single scenario marked in the red circles, along with the odds of each happening.

There were sixty-four different bets one could make with the word "death" in it.

CHAPTER SIXTEEN

SHADOW GAMES

G arlenna's heartbeat quickened under the press of time.

As soon as the masons left the Dregs, she went to the dilapidated stables adjacent the inn and saddled her horse. They were mounted, which meant if they rode from town at a gallop, she'd either lose them or have to gallop after; a poor prospect if she wished to remain unseen.

Dust swirled around hurried feet. She tossed a bronze wheel onto the sleeping stable boy's chest, mounted her horse, and then trotted out into the muddy streets.

Luckily, the masons went at a leisurely pace. She slowed, giving them ample lead. As they approached Digtown's fountain, she turned down an alley. Shadows swallowed her.

A pair of old starving men bickered over a sack of half-rotten apples. When Garlenna rode by, they fell momentarily quiet, but resumed shouting once she turned the corner at the alley's end. She brought her horse to a gallop around the building, rode past it—past the next as well.

She drew her destrier to a halt. She waited, leaned out to watch the main road. The masons trotted by. Garlenna counted to ten and then followed.

Daylight pierced the cloud cover. Steam uncoiled from the mud. She emerged from the alley. Her targets angled toward the town chapel, a slender structure atop which sat a wooden icon of the Sempyrean—four arrows jutting skyward and a fifth pointing down. Garlenna brought her horse to a stop, dismounted, and then hobbled it before ducking into a cooper's workshop.

An aging toad of a man with a fringe of white hair over each ear looked up from a band of wood in his hands. Rheumy eyes with wet corners seemed to light up at the sight of her. "How can I help ye'?"

A few barrels untouched by the hand of time sat at the back in the shadows. "I'll look at those."

"Neh. Thems for some'n."

She threw the man a silver wheel, and his face split into a broad, gap-toothed grin. He fumbled it, stooped forward to retrieve it, and as he did she noted a series of scabs covering the inside of his arm.

One of yours, Barodane?

"Well, I make 'em pretty fast. Gander if you like." His eyes roamed over her. He licked his lips. "Stay the night if ya' like, too. I've got a cot in the back."

I am no fly, toad.

She swept past the toadish cooper to position herself in the darkness and watch the masons across the street.

The chapel's front door shuttered against the exterior wall. Eustus stepped out to speak with the two mounted masons. He wore a leather cap and cast a long shadow. So tall in fact that he looked over the thoroughbreds of the masons as he approached. In a fight, his reach would be a problem. Nothing Garlenna hadn't dealt with before, but combined with his cool demeanor she assumed him a capable blade. *Better to fight him one on one if possible.* Given what she was seeing, she doubted she'd get the chance. The masons were gathering strength. Working out strategy.

Each carried a hammer and had a small shield slung across his back. Eustus wore a dagger across his chest and on one hip—a long sword rode the other.

Here they come... Her prince would need to be ready to fight for his life. *Damn it Barodane. Here they come.*

The moment she'd seen Barodane at the Dregs, fourteen years of feeling punched her in the heart. And yet there was some relief that came with it as well. *He lives,* she had told herself. *By the gods of the Sempyrean, my prince lives.* A dozen memories of friendship and service had filled her like a warm wind, right before a sense of betrayal had come along to slap the air from her lungs. *Why did you hide?* she accused. *Why did you hide from me?* Guilt had fought for purchase. *I was your prosort, your guardian...your friend.*

It had taken years of prayer to stop blaming Barodane for orders she'd followed. Yet the old story emerged from its slumber like a hungry dragon the moment she'd laid her eye on him. Sitting there. Slugging back godsbrew like water.

It was my duty. I did only my duty! It had taken a moment to see the lie. She'd hidden behind her oath long enough. She would not use it to hide any longer. Like her father had.

She winced.

A friend would have stopped you. A friend would have saved you from yourself. Like Kaitos. At least he tried.

A small part of her worried Barodane was no longer salvageable. But it was weak, easily cast aside by her conditioning. She grit her teeth and breathed. Slow inhale, the soothing touch of Srah. Slower exhale, to calm Ozoi's flames. She performed the prosort practices of mind and body as though each were a daily gift to the gods themselves.

Nothing will dissuade me.

She continued inspecting barrels as she watched the masons from the corner of her eye. "Do you see who comes and goes from that chapel?"

The cooper cleared his throat. "I do." His lecherous smile soured her stomach. She turned her attention back to the masons and the placid-eyed Eustus. "The tall man in the leather cap? Have you seen him there before?"

"What's it to ya?" He smacked his lips as if he'd just snared a fly. Certainly, he hoped for more silver.

Garlenna's stomach lurched. The man was detestable. She would give him nothing. "You buy your godsthorn from Kord?"

The toad turned on its toad stool, eyes narrowed.

"I'm Kord's friend," she said. "These men mean him harm. See their honor plates? They are the Crown's Justice from Breckenbright, come to root out and destroy Digtown's godsthorn supply."

The cooper gaped. "I guess that explains why they been in 'n out of that chapel so much. That angular shit heap attached to it is the jail."

"Really?" Garlenna squared to him.

He nodded. "The tall one's been comin' and goin' the last few days like he owns it. I didn't mark him as the prayin' type. Although he's got the serious look of a gods-fearin' man."

"Has anyone else been with him?" Garlenna thought of Hyram Olabran. "A bull-necked man, broader across the chest, perhaps?"

The toadish cooper shook his head. When he sensed she needed nothing else, he asked, "How'd you lose the eye?"

Instead of answering, she motioned for the cooper to look away from her as she slid deeper into the shadows.

Eustus mounted a horse and led the men down the road out of town. Garlenna stepped into the light, blood rushing through her. "If you tell anyone I was here, Kord will die and the godsthorn will be gone. Do you understand, old man?"

He stared up at her, eyes as large around as silver wheels. "There's no need fer meanness nor name callin'."

The sight of Eustus and his men conspiring against Barodane brought the warrior inside Garlenna to the fore. Any who meant her prince harm would die. Her protective instinct was the measure by which the Sempyrium selected priests and priestesses to serve its militant arm. But it was her intellect and her capacity to do whatever necessary in service of her charge that elevated her to the rank of prosort.

She grabbed the toadish cooper by the collar and lifted him from his seat, "And if the fear of losing your godsthorn doesn't keep your slimy mouth shut, I promise

I'll bleed you into one of these barrels if you say a single word to anyone. Do you understand?"

Horror etched the creases of the cooper's round, weathered face. "I'm sorry." He proffered the silver wheel she'd given him. "Here! Take 'er back!"

She released him. "All yours." She was tired of Digtown's predation but let him keep the silver anyway. He deserved something. After Barodane had slipped her the first night she'd arrived, few citizens of Digtown had been willing to offer information on his whereabouts. She'd troubled with Meckin the innkeep for all of a minute before realizing the man would lie endlessly to keep Barodane safe. He'd been forthright in declaring loyalty to his friend and telling her to piss off.

For that, Garlenna decided Meckin was her friend as well.

Next, she'd gone to the Gem Loft. In her experience, whores made the best informants. So when Jennim had told her of Barodane's history there, she thought she'd struck some luck. To her surprise, they'd been no help at all. They'd been a lot like Meckin, protective of their "Kord" and not afraid to show it. They shot down Garlenna's inquiries with open hostility. An older Kurgish woman even had the gall to usher her from the premise with a hand on her back. If it were not for the Kurg's age and a single eye to match Garlenna's, the old woman may have parted ways less the offending hand.

Digtown is as loyal to Barodane as he is to it.

She looked from jail to chapel—chose the jail. She rapped gently on the door. Within, a chair scraped across the floor. Lazy footsteps followed.

"What now, Eu—?" A short man with blond mutton chops opened the door, iron-ring handle clinking. He blinked. "What—uh—what's the problem? Sorry, you surprised me."

"How did I surprise you?"

"Oh—I just..." The man scratched a blond tufted mutton chop as he peered over her shoulder at the street. "Just meant I didn't expect to see you here."

"You didn't expect to see *me* here?"

The man froze. Their eyes locked. Then, he let out an abrasive laugh, as if he could expel all his nervousness in a breath. "No. Of course not you. I meant *you* as in *anyone*."

Garlenna looked over the top of the man's head. The inside of the jail was more of a shabby shed than any true law establishment, with only enough room for a constable's stool and a pair of banded beams running along the back wall. Vacant shackles hung from the beams, their claws lying open on the floor. A boy played in the corner where a couple slats of wood had been torn away. The hole was big enough for a slender man to fit through—exactly what Garlenna suspected had happened. That it was never repaired, in a jail of all places, told her all she need know of the constable.

"I'm Lairton." He brought fist to shoulder in salute. "Never served myself. What—uh—what stronghold you belonging to?"

"I'm no holdguard."

"Back then I mean." He glanced at the street again. "Clearly, you ain't with a hold now. Shadowguard?"

She ignored his weak attempts to gather intelligence. "Lairton, help me understand how it is that in a town with as much crime as this one, you have no one in your jail. Each time I step outside, I see violence and drug use."

The man's mouth parted. He searched the floor.

"To make matters worse, you seem to be the only law enforcement in Digtown. One man for nearly a thousand citizens." Rotted wood crumbled between her fingers as she picked at the door frame. "Please...explain."

Lairton found his spine. "I think I will. You're not from here. That makes you ignorant, and ignorant folk can have a hard time...adjusting. In Digtown, it's a worse crime to not be a criminal so I let people handle things themselves. I'm only here to call the Crown's Justice from Breckenbright when something..." An unnervingly smug smile crossed his lips. "...interesting happens."

Garlenna counted at least two missing teeth. "Interesting?"

"Yeah," Lairton said, "you know, like if something happens to someone important. Like someone with highborn blood."

The message was clear enough: anyone who harms Hyram will face the Crown Justice.

If only the man knew who he vied against.

It would be easier if Barodane could simply reveal his identity. But after fourteen years missing, the truth would be absurd, unbelievable, even to Barodane's closest friends. Given what her father, Gyr, had said in his message, whoever attempted to betray Namarr played shadow games well. That meant they could make unbelievable truths disappear.

Until Barodane has the Slave Banner in hand and enough allies to take control of the Collective, he's vulnerable. His identity must stay a secret.

If she failed to convince Barodane to leave, they'd have to fight. On the slim chance they survived, Lairton could call the full might of Breckenbright down on them in retribution.

May Nacronus keep this little bastard in the afterlife. She surveyed the street. Merchants down on their luck and a handful of drunken citizens trickled over the main thoroughfare.

"Reconsidering your side, then?"

She looked back at a smiling Lairton. *Perhaps, if I kill him now...*

An urge to slip the dagger strapped to her chest came and went. She took a deep breath, followed a different course. *I must do whatever necessary.*

She called upon words, both regretful and effective.

She pointed her chin at the little boy playing naked in the corner—Lairton's son, she assumed. "I wonder if a dead constable and his dead son would interest the Crown Justice."

Lairton chewed furiously at the inside of his lip, a shaking hand fell to the ax slung through his belt. "Now why would you say something like that?"

She didn't mean she would be the one to kill them, but Lairton didn't need to know that. *Let him fear what I may do.*

"You don't know me, which makes you..." Garlenna glanced at the ax at the constable's belt, snorted indifference. "Ignorant. You may think you know the men you work for, but if you displease them, they *will* kill you and *will* kill your son."

Lairton glanced back at his son. The boy had stopped playing and now watched them, eyes as big around as eggs. The constable's tongue flicked over dry lips. "Boy, go into the chapel now."

Darting through the break in the wall, Lairton's son disappeared. Good survival instinct.

The pressure in the space between them rose. Sweat spread between Garlenna's shoulder blades. She stepped close to the constable and raised her voice, hoping to break him down. Feed him misinformation.

Though she detested Father Alcor—Archprelate Alcor now—his words filled her ears.

We must work in layers of victory. At all times, you must be a weapon aimed for the killing stroke. You must do whatever is necessary. For the Crown and the Sempyrium. For your duty. For your gods. Lie, kill, steal, expose, betray...

She leaned forward. "These men you work for cannot be trusted. If you fail, they'll kill you, and they will kill your son. And you *will* fail. Kord has many more retired soldiers just like me throughout Digtown. More shadowguard. Ready and waiting."

Lairton's eyes narrowed.

Garlenna spoke quicker, every word punching the air. First thoughts were fearful thoughts. Second thoughts, suspicious thoughts. She could leave him no space to question as she spun her lies. "Look into my eyes if you dare dispute it. When I came to town, the others came with me. Some I've planted in the slums. A half dozen more wait for Kord's signal in the hills beyond. Even now, they search for Hyram and his men."

"You think Kord is a fool, don't you?" She tapped one of her temples and smiled knowingly. "He's from Alistar. He knows how to handle worse threats than Hyram Olabran."

"I ain't seen anyone new in town but you." Lairton hesitated. "Jennim said Kord came from Nine Lakes."

Garlenna forced a laugh. "Listen to me, Lairton. Jennim also said Kord would sell his godsthorn operation. He was wrong about that. He's wrong about this too. And you know where Jennim stands with Hyram now, don't you? Is that really the man you want to stake your life on? Your boy's life? You want to be like Jennim? I'm trying to help you survive this, but I can't do that if you don't listen."

Beads of sweat sprang onto Lairton's brow.

"Now you're thinking with me," she cooed. "You're thinking smart. Here's the truth. You can ensure your safety on both sides of this thing. If you tell Hyram about the men—"

"Why would I do that?" Lairton's voice had become husky.

"Let me finish. Telling Hyram about Kord's men doesn't hurt Kord at all. Hyram won't know where or who they are, but it could save him from rushing into a fight he can't win. For you—for you, it does a lot because you get to be Hyram's savior. If it's true, he won't kill you and he won't kill your son. Here's the next step. You tell me where Hyram's camp is."

Lairton shook his head.

I press too hard. Do not lose him.

Backing away to give the constable the feeling of more power, Garlenna continued. "You're not giving anything up. I already know where it is. I just need you to confirm it so I know I can trust you. Then you can tell Hyram about Kord's men. That way no one will kill you or your son."

Lairton reeled, rubbing a mutton chop. Flakes of dry skin swirled in the air. "I—I don't know."

Confusion. Indecision. Uncertainty. The elements necessary to cultivate misinformation. She pressed him again.

"It's very simple, Constable. If you tell me where their camp is now—prove you're trustworthy—I can end this for you. You won't have to worry any more. You can go back to the simple, easy way of things as they were." She paused. "I'm here to help."

Lairton flinched. Distrust clenched across his brow.

Damn. I should have known. Altruism is the thing least trusted in Digtown. Jennim warned me of that.

The constable's eyes narrowed around a point on the floor. He grunted and shook his head. "Nah." Rolling his shoulders, he stared her full in the face. "I ain't playing your game."

For a moment, she considered bribing him, but that would be fruitless. Hyram not only had the coin to beat her, he had the prestige. If she touted any more money, it could give away her identity. With one eye and an imposing figure, those who knew her might match her description with a somewhat renowned prosort of the Mad Prince.

"As you wish." The ally's facade disappeared. A menacing tone tinged Garlenna's words. "You've been warned."

In truth, she thought it unlikely that Hyram would find reason to kill the constable or his son. It seemed Lairton had looked past the fear of Garlenna's mind games to conclude the same.

The hard way it is.

She mounted then spurred her horse out of town in search of Hyram's camp.

CHAPTER SEVENTEEN

HOW TO SEE

T he people of Jarik should not see their princess holding hands with a Scarborn. Walking together already pushed the limits of what was acceptable.

Ishoa pulled her hand free. "If I were anyone else…"

Lodaris nodded somberly.

Chickens fled across their path, chased by a group of giggling children. One fell, but before Ishoa could help him up, he darted off after the rest. A butcher slapped a knife into a block. Racks of lamb sagged on hooks along the shop front. A pair of bakers from Prav called to passersby, "Sweet breads! Savory breads! All fresh!" Some loaves were oblong, others round, crusts both light and dark, hard and cloud-soft. Ishoa gave them a handful of copper wheels and took a roll just big enough to fill her hand. It was not as warm as she'd hoped, but the sweetness of the powder covering it was pleasant. She offered to buy one for Lodaris.

He refused.

They navigated the tight streets, hedged in on either side by hovels and storefronts. Once, they accidentally took a wrong turn down an alley and stumbled into a shared living space, coming face to face with a sow and an unhappy, toothless grandfather.

Forced to go back the way they came, the knight of Jarik suggested he take the lead. "If your Highness tells me where you wish to go."

"Her highness and her friend are going where they please," she said. "The great hog of Jarik is merely one of many such attractions we plan to—" she laughed through her last sentence, unable to complete it as Lodaris joined in, "to—ahem, visit today."

The knight grumbled and offered no more suggestions.

After another wrong turn, they found their way onto a dirt-packed road that fed into a broader avenue. Whores shouted down from second-story windows. Bahna drummers thumbed and slapped their instruments as their child companions proffered leather caps for handouts. Beggars accosted passersby on every corner, coughing for sympathy or offering ancestral blessings in exchange for a copper wheel.

Jarik was the oldest city in Namarr—at least the oldest that wasn't a Kurgish temple—and so it had grown atop itself in the least clever of ways.

"Packed tighter than a fishing barrel," Wolst once said of it. On the rare occasions when Ishoa went through the city proper, a sea of faces crowded it. Even so, they did their best to give her space to walk unimpeded. For once, she was grateful to have the knight of Jarik and crownguard shadowing her.

A fountain sat at the center of a massive, busy square. Three wells ringed it. Maidens pulled buckets of water while a troupe of dancers twisted and turned in unison on the lip of the fountain. When their leader spotted Ishoa and Lodaris, he halted the dance and bowed deep. Ishoa tossed them a silver wheel to continue.

"I want an apple but see no fruit stands," she said.

Lodaris gave a mirthless laugh. "Because the Golden Silos charge extortion rates for us to import them."

"Oh...I suppose we could get some sweet root instead."

"You won't find that either," said Lodaris. "The price of that, too, has been raised by Haydees Cotter and the rest of the greedy Peladonians."

Ishoa watched Lodaris expectantly. *This is what Grandmother wishes to hear.* "You know more than I."

"With Syphion Muul around so much..." Lodaris shrugged. "The man rants endlessly."

"How do you feel about him?"

"He let his own daughter starve to death to spite Namarr—I hate him." Lodaris fixed her with a serious look. "But that doesn't mean he's wrong, Ishoa. Before Unification, Anjuhkar benefited from its own goods—like apples and sweet root. Now, only orchards and croplands approved by the Crown can manage without going in debt. In fact, they become quite rich. That is not just, Highness."

For the first time, Ishoa felt a wall of defensiveness rise against Lodaris. "What we sacrifice in individual freedom, we gain in security and stability. I hear you. And I'm sure there's a better way. Namarr is still a young nation. We all play a role in keeping Scothea at bay."

"I suppose," Lodaris said.

Before he could say more, shouts carried across the square. The jostle of arms and thunder of hooves sent vibrations through Ishoa's feet. They weaved through the crowd toward the main road leading up to the Gate of the Tiger. A heavyset smith struck iron on an anvil nearby. Sparks showered the air amid a light fall of snow. The smell of molten ore mingled with coal dust stung Ishoa's nostrils. She wrinkled her nose and shied away, but Lodaris motioned her closer so they could see which hold approached.

A knight rounded a bend in the avenue, decked head to toe in burnished plate and carrying a banner depicting a black anvil surrounded by pink and orange embers.

"The smiths of Summerforge," Ishoa muttered.

The blacksmith stopped working and came to stand beside Lodaris, a greasy fist held to his chest.

Following behind the banner bearer were a pair of familiar faces. *The Omenfaen twins.* Though only a couple years older than Ishoa, they seemed far closer to adulthood. A thread of self-doubt sewed her stomach into knots as she considered the Trials. *How can I compete alongside that?*

Dragga Omenfaen looked every inch a hero. With a lantern jaw and a mop of tight black curls, his polished smile claimed the crowd. A darksteel blade hung at his hip. A steel embossed shield slapped his warhorse's flanks. Tongues of flame were etched into the enamel of his breastplate, and the anvil and embers of his family crest decorated his pauldron. Someday, he would be trained as a knight in Alistar and wear an honor plate emblazoned with the fist and chain of Ironlight.

While Dragga beamed his twin sister Stirrma, brooded. A dark and surly cloud. Focused implacably forward, she ignored the crowd. Sharing the same powerful jaw, dark eyes, and onyx curls as her twin, Stirrma Omenfaen still found ways of setting herself apart. Midnight ringlets were pulled back into a fat ponytail, highlighting swaths of clean-shaven skin above each ear. A pair of thick nose rings adorned septum and eyebrow. Instead of plate protecting her legs, she wore an Anjuhk warskirt. Dragga's cloak was lined in the gray fur of a storm bear with orange trim. Stirrma's the black fur of a wolf. A warhammer with a darksteel head wrought into the shape of an anvil was slung across her back—a menacing thing.

"Stirrma carries no shield," said Lodaris. "Less cautious than her brother, maybe?"

Ishoa nodded. She thought the scion of Summerforge dressed more like a Scoth than a Namorite.

A score more holdguard decked in Summerforge steel and chain followed, bronze honor plates flashing in the midday light as they escorted a drawn carriage.

A moon-round face poked out from one of the windows, a woman of middling years. When she spied Ishoa, she called the column to a halt. "Smiths, bow to her highness, Ishoa Ironlight." The mounted men bowed as deeply as they could from the saddle. The allegiance of Summerforge to the Frosts had always been one of the strongest in Anjuhkar. Unsurprising given their utility. They'd learned to rework Scothean darksteel, a task that took many years but yielded substantial profit.

"Greetings, Lady Hilkka." Ishoa dipped her head. Dragga doubled back, brought his horse alongside the carriage. Stirrma offered a stiff bow but kept her distance. The citizens clustering around Ishoa made space when they discovered who she was.

Hilkka's round cheeks shone a slight cherry and tightened mirthfully. As far as physique was concerned, clearly the twins took after their dead father. "You've grown into quite the young woman since I last saw you, Highness."

Stirrma snorted.

She does not belong. Like Lodaris. Like me.

"My children have also grown." The Lady of Summerforge gestured at Dragga. "As you can see."

At this, Dragga swung a leg over the saddle and leaped onto the cobbled street. Though fully plated, his armor seemed to impede him not at all. At sixteen, Dragga was every inch a man. Nearly as tall as Othwii, he was half a head taller than almost any knight of Jarik and broader through the shoulders than all but Wolst. Like something out of legend, his face held an angularity and fullness to it that would melt ice from the heart of the bitterest of crones.

He took Ishoa's hand and knelt. "I am honored to be a Claimant in the Trials alongside one so beautiful as you, Highness." He winked and rose.

Lodaris bristled. A hand shot out to take Dragga's forearm. "Well met, Omen-faen."

Dragga seemed to squeeze back as he clapped Lodaris on the shoulder. A smile rode his angular face, but his eyes narrowed some, as if considering whether the red-maned Scarborn was actual competition.

"Well met, Warnock. I congratulate you on being the first Scarborn to attempt the Trials." Dragga showed himself to be deeper than a heroic face. Diplomatic charisma oozed from him. *He knows he's better than Lodaris...than everyone.* Dragga's expression turned solemn. "I know you have faced many challenges on account of your lineage, but I for one, am rooting for you."

Ishoa glanced at Stirrma. She watched her brother's exchange dispassionately.

She lives in his shadow. She hates him for it.

"I—I thank you." Lodaris pulled his hand away, brow furrowed.

"Princess." Dragga gave a deferential bow, then smoothly mounted his stallion. Jealousy poured off Lodaris. A bead of sweat broke across his brow. He chewed at the inside of a cheek.

Ishoa couldn't decide if she liked Dragga or hated him. Certainly, he was impressive, respectable even. Something about her exchange with him was off. Forced.

What does he want from me?

Hilkka Omenfaen's expression brought things into place with terrifying clarity. "We look forward to further conversation, Highness." Triumph lined her face.

Oh no...they want me to marry him.

As the retinue headed for the Gate of the Tiger, Ishoa chided herself for being slow-witted. In truth, she found herself more drawn to Stirrma. At least they might be able to relate.

To the people of Anjuhkar, however, Dragga Omenfaen would be a perfect match for the last Ironlight. Their princess.

She crossed her arms as a shiver raced up her spine.

Dragga was handsome, charismatic, and strong. Yet the thought of marrying him didn't intrigue Ishoa in the slightest. *Shouldn't I be at least a little swept off my feet?* When she read love stories, the men almost always resembled Dragga. Even the book her grandmother wrote about Danath cast him in a similar light.

The insidious hands of shame pulled at her. *If it's best for Namarr, why shouldn't I want someone so...perfect?*

That was it.

Boringly perfect.

She looked at Lodaris, red faced and glaring daggers into the young lord of Summerforge's back. *Besides, I do not love Dragga.*

"Mind your stare, boy," came a gruff voice.

Ishoa whirled to find the smith grimacing at Lodaris. The anvil and ember of Summerforge was sewn into his soot-smeared apron, the only thing covering the man besides trousers and an unsavory amount of oily body hair.

"Mind your business, fool," said Lodaris. "I'll look where I please."

The smith hacked then spit, a hammer jumping in his hand as he changed grips. "I won't have some fucking Scarborn trash disrespecting my hold."

Red rage crept up Lodaris's neck. He laughed meanly. "Fuck Summerforge." He whipped aside his cloak to reveal a sword at his hip. Though the smith was a head taller and a couple of buckets of nails heavier, Lodaris wielded the confidence of invincible youth as well as the skills of one trained by Captain Korpa and Lodecka Warnock.

Ishoa found her voice. "Both of you will stop right now." With a jostle of steel her crownguards formed up behind her. The knight of Jarik laid a hand on her shoulder to guide her away, but she twisted from under it.

"Give us space, Highness," said Lodaris.

She would do no such thing. She stepped before Lodaris. "Do not ignore me!"

"Ah," said the smith. "See here, Highness. Scarborn have a black mark on 'em. You'll get as much respect from a rabid dog. Best you let me do away with him for ya. Can't let these scum mix their traitor's blood with real Anjuhks."

Shaking with anger, Lodaris yanked his sword halfway from its scabbard.

Ishoa grabbed his arm. "Lodaris! Get your hand off your sword. Smith!"

"I'm honor bound, Highness." The smith glared. "He insults Summerforge."

"You are honor bound to me, smith. Go back to your work or..." Uncertainty slapped the words from her. She'd never faced a conflict like this. She hesitated. *What might Grandmother say?* She jabbed a finger at him. "Since you love your anvil so much, I'll have my guards tie you to yours—naked."

She would say something like that.

It had the desired effect. The smith turned his back on them, rolling a shoulder, then retreated into his smithy. Lodaris spit at the man's back, but it fell short. "Fuck Summerforge."

A tense moment passed before the sound of steel rang against anvil through acrid air once more.

Wolf fur bunched under Ishoa's hand as she dragged Lodaris into a nearby alley. It was so narrow, her uncle would struggle to enter it. When her guards made to follow, she threw a palm in the knight's face. "Leave us be."

His chin lifted. "I cannot, Highness. Not unless we disarm the boy first."

"Leave us be or I'll have my uncle throttle you."

The knight shook his head. "He'll throttle me if he hears I allowed it. Weapons first."

"Two threats in one day." Lodaris handed over a sword and dagger. The knight and holdguard drifted back. "Suddenly you're a real princess."

Anger and the rush of danger had set Ishoa's heart to racing. She recalled her uncle's training. A slow breath in—*think of ice*—a slow breath out—*think of steam*. She repeated it thrice more but felt only slightly better.

"You should have let me fight the man. When my mother hears of this, she'll…" Lodaris swallowed, looked away. "It will not be kind."

"You cannot kill a man simply because you face a lecture from your mother." Emotion boiled to the fore. "And—and you cannot disobey me in front of others like that."

"You give me a lecture?" Lodaris's eyes narrowed. "Syphion was right. You really are naive. You think the smith wanted me dead because I glared at Dragga? You are blind."

"Oh." Ishoa shrank back. "Because you're Scarborn?"

"Yes! Because I'm Scarborn!"

Different. Alone. Outcast. *I know that pain.*

"Lodaris, I know—"

"What do *you* know of what it's like to be me—to be Scarborn?" he sneered. "When was the last time you were forced to live at the Fringes, fighting C'Dathuns for food because your own people hate everything that you are? A forgotten order of grain here, a delay in meat there… prejudice is the only truth in such exchanges. When was the last time you rode down the streets of Jarik to the sound of spit and insults? It happened when we arrived. But you didn't see… you were too busy buying sweet bread and tossing coins to dancers." He stepped closer. His breath was hot…suffocatingly hot. "When was the last time you were beaten by your parents for not killing a stranger, Highness?"

"My parents are dead." Her heart skipped a beat. She glanced sidelong at the thoroughfare. Her voice fell to a whisper. "Give me your scars, your spit, your insults. If I could meet them for just one day, I would trade you for all of it. Stories, Lodaris. Pictures." She looked at the ground. "Illusions of people who loved me. That's all I have."

Lodaris pressed his back against the wall. "I—I am sorry about your parents." The alley was as quiet as a grave. A man walked toward them from the other end of the narrow lane, whistling. Once he saw the seriousness of their expressions, he turned on his heels and whistled back the way he'd come.

Lodaris cleared his throat. "Perhaps it's better that they are dead. At least you don't have to see the way you displease them. But perhaps your parents would be kinder than mine. Perhaps they wouldn't give you all their pain." A fist trembled at his side. "You're free, Highness. Truly."

Before he could walk away, Ishoa grabbed his hand. "Lodaris. I don't think Scarborn are bad. When I'm crowned, I'll end the scarring ritual. I swear."

Lodaris watched her hand where it held his own. "Still, you do not see it." Wet jewels gathered at the corners of his eyes. He squeezed them gone and stiffened. "You do not see it, Princess."

He jerked his hand free from Ishoa's. The knight of Jarik gave him back his weapons, and then he walked toward the Gate of the Tiger. As he went, his black cloak trailed in the muddy street. It did not take long for her to see...

For the first time, she truly saw.

The people of Jarik watched him with furrowed brows. A heavyset slattern turned her back to him with a sneer. A youth's snowball burst harmlessly at his heels. Bakers and cheese mongers fell silent as he strode by them, only renewing their attempted sales once he'd past. A crownguard slapped the chest of his comrade, pointed, shouted an insult, laughed...

Laughed. Laughed. Laughed at Lodaris. *My Lodaris.*

Alone, he walked up the street, black cloak trailing, three scarlet blood drops dancing in the wind, proudly declaring a lineage of pain and oppression.

Hatred walked with him, surrounded him, dogged his every move, greeted him in the eyes of every passerby.

I am too late.

Bloodshed was inevitable.

CHAPTER EIGHTEEN

MAKING SPACE

Ten days come and go.

Ten days of my foot kicking Akyris's backside. Ten days of groaning protest, of the boy kicking at the dust with me hobbling behind. Ten days spent sitting beneath the elm tree staring into the face of our only chance against the Arrow of Light and his ever-stretching shadow.

I see them through the jeweled eye of time...

A legion ten thousand strong. The smoky glimmer of darksteel axes, breastplates, and plated warskirts. But their eyes are harder than any armor. Hate tempered with determination. Emboldened by a leader who calls them chosen, who would give them the world, who brings annihilation for all others.

Hundreds of voar rumble over bloodied turf, bellowing and bludgeoning, steel rods casting off gore as they render Namorite faces into pulp. Cracked armor and rag-doll bodies mark their going...and the raek calvary's coming. They worm along behind the charging grotesques. Hiding. Waiting.

The rustle of scaled bellies is a rock slide of doom. The defenders of Namarr pale at the sound. They curse, sweating like pigs in the slaughtering line. Little to be done but feel terror and hold their weapons tighter. The raek knights come, and scything death comes with them.

The Arrow of Light's army will be a juggernaut, but it is his other agents I worry over most. Silhouettes, mad with power, stalking the River for prey. A shroud surrounds them—a blind spot. All I know is that they mean me harm. Akyris too. For their master, they will hunt and hunt and hunt. They will never stop.

Violence awaits. Our future is red with it.

Akyris must be ready.

Ten days, he acts a child. Not unexpected.

Children always rail against change, but it is this very thrashing resistance that serves as a sign post for his progress.

For ten days, I watch the change. Stillness grows within him, the flowering of potential and possibility.

Ten days of calm sigh across the boy's brow as he sinks deeper into himself.

Ten days of Akyris finding what was never lost, only held at a distance.

Ten days of watching righteousness, impulsivity, and despair retreat from his eyes.

Ten days of cultivating our single seed of hope.

Ten days. A drop in the River. The River in a single drop.

At first, it's difficult for him. Arms flop to his sides in resignation at the end of every session.

Nevertheless, each day my foot finds his backside and then his backside finds the stump.

Another step.

Then another.

Onward toward our salvation.

Onward toward his annihilation.

Before me he sits. His Locus expands into the nothing of space created, roars to life in the silence observed.

The tenth day will be over soon.

It's amazing what sitting calmly can do for a relationship. My grandson despises me. That damage is done and may never heal before the end. I also see a morbid sense of appreciation dawning in him. He understands that what he's doing has merit. And I am its facilitator.

Besides, I gave him free reign outside our sittings. I no longer sting him with pointless chores or meaningless hard labor. Now his time is his own. The choice that mattered most has been made. Control was the tool of yesterday.

At first he avoided me as if I carried a disease he might catch by sight alone, fearful I might snatch the deal from him at any second. Now when I sit on the porch watching the sun make its rounds, he acknowledges me with a dip of his dark-haired mop before scurrying into the cottage.

When he thinks I can't hear, he speaks with my daughter like a spy entrusting secrets. "It's really weird...what we do," he tells her. "I just sit and...something happens. She's nicer now too."

My daughter says little, just as I have instructed her to do when it comes to the boy's training. It's enough. The boy speaks mostly to test his own thoughts aloud. Mothers are patient and convenient targets for such.

"I feel better about myself," Akyris says. "Sima's talking to me again. She says I'm different. Calmer. More confident."

"Good," my daughter says. "She's not all bad then, is she?"

"Maybe." His tone is dubious, less than totally convinced.

I've taken Magomedes's advice. At the end of every sitting, I look him in the eyes. They open, serenely present, like a baby seeing its mother for the first time. I praise his efforts.

"You're doing it."

"You've done it yet again."

"You're improving."

He does not smile, but neither does he seem upset. From the space within, from his Locus, he exudes curiosity about all of it. I see him questioning preconceived notions about both of us.

On the fifteenth day, I praise him before slowly rising from the stump, a fist pressing into my low back for added support. My place of solace upon the porch beckons. A pair of steps and heartbeats pass before he calls to me. "Grandmother?"

I look back. A faint smile plays at the edge of his mouth. "Thank you."

Gratitude. The benefits of our work together are not lost on him.

The work continues. My daughter tells him he's acting more mature of late. Where once he bemoaned every inconvenience, he helps without being asked. I no longer need to wake him in the morning as well.

The next day, I hobble my ancient ass to the tree to find him already sitting beneath it. "The time does not start until I say it does," I remind him. "Thirty days is thirty days. Ten hours in one day won't get rid of me faster."

"That's okay." Akyris shrugs. "I think I'm starting to like it."

"Oh, do you now?"

"Yes." A grin pushes through whatever bad blood he's felt toward me. "People say I'm different. In a good way. Sima likes me better since I've been doing this."

Pride mingles with sorrow in my breast. The joy of his newfound transformation will be short-lived.

"You told her what you're doing?" The last thing I need is Akyris's childish love bothering our work.

He shakes his head. Dead leaves skitter over an exposed root. The elm is losing its foliage, marking the passage of time in the beautifully sad way only nature does. They sit for a long, silent minute in appreciation of their surroundings.

Akyris breaks our shared reverie. "You don't call me 'little fly' anymore." He cocks his head. "That must mean something. Maybe *you* see a difference, too."

Perceptive. I laugh. "Flies make an annoying buzzing sound. But you, Akyris, you circle life's shit in silence now. I'll call you little bird instead, for you still preen for attention. But you learn as quickly as a crow."

His mouth is pursed as internal debate wages. Then he nods as if deciding the winner. "Fair enough."

We both smile.

A burbling in my ears...

"You're growing attached to the boy." Darkhorn's gravelly voice.

"I attach myself to the hope he brings. As we all should."

The Kurg falls quiet. He has a way of using stony silence as punishment. I find the behavior to be utter drivel. I'm capable of waiting out the shaman's impetuous brooding.

Finally, he says, "Just don't let your love of the boy cloud your judgment."

Before I can snap out a response, Mags takes a stand by my metaphysical side. "She's doing what must be done. We're dealing with a child, remember? Let her work in peace if you offer nothing useful."

It appears learning rolls both ways between Mags and I.

"By all means, Darkhorn." My tone drips with cynicism. "Let me know every time something bothers you. Maybe we'll criticize our way to victory. Perhaps that is the Arrow of Light's weakness? The nagging of a crusty old Kurg."

Darkhorn's consciousness retracts. Mags whistles low. "That was a bit heavy-handed. You know he means well."

It's true. Darkhorn is not all bad. He's one of the mightiest Awakened I've ever met and his heart is on the right side of history. The only problem is, I've never met a man who didn't let power feed his ego. Putting them in check with regularity is a necessity for cohesion. Otherwise, their egos grow until they become the stuff monsters are made of.

"He should learn a better way of meaning well." I leave Magomedes in the River, then return my attention to Akyris who watches me intently.

After a moment, I realize he sees something.

Me. He sees me.

"You're worried." His mouth splits into a knowing grin. "It's very loud."

I look away, grumbling at my stupidity. "The frustrations of an old hag should not concern you, little bird." Not yet. He's not ready.

Akyris stands, eyes narrowed. "Where were you just now?"

I feel my brow draw into a glare. "What do you mean?" Perhaps I'm wrong. Perhaps he is ready. "I'm sitting right here." I massage my lower lip with my tongue as I wait. I've thrown a hook. I wait to see which fish takes the bite.

"You've done what I'm doing—done it a lot." He's unraveling a puzzle he's long worked to solve. "You do it still. That's why you sit on the porch every day." He points at me, lips parted, head cocked. "Just now your lips were moving. You were somewhere else. You're strong with silence. But just now, something in your head...it got very loud."

Something between a laugh and a grunt escapes me. "You're right, little bird. Well done."

With a gnarled hand wrapped around an equally gnarled staff, I rise from the stump. I get only five steps before Akyris is beside me, his hand resting softly atop mine. I glance at it. He pulls away. Softness between us is still a fleeting thing. I like the kid. He can be a little bastard to be sure, but the apple, as they say, hasn't rolled very far.

Not far at all.

"Aren't you going to tell me what happened?" Innocent green eyes bore into me. It feels like I'm the one on the defensive for once.

"An old woman has secrets." I shrug my shawl higher onto my shoulders. "Best if I keep them for now."

I start to go. He grabs my arm more firmly this time. "Haven't I earned it?"

"Earned?" I say with disgust. There it is, the privilege of youth. The hardest back of all to break. "You may not be a little fly anymore, but you're still only a bird with hollow bones. What weight can you bear besides your own?"

He stammers.

"I'll tell you my secrets when you're strong enough to bear them." I leave him in the dust, scratching his head. He's onto something, he just doesn't know what yet. If I tell him too early about who I truly am and what's truly at stake, it could jeopardize the future of everything.

Regardless, I smile as I take my place on the porch to watch the sunset. The energy has shifted. I'm no longer pushing him where he needs to go. He's racing ahead to meet me there. Together, we pry open the possibilities together. I lure him to the abyss's edge. Soon, he'll fall in.

Until then, I'll need to bear the burden of secrets for both of us. The thought makes me weary.

So much work yet to be done.

On the twenty-first day of our training, I receive a pleasant surprise. Akyris stands over my bed. He nudges *my* backside with a barefoot. "Come," he says. He helps me rise, even retrieves my staff for me, then offers his arm to lean against on our way to the elm tree.

CHAPTER NINETEEN

THOSE UNEXPECTED

A thin line of drool connected the man's slack jaw to his bare chest. He shambled into a haphazard lane, barring Garlenna's way. She did not stop. Glazed eyes regarded her as she maneuvered past him. As she suspected, the man acted more out of a childlike curiosity than ill-intent. Lost. Ascending on godsthorn.

Others straightened from under patched canvas tents to watch her travel through the slums at the edge of town. This camp was bigger than the handful of others she'd seen. Unavoidable if she wanted to quickly reach the north hills. Hyram's men might see her if she left by any other route.

Flies worried at a woman's corpse beside a scattered fire pit. From the smell and deterioration, she guessed the body had been there a while. *Do they wait for the rain to wash it away?*

She glanced back. A pair of women with scabbed faces stared at her. The drooling man scratched his naked chest before continuing his purposeless shambling. The slums of Digtown offered a life both harsh and brief. *They're going to need a lot more rain.*

She snapped the reins. Her horse heaved forward into a gallop.

She searched the barrow hills and covered the ruins of Rainy Meadows. But signs of wagon wheels or horse droppings or tracks of any kind eluded her. The morning hours slipped by. Wasted.

She turned northwesterly toward Breckenbright. The sun was at its peak when she came across a shallow ravine bordered by maples and oaks. Squirrels darted over the thick duff from tree to tree. She followed the ravine until it opened into a rock quarry. Still nothing.

The sun peeked from under the thick paste of clouds like a glaring eye.

They are here, and I will find them.

She searched through midday as the sun swooned toward the western horizon. She considered pushing through to nightfall, but the thought of sleeping under the stars with a camp of hostiles somewhere in the vicinity dissuaded her. As much as she welcomed a night spent anywhere besides Digtown, it was foolhardy. More so after her failed gamble with Lairton.

They'll be on high alert now that they know I'm searching for them. Best to get back.

She compromised with herself to continue the search as she headed a different way back to town. The decision rewarded her almost immediately. Near the lip of the quarry, she found a linear depression in the earth and footsteps spaced at length alongside it. A handcart carrying a heavy load. Following the tracks, she discovered a pile of dog shit further along, a surprise considering the amount of rain the valley saw; two days at most had past since it had.

The trail led straight west from the ravine, sometimes as one line, but more often in rain softened earth it became two, a sure sign of wheels. The earth sloped upward. The ground hardened, causing the indentations to wane. She spun in a circle, then picked up the trail again. Vegetation became so thick it forced her to mark the last sign of wheel tracks and then take her horse in a wide loop around before resuming.

A pair of broken branches.

Leaves turned light side up. An overturned rock a few steps past that.

Displaced clod of mud—a tripping boot-heel?

She sped up her pursuit, heart quickening. *Slow yourself, Garlenna. This is dangerous.* Following her own advice, she tugged gently at the reins. To proceed without caution was to risk an ambush.

Ducking over her horse's neck, she followed the spoor. Evidence came more frequently. More upturned leaves, more broken branches, and stones facing muddy side up.

A wax wrapping for hard cheese.

She sniffed at the air. Hyram's group might smell sour or musty from the wet climate. If they didn't expect anyone to be looking for them, they might even use cook fires without concern.

But she would have no help from Srah. The wind was dead. She smelled naught but wet dirt.

The path left by the cart came to a half in a clearing. Garlenna dismounted at its edge, then drew out a length of rope to hobble her horse. She gripped the leather handle of the mace at her belt, doing her best to step lightly as she cut a line to the clearing's center. Two deep depressions sat at the head of the grooved lines from the handcart's wheels. *You stopped here.*

Why?

She glanced around. Muddy cast off and hoof prints came from the direction of Digtown. More still coming from the west—Breckenbright. *So this was a rendezvous point.*

The drover of the cart had arrived first and been forced to await the mounted men from Breckenbright and Digtown. She made mental boxes around the hoof prints in her mind and counted the tracks within. At least three riders had come from

Digtown. Three more from Breckenbright. The drover and perhaps four more on foot had come from Unturrus.

So, there are at least ten of you. Mostly mounted. And a dog.

Eventually, the group had moved off to her left. She followed it to a log with muddy footprints and chipped bark where shod hooves had clipped it during a jump. She drew her mace and leaped over.

At a hundred yards, she heard them, garbled and incoherent. At fifty, she smelled them, horse and hay and smoke and pungent, unwashed bodies. She flipped around to place her back against a broad oak, then drifted her good eye out to watch them.

Seven men sat around a dead fire pit on downed pines playing a game of cards. A canvas lean-to was strung to a tree on either side of them. At the camp's outer edge, she spotted the small cart that had led Garlenna to them. Out of view, she heard another man as well. She thanked the Sempyrean they had no archery equipment. Some wore leather armor and carried swords. Hired men, like Eustus. Two wore the livery of Breckenbright masons. Bronze honor plates marked them as holdguard. They wore gray cloaks bearing the sigil of the Masonry: crisscrossed hammers framed by laurels. War hammers rode their hips and none of their half helms or bucklers were far from reach. Well-trained professionals. Most likely hand-picked men.

This could never escape the Hammer's attention? Is Roddic Olabran the traitor my father seeks?

As the Magnate of Lah-Tsarra, he had money enough to rival the House of Saud. What he lacked was the influence necessary to turn votes in his favor. The Lord of Breckenbright was respected, but few would stomach him as their leader.

Which means he's not alone. The thought chilled her. *Namarr needs you, Barodane.*

A horse whinnied. She craned forward as far as she dared. Horses stood in a line on the far side of camp. Something moved around at their knees...

Garlenna swore.

A dog, as thick in the chest as a man and a jaw half-again as wide as a common hound, padded into view. Muscle and fur from thick snout to stub tail—a bearhound. Bred primarily for defending the stables of the rich, they were occasionally commissioned in foreign wars or other violent endeavors. Compared to other dogs, bearhounds weren't swift enough to hunt, but they were massive, vicious, obedient, and felt no pain at all. Only highborns could afford such dangerous weapons, for they required a trainer to always be with them.

The bearhound's head swiveled in Garlenna's direction. Panic jolted through her. Slow and quiet, she retreated, chiding herself for not being more cautious. *A common hound is one thing, but this is quite another.*

Upwind already, she gave a prayer to Srah, the goddess of winds, for added protection. Once behind a tree further from camp, she peeked out again. The bearhound continued to sniff the air. A mason with a blond bowl cut watched it—likely the hound's master—then he too began surveying the trees.

Garlenna's grip tightened around her mace. There was no doubt she could reach her horse before they could get to her. If the bearhound caused a ruckus though, she'd find herself in a running fight with seven mounted men. *And the dog would be on me in short order.* All it would take was for the beast to dodge her mace once and then snare her arm. The men wouldn't be far behind.

Even if I hit it clean, would that stop it? There were stories of bandits firing crossbow bolts into the monsters' chests only to have their arm torn from its socket seconds later.

Exhaling slow, she focused her attention on her feet planted firmly on the ground, then shifted it to her hand choking her mace. *It's just sniffing. The Sempyrean watches over me.*

Her heart thudded. She stared at the bearhound. Waited. Sweat trickled down her nape, soaking the collar of the padded surcoat under her leather armor. She forced her breathing to slow.

The Sempyrean watches over me.

Suddenly, one man slapped his hands on the fallen pine and stood, fists flying overhead. "Woe to you, bastards!" he laughed. The dog's head jerked toward the commotion. In answer to the excitement, it snarled and barked as if the camp were under attack. The bearhound's master sneered at the victor in disgust as he shook his head then silenced the beast with a clipped command.

Garlenna crept back to her horse. In the clearing, she erased any trace of her presence before returning the way she'd come. In a pair of mile-long loops, she doubled over her tracks for good measure.

She returned to Digtown at dusk. Almost on cue for its nightly appearance, the rains began.

As Garlenna approached the Dregs from the back, she couldn't help but notice movement in the window of a darkened room.

Her darkened room.

Lyansorca drank like a man. At least, that was what men said. She always thought she drank like herself. Her free hand hung in the air, a single finger waving as she threw back another tankard of Meckin's finest. Most of the men huddled around her cheered; a few gaped in awe. Women less pretty than herself, glared from the periphery. A thing most expected and familiar on busy nights at the Dregs.

"Another for you, Lyansorca?"

"Just one," she said with manufactured smoothness. She bit her lip as she breathed in deep through her nose. As she exhaled, her eyes rounded. This made men swell. Madame Gratha's trick. It signaled men that she was so excited she could barely contain herself and that it was them she was excited for. "Wider eyes draw more flies," Gratha always said.

Lucky for these fellows, Lyansorca was only a little thirsty for blood.

Two of the men immediately ordered another round. Lyansorca didn't worry about drinking too much. She would vomit up the contents in private before heading to anyone's room. A necessary indecency for the business at hand and one easily remedied by the mint leaves in her pocket.

The men contended for her attention as they drank. They matched stories—lies certainly—of bravado, importance, even intellect in one case, which surprised Lyansorca.

"You're from out of town, I take it?" she said after the intellectual man used the word, "deleterious."

The others laughed. The intellectual blinked. "Why do you ask?"

False bemusement. A hooked finger resting on her lip. She giggled. "It's just—you must be careful using big words like that in Digtown. You'll melt their brains." She inspected the ear of the man sitting next to her. "Here, I think I see some dripping out now."

They smiled. They laughed. All except the man she mocked. He jerked his head from her hand, snatched up his drink, and left.

Lyansorca pouted. "Poor little dunce. Couldn't handle a joke. Men rarely handle my humor well." She leaned back, spreading her legs suggestively. "Or any part of me for that matter."

She stretched a foot under the table, found the intellectual's inner thigh. "Here with anyone?"

He gulped. "I—uh." He looked at the others.

They huddled into themselves, grimacing into their drinks in defeat. As Lyansorca stared at her prey like a cat watching a mouse, they slowly dispersed.

The mouse wiped a bit of sweat from his brow. "I'm on—uh—business."

"Oh? What business?"

He puffed up. It was almost too easy, playing their egos like a flute. A finger held down here to emit this, a little blowing there to elicit that. It turned out he was a musician too. Though they played far different instruments.

A learned man whose father was a wealthy merchant. He himself was without direction.

She groaned inwardly as he babbled on. "So I thought, I have but one life, I might as well use it to make beautiful sounds that inspire others."

"Such purpose," she purred. "I imagine the world will be grateful for your daring leap into the life of a bard when your songs carry the night in every house in Namarr."

Yes, nothing inspires like a rich son's risk-free venture.

"I can play for you," he said. "I see no other performers tonight. Perhaps a ballad—"

Lyansorca sucked in a breath and leaned forward. "A tumble would be better." She was eager to avoid the tedious experience. Besides, he'd like her performance much more. "It's a silver wheel, but I assure you that you'll never buy another thing so worth the value."

She drew her lips into a smile like a bow pulled taut and ready to sail toward its target.

His chair skid backward as he shot to standing, adjusting his pants as he did. "After you, milady?"

The smiled faded, leaving only predatory eyes. "Don't call me that." She patted his shoulder, then gave his ass a squeeze as she slipped past.

He hurried up the stairs after her. "It's early."

"Never too early for what awaits you. Come quickly now. I'm eager."

His step quickened.

He motioned to a door on their right. "My room."

Lyansorca marked the door of the room Kord's woman was staying. She'd watched the big woman the day before, had her room confirmed by an indifferent Meckin. Unlike Imralta, Meckin cared little for his customers' confidentiality. Unless, of course, their name was Kord.

"A moment," she said. "I must wash. Be back shortly."

He nodded vehemently. "Of course, of course. Take your time. I'll be waiting right here." He winked then entered his room. This man, she decided, she would abuse a little. The surprise on his tender face would be oh-so satisfying.

She slid over to Gyra's room and produced a lock pick from a pocket beside her breast. In a matter of seconds she heard a pleasing click. A sigh of cloth and creaky hinge later, she was inside.

She was careful not to disturb anything and even made sure not to wear potent scents that might linger.

Above all, Lyansorca was a professional.

A rucksack sat near the window. She opened it, then rifled through the contents...

Garlenna stood outside her room, mace drawn, back pressed against the wall. She waited. A sorely out-of-place looking man, clean from crown to naked toe, poked his head out from a room a couple doors down. Being that he wore naught but undergarments, and given Garlenna's serious disposition, his eyes widened before he frantically closed the door, saying "pardon" and "sorry" as he did.

She turned her attention back to the door of her room. A minute skipped past. It opened. A woman crept out on silent feet. She was partway through the door when she noticed Garlenna. Dark-brown eyes flashed sudden fear.

Garlenna clasped the woman's lean throat in an iron grip. A strangled cry. A gurgle. The muffled swish of cloth. Garlenna pushed her inside. The woman hovered, toes scraping the floorboards. She clawed at Garlenna's forearm like a raccoon trapped in a bear's maw—a futile effort. The woman's face contorted, a swirl of horror and rage as a purple hue spread into her narrow, desperate face. Her hand disappeared behind her back. A knife whipped up toward Garlenna's elbow.

The prosort was already moving. The handle of her mace met the woman's knuckles. The knife bounced and skidded across the floor. Garlenna threw her down. With a pained grunt, the intruder landed hard, then scrambled onto hands and knees after the knife.

Too late.

Garlenna bore down on her, forcing a knee into the small of her back and taking hold of a fistful of nut-brown curls. "Fucking bitch!" the woman hissed. With her other knee pressed onto the woman's arm, Garlenna clamped a hand around the intruder's mouth, silencing her. Then she yanked her hair back. The woman struggled, but the effort was fleeting. Garlenna increased the pressure. The intruder whimpered as her spine bent painfully backward. "Keep fighting. It'll get worse."

The woman froze, sucking heavy breaths in and out of her nose until she relaxed into obedience.

"That's better. In a moment I'm going to release your mouth. When I do, I'm going to take my hand and place it around your throat." Garlenna spoke at a measured, instructional pace. Flat and direct. "My mace is right next to me. At any time I wish, I could grab it, calm as an ice tiger, and crush your skull. You understand that?"

The woman nodded.

"Good. Do you see your knife over there?"

The woman nodded.

"You understand that it's too far then. I'll still have your hair and throat in my hands. When I slide my knees off your arm and back, they'll straddle you on either side. At that point, I'll apply force in a way that invites you to turn over and look up at me. I suggest you do that without resistance. Understand? Good. I'm then going to add my other hand to your throat. Do you understand what that means?"

The woman paused a moment then nodded vigorously. The intruder's shoulders shook from the strain of bearing Garlenna's weight.

"One last thing. You understand that at any time I can crush your throat with my hands, right? If you doubt me, know that I have done it to men—big scary ones. Here..." Garlenna squeezed. The woman purpled and began to thrash. "That's little of my strength. It would be easy, like crushing an egg. I'm not trying to scare you, nor hurt you more than need be. I simply want you to understand the situation clearly so we can have a nice conversation." She leaned down to whisper. "But if I were you, I *would* be scared. Very scared."

Garlenna flicked her head, tossing strands of lank hair from her face. "Now, are you going to scream?"

The woman shook her head.

"Smart," Garlenna said. "We're going to start in a second. Any motion from you that I don't lead will be met with violence."

Let that sink in.

"I'm starting now," Garlenna said. "Slowly now."

She released the intruder's mouth, hand hovering nearby as the woman sucked in tremulous breaths. She slid her knees to the sides of the woman's torso and pulled her hair while also fixing her other hand around the woman's throat.

"Look into my eye. Yes, like that." The prosort kept steady pressure around the woman's neck until she lied flat on her back. "Now, what's your name?"

"Semalda." *A lie.*

Asking a name was always Garlenna's first question in an interrogation. If the person seemed more intelligent than a dog, they always lied, which gave her a baseline for all subsequent lies. Semalda's lips twitched as if resisting the name tumbling forth. The words were spoken flatly, lacking the casualness of one who'd said her name a thousand times throughout her life.

A great liar, this one.

"I'll give you one free lie, Semalda. But lie to me again and I'll sew your mouth shut. Then I'll do things to you I would not be proud of. Things you wouldn't enjoy. You saw the field sewing kit in my rucksack, right?"

Semalda gulped.

"Good. Next question. What brought you to my room?"

"I—I wanted..." Garlenna choked her a moment, then released. Semalda gasped.

"Do not hesitate and do *not* lie."

"I came for information," Semalda said in a rush. "I wanted to know if you traveled alone or had others with you. Maybe even figure out who sent you."

"You didn't come to kill me?"

Brown curls bounced as she shook her head.

"How much were you paid?"

Semalda frowned. "Two gold wheels."

Only Barodane or Hyram could afford that.

She released the spy. "Tell your employer I travel alone."

The woman claiming to be Semalda rolled to her side, then stood. Her eyes flickered to the knife then the door. Ignoring her, Garlenna made her way to the cot to sit. She brushed a meaty hand through matted, ruddy hair and shook free some tangles.

Semalda panted, nerves and breath racing to recover control. "You're letting me go?"

Garlenna nodded.

"Why?"

"You're not here to kill me. And I wouldn't hold back information from your employer anyway," Garlenna sighed. "I only wish he would have asked me himself."

Semalda stood and smoothed her dress. "But I didn't tell you who employed me."

"You didn't have to. You're a whore from the Gem Loft. I've known Kord a very long time, and there are only two men able to spend gold wheels on a spy. Though I dare say he overpaid."

And if it were Hyram, he would have sent his own men to deal with me. It would have been knives in the night. Not a sneaking whore at dusk. If her estimation of Hyram was correct, she figured him as a man that looked down on the "gentler" sex. He wouldn't trust a woman with such a task.

Semalda's ego looked hurt about being referred to as overpriced. Her chin jutted slightly, lips pursed together. "Well...it's only a secondary profession anyway, and I did drive up the price."

Garlenna snorted, nearly a laugh. "Good for you." She pulled a gold wheel from her belt. "Would you like more?"

A smile twitched across Semalda's expression. "This has certainly taken an unexpected turn."

"Unexpected. But fortuitous for both of us, I hope."

The whore's eyes narrowed, waxing suspicion. She looked Garlenna up and down, then shook her head. Garlenna waved the gold wheel through the air. She shrugged then made to replace it in her purse. "I suppose I misread you. I suspected you an opportunist. Not a coward."

"What am I to do?" Semalda said. "Moments ago you were set to kill me. Now you offer me a deal. I may lack morals, but that doesn't mean I trust lightly."

"Nor should you." Garlenna paused, gold wheel hovering between thumb and forefinger. "But consider what the alternative might have been. Is sparing your life worth nothing? A foundational first step for any relationship built on trust."

Semalda crossed her arms and sniffled.

"They say a crow knows to hide its hoard because it steals from the hoards of other crows," Garlenna said. "Perhaps you hoard trust because you so often rob others of it."

The woman cocked her head haughtily. "I suppose that means you give others wisdom because you need it yourself then."

The words of Garlenna's father tiptoed through her mind. *The shadow of falsehood flees before the torch of truth. Will you, my daughter, bear these flames and challenge the darkness in others? Will you call forth the light of the Sempyrean in all who cross your path?*

Garlenna brought elbows to rest on knees, gold wheel rotating between her fingers. *I give only the wisdom that what was given to me.*

The failed spy's arms flopped to her sides. "Fine, I'll take the wheel. What do you want me to do?"

"Keep an eye on some men—should be easy for you. Masons of Breckenbright and any one with them." She flipped the gold wheel with a thumb. It struck the floor, rolled to the woman's foot. She scooped it up in a flash. "I want a report of their movements. You'll get two additional silvers if I'm satisfied at week's end. Now, what's your name?"

"Lyansorca," she said. "And it's a gold wheel at week's end."

If we survive a week. My lie about Barodane having extra muscle won't make Hyram hesitate long.

Garlenna rose and crossed the room, picking up Lyansorca's knife along the way. Compared to a man, Garlenna was broad. Compared to a woman, especially a lean one such as Lyansorca, she was a veritable giant. This fact wasn't lost on the whore. Garlenna leaned close, raising the knife between them. "You'll already have trouble justifying your fuck up to Kord, so tell him the truth. Tell him exactly what I've said. Tell him what I've paid for if you like. I *want* him to know. And remember," Garlenna slapped the knife into Lyansorca's palm. "Others you run across might not be so kind as I."

Lyansorca cleared her slender throat. "I understand."

"It has been an evening full of understandings." Garlenna turned her back. "You may leave now. Return in two evening's time with the information I need."

At the door, Lyansorca lingered. "Why?"

"Why do I want these things?"

Lyansorca nodded.

"Why do *you* do what you do?"

The whore smiled. "Money, of course."

"You and I both know you have plenty of money. A girl like you in a place like this. Why do you really do it?"

Lyansorca wistfully traced a finger along the door frame. "A thrill. Life is boring, you know."

"You underestimate the joy of a boring life. At this point, I would give a great deal for it."

Bawdy laughter drifted up the stairs from the taproom, reminding Garlenna of just how weary she was. Yet the comfort of hearing people enjoying themselves warmed her.

It was the very thing she fought to uphold. *Peace and joy for the United Lands of Namarr.*

Garlenna studied the spy. "Do you imagine you truly have a choice, that you could stop yourself from chasing thrills even if you wanted?"

"Oh, I don't know. Never really wanted to."

Garlenna nodded. "So it is. We are simple creatures. Capable of great deeds but oriented toward the most meager pleasures. Slaves to what validates us." *Whether it's service to the Sempyrean, our own misery, or gold, or a Crown.* "It seems we're fated to do what we do."

Lyansorca flinched. "Like animals."

"Yes. Just like animals. Now go."

The door opened and Lyansorca hurried out. A second door out in the hall opened. A man's questioning voice followed by a hushed conversation. A sharp slap. Footsteps thundered down the steps. It sounded as if the man were stifling pained sobs in the hall.

With her room violated, Garlenna found sleep difficult even after locking and securing both door and window.

But sleep never came easy.

The day tumbled through her mind's eye. Hyram's men were gathering. Pawns like constable Lairton were being activated. Her own prince moved against her.

Comfort in sacred duty was the only bastion left.

No matter what it takes. No matter what I have to do, Barodane will hold Solice-rames...he'll be Prince of Namarr once more.

CHAPTER TWENTY

LEVERAGE

D rummers and flutists lined the High Hall, playing a low tune for the feast. Braziers and torches cast a ruddy glow over the holds and their retinues, birthing shadows under arms, tables, and huddled brows.

Ishoa jumped as Wolst pounded the table to the tune of a banha drum. *Poorly.*

He wore a merry grin. "Your uncle Barodane was a damn fine drummer, you know?"

She did. It wasn't often she thought of her father's brother. Without parents to tell of him, she relied on bits of information sparingly doled out by Wolst and her grandmother. But these came too infrequently to overcome the murmurs of history. The Mad Prince, they called him, a divisive figure. Hero and villain both.

Two stories competed for Ishoa's opinion of the man. The foremost was his heinous act at Rainy Meadows. The other brought a sad smile to her lips. When it was announced that Ishoa's mother was pregnant, Barodane had filled her chambers with a thousand baby dolls. As Wolst told it, the sight of Malath Ironlight wading through a sea of stitched mouths and button eyes while cursing and laughing was riotously funny.

Perhaps Barodane was always a little mad. In a fun-loving kind of way.

Godsbrew and mead circulated the room on servant's platters. Cups sloshed in roughened fists. Amber beads collected in the beards of savage mouths. Ishoa sampled both types of drink. The bitter taste of the godsbrew made her nose bunch, and the mead had a tang to it as if made from her uncle's armpit. That didn't stop Wolst from offering her more of the wretched liquid. Seemingly, he enjoyed her disgust. Each time she waved the putrid liquid away as if a viper hid in the cup, Wolst gave a hearty laugh.

Ishoa scanned the room for the third time in as many minutes. Lodaris and the Scarborn had yet to arrive.

Ollo Bael, the Lord of Baen's Handle, caught her gaze. A stout man with a gray neck beard and a balding pate, he raised a cup and bowed his head.

Anjuhks ate meat. Seal, whale, storm bear, lamb, mutton, veal, snow bison, and a litany of fish. Although they didn't eat ice tiger, Ishoa struggled eating animals since she'd gotten Rakeema. So when a platter of braised bull from Ollo Bael's private stock slid from a servant's hands onto the table in front of her, she had to stifle a grimace.

While Ishoa always found it funny that the other holds called him the Cattlewarden, Ollo Bael was not one to slight. As Magnate of Anjuhkar, he was second only to Belara Frost in power and sat the Collective in Alistar.

He's watching me. Stomach recoiling, she talked herself through it. *Smile. Look enthusiastically at the steaming slab—don't gag. Cut. Bite. Chew...yes. All in the name of Namarr.*

With a crackling purr, Rakeema rubbed her lithe frame against Ishoa's knee.

I'd do anything to stop eating this. All the same, she chewed, swallowed, smiled. To stem the budding guilt, she slid back her chair and stroked Rakeema's ears.

An elbow in her ribs drew Ishoa's attention to Wolst seated beside her. Bits of food tangled in his smoky beard. He thrust it at a group filing in at the back of the High Hall. "The hunters of Twilights Cape."

They looked to be nearly beasts themselves. Bedecked in the pelts of wild storm bear, Ishoa imagined how fierce they looked knifing through the icy shoals of the Eastern Fjords hunting seal. The sharp, cannibalistic teeth of C'Dathun trolls clacked together on leather thongs around their necks and black ink covered their faces from nose to throat—once merely a camouflage they used for hunting, now a ritual tattoo.

All were stunning to behold, but it was the Lady of Twilight Cape, Enkita Vulkuu, Ishoa fixated on.

"What do you think of her?" Wolst said.

Awe filled Ishoa's voice. "She's unlike any lady I've ever seen."

"Don't let Enkita hear you call her that."

"A lady?"

Wolst nodded emphatically. "Diminutive in stature but titanic in spirit. That's a woman to shape yourself after. Enkita Vulkuu didn't earn a hold through service in the Great Betrayal. Nor did she buy her way in through financial means like some of these others. She grew up in a family of seal hunters in the Fjordlands. Long stretches of dusk and deep snow forged her soul into iron. When she was eleven, her father was killed by a storm bear. A year later, her mother met the same fate. For nearly a decade she drowned her woes in piracy, razing villages along the coast of western Valat and southern Namarr." Wolst shrugged. "It wasn't long before the Crown's Justice hunted her. Drunk beyond reckoning and with nowhere to go, she fled to Unturrus to make the sacred journey or die trying. She Awakened. Dominarri arrested her, of course. Five years she spent in manacles at Deephollow prison. But she was strong, fearsome, capable. Belara could have quashed the vote at Twilight Cape that gave her the hold, but she didn't."

Ishoa pressed a knuckle to her lips. "Was it a close vote?"

In Anjuhk society, being an Awakened made Enkita Vulkuu an outcast. Unlike the rest of Namarr's populace who both feared and respected Awakened, Anjuhks saw them as unnatural, evil creatures meant to be shunned. Most referred to them pejoratively as "ghosts." The line between criminal and Awakened was thin, which placed them just beneath Scarborn in the social pecking order.

Wolst threw back a tankard of mead, then wiped his mouth with the back of a furry arm. "The Fjordlands are no easy place to live, so they vote by simple logic. Merit. Who is best at the thing that helps them most? No one is a better hunter than Enkita Vulkuu."

The lady of Twilight Cape showed herself to match every bit of the myth surrounding her. Shorter than every man in her retinue and scrawnier than Ishoa, she looked feral as she grabbed a passing servant. She forced him to drop his platter before her, and then tore into a rack of seal ribs. Every hunter at her table turned red with laughter when she slapped the servant on the backside. The woman seemed to have no care for prestige or power. Nonetheless, there it was.

The power of an Awakened.

Regardless of status, the other Anjuhks steered clear of Enkita Vulkuu's table.

Throughout the evening, Claimants approached Ishoa's table to pay their respects and their tithes for the Trials to the duchess. Most wished Ishoa good fortune and spoke of the honor it was to partake in the Trials alongside an Ironlight.

Dragga Omenfaen kissed her hand, while his twin sister, Stirrma Omenfaen, barely made eye contact. "Honored," she said before returning to a support column in the shadows. For the rest of the evening, she leaned against it with her arms crossed.

I don't know why her brooding makes me smile, but it does.

Wolst leaned over, a dwarfed apple in his titanic hand. "This one talking with Belara is Megalor Bog. Three years the Lord of the treekin of Shadowheart."

Megalor Bog was like a pot of ink poured into a man. A scruffy dark beard covered a narrow chin. He bowed to the duchess, then moved to stand before Ishoa, speaking with grim indifference. "I hope you teach my little brother a thing or two during the Trials, Highness. As is, he's nearly useless."

Ishoa laughed. "I've high hopes, Lord Bog. Who's that there with you?" A black and gray fox sniffed at the platter of braised bull.

"Aht!" Megalor hissed. A slap on the fox's snout followed. "Apologies, Highness. My anjuhtarg, Fang, a little devil."

The show of abuse caused Ishoa to tense. "Well, maybe I'll have the honor of learning something from your brother too."

"Doubtful." Megalor bowed, then moved on to greet Wolst. As soon as Megalor's back turned, Fang darted over to snag a bite of bull off her platter. The fox choked it down greedily, then slunk after his master to a table full of treekin from Shadow-heart.

There's a man worthy of my dislike. And an anjuhtarg I'll not soon forget.

A boy bearing a blightwing hawk on his arm came next. Given the sigil sewn into his doublet of a bisected oak tree mirroring spring and winter—and that he looked only slightly older than Ishoa—she assumed this to be the younger brother, Unalor Bog.

The blightwing hawk regarded her, fleshy lids lapping over golden eyes as it blinked. Its back and crown were forest green, the wings striped through with oaken brown. But its belly, throat, and sharp talons were black as night.

"She's called Frenzywind, Highness," Unalor said. "Wanna pet her?"

"Certainly!"

Ishoa reached for the hawk. Just as her fingers were nearly on its head, Unalor shook his arm and gave a guttural shout. Frenzywind flapped and opened her black beak to screech. Ishoa gasped, heartbeat frozen as her hand shot back to her lap.

One hand holding his belly, Unalor laughed uncontrollably.

A flush crept up Ishoa's neck. Shock held her tongue from harsh reprimand. Only later would she be proud of herself for having the grace not to respond aloud. *A whole family worthy of dislike. I hope Frenzywind pecks your eyes out.*

A pair of Omenfaen knights and the table of cattlemen from Baen's Handle glared at Unalor's shameful behavior. But the sparsely mustached boy appeared immune to social graces. He moved over to Wolst...

A squawk of pain brought Ishoa some small satisfaction as her heartbeat steadied to normal. The fool, Unalor, shook hands with Wolst. Her uncle had also witnessed the uncouth act and found it less than humorous. "Best not to toy with beasts, boy." Sweat shone on Unalor's boyish mustache. "They might not find your antics so amusing."

Wolst squeezed the Claimant's hand to approving jeers from the feasting table of Shadowheart. Megalor Bog approached his younger brother, now gulping with pain, and took him by the ear. "Unalor, meet the Beast of Anjuhkar." Through grit teeth, he added, "Foolish little twat," then dragged away the whimpering boy. The blightwing hawk on his arm flapped for balance but otherwise showed no concern for its master.

A pity such a beautiful anjuhtarg should be wasted on that cretin.

Wolst reached over to tear a strip of braised bull from the platter before Ishoa. As he chewed it, Ishoa locked eyes with her uncle and playfully shook her head.

He swallowed. "What? You'd let it rot." Pushing aside a wooden bowl of stripped bones and apples cores, he took the entire platter of bull and encircled it in monstrous arms. Within seconds his smacking lips were covered in grease from the golden brown meat. "I've a long way to go if I'm to be the Barn of Anjuhkar."

"Wishful thinking, Uncle." She cleared her throat. "A couple more bites should do the trick."

Their laughter mingled with the joyous clamor swirling about the High Hall, then trailed off. Wolst turned to talk to Arick on his other side.

For a few dreadful minutes, Ishoa sat quiet and alone—alone but for the sea of eyes watching her every move, judging each of her conversations, measuring her against those who came before.

My betters.

Panic set her chest to pumping, her breath to shallow sips. She didn't move as her eyes darted from face to face. She swore her name rode their lips. "Ironlight," they mouthed.

"The last."

"A disappointment."

"Weak."

Loneliness embraced her like a storm bear's maw. The image of her parents pushed to the fore of her racing mind. She wished their expressions could be any but the ones they always wore—wished she could see them smile. See any kind of approval as they looked down at her.

That will never be.

She inhaled sharply. Heaviness smothering her heart like a stone ballast. *I wish Lodaris were here.* She wanted to apologize, to make things right between them, to hold hands where no others could see.

To hold hands openly without threat of scorn.

Frustration followed powerlessness.

But have I offended him too deeply?

She looked to Rakeema for comfort. The ice tiger's tail twitched as she intently watched the blightwing hawk perched on the treekin table. *Sorry, girl. Sometimes we want things we can't have.*

Ishoa was wondering when she might be allowed to leave for the night when another young male approached her grandmother. He was like a scarecrow come to life, except more frightened than frightening. What looked to be his father trailed him, a hand on both the boy's rail-thin shoulders. They were dressed lavishly in the style of Peladonians. Pelts of gray wolf fur, pristine in their cleanliness, draped over the right sides of father and son. The dancing wolf sigil of the furriers of Ghastiin dangled on chain necklaces wrought from gold. They wore doublets of such a deep purple that Ishoa had never seen a color so vivid. A black wolf stood at the father's hip, staring forward in rapt obedience.

"Highness," the bald man said. "You remember my son Yurm."

"How could I forget one so strapping?" Belara Frost lied. Any fool could see the boy was quite the opposite. "Yourself, however, I cannot place."

The lord of Ghastiin stepped forward, then knelt suddenly, bald head bowed. "Alas, it seems I've proven myself quite forgettable. I wonder how I might rectify this, for nothing brings me greater joy than knowing I am regularly on the mind of one so wonderful as you." He stood, a coy smile playing across clean-shaven face. "Perhaps the gift I brought will help the Ice Maiden to never forget me again."

The man's son, Yurm, gulped. A bolt of cloth fumbled from his hands, and he scrambled to retrieve it. Distended throat apple bobbing, he handed the folded bolt to the duchess.

With a broad grin, Belara untied the silk rope holding the material in a tight roll, then ran a hand over the surface which shone like armor. After a moment spent in quiet thought, Belara gasped.

Wolst was at her side in an instant.

"You have done it indeed," she said. "I shall not soon forget the name of Joffus Kon, Lord of the furriers of Ghastiin. You wouldn't dare gift me with raek skin. So what is this?"

Joffus laughed. "Correct, Highness. This is from the jungles of Mimbor."

"Jungles?" Ishoa leaned across Wolst to run a hand along the skin. It was so smooth as to be soft. Hard but without texture. Her fingertips glided over it.

"You've grown, Princess," Joffus said. "You might not remember me... it's been some years, but it is good to see you all the same." He turned his attention back to the duchess. "Yes, Highness. Mimbor...jungles *and* swamps. How else could I get the skin of a dragon's whelp?"

Everyone in the vicinity of Joffus Kon fell silent, heads craning to hear the exchange.

Belara Frost raised a thin, snowy eyebrow. "While I appreciate the gift, Joffus, I believe I'm owed an explanation. I value the humor we share, but if this is a joke, tell it true now."

Dragon skin.

Joffus became serious. "No jest, Highness."

"How did you come to own such skin?" Belara said.

A wave of silence had moved through the tables closest to the duchess. However, at the back of the High Hall, the hunters of Twilight Cape still japed and cajoled bawdily. With hands crossed behind his back, Joffus Kon threw an amused look over his shoulder. He whispered, "A gamble, nothing more. Dealing in furs goes as well as ever for Ghastiin but if I'm ever to convince you to take White Plains from the Hines and give it to me, well, I must show you I am worth more than our simple flirtations."

Sickness pooled in Ishoa's gut. Her grandmother was over eighty, Joffus Kon at least thirty years her younger. It was clearly a joke between the Ice Maiden and her hold lord, but still. *Disgusting.*

Belara leaned forward. "That still doesn't explain the skin."

"Ah." Joffus patted the anjuhtarg at his side. The wolf glanced at him expectantly a second before returning to its statuesque repose. *I'll have to ask him how he trained his wolf so well.*

"I assure you I did not gain the skin without sacrifice, Highness. My hold has been living on old bread and rationed meat for over a year now. My boy, as you can see, has been half starved." The last was a joke, but none laughed. "Cutting those costs allowed us to invest in more exotic expeditions. Allowed us to hire better ships and contract pirates and guides to get my trappers in the right place to bring down more exotic prey."

"Dangerous." Belara rubbed a palm against the skin. "But if you think this gift will forgo your tithe, you're wrong."

The lord of Ghastiin dipped his head. "Of course not. It is but a gift. Though I must tell you one dragon whelp's carcass provided four such bolts. I've sold the other bolts to three Lights of Malzacor's Imperial family. What you hold is worth ten tithes for the Trials."

Wolst whistled low.

"How can that be?" Ishoa blurted.

Joffus cocked his head. "My trappers are the best at what they do. The jungle of Mimbor, as you can imagine, is perhaps the most dangerous place in the world. And a mother dragon..." Joffus shrugged. "Ferocious. It cost me nine men to get that one skin. Even the locals are not foolish enough to hunt the monsters."

"Nine men for one skin." Wolst shook his head. "Foolish indeed."

The warmaster's condemnation deterred Joffus little. He smiled. "What no one has done before is often seen as such. Yet with a second skin on its way to Ghastiin now, I'll soon have another fortune in my foolish grasp."

"Impressive," said the duchess. "I do admire your ambition, Joffus but you and I both know the rules. Power over the holds is voted on by the people of each city. If the Hines were to fall to ruin, effectively threatening the livelihood of the stronghold under their care, things might be different." With what seemed like an afterthought, she added, "With such fortunes on the horizon, it sounds like you are doing just fine."

"You are right." Joffus bowed, invited Yurm to do the same. "Great suffering amid great risk are the cornerstones Namarr was built upon. I cannot help but give gifts of gratitude to you and your great-granddaughter. Your family has provided me the opportunity to serve a nation I so love. I will not ask for more again."

Belara gave Joffus Kon a nod of dismissal.

Next came the Narls, a small hold of bakers from Prav who'd fallen on hard times. Their gift, when compared to the Kons, was of woefully low worth. Along with a small chest of gold wheels for the tithe, they gave a decorated basket of fine breads.

Their Claimant was a heavyset boy with a vacant stare, and his father, Golthius Narl was immensely fat, a grinning sack of powdery dough.

"What a lovely gift, Lord Narl," said Belara. "Unfortunately, I do not eat bread. Thankfully, my warmaster has the hunger of ten men."

The double chin of Golthius Narl shook, one of a few barely concealed indications that the man was abashed.

Belara seemed to notice the gluttonous lord's displeasure. "When my warmaster is happy, I am happy. My many thanks to the illustrious bakers of Prav. Your skill precedes you."

The heavy-set lord was not to be dissuaded from insult. A dark look fell over Golthius Narl as he and his son gave stiff bows then left the High Hall.

Ishoa watched the door. Still, the Warnocks did not come.

Where is Lodaris?

The hair on the backs of her arms stiffened. She wondered if Lodaris suspected her of trying to use him. *What have I done?* Worry gnawed at the back of her mind. Had she lost his trust in addition to alienating him? If so, that meant she'd failed her family.

Failed Namarr.

Right before the Trials start. Perfect.

CHAPTER TWENTY-ONE

THE CORPSE GATE

S leep had never been a friend to Thephos. Then again, nothing had.

Unturrus blotted out the moon's light. Torches and braziers lined the mist-strewn lanes, flickering guides for Thephos's wandering. Three wide thoroughfares spreading out from Danath's statue connected a network of half a hundred alleys and side roads to form the settlement of Eastshadow. Despite it being the dead of night, many stalked the streets. Mostly drunk. The settlement had the feeling of an ongoing party once the lights went out.

Work all day, drink all night, repeat.

A pair of singing men strode by, arms wrapped around one another. A young couple pulled at each other's clothes as they kissed their way into a dark alley.

The intimacy of Eastshadow's people made him shudder.

He turned up an alley, seeking solitude. It angled upward and kept going, all the way to the base of the curtain wall. Torchlight and the dull murmur of merriment faded behind. Thephos ran a hand along the wall. Fifteen feet of sheer stone, marred here and there by gaps and grooves.

I couldn't scale this. A well-trained climber or superior athlete might be able to. I'm neither.

There were times back at the pig farm when one of his younger brothers bested him in a wrestling match. Of course, they only played like that on the rare occasion when the old devil wasn't around. As soon as they heard his approach, they scattered like cockroaches and took up whatever task they hoped might stay his wrath.

Strength was not his strength.

Chill, damp air entered Thephos's lungs as he slowly inhaled, then exhaled in a rush of steam that dampened his cheeks and the tip of his nose.

Why Unturrus?

The question suggested by the drunk priest gave him pause. An ache started behind his eyes. The hollow place in his gut stirred, sent a stab of sensation from belly button to spine. *That question is best answered by those with something to live for. Not the doomed.*

He recalled the betting board at the Numbers.

After the old drunk had finished feeding him scraps of information about the gambling stakes, one of Syn's men had led him to a tent set aside for Ascendants. Thephos had come to Eastshadow fully expecting to sleep outside, so the news had been welcome. Upon entering, a Sister of the Rose invited him to strip and took his possessions and clothing before giving him a ceremonial white smock. "People must know you're an ascendant. If you don't wear it, you won't be allowed beyond the Corpse Gate."

"Corpse Gate?"

"The place your journey begins," she had said.

"You mean where it ends?"

A sad smile tugged a corner of her mouth. "Aren't they the same?" She turned away, laying neatly folded linens on a cot. One of ten in the large tent.

The white Ascendants smock was the finest piece of clothing Thephos had ever worn. The feather-soft feel of it summoned memories of his mother's hands from when he was very young. Warm too. The smock reached down to his ankles, just loose enough that he could move freely and just tight enough that the frigid night air didn't creep into his bones.

Once he left the Ascendants' tent, Thephos had turned in a circle. The head of Danath hovered over a row of buildings a few lanes distant. The Corpse Gate was a gaping hole in the wall fifty further up slope. When the tenth member of their group arrived, Thephos would enter it. The old drunk at the Numbers had done his best to explain its magic.

"Now if ye' get to bein' a Ruptured or Awakened, you'll come right back down through the Corpse Gate, same way you gone up. If that weren't the case, the Dominarri might have a hell of a time chasing down the mad ones needin' to be killed. But, as luck has it, you'll be like a moth to flame. If you get powers that is. Come right back, you will..." The old man shrugged, trailed off, then resumed louder than before. "Like if I drop this 'ere mug 'o godsbrew, it'll fall, and when it strikes the ground it'll eject its liquid on ye'. It's just a matter of fact like that. Enough people observe a thing enough times, and it makes it true. Course my momma always said I'd be a drunk like my daddy and—" The old man had winked and took a playful sip. "That ain't so, eh?"

Thephos was nothing like his father—he'd made sure of that. All the same the old devil's words slashed Thepho's soul, telling him who he *was*—a matter of fact.

I hate you.

You're a pathetic worm.

You have no fire in you, Thephos.

I'd fucking kill you...

Thephos's head dropped backward, skull knocking against the stone wall. He barely felt it. Then, like a cup of godsbrew in an old drunk's hand, he was pulled down by forces that simply...were.

The damp earth soaked his white smock, spreading coolly as he lied on his side—an unavoidable shame, for it was a fine piece of clothing. He hated to ruin it.

Do I want to die because the old devil told me I should? Will it be his voice whispering, "I told you," when the demons kill me?

"Do not move!"

Thephos froze, heart beat thudding. He craned his neck in the direction of the shout—from above. A wood tower just inside the wall a stone's throw away.

"Slowly exit the shadows," the voice commanded.

Crownguard.

A second man sprinted from the lanes and up the hill toward Thephos.

When he seemed to notice what Thephos wore, he gave a breathy groan, then shouted, "Ascendant!" to his peer in the guard tower. The crownguard leaned on his spear, chest heaving for breath.

"Shit." The self-reprimand from the crownguard in the watchtower was muffled, a mild echo pushing the night air.

They tried to time their arrest. Even as a suspected criminal, I'm a disappointment.

"We thought you were a thief," said the one in the lane. "Wasted my one dash for the night on a false alarm...fuck me."

"Thieves go over the wall? Why?"

The crownguard laughed. "More so near Northwilds...more still at Westlakes where there's no wall. Less often from Eastshadow, hence my lack of conditioning. But at Northwilds it's a steady business chasing down drug runners. Crownguards be thinner and younger there for a reason. A silver wheel for a bundle of twenty godsthorns is a good living for the desperate types. But I'm too old for such strenuous activity. I'd rather do the daily runs for the holds. Nice and safe."

Thephos stepped down slope. "The daily runs?"

"We take the brewers for the holds and the Sempyrium inside the wall to harvest." The crownguard waved a hand. "Harvesting ain't dangerous until you get up around the Cusp. That's when the demons start appearing. Sightings are more common the further up you go."

The Cusp. A little dread swept down Thephos's back, evoking a thin lather of cool sweat. *No, that's what I want, the only way I can hope for Vaniton's Gasp.* "Why don't drug runners just gather—"

"I know what you're going to say, kid."

Thephos was not quite a kid, but neither did he take up space as a man.

"No sense to it, but godsthorn gains its psychoactive properties around the Cusp. For brewing purposes, the lower slopes are fine. If someone wants the real deal though..." he sucked at his teeth. "It's like the drugs and the demons are linked."

A sudden realization seemed to come to the guard as he eyed Thephos. "You didn't steal that smock did you?" He leveled his spear. "Some kinda clever drug runner, are you?"

Thephos stepped back. "I'm only curious." Despite the threatening posture, he didn't think the man was about to hurt him. He knew those signs all too well. "Since I'm to go up soon."

"Ah well." The butt of the spear sank back into the earth with a muffled thud. "I didn't think so. Can't be too careful. Good luck to you, kid. However you end up, I wish you peace."

"You as well." Before the crownguard got too far, Thephos said, "Are you a father?"

The man hesitated. "That I am."

"I—I." Thephos stammered. "I bet you're a good one."

Three heartbeats of awkward silence passed.

"I'd like to think so." The crownguard sighed. "What's your name?"

"Thephos."

"Well, Thephos, I'll be sure to put a bet a on you becoming Awakened. From what I see, you don't deserve to die. I'll pray to the Sempyrean for you." He nodded then walked back down the lane.

Why did I say that? I'm a pathetic worm and I've just lost that man's hard-earned money. Taken food from his children's mouths!

Thephos folded his arms over his stomach where a knot tightened. It didn't feel like the pain of hunger, which he'd grown used to on the long road from Carthane.

Tears clogged the back of his throat, filled the hollow place inside. Vomit threatened. He stumbled the way he'd come, back to the Ascendants' tent.

Sleep. I need to sleep.

Numb was good. Unconscious was best. A fitful night's rest deadened the pain of the past. But sleep never came easy.

Inside the tent, seven others lied on cots, mostly fidgeting, muttering, or crying to themselves. A gray-haired woman sat in relative silence, breathing rhythmically and looking tranquil. A girl slightly younger than Thephos stared ahead with vacant eyes. Her hair was matted, her face smudged. If Thephos were to bet, he assumed the grimy girl already touched by madness.

At the center of the room, the Sister of the Rose waived a bundle of burning dry leaves in the air, giving the room a pleasant aroma. She wore scarlet robes with a white rose embroidered over the heart and at the cuffs. When Thephos sat on his cot, she placed the bundle of leaves in an iron pot at her feet and then offered him water from a pitcher. "Are you comfortable?"

Thephos nodded unconvincingly. The sister cocked her head and smiled, imploring honesty.

"Sorry, I'm...uh..." His face twitched. He couldn't meet her stare. "I'm very hungry."

She patted his leg then produced berries and dark-crusted bread. He'd been hungrier than he thought. It took only a minute for them to disappear. With a full belly, he fell soundly asleep.

At some point in the night, the Wordfox entered the tent, mask tucked protectively under one arm. Thephos woke to the man coughing dramatically as he stood with his rich man's shoe inside the tent and the bare foot outside of it. "I shall sleep beside the door. Where the air is...untainted."

Thephos got the sense they had ushered him into the tent because right after the Wordfox entered, another man followed who Thephos hadn't seen before.

"We have ten Ascendants," the sister declared. Doom rode the honey-sweet calm of her next words. "In the morning, the shamans will receive you at the Corpse Gate."

After that, Thephos couldn't sleep.

To his brothers back in Carthane, he said his goodbyes. It saddened him that he wouldn't miss them as much as he hoped. Loving anything under his father's roof was a dire mistake, a recipe for deeper suffering. They were a prison of his past, a shackle to the horrors he failed to shake free from.

Into the hollow place he cast them.

Those who entered his mind in the final hours before ascent, surprised him.

The Kurg most of all. A rapist, a murderer, and a robber. *You protected me from shame and pain. Nobody ever did that. And you blessed me. No one's done that either.*

The old man at The Numbers whose name Thephos never got. *You took a moment to be helpful.*

And the crownguard, the good father. *I would have liked to know you, I think.* An odd tingly feeling entered his chest. As quick as it came, Thephos retreated from it.

Syn Backlegarm's untamed visage arose last, beaming and jovial. There was no questioning the man's ulterior motives. He would profit from Thephos's death. Regardless, his presence lifted his spirits. *Thank you for treating me like a friend. I hope I don't disappoint you.*

Sleep lurked at the edges of his consciousness like a wolf. Light filtered in through the slit in the tent. More light followed. The flap opened quietly as Ascendants came and went. The bustle of activity outside started as errant bursts of sound then transformed into a steady hum of clattering wood and bawling foremen. Eventually the tent flap was whipped aside, over and over, with dwindling care for those resting.

The Sister of the Rose and her helpers prepared.

Finally, Thephos rose from dissatisfied slumber. The other Ascendants too.

All rose to meet their doom.

For a person who felt little, fear was the last feeling to leave. Thephos was no exception.

A crowd gathered at Danath's statue in silence. They lined a roped-off path leading up Unturrus to the Corpse Gate. Besides white ceremonial smocks, the Ascendants were given only a waterskin.

Little difference it will make.

The number of eyes watching Thephos unnerved him. Rarely did anyone look at him. In fact, he thought he looked so meek he long assumed others saw it as some kind of disease they feared contracting if they made eye contact with him overlong. So he'd gotten used to being ignored. Now hundreds of eyes crawled over every inch of his sweating skin.

He shivered.

A trio of cloaked Kurgs emerged from the mists creeping around the Corpse Gate. They descended to meet the Ascendants.

"Shamans," said the gray-haired woman. "One from each of the major enclaves."

Thephos marveled at the intricacies of their ceremonial garb as the ten Ascendants inched upward, a swaying, shuffling pace.

The pelt of a white lion draped over the shoulders of the shaman from the plains enclaves, its upper jaw resting along the crown of his head. The Kurg's only other piece of clothing was a loincloth wrapped tight from thigh to belly button. Smooth gray mud caked his exposed face and arms.

The shaman from the forest enclaves bore a cloak of crow feathers, but aside from that he wore more common Namorite garb: tunic, trousers, and boots. His people had been subjugated most harshly when the Scoths had gutted Al'Ushari—the Ardent Heart—during the first invasion. The savagery of the shaman appeared undiminished by history. A rectangle of black paint covered the area around the Kurg's eyes, giving him an unsettling stare.

The last shaman was a female from the mountain enclaves. She was taller and more lithe than her male counterparts, a commonality for the Forgotten People. Shadows marred the features of her face sitting within a giant ram's skull. Sinewy, lean-muscled arms sprouted from a leather vest covering golden-hued breasts. She wore a skirt of boiled leather.

All three held spears and obsidian daggers sheathed at their belts. Two carried chaswas: short clubs of polished stone wrought in the shape of a foot.

While Thephos studied the shamans with morbid curiosity, he sensed their presence affected the group at large in a more primal way.

Guides to our death.

Fear wound its way among the Ascendants, sending up sniffles and strained coughs. A few glanced furtively about as if questioning whether they should escape the dark guarantee of their end.

In the face of that doom, Thephos felt the burden of his most recent regrets. How could he leave his brothers? As the shamans called the group to the Corpse Gate, he wondered what he could have possibly done differently to help them.

What could I do? I am nothing. No one.

They needed a man like the fatherly crownguard. Someone with enough heart to chase a drug runner or enough spine to point their spear at a liar.

I did what was best for them. Now I do what's best for me.

Searching the faces of those he passed on his way to the Corpse Gate, he noticed a mix of sadness. A hardness too meant to keep tears at bay, he supposed. When he met their eyes, he knew they thought ascending was a courageous thing.

If it was, it was the first in Thephos's life.

Followers of the Sempyrean offered the Ascendants prayers of peaceful rest. A smattering of unimists touched thumbs to heart and then index fingers to forehead. Others gave grim nods or glanced away, unable to meet the eyes of the willful dead. A few showered the Ascendants in the wisdom drunks.

Respect. They are showing us respect.

Even when he stole the pride of it from himself by thinking, *You're not courageous, just stupid, a pathetic worm,* there was still a little voice inside telling him a different story.

The Thephos you knew would be more terrified than you are.

They shuffled onward.

You are called.

A familiar face stood a full head above the crowd. Syn Backlegarm called out, "Hey, Thephos! Hey, come this way!"

Seized by curiosity, the former pig-farmer angled through the group, offering apologies on his way toward the proprietor of the Numbers.

Thephos slowed but did not fully stop as he reached Syn. The two of them walked in tandem, separated only by the rope. Spectators made way for the owner of the Numbers as he went. Morning light shone off the rings in Syn's ears and clean-shaved pate.

Ash struggled to remain at her eccentric husband's side as the towering man came to a stop at the cordon among a handful of disgruntled spectators with unhappy glares. Her hair was short and tousled, as if a team of oxen had licked her awake. Small even for a woman, her demeanor and the blade at her hip shrank Thephos's spine. Danger and its origins were Thephos's life. He sensed Ash was not only very capable of violence but overly willing to dole it out.

Thephos slowed and started lagging behind the other Ascendants.

"I just wanted you to know," Syn said, "I bet five gold wheels on you for powers."

Thephos's lips parted. His brow furrowed. *Five gold wheels is more money than my entire family could make in a decade.*

He tripped, stumbled forward a step before righting himself. Guilt and laughter chased him. *Have I misled, Syn?*

"A foolishly placed bet, I say," said Ash as Thephos drifted further away from them and closer to the Corpse Gate.

Syn rolled his eyes. "Good luck, Theffy. I would have bet on you being Awakened over Ruptured, but I have a policy never to make that choice."

Thephos rotated around to keep the conversation alive despite the slow-growing distance between him and the other Ascendants. "Why?"

Thephos meant "why" to all of it. *Why choose me for anything?* Syn Backlegarm, however, seemed to think Thephos asked "why" to having a policy never to make that choice.

"Because," Syn shouted, arms stretching outward as if he could embrace the world in a hug, "Only an Ascendant can make that choice. Choose well my friend!"

Thephos stumbled again. *Friend?*

Tears filled the back of his throat. The knot in his gut tightened, a braid of two parts. The first, a kindness from a stranger. The second, an impending loss of the same.

The Ascendants stopped before the Corpse Gate and the indifferent stares of the shamans. The rope cordon held back the gathered mob, allowing the Ascendants to continue forward without the crowd. A pair of rooks cawed as they chased a hawk out of their territory. The sight opened Thephos's ears to the buzz of activity around the Corpse Gate, the sound of nature eerily and suddenly loud. Dogs barked throughout the settlement. The shrill battle cries of stellar jays rang across Unturrus's slopes somewhere beyond the wall.

A great thrumming at the edge of hearing underlaid it all.

Thephos searched for the source, found it hovering in a dark veil around the Corpse Gate. He swallowed hard.

Thousands of flies swirled around the rib bones of some immense, unknown beast. Lashed together at the apex by hempen rope, the ribs formed an arched entry point in the stone wall. The shaman from the plains held up a hand covered in gray clay. "Wait."

They did as instructed. The vacant-eyed girl with a touch of madness wept uncontrollably in the silence.

It didn't take long to figure out what they waited for. A ripple of radiant gray light flashed inside the Corpse Gate. Thephos fell back a step and gasped in a unified intake of breath with the others. The monstrous rib bones rattle briefly. Faced with mortal demise and irrevocable decisions made, they gasped in awe of Unturrus's mysterious power.

Wild-eyed and shaky limbed, one man strayed from the group. He blubbered at the Corpse Gate, horrified. Like a deer separated from its herd by wolves, he bolted down the slope back the way they'd come.

"Sacrilege," the shaman from the river enclaves declared. His crow-feather cloak rustled as he hurled his spear. It whooshed overheard, skewering the man through the back of the neck. He gave a sickening wet sputter. His hands wavered over the tattered exit wound in his throat. His seal of mortality broken, he dropped to his knees and pitched forward, spear tip embedding in the earth. He convulsed around a cascade of blood as he slowly slid down its length.

A single shout of triumph erupted from the crowd. Thephos jerked around, found a man celebrating and pointing at Syn Backlegarm—calling for a payout. *A bet won. At least someone may find value with my life. The end of it, at least. Not the crownguard. And not Syn. He'll only win at his own game if I return Awakened...or Ruptured.*

"You have taken your last breath as free people." The voice of the woman wearing the ram's skull boomed over the assembly. "You belong to Unturrus now. You can never turn back."

The crowd chanted in response. "Peace in ascent. Peace in descent. Peace for the ones whose lives were meant."

Thephos watched the man's life spill into the grass. He glanced at Syn Backlegarm, one arm draped over his wife's shoulder. A disappointed half-smile twisted the corner of the gambler's mouth as he watched the Ascendant die. Ash watched too, a stoic mask.

In one way, Thephos envied the Ascendant his quick end.

At least it's not Hemgowwa the Ever-Grasping.

Dying atop Unturrus was rarely so simple as a spear through the throat. But here the man would be buried with little fanfare. Thephos still held a shred of hope he might become a mirrored statue, forever glittering under the eerie splendor of moonlight. Forever frozen in time and admired from afar. Yet here was this man, a reflection of opportunity lost, his life dripping away into a scarlet puddle before him. Thephos wondered if the man saw his own reflection as the darkness took him.

The Corpse Gate loomed ahead.
Thephos passed beneath it. Surrounded. Alone.

CHAPTER TWENTY-TWO

FEVERED DREAMS

B arodane tossed meekly, a moan of pain reaching no ears but his own. Despite parched lips and a desert-dry throat, the bed was soaked. He coughed, tried opening his eyes, but the light felt like pincers under his lids. He let the comfort of darkness swallow further efforts.

Sickness has a way of breaking its victim more easily than any torturer, though it is certainly of the spirit more than the body. Unseen, it renders one defenseless, worms its way into their vulnerable places. It weakens, sating thirst on fevered sweat. Its burning hunger feasts on one's longing for death's escape.

And when one longs to die, they have little guard left, nothing to keep them from their darkest, most-feared thoughts.

They are naked. Exposed.

The sickness drags into the light what should be kept chained in the deepest parts of the mind. So came the fevered dreams to take from Barodane what they would...

Rain pounds against the command tent. In the yawning silence of portending tragedy, they wait.

Garlenna fills one corner, head lowered in prayer. Barodane watches those assembled. Lords from the major holds surround him. Some are friends. Marus and Malus D'Alzir speak in hushed tones with Gyr Renwood—Garlenna's father. A covered brazier at the command tent's center lights Kaitos Barabi's bronzed face as he paces nearby, thumbs hooked into his sword belt. Others are not friends but are important nevertheless.

Necessary.

A pair of envoys from the Dominarri sit on a bench on the opposite side of the command tent from a group of Sempyrium paladins who sit stiffly, resplendent in their gleaming plate armor. The two groups glare at one another with open hostility.

Barodane sits in a fur-draped chair, anxiety grinding through him. Word had it the Crown's army was destroyed at Golden Beach. The "Bloody Beach" some were calling it. His father, Kordin, and brother, Malath, had led the holds of Peladonia along the coast of South Setton right into a trap. A slaughter.

Word had it the survivors were few.

It's the first time Barodane feels himself contracting. Escaping reality. In that hollowness, he waits.

An Awakened by the name of Warro Herd approaches a table to Barodane's left. Some call him the Void, others the Black Hand Marionette. The man brushes back greasy dark hair with an ink-black hand that appears to have been dipped in tar. He's stout with the shoulders of a wrestler draped over the gut of a drunkard.

Warro Herd pours a flagon of godsbrew into a cup then offers it to Barodane. "Want some, fella?"

Barodane shakes his head. "My stomach is a bit sour at the moment."

Warro shrugs thick shoulders, places the cup back on the table, then slurps directly from the flagon.

"Respect our prince, Herd." Garlenna stands behind the Awakened, fists balled at her sides. "Address him as, Your Highness."

Warro looks to Barodane, eyebrows raised. "I mean this with no offense, Prince..." He turns back to Garlenna. "But fuck yourself."

The words slide over the prosort like quicksilver. "Your Highness, why do we employ this man? He is without code, moral compass, or basic decency. Can we really trust someone guided only by gold or—" She reaches out a gauntleted fist to pat the Void's potbelly. "Gut."

The Awakened laughs then makes an odd face. Like he's revealing a secret to a group of kids. "Here, look at this." He holds up his char-black hand. Darkness pools into a spinning sphere above an upthrust finger. Energy crackles as it gathers. His eyes ooze vaporous black mist. "I've got things you ain't got. Talents you never fucking dreamed."

"Herd," Barodane says peremptorily. "Return to your own tent. This is no place for children. I'll send someone for you when you're ready to act like a man."

Warro Herd laughs then makes to leave, but not before Garlenna snatches the flagon from his hand. "We'll need you sober when the time comes."

The Awakened protests, eyes filling once more with shadow as he sets his feet apart, prepared to fight for his drink. The less cool among those assembled draw steel. One of the Dominarri stands bolt upright, incandescent gray mist trailing from her eyes.

Warro Herd hesitates, opts instead to make a noise like that of an old man dismissing the rantings of a pestering wife before whipping aside the tent flap and exiting.

Deep foreboding probes Barodane's stomach.

Animosity is not usually preferred, but at least it distracts from the oppressive wait, which resumes, tension redoubled. Garlenna is at his side. "Not much longer, Your Highness."

Barodane has waited long enough. "They make their way here, do they not?" All eyes turn to regard him.

Garlenna frowns. "Yes. The last of the Crown's army, Your Highness."

Barodane clenches his teeth. Time slips by...

In another place, he heard himself moan in his sleep. He gasped, saw piercing light, felt heat racing through his veins. A moment of consciousness like the surface of water breaking over head as he came up for air.

He wondered how close to death he was, how long before the fever exacted its merciful toll.

Darkness fell once more, dragging him back into a time forgotten...

Onai Saud's diminutive stature is pronounced to the point of a jest while standing beside his prosort, a hulking, bald bull of a man. But at the moment nothing about the Duke of Peladonia's presence is humorous. The shrewd politician sweeps the room with his beady eyes, salutes, then speaks. "Your father and brother are dead, Your Highness."

Even though Barodane expected the news, hearing it was distinct, a stunning revelation one could never plan for. *How can they be dead?* A memory of a hunt he'd gone on before the war started six months prior flashed across his mind. They sat horses together. Malath led the conversation, speaking fondly of his newborn daughter's incessant crying. "She'll have a gift with words, I'm sure."

Their father, Kordin, had joked, "For your sake, Malath, you best pray she takes after Ishra on that count. Otherwise, she'll drive you mad before she's fifteen."

A smile tugs at Barodane's mouth in remembrance.

They cannot be dead. I loved them...

Anger strides forth in defense, turning aside unbearable truths. Barodane scoffs, looks Duke Onai up and down. Hate. Hate burns through him. It leaves naught but ash.

He points with his chin at the Lord of the House of Saud. "You are clean. You are alive. Perhaps they might live had you the courage to put your blade before your life."

"Well..." Saud says in a monotone voice. Caught off guard, he trades glances with Duke Malus D'Alzir and then Garlenna. Barodane's closest friends. The gesture is not lost on the prince and serves only to enrage him further. Onai Saud cocks his head to the side, deliberating something. "Your Highness, maybe it would be best to take a moment to yourself."

"What are you afraid of, Duke Saud? Seems a fitting conversation to have in the midst of war. If we aren't to discuss loyalty, valor, courage, what are we to discuss? Perhaps strategy—that seems a timely topic. What about we discuss how to win this war and not have an entire army annihilated. Maybe we should have done *that* before losing my father and brother!"

Saud's eyes narrow, not in suspicion nor anger, but like a child inspecting an insect. Barodane knows the look well. Before this moment, he respected the man greatly for such placid observation.

Now he passionately despises it.

The Duke of Peladonia speaks in a slow cadence. "There are times for courage and there are times for compassion. I think it no small wisdom to fear a powerful man in the moment they are receiving painful news. I do not take your words personally, Highness. I can only offer my utmost respect and condolences. This loss weighs heavy on the entire nation. But you are right. We must plan a more calculated retaliation if we are to defeat the Scoths. It was an impetuous choice for us to attack at Golden Beach. If we are to expect a different outcome, our next attack cannot be driven by emotion alone."

Barodane stares at the man. A halo of black hatred surrounds his every thought.

"My Prince," Garlenna says. "Duke Onai has done nothing wrong."

"I am the judge here." Barodane slams a fist against the arm of his chair. His voice falls low, "Do you hear me, Saud?"

Onai gives no reaction. He meets the eyes of those assembled. *Caution. Danger,* he seems to tell them. Then his gaze finds Barodane's. "You are indeed the judge, Highness. I'll leave you to it until the morrow. Be gentle in your grief tonight."

Before Barodane can muster a reply, Onai Saud salutes quickly and then leaves, his monstrous prosort dogging his heels.

Slowly, others bow and filter from the tent. Kaitos Barabi remains, unblinking as he stares into a brazier.

Garlenna's hand comes to rest on Barodane's shoulder. He doesn't feel it. "I am so sorry."

He barely hears her. Vengeance consumes his every thought. All of them would die. Raeklord Sahuhd. Acramis the Twice-Burned. Every Scoth...their bloodlines, eradicated.

Every. Single. Scoth.

"Garlenna. Kai. With me."

Barodane rises.

Kai asks. "Where to?"

"I want four hundred men ready to ride in the hour. They are under orders to speak no word of it. Once the command is given, you won't speak of what we do either. Understand?"

Kai frowns. Garlenna steps close. "Your Majesty, is this wise? I know you grieve but—"

"It is Scothea that will grieve," he hisses. "Be sure of it. Now do as I say."

"Your Majesty—"

"Stop calling me that! They've not been dead for a day. I am not yet—" The words falter. She's right. He is. He is the Crown Prince of Namarr. King of Kania's ruins. The Arm of Solicerames.

Garlenna takes him by the shoulders. "I'm sorry, but you are the Crown Prince now. You cannot flee your army. We must prepare. We must collaborate with our commanders. If we do not—"

With a vicious shrug, Barodane casts off her hands. "*I* am the Crown Prince. I give the commands, not you. You heard my orders, Prosort. Now follow them."

They ride out of the Ardent Heart in the middle of the night, a file of guttering torches worming its way toward the Dawn Vale. Barodane sets a tone for the men as they proceed in silence for a full day east. The only sound is the constant rustle of arms and armor. Garlenna looks to Barodane regularly—questioningly. Kaitos huffs and sighs, clearly frustrated.

Barodane refuses to meet the eyes of either.

On the second morning, as darkness shifts to twilight gray, they crest a hill overlooking the town of Rainy Meadows, a settlement for those of mixed Scoth lineage. The steam of four hundred panting men and their horses hangs forms a cloud over them. The warmth causes sweat to pool beneath men's helms. Glistening beads race down their cheeks.

Barodane feels little but the chilly hollowness inside. A cold absence of things taken.

I am the judge.

Candlelight springs to life in the stone and thatch homes of the people of Rainy Meadows as they begin their day.

"What are we doing here?" Kai casts a dubious look back at the assembled knights.

"There are spies in that town," Barodane says. "Rainy Meadows is a well-known bastion for half-bloods. Would you not look to your largest Scoth settlement as the breeding ground for enemy loyalists?"

Garlenna watches him, a tightness to her lips.

Kaitos shakes his head. "So we brought a battalion to interrogate a—"

"No interrogation." Barodane rounds on Kaitos. "Leave no one alive. Burn Rainy Meadows to the ground."

As though it were a joke he doesn't comprehend, Kaitos Barabi emits a timid laugh. "Hilarious, but why did we really come out here?"

Emptiness gives way to hate. Barodane stares into Kai's nut-brown eyes. All he can think of is the man's smile, the smile of one who cannot know his loss. Loathing, jealousy, and rage dance together in Barodane. He raises his voice to address the entire column. "The town of Rainy Meadows is hereby deemed a threat to Namarr. It is recognized as a haven for half-blood spies and Scothean loyalists. These are the scum responsible for the murder of my father and my brother, the Prince and Crown Prince of Namarr."

"You don't know that!" Kaitos snaps. "There could be no such people there. These *are* Namorites, Barodane. Our people."

Barodane jerks the reins of his horse, wheels around to face the column. He looks Kaitos Barabi up and down. Although the man is armored for battle, he's richly dressed. A wolf fur drapes his shoulders and chest over plate, gauntlets, and twin swords from the best metal workers in Alistar. His hair and beard are oiled and beset with glass beads. He has a stallion as good as any lord. His honor plate proudly bears the fist and chain of Ironlight, the most prestigious garb in all of Namarr.

Ungrateful. A leech.

"You are no patriot, Kaitos Barabi. You do not deserve the honor of riding with this company—with true Namorites."

Kai jerks the reins of his horse, pointing away from Rainy Meadows. "You're not in your right mind, Barodane."

The Crown Prince brings his horse abreast with Kai's. "Are you disobeying me? You will lead this column down into the town of Rainy Meadows and you will—"

"I will not. You—you're not yourself, Barodane." His tone is pleading. "I'm begging you. Don't do this."

"What you should beg me to do is spare you shackles. I raised you up, treated you as a brother, made you a knight of Alistar. Now my father and brother are murdered by Scoths and you repay me with treason? Shame on you."

A tendon jumps along Kaitos's neck. "If you think you need repayment, then you're no friend. No brother. I'm trying to help you, Barodane. I stand against it, *for you*!"

"You do it for yourself, coward." Barodane spits. "For *me*, you will lead my knights down into Rainy Meadows and eliminate the Scothean threat."

Kaitos rises in the saddle, chin thrust outward. "I'll do no such thing."

"Fine then. Leave us. Go back to Onai Saud and the army. Tell them I deal with insurgents and that we go from here to attack King Acramis directly."

"My Prince," Garlenna snaps.

Kaitos laughs. "You've gone insane."

As one, the men shift in their saddles, discomfited.

Barodane continues. "Tell them to meet me there if they wish to partake in the victory."

"Your Majesty, we are four hundred," Garlenna says. "Even if Frost's army bleeds the Scotheans, they'll outnumber us twenty to one."

"Not if Kaitos does his job." He turns his attention back to his former friend. "You may leave us. After you tell Saud and the rest, go back to Alistar and await my return." Darksteel scrapes from the scabbard at Barodane's hip. "And my judgment."

Gathering the reins, Kai says, "I depart with great pleasure," and then spurs his horse.

Someone shook Barodane awake.

"What?" he croaked, sounding like air forced through a ruptured bellows. Eyelid parted a sliver, he made out a mousy teen. One of Meckin's serving girls, Vey.

"Drink," she said. "Meckin's orders."

Pain shot through Barodane's back as he tried sitting up. Vey grabbed at a shoulder to help him, but the jerkiness of her attempts brought on worse. Finally, he posted up on his elbow and drank. Cool liquid swept down his throat, so quick and so cold it made him sputter and cough. A few droplets landed on Vey's face. "Oh—uh...I'm so sorry."

Eyes pinched shut, she wiped her face. "It's okay."

He handed her back the cup. She glanced at the door.

"What?"

"Well..." she tapped the rim of the drinking cup. "You were crying in your sleep."

Barodane flopped back onto tepid, wet sheets. "I say anything interesting?"

"You said the names of the dead princes...the ones who died during the Great Betrayal."

He raised an eyebrow. "What else?"

"You kept saying you were going to kill them all. That they'd pay." Sudden courage seemed to kindle to life within her. "Did you fight, Kord? You look like you could have been a soldier. I know you have a shadowguard's honor plate, but lots of folk around here do. Stolen from battlefields and barrows and the like."

A wave of nausea forced his eyes shut. All he wanted was to pass out. But he knew if he didn't give the girl something to calm her query it could lead to the spread of undesired rumors.

Near-truths, he'd learned, made for the best lies. "I served under Prince Malath at the Bloody Beach. We were betrayed by Scoth loyalists. Slaughtered. The Ironlight princes too. I don't like talking about it."

Rest. I need to rest. Desperately, his body called for it. The girl remained. A part of him was grateful; as long as she stayed, the nightmares were kept at bay.

"That must be why you're sad all the time," she said. "I understand...I was only a baby when it happened. My mom says that's where daddy died—the Bloody Beach. Sometimes I think she just tells me that because it sounds better than whatever the truth is. He was probably a drunk or a gravedigger like everyone else."

Barodane's lids grew heavy. He couldn't stave off sleep much longer. As he drifted off, the last thing he saw were Vey's eyes.

He'd never noticed their color.

Green with flecks of brown.

Familiar but different...

A boy staggers toward Barodane from the doorway of a chapel. Its support beams falter as he leaves. Devoured by flame, the eaves cave. Yet the boy cannot be numbered among the lucky. It seems to take hours for his feet to bring him before Barodane—but only a second to step onto the altar of the Mad Prince. Blood runs down the boy's face from a wound along his scalp. He's shirtless, exposed, a ready sacrifice to a sacred rage.

"Help me," the boy says.

There is no thought. No mercy. Only reaction.

Hate and its momentum.

His blade snakes forward to steal the boy's life. Barodane notices his own hand wrapped around the hilt. *Is that mine? It can't be mine...* But it belongs to no stranger. And it is no dream. Only memory relived.

As soon as it happens, Barodane wishes it hadn't. He would give anything to give the boy his life back, to tear cloak from shoulders and swaddle the boy, to tell him, "It's okay. You are safe."

Instead, he watches once more. From the infinite circuit of horrors lived, he watches the light and life drain from the boy's eyes.

Green eyes with brown flecks.

Familiar but different.

The boy's body shudders around the blade in his chest like a small, wet, dog. The tone of his skin grows paler with every heartbeat of blood pumped onto the cobbles.

He whispers something. Perhaps, "Please," or the name of a loved one. No matter how many times Barodane has heard the mumbled word, he's never comprehended it. The boy slides, a weighted nothingness, to the ash-covered ground.

The thud is cruel to the ears, a drumbeat of doom.

It's easy, this kind of killing. So simple as to be casual.

Barodane walks the streets of Rainy Meadows with limp arms, darksteel sword tip scraping over cobbles as he drags the blade behind.

Never has it felt so heavy.

Smoke and screams consume the senses. Tongues of fire pull down the roofs of stone buildings. The burst and sizzle of fat from nearby pigs, unable to escape their pens, dissolve in Barodane's ears. Foundations crack. Wood groans. The few windows in the richest buildings burst, raining thin glass onto the cobbled lanes.

And screaming. Always screaming.

Grim-faced Namorites stalk the streets. They have the decency to be ashamed, turning away their faces as they skewer young and old alike. Indiscriminately, they stab, swing, and slay anyone without the fist and chain of Ironlight riding their shoulder. Torches arc through the air, land with a splash of embers as they catch roofs. Mothers who stumble forth hacking smoke are met with the quick end of a blade. Their wailing babes too. More than a few knights stop at that though, their soot-covered faces marred by tears as they wait for those more caught up in the moment to execute the horrible deed. They turn hard eyes on Barodane as he passes. They look away quicker still. They do not wish for further commands. Not from him.

The only one that matters was given.

Put the town to the torch, its people to the sword. Leave no Scothean loyalist alive. Leave no building standing.

Lay Rainy Meadows in its grave.

In this, Barodane is not passive. He feels a coldness, a void, and he fills it with troughs of blood, blood that he takes without discernment. For the tumble of every head he strikes from shoulders, he screams the names of a father and brother forever lost.

"Malath!"

"Kordin!"

By night's end, only char and dark stains remain. Crown soldiers drift through the lanes like ghosts.

Seated, Barodane watches the town jail burn. Oily smoke rolls from the entrance, as eager for escape as anyone in Rainy Meadows. A sign over the door reads, "The Crown's Justice." The rope holding up one side snaps. It clatters violently against fire-scorched stone. Wind sets the flames to guttering. The sign twists and turns, dancing above the chaos.

Dancing...

Barodane wonders how long it will take the other rope to sever, how long it will be before the sign falls to the dirt and ash-strewn ground below.

"Your Majesty. We've...carried out your commands. Your first as Crown Prince." Garlenna clears her throat, breaking his reverie. "No spies or loyalists are left alive."

He looks up to find her standing over him. As soon as they lock eyes, she breaks from the intimacy of the contact. She drops to a knee, head bowed. She's not done this since her initiation as his prosort.

Shame lodges in Barodane's throat. *I am so sorry, Garlenna. I had to make them pay.* He says nothing. His body clenches, unable to release. King Acramis and Raeklord Sahuhd still live. Scoths still stand on Namorite soil.

The sign over the jail bangs against the stones.

For a handful of minutes, Garlenna humors his silence. When it becomes clear he means to stay that way, she breaks it, "Your Majesty?"

He turns and spits the word, "Majesty," as if reiterating the punchline to some cruel joke. A flame sprouts along the length of rope holding the "Crown's Justice" sign aloft, and with it, a thin tendril of smoke slithers upward. "How many?"

Garlenna sniffles, answers painfully slow. "Well over a thousand, Your Majesty. It's—it's hard to get a clear count. Less than a dozen brave and loyal Namorite knights were lost in the slaughter. They'll be honored as war heroes...if it pleases, Your Majesty."

The sign over the jail plummets to the ground, smoke trailing.

Your Majesty. Every time he hears it, a wave of sickness fills him where numbness should be.

"It does not please his Majesty," Barodane says. "There are only villains here. Leave the dead. We'll deal with them later. General Sahuhd and King Acramis are still alive. We must move quickly if we're to—"

Kaitos Barabi materializes out of the gray, riding toward them in a swirl of smoke. He stops short of Garlenna, stallion rearing. His face is a visage of disbelief. Stricken, he stares at Barodane and Garlenna, near unrecognizable in their blood-covered cloth, their grime-streaked masks.

Bringing his mount to a walk, Kaitos closes the remaining distance as if approaching an injured wolf. "Barodane, what have you done?" His voice is low. His lips tremble.

"Kaitos..." Barodane savors the word. "I thought you would be cozened up with Onai Saud by now, warming your feet over a fire."

The former knight of Alistar scans his surroundings, mouth open. Tears coalesce in unblinking eyes. "I—I did not believe you capable of this."

"A Crown Prince must be capable of dispensing justice. We are at war. Difficult decisions must be made for the good of Namarr. I did my duty. You, on the other hand, have forsaken yours."

As if waking from a dream, Kaitos blinks and then locks gazes with Barodane, brow bunching. "Justice? The good of Namarr? What lies. These people were innocent!"

No one is innocent. "These people share a lineage with Scothea. With Acramis!" Rage fills Barodane. "They are guilty by blood. Every one of them was a descendant of murderers and slavers—those who tore your ancestor's backs to ribbons or hurled them into ditches when they could mine no more. You think they do not have the memory of it in their bones, the itch to subjugate their perceived lessers, a thirst to *kill* Namorites? They would have taken up the whip tomorrow if Scothea defeated us. I say they are a danger. Or would have been if I'd given them the chance."

"Blood pays for blood then? Yes, that solves everything." Kaitos's eyes flit between Barodane and Garlenna. "These people didn't kill Kordin and Malath."

"This is *war*, Kaitos!"

Kaitos laughs meanly, spits onto the ash-blighted earth. *"This* is not *my* war." From somewhere beneath the wolf skin draped over his torso, he draws a knife from a hidden sheath. Naked blade barred before her prince, Garlenna steps forth, mace whirling into her hand. But the Lah-Tsarene man is only placing the knife's edge under the chest-strap that fixes his honor plate in place. He cuts outward, then slashes the other strap holding the pauldron with the Ironlight fist and chain to his shoulder. He chucks the steel slab into the dirt at Barodane's feet. "And you are not *my* prince."

Even in his unquenchable hatred, surrounded by flames and those dead by his own command, Barodane can't help but feel another dagger of loss enter his heart.

Kaitos turns his attention to Garlenna, a hand beseechingly extended. "Come with me."

She shakes her head. "I—I am sworn to protect him. I cannot. I will not. His Majesty is my duty."

Barodane blinks, noting she no longer calls him, "My Prince." That makes little difference, he decides. All that matters now is the vengeance playing out in his mind's eye, rotating over and over. A sword thrust into a face.

The face of King Acramis.

Nudging his warhorse forward, Kaitos leans down from the saddle. "Garlenna, my friend, you swore to protect Barodane Ironlight. Not this man. Your duty is not worth your soul. Come with me."

"I am sworn, Kai!" Her chin drops. "By the Sempyrean, I will not abandon him. Not now...not ever."

"The man you swore yourself to is dead. Abandon, Garlenna Renwood." With a last glance at Barodane, Kaitos says, "Abandon...before it's too late."

To the clatter of hooves, the man who'd been like a brother to Barodane disappears down the street through a veil of smoke. He watches him go knowing it's the last time he'll see the man. He doesn't care.

There is nothing left to care about.

Not even his own life.

"Garlenna, go with Kaitos."

She protests. He tells her if she doesn't, he'll strip her of her status as prosort—make her a failure to her gods. At this she bows and then leaves.

Barodane dispatches orders for advance riders to locate Acramis's army. The man who takes the orders does so with pursed lips and a brisk salute. He knows it is a suicide mission.

But death is the only thing that will bring Barodane peace.

CHAPTER TWENTY-THREE

SACRIFICES

From the look of Othwii, Ishoa knew he and the duchess had been busy in the days since the last counsel meeting. Dark circles clung to the seneschal's eyes as if he'd been awake ever since. Rather than his usual upright posture that exuded dignity, his rangy frame collapsed around his chest, making him look ever more a bookish vulture than a man.

The duchess invited him to report.

Othwii adjusted the hummingbird brooch at his neck then cleared his throat. "The Scarborn were busy in their absence from the feast. They called upon every hold, regardless of their loyalty. They even sent messages to Hilkka Omenfaen and Joffus Kon. The intent, I believe, is to screen their true intentions and fracture our focus and resources."

"And waste their own time," said Wolst.

"Besides Hilkka Omenfaen, they called on Ollo Bael the most. He refused them—all three times. In fact, all holds refused them. All except two."

Belara tapped her teeth with a fingernail. "Who?"

"Megalor Bog returned a message. He wished their boy luck then went on to congratulate the Warnocks on their recent successes, adding some choice words about the Keelers. He went so far as to suggest they dispose of the entire family...permanently."

"Megalor Bog is an ill-humored fellow," said Belara Frost. "I daresay his father's feud with Torst Keeler is the motivation here. Megalor isn't one to step over a downed enemy when he has a perfectly good vantage for a kick or two. Petty hatred hardly indicates alliance. Besides, we've just given Shadowheart our ship building quota. He'd never risk that deal. Who else?"

"The Narls."

Belara rolled her eyes. "Predictable. And foolish. Golthius, that lumbering hog, may as well have announced his intentions to me at the feast."

"The Bakers of Prav are a poor hold," said Arick. "They're desperate. That makes them dangerous."

"So be it. I'll boost his competitors after the vote. He's sealed his own fate." Belara stood before the hearth. Ruddy flame cast threads of shadow in every wrinkle. "What of your task with Lodaris Warnock, Ishoa?"

Five sets of eyes regarded her.

It's terrible. He hates me. I'm failing. She brushed back a lock of brown hair as she straightened. Whatever confidence she'd momentarily felt seemed to be forming a bubble in her throat. Her voice sounded strained. "I overhead Ularis telling Syphion Muul to trust Lodecka. He said, 'the long game is ours.' Syphion seemed to think they moved too slowly."

Silence followed, gnawing at Ishoa's insides.

An ember burst from the hearth onto the floor, orange glow pulsing. Belara ignored it as she stared into the fire. Wolst shifted his weight, leather studded warskirt creaking. Othwii leaned forward onto elbows over the horn table. Arick sat back, spine as stiff as a spear.

Ishoa's back broke into a sweat. Her silk tunic clung to it. In an attempt to peel it off, she shrugged—to no avail.

"You did well, Isha," Belara turned from the hearth. "Very well."

Why doesn't it feel that way?

"They are not in complete accord on how to proceed." Belara stared at the floor, a smile stretching the skin in one place only to bunch it in another. "Syphion pushes for a fight they cannot win. Ularis heeds caution to a fanatic who refuses it. And Lodecka..." the duchess mused, "...thinks they can wait until I die... 'The long game,' as Ularis put it. Once I'm dead, they'll be maneuvering against Ishoa. It's even possible the lunatics think they can marry Lodaris to her once he completes the Trials and gains a highborn status as well as a vote."

Marry Lodaris...

A clipped laugh escaped Ishoa. When she realized her grandmother was serious, the room started to spin. Blood rushed from her face.

Marry...Lodaris?

Vaguely, she thought she heard someone asking her a question. Her mind emptied. There was a stabbing pain in her chest, a bitter taste in her mouth. It was all she could do to keep herself sitting upright. Hands trembled, brittle leaves.

Fingers snapped near her ears, more muffled than it should be.

Her grandmother's creased brow came into focus. "Ishoa." The duchess snapped again.

"Yes." She inhaled sharply. "My apologies."

Belara lifted her chin in the way of those about to deliver a much-needed lesson. Her tone reflected as much. "I know you care for the boy, Isha. It's a good thing, really. To do this work for Namarr, you must have the best intentions at heart for all its people, even when forced to take actions that could cause pain for some of those others under your rule." Belara sucked her teeth. "I once passed a decree I knew would starve dozens of families. In my heart I knew it was necessary to keep thousands of others from certain death. Did I still care for those children who died? Of course I did...of course. I wept for them like my own grandchildren. Some nights, I still do." Sorrow flickered behind Belara's eyes, and her lips quivered. "You *must* care, Ishoa, and you must command, but you must never look back at your choices. If you do, you'll drown in the guilt power brings."

"Decisions *must* be made. Swiftly and without hesitation. So keep your compassion for the Scarborn, but don't let it consume you nor direct you in your service to the greatest good. If you do, then it is no compassion at all...only fear...only shame...only selfish worry that you won't be loved by all your subjects. Such a thing is impossible anyway. You have to be the one to pick those whose love you can bear to lose as long as it leads to peace and prosperity for the greater whole. The United Lands must come first." The duchess reached down, thin flesh writhing over a bony finger to tap the horn table with a loud clicking. "Do you understand, Isha? Do you understand a ruler, like a fisherman, must hook innocent worms if they're to feed their family? Never forget, your family *is* Namarr. Not the Scarborn. Not Lodaris Warnock." The last rang with finality. "Be honest now. Does the boy play you? Is it he who is the worm here? Or is it you?"

Darkness lingered at the edges of Ishoa's vision, her heartbeat little more than a disjointed succession of hollow thuds...

Suddenly she was back in Jarik proper. Snow worked its way from the sky in lazy drifts. Lodaris stood close, breath warming the space before her lips, telling her she was the most lovely of all. A strong hand fell into hers...then he was pulling her alongside him, nothing mattering at all...

She forced a shuddering inhale.

The room steadied as her breathing leveled out. "Lodaris dislikes his parents a great deal. He made it sound as if they beat him."

Wolst bristled. "Perhaps I should give Lodecka and her weasel husband a thrashing. See how they like it."

"We mustn't forget it could be a lie," said Belara. "A hook for Ishoa's sympathies."

Tightness clamped Ishoa's throat. She briefly considered remaining silent, but her emotions got the better of her. "I disagree."

"Do you?" Belara cocked her head. "Why?"

"Lodaris was jealous of Dragga Omenfaen. He couldn't hide it." Ishoa interlaced her fingers beneath the table, thumbs dancing together. "I don't think he's capable of masking his true feelings."

Belara searched the room for opinions. When none were forthcoming, she spoke with sarcasm. "Maybe the Warnocks simply wish their son a friend, is that it? A friend who just so happens to be the last Ironlight?"

Though his tone was matter of fact, Arick Quinn skewered Ishoa with a possibility she didn't wish to consider. "What if Lodaris is better at these games than Ishoa? He is a Scarborn living at the Fringes. Survival instincts must be sharper there. Ishoa claims he has animosity with his family. That is the exact thing he could be trained to portray, and what we should fear most. How much different can he be from his parents? They share a bloodline."

What do bloodlines matter? I share one with Danath and have a fraction of his courage or capability.

"Here's what will happen." The duchess pressed her hands together then brought fingertips to weathered lips. "Before the Trials begin, you will meet with Lodaris and you will tell him you love him."

Ishoa went rigid, mouth falling open. *Tell him I love him?*

"What's wrong?" asked Belara. "You have the foundation laid to say this, do you not?"

"I—uh." Sand filled her throat, dry and thick. From the corner of her eye, Wolst watched her, bushy eyebrow raised. Arick's azure gaze stared through her.

She thought of her parents. *I'll prove myself to you soon enough.*

"Foundation...yes." At last, Ishoa managed to swallow. "I daresay it's a stretch."

"So it is. Belara's ice chip eyes bore into Ishoa's. "Nevertheless, you will do as needed. For the good of Namarr."

They concluded counsel with the words of Danath Ironlight.

Though they were words Ishoa had recited a thousand times, they were strange in her ears. One line in particular chased her like an avalanche the entire way back to the Sister Keep. When she finally flopped down next to Rakeema on the bed, the words caught up. Buried her.

My Sons and Daughters of Namarr, you cannot die but once. Let us live, boldly and without fear!

Whether it was the fear of lying to Lodaris about loving him or her fear that it wasn't a lie, Ishoa could not be sure.

For the second time since the counsel meeting, Lodaris denied Ishoa's invitation. In one way, it brought relief from a duty she abhorred. Expressing love in order to manipulate was dishonorable.

Regardless of whether it's true or not.

In the shadow of a duty failed, she threw herself into last-minute training for the Trial of Crossing. It was her last bastion to prove herself and help Namarr by earning a vote in the court of Anjuhkar.

She glanced at the portrait of her parents on the wall. *In this, I will not fail you.* She bowed to them then stripped to her small clothes.

A tub of water was brought to her room. A chunk of ice bigger than Rakeema's head bobbed on the surface. Ishoa started the furnace-breath technique Othwii had showed her, focusing on fast repetitive exhales while pulling her chin toward her chest as she reached a toe over the tub's lip. Everything in her screamed to retract the toe, but she held it there and continued to breathe. Slowly, forcefully, she lowered herself into the chill water.

Cold shock stole her worries, thrust her into a panic of icy-pain. She fought to maintain the furnace breaths, faltering twice with sputtering gasps before resuming the technique. As the tub swallowed her to the neck, a fuzzy feeling spread from crown to hips. The room darkened. With a last gasp, she slid her head beneath the surface. Numb warmth slowly suffused her—a paradox that felt both eerily wrong and somehow peaceful.

Under the water, she worked her eyes open into a squint—found a distorted figure looming over the tub. Ishoa surged upward, sputtering. Water sluiced onto the floor. Othwii, his aspect serious, was unmoved by the eruption of frigid water now drenching his slippered feet.

"I'm in my small clothes!"

Othwii nodded then turned his back. "Just a body, Highness. A female one at that, which I have no preference for."

"Still!" She dried herself. The towel was uncomfortably rough despite the armor of numbness covering her skin. She glared at Othwii's tent pole back. "What do you want?"

"The task you've been given with Lodaris is difficult. I came to offer reassurance."

The window was bright, full of light. For a moment her eyes lost focused, and she felt as though she crumbled inward. Her towel strokes slowed, sluggish and despondent. "Doesn't really matter now, does it? The Trials begin tomorrow and he's rejected all of my invitations."

"There will be other chances," the seneschal said. "Days separate each trial. You must have hope, Highness. One's duty cannot be fulfilled without it."

You are strong. Stronger than you know.

Where she once drew comfort from her friend's words, they now only seemed to amplify the void at the pit of her stomach. She dressed, then took a seat on the edge of her bed.

Othwii turned to face her. "I told you how I once failed your grandmother, but..." he paused, swallowing hard.

The energy in the room shifted. The somber tone and faltering words of a man so integral to Ishoa's life pinned her in place. She saw it then, the redness rimming his eyes, the dolorous affect.

He's suffering.

"Apologies, Highness. I wish to share something I've never shared with anyone before. I want to—no, I must tell you what happened because it could help you." He choked down the words, coughed. "Allow me to sit."

He drew up a chair within arm's reach. "During the Great Betrayal, we all had a role. Wolst and the rest of your uncles fought the Scoths directly as matched their skills. Meanwhile, I was given a task much more fitting to my abilities. I'm no fighter, but I have other skills the duchess found useful during wartime."

He stared out the window, shoulders dropping away from his lithe neck. Though he seemed to savor no part of the story he told, he spoke with a methodical, deliberate cadence. "There was a man your grandmother wanted me to watch, a half-blood of mixed Scoth and Namorite descent. So I did. When I discovered he was training a militia of other half-bloods loyal to Scothea, your grandmother asked me to get close with him, so I did. I began working at a tavern he frequented in the hopes of cultivating a relationship with him. What began as jesting over drinks became something more. He was passionate, loud, worry free—many things I am not. Despite knowing him to be an enemy at an intellectual level, I found myself respecting him at an emotional one. Admiring him, you could say…"

It was as if Othwii spoke to himself as he stared out the window and into the past. It seemed right somehow, so Ishoa remained a silent witness.

Othwii's thumb and forefinger rubbed together in his lap. "Eventually, we became very close. I did what the duchess asked. I did exactly what she asked…everything and more. You see, I admired this man for what I wasn't. It didn't take long to realize I loved him, for in one important way we were exactly the same. In our minds and hearts, we were dedicated to a cause beyond ourselves, even if those causes were directly opposed. In that we shared a core piece of who we were. Our very souls. Though he never knew it…"

Othwii grunted, suffocating a sob. "Scothea concealed their approach well. Even the man I loved didn't know what was coming until it happened. After six months of war, one would think Namarr would be better prepared. But it didn't matter. I'd already been given my orders. If my mark was in a position to lead half-bloods against Namarr, I was to deal with him. I knew what it meant…what I had to do. I'm not skilled in martial combat, but I know my poisons. He drank enough godsbrew to flood a cellar. A drop of death dealer at the end of the night would go unnoticed."

Othwii shook, eyes glossy. No tears came. Again, he swallowed the pain.

Why does he tell me this? The horrible truth was alive inside him. In his words. In the act of sharing itself. Othwii's duty never stopped. His mission was never complete. *He tells me out of duty. Duty to Namarr.*

"You didn't do it," she said. "You let him live."

As if slapped, Othwii stared at her, eyes wide. He shook his head. "How could I?" His tone softened to a whisper. "How could I kill him? I loved him. But—I—I am so so sorry, Isha."

He crossed his arms, rocked back and forth with shame.

From over Othwii's jutting shoulder, her parents seemed to watch them. Ishoa's chest tightened, expectant.

"The man I failed to deal with led a raid of loyalists against the port at South Setton. That's where Scothea landed. They killed over a hundred Namorites there. The man I loved was integral in securing the port where King Acramis landed." He ran a shaking hand over his face. "It made the subsequent assault that killed you father and grandfather a success."

The words slid through her, hollowed her out. Her father watched from the painting. "The Bloody Beach," she muttered.

"Yes."

He sees himself responsible for their deaths. How could he have known? Ishoa felt none of the anger she thought the seneschal expected from her.

"Othwii." She glanced furtively at her mentor. "I forgive you."

"I do not ask for forgiveness." His chin swept the air. "And I will not accept it. Only my actions can pay for the blood on my hands. I tell you this in the hopes that you understand." He stabbed a finger against his own breast. "I failed to do what was necessary for Namarr and I regret it every day of my life."

The bags under the eyes, the ceaseless work. This is why he never rests. He can't say no to his duties. Not anymore.

Othwii leaned forward. Tears pooled at the corners of his eyes. "Remember this, Isha. Love waxes and wanes as quick as the season's turn. But failing in your duty, that is something you can never go back on. You'll carry it...forever."

CHAPTER TWENTY-FOUR

ONE CHANCE

I've known my fellow Awakened for longer than I care to admit. One might think that with time, all things improve—that all relationships heal. I wish it were so. I'm a mean old hag, yet compared to Darkhorn's tempestuous disposition, I'm a sweet little rain cloud.

"You have been with the boy a month." The shaman is all accusation. "You must do something. Scothea is on the verge of collapse. Begin his training. Now!"

I smack my lips. "Darkhorn, not everything is a corpse for you to manipulate. In the matters of the living, leave it to me. Sometimes you have to go slow at first to ensure things go smooth thereafter. And the smoother it goes, the faster it goes."

The Kurg's grumbling echoes throughout the River. "Namorite children have no sense. If it were my grandson, he'd be atop Unturrus now. An Awa—"

"Your grandson would die, fool. You know you cannot rush Awakening through sheer force of will. This isn't about respecting elders, nor placing duty above self. It's about Akyris. Who he is. The blood in his veins. The pain in his heart. The potential for power riding the edges of his consciousness. He needs to know himself." I scoff. "He'd already be atop Unturrus...pfah! Pompous drivel."

"You dance to a dangerous tune, Locastrii. Time, as you know, is not on our side. There is a cost."

"Please," Magomedes says. "We waste time. You are both right, it is urgent for the boy to be prepared, and essential that he is properly trained. We have but one shot. The Arrow of Light speeds toward his target."

A tone of regret enters Darkhorn's thudding voice. "We should have had Tahmyrus kill him when we had the chance."

"The Arrow? What chance? She abandoned us," I say. There was a time when Tahmyrus could have killed the prophet, when his powers were still new and he was known as Siddaia. Darkhorn blames me for not seeing the future soon enough to use Tahmyrus. As if I can control what the River allows me to see. I get but sips from a vast, rushing future. "We are all that's left." In truth, there is still Hashuuk, but he's shackled in an Orenese prison. Unreachable for now.

Our bodies are tethered to locations hundreds of miles apart, yet I feel some of the fight in Darkhorn ebbing as if he's right beside me.

"There is news. Unpleasant news," he says. "The boy's followers have begun plotting a coup despite his urgings for peace. They would see him crowned king."

"Not long now." Magomedes stifles most of her fear. I barely notice her trembling. "He's beginning to fully understand his abilities. Soon he'll have the might of Scothea at his back. And then—"

"He'll die." I'll brook no alternative. "Just as we've planned. Now I have training to attend to." My consciousness retracts, returns to my Locus at the center of my being. I come to inhabit my vessel once more. A tingling warmth flows through my body.

Before me, Akyris sits in silence, shoulder blades pinned back, eyes closed, chin upraised.

He's improving.

A minute passes before his eyelids flutter open. "What is it?"

I assume my expression betrays worry. I deign it necessary to ignore the question. "You're getting better at this. Only a few days left now. Then you'll be rid of me."

"Yeah." His lips purse. He studies a point in the distance. "I suppose I will."

I seize the moment, for I too feel the sadness. "You can come with me, you know? I promise we won't be gone forever." The last is a lie.

He shakes his head. "I—I could never leave her."

My daughter. His greatest obstacle. The woman is too damn good a mother. Bitterness clogs the back of my throat. Resent fills me. I wish I'd been half so caring, half so good to her as she is to the boy.

It's too late for sentiments like that though. I am what I am. Hopefully it is enough.

I laugh at the irony of it all. Who could have guessed an exceptional mother might be the downfall of humanity?

The next day comes and goes in silence. The one after that too. Akyris helps me out to the elm tree, even offers a hand to support my descent to the stump. I wave him away. There's a thin line between support and coddling.

We speak no words during our session.

Afterward, he ushers me back to the cottage and then returns to the elm tree alone for a second interval. I imagine he thinks it will impress me, an unspoken message inherent in the act that says, *stay, Grandmother.*

Oh, youth, how they love to prove themselves. In truth, I admire the behavior. If I had any such inclinations to impress, I might have better relations with my loved ones. More often than not I see who I might rankle instead, an impish delight only age, wisdom, and a touch of childish surrender lets me appreciate.

From my place on the porch, I watch a pair of geese flap lazily across the horizon, barely more than shadows in the soft light of the setting sun. A frigid gust chases them.

Akyris returns, arms crossed and rubbing bare shoulders. He wears a somber half-smile. I'm pleased too. He's progressed faster than expected. "Where I grew up we didn't have porches." I pat the space beside me. "Didn't know what I was missing out on."

Taking the seat, Akyris and I watch night descend. The constant need to speak, it seems, has melted from him. Burned away by the fires of silent discomfort. Forged anew by the immutable Locus within.

"Thirty days," I chuckle. "Nacronus take me. You actually did it."

He nods, smirking. More geese fly past, honking. I wait, giving the boy time to look within, to find final words to send me on my way. In the cottage, my daughter drops something as she prepares the evening meal.

"I didn't do it to get rid of you, you know," he says. "Well, I mean I did, but then later...I didn't." Warmth pours into my chest, seeps into my belly. "That only motivated me the first twenty-eight or twenty-nine days."

Our laughter trails the fading sunlight. Shadows stretch beneath our feet, mine swinging freely, his dragging through the dirt.

"You don't have to go, you know." His tone is serious and flat. "You could stay."

I place the butt of my staff in the dirt and rest my chin atop the backs of my hands folded over its twisted top. "It's good to hear you say that. Unfortunately, I have important business drawing me elsewhere. You sure you don't want to come?"

Chin dipping, he stares at his feet a while.

The wind picks up, forcing me to pull my shawl tighter about my neck. My bones ache from the chill. Srah is my least favorite of the Sempyrean gods. "I'm getting cold and need to be up early. I have a long journey ahead." I pat his leg firmly. "Sleep in your own bed tonight. You've earned it."

"No. You're the guest. I want you to—"

"Agh!" I blow a raspberry. "You're a sweet boy, little bird, but I'll hear no more. Right here is just fine for me, I think. An extra blanket wouldn't be out of the question though."

I grunt as I roll onto my side, then curl up to watch night bleed my vision to a blackish haze. Akyris is prompt to comply with my request, bringing not one but two blankets. A far better idea.

I thank him. He nods, hesitates at the door, then sulks back into the house like a whipped dog. How things have changed since that first day. At first his shoulders sagged because of my arrival.

Now they sag at the thought of me gone.

Right where we started, I stand over him. A juxtaposition of things changed. Time has a tendency to offer such repetition as we move through it, a swing of the pendulum you might say. It brings us back to places both familiar and different. What we think we leave behind only lies in wait to teach us anew.

My hope is he has learned.

"Akyris."

He rolls onto his back, smacks his lips, notices me. With some effort, a single eyelid lifts, revealing a sliver of shadowed green beneath. Seeing me, he sits bolt upright, suddenly awake. "Are you leaving now?" he rubs his eyes, reaches for his clothes. "I'll travel with you a short while."

I pin his clothes to the floor with the butt of my staff. "Slow down, little bird."

Slow. I must move slow to create space for what needs greatest speed. I embody the principle, adopting a measured speech pattern, a lilting and soft tone. "Before I go, I wanted to give you something."

It's heavy in my hand. The weight of my deepest fears and insights rest within. The struggle of all humanity lies scrawled across the pages. The leather-bound cover is warm, smooth against my skin. Dust-dry and wrinkled by time. Gilt letters catch the light, flash at me from the cover.

Now. And then.

"A gift," Danath Ironlight had said, "I thought the beauty of the pages inside should be equally reflected in the beauty on the outside." Danath's own scribe produced the book. His own hand had presented it to her.

That was decades ago. When the world was still bright. When the future was paved by the actions of those acting for the good of all people. Now coffers bursting with riches feed the place where a soul should be.

Power is ever a game of the privileged few.

Still abed, Akyris cocks his head. "A gift?" He reaches up to take it.

I chuckle. "Just a little something I wrote long ago. Thought you might like it since you've already practiced some of its principles."

"You wrote..." He trails off, runs a hand over the cover, then reads the title. "The Path Illuminated...by Locastrii, Mistress of Time." Bafflement, complete and utter.

I meet his shock with a wicked grin. "My grandson, it's been a pleasure. I wish you well in your journey." I kiss my fingertips and then trace them in an arc through the air as if knighting him on each shoulder. "Akyris."

I limp from the cottage, touching the insides of the walls as I go. I whisper a message to Mags and Darkhorn. "The moment of truth has arrived."

I've barely stepped from the porch by the time Akyris flies out of the house, yanking on a belt and fumbling to keep the book I've just given him from falling into the dirt.

"Wait! Wait!" He licks his lips as he passes me and then blocks my path. Darting eyes traverse my entirety. His brow knits. "You—you're lying. Why?"

"About?"

He looks at the book then back at me. "You're Locastrii? The Locastrii who wrote this?"

"Indeed." I poke his chest. "The very same." I shoulder past, knotted staff kicking up puffs of dust, bad hip causing my foot to make an extra dragging sound through the dirt.

Moving slower than usual from a night of poor sleep spent on the porch, it takes me a minute to reach the end of the lane. In that same time, Akyris retreated into the house and then raced up behind me once more. He carries a pack stuffed with his belongings. A rusted knife is jammed through his belt and my book fills his hands.

"You look foolish." It's my turn to look him up and down. "Exceedingly so."

"No, I don't." He frowns, shuffles. "And I'm coming with you."

It's happening. A smile pushes forth. I can't contain it. I pat him on a thin bicep, eyes and hands lingering there. Such a frail thing. So young—too young to die. "You're willing to leave your mother?"

He looks back at the house, nods.

"Your friends? This town? Sima? Leave it all behind?"

He hesitates. Nods again.

I draw the knife from his belt with thumb and forefinger like it's a fecal rag. "You don't even know where we're going."

"I don't care." He puffs out his chest. "I'm coming with you. I want to learn more. I *have* to learn more."

To Magomedes and Darkhorn, I say, "Our future has a chance yet." The pieces are in motion to defeat the Arrow of Light. I want to laugh.

And then I want to weep.

With his own words, my grandson has sealed his fate and bound it to my own. Emotion swirls through me like Srah's dubious winds. It's all I can do to keep from running back to the house, getting down on one knee, and begging my daughter's forgiveness.

Then again, what is one life measured against all life? Blood ties or not, I cannot justify sparing him. Not for the love of my daughter. Not for my love of Akyris.

Not for all the love in all the world.

Akyris must die.

"Well done, Locastrii." Darkhorn's voice is hollow. Gone is the bitterness. Duty has been carried out. For him, it seems, that is enough.

Magomedes is somewhat more compassionate. "You should be proud of yourself. You've given us all a chance." Her words encircle me. "Your daughter may still live. Take comfort in that."

I try, but the contentment she offers feels out of reach.

"I'm proud of you, Akyris." I pull him down roughly to kiss his forehead. "Come. Let's begin your real training."

I toss his rusty knife into the bushes, then pivot, heading once more to the elm tree.

"Where?" he asks. "I thought we were leaving?"

"We are." I suck at my teeth. "Feet are only one way to travel, but I daresay a very limiting one. Our adventure begins within."

CHAPTER TWENTY-FIVE

SOUR WINE

I n the fugue state between dreams and reality, blood leaked from the rafters. Barodane sat in a chapel consumed by flames, filled by smoke, surrounded by the screams of the dying.

Trapped.

He saw the boy. *Help me.*

Help me...

Sudden as shattered glass, Barodane's eyes flew open. Blood and fire and the screams and the boy disappeared, leaving him in a soggy mess of his sweat. The dampness, he noted, was not near as bad as it had been. Still, a change of clothing was in order. *If shit could talk, it might say it feels like me right now. Yet somehow, I feel better than before.*

The ache in his head doubled in intensity as he loosed a mighty cough. He wheezed like a punctured bellows. Thankfully, hot pincers no longer clamped around his joints and spine.

How long have I been out? Vaguely, he recalled Vey and Meckin forcing water down his throat a handful of times. If memory served, Madame Gratha had pressed a vial of something bitter to his lips.

It had tasted wretched. Like the past. Barodane wanted to cut it all away like fat from marbled meat. That was a hopeful thought. And hope was not something he deserved.

To his miserable delight, the voices of the dead had stuck around. *If this could last forever, it might be enough to repay your debt of suffering.*

Ambitiously, he tried to rise. A rush of blood and pressure filled his head. He groaned and faltered back onto his elbows. That was when he noticed the intruder seated at the foot of the bed.

He worked his tongue between gum and lips to free his mouth of dryness. "It's you." He was careful not to say her name aloud.

"You sound terrible." Garlenna went to the open window and threw open the shutters. The light of day sent daggers through his skull. He squeezed his eyes shut.

Choice insults burbled to mind as he prepared to rebuke his former prosort, but all he spit forth was a weak rasp. He grimaced and raised a warding hand.

"You mean I sound like death," he said. "Feel that way too. More so now. Thanks to you and the wretched sun."

"Apologies." Barodane didn't think she looked sorry at all. She rolled her shoulders and then crossed her arms. "The sickness has not taken kindly to light, which means it's either the crimson curse or the withers. Since you've been in and out of sleep for two full days without a drop of blood leaking from your lips or nose, not to mention the lack of blood in your coughs, I'd say it's the withers. That means water and rest. It probably feels like you're dancing in the Maw Eternal with Nacronus himself, but a moist climate helps. Who knew living in Digtown would be a stroke of luck that saves your life?" The edge of the bed caved as she took a seat beside him. "The old whore—the Kurg—came by while you slept. She said she gave you something to help, but I did not trust her and sent her away."

"Madame Gratha is a good healer and a..." the word "friend" lodged in his throat. Garlenna must have felt it. A quiet somberness fell over her.

"She's trustworthy," Barodane rasped.

"That is good. You have people here. People you trust."

Silence dragged between them. He scoffed. "So you want us to sit here and talk about the past, is that it? I have a better idea. You could leave. Leaving would be good. You'll stay more alive that way."

"I'm not leaving. Not without you."

Help me...

Anger shot through him. *Damn it, Garlenna, why didn't you stop me?* He wanted to tell her he needed her then, that she could have saved the people of Rainy Meadows if she'd stood with Kaitos.

You were the one with all the power, the voices reminded him. *And you did nothing with it but evil. Woe, Barodane Ironlight. Woe to any who cross your path.*

Kaitos tried and failed. But Garlenna...her folly was in loving him too much. Being too loyal. For that, Barodane had made her pay with a piece of her soul.

For what I've done to her, she's the last person who should care about me.

He spoke tersely. "You don't understand, do you? I'm not going with you. I'm meant to die here, and that's exactly what I intend to do."

"And sooner than you imagine." Garlenna glanced at the door, voice lowering. "Hyram Olabran has gathered masons and assassins in the foothills. I've done what I can to slow them, but even so it won't be long. If I were them, I would have struck already."

"I don't care and neither should you. In fact, why are you here, really?"

Garlenna took a slip of paper from within her leather vest and handed it to him. He read the note from her father, Gyr Renwood. *Maybe it's best if the entire nation falls apart because of me. The voices would be satisfied.*

But the idea of a third Scoth invasion shattered his numb self-loathing. Cold anger filled him as he imagined sinking his blade into Acramis's chest, filled him as he felt the shudder of the man's life through the handle of his blade.

Jaw clenched, he looked away. "None of this matters now. Prince Barodane is gone. I can barely unite my bootlaces now, much less a nation."

"We need you."

"After what I..." He lowered his voice. "Listen, I abandoned the crown for a reason. A very good one."

Help me...

"You've seen the truth." In his mind's eye, the boy staggered close. "I'm not to be trusted with power."

"This is bigger than your fear of power."

That stuck like a well-aimed arrow.

She went on. "Namarr's neck lays stretched beneath a Scothean ax. We need an Ironlight to head the Collective, or it will fracture. If that happens, we're all at risk." She adopted a chiding tone. "Is your petty self-hatred so strong that you'd willingly let our nation slide back into Scoth hands?"

Barodane's cheek twitched.

"Ishoa won't survive long if Revocation passes. She'll be deposed. Exile is the best she could hope for. Execution, the most likely." Palms upturned, Garlenna pleaded. "Unless you take up Solicerames and announce yourself at the Collective."

She does not know you. She thinks you care about others. But you only care about yourself. She thinks you're a good man, incapable of watching Scothea burn Namarr or letting your niece die. But she's wrong, isn't she?

A dull ache started at the base of Barodane's skull. Since he'd stopped taking god-sthorn, the intensity of the voices had increased. He shook his head, chin hovering at his collarbones, hands limp in his lap.

The muscles around Garlenna's blue eye tightened. "I feel cheated. Fourteen years you've been gone. Fourteen years stolen from our friendship. I thought I would serve you forever. Help you make Namarr a stronger nation. Fourteen years and I finally find you..." She wrinkled her lips as if tasting rancid meat. "Like this." She rose. "But only death will stop me from serving you. For the rest of our years here, I can be Gyra and you can be Kord. It doesn't matter. I'm going nowhere. So kill me or live with it. Your choice."

Barodane glared. "I'm getting what I deserve for what I did. You may too. You are a force of nature, Garlenna Renwood, but even you cannot stand up to what

Hyram will bring. You'll die defending a fallen prince not worthy of your spit. A prince you hate."

"I do not hate you, Barodane. I pity you." She patted his leg. "Isn't that what you want? My pity? I'm so sorry for you and your sad little life. What turmoil? What misery?"

"You know, you can be a real shit head." Barodane gave a grim smile. "I thought the Sempyrium scorned mockery?"

"In the name of serving a higher good, I could put literal shit on your head and the Sempyrium would permit it. Though by the look of you, an army of lice might overtake me if I tried." This coaxed a clipped laugh from Barodane.

Garlenna laughed, too. "I have long missed such moments."

Barodane scrutinized her. He cursed himself for enjoying her presence. She had always known how to work his moods. She wielded the skills of manipulation trained into her by the Sempyrium with expert precision.

Barodane had to remind himself that in addition to being a devout priestess, guardian, and friend, Garlenna Renwood was a dangerous spy. *Don't let her get close. She'll take you from us!*

He set his jaw, stifling mirth. "Go, Garlenna. Leave before the masons kill us both."

"They'll kill Tyne's son first. The one you helped raise."

Jennim...

Silence roiled between them like choking smoke.

The prosort loomed. "You loved her, and you're going to let them kill her son. They'll kill Meckin too. They won't stop killing until they have you, and that I will not allow." Her voice was deadly serious and full of steel. "Abandon this place, my Prince. Namarr needs you. You must raise the Slave Banner. You must be the arm of Soliceramcs once more."

The muscles in Barodane's jaw slackened. *I remember the way it felt, the iron-hard wood in hand. The weight and balance of it. Heavier than expected. So heavy. How incredibly strong had Danath been?*

They stared at each other, dark pasts colliding with righteous intents. He balled blankets into a fist. *Why can't I be stronger?*

The voices answered for him. *You. Are. Nothing.*

From outside came a shout soaked in contempt. "Kord! A gift!"

Garlenna held out a hand, beckoning Barodane to remain abed. Her mace was held aloft in the other. *I didn't even see her draw it.*

Feet thudded up the stairs. Garlenna moved without sound into position to one side of the door. Barodane spoke to her with his eyes. A key turned the lock, admitted Meckin into the room. As soon as Barodane saw who it was, he shook his head so Garlenna knew there was no threat.

"That uppity asshole rode through a bit ago with a couple other assholes in mason livery. They left a barrel with a note on it..." Meckin whirled, found Garlenna standing behind him. He gasped, slapping palm to sternum as he bent forward to breathe. "Fuck me! You about stopped my blasted heart!"

"Help me up," said Barodane.

Garlenna pulled him to his feet and ignored his wincing as she slung his arm over her shoulder. Blankets crumpled to the floor. A gust of wind slapped the shutters and set Barodane to violent shaking. "By the gods, get one of those blankets on him," Garlenna barked. Meckin hustled to it, but not without muttering his displeasure about being bossed around.

Garlenna bore Barodane down the hall, feet dragging slowly and gingerly as if he might fall apart if jostled too much.

Fuck, I'm weak.

Garlenna's strength had not waned in fourteen years. Slabs of stony muscle writhed under cloak and leather. Barodane felt the unyielding strength of her trunk each time he bumped against it. A moment's competitive spirit swept through him. Though he'd never been Garlenna's match, he still noticed jealousy rise and fall within.

Perhaps I should begin training again? The fact of his current situation dealt him a sharp dose of reality. *Soon you'll join the dead. And the dead do not train.*

The first step down the stairs came at Barodane unevenly, a flash of pain made him hiss. "Easy!"

Garlenna grunted. "The godsthorn has made you fragile."

They struggled their way to the bottom of the stairs then across the tap room. Before they emerged, Garlenna waved Meckin near. "Take him."

Drawing her mace, she stepped to the inside of the door and then to the other side of it, checking for ambushers. She inhaled sharply, breathed out slow, and then stepped out.

A ring of people formed in the muddy street around a barrel. A knife pinned a note to the lid. No one went near. Squinting, Barodane adjusted to the stabbing light as he stepped out of the Dregs.

One glance at the barrel told what gift to expect. A pang of sadness anchored his heart.

Garlenna looked back at Barodane. He gave a nod.

"Stand aside," she called as she strode through the crowd, pushing aside drab-clothed drovers, ill-fortuned merchants, and the occasional shirtless denizen of the slums with the backs of her hands. There were men taller than Garlenna amid the dozen or so who'd gathered to inspect the barrel, but her breadth and strength moved with her like an unspoken command.

None gave quarrel. All retreated before her in silent resignation. Conjecturing whispers passed freely from lips to ears.

"Kord's muscle," someone said.

"Dead boy," said another.

"Turf war comin'," the last was hollered with a tone indicating both excitement and warning, as if the woman wanted everyone to share her insight.

Garlenna yanked the knife free and took the note. The paper crinkled as she read it.

Once finished, she wedged the knife into the crack between barrel and lid, and then worked it loose with a pair of upward lifts and downward pulls. It popped free. She looked inside then replaced the lid.

Turning on her heels, she said loudly, "No one touch it."

She handed Barodane the note. "Jennim."

Guilt burned at the back of his throat as he read, a cold, unquenchable fire.

Dearest Kord,

Please enjoy this token of appreciation for entertaining my offer. Like any wine, it is full bodied and gets sweeter with time. I do hope it suits your tastes more than it did mine. I encourage you to accept this gift as payment for your supply, all operating capital, and your territory. I also require you to disband those in your employment, or turn them over for questioning. Further bloodshed isn't necessary. Nor will it favor you.

Cordially, H.

P.S. - If my offer is spurned, I have more empty barrels to fill.

Barodane motioned with his chin. Meckin helped walk him to the barrel.

"Get to whatever you layabouts do in a day!" Most followed Meckin's command and sauntered away with an indifferent shrug. Others peeled from the group slowly, glancing backward at the barrel as they went, morbid curiosity too stoked to quit.

"The lid please, Meckin," Barodane said.

Licking his lips, Meckin reached a shaky hand forward. "You sure?"

Barodane gave a curt nod.

The innkeeper's hand halted inches short. "I can't. I—I'm sorry, Kord."

Meckin appeared a hard man to most, but over the years Barodane had come to perceive a soft-heartedness in him. A quality woefully out of place in Digtown.

"It's okay, Meckin. No one should be sorry but me. I did this." Barodane unlimbered himself from Meckin's shoulder. The lid slid off, wooden slats thrumming for a few seconds as it struck muddy earth. Haloed in a blueish tinge, Jennim stared up at him from dark liquid, a frozen and sorrowful plea twisting his mouth and eyes. A couple of fingernails and tracts of peeled skin hung from his upthrust hands.

He attempted to claw his way free. Barodane sighed. *Don't we all?*

He recalled times they'd played together in Tyne's room at the Gem Loft. The time Barodane had shown Jennim the horse he got his mother. Jennim had looked up at him in wonder as if to say, "Why do I deserve such kindness?"

Far different than the one he wore now.

"Aye," Barodane said. "No one to blame but me."

You cannot change who you are, Mad Prince. You are a beacon of misery. The past is the present, and it is the future. Just like the boy you stabbed. Just like this boy you drowned. You will never escape yourself!

The words of the dead rang hollow. Rage echoed. Prickles swept up the backs of his arms. For the first time in a long time, he didn't want his misery, regret, or self-hate.

No, those would only slow him down.

Anger turned his internal eye to his sword. He saw it whetted with blood, dripping where he stood over bodies freshly separated from their souls.

To feel anything but anger now was a liability to that purpose.

There was no way Hyram would leave town without first killing him. And he would. There was little doubt in that, but if the voices were right, and the past was the present and the future...

Perhaps he could make one final suicidal charge like the one he'd done to slay Acramis. Perhaps he could lay down his own life and kill Hyram Olabran. This time he hoped to good and truly die in the process.

He turned from the barrel.

The barrow hills surrounding Digtown watched him approvingly. Meckin slid back under Barodane's shoulder. Beside the door to the Dregs, Garlenna leaned back against the wall. "Let me help you, Kord. One is already dead. You know there will be more."

"Thank you for the offer. But I refuse."

She smiled. "And I refuse your refusal."

They passed her, and she followed them into the taproom. "You need me or more innocent people will die."

Barodane stopped. If Jennim were in front of him, he would have struck the young fool. But Jennim was dead. So Barodane laughed instead, a harsh, laconic thing. "You are wrong to think that any here are innocent." He motioned with his chin back at the barrel as Meckin's stable boy was securing the lid to move it. "Jennim misunderstood. And misunderstanding in this place is a death sentence." He sucked at his teeth. "Like you, he thought he could call upon old sentiments to sway the mind of a man who no longer exists—maybe never existed. By his own hand he gambled his life away. Misplaced optimism you could call it. Suicide in a world such as ours."

"Resignation is the cure then?" She laid a hand on his shoulder. "Please, we have a better chance of surviving *together*. As your friend—"

"I've told you I have no friends." Barodane deflected her hand. "And I am no innocent worth saving."

He looked her over. "And neither are you. Come on, Meckin."

The tap room was silent but for the slurp of drink in the hand of the watching harpist. A few others acted as though they weren't paying attention. Tankards of godsbrew rose slowly to their mouths and then lowered at the same distracted speed.

Floorboards creaked as Garlenna left.

Meckin helped Barodane up the stairs. Sweat poured between his shoulder blades and made a swamp of his brow and the area around his neck. A misstep—they stumbled. Barodane cursed more loudly than was called for and pulled at Meckin's shirt collar to right himself.

With a growl, Meckin shoved Barodane to arm's length in agitation. "Here. You want to be a bastard about it, do it yourself. I'll not have you take out your frustration with the woman on me."

Barodane grunted under the burden of his full weight becoming his own.

"Fine," he said through gritted teeth. Using the wall for support, he came to stand on fever-weak legs then hobbled to his room alone.

CHAPTER TWENTY-SIX

THE TRIAL OF CROSSING

T he Blue River crept past Jarik like a thief. Ishoa turned from the frigid coursing to the sloping hillside outside the Gate of the Bear.

The hold encampments seethed with activity as they made their way to the river's
banks to watch the Trial of Crossing. The largest among these were the cattlemen of
Baen's Handle, their sprawling territory required three banners to unite them. The
bull's horn crossing with a maul over a brown and white checkered field snapped
and fluttered in the wind.

The smallest were the hunters of Twilight Cape, sporting a single gray banner
with a trio of black spears thrust through a crescent moon. Unlike the other hold
lords and ladies, Enkita Vulkuu refused to stay in the guest towers, choosing instead
to sleep among her score of holdguard and their storm bears. To Ishoa, it made
perfect sense. Enkita was an Awakened who spoke mostly Fjordsong. The common
tongue was as scant as any other common ground she might have shared with the
other highborn.

The prize for most impressive camp went to the Scarborn. "I see," Belara Frost
had said under her breath as she reached the Blue River's banks. "Clever."

By arriving before the other holds, the Scarborn retinue had shaped a message for
all to see. That they had taken the highest vantage point on the slope. *We are less
beneath you than you think,* it seemed to say.

Wolst grunted. "The high ground."

From what Ishoa had seen, the Scarborn were not the type to let good boredom go
to waste. Their camp had leveled lanes, earthwork defenses surrounding its entirety,
and an orderliness sorely lacking in the other camps. They seemed to be of a singular
mind with a singular goal: show other Anjuhks who was better.

Lodaris's words assailed her. *You do not see it, Princess.*

I see it now, Lodaris. Very clearly.

Hundreds gathered on the banks of the Blue River for the opening ceremony
of the Trials. Ishoa's chest throbbed in anticipation as she looked down the row
of Claimants. A dozen youth from minor holds filled in between the major ones.
Dragga Omenfaen with his ship's prow jaw whispered to his sister. Stirrma who

wore a permanent glower, snorted at whatever he said. Unalor Bog appeared to be chattering incessantly at Yurm Kon, who looked bored by the interaction but too uncomfortable to step away from it.

At line's end, Ishoa caught sight of a mane of red hair—Lodaris's red hair. Her heart skipped a beat. A flush of rage made her skin tingle. She wanted to walk down the line and scream in his face. After her difficult conversation with Othwii, she'd sent him a message asking if he cared to spar in the yard, but he'd rejected her yet again.

More accurately, his mother had rejected her. Lodecka had intercepted the letter and wrote a brief one in return, stating that Lodaris was already out training and needed to focus on the Trials.

A load of snow bison shit!

Lodaris returned her gaze with indifference. The scars on his cheek were as she remembered them: three thin white lines with the topmost scar being fatter where the Jurati's steel claw had snagged. What Ishoa didn't remember was a dark splotch along his jaw...a fist-sized bruise.

Her agitation ebbed as guilt flowed. *He was embarrassed. That's why he didn't want to see me.*

Lodaris spat, then looked away.

She huffed, anger returning to a boil.

That was when the Trials began.

Chosen as the master of ceremonies, Arick Quinn ascended a wooden platform overlooking a bank of the river. Her cousin was a boring choice. *Enkita Vulkuu would have been far more interesting.*

Arick summoned the crowd to gather around the line of Claimants. Ishoa felt blood inside her cheek and stopped chewing as her cousin explained the history of the Trials.

Right now, Lodaris doesn't matter. I must prove myself in the Trials.

"...every few years in autumn. As we assemble in peace to encourage those Claimants who seek the old honor, we must give thanks to my aunt, Belara Frost, for reviving our customs after Scoth occupation. To the Ice Maiden, a hero of the Unity Wars. Without her, the Trials could not be."

Everyone in attendance, including Ishoa, bowed deeply to the duchess. Syphion Muul's bow was quicker than most.

Arick continued, his tone void of emphasis. "Today, we test our young with the Trial of Crossing. Though not so dangerous as the Trials of Summit or Quelling, there is risk here."

Blue eyes, striking for the pale skin and white-braided hair around them, found Ishoa's. "But that is what it is to be an Anjuhk. You must be one who faces danger and death willingly. To test your mettle. In the courts of Peladonia and Lah-Tsarra, they simply buy their votes—"

"Like they buy their loyalties," Syphion Muul shouted. The crowd muttered and glanced around. A few hurled abrasive insults at the pig-eyed fanatic. He laughed.

Arick raised his voice to cut through the roused murmuring. "But not Anjuhks. We *earn* our voice." He fixed Syphion with a cool stare. "Most of us anyway."

Hesitant laughter followed. Syphion shrugged, unperturbed by the derision of the crowd. Not every hold was as vocal in denouncing the man as Ishoa would have liked.

"Today you do not simply gain a vote at the court of Anjuhkar. You gain the power to influence Namarr's future," Arick said. "What say you? Are you Anjuhks?"

The Claimants shouted as one. "We are!"

"Are you true Namorites?"

"We are!"

When it came time for everyone except for the Claimants to bow, Lodecka Warnock stared ahead with impassive defiance. Ishoa threw the woman a venomous stare. Twin braids of blond hair were tied into a single knot at the top of Lodecka's head, pulling the skin of her angular face taught. In the frigid autumn air, the self-inflicted scars riddling cheek, jaw, and forehead were a purplish hue.

She dipped her chin mockingly at Ishoa.

"Let us say the words of Danath Ironlight," Arick said.

Ishoa's pulse quickened. Minutes remained before she was in the thick of the Trial of Crossing, exposed for all to see. Her bowels felt empty and full at the same time. *Am I too young? Am I worthy of the Ironlight name?*

Doubts swirled over and over like the eddies of a rushing river.

Wolst's plate-sized hand clapped gently over one of Ishoa's shoulders. A chorus of voices rose in the air, but her uncle's boomed, drowning out the Claimants to either side of her as they recited Danath's words:

"Shackles only hold those who allow it.

"One who does not seek to break their chain is already broken by it.

"Here and Now.

"Free your swords! Free your souls!

"My Sons and Daughters of Namarr, you cannot die but once. Let us live, boldly and without fear!"

The last word of Danath's call to war rang in Ishoa's ears.

Arick Quinn bowed to the line of youth. "Claimants, may your ancestors be with you."

They stripped down to their small clothes. Anxious sweat met the cold, chilling Ishoa to the bone. She crossed her arms over budding breasts and stepped through the mud and snow to the edge of the rocky riverbank.

Wolst whispered in her ear, "Good luck, Isha. Remember your breathing techniques." Then he rejoined the crowd.

Claimants rarely died during the Trial of Crossing—a meager reassurance. A few close calls over the decades had resulted in the need for resuscitation by a Sister of the Rose. One stood nearby, scarlet robes stamped with white roses, stirring in the breeze.

Most often a Claimant would fail the crossing too many times and spent overlong in the icy waters. Nothing a fire and some furs wouldn't cure if they were given quick enough. If left untreated, the deep cold could kill.

Dragga Omenfaen stood beside Ishoa. He leaned out over the water and laughed. "A little morning dip to wake us up, eh, Highness?"

Though Dragga was difficult to suffer, Ishoa could not look away from his exposed figure, a thing of art. Not allure. Slabs of muscle on his shoulders were tight from the cold, giving her an intimate view of every twitching fiber and indentation. More impressive still was his torso, where it looked like slate rock had been stacked one atop the other in eight perfect rows. "This should be nothing for someone like you," he said.

With a nervous laugh, Ishoa glanced down at her own exposed stomach. Normal, neither muscular nor thick with fat.

"But if you are swept away, do not worry. I'll be here."

Stirrma's velvet voice spun Ishoa around. "Dragga, if you're swept away, we'll gladly let you go."

To Ishoa's surprise, Stirmma was nearly as heavily muscled as her brother. With hips and shoulders broader than a barrel lid and legs thicker than a birch tree's trunk, she looked like the anvil on her warhammer come to life.

She snorted derisively at her twin. "It would save us all from your mindless nattering." She looked from Dragga to Ishoa, brow dark and furrowed.

An unsure smile tugged at the corners of Ishoa's mouth.

Tossing her thick pony tail behind a shoulder, Stirrma said, "My brother fancies himself a prince. Only, he has no princess to make him one."

"I—uh. I guess I'm flattered."

"Don't be."

Dragga's smile lost some mirth around the eyes as he addressed his sister. "Stirrma, you know I love you but—"

"But. Always a 'but' from men like you, brother. Certainly, you've got the ego to be a prince." Stirrma turned to face the rushing river. She found a stone as large around as her head and hefted it with little effort. "You probably *should* marry him, Highness. Anything to bring and end to his overblown declarations."

Dragga leaned down, speaking to Ishoa in low tones, "My twin shows love in peculiar ways. Some of them come across as cruel. She has a good heart deep down though." He stood straight, then quickly dipped back down to Ishoa's ear. "But maybe she's right about the idea of our marriage."

He winked, then retrieved his own ballast, a monstrous thing he hefted onto a shoulder.

Ishoa cringed. *I am no stone to be slung over your shoulder.*

When she went to retrieve her own stone for the crossing, Ishoa saw Stirrma wore a twisted smile.

"Claimants," Arick shouted. "Prepare!"

Ishoa hurried to find a ballast, picked one that was too heavy, and then grabbed another. They had to be weighty enough to hold a Claimant to the river bottom, but not so heavy it made them slow.

Had Ishoa entered the Trials at fifteen, she would have felt far more prepared. Today, the holds would watch her closely, awaiting any opportunity to praise or condemn her performance.

Lodaris is also under great scrutiny. I wonder how he's handling the pressure.

She glanced down the line. The Scarborn's pale skin flushed red from the cold. He was not so cut from stone as Dragga but looked powerful holding a stone. Strong. Determined.

As much as his earlier indifference stoked Ishoa's wroth, she wished him success.

For herself, she hoped to finish in the middle of the group. While she was no weakling, the other Claimants were older by at least a year, and most were males. Training hadn't been as rigorous or consistent as she'd liked either. She spent more time working with weapons or Rakeema than preparing for the Trials.

Affording a last glance in Lodaris's direction, she started her furnace breaths.

You are strong. Stronger than you know.

She hoped—

"Begin!" shouted Arick.

Thought crashed into oblivion.

Claimants shambled into the river, ballasts cradled over bellies. Ishoa gasped at the rushing cold swirling around her ankles. It climbed up her thighs, then pierced the sensitive skin beneath her small clothes. Pain shot up her leg as she stepped onto a piece of jagged slate. Careful and firm, she waded in to the waist, huffing furnace breaths like a bellows. To either side in her periphery, Dragga and Stirrma flew forward in a white-capped crash. Cheers erupted along the banks as the names of holds were shouted in support of their respective Claimants.

The last unmuffled sounds.

Lips gulped for a final breath of air as the Blue River slurped down Ishoa. Darkness and river rock. The pounding of her quickened heartbeat in her ears. Distorted shouts somewhere distant. The cold lasted only a few more weighted steps before it was replaced with surging adrenaline. A furnace burned within her, fueled by an implacable need to finish. The pressure caused her breath to be shorter than normal.

But time in the Trial itself was a dilated thing, unworthy of trust.

At the river's bottom, the coursing waters weakened. Danger shifted, became the treacherous slime coated rocks threatening her balance. Her foot slipped, her hand too, nearly costing her the ballast. If she had dropped her stone, she would have been forced to swim back to the bank and start over.

Something slick and soft caressed her foot. She bore down her weight on the patch of mud, found purchase, and then hurried across. A handful of dark and muddled seconds later, she breached the surface on the other bank. An eruption of sound greeted her and she added her own gasp to the cacophony. Overhead, gray light, brighter than she remembered before the darkness of the river. Her lungs, screaming to be filled, sucked greedily at the air. She chucked her ballast; it clattered across the stony shore. *I need to catch my breath before the return crossing. The last thing I want is to have to start over because I was too hasty.*

In the heaving interval, she turned to see the progress of the others.

Yurm Kon, or "the Worm," as the other Claimants were referring to him, was still on the starting bank retrieving a ballast. Presumably because he'd dropped his and had to swim back. A fate he shared with a handful of others, though none looked so miserable in their setback. Lodaris was entering the river for his return. Neither Omenfaen were visible.

Breath calmer, Ishoa snatched up her ballast and entered the river. The second time wasn't near so shocking as the first. Her body was acclimated now. Given her glimpse into the progress of others, she thought she had a chance to finish in the top third. An impressive feat at fourteen.

They won't expect that!

Hubris was a distraction that cost her dearly. Her foot clipped a rock. She stumbled, pain lashing the top of her big toe. If she hadn't pitched her ballast at the last second, it may well have crushed her other foot. She ascended to the surface, cursed, and then swam back to restart from the second bank.

Exhausted, with muscles so tight they felt numb, she sought the water a third time but paused as shouts of "Victor!" rose from the distant bank.

Of course.

Dragga claimed the title. Lady Hilkka stood on tiptoes to plant a kiss on her son's forehead while Stirrma crawled onto the shore in second place—no one seemed to notice.

Ishoa took a deep breath and then lurched into the river. Every step with her injured toe, sent daggers up her ankle. Forced to accommodate for the injury with shortened strides, the left side of her low back burned with effort. Tighter, tighter, tighter—like a crossbow's winch. Light refracted overhead. Blurred figures swarmed the shore. Her heartbeat filled her ears, ached in her chest.

The ballast started to slip...

She pushed through the pain in her injured toe, racing the last few steps, and rolling the rock before her onto the finishing shore just as she sputtered free of the river. She collapsed, legs rubbery, one arm draped over the ballast.

Well over half the Claimants had emerged before her. A handful, including Yurm the Worm, lagged. Gouts of steam rose in the air over Ishoa's face as she flipped over onto her back then sat upright. A girl from a small hold succumbed to the deep cold and had to be rushed off in blankets by a Sister of the Rose.

On hands and knees, Unalor Bog spewed up water a ways down the bank. The sight brought Ishoa a shred of heartfelt satisfaction. *At least I am not last.*

She gained shaking legs, then turned. Between her and Lodaris, a dozen Claimants enjoined by their supporters cluttered the space. He'd made his way from the riverbank and back onto the road leading into Jarik. He no longer breathed heavily, a sign he'd finished near the top of the pack. Syphion Muul and the Warnocks congratulated him. Ularis was the only one to give affection in the form of a singular pat on the back. Lodecka kept him at arm's length.

"So, I'm not the only one," said Stirrma in her velvety, hushed voice.

Like some spirit of the river, covered in steam and dripping wet muscle, Stirrma stood a spear's length away. Along with Ishoa, she watched the Scarborn celebration.

"What?" Ishoa said.

"Dead parents don't make you an orphan. For some of us—like him—it's worse than that. Do you think the love you never had is worse than the love they willingly withhold, Highness?" Stirrma's granite chin lifted toward her mother.

Hilkka Omenfaen had finally parted from Dragga and now made her way gingerly over the slate riddled bank toward her daughter, fur-lined skirts bundled into each hand. "Or the love they reserve for those deemed worthier."

"Isha!" Wolst bellowed as he descended toward her.

Ishoa's throat burned. Numbness leeched away, leaving her skin tingling with sensation once more and her toe hot with searing pain. "Even a little love is better than none."

Stirrma scoffed. Just as her mother drew near, she stepped close, dropped her voice to a whisper. "Then you, Princess, have never felt the desperation that comes to those living in the shadow of another's glory. It is a misery only death can satisfy. Yours or theirs. Your Warnock boy knows it all too well."

"I'm an Ironlight," Ishoa said. "I was born into the shadow of my betters."

Stirrma's brow seemed to soften as she picked over Ishoa with unconcealed judgment. A smile crept up one side of the Omenfaen twin's mouth. "Then you above all should know the lengths one will go to feel worthy. Be wary of him, Highness."

CHAPTER TWENTY-SEVEN

WHAT FLIES, WHAT WORMS!

- UNTURRUS -

F lies could not enter the Corpse Gate. The ferocity of their buzzing vibrated in Thephos's ears. On the settlement side, that is. The side with Syn and Ash Backlegarm. The side with the fatherly holdguard and the bawdy priest who drank his profits. The side where the past lay.

As soon as they crossed the Corpse Gate's threshold, the flies' buzzing ceased. The sudden silence was disorienting. *I only wish my past had been silenced as well.* To keep from falling into unpleasant places in his mind, Thephos focused outwardly.

A forest should abound with activity, especially this early in the morning. Where Thephos heard stellar jays, dogs, crows, and the hum of insects a moment before, now he heard nothing. Only the scuff of the shaman's boots over stones and the panting of Ascendants. They too seemed to notice the unnatural absence, the dull throb in their ears. The white smocks of more than a few were already damp with panic-fueled sweat.

"Please, I beg you," The vacant-eyed girl clung to the white lion pelt of the plains Kurg. "I—I don't want the demons to get me. I chose wrong! Mercy!"

The shaman nodded at the female wearing the ram's skull. She stepped up quietly behind the girl and drew the foot-shaped stone chaswa from a loop of rope at her waist.

Thephos turned away.

There was a wet thud—a grunt—then the thrashing of feet on turf and a desperate sucking for air. Once her dying quieted, Thephos turned back, found the girl's life had become nothing more than a crimson blot on Unturrus's slope.

A withered, toothless old man laughed. He reminded Thephos of the old devil. Harshness spewed from the man like a geyser. "Didn't getta see the sights! Foolish girl."

The gray-haired woman rebuked the man. "She chose the only thing she could have chosen."

The withered cretin smacked lips over barren gums. "Eh? What ya mean?"

"Fate. Destiny. Divine—" the woman's soothing message ceased abruptly as the old man squatted to urinate.

"Fate and destiny. Blaggy and blarny. Divine horse shit. Divine gold in my pockets. That what they say?" He grunted out a fart. "I think what ye' mean is a stupid woman is fated te' make stupid choices."

The gray-haired woman snorted disdain and took measure of the man. "I see why you're here."

He cocked his head, grinning broadly. "Eh? Well, it'd be fuck-all amazing if you didn't seein' as I said so already. I come for the sights, ye' dumb twat."

"I grieve the mother's love you clearly were denied." The woman took notice of Thephos. "You seem a gentler soul. Why have you come?"

"I..." *I had no mother's love. Only a father's hate.* "I—uh." The sun rode high over the shoulder of Unturrus. Fir trees crowded around the Ascendants like pigs around a trough. Eagerly, they seemed to wait for the eight lost souls who remained, as if they were a bucket of slop in their master's hand. Finally, Thephos shrugged. "It seemed the only thing to do."

The woman nodded knowingly. She had the same feel about her as a Sister of the Rose. Thephos wondered if she'd been one before she became an Ascendant.

"Desperation. Escape from the trap of a life lived in pain. I've studied every book I could find on Unturrus, and what you describe is a common malady for those who seek awakening."

Thephos wasn't so certain he described anything like that. Still, he wanted to be polite no matter his circumstances. His father's fury had often ignited at poor manners—except for his own, of course. "Why have you come?"

She pounced on the question like she'd been waiting to be asked. "To save the world! I will gain the power to heal others and serve as a boon to every person of every nation. The eradication of sickness—even death. The fear of dying motivates humans and Kurgs alike to commit to a life of scarcity and atrocity. I will end that."

The head of the Kurg cloaked in crow feathers from the river enclave snapped to attention. If Thephos had to guess, he thought it might be because the woman separated humans and Kurgs into different categories.

The woman, however, missed the affront. She bent to pat the earth fondly, like a lover. "If Unturrus deems me worthy of such power, which I hope she does, the Mother will help me bring peace to the world."

Thephos nodded. *If this woman had seen what my father did, would she think he deserved peace too?*

The Kurgish shamans beckoned the eight Ascendants to follow. As they went, the healer woman talked with whoever would speak to her. Thephos was grateful for the woman, Radea, for stirring up conversation; it distracted him from darker ruminations.

Being in the company of so many people was an odd thing.

In eighteen years of life, Thephos hadn't known anyone well outside of his father or brothers—and them sparingly. Even his mother was a hazy specter in his memory. All of them were born in Carthane, and all but Thephos were like to die there.

The other Ascendants came from all across Namarr. Each had different reasons for deciding to make the one-way journey.

A young unimist monk named Olthr wished to join the Dominarri. Like Radea, he'd dedicated his life to studying Unturrus.

A caramel-skinned crabber from the island of Kania had a lethal disease that caused him endless pain. "A pain I'll conquer or see ended."

A quiet, brawny Anjuhk woman with a scarred face wanted power so she could torture and kill her violent husband.

Having already questioned the old man and Thephos, Radea only had the Word-fox and one other left, but the Anjuhk woman's answer muzzled any further conversation.

Hours passed before anyone spoke again.

They stopped for a rest.

The Wordfox's outraged pleas shattered any chance of it being a peaceful one.

The lion pelt of the plains shaman jolted as he pulled at the fox mask clutched in the poet's hands.

Screaming like a teenage girl, the Wordfox leaned back with all his might. "It's mine!" Spittle flew from attenuated lips as he whined and snarled, his pinched together eyes as black and hard as obsidian. "You cannot take it!" Gone were the lavish words and elegant tones.

The Kurg remained stoic. In the way he held tight the mask with one hand, while pressing the haft of his spear lengthwise into the Wordfox's narrow chest with his other, it was clear who was the stronger of the two—and by a wide margin. The crow-cloaked shaman approached and attempted to pry the Wordfox's spidery fingers back.

The river shaman grunted as the Wordfox snapped forward, biting down on the Kurg's fingers with crooked, graying teeth.

The mountain shaman drew her chaswa. This time Thephos forgot to look away. Instead of bludgeoning the gray mushroom cap of frizzy hair, the Kurg brought her club down on the center of the mask, cracking it in two.

"No!" the Wordfox fell to his knees, fumbled the pieces. "No! No! No!"

"It is forbidden," barked the plains shaman.

"I don't give a damn about your savage customs," hissed the Wordfox. He regained his feet, fists balled at his sides. He pointed at the fox mask. "You'll all die for that."

The shamans shook their heads.

At nightfall they approached a contiguous ledge of stone nestled on the slopes like some ancient, weathered crown. There was little possibility of Thephos climbing it, so he hoped there was a path through.

"Sleep," said the shaman with the feathered cloak.

"Take this," said the one with the lion pelt.

He proffered a handful of thin, twisty roots to each Ascendant, and each of them took a shred, chewed it, then chased the bitter flavor down with a gulp from their waterskins.

The Wordfox refused. Lying on one side in the dirt, he chewed the root a moment and then spit it back at them. The plains shaman eased down into a crouch before the Wordfox, menacingly slow. Corded muscle rippled across the holy man's haunches. "Eat it or I smash out your teeth."

With hatred unbridled, the Wordfox complied and popped a tiny root in his mouth. The shaman placed his club under the Wordfox's chin. "Chew." The Wordfox jerked his face away but did as commanded, eyes locked with the shaman's.

Stars wheeled overhead. Thephos felt drowsy. The light of the stars became fuzzy...fuzzier by the second. The stars bled into streaks of glittering paint whenever Thephos turned his head from side to side. Others, too, must have felt similar effects. One by one, they drifted to their sides beneath the stone overhang in an attempt to grasp some sense of stability. The Kurgish shamans remained standing. Silent sentinels.

Watching.

By morning, the Kurgs were gone.

The creak of fir trees swaying in the wind greeted the waking Ascendants. The Wordfox too had disappeared. Some thought him taken by the shamans. Thephos thought he'd just woken first and wandered off.

Groggy and disheveled, they rose and set about finding a path through the crown of stone.

Or, as Olthr identified it, the Cusp.

Beyond what most already knew of Unturrus—Awakened and their powers, godsthorn and its use as a drug—Thephos knew very little of what occurred during ascent. Thankfully, Olthr and Radea knew everything there was to know about the Mountain of Power.

"They always leave at the Cusp," said Radea.

Olthr nodded. "From this point on, the strength of godsthorn increases tenfold. And..." The young monk exhaled slow, attempting to calm panic. "...the demons appear."

Some of them, like Thephos, were unmoved, while others' knees shook beneath their smocks.

I wish for a quick death and a quicker departure from the stains left by the old devil. A thread of anger arose at the injustice of needing a demon to kill him so his father's contempt might cease. He recoiled from it, back into the comfort of the numb, hollow place.

They searched for a path through the Cusp and onto the demons' doorstep like worms willfully seeking the mouths of fish.

The Kanian crabber found a narrow tunnel with a sphere of daylight at its end. Mist swirled around them as they filed through. Thephos had to bend at the waist to clear the last stretch. They stepped out onto a winding trail marked by wooden poles at intervals, each one adorned with grotesque facial carvings. A line of perfectly smooth, rounded stones ran flush alongside the trail as well. Dense forest welcomed them forward.

"We're in it now, eh!" said the toothless old cynic. His mirth resembled the warning bark of a dog than anything joyful.

Knots of steam curled about their legs as they journeyed onward. No leader had been selected, but they were humans facing death and so stayed together to await the next whim of whomever sounded most confident about where to go next.

Hours passed. Little in Thephos changed, though he realized he should be experiencing some fatigue. The fir trees thinned. The carved poles and winding line of rocks dotting their path also came with diminishing frequency.

"Wait. The sun..." The Kanian crabber blinked rapidly. "The sun hasn't moved all day."

Despite the passage of hours, it was as the man said. The departure of reality dawned on Thephos. Dread sank into his bones. He glanced back, half expecting to be greeted by the old devil's wrath-lined face, for he'd been trained to experience terror in tandem with seeing the man.

All he saw was a thick fog rolling up the mountain toward them. *It's following us...*

"Is that the gate?" said one of the men Radea had yet to question. He pointed the way they'd come. Back toward the fog, which glowed with a faint, unsettling light.

"Impossible," said the Kanian.

"No! No!" said the man. "That's the gate. The Corpse Gate. I swear to you! I see it."

"It is not the gate," said Olthr. "You're seeing an aberration."

The man cursed. "You're all fools! By the Sempyrean I'll prove it!"

He disappeared through the fog, followed moments later by his silhouette. They all stared after him without speaking. They waited.

Waiting for something...

Thephos watched the sun. It did not move.

The man did not return.

"Ack!" said the old cynic in disgust. "He's fuckin' gone."

With a somber expression, the Kanian crabber turned uphill. "Let's go."

The trail peeled away, became a steep and rocky climb. Forced to use their hands they clambered upward. Radea struggled over as others passed her, indifferent. Thephos offered her help, but she wiped sweat from her brow and huffed out a refusal.

The toothless cynic, however, asked for a boost which Thephos gave, but for which he received no thanks.

The Kanian crabber gained the crest and pulled Radea up after him without asking. She too gave no thanks. Kindness and manners, it seemed, had no place among the-soon-to-be dead.

Thephos was last to climb over. He heard their stunned murmuring before he saw the source of it. Excitement sparked in his gut. He quickened over the lip of earth. The Ascendants had spread out across a large grassy basin, a single dead tree twisting to one side at its center. The basin was ringed by hundreds of the most beautiful flower bushes Thephos had ever seen. Broad, luminous triangular petals shimmered a multitude of vibrant colors. They bloomed from gray roots an inch thick and covered in long, slender thorns. Sunset pink and orange. Indigo. A yellow more dazzling than the sun.

The Ascendant's faces, the surface of the pond, the reflections in their eyes—all lit with color. Frozen in rapture.

"Godsthorn," Radea breathed.

In all the world, there was nothing like it. A coveted resource without equal. A drink, a drug...a source of mysterious power.

No one talked about its beauty.

Throughout history, a handful of Awakened had chronicled their experiences on the Mountain of Power. Most had wildly different stories of the journey, but two things marked the account of every Awakened throughout time with deadly certainty.

One: when Ascendants encountered godsthorn, reality changed.

"Beautiful," said Radea.

"Dangerous," said Olthr. "Stay clear of it."

"Won't matter," said the toothless man. "You act like ya' expect to survive this. Enjoy some thorn before Hemgowwa the Ever-Grasping Worm gets ya', I say."

Two: godsthorn heralded demons.

Thephos looked back at sun hanging trapped in the sky. It shifted lazily, teetered a moment, then plummeted, racing toward the horizon at an incomprehensible speed.

A ringing built in Thephos's ears. His heart swelled, euphoric. An unfamiliar feeling tingled through the hollow place...

Pleasant pressure filled his face. A smile and then tears of joy devoured his confusion—it didn't matter. The others wept as well. Glistening gobs of falling tears. Falling.

Falling like the sun.

Olthr shouted his thanks. The Kanian crabber fell to his knees to kiss the earth. Radea threw her arms up and ran wildly in circles. "It's a sign! A sign we are chosen!" She stripped off her white smock and let her shriveled dugs dance freely, dark nipples standing pert before the wind.

Time seeped through their hands, a cracked cup. The world was alive. Panes of light found a loving face or a pure blossom. Color burst inside Thephos's mind, a sound so sweet he cringed with pleasure.

He giggled, the blissful resonance ushering more of the same.

Every hue imaginable twirled around their eyes. Every line of definition on his fellow Ascendants' faces made Thephos wax ecstatic. They joined Radea, removing their smocks to dance at the edges of the pond near the twisted tree.

There was a thudding in Thephos's brain. He saw a godsthorn bush as big as a tree suddenly looming over him at the center of the basin. It called to him, told him to dance, to love, to enjoy. It brought him here, called him here. He was meant to be. Meant to be here.

The voice whispered, sighed contentment.

All he felt was his body and the bodies of the others as one, leaping, laughing, crying for the sublime. His insides bulged and simmered at the intake of everything so distinct and clear.

Everything...

Moved like insects writhing in unison, their colors the color of the thing he looked upon moments before—delayed. And he stared and stared, letting the beauty and being of it all soak and bleed through into a thought deeper and more astounding than anything he'd experienced

and in many ways it called to mind his father because it was a thing imprinted, a thing so pervasive in one's memory he cannot shake it if he tried and that which is immediately summoned in the body when the mind snares it

there was a tree at the center near the pond and he went to it with Radea who would save the world beside him as well as another person he didn't know...very old...but the sun was gone...and there he was naked

so cold

the sun slid into an unreal dusk where they were a tribe of people. forever. never to part again

here for eternity—

all fake. yet the most real

his father his past his self his pain his worries the emotions and thoughts observed through eyes filtered by a singular fear...

the pervasive thought one could not escape...never escape...always trapped in fear

the true pain the anticipation of pain

he stares at a fire...darkness ringing him...the flowers and the beauty and the color all gone—

unfamiliar faces staring at him horrified with the knowing that they are horrified but unable to admit the horror in their face or the horror in the faces of others—

trapped like the sun in a loop that burns and burns and leaves them lonely in the cold

do they see the coward—a void of passion or fire or the ability to love or be angry or be anything but a worm—

he is a worm...

thephos the worm!

Wriggling in a sexy dance of confusion for demons on life's hook and a devil gone but still here...

so he finds himself lying as flat as possible on the cold ground with darkness creeping in

while someone's feet sway as if tracing the sun in the air overhead

feet circling the sun...

going in circles...

tracing the sun—the feet—telling them where the sun was in the sky but disappeared now...

gone forever

the sun—the son
only cowering faces now and they're all him—a worm
a nothing
scrimping across cold earth until still—dead
like feet swaying in the shape of suns and sons
trapped and dead nothings
nothing but dead swaying feet
only darkness now
trapped in sleep awake—but not awakened
fold into death to escape the earth—
into earth to escape death
sleep worm...sleep

Chapter Twenty-Eight

OPEN WOUNDS

M eckin swayed in the hallway, a tankard of godsbrew dangling from one finger at his thigh. The lock to Kord's door was gray and fuzzy looking—the key in Meckin's other hand too. He glanced in either direction, rocking drunkenly from toe to heel to toe. A few patrons remained in the tap room. Passed out or on their way to it. Vey had been tasked with the nightly clean up, giving him the freedom to get as drunk as he wanted.

Head cocked, he listened intently at the door. From inside, Kord's ragged breaths were all he heard. He stabbed the wood beside the lock with the key a few times, then huffed and stopped. He placed a hand against the wall, gathering himself for another attempt.

Damn. So drunk.

It was right around the time a mason with a boyish-smooth face, chestnut braids, and a disposition like curdled milk entered the tap room that Meckin had started drinking in earnest.

A bronze honor plate bearing the golden hammer and laurels of Breckenbright sat on one shoulder, marking the man as a holdguard. A soiled cloak—once white—was slung over his other shoulder. The man had stomped through the door, mud tumbling from his boots in all directions. Looking down, he'd chuckled at the mess.

He raised his porcelain face, meeting Meckin's gaze. "Sorry." He flashed a hooked smile then stomped his feet harder. Mud flew. Nearby patrons grumbled about disrespect, but they were summarily ignored.

The holdguard made straight for the bar.

Meckin poured godsbrew for the harpist. The fool grinned as the tankard slid across the board and into his talentless hand. Meckin stared at his own beneath the bar; it trembled.

He tried calming himself as the mason drew closer. His chest tightened instead as if all the air in in his chest had clogged up. Then he puffed out through pitted cheeks. His hand kept shaking as if it had a mind of its own. He cursed it.

"What do you have there?" The mason leaned onto the bar.

"Nothing," Meckin balled the hand into a fist then poured himself a drink. His throat made a loud gulch as he threw back godsbrew—drained half of it.

The mason raised an eyebrow. He looked mean with that damn hooked smile. Ready for cruelty. He watched Meckin leisurely drain the rest of the tankard.

"What's the occasion?" The holdguard scanned the crowded taproom. "I see no wedding chattel. No bride or groom. Perhaps..." The smile hooked further up his cheek as he leered at Meckin. "A funeral? I hear a boy died."

The threat in the mason's tone made the hair on the back of Meckin's neck bristle. He smacked his lips, snorted, trying to look unafraid. Meanwhile, Jennim's pale face stared up at him from the wine barrel. The image struck him in the gut like a fist. "No man needs a reason to drink. We've all got plenty." He poured another, then twisted the spigot closed, so hard it squeaked. "But since you're searching for one, I'd say listening to your boring ass is reason enough."

Menace, the relaxed kind, settled onto the man's brow. The hooked smile remained. "I've got a mighty hankering for some wine. I hear you had a barrel of Breckinbright's finest sent over earlier today. Or are you just serving yourself tonight?"

Rictus and horror framed by red hair, splayed out and floating. It looked as though time had frozen around Jennim the moment he'd meant to leap from the barrel. *The moment he'd watched his doom sealed overhead.* Meckin wondered if the last thing Jennim heard were nails hammered into wood.

"Something wrong?" asked the mason.

"Speak your peace. Then leave." Meckin curled his lip at the mason's braids. It was a common style for men of Anjuhkar but for those of Lah-Tsarra and Peladonia it was uncommon. "And take your stupid fucking hair with you."

A pang of pride rippled through Meckin as the mason's smile wilted. Running a hand over his hair, he snorted, stepped back from the bar and whipped aside his cloak. Malice twitched in the muscles around his eyes and in his fingers as they hovered over a hammer at his belt.

Sweat lathered Meckin's palms, dappled his brow.

The harpist cleared his throat. The mason shot the man a withering look, then seemed to think better of killing Meckin on the spot. He jerked his cloak back over the hammer.

Relief shuddered through Meckin.

Nostrils flaring, the mason ran a hand over his braids once more and then leaned back onto the bar. "I'll not forget that insult, innkeep. Lucky for you, I am a professional. I'd like nothing more than to turn your pouring hand into a bloody—"

"Get on with it and say what you want to say, professional." Meckin growled. His words were daggers meant to agitate. *At this rate, it'll be my fool ass in the wine barrel.*

But the godsbrew was already doing its work. He poured another tankard and then grinned mockingly as he drank it.

"We know you harbor, Kord. For that, Hyram has set aside a wine barrel just for you." The man paused, presumably to let the implication sink in. It did. Meckin was scared, but he didn't let the bastard see it. The trembling in his hand spread to his knees. His heartbeat went from trot to gallop.

"We know about the Kurg, Danuuk. We know about the Redhand brothers. The big woman has been an unpleasant surprise, but she'll be dealt with all the same. We've mustered plenty of men, but Hyram wants to make sure we've got just. The. Right. Amount." He punctuated the last word by poking a finger at Meckin's face. "So how many others does Kord have lying around?" The mason's braids fell over his steel honor plate as he turned to survey the taproom. "You see, the boy in the barrel turned out to be horribly incompetent, so we must get our own information now. Between you and me, I can't understand what Hyram wants with this shit hole town, or its shit hole people. But then I think about who Hyram is and it all falls into place. Let me put it this way, if you say your floorboards are brown and Hyram says they're red, rest assured, he'll cut your family's throat over them before he lets you be right about it. If you say the sky is blue and Hyram says it's orange, rest assured he'll set your inn on fire before he admits he's wrong."

"Oh!" The mason pushed off from the bar and snapped his fingers with a punctuated laugh. "I almost forgot. We'll also need to know where Kord's supply is. Hate to kill him and all his friends before we find out. You've got a trustworthy reputation in this town, Meckin, so if you tell us what we need to know, Hyram will have my brethren break apart the wine barrel we reserved for you. Before you give a hasty answer, I must tell you that this is the one and only time he'll make this offer. Otherwise..." The mason held the back of his hand to the side of his mouth and whispered. "...it's the barrel."

Damn your pride, Kord. But as much as Meckin blamed his friend, he understood him to the bone. There were things in life a man had to hold onto. Even if it meant death. Meckin wouldn't sell the Dregs. Not for any price.

Suddenly, Imralta stared back at him from memory. *For you though, I'd throw the first torch in a heartbeat.* He missed having someone to love. In a way, the Dregs was only a stand-in for that missing piece. Since Imralta left him, little felt right but his inn. And before her, the gaping wound left by his son's death.

He fixed the mason with an icy gaze. "No."

"You say that now, innkeep," said the holdguard. "But I suspect you might change your tune, which is why I'll be back. Hyram likes giving people time to consider."

The mason stepped back, eyes meandering the stairs leading to patron's rooms. "Do you want to know what I'm seeing right now, innkeep?"

"Given your hair, I'm guessing it ain't a mirror."

Cruel laughter. The hooked smile. Raising his hands, the mason wriggled his fingers. "Flames." He turned to go. Two more masons were mounted and waiting for him outside. They conferred then left in three different directions.

The rest of the night, Meckin cursed Kord and Jennim and the masons and Hyram. He cursed them all and drank a tankard for each. It wasn't long before he found himself outside of Kord's room, staring at the key in his hand that couldn't find the lock.

Last, he cursed himself.

Come on now, Meckin. Imagine it's Imralta.

The yearning sobered him some and brought reality into focus. Metal clicked satisfyingly into place, admitting him to Kord's room. *I'd put it in you good like that, too, Imralta. You know I would.*

All sexual thought was dashed at the smell of tangy sweat and trapped air. Meckin gagged, staggered to the window, wrenched it open.

A stool bounced off uneven floorboards as he dragged it to Kord's bed and sat. The linens surrounding the man's pale face were dark with wetness. Asleep, Kord wheezed like a dusty old crone. Meckin squinted and leaned close. His friend's lips were moving, eyebrows twitching with conflict. *A nightmare.*

The room spun. Meckin grunted, hand to his head, then gripped the edge of the bed to steady himself.

He sighed. "I ever tell you how my son died?" Of course no reply came. He nodded as he considered waking Kord, but he cursed the thought as drunken selfishness. "Sometimes in a friendship, it's natural for a man to tell another man about...ways he hurts. I know we've been friends a while, but I think we've had an unspoken agreement between us that made it work. We don't talk about the our pasts. And...well..."

When he looked at Kord he saw Jennim clawing for a way out. Meckin's trembling hand sought Kord's, but he pulled back before the touch of skin. "Shit. I wish you were awake for this." He grunted. "Ack, I know I couldn't do it if you were. I'd feel better telling you if I knew anything real about you, but our days are numbered, and there's no glory in being second to share. So I'll just say it then."

He inhaled, breath sharp against a lump in his throat. "I got my son killed."

A breeze from the open window guttered the candle beside the bed. Droplets of rain gathered on the floor in a murky pool. Tears formed in Meckin's eyes. He barreled past them.

"I ran a place called the Scarlet Queen in South Setton. An inn far more successful than this one. I was rich. Money's always come easy to me. We got a lot of Kurgs from the plains enclaves in those days, before the Great Betrayal of course. A lot of men from the Golden Silos...the House of Saud too. Despite all the money, my son was my proudest achievement. I had a daughter as well, but she took a stronger liking to her mother so we were never close. Barely talked outside a few words here and there. You know how I can get quiet.

"But my boy...anything he asked of me, I gave. I used to even let him sit on my lap when I'd go to fetch the godsbrew from the brewers. He'd make up these fanciful stories that kept me in awe to think he was mine. I gave him everything I could to keep him telling me those stories. I'd give anything to hear another."

Meckin hunched his shoulders. "Money...I gave him that especially. See Kord, when you grow up with nothing, all you think about is how you'll make sure your kids grow up with everything. For the ones we love, all we really hope for is less of the shit we suffered when we were young." Meckin looked at Kord. "Turns out that don't work. Life's got a way of 'hiding the knife' you could say. You never see it coming until it lands between your shoulder blades."

He swallowed hard. "It wasn't long before my boy was using what I gave him to buy godsthorn. Life had come so easy to him, he wanted to keep it that way. We all get the choice. Either work a whole day for only a glimmer of pride at its end or cut a purse and make the same, but with enough time to spend our days happy and high. My boy chose the latter. Over and over he chose it..."

"And I just kept feeding into it like a damn fool," Mecking growled. "I never said a word about the drugs or the thieving. It didn't take longer than a few years..."

Linens rose to meet Meckin's face as he slumped, sobs breaking from him. Kord stirred—stayed asleep. With his eyes rimmed red and puffy with unspent tears, Meckin straightened. "The Crown Justice hung him. I never saw it. Never wanted to. But that boy today—Jennim—was about the same age."

He blinked hard.

"After my son died, I decided I'd rather dig graves for the Mad Prince. I left my wife and daughter the Scarlet Queen Inn and moved to Digtown." His voice took on a lazy, matter-of-fact tone. "Saw pretty quick that the men needed somewhere decent to drink. A way to forget themselves and their pasts like you and me. Then I fell in love with Imralta. Loving the loss of her keeps me going, you know. Keeps me from feeling that untreated wound festering beneath the surface. When you've got enough pain, you start trading the lesser hurts for the greater ones despite it never changing a thing. My son's still dead—"

Jennim stared upward, haunted and pale, drowned in a sea of maroon shadows. His stricken gaze seemed to judge, to condemn, to damn.

"And I killed him!"

Kord woke, all blinking confusion. "Meckin?" Air passed through the parchment dry tunnel that was his throat. "What are you doing?"

"I killed my son," he moaned.

Kord struggled onto elbows. "Wha—are you drunk?"

Shame swallowed Meckin. "What?" his voice was gruff.

"What's happening here?"

Meckin set his jaw, tone bitter. "You lie in one of my beds questioning me? Masons prepare to kill us and burn my inn down and you question me? Some friend you are. Selfish fucking bastard."

Meckin shoved to his feet. Given the visit from the mason earlier in the night, he felt justified and cared little if Kord was baffled.

Kord coughed. "Meckin, wait. You were saying something about—"

"Look here." Frantic to end the conversation, Meckin snatched up a pitcher by the bed and flipped its contents full in Kord's face. "Your fever's broke."

After the sharp exhale and sputter, Meckin held few doubts the sick man was fully awake now.

"By the Triune God, have you lost your mind?" Rivulets of water raced down Kord's face. He swiped them and blew them from his lips.

Meckin staggered toward the door. "The only thing I'm losing is you. I want you out, Kord. Out of my inn. Out of Digtown. You're not welcome here anymore."

Meckin's heart was a stone, but even drunk he knew it might be the only way to save his friend. He opened the door.

"Wait."

Meckin paused, leaning against the door's frame to catch his breath. He swayed a moment then pressed into the inky hallway beyond.

Run, Kord. I hope you're smart enough to do that at least.

The last thing he wanted to see was his best friend's face, pale and dead, staring up at him from a wine barrel. He'd had his fill of tragedy.

CHAPTER TWENTY-NINE

ASSASSIN

At dusk on the fourth day, the fat, crawling file of Anjuhks arrived. A thick mist hid the Ice King's craggy tor from view and a heavy snow whipped cold, stinging flakes at Ishoa's face. She turned in the saddle. Five columns stretched across the blanketed white tundra, wide and never-ending, splashes of colored tabards, rippling cloth standards, jostling steel, and furs lifting in the wind. All holds combined, two thousand Anjuhks had traveled from Jarik and along the Prince's Highway to the Ice King's base.

The order to halt came, a series of horn blasts. Motion rippled down the lines of mounted knights, supply wagons, and holdguard.

The Trial of Summit was about to begin.

Ishoa's foot still ached from her injury during the Crossing, but it no longer bled, nor did it cause a limp when she walked. *I hope it doesn't slow me tomorrow. I'd like to finish higher than middle of the group.* She thought of her parents. She found it funny she wished to perform best for those who couldn't celebrate her.

Squinting through the flurries, Ishoa searched the procession for the Warnock banner. Bloody red and black came into view a moment from the very back of the winding columns.

The holds set about constructing their camps.

As night settled, the Claimants came to attention in a line, the rest of the Anjuhks encircling them. Torchlight shimmered on the brittle, snowy crust.

Arick Quinn broke from the crowd, torch in hand. He led his steed into a gallop, churning up gouts of white powder that dissipated when the gale winds caught them. The frosty-haired young knight wheeled to address them, pale face aglow. "Claimants, you have until morning to prepare yourselves. You will begin the Trial of Summit at first light." He raised his voice as high as Ishoa had ever heard it. "Heed what I now say, for your life depends on it. Tomorrow, do not leave before the sun breaks the horizon. Do not harm another Claimant. If you do, your entire hold will be responsible. The consequences will be dire. Do not return without a sentry rose. If you do any of these things I have warned against, you will have failed. You will have gained no vote at court, and your tithe will be forfeit."

His horse shook its mane, casting off droplets of condensation from steaming nostrils. "But most important of all, do not start a fire."

Silence fell over the crowd. They knew what a fire might bring to any Claimant who dared. C'Dathun trolls roamed the Ice King, hunting snow bison or preparing to raid a small village. Every decade or so, a Claimant went missing during the Trial of Summit. Sometimes, others heard prolonged screams on the wind, letting them know their missing peer had not simply fallen through ice.

"May the ancestors be with you." Torch-flame guttering violently, Arick rode back to join the masses.

Chill slithered into Ishoa's clothes as the sun sank behind the Ice King.

My parents are with me. I will succeed.

The thought didn't stick as she hoped it might. She thought back to what she'd said to Stirrma Omenfaen about being born into the shadows of her betters. Of all the Ironlights to rule, only her uncle Barodane had deviated from a path of respect. Despite his error in judgment, even he'd won the favor of most Namorites by sacrificing his own life to slay King Acramis.

I'm no fighter, no philosopher, no sage, and certainly no hero. I have the sharp tongue of my grandmother, but even that sometimes fails me.

As a Claimant, Ishoa would get no help that befit a princess. Not from the Frost holdguard. Not from the knights of Jarik, they'd been advised to let her fend for herself.

A lonely process.

I miss Rakeema. Since the Trials began, the anjuhtarg had grown irritable and jealous in response to the sudden neglect. With a heavy-heart, Ishoa had needed to give the ice tiger into the care of Othwii, who stayed behind with Belara Frost. Syphion Muul too had sought fit to remain in Jarik, along with a handful of hold ladies and lords.

Politics never rests, does it?

"I will be busy while you're gone," Othwii had said as Rakeema rubbed her body against the seneschal's knee, "But rest assured, she'll be in great care."

"Two weeks." Ishoa patted Rakeema's hindquarters. "We haven't been apart longer than a day since I got her."

A smile had fluttered across Othwii's face. "We must all make sacrifices if we are to grow."

Ishoa strode past a pair of knights stationed outside her tent. Come morning, she'd have no more protection.

She checked her pack and waterskin for tears, as well as the rest of her pack: a wheel of hard cheese, five strips of smoked perch, and a half loaf of bread, one of those given to the duchess by Golthius Narl. An extra wolf pelt, wool socks, and fox fur gloves were essential given the bone-shattering cold she knew would meet her high on the Ice King's slopes.

The roll of treated walrus skin meant to hold a sentry rose was small enough to fit in a pocket. Ishoa imagined herself kneeling before her grandmother, the azure flower alighting her palms. Triumph and honor for her family, a duty to her country fulfilled, and best of all, a sense of worthiness to bear the Ironlight name.

As she lay down to sleep, her imagination shifted to darker possibilities.

Stepping through false-ice and earning a wet leg...building a fire to fight off the deep cold and certain death. Manlike silhouettes with hungry faces and crude weapons...waiting just beyond the fire's light.

She pulled her sword closer, cradling it tight where Rakeema should be. Her heart kicked at her breast bone. *I have to focus on better outcomes.* But her heart only raced faster as images of danger and death flitted around her mind, birds of prey hunting mice.

She begged for more courage, more wisdom, more control. When that didn't help, she cursed herself to sleep. *For once, I wish to feel courage like an Ironlight should!*

In the middle of the night, she woke to howling wind against her tent. Her name was absent. Empty. She knew only the full-bodied lightening of fear. A foreboding chill running through bone and blood and flesh.

She slept none and waited for dawn.

Tundra sparkled with the morning's first light. Lazy mist rode the faintest wind currents. Ishoa slung her pack over a shoulder and made her way through camp. Wolst waited at the edge of their camp with a pair of Jarib knights and a host of holdguard who saluted her as she went.

Halfway across the glimmering white plain, she spotted Yurm Kon. They waved at each other, left trails of divots on their way to meeting. Belara Frost had advised Ishoa to partner with the Claimants of their staunchest allies, primarily Yurm Kon and the Omenfaen twins.

"Greetings, Yurm."

His face contorted into a panoply of nervous twitches, as if he didn't know whether to smile, scowl, or relax. His eyes were everywhere but on her. "Yes hello...Princess." He drew himself up, puffing his chest out. Skinny as he was, it shocked her how tall he was.

Taller than Dragga, but a strong wind would blow him off the mountain like a dead leaf.

"Have you picked a path yet?" She glanced around. "I thought we might work together."

Unalor Bog approached, the Narl boy in tow. The first grinned at her like a fool. The second stared vacantly from beneath a thick, singular brow.

Bile rose at the back of Ishoa's throat.

"You're coming with us, Princess?" Unalor's sparsely haired upper-lip somehow defied the cold with a sweaty sheen. It stretched into a grin. "I'm okay with that, so long as you don't startle at every moaning wind and creaking tree."

"How hilarious." Ishoa gave a fake smile. "It wasn't your hawk that scared me in the High Hall, it was your verminous face come too close."

A crease formed at the center of Unalor's forehead. He blinked dumbly, stabbed a finger at the air as he brewed up a retort. Yurm placed a hand on the heavier boy's chest. "Best to let it go. You look foolish as it is."

The boy from Shadowheart shoved off Yurm's willow arm. "Fuck off, Worm." Nevertheless, he kept his mouth shut, which surprised Ishoa. Yurm seemed a decent young man despite his physical weaknesses. Typically, when one such as Yurm Kon found the company of boys like Unalor and the dead-eyed Narl, they were more likely to be the recipient of harshness rather than a defacto leader.

"You think you can talk to us however you want because of your blood?" The voice of the Narl boy was hollow as a gutted log, and it sent a stab of dread into Ishoa's belly. A set of fat lips and a fat mop of dark hair, cropped on the sides and left long in the back, made him look more overgrown grub than human. Whether he grinned or glared, the area around his eyes stayed eerily the same.

"Gestryn..." Yurm cautioned as Gestryn stepped toward Ishoa.

"My name is Sweet Ges. Say it right, Worm."

Despite the heavy pack on Ishoa's shoulders, she drew them back and straightened. "Gestryn Narl, you—"

"Sweet Ges," he corrected.

Rather than back down, Ishoa stepped to meet him, her nose mere inches from his own. His breath smelled like fish. "Sour Ges. Bitter Gee. Rancid Ges. I give little damns what flavor you demand your name follows. I don't know why you deem me worthy of your menace, but it stops now. Or I'll have you thrashed."

"Do it yourself." The wetness of his lips made a gentle plop as he savored the last word. "Bitch."

Unalor glanced furtively at his feet. Yurm stepped between Ishoa and Sweet Ges. "Stop this, please." He turned to Sweet Ges. "You—you have to leave."

"It's fine. Keep company with this slug." Ishoa curled her lip. "I'll find my own way."

Sweet Ges's laughter dogged her as she traveled parallel with the tree line. She ascended the western slope. Most chose the more direct path straight up the southern.

Once out of sight from the trio, she picked her way up a steady incline. *Alone it is. Like always.*

The first rows of trees came and went...

A hand shot out, caught her wrist. Her assailant jerked her into an embrace, and an icy hand clapped over her mouth.

"Ishoa," a voice said.

In an attempt to get free, she drove into her feet and arched her back, but the hold was too strong. She fumbled for her blade—

"Cousin!" This time familiarity edged the voice. She ceased her struggle. Slowly, he released her mouth.

She licked her lips, breathless, then massaged her mouth. "Arick...what are you doing? This isn't allowed."

With a hood pulled over his head, her cousin's telltale white braids were covered. Palm pressed against a tree trunk, he looked back toward the camps. Claimants were at various stages of ascent. Most had made it to the Ice King's heavily forested lower reaches.

"I come with an urgent warning. Trust no one. When your life is on the line, you have no friends. You must be prepared to save yourself at all costs. And beware that one." Arick indicated a red-maned figure cutting a trail from the distant Warnock encampment.

Lodaris...

"Othwii has sent word. There's reason to suspect there may be an attempt on your life. Steer clear of Lodaris. He is confused—manipulated. A dangerous pawn."

Ishoa eyes went wide, her jaw slack. "But...he wouldn't."

Arick continued, tone matter-of-fact. "Keep your blade close, Isha. Trust none but the Omenfaens."

Without another word, he glided through the shadows, silent as a wraith, absent the crunch of snow under booted foot. For a few long seconds, she watched him weave between the trees. Then he slid behind one and never emerged. Gone. She turned, spotted Lodaris in the distance as he reached the Ice King's southwestern slope. He would be close. But not too close.

I don't believe them. Lodaris wouldn't do that. He couldn't.

Tears welled. Sobs worked their way through her chest. She threw out her palm for support. Frustration formed her hand into a claw, nails dragging and scoring the bark.

Othwii's words scraped the back of her mind. *Information is the shield...knowing your enemies, the killing blade.*

"I don't understand." She sniffled. "I don't understand at all."

She gave a meek exhale, breath preciously scarce, then adjusted her pack with a shrug. *I have a sentry rose to acquire and a duty to fulfill.*

She turned to go...and nearly collided with Dragga Omenfaen's chest.

CHAPTER THIRTY

THE MADNESS

A scream jerked the worm that might be Thephos from his stupor. He sat up, shivered, cast about. There was a disconnect, a lag in time he now occupied—alert without yet being conscious.

Seeing before comprehending.

Feeling before knowing.

Nothing before being.

His smock lay in a soiled pile just out of arm's reach. Others too now crawled or slunk toward their tattered clothing, shame-faced and wary, the horror of unreality still clinging to them. Thephos knew the garb well; it was not the kind one casually removed.

I have worn it all my life.

The five remaining Ascendants sat on logs surrounding the corpse of the cynical old man. Overlooking the pond, he hung from a tree, purple lips twisted into a leering grin around an outstretched, blackened tongue. Blood-rimmed eyes bulged, unflinchingly staring down at an angle.

Olthr wretched. Thephos too felt his gut turn. The body was bloated as if it had been there far longer than a night.

"How?" Radea gulped. "How did he get up there?"

"Where did he get rope?" asked the Kanian.

Thephos shook his head. "Does it matter?"

"Maw Eternal...I...I'm not sure if *we're* still here." The Kanian stared into his callused hands. Hands once used to catch crabs, to tangle them in rope nets before killing them. "Are we...already dead?"

Thephos's heart skipped. He shared the fear but refused it with a slow inhale. "I think I'm here. Alive. The godsthorn is still working out of our system. That's all...I think."

Radea wept with relief. "Thank the gods. Thank the gods." She trembled, sucking in ragged breaths.

The bronze-skinned crabber wasn't persuaded. "You sure?" He whipped his hands in the air like a cat flicking water from a paw.

"No," Thephos said. "I only know the ground is beneath my feet, the sky over-head, and my lungs full of air. Anything else, I'm only guessing."

Olthr added his worry to the fray. "What if we were killed and can't remember? What if we are in the Abyssal Sea right now, trapped eternally in our own fear and suffering?" He started to cry hysterically.

Eager to move on from the conversation, Thephos stood and donned his smock. The old man's corpse twisted gently in the wind. "We—ah—shouldn't linger here."

"What about him?" said the Kanian crabber. "We should say a few words."

"Did anyone know his name?" said Radea.

The scarred Anjuhk woman stepped close to the dead cynic, fists balled at her sides. She studied him as if his existence had been a great injustice of the universe. As if hate were a wish, a magic thing capable of killing.

Like my father looked at me.

The crabbed gaped at his hands. "How do I know any of this—or any of you—is real?"

Radea approached him, paused, then slapped him. "How's that?"

He touched the fast-forming welt, pulled his hand back to stare at it, then touched his cheek again. "Thank you."

Through tears, Olthr said, "I can say a prayer, if you don't mind—"

"Not for a man like him." The Anjuhk woman spit in the old, dead cynic's contorted face. Foamy specks dappled a gleaming eye while the bulk of it oozed down a sunken cheek. "Bastard. Woman-hater. He got what he wanted. He gets to see the sights now. Forever."

They followed Thephos around the pond. Some raced ahead of him on frantic legs, as if eager to find a place to relieve themselves. Others moved ponderously, yoked to the contemplations of a life full of regrets and a death near at hand.

Olthr fell in beside Thephos. "They say the visions can come and go from this point on without warning. I've never..." He wrung his hands. "I've never seen anything like that."

"I have." Radea walked a dozen paces behind them. "To prepare for the journey, I regularly used godsthorn to ascend. Hallucinations, enhanced senses, a feeling of godlike power. The unfolding of emotional pain too."

The woman who sought to save the world watched her step as she went, ragged hair shielding her face. "Godsthorn takes what is already there and makes it real. The process is not too discerning. It could be the best day of your life and a foul smell could invite an onslaught of heinous visions." She stopped. "But last night...that was more potent than any journey I've had. A great deal more potent. Locastrii talks about godsthorn being stronger on Unturrus's slopes." Radea covered her face and wept, chest jolting. "What a fool I am. I could never have prepared."

The Kanian, Olthr, and the Anjuhk walked on ahead, leaving Thephos to wait for Radea. After a moment, she patted his shoulder in thanks. "Can I tell you something that I do not wish the others to hear?"

Thephos cocked his head.

"I feel I made a mistake coming here. After last night, I..." Her weeping redoubled. "I worry I've lost faith in myself."

They started walking.

Anything faith-based was a fool's endeavor from the start. It was the one subject he and his father had agreed on. To Thephos and his brothers, their father was a living testament that the Triune God of unimists or the Sempyrean gods were nothing more than a game the rich played to mislead the poor. He'd never found any safety in gods, nor good fortune for doing right. There was only luck and a lack of it. Some people had mothers who loved them. Others had fathers who killed them.

Such was life. A godless world. People's foolish faith in it was unearned. "You really believed you were going to be Awakened?"

A half-hearted smile came and went. She sniffled. "I've done everything the books said to do, just as they said to do it. But I can't shake the feeling of last night. I thought I'd be ready...if I died. Seeing that bastard in the tree though...I saw myself. I saw that he deserved it, even felt gratitude for it to be him dead because of the way he spoke to me. But mostly because it wasn't me. I do think he deserved it, but maybe we all do."

"I've never thought about it as something deserved." If it was deserved, Thephos's father would have hung long ago. *He never would have died peacefully in his sleep. Death skips the deserving all too often.*

Radea fell silent until they caught up with the rest of the Ascendants. The mood was lighter than the morning. Olthr managed a smile and attempted to engage in conversation with the Anjuhk. The Kanian crabber chuckled every so often as he listened to them.

They mask their true feelings.

They used each other as distractions. A weak attempt at returning to what felt normal. Thephos didn't blame them. It was human to desire distance from the terror from that morning or the imagined terrors lying in wait ahead. Luckily, Thephos was only a worm. He saw through it all.

Whenever the Anjuhk woman spoke, Olthr glanced back at the rest of the group, lips counting their number. Between chuckles, the Kanian crabber stared at his hands, brow knitted in puzzlement. The Anjuhk spoke flatly, resigned to a bitter fate. Radea retreated into silence, an island of barely held together fears.

They walked for what seemed hours. Again, the sun did not move. Oddly, Thephos felt neither ache nor strain in his legs. On the Prince's Highway, he had stumbled into camp at the end of each day exhausted and malnourished. On Unturrus, they traveled at an incline for just as long, yet he never tired.

Just when he was about to bring up the oddity, they sighted a waterfall. Thephos wandered last into the basin.

The Kanian crabber ducked under the falls, then shook the excess water from his gray streaked hair and beard with forced enthusiasm. "There we go!" He looked at his hands, his expression slowly melting from satisfaction to doubt. "No...yeah there. There we go. That's right. That's right." He flexed his hands, lip twitching into a grin.

After filling his waterskin, Thephos sat on a waist-high rounded stone, one of many covering the rocky shores on either side of the stream. The falls pounded steadily into a shallow pool, then trickled away beneath overhangs of clustered deadfall. Tranquil forest stretched out in every direction.

If they were anywhere else but Unturrus, it might have been a pleasant place to stay.

Seated on a stone near the waterfall's base, the crabber muttered, "That's right. That's right," under his breath, alternating between smiling and frowning.

Olthr stood—the only one of them to do so. He paced the stream's edge. "I didn't want to scare you all but I must be honest, yes, I must. That's who I am. An honest man." He glanced furtively about. "So here it is. I saw a dark robed...man. A bit ago, in the trees, I saw him. He had a white face and carried some kind of blade."

The Kanian crabber looked at his hands, laughed. "You're seeing things, fool. Just the godsthorn." He pointed at Thephos, studied his finger in the air, voice falling to hushed tones. "Like he said."

"I saw him!" Olthr sucked in quick breaths. "Every time I looked. I saw him. I saw him!"

"Olthr be calm." Radea surveyed the woods, wetting nervous lips. "The godsthorn vapors haven't cleared your system. It can take time to adjust. Rest easy now."

Rest easy? There is nothing to rest easy about. They lie to themselves to feel safe.

Growing up in Thephos's home, life was full of truth. Truth so harsh and brutal, none escaped it. Unturrus was no different. It stunned him how comfortable he'd become, how fearless he was in the face of impending death. He never imagined his upbringing might prepare him so well for something like the Mountain of Power.

Olthr gave a nervous chitter, then forced a guffaw. The trees swayed with a sudden gust. "Maybe you're right. Just the godsthorn." He chewed his fingernails. Watched the shadowed woods. "Thank you...friend. Wise woman, you are."

Thephos wondered if they were truly friends. Syn Backlegarm was the only one he'd ever had. A pang of sorrow made Thephos wince. *I wonder what it would have been like to have a friend for a while.*

Color drained from Olthr's face as he went rigid. Like a landed fish, he gulped for air. "I—I swear to you, I just—just saw him."

All eyes turned the direction he stared. The skin on the back of Thephos's neck stiffened. River stones clacked against one another underfoot as he and Radea stood.

"Oh, it's a *him* now," the Kanian crabber laughed as he dragged palms down his cheeks. "That's right. That's right. There they are. I feel them now."

The collective desire for Olthr's stalker to be fake pushed its way through Radea. "You saw all this through the trees? That's keen eyesight considering no one else saw anything."

"Where is he now?" asked the Anjuhk.

"I—I don't know. I see him and then he's gone. Just disappears."

"Liar," the Anjuhk scoffed.

"Maybe he did see someone," said Radea. Something about the way she wrung her hands told Thephos she knew more than she let on. "The man who went into the fog. Do you remember the man who thought he saw the gate? We haven't seen him since—"

"He said black robes," the Kanian crabber snarled. "A white face."

The Anjuhk stood. "Was this man running as if to catch up with us?"

Olthr stammered. "He—he wasn't running. He was walking alongside us like..." The unimist monk trembled violently. "...a wolf stalking sheep."

"It's okay," said Thephos, "Breathe, Olthr."

The energy around the tiny falls and runoff creek was palpable. Racing horrors so thick it choked the back of Thephos's throat. Since the night before, with the godsthorn, Thephos vaguely realized that he *actually* felt the other members of the group. He felt their fear now as clearly as his own. Olthr shook violently. The rest searched the woods for a sign of their imagined stalker.

The Anjuhk stepped toward Olthr. Her shoulders were so broad they stretched the fabric of her white smock. "What are you doing?" Hard eyes trained on the monk.

Olthr balked. "What do you mean?"

Chin jutting, fists clenched, she growled, "You know you didn't see anything, so why are you lying?"

Rock clattered as Olthr backpedaled. They drew a collective breath, as if the sudden sound might summon a demon down upon them at any moment.

"I'm sorry. Maybe you're right." Olthr shook his head, then stared at the ground. "Truly, none of you are seeing him?"

If any of them were brave enough to go in search of the figure, they did not show it. When Thephos was a boy, fear set the tempo, confining his actions, limiting his words, his thoughts, his feelings. Only when the old devil had died was there any kind of reprieve.

Now it all came rushing back, more terror than he'd ever managed. More than just his own.

Maybe I'm going mad.

Death was an end to the suffering. Madness though seemed the opposite. Madness dangled from the strings that the hands of suffering controlled. He looked at his palms, saw traces of luminescence, as if spirits haunted them.

He looked up. The Kanian crabber watched him, bronze skin pulled tight into a mean sneer. "That's right. That's right," he mumbled, laughed, looked away.

Thephos crossed his arms, hiding his hands in his armpits.

The sun suddenly disappeared, leaving them in the gloaming gray before nightfall. Wide eyed silence followed.

Something was coming. They felt it.

Radea broke. Tears streamed around the fists pressed to her open mouth.

We are going mad.

The Anjuhk woman stumbled back and landed hard on her ass. Radea screamed. Panic shot through Thephos, pinning him in place. Slowly, he craned to look back over his shoulder...

A figure wrapped in black robes materialized behind him, close enough to touch. Thephos's insides went icy cold. He shook so hard his jaw hurt.

The face of the creature that would kill him burned into his mind. Lips the color of coal split into an unnaturally wide and lecherous grin, exposing sharpened teeth poking from black gums. It loosely resembled a man, but it was nine feet tall and with skin whiter than driven snow. Wisps of ashen hair, like spider legs, clung above his ears and to the back of his skull. Folds of pale flesh sagged beneath engorged eyes.

The demon's tongue wormed over glistening black lips as it stared at Thephos.

"It's the Madness!" screamed Radea.

Olthr fell to his knees, summoning faith. "Triune God save us."

It brandished an onyx sickle in clawed hands. Thephos locked eyes with the creature. When the Madness rested the tip of the sickle against Thephos's forehead, he felt a bead of blood race down the bridge of his nose, tickling his upper lip.

Thephos felt suddenly warm. Calm even. *Peace awaits.*

His final wish before he died was to go some place other than wherever his father had gone.

Vaniton's Gasp was too much to hope for.

The blade gleamed menacingly in the twilight as it rose overhead. *This will have to do.*

The Madness's cruel, wild laughter echoed around the falls, severing whatever shreds of courage remained to the gathered Ascendants.

Thephos sighed.

The sickle descended.

CHAPTER THIRTY-ONE

DISTANT, THE SOUND OF FIRE

S tars glittered, the scattered embers of a kicked fire. It was, Barodane realized, the first night he'd spent in Digtown with a mind clear of godsthorn.

Fourteen years...by the Triune God has it been that long?

Behind him, the front door of the Dregs creaked in the wind. The serving girl, Vey, moved to close and lock it for the night. He stared past her to the man draped in the ruddy glow of the hearth—Meckin.

A lump formed in Barodane's throat. Meckin's words tumbled through him. *The only thing I'm losing is you. You're not welcome here anymore.*

After Meckin had doused him, Barodane changed his clothes then went downstairs on unsteady feet. Meckin knew he was there but kept his back turned, face deep in his cups. A poignant gesture, Barodane thought. *He was right about the fever breaking though.* Barodane suspected the worst of his sickness had passed sometime earlier in the night.

Vey spotted him staring and waved a meek goodbye. The door to the Dregs closed with a click, locking Barodane out of Meckin's life. Forever if the man was lucky.

You should lose everyone and everything. Like we did.

Gray light haloed the horizon to the east. Barodane stepped into the mud and circled around the back of the Dregs to the stable.

He coughed. The sound of phlegm breaking up in his chest was a welcome one. His fever had broken, and he felt markedly better, though it might still be days before he was back to normal.

He slid open the stable door. Within, a stable boy slept soundly on a pile of straw. Mildew and the scent of horse hung thick.

He surveyed the line of horses from the entryway. A shrill whinny came from a scrawny palfrey belonging to the harpist. *You and your master share a gift for splitting ears.*

A horse of his own huffed gouts of steam in the stall beside it. It wasn't his riding preference; that honor belonged to his once-dead mount, Scab, in the other stable. But if he didn't take this one, he knew Meckin might wake up, still drunk, and sell it. After all, there was a precedent. Whenever a patron caused damages to the Dregs or hurt one of the serving girls, Meckin exacted a hefty price from the perpetrator. Usually that meant locking them out of their rooms and selling their possessions.

Such a loyal man.

The idea of losing Meckin made Barodane sick to his stomach and brought with it images of Garlenna and Kaitos. *Is it my fate to relive the past at every turn?*

His hand balled into a fist at his side as he considered returning to the Dregs, kicking the door down, and telling Meckin everything. *I am the Mad Prince, Barodane Ironlight. The Arm of Solicerames. Son of the Ardent Heart. Heir to the Crown of Namarr.*

Raising his fist, he studied it. He'd not held the sword engraved with Danath's pledge in fourteen years. The last line read, "Let us live, boldly and without fear."

A hand that slaughtered innocents! Never hold it again! A wave of nausea flooded him. He stumbled, one palm pressed against the stabbing feeling in his temple while the other found purchase against the stable wall. He drooped, barely managed to keep his feet. *Yes, tell him, fool. Tell the entire city. You laid the foundation of bones that built this place. Their misery is their's, but the fault will forever be yours.*

"No." He labored to breathe. A part of him was ashamed for rebuking the voices. Another was angry. "You're wrong." He grit his teeth and doubled down. "They have a choice."

He waited, expecting a cascade of derision for speaking out against the dead. When none came, a void of discomfort grew at the pit of his stomach. A silence completely unfamiliar.

Fourteen years...

Without Meckin or Tyne, he never could have made it so long.

Meckin's voice crashed through his memory. *I killed my son.* The words hung in his mind like dense fog. When he'd first woken to his friend's sobs, he thought himself dreaming. The prickling energy of the admission, however, shook Barodane to the roots. Sorrow opened him, fell like a hammer against an embittered and brittle soul. *I killed a boy too. Not just Jennim. The boy at the Rainy Meadows chapel. Yet here I am, a worthless cur.* So much of who he was lay buried in the shame of misdeeds. Rotted under earth and stone in the barrow hills.

Barodane slipped through the shadows past the sleeping stable-boy. He hushed his horse as he saddled it.

Outside, the veil of night diffused. Dawn blossomed by the minute. The cover of dark wouldn't last much longer.

I need to find a place to lay low.

The horse's neck was soft. He spoke in soothing tones as he patted it. "Sorry I've not seen you in a while. I should have paid the boy to ride you more. I pray everything still works."

"I've prayed much the same for you."

Barodane whirled to his right, hand reflexively gripping the hilt of the dagger strapped across his chest.

"Many times I've prayed." Garlenna stood beside the stable's entrance. "Because if you don't mean to ride out of town with me right now, you're going to need the might of the Sempyrean to survive what comes."

Waning moonlight shimmered in her piercing blue eye. He looked away, his cloak feeling as heavy as iron. *Why must anyone care about me? Why must good people foolishly throw their lives at my feet? There is no justice!*

"While I admire your dedication as much as ever, I hoped you would have given up by now," Barodane said. She stepped closer. The horse's hot breath warmed the air beside their faces as it sniffed her. *I don't want to lose any more friends. One was enough.*

The horse flicked its head, sidestepped. With a soothing hand and low hushes, he calmed it.

"Where did you bury it?" She gestured at his sword, noting the fact he didn't carry the blade of his heritage.

"If I tell you, you'll dig it up."

"It is not mine to dig up. That burden is yours and yours alone."

"You think you know my burdens?" Barodane scoffed. "Have you ever thought for a moment that I did not wish to be born a prince? Who could know what it is like but a handful of souls across the span of decades? It is a poison without antidote that few taste. And it corrupts those it doesn't send to an early grave."

"Like your father and brother?"

A cool breeze rifled his hair. The stable door shrieked on rusty hinges. His horse jolted, raised its head, nostrils flaring as it inspected the various scents of dawn.

Garlenna was stoic. "And when Hyram Olabran's masons take you and torture you or kill you, what then?"

"I'll probably be dead." Barodane pointed at the barrow hills a half mile off. "So long as it's here, where *they* can see it, I'll do so happily."

She raised an eyebrow. "And what if it is Meckin they torture and kill?"

Barodane hesitated. His own death wish came from a desire to escape a doom-swept past. *I killed my son.* "No one is innocent."

"Do you care for anyone but yourself? You once loved Omari, yet you've not asked how she fares since you abandoned her."

Barodane shrugged to disguise the hurt. At the time of his father's and brother's death, he'd been engaged to Omari D'Alzir. What happened to her after, he'd made sure not to know. He still loved her, his heart aching at mere mention of her name. "It was for the best. Her best. Yours and mine too."

Calm, granite in motion, Garlenna stepped so close their toes almost touched. "For the best?" Her silhouette was darker than the night sky and blotted out hundreds of stars. Barodane frowned.

She hushed his horse, patted its neck.

She turned a cold eye on him—her fist followed.

The world exploded. A deluge of shimmering light. Numbness washed over Barodane, left little else. Ears ringing, he sensed himself stumbling backward, limbs flapping uselessly like a marionette with its strings slashed. He dropped and skid across the ground within the stable. Mud and straw piled around him, stalks jabbing at his fingers and cheeks. His head lolled as he fought to sit up all wooden, jerky, and non-compliant.

Before he could gather his senses, Garlenna was pinning his arms to the earth with her knees. "Surely, you dream and I must do what I can to wake you. It's for the best."

Slaps thudded against Barodane's cheeks. Not the stinging slaps of a maiden either. These were hands that had broken the strongest of men. After the first two, the world teetered on the edge of the abyss. Garlenna's palms swept his face, heavier than a maul's handle, locked fingers unflinching against his jaw. Tingles sprouted on his face, the base of his skull, spread to his fingers and toes. Tingles dissolving...

His body grew distant. Filled with cotton and dust. Warmth leaked away with thoughts and left nothing.

Darkness swallowed him.

Muffled sound.

Awareness seeped back in, drip by lazy drip of it. Globs of gray light opened, became the hazy outline of two figures.

Garbled words, spoken as if underwater.

Seconds limped by. A stabbing, tingling pain in his jaw resolved as color entered his vision.

Garlenna exchanged whispered words with the stable-boy and then sent him away. She spotted Barodane stirring. He sat up as she approached and jerked him to his feet.

He winced and placed a hand against his throbbing temple. The veil of night still hung over his horse beyond the stable—he hadn't been out long. "So." He smacked his lips, tasted warmth, salt and copper, sweat and blood. "You'll pummel me into submission, then?"

"Please Barodane, I don't wish to see you die." Her tone was pleading. "What happened to you? Where is the man I loved?"

Chills crept down the backs of his arms. *Abandon, Garlenna Renwood. Abandon before it's too late.* Tightness formed around his heart. "Like I told you." He made to shoulder past her. "The prince you speak of is dead."

"Good," she said, now all harsh and cutting. "Clearly he was a fool. A man who would kill innocents to escape from his own suffering."

He whirled, fists and jaw clenched.

Garlenna scanned him up and down. "All I see before me now is a sad craven. Truly, I wish it weren't you I needed, but it is. Give me any other man capable of raising Solicerames. Give me a man worth spilling a thimble of blood for." She scoffed. "No such luck. Fate would have it different. There is only you...Kord. And I'm to muck away my final days in this filthy, woe-begotten place waiting for you to be slain. Myself along with you. A miserable charge indeed. It would have been better if you'd died like your father and brother at the Bloody Beach. Danath would spit on you if he saw you now."

Barodane shook with fury as he drew his dagger. *She's right! You're no true Iron-light. You've brought only shame to crown and country.* "You're right. Danath would see Kord."

She flung her arms wide. "Come then. If you're no Ironlight, kill me. Kord would! He has no friends. No honor." A mean smile bunched against Garlenna's cheek. "*I* will not abandon my prince. I did it once before—never again. Unless parted by death." She slapped her chest. "Slay me now and we'll be done with this! Go on being Kord. Forsake Danath. Kordin. Malath. Forsake your family. Forsake Namarr." She watched him through lank strands of auburn hair, her voice low and goading. "Kill me."

Barodane worked his jaw, heard a click. *You can end this. You can be with us forever!* He stepped forward hesitantly, his stomach a sickening stew. The dagger trembled, the hand holding it slick with sweat. Another step carried him into striking distance. Licking dry lips, he searched the straw for something to say, his grip weak as he hefted the dagger.

The faces of the loved ones Garlenna named. Tears came unbidden. He blinked them away and swallowed hard, feet rooted in place.

Garlenna let her arms fall, her voice a hush of silk covers. "The blood on my hands is the same as yours. I have sacrificed my honor—for you. I have sacrificed a thousand nights of peaceful sleep—for you. I have gone against the prosort's creed—for you. For all of that, you can't be honest with me. You can't even be honest with yourself."

"I'm sorry." The knife dropped with a thud against the hard-packed earth. "Damn! What do you want from me? What do you want me to say?"

Garlenna shot forward and grabbed him by the face. He struggled against her but her hand was like a vice, her fingers like a smith's tongs. "Gah!" he winced, jaw tender from the thrashing she'd given him.

Her lips brushed against his ear as she spoke in menacing tones. "Say the truth." She pointed his face through the open stable door toward the barrow mounds. "Say 'Garlenna Renwood speaks true. I am Kord, a cowardly, unworthy wretch.'

Renounce the Ironlight name. Forswear your father and brother." An invisible hand squeezed the breath from his chest. When he hesitated, Garlenna shook him and hissed. "Jennim. Omari. Your friends...me. Forswear us all! Condemn your niece, Ishoa. Curse Danath's name. Renounce your family!"

A shadow rose before his mind's eye and silently watched him from a thousand sets of eyes. He was trapped in this starving spider's web. Terrified, every part of him wanted to flee, but a voice he'd not heard in a long while held him fast. *If you keep running, they will never rest. You will never be free.*

"I—I can't."

Garlenna released his face. "I thought not." Her single eye met his. "Because it is *not* the truth. You are not here to honor the dead as you claim. You hate them. And every day you get to be reminded of that hate because it's better than being reminded of the pain. The pain of losing the people you loved—the ones you love still. The pain of tainting your family's name. The pain of being alone in your guilt." She stepped back and fell to a knee. "But I am here, my Prince. I will bear it with you."

Warmth flooded him, the tension around his heart bursting like a dam. He wept.

A rustle of cloth told him Garlenna stood. Then she pulled him into an embrace. "They are gone my Prince. But you are not. You are here. You think of yourself as Kord, but it's a lie. A mask you hide behind to keep you safe."

Heat rose from his collar. Sweat broke out across his skin and dampened his underclothes. "I—"

The scorn of the dead was an icy wave, a leech that burrows deeper when threatened. *You're Kord! A selfish coward and criminal! Nothing more!*

Garlenna pulled back to gaze into his tear-streaked face. "You *are* an Ironlight."

A shuttering breath escaped him.

Glass shattered—not too distant.

Somewhere someone shouted, "Fire!"

CHAPTER THIRTY-TWO

WHERE THE RIVER TURNS

I watch Akyris through the jeweled eye...

He watches me back. "You said you had a long journey, didn't you?"

The elm tree's branches stir overhead. He stares at the ground. Doubtful. Resigned. "Shouldn't I go say goodbye to Mother?"

"There's no need." I open my eyes slowly to regard him. "She'll be around."

"So we aren't going anywhere? I don't understand."

My consciousness creeps forward, tendrils of energy probing his essence in the River. I'm no expert in using my Locus in this way. Not nearly so good as Mags. Or the Arrow of Light for that matter. Nonetheless, our relationship and our shared bloodline amplifies my ability to sense Akyris's thoughts and feelings.

There is so much more to being an Awakened than a singular power.

So much more.

He's hesitant, confused, dubious. Expected. I probe more strongly—clumsily. His consciousness contracts like a stabbed muscle. He's sensitive to the unknown presence touching a part of him. A part he thought solely his own.

I don't hold back. I pierce the surface.

Slowly, trusting in me, his mind relaxes enough for us to join in the River. Together, we slide beneath the troubled waters of the surface to the smoother, denser, quieter place.

The place of truth.

He's eager. A desperate curiosity drives him. He's come to like me more than he cares to admit, and he senses my power. Where other eyes are blind and unable to pierce the veil—that sinewy layer of protection all beings must shroud themselves within—he sees many things.

For now, I only give him a sip of it.

I retract my probing energy. Akyris exhales. In the brief span of a morning, he's gone from thinking me his quirky grandmother to wondering if I am in fact a god.

I am Locastrii, Mistress of Time.

But such labels are worth less attention than the passing of grains of sand from dune to dune.

His conscious mind struggles out of the depths, eyes vacant. A thread of drool glistens on his lip in the rising sun's rays. Finally, he recovers—blinks dumbly.

"Not all journeys happen in the body. Most, you will find, happen first in the mind, then in the heart." My tone is soothing. "And then if it is your Path, then and only then, do they enter the body."

A shudder runs up his spine. "What..." He shakes, blinks again. "What was that?"

I lean forward onto my staff. "That, my boy, is where we're going. That is what we call the River."

"We?"

I wave away the question. "Forget about the 'we' for now. Just know the River is where your learning occurs. Where the answers lie."

The muscles of his prominent brow tense. "I don't even know what question I should be asking to get any answers."

I lick my lower lip. "If I were you, I'd ask, 'Most lovely grandmother, what is the River?' Just like that."

He frowns and nods. "What is the River?"

"I don't know."

A warm wind sends a dead leaf spiraling to the earth. It lifts and then falls like a horse with a broken leg fighting to stand until eventually it stills.

"Well great," he says. "If you're not going to tell me—"

"Do you need to be told everything? Do you need me to tell you that you sit on a stump? That the sun's rays warm the back of your neck? That your heart beats in your chest?"

He leans back from me. "No. I just don't know—"

"Lie," I snap. "Lying. Liar."

Eyes narrowed, he fights down frustration. I don't blame him. I'm shaking him free of what he was. The process is anything but pleasant. "Why are you being like this?"

"Like what?"

"You're being..." He hesitates, worried the door to an extraordinary future will be closed if he offends me. Fortunately, he chooses truth anyway. "...like you were before. You're being a mean old hag."

"I *am* being that way, aren't I?"

"Yeah." Anger edges his tone. "You are."

"So it is. I am being that way." I raise my chin and tap my lips with a finger. Hopefully he gets that my rude behavior is leading him somewhere. "But how do you know I'm being that way?"

There's a shift, a sudden alertness through his face and body, a wolf picking up the scent of prey. The muscles of his face relax as his Locus turns away from my abuse of him and instead seeks an answer.

He shakes his head. "I guess I know because you're doing it to *me*."

"Your guess is precisely correct." I chuckle. "Because you are the one experiencing it, it is so. It is what is true. The River is exactly that."

"The River is truth?"

I wobble my head, ears bending toward each shoulder in a back-and-forth motion. "In the broadest sense you could say that. More accurately, I would say the River lies behind a gate you need a key for. Truth *is* that key."

One of Akyris's fingers shoots into the air. "It's time!" Then, sheepish and a great deal more quietly, he adds, "The River is time."

Reaching forward, I pinch the tip of his finger and wiggle it. "Not at all."

"Oh."

"But that is an important part of the River. Time forms the foundations on which the River flows. It's the ground the gate is planted upon, the banks the River turns and travels along. It gives the River a place of being."

The last part, I sense, goes past him entirely.

"Don't chide yourself too harshly if this is lost on you. I am your teacher here, the one responsible for your learning. If you lack understanding, the blame is shared. Let's save time for another day. Next question."

Arms crossed, he taps a finger against his bicep a while, then says, "So what *is* the River?"

"The River is the flow of conscious reality." I let the words sink in. I want him to look for the River when we're not together. I want him to see it in everything he interacts with. So I repeat the most important thing he'll ever hear. "The River is the flow of conscious reality.

"The flow of conscious reality is formed by experiences, both individual and shared. One creates all. All creates one. Think of your life as being a jewel. Each plane reflects light in a single, unique direction, whereas all planes together create a unified perspective—the jewel itself. Without the adjoining planes to support it, there can be no single plane. Even if you were to crush the jewel, over and over into smaller pieces, the variety of planes would still exist, but only ever as part of a whole. One creates all. All creates one."

A slight twitch between the brows tells me he's lost. He nods with conviction in an attempt to act like he understands. He doesn't. I see through the bluster.

Looking at the roots of the elm, I notice a web glistening with morning dew. "Here. Think of life as a great web, and each of us as a single strand."

He takes in the web strung between exposed roots. Its spider is nowhere to be seen.

"A web works poorly to keep the spider alive if it doesn't have all the strands necessary to hold it together," I say. "Such is the River. Our conscious reality is a series of individual strands holding together an immense shared web. The one we call life."

A fly swims through the air overhead with aimless enthusiasm and attempts to alight on Akyris. The boy swats, misses, sends the fly hunting for tamer places to land.

"Grandmother—should I call you that or...?"

"That's fine. Locastrii works as well. But call me Granny and I'll thrash you." I shake my fist.

Akyris laughs. A fleeting thing. "Aren't I already a part of conscious reality? Why would I need to train for it?"

My whole body shakes with laughter. "Like most people, I would say, 'barely.' The majority go their whole lives being swept along by the River, unwitting and without agency. Awakened and some few others learn to swim against the River's current and touch its power. A rarer breed still have grasped how to stand in the River at will and let its waters rush past them. You, my boy, will do the last."

"Me? How?"

With a groan, I rise. "That's enough for one day. Might I suggest sitting in silence for a while to consider all I've told you. We'll pick up bright and early tomorrow for another lesson."

The difficulty of the concepts have not deterred Akyris's excitement, it seems. He pumps a fist in triumph, eager for another lesson.

A moment later the barest glimmer of madness climbs within him, subtle disbelief. He searches his hands for reality, mouth twitching. I promptly press his hands down with the butt of my staff.

"Now that you're well-trained in the way of silence, I advise you to practice it. It will keep you grounded and strong in yourself as we go. For the nature of our work, both are required."

He nods. The fly zips past my ear, then lands on my shoulder. "One last thing before I go. A warning."

Deep set emerald eyes snap to attention at the word.

"If you speak of this to anyone, I will kill them."

He smiles, waiting for the punchline of the joke. There isn't one. In this matter of secrecy, there can be no misinterpretation. "That includes Sima."

His mouth gapes in horror. The fly takes off from my shoulder, swirling between us in maddened haste. Too much haste.

It does not see...

Plummeting, it comes to an abrupt halt in the spider's web. Frantic buzzing. I hear them as screams. From nowhere, the spider races toward its hapless victim. The fly's legs churn the air. Desperate. Fruitless.

The butt of my staff sinks through the web. I swirl it, wrapping the whole thing in a thin paste around the knotted oak. The buzzing stops as the fly returns to its lazy flight pattern, freed. Stunned, the spider walks jerkily along the remnants of webbing on my staff—perhaps I've injured its leg.

"Why'd you do that?" Akyris says.

I wish to tell him of the dangers ahead. Of those in the River who, like spiders, lie in wait, hungry for unsuspecting flies. But I've given him enough to worry over for one day. Our mission and its mortal consequences are better saved for later.

When he's ready.

I bring the staff toward my thumb and middle finger, which are locked together. "Because." I flick the limping spider back toward the tree. "Sometimes even flies must be spared a spider's hunger. Nature be damned."

CHAPTER THIRTY-THREE

THE TRIAL OF SUMMIT

- ASCENT -

C onversations with Dragga Omenfaen had a way of devolving into a contest, one which he sought to win by finding gaps or leads he could leverage to demonstrate his exemplary being.

No matter the topic, his ego indulged.

Meanwhile, Ishoa rolled her eyes so many times they nearly fell from their sockets.

She told Dragga about her interaction with Sweet Ges, Yurm, and Unalor. "They seem doomed to fail, don't you think?"

The Omenfaen scion paused, proud fists planted on proud hips. "I don't know, Princess." Perfect words from perfect lips. "An unlikely team indeed, but I've always held firm with the value of never underestimating people."

"Yes, that's probably a better way of looking at it." *I only wished to share a laugh, not a life lesson.* "Speaking of underestimating people, where is your sister?"

Dragga's smile took a coy turn. "Stalking shadows somewhere close by, no doubt. She likes keeping an eye on her competition." He inhaled through his nose as if the mountain air were lavender or rosewater. "Such is her way."

Ahead of them, mist coiled off a sheet of untouched snow. Its top crust had melted into a crystalline gleam under the mid-morning sun. Dragga directed them around the icy sheet to a bank of trees, clear of drifts beneath their canopy. "Easier terrain." His voice sank into silky tones. "Besides, I wouldn't want to destroy something so beautiful."

Ishoa held her tongue. Clearly an inroad to receiving some unwanted compliment. "I'm surprised. You don't seem to be in a hurry to finish first as you were at the Trial of Crossing. Aren't you worried Stirrma will beat you?"

"Not at all, Highness." He laughed. "I wish my sister the utmost success. I'm afraid it is solely she who perpetuates our rivalry. If she finishes ahead of me, so be it."

Oh yes. You're the most humble man.

"And if I place dead last, it matters not and effects me little, so long as I finish," he said. "My pride is that of an anvil. Strong. Unbreakable."

Like I need such a simple metaphor explained to me. Ishoa whirled. "And if the sentry rose eludes you? What then?"

Downslope, Dragga stepped up to meet her at eye level. The towering Claimant brushed dark curls from his face and grinned broadly. "Impossible."

Ishoa frowned. "Why is that?"

"Because, Highness." He affected a softness around his eyes, a playfulness around a full-lipped mouth. Like a mother's enamored whispers to her newborn or a stable hand inciting a horse's calm, or a young man attempting to woo a maiden, he breathed, "I have one I would give my rose to when finished. Naught but death will keep me from her."

Well, I think you're full of yourself, and it repulses me.

"Please," Ishoa turned back to the mountain slope, frustrated that his romantic lip-service had probably worked on dozens of Summerforge maidens. "You don't even know me. To you, I'm just a princess."

But Lodaris saw me. He glimpsed the person behind the title.

Arick's warning about her friend sapped the pleasantness from her. She trudged upward.

When she sensed Dragga made no move to follow, she looked back and found him watching her with a half-wrought smile. "Then I shall get to know you...Ishoa."

She was terse. "If it is my choice, and I believe it is, I'll not marry you."

Despite a chipper demeanor, the arrow found its target. He blinked, a flicker of despair. His shoulders lost their skyward swell and sagged slightly.

Ishoa felt only a little bad. "But I will allow you to speak plainly. You may call me Ishoa. For now."

He brightened, a dog given a bone. "This way, Ishoa."

Immediately, she regretted her kindness.

Shadows grew long as they wound up the western slope of the Ice King, temperature dropping by the minute and chilling Ishoa in the places where sweat had gathered from the climb. The wind didn't help. As the sun drooped lower, gusts came with increasing frequency, just as it had the day before. They stopped to rummage through their packs, each drawing out another pelt for warmth as the sun set.

It wasn't long before Dragga grew bored of not hearing his own voice and took up the song of courtship once more. *Does he not fear the Trial of Summit at all? How can he be so stubbornly devoted to speaking of marriage when danger lurks at every turn?*

Considering Stirrma's attitude, Ishoa wondered if the denial of fear was a common Omenfaen trait. They crested a hill lined with winterberry bushes then descended a steep slope that led into an earthen depression ringed by trees.

"I know what you think of me—of my ideas about marriage," Dragga said. *Of course! Because I told you!* "But there is something I wish you to consider. I've trained against knights of Summerforge since I could hold a sword. Now only a few might avoid embarrassment if they stood against me. I also delayed my entrance into the Trials so I could attend the Academies in Valat for a year. My scores were top of the class."

They started across the bowl, Dragga's chiseled, imploring face dogging her a dozen steps behind.

"I do the Trials in order to have a voice in the court of Anjuhkar, for that is my duty as a young man with the means to help steer the future of Namarr." Dragga's next words were theatrically composed—likely during their silent stretch of the journey. "But I say, damn the vote. I came here for *you*, Ishoa. You alone." Ambitious declarations chased her, a fox hunting a hare. She quickened her pace. "I will marry you. I will prove myself to you. Over and over, if I must. We are meant to be together! The bloodline of Omenfaen and Ironlight will birth children the world yearns for. I promise it!"

Frustration bled into rage. "You promise to force me to do what I don't wish to? What a grand relationship. Frankly, Dragga, I'd rather marry your sister."

A cracking sound slapped the air.

Ishoa stumbled forward as if struck from behind. Hands and knees bashed down onto an unyielding surface—harder than snow. *Ice.* She whipped her head around. Brow knit with alarm, Dragga stared at his feet.

Another crack. The ice gave way. Dragga plummeted.

Lightening quick, his hands and a knee flashed outward, saving the Claimant from falling through the surface completely. One leg, however, was fully submerged.

Wide-eyed, they stared at one another. Dragga cursed, pulled free, painstakingly slow until he was prostrate on the ice. Weight evenly distributed, he rolled toward solid ground a hundred feet away where the bank sloped upward. On hands and knees, Ishoa crawled to the tree line ringing the hidden pond, then ran to Dragga.

Ishoa gasped. One leg was drenched all the way to the crotch. He was wet up to mid-calf on the other leg as well.

A death sentence.

"Dragga," she said. "I'm—I'm so sorry."

"Do not fear, Princess. I'll start no fire." Grim confidence turned his face to hard lines.

"Dragga..." she searched for words that never came.

"All is well." He cinched his pack tighter to his back, then dropped to one knee to wring the moisture from each fur-lined trouser leg. "However, I must abandon you. It pains me to do so, but it is necessary."

"Dragga, you're wet. It's too far to the tor, and if you turn back now—"

Dragga's laughter boomed across the glade. "Turn back? If *that* is the man you think I am, it's no surprise you refuse to marry me. I beg you to reconsider, for I, Dragga Omenfaen, am no such man and I'll do no such thing."

"What are you saying? You can't start a fire. It could bring *them...*" C'Dathun trolls.

"Of course you are right, Ishoa. My sister said you were intelligent, and I trust my sister more than anyone in this world." This gave Ishoa pause. It surprised her to know Stirrma spoke well of her, but even more that the twins were closer than they appeared.

"I could not risk hurting you or our fellow Claimants. I must be fast if I'm to survive. The cold cannot catch me if I never stop moving. Wish me luck, my Princess." With that, Dragga left her in a mad dash to the top.

A race against death.

She watched him go. For a while, she followed behind, keeping pace, fearing to be alone. When she slowed, Dragga maintained his inhuman pace. When she finally collapsed to her knees to rest, he seemed to go faster still. Onward, upward, inexorably, Dragga sprinted.

Never did he slow.

Breath, sharp with cold, pumped through her lungs. Dragga dwindled, became a hazy dot somewhere in the distance. To any other Claimant, a whetted leg meant certain failure. To Dragga Omenfaen, it was a mere challenge to be laughed off.

He is no youth. Not even a normal man. He's something far stronger.

As the shock of his stunning prowess wore off, Ishoa turned in a circle.

Alone. Completely alone.

The wind moaned. A tree creaked. Arick's words scraped across her mind like a dagger striking bone.

...there may be an attempt on your life. Steer clear of Lodaris.

Inside her dugout snow shelter at the base of a tree, sleep came in fits. Every time she slipped into a dream, the whistle of wind through scrabbling branches brought her bolt upright. Her stomach too did its part in keeping her awake. In the middle of the night, she was forced to eat a chunk of hard cheese and a few bites of the Narl's bread.

She woke weary and dragged herself to standing. Coughing the cold from her lungs, she felt her muscles reluctantly loosen as she resumed her journey up the Ice King.

The wind had dwindled, more errant bursts than relentless onslaught as it was the evenings prior. Heavy snow and wind in the night were enough to erase any trail Dragga might have left.

By midmorning, sunlight pierced the veil of hazy cold. Twinkling droplets of melted snow dripped from branches and pattered Ishoa's face. A few slid along her cascading hair then trickled down the back of her neck, dampening the wolf pelt.

Give me the shock cold of the Blue River any day over the Ice King's slow, sodden misery.

Up she went, chasing the rising steam of her own breath. After a while, she found a rhythm where forging ahead felt better than the idea of rest. Her body flowed, no longer inhibited by trivial worries or complaints born of the mind. Soreness melted from her shoulders and thighs. Warmth filled her lungs. The dull ache in her foot faded. Hunger came and went, more a thought than a need.

What I need is a sentry rose.

She drew comfort from the tightness in her stomach where it sucked against her spine. Warm sweat pasted her clothing to her back. Heat gushed from her collar with every stride.

Hours passed. The sun reached its zenith and began its descent.

I'm enjoying myself. The realization shocked her. With the fear of failure and death sequestered at the back of her mind, and utterly alone, Ishoa noticed an increased sense of inner strength. Her pace quickened. *Is this what it feels like to be Dragga?*

For the first time ever, she *felt* like a real Anjuhk. Felt she might be worthy of the old ancestral honor. Maybe even worthy of the Ironlight name. Her heart swelled, fueled her onward.

I need a sentry rose.

As if in answer, a snort to her left caused Ishoa to freeze. A flicker of motion in her periphery. A gray-blue blur.

Another snort.

She peered through a copse of birches.

A pair of snow bison grazed, snow mounded around their snouts as they dug for sweet roots and damp grass. Ishoa crept toward them, pulling herself along, each tree bole a rung on a ladder to success.

Light gleamed along bone-white horns. Compared to the livestock in Ollo Bael's massive pens at Baen's Handle, whose shorn fur gave them a grayish coat, these wild bison were far shaggier and looked almost blue. With snow clinging to their eternally clumped strands of fur, they had a natural camouflage against predators. More importantly, snow bison were the heralds of sentry rose. They grazed close to areas where the winter flower bloomed and ate the bush's roots.

Ishoa scanned the area for a glimmer of azure pedals. But more of the herd emerged from the far wood: cows, calves, and the infrequent bull, blocking her view.

She skirted the herd, hoping they followed a path strewn with sentry rose bushes. Dense foliage lashed her face and legs as she burst through a line of trees. A clearing, similar to the first, sat on the other side. A cluster of bison hemmed in spokes of green that culminated in azure blossoms.

Ishoa punched the air in triumph and plotted how to get a rose.

Foolishly, she thought if she crept among them, the bull's might ignore her. There were stories of Claimants doing such though no one had ever witnessed it first hand. When Ishoa got too close, a bull bellowed, inviting her to creep back the way she'd come. She chided herself for taking such a dangerous risk.

Greedy bastard aren't you?

With minimal cover, a bull would outrun her in short order, and she was less than confident about winning any manner of direct conflict with the beast. But waiting wasn't ideal either. The longer one remained on the Ice King, the greater the risks of the deep cold, injury, or worse.

If I'm too bold, I die. If I'm not bold enough, I die.

While she considered what to do she took a seat on a stump then pulled the smoked perch from her pack. As soon as it touched her mouth, hunger returned. The rest of the fish parcel disappeared, leaving her with only half her hard cheese and bread.

The herd filtered endlessly into the clearing. Endlessly filed out.

Filing in...

Filing out...

She shook her leg impatiently, blew a strand of hair from her face.

Filing in...

Filing out...

She pulled the roll of treated walrus skin from her trouser pocket and rose with an exasperated sigh. Fox-fur brushed her forehead as she blocked the sun with a gloved hand. In less than two hours it would be dark. Ideally, she'd be on her way down the mountain by then.

I can't wait any longer.

She searched under the snow until she found a pair of large stones. "Here we go..." She took a breath, grimaced, then clacked them together. At first the herd merely swung their heads her direction. A puff of dust kicked up from the second collision, harder and louder than her previous attempt. A jolt rippled through the herd's heavily muscled shoulders. Snow cascaded from shaggy blue coats. A bull bellowed and stamped. Calves bleated and trotted to the safety of their mothers' sides.

Ishoa's heart sped to an aching rhythm, the smoked perch in her stomach gurgling and threatening to come up. Like a champion peeling from a battle line, a bull moved to the edge of the herd.

Come on now. There are other patches of sentry rose root for you. Go there!

A snort of warning.

The bull charged. Ishoa's throat went dry as it hurtled toward her. But she held her ground, smashing the stones together a third time. At twenty feet, the horned snow bison shook to a stop. A false charge. A trickle of urine escaped Ishoa's bladder, warming her leg. But she wasn't ashamed, quite the contrary.

She was determined.

I'll wet myself all the way if I must.

She stepped forward and spread her feet. "You go! Not me! You!" Stone met stone three more times in rapid succession. A tiny bit of sediment stung her eye. She squinted, voice cracking. "Go!"

A rumble traveled up her legs as the herd fled, a prehistoric mass of muscle snorting gouts of damp, vaporous breath.

A thousand feet farther down slope, they rumbled to a stop.

"Yes!" The thrill of success made Ishoa light on her feet. She forgot the injury she'd gained on top of her foot during the Trial of Crossing as she raced across the snow and plucked an azure sentry rose, one of three remaining on the cloistered bushes. She rolled it up in the treated walrus skin and placed it in her trouser pocket.

As she made to go, she hesitated. Two other green stalks looked as though they'd already had their roses pinched—recently. *Dragga perhaps?* She looked around. *Who else shares this patch of the Ice King with me?*

She thought of Lodaris. Sadness sapped the joy from her quicker than any icy wind. Her cousin's words slapped her. *Trust no one.*

Yet the betrayal she'd already enacted upon her friend lodged in her heart, a bitter poison. She had a duty, a family to appease. Pride, however, was difficult to grasp. Completing the Trials and gaining a vote in the court of Anjuhkar should have given her a sense of belonging, but all she found when she turned within was a fading feeling, a part of herself drifting further and further away, a boat without anchor on a restless sea.

When the Trials ended, the vote for Revocation began. When that ended, the Scarborn would leave. And with them, would go the only person who understood her.

She'd be alone.

She rolled back her shoulders, took a breath. *I can succeed alone. I don't need Dragga or Lodaris or Wolst or anyone. The sentry rose in my pack proves as much.*

The wind picked up as night closed in. Howling gusts pulled at Ishoa's furs, stung her face, and forced her eyes to knife's edge slits. Even so, she found a thick stand of pine, spruce, and cedar trees. A solid place to dig out her shelter and rest.

As she trudged toward the dark cluster of trees, she heard a sound...from behind. She whirled, hand slapping sword hilt.

Throttled by relentless, cutting gales, the boughs dropped their accumulated snow. Nothing else moved. A flush of heat spread across her shoulder blades. Sent tingles up her spine. She cast about, all rational thought fleeing, panic taking hold.

She was vulnerable. Never had she wished more for Rakeema to be at her side. Or better yet, Wolst.

Her mind sped toward worst case scenarios. Sharp, cannibalistic teeth. Bronze axes. A spit slathered with human grease...

I need cover.

Adult ice tigers sometimes hunted near the tor of the Ice King. Trolls and other creatures too.

Furnace breaths pumped through her chest as she attempted to gain control of her dark thoughts.

I need to calm my nerves. It's just the wind. No one is there.

She hated the fact that Unalor was right. She was being jumpy. Nothing more. Being alone wasn't always a bad thing anyway.

Once she reached the cover of trees, the fearful thoughts slowed. The Ice King was plentiful in prey—no natural predators would prefer her. And C'Dathuns were exceedingly rare.

The copse was dense, its evergreen canopy bringing with it an earlier night. There were tree wells and an abundance of fallen branches. Twigs covered in pine needles lay everywhere, ideal for a shelter.

"Nothing but the wind and imagination," she said.

As she bent to retrieve a wrist-thick branch for the center pole of her shelter, snow crunched under foot nearby.

She spun to the sound.

A shadowy figure...

She fumbled for her sword and backpedaled as it slunk closer. Her heel caught a branch. She tripped and fell onto her backside, arms splaying out behind her.

The shadow stood over her.

Her blood went cold.

"You were very loud up there, Princess." The voice was familiar. Never had she heard it drenched in so much hate. "You've drawn unwanted attention."

"Lodaris?" she gasped.

Naked steel in hand, Lodaris Warnock stared down at her, hard eyes promising violence.

A hollow despair jerked the warmth from Ishoa, consumed all feeling, all thought. All but one.

I'm going to die.

CHAPTER THIRTY-FOUR

YOU CAME TO KILL

Thephos was ready for death.

He closed his eyes, heard a grunt, and felt a whoosh of air. His heart threatened to beat out of his chest...

And continued beating.

His eyes twitched open. The black sickle hovered the breadth of a fly's leg from his forehead, a pouting demon holding it.

"Not even a gasp." The demon's voice was high, gravelly. "You're supposed to be terrified. Come, let's try again. I raise my sickle—" He raised it, maniacal rage tensing across a broad, ghostly face. His voice became strained, more fitting of an elderly crone than a demonic executioner. "And when I bring it down, you scream. Then I end the scream by cutting your head in two. See, if you hit it just right, you split the voice box and it makes a funny little sound. Well, I mean, I hit the voice box. You just kinda..." The Madness shrugged. "...fall apart."

Numbness tingled down Thephos's neck and into his shoulders. He had been prepared to die—expected it—but now he gaped, mind reeling from the unexpected turn of events. It was as if his soul had already departed but forgot something and had to make its way back to the start.

Fat black lips curled in disgust. "I give you sorry thespians advice worth more than gold and you can only stare at me like a patch of...cabbages!" He cast about in search of a more fitting word. Drool hung from the corner of a mouth fit for a deep-sea fish. "No! Fucking eggplants!"

He strolled past Thephos, tapping cannibalistic teeth. No one dared move.

Olthr wet himself, invoking the Madness's attention. "You've a nice set of eyes on you." The demon blinked out of existence—reappeared before Olthr. The monk's lips quivered, gaze fleeing the sight of the looming demon.

The Madness snatched him by the neck like a puppy then pulled the monk's ear close to centipede lips. Olthr's feet dangled, a limp pair of lamb shanks.

The Madness shouted. "Don't ever lie about what you see!"

"But I didn't!" Othlr keened, eyes clamped shut. "You—you—you were ra—really there!"

"Oh...right." The Madness frowned and scratched his blue-veined pate with the tip of his sickle. He jabbed a clawed finger in Olthr's face. "In that case, don't ever let others tell you you're crazy! That's weak shit, and I don't like it!"

The monk nodded vigorously. The Madness dropped him to his knees. "Pray, fool." He positioned himself for another killing blow.

Words blubbered from a stricken Olthr. His hands and knees shook too hard to comply. Little of what he said sounded like prayer.

The sickle rose overhead.

Otlhr's mouth opened. Closed. Like a hooked fish, he gulped for any reality different from the present one.

The sickle descended—halted mid-swing.

"Fuck!" The Madness twisted away and booted a stone. "Fuckity, fucking, fuck. You stupid little thespian. I told you, you're supposed to scream for the sound to—agh—fuck it! I guess I can live a thousand years and still be surprised once in a while. Pissers are almost always screamers. Gaspers also piss, but you fucking eggplants..." He sputtered in disappointment.

I'm sorry.

The Anjuhk caught the demon's eye next. "Nice scars."

Somehow the woman pushed terror down enough to grab a rock. She raised it before her as if she meant to strike the demon if he came near.

The Madness met her defiant act with a leer. "You ever been fucked with a sickle?"

She dropped the rock quicker than if it were a poisonous snake.

"Oh, it's okay, ma'am. I only jest. Sex is an unsavory business, even when you class it up by bringing a sickle into the mix." The demon's smile returned, broader and more lecherous than before. "To tell you the truth, I'm more in the mood for some—"

A deafening tearing sound. A wink of darkness. The Madness disappeared.

Somewhere out of sight, rock tumbled. Thephos spun around.

The Madness was already in his upswing. "Kanian!" he snarled.

Head swiveling, the crabber screamed. The sickle passed between upraised, useless hands and cleaved the man's head in two with a wet, metallic ring. The Kanian's scream terminated abruptly with a punctuated wheeze.

"Heehee! Sweet music!"

Gore sluiced across the moss-covered stones. It reminded Thephos of when he used to throw buckets of suet to the pigs. The Madness bowed to each of those yet to be slaughtered in turn. The Kanian's hands twitched violently as the corpse slumped forward over its knees, sickle blade buried deep, down to the dead man's navel.

The white Ascendant's smock blossomed scarlet.

"Now that was a performance, people. Take note. Your friend here was a true thespian. Dedicated to the—damn it to fuck—why are Kanian's so fucking sticky?" The Madness worked to pull his sickle free from the crabber's torso. "So. Fucking. Sticky!"

A few seconds passed in silent horror until Radea overcame her shock and scrabbled across the rocky banks in flight.

"The lesson is not over!" the Madness shouted after her.

The frantic-eyed Olthr bolted after Radea. The Anjuhk heaved into motion, sprinting in a different direction. Legs like planks of wood, Thephos could only sit, watching the Madness heave at his sickle. He propped a foot against the Kanian's shoulder blade like a lumberjack who'd lodged his ax in a stump.

I should run.

He couldn't. Thephos watched as if outside his own body, feelings and action becoming concepts out of reach. Only the persistent beat of his heart and the convulsing tension in his gut told him he might still be alive. *Why aren't I dead?*

Flustered, the Madness stepped back from the crabber's body. "Fucker." Dark veins reached toward midnight irises at the center of bulging eyes. He wheezed, fat gobs of saliva dripping. The mask of rage turned to curiosity when he noticed Thephos watching him.

I should have run.

Thephos thought of Syn Backlegarm and his wife, Ash, and the guard he'd spoken with outside the curtain wall. The worst part about dying was that they would lose their hard-earned money. They were good people. They didn't deserve to be dragged down by Thephos's disappointing death.

"You're still here?" A sound like ripping fabric preceded a flash of black smoke, and then the Madness loomed over Thephos once more, his sickle miraculously filling his hand. Thephos glanced at the crabber's body, the blade now absent. "Why didn't you run off with your friends?"

They left me. Are friends supposed to do that?

Syn's smiling face rose, towering above all others in his mind's eye. With disembodied calm, Thephos said, "They're not my friends."

Is this what courage feels like? His father's voice crushed his own. You have no fire in you, Thephos. You're a pathetic worm. You are nothing.

But it was being nothing that allowed him to converse with the demon. If nothing died, it was no problem at all. He met the Madness's stare. The demon watched him expectantly.

"Why did you act like you couldn't remove your sickle?" The demon's attention was oppressive, like the crush of rock and darkness in the bowels of a cave. Thephos knew it well. His father's was similar. "Why didn't you kill me?"

Silent and impassive, the Madness continued staring at Thephos. In the distance, the other Ascendants' screams faded to faint echoes.

Whispers.

"Don't you hate me, Theffy?"

Thephos flinched, stumbled back as his father's words stabbed through him. "What?" He licked nervous lips. "Why—why did you say that?"

Without a word, the Madness shot forward, a blur, a phantom of light and shadow. He grasped Thephos's face in a clawed white hand and hoisted him in the air, ice-cold palm wrapped around his chin. Unlike Olthr, Thephos struggled wildly against the demon's grip. He kicked until his toes flared with pain and pounded and clawed at the Madness's arm. The tremors of his thrashing moved no further than the demon's wrist. The Madness was a stone statue.

Sharp nails pressed lightly against Thephos's temples. He froze.

The demon rotated Thephos's face to one side, then to the other. "I can see him right through you...Theffy. You can't even feel him in there, can you? You want him to be a ghost, a faded memory, as unreal and distant as the dark of the night sky. But he's right there, alive as ever, firmer than the bones in your hand."

The Madness released Thephos to fall hard on the rocks. "There's a devil in you Thephos. You didn't come here to die. You came here to *kill*."

"No," Thephos breathed. The air in his lungs had left him and his low back spasmed with pain. He shook his head as he gained his feet. "That's not true."

I hate you.

You're a pathetic worm.

I'd fucking kill you.

He closed his eyes, let the words repeat. A viper's bite that comforted.

The Madness laughed. "With eyes like these, you don't believe me? I could see the inside of a hen's cunt in Malzacor from here. And just as easy, I see the old devil in you. You came here to drink blood! To crush skulls! To sear flesh from bone!"

He pointed at Thephos, damning him with a roar. "You, *Theffy*, came here to kill!"

Horror strangled Thephos, sought to drag him beneath the surface of sanity. Feeling finally returned. He could not stop it. He folded his arms around his torso and hunched protectively over his belly.

Numbness peeled back, exposing him, an open wound to salt water. Fear flooded every inch of his body, seeking escape by any means.

The pressure. So much pressure!

"That's not true!" Rage burst from Thephos like lightning. It rang clear, truth echoing across the rocky banks surrounding the falls.

When he looked up, the Madness was gone.

Numb in the way of those who've had insights better left unseen, Thephos carried himself across a slope of loose slate. He worked his way upward to a narrow path along an escarpment and followed it.

Darkness fell by layers, each one swallowing what lied ahead by greater degrees. He wondered if he might eventually walk straight into the mouth of some monster, the dark itself but the back of its waiting throat.

That was too easy. Too much to hope for.

You came here to kill.

He looked back, half expecting the Madness to be stalking him. Only stars watched his forlorn escape. *Escape from what?*

He scraped forward, untouched by the cold and with but a halo of visibility in any direction. The old devil's words chased him. *I'd fucking kill you. Pathetic worm.*

Fire kindled to life in Thephos's chest. Heat crept into his shoulders and jaw. He wanted it gone. He tried pushing the feeling away like he'd done thousands of times before, but the more he tried, the more it burned. Like a wildfire, it burned.

More agonizing than the jolt in his hands from the shovel's shaft as it sank into the dirt of his little brother's grave.

A sharp pain lanced through one side of his jaw. He clenched his teeth to stop it but only made it worse. His fists ached with strain.

He's the devil! Not me.

Fists pressing his cheeks, he paced along a ledge of rock overlooking a sheer slope. To continue any further in the dark was to court injury or a fatal fall. He saw it clearly in his mind: a misstep followed by a moment of arm-flailing panic as he plummeted into empty space. Momentum would carry him down the rocky scarp, his body broken by sharp, unyielding stone.

Then the peace of silence. The silence of peace.

From the back of his mind, his father watched him. *I hate you. Pathetic.*

Somewhere, the Madness laughed.

For what seemed hours, Thephos's feet slapped the ground, a furious pace, back and forth. Back and forth. Wind howled and snapped at him.

You came here to kill...

"I didn't!" he roared. The wind answered, blowing him back a step. He faced it and screamed at it to be silent. Nothing changed. Nothing would ever change. Evil persisted, inside and out. Devil's die long after they should. Their victims are left to crawl through life with bloodied knees.

You came here to kill.

Thephos's arms fell limp and hopeless to his sides. The steep descent and dark chasm beyond beckoned. The hollow place filled with lead. Its despairing weight dragged him to the edge.

"You're wrong!" A piteous cry. "I came here to die!"

Thephos shuffled forward until his toes kissed empty air then reached his arms wide. The slope peeled away beneath him. Closing his eyes, he watched himself leap outward, replayed the image in his mind a dozen times. The fire in his chest burned, unbridled wrath, a ravenous beast.

And it begged him not to go.

The wind died.

A faint thumping filled his ears. The anger remained, a steady presence in his breast. His heart calmed like an ocean wave sighing across the sands. Thephos listened. In Carthane, he could step into the night and hear the sounds of a half-dozen different animals. Now he heard nothing except his own pulse. As the rage inside came alive, the outer world fell quiet, as though there was a rightness to it. A mote of tranquility at the pinnacle of hate.

The eye of the storm.

Thephos backed from the ledge, toes finding cool earth. The notion that he could be enraged and calm at the same time sent him spiraling down a harrowing line of thought. *What if I become Ruptured?*

He stared at a hand hoping to find it normal. Calluses rode a wraith's palm—not his own. Horror descended like a canvas sack overhead. He turned the hand over; it had struck him too many times not to know its owner.

The old devil's hand...my father's hand.

Thephos turned in a circle, trying to catch the moonlight at a more favorable angle.

A trick of shadows?

Light glimmered in the distance, breaking him from his plunge into madness. He slapped palms to cheeks, shook his head, and then squinted at the luminous speck.

At first, he crept slowly, careful of the treacherous footing. But as the light brightened, a whisper spurred him onward, drawing him toward it at a dangerous pace. Legs pumping, he threw a hand to one side, fingers brushing the rock wall for balance.

I must know what it is!

He slipped, cursed as he felt the sole of his foot split against a hunk of razor-sharp slate. Warmth spread under foot. Sediment stuck to the bloody wound. Thephos didn't care. He'd never desired something so badly. The thought was a depressing one. Other Ascendants had glorious aspirations, like the Wordfox and his poetry or Radea who would save the world. All that existed for Thephos was this moment, his aspiration a passing curiosity on a haunted mountain scarp.

He looked to the moon then back at the glimmer. Excitement encircled awareness. There were only two possible sources of light on Unturrus: the moon and the
mirrored statues.

Or Vaniton's Gasp.

But as he drew closer, he discounted the idea that it could be the demonic,
mirrored river. The luster Thephos saw was a point, not an undulating wave of
shimmering brilliance, which was what it would have been if it were Vaniton's Gasp.
Olthr had said the demon reached sizes as large as a few acres but never so small as
whatever lay ahead.

Thephos left the scarp and hurried into a stand of trees. A bush snared his
Ascendant's smock, tearing it at the hip. Branches whipped at his face, stung his
eyes until the dense vegetation spit him out into a clearing. He stumbled to his knees
then looked up...

At the top of a barren knoll, a hundred feet away, a mirrored statue shone like a
beacon.

Thephos scrambled forth, ignoring the pain shooting through his foot. Nothing
mattered. What he wanted was possible. He saw that now. The evidence was just
ahead.

A dozen feet from the statue, he dropped to his knees.

It was a young man. Slightly shorter than Thephos from the look of it. When
Vaniton's Gasp had overtaken him, he seemed to have been in the middle of turning
around, with only enough time to raise a single hand in warding before it swallowed
him and left him frozen in eternal repose. Shoulder length hair jutted behind him,
shining stalactites splaying. The young man's other hand was forever balled into
a fist at his side. Every contour of the statue's frame was perfectly smooth. The
detail so clear, he wondered how thin the layer was that killed the Ascendant. In
his dreams, Thephos imagined it would be thicker, messier, not nearly so defined.
A twinkle of light rippled across the young man's shoulders and hawkish nose.

Tears raced down his cheeks. *So beautiful.* The admiration, however, was fleeting.
Jealousy snared the joy from him, carried it away like a barn cat with a mouse. After
a moment spent sobbing, he beat the earth with a fist. *That should be me!*

Destiny preferred him to suffer. To feel the rage, the hate, the horror of evil desires
inside. For whatever reason, he knew it in his bones that he would never die by
Vaniton's Gasp.

A more deserved horror then.

He wiped away his tears and approached the statue. A familiar face materialized
out of the darkness from behind it.

"You live," Olthr said flatly.

Radea appeared a second later. A single glance was all Thephos needed to see to
realize the woman didn't believe he truly existed. She shied away from him and took

a seat on a patch of dead grass. He didn't blame her even he thought it impossible he survived.

On the ground, Radea curled up into the fetal position. Olthr paced, just like Thephos had atop the scarp. The track insanity traveled.

Back and forth. Back and forth...

Thephos rested his back against the feet of the statue. He took in the expansive slopes of Unturrus still ahead, an endless canvas of rock, tree, and misery.

"I think I'm becoming more myself," Olthr said. "I'm telling you, this is good. This is fantastic. The Madness challenged my cowardice—I've always been a coward. Always saying yes to others without thought of my own wants or desires because I'm afraid of...I don't know what." He laughed. "If I'm being truthful, and this is frightening to share, I became a monk out of fear that I'd disappoint my family if I didn't. But I'm sharing it now because I want to face my fear, just like I faced the Madness. See? I'm really becoming more myself."

Branches gave way to something large in the bracken. All three turned in time to see the Anjuhk woman shamble into the clearing. Wordless and stoic, she took a seat near Thephos. Neither Radea nor Olthr responded to her presence with more than a relieved sigh. She was not a demon.

That was all that mattered now.

Thephos wished it had been Vaniton's Gasp.

Heedless of the Anjuhk, Olthr continued ranting. "And when I face my fears, I become more me. I prove to myself I can overcome them."

All the books in the world could not have prepared him. He didn't even realize how afraid of death he truly was until he ascended. The man's expectations were nothing but wind, a fleeting sigh.

The Anjuhk stared at Thephos. A chill ran up his spine as he met her vacant eyes. It was like she'd been hollowed out.

Has she withdrawn to protect herself from the horror and insanity of it all?

Olthr ranted. "I'm becoming more myself..."

The Anjuhk began singing in a haunting tone. An old Peladonian farming song Thephos knew.

"Plant all the rows and strive to survive. Bend and drop, bend and drop...

"The rains will come and your work is yet done. Bend and drop, bend and drop...

"Wife and kids call but there's wood to be chopped. Bend and drop, bend and drop..."

Olthr whirled, fists clenched at his sides. "Will you be silent? I'm saying something important."

The Anjuhk threw an empty look at Olthr as her singing dwindled.

"Where was I? Oh yes, becoming more myself. The books all say that's what happens right before you become an Awakened—"

The Anjuhk took up her song. "A seed that is planted is a task that is done. Almost there, almost there, almost there...

"Watch for decay and pray for good growth. Almost there, almost there, almost there..."

With a childish frown, Olthr strode toward the Anjuhk. He swayed over her, attempting intimidation. When she gave no sign of worry, he slapped her. She paused then gave him a questioning look, void of emotion. Blank.

It offered Olthr nothing but his own reflection.

With a screech, he brought the back of his hand in a downward arc and dealt her a glancing blow across the brow. Then, he turned away, smoothing his smock before resuming his speech. Thephos wondered if the unimist spoke to anyone in particular or just himself.

"Like I was saying, I have to become more myself. What is the self? Who am I? That's what I'm meant to discover." His voice became an enthusiastic crescendo. "That's what Unturrus wants from all of us. That's what the Triune God wants, the Sempyrean gods too! Haha! They want us to see who we are so we can awaken!"

The husky voice of the Anjuhk returned. "Inside you are safe. The work is done and the rains do come. Go to sleep, go to sleep, go to sleep...

"The fire crackles and the harvest abounds. Go to sleep, go to sleep, go to sleep..."

Terror passed over Olthr's expression. He left the clearing, casting backward glances at the Anjuhk as if she were a wolf hunting him.

You came here to kill.

Thephos met the Anjuhk's flat stare for a long time. Then he curled up beneath the mirrored statue of the lucky young man and fell into something that was not quite sleep.

More, an interval between the world of the dreamers and the nightmares of the living.

Chapter Thirty-Five

LIES

Disbelief gripped Ishoa by the throat, silencing her. *How could you? How could you do this?*

Lodaris scanned the surrounding moonlit woods, blade menacing at his side, lethal edge shining in the reflected light of the snow.

Ishoa fought down her fear to find a single word that came out with a quiet puff of steam. "Why?"

Then she remembered the sword at her hip. She made to stand, one hand outstretched, one hand moving slowly toward the hilt. "You're a better blade, but I'll not make this easy."

Lodaris frowned. "Do you think so little of me, Isha?"

Gloved fingers froze around her sword handle, waiting to draw. *My first cut must be quick—fluid—a single motion from scabbard to swing.*

"Come with me." He extended a hand. *Danger*, her mind screamed.

She hesitated.

"Trust me," he said.

She stepped back, recalling Arick's words. *Trust no one.* The tip of Lodaris's blade scraped the top crust of snow as his shoulders relaxed. "Please. You're not safe here, Highness."

Danger!

"Quit with the formalities, Lodaris." Her tongue darted over nervous lips. "Why are you here? And why is your sword drawn?"

"Like I said, you're—"

"Not safe." Her blade shrieked free from scabbard. "I heard you." Darksteel reworked by the smiths of Summerforge rippled in the waning gloom light. "But all I see is an angry Scarborn with a weapon, so you better explain."

Lodaris glared but made no move to strike.

Far to Ishoa's left, a twig snapped. They whirled toward the sound. *We're not alone.* She shifted her weight from foot to foot, half facing the sound while still angled toward Lodaris.

For reasons unknown, he didn't seem nearly so surprised nor worried as she.

"What's going on?" she hissed. A banha drum played in her heart, her ears, her stomach. Her insides pulsed. Her fingers tingled. "Is—is it C'Dathuns?"

Ignoring her, Lodaris brought a hand to the side of his mouth and shouted into the darkness. "Narl! I know you're there. You'd better leave off."

Narl?

The dull voice of Gestryn Narl called back from somewhere in the dark. "Fucking Scarborn." Distant but still too close for Ishoa's liking. She searched the shadows for movement, found naught but quivering branches in the wind.

"You can't help your traitor's blood can you?" Sweet Ges shouted.

"Leave us," yelled Lodaris. After a moment's pause he added, "Or I'll kill you."

"Not me you should be killing, scum." This time Sweet Ges's voice sounded farther away. "Why don't you hurry down the mountain? I'll make sure the princess returns safely."

"I won't warn you again, Narl. She's with me."

"I don't need your protection." As soon the words left Ishoa, she realized they weren't entirely true. She was glad to have him there. If she were alone, she wasn't sure how a conflict with Sweet Ges might go. He was taller than Lodaris by a head, though soft-bodied. He didn't strike Ishoa as one well trained. Lodaris however was more than capable of teaching the boy a lesson. Of that, she was sure.

But with the two of them together, Sweet Ges stood no chance.

How did he know Sweet Ges was stalking me? How did he know he meant me harm?

"Sleep easy tonight!" Sweet Ges's voice came from far off now, hundreds of feet away and barely audible above the gusting winds. His final shouts of "coward" and "traitor" were little more than harsh, punctuated whispers.

Lodaris squinted, leading Ishoa to believe he had been able to see the boy from Prav the entire time. "Come, we need to find another place to sleep. We'll have to move fast if we want enough light to build a shelter. The dark will play against him as much as it will us but—"

Ishoa's blade rustled against the sparse beard hair covering Lodaris's neck. "Explain yourself." She lifted her sword, forcing his chin upward. "Tell me why you've been ignoring me—why I'm considering you an enemy right now."

The apple of his throat rose then fell. "Please, we must hurry."

"Then hurry." She stepped closer, bringing them into the sphere of each other's breath. His gaze traveled the length of her blade and came to rest on her face. He looked away.

Shame?

"I—I saw him following you up to where you got the sentry rose," he stammered. "I thought he meant to hurt you. I've heard stories about him that—"

"So you were following me too?" She pressed the blade firmly against his jugular. "Why?"

"Does it matter? I just saved your life and plan to keep it that way. Let's find a place and then talk. Here—" His sword tumbled from his hand.

After a moment, she sheathed her own. "I suppose if you were going to kill me you could have let Sweet Ges try it first."

A subtle smile played across his lips. "It's good to see you, Ishoa."

"You too," she said brusquely. *You look too much like your father and sound too much like your mother for me to trust you.* If not for the threat of Sweet Ges still lurking, she may have slapped Lodaris and set off alone.

"Let's go." He retrieved his sword, sheathed it, and then exposed his back to her. *A decent first act to rebuilding trust.*

Together they made their way out of the wood traveling parallel rather than downslope to avoid crossing paths with Sweet Ges. By the time night settled, they found a small thicket of tightly clustered evergreens. Sweet Ges would be hard pressed to find their tracks or their hideout in the dark.

They erected a shelter over a tree well and then hollowed out more space for them to curl up for the night. As darkness overtook sight, and the temperature plummeted, the barrier between their bodies faded.

Ishoa's teeth chattered. Her nose and ears ached. They inched closer to one another until, just after midnight, the cold forced them into each other's arms.

The heat of Lodaris's breath and the touch of his hands reminded her of that first moment beside the Blue River outside Jarik...

She shook her head. *No! He lied to me.*

And yet she'd done the same to him. *I'm no victim and he is no villain.*

"The lies must stop here, Lodaris," she whispered. "You are my friend...my best friend. Before you left me in Jarik, you were good to me."

Wind whistled through the boughs, setting the claw like branches to clamoring. The Claimants shifted into each other more, every part of their bodies molding together. There was no effort needed for them to hear, and so, they spoke in soft tones, mouths mere inches from ears.

As close as they were, Ishoa could feel Lodaris's internal struggle. Breast pressed into breast, heartbeats thudding in tandem. Thought escaped her. It was good to feel him, to be near him again.

He sighed. "I knew Gestryn Narl wished to kill you."

A sudden rush of blood set Ishoa's ears to ringing.

"My mother has been corrupted by Syphion Muul." his voice shook. "But Isha, please believe me when I say I knew of the plan and had no intention of allowing it to happen."

Venom laced her words, "You knew?"

He tensed. "Sweet Ges volunteered. Your grandmother slighted the Narls in front of the other holds. She's slipping in her old age, and it nearly cost you your life.

Atop the Ice King, with no witnesses...it would have been a perfect plan if he'd been successful." He sighed. "You're upset I didn't warn you. Did you see my face at the Crossing?"

Through grit teeth, Ishoa whispered, "Yes."

"Then you know what stakes I play even within my own family. I received a beating for failing to kill a man who insulted me. The smith was a bastard and I was angry, but he didn't deserve death. What consequence do you think awaits me for stopping Sweet Ges?"

"But..." Ishoa let go of her response. Whatever she said next came from the place of life differently lived. *You do not see it, Princess.* His words struck harder than a smith's hammer.

Anger ebbed, diluted in a river of compassion. "Why do they do this to you?"

Lodaris's body melted against her own. "My father says it is because I grew up soft. Like a Frost. Most Scarborn must fight for every scrap they get, but I've had a unique experience as the first Scarborn child birthed into hold life. In all but technicality, I'm highborn. Syphion says my status has made me weak. My mother agrees."

"No, Lodaris. You are not weak. You are strong." *Stronger than you know.* "Refusing to let a friend be murdered isn't weak. Refusing to save them *is*. To be honest, your mother terrifies me. I wouldn't have the courage to cross her. But you *do*. You have the courage to do anything. That's why..." she choked back a swell of emotion. *What am I doing? What have I done?*

Hot tears burst forth, racing across her eye line. Though she knew Lodaris felt her crying, she was grateful for the cover of darkness. *He refused to betray me, even when forced. Me on the other hand...I'm the weak one.*

Sobs wracked her. Lodaris held her tight about the shoulders, drew her hard into his chest, compressed her thighs within his own.

A distant screech told them of an owl or blightwing making a kill. The night's silence stretched for long minutes as she wept into Lodaris.

He stroked her hair. "I'll need muster all the courage I can get. Narls are nothing compared to my mother. When she finds out what I've done, well, I plan never to return to the Fringes. After the Trials, I'll go wherever I choose."

Wiping tears and snot onto a fox-fur glove, she asked him where.

"Perhaps Alistar. One day I may save enough for the training to be a knight. Or I could start my own business as a caravan guard. I have my parents name, their blood pumping through my veins."

Going into competition against the Warnocks seemed foolhardy enough without adding Lodaris's age and height to the equation. The latter should not count against him, but she knew the shallow hearts of frightened merchants seeking protection.

On sight alone, most would take a worthless giant over a shorter man with greater skill.

She couldn't bring herself to say as much. Instead she said, "I'll pay for the training."

Lodaris stiffened.

"I will. I'll do whatever I must to get my grandmother to help. In fact, she would relish the idea of thumbing her nose at your parents." Her voice took on a somber tone. "I don't want you to be gone forever. Recently I've found that what I want and what I need don't always meet up. More than anything, I need you to be happy."

Equal parts shock and gratitude laced his words. "Ishoa. I—I don't know how to—"

"Wait." She chewed her lip. "Before you thank me, there's something you should know. I lied to you Lodaris. For that, I am sorry." *But do I tell him specifics?* Arick's words haunted her. *Trust no one...*

Lodaris cleared his throat and waited.

A dull ache started in her chest and reached up her neck into her jaw. Her duty was to Namarr. To the memory of her parents. To Wolst and Grandmother and the counsel that entrusted her with the safety of Anjuhkar.

To the lineage of Ironlight.

Her breath caught. The words limped forth to her throat as mere whispers. She choked them back, but they returned louder and stronger than before.

They shouted for release. Begged to be heard, a final gasp of hope before dying...

"I love you," she breathed. When the words finally came, Ishoa questioned whether they were truth or some clever trick. A ruse to avoid giving the enemy crucial insight.

Either was terrifying.

"Ishoa..." Her name was a sigh in Lodaris's mouth.

The world raced from groin to quivering lips. She exhaled slowly, wishing she could see through the swamping blackness. Lodaris's chest heaved. His breaths rapid. A tentative hand slid to the back of her head. The gap between them dwindled as she was drawn close. Warmth swam between them as his face inched nearer.

Nearer...

Whether Lodaris said "I love you" back, Ishoa couldn't recall. Only her own words echoed through her mind as darkness and cold and threat of bloodshed clouded the air around them, condemning their embrace, and damning them.

Right up to the moment their lips touched.

A press of warmth. A surging rush. Damp. Smooth. Soft. Pressure both gentle and firm.

A door inside Ishoa was thrown open, revealing her. Allowing him. Her cheeks flushed. Her stomach fluttered. Everything in her crashed into place, a ripple of joy and sorrow riding her lips. Then it filtered back into her as she pried herself from him, the cresting wave of bliss coming to settle.

Lodaris's chin rested against her forehead. Breaths rose and fell in rhythm. Their kiss heralded the sweetest and shortest night of sleep Ishoa ever had.

CHAPTER THIRTY-SIX

BLOOD BROTHERS

Garlenna's mace hissed from its leather throng as she whirled toward the yelling coming from the Dregs. *My lie has met its limit, it seems.*

"That was Meckin," said Barodane.

They raced from the stable around to the front of the inn. Smoke billowed from one of the windows. "My room," Barodane said.

"They mean to draw you out. Or burn you in your bed."

Barodane launched himself at the door with his shoulder. Upon impact, it shuddered but didn't open. He stepped back to do so again, but just as he was about to hit it, the door flew open. Vey sidestepped him as he fell forward into the tap room. Garlenna followed him in.

At the top of the stairs, Meckin had just rounded the corner with an empty pail. "I need help!" A second serving girl was on the innkeeper's heels. A pair of patrons were coughing, wearing nothing but their small clothes and lugging packs of their belongings down the steps. The harpist looked like a wild animal with tousled white hair as he sought to escape.

"I saw 'em," Vey said. "Two horsemen chucked torches through the window then took off down the street."

Barodane stumbled forward, his feet barely regained. "I'll help Meckin! You—"

"I know what to do," Garlenna turned.

Out in the street, gawkers had gathered to watch the blaze. Garlenna strode past them. A pair of shirtless men hustled toward the inn, buckets of water jostling at their sides. A bell rang to summon more able bodied people to the firefight. She sent a prayer to Ozoi to calm his flames then to Maletha for abundant, cooling waters.

Foregoing her horse, she broke into a jog. A mount at this hour of night would be loud and make her a target. She needed to be swift. Secretive, even more so. *They'll either leave town at speed, or if I'm lucky they'll meet at the chapel first.* If they left town, they were already well away, and she could easily stumble into a trap rushing headlong after them. If they headed for the chapel first, she could possibly take them off guard.

If they were to have a fighting chance, she'd need to start picking the masons off. Even with Barodane coming back into himself, the odds would be near impossible to overcome once Hyram figured out they had so little muscle. Danuuk seemed good for a knife in the back, but man to man, shoulder to shoulder, she didn't think him worth a silver wheel.

If the Redhand Brothers arrive soon we may yet have a chance.

The ringing of the bell grew quieter as she ran, puffs of breath trailing into the cold morning air. Shouts dwindled, as did the number of those responding to the alarm bell who passed her. She slowed, angling toward a man sitting in a coat of furs under a shop front. "Have two horsemen come this way?" She inhaled slow, managing her breath.

He pointed a smoking cob in the direction she'd been running. "A bit ago...rode through blisterin' fast."

Without another word, Garlenna resumed. It wasn't long before she passed the town fountain. She stuck to the fronts of shops now, apologizing to those she disturbed at such an early hour. Few responded, though one older woman cursed under her breath. By the time Garlenna had the riders in sight, the sun was poking over the horizon, leaving the topmost half of Digtown in light and the bottom in shadow.

To her surprise, the riders came to a stop outside the Gem Loft rather than proceeding to the chapel. She dipped into an alley and made her way around the building.

Stopping, she pressed her back against the wall of the Gem Loft. The riders' voices found her ears. She brought her mace to her lips, kissed it, and then with a calming breath glanced out with her good eye.

So much for catching them off guard.

Mounted, Eustus and two more cutthroats on foot emerged from an alley across the way to join the riders. Luckily, the shadows were still deep enough for her to spy.

An older, bearded mason who she'd spoken with at the Dregs days earlier dismounted then approached the Gem Loft's front door. He held a note and drew his hammer.

Another mason with long braids in the style of an Anjuhk brought his horse alongside Eustus's. "The shit hole is in flames. My only regret is I didn't get to cave that smiling innkeep's face in. What about you?"

In the distance Garlenna heard the trundle of an approaching wain.

"It's done," said one of the cutthroats. "Found the bastard drunker than a Val passed out at the cooper's place."

The other footman made a throat-slitting motion. "So drunk he barely moved when we cut him. We thought it'd be fitting to give him a joker's smile."

The first man said, "That wasn't no joker's smile you damn fool. That's when Kurgs break the jaw off. Eustus just pulled his tongue out his neck."

Danuuk is dead.

Garlenna cursed inwardly.

The wain squealed to a halt. Garlenna peeked out. From her vantage, she only saw Eustus and his assassins as they turned to regard the drivers.

A high-pitched voice carrying threat addressed Hyram's men. "Who's this you be braggin' about mutilating in the streets of Digtown?"

A second voice, deep and menacing. "I don't think we know you."

The mason with braids snorted contemptuously. "Be on your way, strangers."

The bearded man began hammering a note to the front door of the Gem Loft.

"You get Imralta's permission to go hammerin' like that at this hour?" The high-pitched voice.

"Mind your business and we'll mind ours. You may pass." The mason with braids. The way he spoke, Garlenna could almost see the smile on his face. "For your sake, I suggest you do so quickly."

Laughter. The mean kind. The high-pitched voice said, "Threatening the Red-hand brothers is about the dumbest thing any man does once."

What rotten luck.

The bearded mason stopped hammering. He stamped down the stairs of the Gem Loft's landing. Someone else—one of the brothers Garlenna assumed—jumped down into the dirt with a heavy thud.

A sick feeling eased into Garlenna's gut. She'd heard the voices of men aiming for violence more times than she could count. This night would end in blood. And soon. *Three against five.* A knuckle popped as she tightened her grip on her mace. She took a steadying breath. *I have the element of surprise. Eustus first.*

She craned her neck farther than before, trusting Hyram's men were now fixated on the Redhand brothers.

One of the brothers stood in front of the wain, an ax slung over a shoulder. Heavy set with fiery hair and a whistling wide gap in his teeth. The other brother stood in the seat of the wain, broad of shoulder, long of limb, and dark-haired.

The heavy-set brother raised his high-pitched voice, "One of you cowards best start talking or we're going to have an issue right fuckin' now!"

With a sneer, the mason with braids leaned over the saddle horn. "Fool! You're outnumbered five against two."

Unlimbering his ax, the heavy-set brother slapped the haft against a meaty palm. "We never been good with sums."

"Ain't no number of cowards who kill drunks in their sleep will scare us," called the rangy Redhand from the cab.

Not now. Not like this. Teeth clenched, she shifted her weight and wrung the handle of her mace. *If I attack and they can't muster a kill between the two of them, it'll be five on one. I'll die and Barodane will be alone.*

She shook her head in frustration.

"You know," said the red-headed brother with the ax. "I bet these guys are why Kord wanted us back."

At mention of Kord's name, the masons looked to Eustus. The assassin nodded. They drew hammers and pulled bucklers into their hands. The two afoot unsheathed swords.

"Spot on." The dark-haired brother spat into the mud.

The heavier Redhand turned around to address his brother. "What you think..." he said as if starting a thought. Then he whipped back toward Eustus, ax suddenly cocked back in both hands, and hurled it twenty feet into the chest of Eustus's courser. The horse screamed, staggered. Eustus leapt from the saddle and landed hard on his shoulder in the mud.

Garlenna hesitated. *Now. Charge now!* But something felt wrong.

A moment later, her intuition was validated when two more men previously out of sight rushed in at the flank. *They must have been in hiding on the other side of the Gem Loft.*

Still she wanted to help, but her voice of wisdom held her fast. Without shield or steed, seven was too many, even for her. She couldn't risk it. She'd have to watch and pray for the best.

The rangy Redhand reached under the canvas covering of the wain and came up bearing a rusty long sword. He twisted around just in time to boot a cutthroat in the face. The foe stumbled back, nose gushing blood. The other took a cut at the dark-haired brother's legs, but he leapt out of reach into the wagon bed. He popped up as his opponent followed and cleaved a scarlet trench through the man's head before he could swing again.

The mason with braids spurred his steed forward to meet the Redhand brother in the wain.

The bearded mason and other two cutthroats turned in all directions, ready for an ambush as they kept wary eyes on the Redhands.

This would not play out favorably. The brothers had a nice little surprise attack, but they were ill-equipped, outnumbered, and if she judged rightly out-skilled.

We needed you, fools!

The Redhands' courage, or perhaps stupidity, was anything but lacking. The brother with the fiery hair had drawn a dagger and rushed at Eustus on the ground. One of the footmen pounced forward, leveling a cut at the brother, but the Redhand bulled forward, miraculously blocking the man's sword cut with his dagger and then knocking him to the earth.

Meanwhile, the mounted mason brought his hammer down against the blade of the rangy brother in the wain. Dark hair swept across his face as he struck back, attempting to skewer the horse. But the mason turned his steed aside and rained down two vicious blows. The first was deflected. The second came at him sideways and caught the Redhand in the ribs. He grunted, slaver flying from his mouth. The mason smiled cruelly, tossed braided hair over a shoulder, and then casually bashed in the man's skull. Chunks of glistening pinked bone flipped into the air. The brother's eyes rolled to white. With the mason's hammer lodged in his crown, he flopped face-first into the dirt.

The remaining brother jumped on the injured Eustus, dagger driving toward the stoic man's chest. But Eustus was long and seemingly just as strong as his adversary. By throat and wrist, he held the Redhand at bay. An assassin drew back his sword to skewer the gap-toothed brother, but Eustus growled, "Mine."

The mason with braids was working his hammer out of the rangy brother's skull. Seeing the fight with Eustus, he shouted, "By the look of your brother's brains on my hammer, I'd say you really weren't too good at sums. It's now seven to one. You're dead now, you fucking ingrate!"

This only enraged the Redhand struggling with Eustus. Spittle flew from his mouth as he thrashed wildly and forced his dagger downward another inch. Eustus shifted, cat-quick, hand flying from his foe's throat to grip the thick man by the jaw. The Redhand bit down savagely. Eustus remained calm and jerked him to one side.

The Redhand rolled in the mud, came to his knees, an enraged bull. Calmly, Eustus stood and drew the sword at his hip. With a grunt, he motioned for one of the assassins to give the gap-toothed brother their sword.

A blade skidded to the Redhand brother's feet.

Brandishing his new weapon, he said, "I want that one!" and pointed at the mason with braids who smiled back.

Eustus tapped his own chest with a thumb as if to say, *you get me.*

The Redhand cursed then charged.

A mighty stroke, a whoosh of air. The tip of the Redhand brother's blade bit dirt. Eustus had sidestepped. In passing, he flicked his sword, lopping off three of the Redhand's fingers. Blood gushed from the fat stumps. The wounded man raged, looking more like a wild pig than a man. Face splotchy and pale, neck tendons jumping, he ran forward hacking and spitting and making an angry show of it.

"Look at him go! Such a big, tough man," called the mason with braids and a cruel smile. "Oh, watch out now, Eustus. I think he's going to get you!"

Blades met high, then low, Eustus laughing and moving with lazy calm. He saw the oafish chops before the Redhand even knew he was making them.

Garlenna's chin fell to her chest, drifted to one side in pity.

Eustus took an ear. Split a knee. The Redhand limped forth and took a slash across the back. The towering assassin spun around him with casual grace, then slapped the wheezing Redhand's sword aside and skewered him through the heart.

The thick Redhand brother jolted like a whipped ox. Death gleamed in the whites of his eyes as his sword clanged to the ground.

This fight was over. Garlenna hoped that didn't mean the next one was.

Eustus yanked his blade free. The meaty man pitched forward like a slab of wood. Blood spread from his center, a sluggish pool soaking the mud.

The mason with braids made his way over to spit into the face of the dying man. "I don't understand why Hyram was so worried about...these." He surveyed the carnage. "It's over. The Kurg is dead. These idiots are dead. Kord's exposed. We should attack. Now."

The bearded mason grumbled as Eustus took his horse. "That's for Hyram to decide. Not us. We've still got the big woman. Who knows how many more they've got in waiting. Lairton said—"

The mason with braids spun his horse. "Even if there are more, they'll be worth-less. I'm eager to be back in Breckenbright, damn it. I'm pushing Hyram to end this thing."

"I ain't pissed in hours," one of the assassins walked toward the place where Garlenna hid.

She peered into the alley stretched out behind her. All shadows and shop-fronts and eaves. Rectangles of orange sunlight gleamed along the tops of the buildings. Garlenna slid her mace into her leather thong then slipped her knife from its sheath. With numbers now woefully in favor of Hyram, their chances of survival were dwindling.

That meant her need to take risks just increased.

Garlenna shrunk back against the wall. *Kill, disrupt, escape.* She was trained for such conditions. Few against many. All at once, her plan fell into place, formed along branching lines of possibility.

The man sauntered over, features lit for a split second as he passed into view, then gone, swallowed by shadows. He stopped before the wall opposite her. A burst of scraggly hairs on the crown of his head were the only bit of him left in the sun's light.

His back was to her as he untied his breeches. She waited for the cover of sound. A splat of liquid. A groan of satisfaction. The violent hum of urine streaming into the earth.

Like a barn cat stalking a mouse, the knife led her forward, elbow cocked and tight to her side. Her other hand was cupped, outstretched at the level of where she judged the man's mouth to be. Quick, efficient. No wasted motion. Just training and reflex.

Kill, disrupt, escape.

A tendril of steam coiled into a pane of sunlight over the man's head.

"Hurry the fuck up, Castor!"

The man grunted, turned his head to the sound.

Garlenna froze. A tingle rushed down her spine. She gave no other response in body or mind. The action was already determined. She need only follow through.

His head swiveled back to his cock.

One step. Two. Even, balanced, silent.

His head snapped up, then cocked as if hearing something distant...

A single fluid motion.

Cupped hand clamping around his mouth, hot breath pouring into her palm, dagger punching into the back of his lungs—five thrusts faster than a striking snake.

He arched his back, gasp drowned by throaty gurgles. A sixth and final stab crunched into the base of the skull. He went limp. Garlenna fumbled the man as he dropped. An arm flopped out into the sunlight.

"Castor?" called the cutthroat from before.

"Fuck!" said the mason with braids.

Garlenna was already halfway down the alley. Leg muscles jolting, she sprinted for a wooden column. She wrapped herself around it and shimmied up like a bear. Commotion ricocheted from behind. Hoof beats, curses, the scrape and slither of drawn weapons.

Fingers latching onto the roof, she pried herself up and over. Once atop the second story eaves, she spotted a half-open window within arm's reach. She crept toward it, careful not to give away her position with loud steps, and then worked her way inside.

A baby rolled over on a bed stuffed with straw. It started to crawl toward her as she crossed the room. She passed it by, opened the door—

A fist flew at her face and glanced off a cheek with a flash of light. She stepped back instinctively, ducking the next blow.

Indecipherable curses poured from a young disheveled man in a night shift as he cocked his fist for another punch. Garlenna stepped forward, snared his wrist and throat, threw a leg behind his hips and tripped him gently onto his back. "Stop," she hissed.

"Geh away from muh daher," he choked.

"I mean you no harm. Men are chasing me. If they catch me, they'll kill me." *I have a father too. He wouldn't want me hurt either.* The young parent calmed some, crimson ebbing from the hard lines of anger in his face.

A floorboard creaked. His wife stood in the corner, shaking.

Garlenna ignored her. *Kill, disrupt, escape.*

A hallway paralleled a narrow staircase leading down to the lower level. Above it, a window. "I'm going to leave through there. I'll be gone in a second. Just stay quiet and I won't hurt anyone."

All the energy the woman seemed to have at her disposal went into a single nod. The man glared as Garlenna loosened her grip around his throat.

She strode down the hall, threw open the window. *Barely big enough.* She paused. When she heard no hurried hoof beats or other sounds of chase, she made haste out onto the eaves on the other side of the building. On her belly, she crawled and peeked out into the street.

Digtown was waking, its main thoroughfare beginning to fill with drovers, hawkers, disreputable merchants and the like. A pair of bloody drag marks were all that was left of the Redhand brothers at the Gem Loft next door.

The clean up of murders happens quick here. I'll remember that.

In her years of service as an agent of the Sempyrium, Garlenna had learned that hiding one time wasn't good enough. Twice was effective but three times was best to avoid being found. Pursuers often doubled back later. Right when it felt safe was right when it wasn't.

Crawling like a lizard, she made for the alley furthest from the Gem Loft. She swung her legs out, flipped around, dropped. No shouts. No horses bearing down. No Eustus. No masons.

Hood drawn around her face, she strolled across the main street. Movement too fast or too slow caught the eye. Into the alley across the way, she went, then into the slums beyond.

Before she could draw too many slack-jawed gazes, she ducked under the nearest canvas. A filthy woman lay curled-asleep. A second later, she woke, gagging with shock. She scuttled backward, all hands and heels.

Garlenna held a finger to her lips. "Mind if I stay with you a bit?" Instead of a blade, she produced a silver wheel.

The woman put a hand on her own chest, then gave a toothless grin.

An hour. Then I go in search of Barodane.

Hyram wouldn't be far behind.

CHAPTER THIRTY-SEVEN

TIME AND TIME AGAIN

- THE RIVER'S DEPTHS -

S econds. That's all it takes.

Tendrils of warmth extend outward, forming deep connections, points of information absorbed and sent to a greater whole. It's like fingertips running over smooth lips, like eyes held in awe by the setting sun, like bare feet gripping at soft grass.

I hone my conscious energy, my Locus, and wrap it around Akyris's own. I shudder at the sensation, a fusion of experience.

And we are spinning. Together, we are spinning.

A ringing in the ears, and then rushing, as if our entire body stands within a waterfall. A deafening roar, the rapid clash of quantity against quantity.

The friction of energy moving through space and time.

We push our way through what is known and meet a wall of resistance. It's always at this point in the process that I see the River as an outraged parent and myself as its obstreperous child. It wants to oppress me, to put me in my proper place, to force gratitude for the reality it has created for me. Like any rebellious teen, I push back and reject the course it chose for me.

I work against the River's current, towing Akyris's consciousness until we are birthed, spit forth into floating void and shadowed depths.

The River's greatest secrets.

Illusion and truth, dark and light, the inconceivable and the undeniable, swirling together. Beautiful chaos in all directions.

My Locus seizes, brings to heel what is, creating a focal point. A rainbow of color vibrates through us, moves like a cresting wave across our conscious awareness. What I consider to be my chest hums with anxious delight, a hollow bliss.

Absence is felt here—more so than standing on Unturrus's peak beneath the empty night's sky. No more than a flicker of limitation at the periphery, the absolute horizon of our being. Consciousness, the beckoning center. A storm of all creation's energies.

The River.

Stillness. Nothingness. The web holding everything.

Akyris gasps, thinking there is breath. Breathing is the last vestige of a vessel to be stripped away during a full jump into the River. We cling to it, our dying breath, our last gasp, the mechanism by which we pump life into awareness known.

Here, breath is but illusion.

"You're drowning," I say.

Akyris cannot respond. For him there is only void. He cannot yet see through the jeweled eye. He cannot see with eyes untainted, untethered, unattached.

But I do.

He reels through the blackness, his Locus gradually being swallowed. "You're drowning," I say again.

A thread of understanding. He wraps his consciousness around my words. "Silence, Akyris. Space through surrender. Quit fighting the experience. Be with it. There's nowhere else to go but here. You are here. I am here. We are here. Do you see that?"

Holding onto me by the tether of consciousness, he relaxes. The horizons of his being soften. Fear has tightened his grip, coalesced around his Locus, become an unyielding guard. The more he strangles the experience, the more the inky maw devours him.

It takes effort for me to maintain our tether, though here it is a fraction of the power I can bring to bear. "Can you let go, Akyris? Just a little?"

He hesitates, coils of awareness contracting defensively.

"Did you come here to cling to your old life or forge a new one?"

His Locus relaxes. By the moment, his grip becomes lighter until eventually he releases. The beacon of fear dims within and the defensive barriers drop. The surging tide of the Abyssal Sea retreats, become lapping waves at the edge of awareness.

I show him the River through the jeweled eye...

His mind opens, stretches to take in what are both images and a lack of them, what is known colliding with what could never be. Here he must observe in a way that transcends eyesight.

He must see with the whole being. The Locus. Pure experience.

"Satisfied with your journey now?" I chuckle. "And you wanted to walk dusty roads and sleep under stars. This is a bit more exotic, don't you think?"

He's shocked by my levity. Awe consumes him. A muffled cry escapes his lips, then sobbing. He's overwhelmed. What he thought of as Akyris is being shed. Souls are a deciduous thing, born to greater extents even in their own dying.

I send forth warm comforting pressure. "There will be more tears in the days to come. To mourn is a good thing. To rejoice and revel in this door fate has opened for you, that is good too. It has likely already occurred to you, but I'll voice it now in case you're dafter than expected. You have a special path, Akyris."

His energy gathers inward, settling around the density of his Locus.

"When we return, I suggest you sit with today's experience and be gentle in your process. I do ask that you save your grieving for times when we're not training. There's a purpose in being here. Time is of the essence."

Fear hovers nearer to his Locus. Concentrating, he pries it away and funnels his energy into mine. Space cleared for the next step. "I think...I think I'm ready."

He's not. Soon though, I hope. He has to be. "Good. Here is what you must know. I've bonded you to me for now. That's what allows you to be here. With enough time and practice, you will stand here under your own power and your power alone."

His Locus drifts outward. "Is this the River?"

"These are the River's depths, yes. The River is everything, Akyris, even you. It flows through and connects all. Life and death, shadow and light, the rainbow of chaos and the order of pure absence. From the beginnings of creation to their end—if such a thing as an end exists."

"Wait...am I actually here?"

"Clearly, but your physical vessel is where you left it. Your consciousness has been directed here by my hand while you and I still sit beneath the elm tree. Here..." In the River, I am capable of creating or destroying any constructs of reality at will. I sense he needs an anchor as life's mysteries unravel before him. My Locus scans passing waves of rippling color, snares and then weaves threads of existence together in order to manifest physical bodies. Akyris's smile is first to manifest as he sees his consciousness forming into what he knows as himself. I do the same, though I do away with the bad hip and a few excess wrinkles. "I thought this might help you adjust."

Floating side by side, I drift a short way from him and then move my staff through the space. Struck matter rolls toward Akyris like an ocean wave, a panoply of swirling hues. Just before it passes through him, his expression is shocked. After, his face is etched with wonderment.

"You. Me. This. That. Everything *is* the River. It flows through all. Threads of conscious reality united as a singular evolving event. And, much like a River, it looks entirely different beneath the surface. Few humans ever dive past their own obscured reflections. Those who use godsthorn, have near-death experiences, or become Awakened on Unturrus catch a glimpse. Of those, many drowned in their unwitting attempts to touch the bottom."

I raise a finger wreathed in ghost-light. "However, with my support, *your* consciousness can survive here. Our first goal is for you to be able to travel alongside me, unaided. That is step number one."

Excitement ripples through me at the idea of Akyris someday rivaling my power or that of Darkhorn. Perhaps, he'll attain Tahmyrus's power of traveling through the River fully integrated with his vessel.

Akyris senses my uptick in energy. "Our goal?" I've forgotten we are linked. "Who's goal?"

I kick myself for the slip. One thing at a time. "There are a handful of others who I communicate with through the River."

"And you have a goal for me?" His Locus condenses, hard as steel, suspicious as a battered cat. "Why?"

"Do you want this or don't you?" I'm more short with him. "We're beyond the point of questioning, Akyris. It's yes or no. Decide now."

He stares at a torus of emerald dust and darkness funneling back into itself as he considers. Time and silence linger. "Yes." The word echoes throughout the River.

Compassion drives a promise from me. "In time, I will tell you of the others...and more. But I need your trust. It'll be good for you to trust me. Some of what you'll see will be painful. Excruciatingly so. Do you understand?"

There's no way for him to know what that means, not really. Stubbed toes and scraped knees and the slaps of teenage girls give him no measure for comparison. Likely, he's thought them all excruciating. The truth is they've been gentle breezes compared to what comes next.

I know he'll say yes. Keep saying yes at every step on the way to his death. I share truths and then find them as daggers of guilt stuck in my breast each time I do. I lay the trap for my grandson to step into.

I march him to his grave.

Yet, I cannot stop it.

He nods. I swallow shame. "I'm going to release you to drift alone. Remember, open yourself to what you see, hear, and feel, as well as what you don't. If you refuse the unfamiliar or fight it, it *will* consume you. Ready?"

The hubris of youth nods. I cannot blame him. Given the same situation, with roles reversed, I would say yes. I always have. Just like Akyris, my curiosity can't be quenched.

The very reason I ascended Unturrus.

I release him. Instantly, the manifested form I've pulled together for him dissipates. The Abyssal Sea creeps in to snuff him out.

I let him drown. There's scant possibility he'll see himself out of it. There is a nominal chance his Locus will be flayed of a sense of self. A horrifying prospect.

It was by this same set of circumstances the world was been cursed with the Arrow of Light. An Awakened with dizzying power and stripped of all humanity.

I feel the edges erode, a breach in the walls of Akyris's consciousness. His awareness is being siphoned away, dragged into the Abyssal Sea. Dark waters drinking him...

My Locus reaches forward to save him from the brink of annihilation.

I return him to the form he's most familiar being. Coughing on his knees, inky energy spews from his nose, ears, eyes and mouth. Neck tendons bulge with imagined strain. "The pain." he moans. "Gods...the pain."

"It will continue to hurt until you can swim in the River on your own." I help him to spectral feet—a silly act. I know it comforts him. "Come. Go again."

Again he drowns. Again I tether him back to himself.

Gasp. Pain. Sputter. Weep. Hands and knees and inky orifices. Shivering torment. "Again."

Again and again, he meets the same result.

After a dozen more attempts to fly, the little bird is worn out. Even with my help, he barely musters the energy to return from the endless dark.

He's gasping, his consciousness worn thin, exhausted to the breaking point. The process has made him stronger. "You're getting better." I attempt levity, hoping to overpower the stink of failure he feels. "But why do you love drowning so much?"

"I can't keep going. My—uh, my mother will worry about me if we don't go back soon." An excuse birthed from fear.

"You think you're failing?"

"Of course," he snaps. "What else would you call it? I'm getting worse. Torture for nothing."

"Just because you stand alone for less and less time doesn't mean you're getting worse. On the contrary, you being willing to continue is what strengthens your spirit. Despite your inability to see it."

Doubt wells in him. He doesn't believe me. "We have to go back...it's been so long. Mother will start—"

"Don't worry about that," I snap. "It's only been a few hours."

This rocks him. "So you can control time?"

"I wish." That would solve many problems. "I can only see through it and move through it. But a small pebble throws wide ripples. We think of time as some external machine, dripping away like sand, or like a hoard of gold one can save. It is no such thing. Time is within you, Akyris. Within me. Within all. It bleeds through our thoughts, feelings and actions. It bleeds through and connects them to the River, which is expressed through you and I.

I poke his chest with my staff. "Time dwells nowhere else but here. It starts, stops, and slows within the turning of our mind's eye. By learning to block out thought, feeling, or action, you can learn to exist outside of time and capture it for a fleeting moment." I lean into him with my eyes. "You can see through it. Even enter it."

"I'll have this power someday?" He hesitates. "What makes me worthy of any of this?"

His path has been chosen by something beyond my ability to comprehend. Magomedes and I are simple conduits just like the others: Darkhorn, Tahmyrus, Hashuuk. Each has a role to play, and each has only the limited understanding to know they play it. The rest of the world, other Awakened included, wake and sleep in the shadow of this truth.

In the shadow of what awaits.

The Arrow of Light.

"You are my grandson," I say. "You share my blood, and now you will share in my power if you so wish."

His Locus whirs, brightens, a brilliant glow outlining his illusory vessel. He pins back his shoulders. "I do."

"Then never again question your worth to me!" I thunder. "What you do with the seconds that float by you dictates who you are and how you'll be remembered. Time reveals the truth in all of us."

My words echo through the River, resonate within Akyris.

"I have seen who you can be. I deem that boy worthy of this training. But this self-doubt you're so attached to is like a ballast." I fix him with a stare that could strip skin from bone. "This is why you drown."

Woe fills him.

A susurration, just out of the boy's ability to hear, enters the space.

"Tell him why." Darkhorn's tone is less ornery than usual. More adamant. Almost pleading. I'd say he's learned you get more from a honey bee than a hornet, but I don't actually believe it will last.

Magomedes is here too. "He's not ready."

"What point is there in him being ready if we cannot get him to where he needs to be when the Arrow of Light comes?" Darkhorn says.

I push back. "What point is there in him facing Siddaia if he cannot stop him when he needs to?"

"He needs to know what we face." Darkhorn says.

"No," I say. "What he needs is training. He'll hear about his role when he's ready. Not a moment before."

Silence precedes the Kurg's condemnation of me. "At the end of the world, I'll blame you, Locastrii."

"If I wasn't going to be dead by then, I'd say you'd be kissing my feet. Righteous, fucking cur."

Magomedes gasps. I don't stick around to process the interaction. There's training to attend.

Much, much more.

Another fifty times, Akyris wades into the River alone. And another fifty times he drowns.

CHAPTER THIRTY-EIGHT

THE TRIAL OF SUMMIT

- DESCENT -

Together, they descended the forested slopes of the Ice King.

"I'm in no rush," Lodaris said. His parents would discover his betrayal when they reached the bottom.

I'd be in no rush either.

The wind died and the snow ceased to fall. The sun returned around midday, churning the cold into veils of heavy steam that curled at their legs.

Snow melted and thinned as they wound down a narrow path with a twelve-foot drop to one side. Lodaris pressed a foot against a boulder as Ishoa locked hands with him and helped lower him down. She grunted under the strain until he dropped the rest of the way. When it was her turn, he bore her weight on his shoulders a fraction of a moment before she jumped, kicking up a white flurry upon landing.

A stream gushed forth from beneath the vast root system of a clump of trees. They followed it, navigating slick rock and frosty beds of packed mud. Hunger gnawed at Ishoa's belly. One glance at Lodaris told her he was similarly famished, so they stopped to eat.

The cold air sapped moisture from them at a faster rate than normal, making each take long pulls from their waterskins. Lodaris flipped open the corners of a cloth wrapping containing hard biscuits.

With her dagger, Ishoa worked at a small, hard wheel of cheese. *This should pair nicely.*

"You'll dull the blade," said Lodaris. "Over time, that is."

Ishoa paused mid slice and wagged the knife at him. "If you insist on dulling my mind with your empty worries, you can start calling me 'Highness' again." They laughed, eyes soft and full of dance.

A hawk passed in front of the sun, screamed, then wheeled away. Robins shuttled from thicket to thicket. One fluttered onto the twig of a bush and sang, head twisting to one side and then the other as it inspected their food. Lodaris tossed it a flake of biscuit. "A beautiful place."

Ishoa smiled as she touched her lips in remembrance of the night before. "Beautiful indeed." *When I'm not fearing for my life.*

She replaced the wheel of cheese and shouldered her pack. "We need to keep moving."

The wind returned as the sun descended, casting an ashen pall over the landscape. They trudged into a wide clearing. By the smooth look of it, the sparkle of an unbroken surface, it seemed no others had come this way. Beautiful. Perfect. Like the one she'd seen with Dragga.

She leapt onto the crusty surface with a satisfying crunch. *There's more pleasure derived from what's broken and blemished.* She looked to Lodaris as he followed suit. Sunlight traced his face, scarred cheeks red from the nip of cold.

She took his hand. Felt the stroke of his thumb against the pit of her palm.

It felt free to do so on the mountain where no one would see. Without judgment of Ishoa's choices. Without harsh consequences for Lodaris. They were free of society's condemning yoke. If Ishoa felt any lighter, she worried she might fly.

She sighed, wishing she could breathe it in forever. Wishing she never had to return.

Could I abandon my duties for my feelings like he has?

Only a child, unfit to rule, would consider it. *I'm not Lodaris.* His was a decision of rightness and necessity. Hers would be a fanciful dream motivated by impulse and emotion. *All of Namarr depends on me. I'm a prisoner to my lineage.*

"What's this?"

Ishoa followed Lodaris's gaze to a wooded area, a stone's throw downslope. Orange light flickered under the shadowed canopy. They exchanged an indignant look.

Fire.

"I wonder who fell through the ice," Ishoa said. Dragga Omenfaen's face swam before her mind's eye. The idea of perfection incarnate starting a fire didn't seem possible. *Nevertheless, I hope he's safe.*

"Do we steer clear?" Lodaris tongued his lower lip as he stared.

Ishoa shook her head. "This close, the fire is a danger to us. We have to put it out. Besides, it may mean they're wet or lost. They need us."

Lodaris scowled. "My bet is it's Yurm the Worm and that fool, Unalor."

They resumed their march, heading for the wood. "I wonder if they know how close they are to the bottom." By her estimation, they were a half day's descent.

Crunch. Crunch. Crunch. The sound grated in Ishoa's ears. *Absolute idiots!*

When they were within a few hundred feet, Lodaris whispered angrily, "The ingrates convinced another to share in their stupidity."

Three silhouettes sat around the fire. *Have they gone mad?* Puffs of hot breath pooled in the sun's fading rays as they drew closer.

A fourth, and then a fifth silhouette appeared.

Crunch. Crunch. Crunch.

A tingle ran up Ishoa's spine. *Such wanton disregard...seems impossible.*

A sixth figure stood. She slowed, peering more intently as her eyes struggled to adjust to the dense, dark understory.

Crunch. Crunch.

They were upwind from the thicket. A light breeze traveled over the clearing, carrying the stale smell of animal hide and roasting meat to Ishoa's nose.

She froze. *Oh no. Ancestors no.*

"Fools!" Lodaris cupped hands to the sides of his mouth. "Douse that fire!"

Crunch...

Lodaris took one more, blaring step. Panic mounting, Ishoa seized him by the pack and yanked him back, nearly onto his rear. He grunted, stumbled backward, but maintained his feet.

Over the group's fire, what looked like a snow bison's leg roasted on a spit.

Ishoa's mouth was dry as dust. Her legs quaked with fear. It was all she could do to make her lips move, to form the word necessary. Meek, incredulous, it dribbled into the space. "Trolls."

Everything seemed to slow.

Balance regained, Lodaris swiveled toward the wood. Six sets of narrow shoulders had risen, now turned in the Claimants' direction. The warband was silent but for a single guttural, alien word.

Lodaris's eyes went wide.

A troll stepped from the copse into daylight. Flame flickered off milk-white skin. It furrowed a jutting brow and stared down its long, pointed nose at them. Bones dangled from its shaggy, ivory mane. A battered and rusted honor plate was roped to its chest.

This one has killed Namorites before.

It lowed.

Bronze axes and short swords leapt into the hands of its brethren. Goat-like beards anchored narrow, lobeless skulls as they drifted like hungry specters from the wood.

"Ishoa..." Lodaris drew his sword. "You—you must run."

She drew her own blade. "I'm not leaving you." Her teeth chattered with unchecked fear. She gasped, vaguely aware she'd stopped breathing only after her body forced air back into her lungs. Light swam in her vision as dizziness took hold. She was breathing in rapid sips—dangerously fast. If she fainted now, she would never wake up. Wolst had told her about this, told her what to do when nerves threatened to overwhelm. First, she exhaled hard, then breathed in through her nose as slow as possible. Repeating the process, thought returned and the disoriented feeling faded.

Ishoa wished Rakeema was there but only for a moment. *She'd only die with us.*

Three more C'Dathuns she hadn't seen, brought their number to nine as they emerged from the thicket. Feet that looked like the trunk of a tree where it meets the earth remained above the icy surface, three gnarled toes gripping it. Ishoa glanced at her own feet, sunk to mid-calf in the snow.

That's bad.

Lodaris's tongue darted, eyes fixed on the enemy. He backpedaled, his voice hoarse. "Run."

Like rabbits who'd spied a fox, they sheathed their swords and plunged through the snow. Thought became slick, fluid, and fell into her feet. Training evaporated, leaving her with naught but instinct.

Instinct and the mad rush of terror.

Lodaris lagged behind, his shorter legs struggling to win free of the deep drifts. But when they hit a stand of dense trees where the snow couldn't reach the earth, he raced ahead of her. A loose rope on Ishoa's pack caused it to jerk against her shoulder; it started to burn fiercely but she ignored it and sped on.

The C'Dathun trolls lowed and whooped and chattered in pursuit. One gave a throaty cackle. *A laugh?*

Horror bled into Ishoa's bowels. *Yes, because they're going to catch us...*

"Faster!" Lodaris reached back for her hand and pulled her along.

They clambered over a fallen snag. Ishoa afforded a backward glance. Reality sank in. The white-furred legs of the C'Dathuns were long and lithe, falling somewhere between those of a human and the hind legs of an ice tiger or goat. These creatures migrated over glaciers, chased down prey on strands of sea ice. This was their terrain. The landscape they lived or died by.

We can't outrun them.

They raced headlong into a sparse stand of birches.

"Lodaris!" she screamed. "We have to fight!"

He looked back. From his expression, he had to have recognized the same. Resolve followed resignation. He stopped, drew his sword, and turned to face them. A split second later, Ishoa whirled around. The leather grip of her sword filled her hand. Darksteel rasped forth. Breath came to her in ragged gulps. At least her teeth no longer chattered. Running for her life had shaken the nerves loose and she settled into a crouch, jaw clenched, the urge to survive at any cost filling her grip with iron.

Sweat dripped over one eye. Not daring to take her hands off her blade hilt, she wiped it with a bicep.

Steam rolled from the C'Dathun's apish mouths as they spread out in a crescent formation. They reeked like an unmucked-stable. Thumb-sized horns protruded from shaggy white hair at the tops of their skulls. Eyes, just as pale as their skin, with black slits for pupils, were nestled deep under in cavernous sockets.

The one Ishoa assumed to be their leader swept the snot from its long nose with the back of a clawed hand then slapped the pauldron it used as a chest plate. Its cheeks puffed as it forced a guttural cluck through a cratered mouth.

It raised a bronze ax at them.

Lodaris dragged Ishoa behind him by the hem of her cloak.

The C'Dathuns advanced. Two of their number paused. Thick brows knit, they sniffed the air.

Lodaris feinted at the nearest troll, then drove back a second one with a series of tight thrusts and slashes. A third C'Dathun lunged, dinted short sword flashing. Lodaris dipped, countered. The troll screamed, a sound half-human, half-beast, as blood sluiced from a gash along its forearm. The other C'Dathun's glanced at each other, then proceeded more cautiously.

"Yes!" Lodaris hunkered around his sword hilt gripped in both hands. "Be afraid!" He rushed forward, leveling a chop at one's midsection. The creature threw its weapon up just in time to block it.

That was all Ishoa had time to see.

Two C'Dathun's leapt into the space Lodaris had vacated. Before training could take over and tell her to yield no forward momentum to her opponents, she backpedaled instinctively. The pair of trolls rushed her, a flurry of white hair, barred fangs, and throaty snarls. Wild slashes split the air.

The misses were narrow and became more so with each blade's passing.

Ishoa leaned quickly to one side, felt the whoosh of one of their weapons a fraction of a moment behind, saw strands of her dark-brown hair jump then drift away.

Do something!

An ax edge plummeted toward her face. She dug in her heels, pivoted to her left, slapped the blow past. The troll grunted, its flank suddenly exposed as it overextended. With gritted teeth, Ishoa drove her blade into the creature's hip. It stiffened and fell shrieking to the snow-strewn duff. The second troll faced her, slitted black eyes unblinking.

Somewhere in the slurry of grunting and clashing metal, Lodaris cursed.

The C'Dathun leader lowed triumphantly.

"I'm cut!" Lodaris's shout was frantic. Icy shards of dread settled into Ishoa's spine. "Run, Ishoa!"

Before she could react, she glimpsed the charging shadow of a second troll behind her. Only the instinct to drop forward at the last second saved her. The C'Dathun still in front of her cut the air where her head had been as she dove into its thin, shaggy leg with a shoulder.

Collarbone met shin. Numbness shot down her arm, causing her to drop her sword. The sacrifice was not without reward. The C'Dathun's ankle made a sickening pop. It keened and fell, entangling with Ishoa in the snow. She fought for position, but even injured the creature was strong with rage. It grabbed her by the neck and slammed her to the ground. Callused hands locked around her throat. It rocked forward, pinning her to the earth. She bucked her hips—to no effect. It sat on her stomach and began to squeeze the life from her, saliva falling in a bead from its apish mouth onto her forehead.

Do something!

Mustering what fading strength she had left, Ishoa sent a fist toward its protruding nose—a glancing blow. It snorted, then raised its head out of reach. She aimed the next blow at its injured ankle, but that also fell short. Pressure filled her face until her skin felt as if it might burst. Flashing dots muddied her vision. She thought of Lodaris fighting nearby. *At least we die together.* She would miss Rakeema. She would miss Othwii. She would miss Wolst.

Images of her parents flashed across her mind. *I'll meet you soon...*

The forest grew darker by the second. A blur of motion bleeding into stillness. Warmth suffused her arms and feet, and crept into her torso. She could no longer tell if she breathed. Vaguely, she knew she'd given up fighting.

Lodaris...

Her arms went limp then melted away. The troll's face faded black.

I love you.

But for a pinpoint of light, abyssal darkness swallowed her.

A muffled thud...distant and near. Something shook her hands.

She gasped. Consciousness rushed back into her in a wave of sensation. She coughed, dry and harsh, lungs burning with the sudden intake of air. Pain flared through her skull, and there were sharp pinpricks in her ears.

The C'Dathun's blurry face entered her vision. Crimson beads raced down the troll's cheeks to patter onto its shoulder. Its tongue lolled, a dead purple worm, as its empty gaze searched the sky. It wavered a moment and then toppled into the blurry backdrop.

Garbled sound. A familiar voice.

A shout repeated, gaining clarity with each command until it resolved into something coherent...

"Highness!"

Not Lodaris. Someone else.

"Highness! Get up!"

Ishoa blinked. Her vision returned like spilled wine soaking through a tablecloth. Her eyelids were heavy and aching. Lodaris stooped over her and grabbed her round the shoulders. He yanked her to a seated position, then heaved at her to rise.

Nearby, an unknown ally fought C'Dathuns.

Blood spattered Lodaris's face. Crimson rivulets streamed down his sword. Evidence of a wound pasted his shoulder. He'd lost his pack. She hoped he'd tucked his sentry rose in his pants pocket as she had.

With Lodaris's aid, she grabbed her sword and struggled onto wobbly feet. She glanced at the dead C'Dathun beside her. The top portion of its skull was stove inward.

"Your Highness!"

Ishoa winced, neck muscles tender as she turned. Swathed in black wolf fur and a studded warskirt, Stirrma Omenfaen was there, the anvil-shaped head of her warhammer singing chaos in the space around her. The C'Dathuns balked, whooping angrily at their new assailant.

"You must run!" Stirrma said. Sound, breath and clarity peeled away the final numb shadows of near death.

"We can't leave you," Lodaris said.

Ishoa sputtered, words failing. She rubbed at her raw throat.

"You must! And you will!" A troll made to circle wide of Stirrma. She swung her warhammer in a low loop, sundering its thin legs, then brought the hammer around and down onto the back of the creature's skull with a soupy splat. Scarlet spewed in every direction.

"You're in no shape to fight. Lodaris, get the princess out of here." Stirrma laughed, a painfully joyous thing. "Tell my brother he'll not have all the glory!"

The C'Dathun troll Ishoa had wounded in the hip leapt forward—too slow—Stirrma sent it hurtling sideways with a shattered face. Its head thudded to the earth first, then the rest of its limp body crumpled up around it.

"No..." Ishoa croaked, but a pale-faced Lodaris was already dragging her by the arm with his remaining good one. He kept the bloody one cradled at his side.

Though it tormented Ishoa's neck to crane around, she had to see...

C'Dathuns converged on Stirrma from all sides. The scion of Omenfaen blocked a stab with a sweep of her haft. Her momentum spun her in a circle. She brought the anvil head back around lightning quick, then released one hand, suddenly doubling her weapon's reach. The head of her hammer shot into the ribs of another troll, doubling it over, eyes bulging as it vomited blood.

Three came at once. Stirrma side stepped, blocked a cut, then another. The C'Dathun leader feinted, ducked inside her guard and scored a slash along her thigh.

Rage filled Stirrma's scream. She sought to return the favor, but the trolls' leader hastened out of reach.

Stirrma was a skilled warrior. Beyond even what Ishoa had imagined. And every bit as courageous as her twin brother. But the reality of her grim fate sank into

Ishoa like an ice tiger's killing bite at the nape. Stirrma Omenfaen was wounded, her mobility hampered, and she faced five C'Dathun trolls.

Ishoa stared straight ahead as they fled.

Full of pride and only a tinge of fear, Stirrma's final war cry pinioned Ishoa like an arrow. "For glory! For Namarr!"

It rang out across the Ice King's slopes. Echoed through Ishoa's memory, the loudest thing she'd ever heard.

Louder than the crunch of Lodaris's boots on snow as they sped to safety.

Louder than all the fanfare that would greet the Claimants when the Trials were finished.

Louder than the songs sung at celebrations that breathed life into legends.

CHAPTER THIRTY-NINE

SWIFTLY THROUGH THE SNOW

They woke to winter stretching from horizon to horizon. To the east, a pink sky bled upward into the underbellies of swollen clouds. To the west it was clear, only a chilly-looking cobalt blue and a brush stroke of ocean beneath. Anything nearer to the Ascendants was deep snow. Life had become a blank canvas.

Thephos blinked, brushed a melting flake from his cheek. *I'm not cold.* He looked to the others for confirmation, a sometimes risky venture. Horror confirmed horror, confusion validated confusion, disbelieving questions begotten by unbelievable answers.

Radea sat up and shook powder from her smock, her hair wild and strewn with snow. Olthr did the same. Neither had blue lips nor too pale a face. "Unturrus does what it will, when it wills," Radea said in bitter tones. The woman who would save the world had lost all the punch of righteous confidence in her voice. She seemed a husk of her former self, a beaten child given over to despair.

Thephos didn't blame her. There were few of them now. The buffer against death had waned. Fate clamped around their awareness like a bear trap.

And we already gnaw at our legs for escape.

Despair threatened, but Thephos plunged it into the depths.

Olthr leapt to a standing position, snow crunching underfoot. "I've got a good feeling about today." With a sharp intake of breath, his chest swelled.

Thephos waited for the man's exhale. He'd never hoped for a cloud of steam before. Never looked for one as an anchor to reality. His heart ached as he stifled a passing impulse to look at his hand in the light of day. Finally, the monk sighed forth a thick cloud of steam. Thephos relaxed.

The Anjuhk moaned in her sleep. Radea went to her. As her hand hovered over the woman's shoulder, Radea seemed to see something. Her mouth fell open. She pulled back. "She broke." Radea's demeanor was bleak. The momentary impulse for compassion gone. "We should go on without her."

"Perhaps." Olthr chewed the inside of his cheek, then forced a smile. "But we will have strength in numbers, regardless of her mental state."

Thephos knew what he meant. Maybe she would die in his stead when the next demon came. But the truth was, the moment they'd passed through the Corpse Gate, their lives were forfeited. *I was dead long before that.*

"What does it matter if she's broken?" Thephos said. "We're all going to die. Why not allow her the comfort of others at the end?"

Radea turned her haunted stare up the mountain. "You wake her then."

The Anjuhk was deathly still, a fixture on the mountain no different than another stone or twisted stump. Thephos knelt behind her sleeping form and grabbed her shoulder then shook her gently. "We're going." Under the thin fabric of the smock, she was firm. He hadn't met many women. Only the Rose Sister who visited the farm and his mother when he was very little. He'd crossed paths with a handful of others before he'd come to Unturrus, but never had he touched one as an adult. His father had convinced him women were a frail breed compared to men—more like Thephos. She should feel softer, weaker. *The old devil lied.*

When she didn't stir, Thephos swallowed an arid lump in his throat and shook her again, more vigorously this time. Knees sinking a half-foot into the snow, he leaned over her. He hesitated. He took one of her hands in his own. Still warm. Vacant eyes stared at the sky as he hauled her over.

Then flickered toward him.

He shot backward onto his rear with a startled cry. The Anjuhk ignored him and began making butterflies in the powdery snow, the act mechanical and mirthless.

Olthr glared at the Anjuhk. Radea turned her shoulders toward the mountain's face. *Leave her*, the motion seemed to suggest.

"Sky," said the Anjuhk. "The sky is red. The sky is pink. The sky is orange. Nothing rhymes with sky."

Cry, lie, die, Thephos thought but saw no purpose in answering the challenge of insanity. "It's time to go."

"Am I home?"

"No."

"Oh," the Anjuhk said. "Pity."

Olthr and Radea started up the mountain, packed snow screeching with every step.

"You need to stand and move." Thephos helped her along. *It's a miracle she keeps her feet at all.* "Come on." She complied sparingly, exerting only enough effort to stumble through the other Ascendant's footsteps. It wasn't like helping an elderly person, for they took much more care and leaned heavily on their supports. More like guiding babies as they learned to walk. Thephos had done so numerous times with his brothers.

He hoped the youngest of them held the hands of a Rose Sister now. He was grateful for the hands that would no longer touch them. The devil's hands. Grinding his teeth, Thephos resisted the urge to look at his own.

I am not my father. I did not come here to kill.

As they caught up to the others, he repeated the mantra to himself, whispering rage barely kept at bay. Helping the Anjuhk brought some small comfort. *My father would never have helped this woman. He would have left her for dead, like Radea wanted me to do. And I am not my father. I'm not evil.*

Suddenly, he felt jaw clenching hatred. The arm he led the Anjuhk with stiffened. He hated Radea for her coldness. He hated Olthr for his self-obsession. He hated the burdensome Anjuhk too. She moved like some stupid wooden doll. He hated the old devil too, but most of all he hated himself for hating all of them like he would have.

The impulse to stare down made him curse. Instead, he looked upward—anywhere but his hands. No birds flew. They at least had enough wisdom to avoid Unturrus. The air was thinner too, which made breathing a trial. Thephos found himself hating Unturrus for its fickle nature; they did not hunger, nor feel cold, but the Mountain of Power deemed it necessary to still impose physical limitations in a handful of other ways. Added cruelty to those doomed to die.

Thephos looked at the Anjuhk.

"Are we going home?"

He didn't respond.

At intervals, he glanced back from the direction they had come. The landscape stretched below, pulling tighter into itself the greater distance up they traveled until it became a two-dimensional abstraction of green, brown, and gray. Detail was shouldered aside by scope and scale.

A trail of dark footprints followed them. Imprints of the past. Little graves waiting to be filled.

Snow blanketed more of the mountain, gave way to a memory long suppressed. He remembered very little of his youngest years. They didn't seem important. Not compared to the years when he was more useful as a worker to his father. When he could carry a slop bucket or dig a post-hole. Those were the days he recalled most often. The dangerous ones. The ones where he needed to live in fear of past experiences in order to avoid future pain.

So this pleasant memory surprised him.

He and his brothers had strapped broken planks of wood from a pig pen together and used them to sled down the snowy slope under the willow. From level ground, it was only a dozen paces to the tree, but he'd been so small that it seemed monstrous then.

Warmth suffused Thephos's chest and arms. He racked his mind for more memories of the same, but it seemed the sledding had happened only once before his mother had died. His father had to have been gone for such fun to take place. Conditions for that single moment of joy had to have been perfect. A star in the vast stretch of black that was his life.

Thephos felt his face twist into a wistful smile.

"I want to go home." The Anjuhk swayed, pulling Thephos off balance. "Please take me home."

"We'll be there soon," he lied. Why make her suffer needlessly before death? "Almost there. Almost there."

Ahead, Olthr kept a frantic pace. Thephos suspected the unimist monk thought he could beat fate to some invisible finish line if he hurried. *Who am I to assume him wrong? Perhaps Olthr will become Awakened.* The thought ran counter to Thephos's deeper intuition. The monk was just as broken as the Anjuhk clinging to a semblance of reality at his arm. It just looked different. While she retreated to a safe place, protected from the horrors she'd seen—or would see—Olthr dashed forward, a naked sprint to outstrip crippling uncertainty.

They trudged toward a forest. Without breaking stride, Radea twisted to look back at them. "If you keep that pace with her, you'll fall behind."

Wind howled across the gray and white slopes. Thephos bent a hand around his mouth, shouted, "Who are we to slow you? Leave us if you must."

Radea nodded grimly.

Obscured by a halo of cold, the summit of Unturrus loomed. *If we make it there, what will we find? What horrors still await?*

The Anjuhk muttered, "Almost there."

The cold struck, a series of intense gusts nipping at Thephos's ears and the tip of his nose. He gasped, inhaling spiky air. Radea and Olthr must have felt it too, for they wrapped arms around their torsos and raced the rest of the way to the treeline. Frigid fog gathered around the skirts of the trees as they stopped to reclaim their breath.

Radea took up a seat on a downed log and stared at the snow pack. With the backs of her hands resting against her thighs, she took measured breaths.

The focused edge Olthr once held in his eyes was gone. Whatever dam holding his sanity in place was now broken. Everything about him sought escape. His eyes darted. His hands twitched. His tongue probed dry lips. But he smiled—a fake thing. Whatever consciousness lived inside him was fighting to be free of his body. Almost as if it sensed his doom fast approaching. "I'm starving," he said. "I haven't eaten in so long." He went to the well of a tree and knelt, searching the ground. Began to dig.

Thephos's spine tingled.

Olthr scooped something to his face as he hunched covetously around it. His shoulders and neck flexed through the white smock as he gnawed at whatever lay in his palms.

Radea wore a wary sneer as she watched the monk. "Let's continue."

With a dead look in his eyes, Olthr hid what was in his hands and took the lead. Radea fell in behind at a distance. Thephos and the Anjuhk followed.

Time passed. Bursts of sunlight told them it was day, but Thephos doubted even that was trustworthy. They followed a path through the trees, moving gradually upward. Light faded, ushering the gray pall of dusk. The temperature plummeted. Thephos's teeth chattered, his hands and feet became numb blocks. After a while, the only tingles of sensation were those he felt when he stepped on a sharp stick or rock.

Olthr dropped back to walk beside Thephos. "Are you hungry?" He thrust a handful of worm-riddled moss under Thephos's nose. "We need to eat to keep our strength."

With his free arm, Thephos shoved the monk back a step. "That's dirt and worms, Olthr."

"Oh." The monk's brow knit together, mouth parted. As if stung, he cast the handful of earth to the ground and frantically wiped his mouth. "I thought—I'm so sorry."

He mumbled as he made his way back to the front, glancing back at intervals as if stalked by some monster unseen.

The trees thinned out as the sharp incline through the forest leveled. They marched onward, a purposeless procession riding the razor's edge of impossible hopes.

Striving upward.

A single direction.

Up the Mountain of Power.

It had become primal since the Corpse Gate, a singular focus without compromise. Go to die, but make sure you do not stop. Go up. Always up.

Ascendants. The namesake is well earned.

The path wound around a cliff side, offering a brief reprieve. To their right, a narrow stream wound down the mountain and then dropped over the cliff's edge, dissipating into the air as it plummeted out of sight. Wind whistled through unseen fissures in the mountain. They went slow, careful of the treacherous footing. Eventually, they picked their way over tumbledown boulders and back onto something resembling a path.

Frosted canopy lied ahead, ringing an expanse of snow-covered earth. The glade fast approached as they hurried to be free of the howling, snapping wind. By the time they arrived at the glade's edge, dusk was upon them.

They panted.

"What's that?" asked Olthr between ragged breaths.

Thephos shook his head. "What?"

"I feel strange," Olthr said. "I maybe...hearing things."

Thephos's ears buzzed as if a bee crept into the back of his skull. "I feel it too." Something about it seemed familiar. "Should we keep going?" Radea and Olthr nodded emphatically. In the shadow of the unknown, a rush of panic seized them. Thephos felt it—realized *they* felt it, too. It eddied in the air...everywhere around them.

The Anjuhk began to sing.

"Plant all the rows and strive to survive. Bend and drop, bend and drop..."

Olthr led them out of the trees and into an expansive clearing of deep snow drifts that looked like uneven smears of butter, or the waves of a troubled sea suddenly frozen. Where once they left footprints, they now left deep gouges, knees dragging to win free with every twist of the torso.

The gray sky burst, releasing a white deluge. Icy wind drove against them, sought to drag their ceremonial smocks from their bodies. Thephos pulled the Anjuhk closer for mutual warmth and closed his eyes against the stinging flakes. Visibility was limited to a couple stone throws.

The Anjuhk stumbled as she sang. "The rains will come and your work is yet done. Bend and drop, bend and drop..."

Thephos struck a quicker pace, body torquing through the frozen waves of thigh-high snow. The Anjuhk's hand was limp in his own, but her voice was powerful—more powerful than the howling wind. He fought to drag her faster.

"Wait!" Thephos called to Radea as the gap between the pairs widened. Lungs burning with effort, he lurched forward—nearly fell.

When he glanced ahead, his heartbeat leapt into his throat. Radea had gone rigid, palms staring up at her. She studied her hands.

All of them were looking for an explanation, an answer to the rush of alien sensation.

All but the singing Anjuhk. "Wife and kids call, but there's wood to be chopped. Bend and drop, bend and drop..."

Thephos stopped. Let the Anjuhk's hand fall away. His own breath, his heartbeat, the blood pounding through his veins...whispered his name. Demanded his attention, all at once, stunningly clear. Warm and full and impossible to get enough of. Infinitely, he could drink the sensations, the air and the blood and the thump, thump, thump of life.

Near a berm on the other side of the snow-drenched clearing, Olthr halted and beckoned them to follow. *He's terrified.*

Here and there, great drifts rose higher than the rest, as if they were a cresting wave. Solid ground, immovable in reality, started to dilate. Rising and falling, sucking in and pushing out, the waves drew Thephos into them. He sauntered toward a snowy swell and kicked it—struck solid. Pain shot through his foot. Something rooted deep in the earth.

Frail snow, like handfuls of sand, caved inward, revealing a secret he'd already known. Brightly colored flowers sank into his eyes. Blood wept from a half-dozen places on his foot. Cut by godsthorn.

Somewhere distant, Radea shouted, but the wind screamed her words inchoate. Despite his threshed foot, Thephos's ears throbbed with pleasure. He looked up.

Olthr stumbled into a thicket of godsthorn. His mouth looked like it was yelling. No one answered. The wind swallowed it all.

Amid the pleasure, Thephos felt their fear rising. Felt his eyes in theirs...all places at once without turning his face to see...

He saw it all.

Saw Radea run toward Olthr. Saw the Anjuhk sitting alone back near the forest's swaying edge, dancing with the wind like an old lover whose hips didn't quite move like they used to but still wanted nothing more than to dance.

Thephos swayed with them, eyes closed until the world spun underfoot and overhead and the feeling of falling was so strong, like memories from childhood—too happy. With love, the wind pushed him onto his back. Cushions of cold welcomed him in a downy embrace.

"A seed that is planted is a task that is done. Almost there, almost there, almost there..."

He sat up.

Laughter. Grin. Ungrin. Grin. Ungrin. His alien mouth's motion pleasant on his face.

He looked.

Emotions of horror gripped his body as he saw a thing that should never be moving dog quick along the berm up ahead.

"Watch for decay and pray for good growth. Almost there, almost there, almost there..."

A worm-like tube of gray flesh as long as ten horses from snout to tail and as tall as a cottage's roof serpentined along the berm. It violated the eyes. Violated the rules of reality. Like an uncut phallus, propelled along by hundreds of human arms sprouting from its length. Elbow joints bending, shoulders flexing and jolting where they inserted into the fleshy worm-body, it loped across the snow.

Turning, sprinting, carried by feet of horror, friends and not friends, Radea and Olthr, eyes like snowballs, mouths abyssal pits that could never suck in enough air to help them escape. As if tongues of flame licked their backs, they ran down the slope...toward Thephos. Going downward when one should never go downward. Only up.

Onward. Ever onward.

"Inside you are safe. The work is done and the rains do come. Go to sleep, go to sleep, go to sleep..."

"Hemgowwa!" Olthr cries to the wind as if it will save him.

Hemgowwa the Ever Grasping Worm has come.

The demon freezes in time, a moment atop the berm in parallel with a fleeing Radea and Olthr. Both are so slow, as if they want to die by a thousand greedy hands.

Like a log, Hemgowwa rolls, hands slapping outward to catch its tumbling, cylindrical form. So much faster than its prey. It rolls over Olthr. The monk is screaming and screaming and screaming, and the Madness would be so jealous to hear it. His friend, the Madness, who spared him out of hatred for him.

You came here to kill...

I came here to kill.

But he could never kill as well as Hemgowwa...the one who could kill like only demons could...somehow that's comforting, the way a demon kills...

here it comes—

screaming in an ungodly way for monks, the shattering of illusions vocalized and of a self that could no longer stay in its body

fate awaiting Olthr in gray arms, gray hands, cracked and soil-caked fingernails...

a handful of hands gather handfuls of Olthr—

arms at the center of the fleshy tube, snatch and then slam the unimist helplessly to the ground, shattering his everything, then flings him casually into the air—

the rim of one of Hemgowwa's end bends upward to catch the falling man, stretching back like lips pulled taut around bared teeth. From within, a circle of greedy arms reach like the stamens of a blooming flower, raised as if in prayer to receive the bounty that is olthr the monk...thephos can't help but remember he himself was a worm once

then olthr passes from one end to the other.

Hemgowwa swallows him—gone—through the hands of hundreds of grasping, prying, clawing and wrenching arms, until blood and offal erupt from Hemgowwa's other mouth at the other end of its fleshy, ashen body—

a much greater killer, a much greater worm

a real demon

olthr says goodbye without being awakened

torn to ribbons by a thousand clawed hands within, but not before a final becoming...red on snow

and maybe he wanted to escape to join the demon—maybe that's what he really wanted—

to be in Hemgowwa—to be in a body that wasn't his body anymore

sprouting like a bloody calf, a stillborn foal, one of olthr's arms becomes the newest arm on Hemgowwa's body...one red in a sea of ever-grasping gray

of hundreds forever claimed

bloody fingers drip olthr's lifeblood from his and Hemgowwa's fingertips

no future ascendant will ever know if it is olthr the unimist monk who tears their flesh or another nameless arm from another nameless ascendant

the world spins, away and then together, bereft of moral perception

radea running...

she will not save the world after all

then it is on radea too, the worm demon and its infinite grasping arms, coiling around her for a moment like a starved snake around a bird's egg

theffy's friend and unfriend moans helpless fear at the filthy nails digging into her soft aged skin—

gripped by a score of hands

maybe one is olthr's new bloody hand

Hemgowwa unwinds with terrible suddenness—uncoils with a wet schlucking sound of dreams taken apart

every piece of the woman who would save the world flings in all directions, a scarlet explosion across the plain

every piece its own spot, its own patch of snow, its place to be unbothered in foreverness

radea and olthr—two little blots of yesterday's life now...

only a pathetic worm so weak and so cold without any fire sees them go so courageously—so quickly—out of death and into the unknown beyond

the one afraid to be a devil shakes, for a thousand and then a million shakes, images unshakeable no matter how many times the worm-demon walks away...

back up the slope it goes and over the berm like some predatory dog having sated its hunger for carnage...

back upward, mist swirling about the bloody dripping rear of it, the ichor slavered anal-mouth, disappearing, and then gone

a child's voice pierces the vigil

"The fire does crackle and the harvest abounds. Go to sleep, go to sleep, go to sleep..."

shaken to the core at sight of the splashes of red that are black in the fading light, of friends who never truly were, only then does she finally stop singing

"Almost there, almost there, almost there..."

thought comes as a shout

...almost where?

so small as to not even hold the weight of a thought, there comes an answer far beyond hearing...

says his name—

Thephos...

then a whisper like shattered glass gouging at the very softest parts of him—

you came here to kill

CHAPTER FORTY

INTO THE COLD

There was nothing else for Ishoa to say. Bleak and desiccated words limped into their ears.

Hilkka Omenfaen wilted into her son's arms, mouth groping for words that could undo what had been done. Dragga held her, jaw set to one side in grim surrender. Pain etched their faces, as if a piece of their soul had been torn away and they were fighting to keep what was left.

The dozens who'd gathered around dispersed with shocked murmurs once they felt the pulse of the situation, leaving only the smiths of Summerforge.

The Warnocks, meanwhile, had yet to greet their son.

Because I still live, Ishoa realized. *And because he stands by my side.*

Gentle yet firm, Dragga pressed his mother into the arms of a knight of Summerforge. "Prepare my pack," he said to a holdguard. "Two days' supply."

Hilkka wailed, a chubby fingered hand grabbing the tail of his orange cloak. He ignored her. For the first time since Ishoa had met Dragga, he failed to smile. And in that moment, it was Stirrma's dark visage sported on his lantern jaw.

Even death, it seemed, could not stay their rivalry. No matter what Dragga did now, his feats would fall short of his sister's sacrifice. Unless he too gave his life.

Ishoa's breath caught. The echoing war cry hung at the edge of hearing, razor thin, anvil strong.

Dragga seized handfuls of Lodaris's soiled cloak and shook him. "Where did you last see her?"

Lodaris managed to grab his fellow Claimant's wrists, turning pale as he struggled against the powerful youth. The wound in his shoulder wept fresh blood. Knights and holdguard moved to break them apart, but it was Ishoa who was nearest.

And she had the only thing that would stop Dragga. Answers.

"The western slope, the same way you and I went up." She pulled at his arm, root-strong and unyielding. "The untouched clearing. You called it beautiful."

Recollection flickered across his expression as he looked at Ishoa. Then he shoved Lodaris onto his backside in the snow.

She continued. "A half day's descent, so it may be farther than that on your way up."

"Less," Dragga sneered.

She hoped she propelled him toward closure instead of greater loss. "We ran into a thicket of birches, downslope roughly half a mile."

Deftly, Dragga checked the darksteel blade in his scabbard, then tightened his belt. "Thank you, Highness. I shall find her."

Sweat dappled Lodaris's forehead as he nursed his shoulder. Dark stains seeped into the collar of his padded surcoat. He was sucking breaths now, his eyes losing focus.

He needs a Sister of the Rose.

Dragga shouldered his pack. "I will be back in a day."

"Dragga don't," Hilkka cried. "Oh! My Stirrma!"

With tears threatening, Ishoa held her chin high. "Dragga Omenfaen..." He regarded Ishoa, his mouth a flat line, his brow a brewing tempest. Never had he looked more like his sister.

Ishoa swallowed. "Stirrma's last thoughts were of you."

His nostrils flared. A single swell of his broad chest. For a silent moment, his gaze fell to the ground. The wind stirred. Knights, holdguard, and Claimants watched the young scion of Summerforge expectantly.

Dragga blinked twice and then set off at a dead sprint to summit the Ice King once more.

Of all those Claimants who went up the mountain, two failed to bring back a sentry rose, which meant they'd be forced to attempt the Trials again in the future.

Only Stirrma Omenfaen perished.

A day came and went. Dragga did not return as promised. There was conjecture as to whether Hilkka Omenfaen had lost both her children. "Dragga? No." She smiled, wrung her doughy hands. "Dragga will return. You will see."

If Claimants failed to return by the morning of the fifth day of the Trial, the retinue would leave a horse with supplies for the ride home. Over time, it had become ritual. No one ever found their way back once the Trial ended.

Despite a second day's passing—the last—Hilkka Omenfaen remained faithful. Even as Wolst ordered the holds to break camp and return to Jarik, she spoke confidently of her son's return. "You will see," she muttered repeatedly. Hilkka's holdguard shifted uncomfortably as they watched their lady stare into the forested hillside of the Ice King.

Ishoa led a horse laden with supplies to the grieving mother's side then took her hand. The woman received it woodenly, acting as though Ishoa had been with her from the start. "Dragga will return. You will see." Her voice trembled like the wind and promises. Her hand wet with sweat. "You believe me, don't you, Highness?"

"Yes." The rest of the retinue likely thought their princess only there to comfort a twice mourning parent. "I do."

Wolst reigned in his mount behind them. "I'm sorry, Lady Hilkka. We have to go. Your hold can to stay, but I would recommend—"

"What nonsense!" Hilkka laughed meanly, eyelids swollen and rubbed raw. "My Dragga? You are mistaken. We'll stay. You leave if you must, Warmaster." She pulled her hand from Ishoa's and fidgeted with the hem of her heavy fur coat.

Wolst cleared his throat. "Once more, my condolences Lady Hilkka. Stirmma saved the princess. She is a hero. Your children have your strength."

Hilkka's lips trembled as she nodded.

The retinue finished its preparations as Ishoa returned. A strong wind kicked up, bringing heavy snows with it. Fat flakes stuck to steel and nestled into beards and hair as if the cold itself sought warmer refuge. She threw a look at the Ice King.

Please be okay, Dragga.

Wolst bellowed the order for the columns to move out. A horn blast followed, alerting the holds farther down the line. As soon as the sound faded, awed whispering arose. The heads of holdguard and knights and highborn alike, swiveled toward the Ice King.

A hulking silhouette at the mountain's base. Marred by white flurries and driving winds. Taller than Dragga. Wider too.

"A C'Dathun!" cried a young highborn.

A holdguard laughed. "That's naught but a storm bear."

"No," said a knight of Summerforge with unbridled cheer. "It's Dragga."

The knight knew his master well.

The Omenfaen raced across the snow, knees driving through heavy drifts, Stirrma's body slung across his shoulders. With one hand, he held her steady as he went, and with the other he carried her warhammer.

"The boy lives!" another shouted.

"Boy!" scoffed the knight of Summerforge. "He's no boy. He's barely human—a fucking god!"

When he reached the columns, Dragga fell to his knees panting and laid Stirrma's body down before him. Hilkka draped herself around her son, peppering him with kisses on his sweat drenched brow. She wailed with renewed vigor, equal parts joy and sorrow for children both dead and alive.

A sharp pang brought Ishoa's hand to her stomach. *Stirrma died to save me. Lodaris wounded because of me as well.* Bitterness filled her mouth.

The entire way back to Jarik, the more Ishoa heard of the ceaseless gossip, the more it twisted the guilt in her belly like a sword.

"Stirrma had bodies all around her."

"She took four of the devils with her."

"Dragga tracked them back to their camp. Slaughtered every last one…"

"I saw a bloodied honor plate in his pack. White hair, too. One of their heads is my guess."

Ishoa's stomach soured. She ate little on the four-day journey back to Jarik.

Ishoa's hair was pulled back into a pony tail. Othwii drew a razor over the space above her left ear. The seneschal didn't want to perform the haircut, but Ishoa had forced him.

"To honor Stirrma Omenfaen. She saved me. Shaving one side of my head is the least I can do to pay my respects."

Othwii advised prudence. "An open show of favor to one hold over the others is ill-advised. The Trials are a neutral ground meant for honoring all Claimants equally."

"But not all Claimants earned equal honor. I'll honor the one who risked far more than political disfavor, thank you very much."

The scrape and slide of the razor over skin filled the silence until Othwii finished. With a towel, he removed the excess oil and soft soap, as well as any leftover hair, and then left.

Ishoa held up a mirror. A fine job. Bare scalp stared back at her above one ear. She let her dark mane cascade across her shoulder, then drew it back again, unsure how to style it. *A ponytail like Stirrma. It has to be. At least until the Trials are over.*

With tears in her eyes, she recalled the events that followed their flight from the C'Dathun trolls. Her hands started to shake, heart beat thudding to life as if it were all happening again. She thrust the images from her mind with a sharp inhale.

Rakeema purred and slammed her bulk against Ishoa's leg. She pet the ice tiger so hard and fast that hair rose in a tiny plume over the anjuhtargs back. "I'm sorry, love. I vow to spend time with you once the Trials end. You've been such a good girl."

Rakeema slid by, leapt onto the bed, and then rolled over to await belly scratches. With a sniffle and curt laugh, Ishoa obliged. She sank her hands into the soft fur. The anjuhtarg's eyes narrowed to slits as she emitted throaty purrs. *Her paws are larger. Her torso, longer.*

"I really am sorry, girl," she said. "At least you can come to the next one."

The Trial of Quelling.

She wet her lips. Tomorrow she faced her final test. Soon she'd have a vote in the court of Anjuhkar. Not only that, she'd prove to all of Namarr she could bear the Crown.

A true Ironlight. *At least, I hope that's what they'll think.*

A cry escaped her. She glanced at the picture on the wall. *I wish they could be at the ceremony.* Malath projected the strength and playful confidence she sought, while her mother stared forward in placid observation as if studying the artist. That was the kind of focus Ishoa needed to succeed.

I miss you. It was odd missing someone she'd never met. *If they were alive, would I defy them? Frustrate them? Make them rue me as their daughter? Perhaps their death makes a fantasy of what our lives together would have been.*

Lodaris's words from the alley in Jarik clutched her heart. *At least you do not have to see the way you displease them.*

Stirrma's death hadn't been the only tragedy the day of the Ice King's descent.

After Dragga had left to find Stirrma's body, Lodaris had gone in search of his parents. Ishoa had followed. She kept her distance and drew the hood of her cloak up so as not to be recognized. Chin held high like the statue of some conqueror, Lodaris strode into the Scarborn camp.

Ishoa had ducked behind a tent. She chewed her lip and peered around it. Exhaustion had begged her to rest, but the thumping in her heart called her to more important matters, namely, the well being of one who she loved. She would face his fears with him. Witness the bravery that made him who he was. A smile came unbidden to her lips at the thought of what he'd done for her. Lodaris Warnock was nothing if not brave.

How could I not love him?

A dozen tents separated Ishoa from the Warnocks as they spoke with their son. Ularis's head bobbed in anger as he did most of what appeared to be lecturing. Lodaris's chin drifted slowly to his chest in defeat. He cradled his injured arm as Lodecka scrutinized him with chill indifference.

Lodaris's head snapped up as he shouted something. Ishoa strained to hear, but it was too distant and crowded out by camp noise.

Lodecka brought a fist crashing down on her son's wounded shoulder. He fell to his knees. Ishoa winced and shut her eyes, debating whether or not she wanted to see.

I could return to my tent and...do what? Act as though my friend isn't suffering?

It was Lodaris's voice in her head that forced her to watch. *You do not see it, Princess.* Lips pursed, she looked.

Lodaris sat back on his heels and swayed. Casually, Lodecka stepped in front of him and took a handful of his red hair. Ishoa clawed the tent canvas into a pile in her palm. For whatever Lodecka did to her son, Ishoa vowed she would exact revenge.

The Scarborn leader backhanded him.

When I am Crown Princess of Namarr, you'll lose that hand.

Lodaris lurched to one side, his good arm keeping him propped up. A strand of blood repelled, connecting mouth to snow. He spit it out and tried to stand...

But Lodecka was already on him, dragging him onto his back. Heavy, open-handed blows rained down on her son. Cold horror filled Ishoa as strikes continued to fall, the force of them reaching Ishoa's ears a split second after they landed.

Eventually, Lodaris lied still.

"What are you doing here, Princess?" A death-rattle voice.

Ishoa whirled, found the tattered face of the Scarborn captain regarding her. Korpa, Lodaris called him. The man's shoulders and hips slanted at awkward angles and the cold suffused his scar-puckered flesh with a purple hue.

"I'm—I'm here to see if..."

He stepped closer, and though he was only slightly taller than Ishoa, he seemed to loom as large as Wolst or Lodecka. His presence was not so much intentionally threatening as it was an objective thing, like a blade or hammer, dangerous utility resting solely in the purpose of its use.

"You see things you shouldn't." He spoke to her as a child, and though she'd just finished the most difficult of the Trials, she certainly felt like one under his flint-hard gaze. "It's time to go, Highness."

She looked back. Lodaris was staggering to his feet. Ularis and Lodecka were gone.

"That's enough now, Highness." Captain Korpa wrapped a battered hand around her forearm. His flat demeanor froze any impulse to resist. "You need to rest."

He escorted her from camp. "The Quelling will be here soon enough..."

Imminent reality snared Ishoa back into the present.

Rakeema sniffed the air, then bounded to the window. Ishoa followed.

At the center of the bailey, a low wooden ring was being constructed for the Trial. A train of wagons entered through the Gate of the Tiger. Each bore the mark of the furriers of Ghastiin, a gray wolf dancing over a trap. Partially covered cages, wrought from thick iron, jostled in the wagon's beds. A frenzied snarl echoed throughout the bailey as one cage shook. A shiver settled between Ishoa's shoulder blades. White, clawed feet shuffled into view where the canvas didn't cover. Tail twitching, eyes rounded with focus, Rakeema watched the cages.

The Trial of Quelling wasn't the most dangerous—that honor was reserved for the Trial of Summit—but certainly, it induced its own anxiety. Tomorrow, Ishoa would come face to face with the most ferocious creature in all of Namarr. *I'll need the focus of an ice tiger.*

A pair of furriers moved from cage to cage, removing canvas coverings with a sweep of the arms. Claws scored the cubicle prisons. Mouths full of yellowed teeth clamped around the iron bars, chewing at them like a dog with a bone.

White wolverines.

Pelts as white as the snows dappling the bailey served as a stark contrast to their blood-red eyes and black gums. They were larger than wolverines found throughout the south of Namarr but still every bit as ferocious. Ishoa was starting to feel she'd need more than an ice tiger's focus. *Its agility would also be welcome.*

She fidgeted with the collar of her dress where wolf fur met linen. The first counsel meeting since their return from the Ice King commenced shortly. *If I tell them Lodaris knew of the assassination plot, I'll never be allowed to see him again.*

Chewing her lip, Ishoa tasted the warm saltiness of blood. Time passed in frantic thought, considering all angles. The Narls were the ones who'd truly been at fault. But the duchess knew they plotted alongside the Warnocks.

He demonstrated his loyalty! He chose Ishoa over his own family. Was she willing to do the same? Was she willing to lie for him?

She reached a conclusion that refused to settle inside. Her sense of right and wrong had become as tangible as the wind. She pressed the stone ledge of the window away. She glanced at the painting of her parents but refused to meet their eyes.

For you, Lodaris. I'll lie for you.

On her way to counsel she found Wolst and his son Hast at the Trial of Quelling arena. They were discussing how to best control the flow of spectators attending the final test. Rakeema pounced on the pale-pink winter blossoms littering the ground at Ishoa's feet.

Wolst eyed the anjuhtarg. "You'll not have that thing at the quelling tomorrow, will you?"

Ishoa punched her uncle in the arm. "That 'thing' is a she."

Feigning pain and wearing a slight smile, Wolst put up a hand in surrender. "I only speak on behalf of her own protection. Training must override an anjuhtarg's instinct. The white wolverine is loud. It's smell, unpleasant. I wouldn't want your kitty prancing into the ring only to be torn to shreds."

"Rakeema *is* well trained. When I wasn't training for the Trials, I worked with her almost every day." She looked at him in mock incredulity. "You are dismissed, Warmaster."

Wolst laughed. "Sorry for doubting you."

"Apologize to Rakeema. Torn to shreds…" Ishoa bent to rub the ice tiger's ear. "You would do the tearing wouldn't you?"

"Aye, even in jest, I won't apologize for the truth, Isha. Keep her leashed tomorrow. The white wolverine is king of the snow. With stealth on its side, a full-grown ice tiger with a clean first strike would get the better of one. They're damn tough creatures. Vicious a hundred times over. Even storm bears steer clear of them." Wolst leaned in. "As for you. When you're in the ring, make sure to—"

The Warmaster peered at something behind her. She turned. A figure stumbled toward them. From a distance, she thought it a complete stranger, but as they came closer the mane of disheveled red hair was unmistakable.

"Lodaris!" she shouted, unable to keep the joy from her tone.

Her uncle, however, sensed something was wrong well before her. "Hast, fetch the Sister of the Rose. Hasty now."

"What?" Ishoa said as they went to meet Lodaris. Only then did she see the answer to her question. Underneath a horse blanket wrapped around his shoulders, he wore only small clothes. His lips were dusty blue, the scars of his cheeks, a deep purple. All else was stark white. He shook, fell to his knees. Ishoa tried to break his fall and gasped at the icy feel of eggshell skin.

"Ishoa," he rasped. The cold had sapped the moisture from his throat. His mouth chattered so violently it made it hard to understand her name as he spoke it.

"It's the deep cold," Wolst gathered Lodaris into his arms with the ease of a mother taking up a babe. The horse blanket flopped aside, revealing the still-healing wound on the Scarborn's shoulder. Wolst strode in the direction Hast had gone to fetch the sister. Ishoa placed a hand on Lodaris's chest. It was like touching a piece of metal left overnight in the Blue River.

"He needs warmth," Wolst said. "What happened, boy?"

Lodaris's eyelids drooped closed. When they shot open a moment later, his gaze found Ishoa's. She tucked the errant flap of blanket under her friend's chin. "What happened?"

The words shook from Lodaris. "I told...them. I was stripped and made to...sleep outside. I tried...tried to show them you could cha—change it, Ishoa." He shivered. "Had to...steal the blanket."

Wolst's broad torso convulsed around an angry grunt. "You've some dastardly parents, boy."

By the time the sister reached them, Lodaris's eyes were closed. The sight lodged a rock in Ishoa's throat. She swallowed hard. *Is he dead?*

She recoiled from the thought.

Inside the infirmary, the sister set to warming Lodaris by covering him in heavy furs on a cot. "Start a fire, a big one." Ishoa went to the wood stack and started handing seasoned pieces to Hast as he placed them in the hearth.

"We'll need that door closed," the sister said. "And you'll all need to go."

Ishoa looked to Wolst. A challenge.

"We do as the sister says," he replied.

Lodaris stretched out on the cot, unconscious. A white-blue corpse.

"No," Ishoa said. "Never."

"He'll be fine, Highness." The sister dragged a fur over him. "I promise. I've handled far worse."

"I'll have clothes brought to him. Frost livery. See how the Warnocks like that," Wolst said. "Come, Isha. We'll return tomorrow. After the Trial."

Lodaris's chest rose and fell under the blankets. *He's breathing.*

"Princess," said the sister. "You have my word. He'll live."

He's not dead.

With a sigh, she left.

The anger flooding her did not. Pacing her room, she couldn't strike the worry from her mind, so she made her way down into the yard to practice.

A holdguard stepped into the practice ring across from her. Where worry fueled little, the fires of anger and hate could conquer much.

She thought of them stripping Lodaris. She saw them cast him out into the cold in her mind. She thought of her own parents too. Jealousy, guilt, rage...even pity. They branched through her. A maelstrom of wounds that could not be healed by any hand but her own.

The holdguard opposite her was surprised at the ferocity of her strokes. He adjusted accordingly, sent blow after blow skittering off a shield before returning wooden sword strokes of his own at three-quarters speed.

He put Ishoa on the defensive.

She focused on Lodecka and Ularis. Smiling, laughing, indifferent, unloving. She hated them. Their righteous and cruel expressions.

Fury guided her blade as she attacked, inciting curses from the holdguard. She didn't try to avoid the burning sensation filling her chest. One could make the case of it being foolhardy to expend so much energy in a training session the eve before the Trial of Quelling.

Ishoa didn't care. With Lodaris in such a state, the Trials seemed of little consequence. The holdguard slapped her training sword from her hands, then sighed relief as he straightened, sweat dripping from a bulbous nose.

Retrieving her wooden blade, Ishoa fell immediately into a crouch. The holdguard frowned. "Ack!" he shot a jet of spit outside the practice ring.

She rushed him.

In her mind's eye, she dealt the Warnocks one last scar before she killed them.

CHAPTER FORTY-ONE

OFFERINGS

Ash drifted from Barodane's hood onto the rug of the madame's suite as he drew it back. The Baroness, Imralta, glanced at the mess but made no fuss. She sucked her teeth and stared down into the street from the second-story window of the Gem Loft.

Soot gummed Barodane's fingernails to black. Sweat and slopped water had cleared some of the char stains, revealing smears of tan flesh. The rest of him was grime and ash. A spotty layer of gray covered his once-black cloak. Smoke nested inside his nostrils. It had taken all morning to quell the inferno. By the end of it, half of Meckin's upstairs was chewed to black and sitting under a gaping hole in the roof.

Fucking bastards.

The dead goaded him to see the brighter side. The justness of it. *They speak your language. Flames and blades for Rainy Meadows, wasn't it? Don't you admire such carnage?*

A velvet cushion met his backside. More than he deserved.

The worst part was he hadn't seen Garlenna since. Why that was the worst part, he wasn't sure. *Wasn't that what I wanted?*

Imralta turned to him, the crown of her head stretched to the Sempyrean, spine stiff as a spear. A piece of rolled parchment was clutched in a finely manicured hand. "In its inception fourteen years ago—when I was in my prime—Digtown flourished for a short while."

A high-vested black doublet with a plunging neckline highlighted the two features the Baroness was known for: large breasts and high cheek bones. Imralta did all she could to promulgate them. A whore's skill at presentation was half her allure, and a woman a decade deep in the life of a brothel madame knew her insecurities and strengths better than any. Livelihood depended on it...usually. For Imralta, the days of hustling cock for coin were long gone.

She took a deep breath, crescent shadows expanding around heaving breasts. She chewed the flesh on the inside of her cheek as she studied Barodane. "As you know, Digtown was created for one purpose—bury the city that was here before."

"I'm aware of the history." *I'm the one who gave the graves a purpose.* "Why did you call me here? I'm...busy."

She tapped the back of her hand with a long fingernail. "Patience is an important quality in a man. Counter to common thought, men are not the more violent sex but ever the more impulsive. A woman's vengeance is like the cold, leeching heat over time. A man's is like a fire and burns rather quickly. That makes patience an essential virtue for men to practice more than any other, you see? Otherwise, you end up like this." She indicated his attire, a swirl of black and gray blotches. "Now, I warn you. If you wish to never know the cold violence of a strong woman, you'd do well to listen carefully."

Barodane tensed. *You wish me dead now too.* He glanced at the door to her suite. Had he just heard a faint creak beyond? Had she cut a deal with Hyram?

Imralta's expression, however, betrayed no such intent, so he heeded her advice instead and listened. "Patience. Of course."

Chin probing the air, Imralta proceeded. "What you're not aware of is Digtown's history from *my* perspective. You see, I came here with my former husband. He was a decent man, a hard worker, I thought. While he dug the graves for those pitiful half-bloods slaughtered by the Mad Prince at Rainy Meadows, I stayed home, managing our hovel at the edge of town and preparing for his return. Every. Damn. Day." Imralta's cheek twitched as she eyed the flakes of whitish ash now ground into the rug by Barodane's boots. "I thought it was my husband's duty to provide for me, and my duty to ensure his happiness. I cooked. I cleaned. Oh how I cleaned! Every day. As you can imagine, cleaning a thatch hovel can be rather tedious. *Can you imagine?*"

Barodane shook his head. "I'll hear this story another time. Truly, I am needed elsewhere." Word of Danuuk and the Redhand brothers' deaths boded poorly for his missing prosort. Images of Garlenna beaten bloody by mason's hammers played over in his mind. He grimaced, cleared his throat.

They're gone, and if I don't run, I'll be killed too. The dead agreed. *To die now is to suffer less. Flee, coward!*

Ignoring his comment, Imralta returned to the oval window. "Of course you can't imagine such a thing. You're a man. An impatient one. Like the rest. Every boy a prince, every girl a servant." The Baroness sighed. "I cleaned the mud from his clothes after he went to bed. I woke the next day and treated his boots with oils so the lye and mud from the graves wouldn't gather and corrode them. Despite my efforts, my workload never decreased. But I took solace in the man I'd chosen. I served a purpose in making him happy. And when he was happy, it made me happy."

She pinned her shoulder blades back and raised her chin even higher. Contempt laced her tone. "It turns out he was only half so hardworking as I imagined. He was here, at the Gem Loft, though in those days it was infamously known as Mound

Diggers. A gods awful name. Nevertheless, my husband was getting drunk and fucking whores, a wholly familiar story for too many women. Instead of saving for us to improve our situation, he spent every wheel of what little money he made working half as many days as I was led to believe. I could have been cleaning a proper cottage as opposed to a mildewed, lice-ridden hovel. I didn't deserve to be treated so poorly. That's what I told myself."

She wagged an upheld finger.

"That was only the first thought. The one that didn't matter. The one where I assumed I *deserved* something different than what I'd chosen. I couldn't really be mad, nor blame him long. I married a ditch digger. Was I expecting some romantic hero? I chose to be a fool and so attracted the same. Now that thought *stuck*." She snapped her fingers as she spoke the last to drive home her point.

"I could have gone the familiar, easy way out and blamed the man for my troubles. A story I find overused by too many. In truth, it only reinforces a woman's idea she isn't worth a damn. If you expect a man to make you happy, you will be unhappy. I learned that the hard way. But do I regret it? No. I simply vowed never to give any man power over me ever again. Within a week, I was working at Mound Diggers. Of course, my husband had proved to be a weak-willed child and tried to force me to quit. Turns out many men become quite chivalrous when they want to bed you, so my husband left Digtown with ample bruises and broken teeth."

She sat beside Barodane on the velvet couch, angling her cleavage at him. *Posture as good as any highborn lady.* "I worked night and day saving every single wheel that crossed my path. I discovered that the more dignified and respectful I was toward myself, the more men wanted me. This room became my source of power over them, like a spider's web catching unsuspecting flies. Meckin was one such. He was a regular at first, but soon he became a friend. When I told him my grand vision for Mound Diggers, he helped me buy it, and I reopened it as the Gem Loft."

She plucked a horse hair from Barodane's shoulder. "Now comes the part you've likely not heard. Meckin is a good man, but close-lipped about his past. He tried to advise me on how to run *my* business. No man tells me what to do. He was only jealous that my profits were greater than his. Rather quick, I became the richest person who isn't highborn between here and Breckenbright. All of Meckin's insecurities culminated in a single desire. He wanted power over me. Like he had when I was a whore. So you see, in the end, that's what life is always, only, and ever, about. Power. How we express it, how we seek it, how we bear it within ourselves."

Palms alighting on her knees, Imralta's eyes narrowed around Barodane. "But you, Kord, baffle me. You have the bearing of one with power, yet you go out of your way to deny it whenever possible. My girls swoon at the sight of you, despite you being no more comely than an above-average man, yet you refuse to bed them. Your godsthorn operation could expand with ease, but you choose to keep it localized to

Digtown. You stand out from others like a beacon with a twenty foot blaze but try to make yourself seem a guttering candle. I've met few men who, presented with the opportunity to take more, refused it."

She rubbed her collarbones. "As you know, I would leap at the opportunity to take you to bed and teach you what I learned in all those years of hard work at Mound Diggers."

Barodane raised a hand, but before he could say anything, Imralta laughed. "Please, I already know your honor runs too deep with my Meckin. Which thickens the plot further still. You actually *have* a sense of honor. Of all the drug dealers I've known, you'd be the first."

Barodane looked away, chin hovering above the false shadowguard pauldron.

"So, you do not disagree that you have honor? That's good. I respect that you're a private man, Kord. Really, I do. Here's the problem though."

He'd forgotten about the tiny scroll in her hand. It crackled as she unrolled it and began to read:

"Dear Madame Imralta. Firstly, let me say you run a fine establishment. It has been a ray of sunshine through dark clouds for some of my men who've had a chance to test its delights. I've yet to visit it myself but plan to very, very soon.

"Believe it or not, I've come to be quite fond of the rich character of your little town. Because of this, I'd like to offer you five hundred gold wheels for full ownership of the Gem Loft. That is a final offer, and it will be an offer no more than thirty-six hours.

"Further, I've come to understand a great deal about you in the past week. Specifically, I am interested in your relationship with Kord, a known criminal and dealer of godsthorn. As a just man, I am seeking any information regarding the whereabouts of his godsthorn supply. We've apprehended one of his agents, which I unfortunately must tell you is one of your own girls. My men say she's known as Lyansorca. Perhaps a trade can be arranged. The requested funds and information I desire in exchange for a writ of ownership and the return of your girl. Unless, of course, you're interested in selling her into good holding, since I'll own the establishment soon enough. Either way. I eagerly await your response. Sweet Regards. H."

The parchment rustled as Imralta let the loose cylinder drift to the floor.

Barodane leaned elbows onto knees. "He knows the Gem Loft is the heart of Digtown. Whether he gets my supply or not, he'll want to use it as a front."

A town sitting in the blind spot of the Crown's Justice, untouched and unclaimed by any hold. Hyram is cleverer than I thought.

"Well." She pursed her lips, pink and heavily furrowed. "I will never sell as I'm sure you can imagine."

"If you don't, he'll kill Lyansorca."

"No, no. I'm not sure you heard me before. No man will ever hold power over me. Not again. Certainly not one who attempts to buy *my girls*. Why do you think I've decided to stay in Digtown, Kord? The weather? Listen, I get it. People come here to bury the past. Meckin, Tyne...you. That doesn't mean you have to be buried with it. For some of us, it's impossible to let go. I could be making ten times as much running this place in a city like Alistar. But I hate the people. I hate the idea of being at the behest of some cunty highborn in his cups who I cannot seek retribution against if he hurts one of my girls." Imralta shook her head. "I will never sell the Gem Loft. Lyansorca violated the rules of this house when she failed to reveal her extracurricular activities with you. She got herself into this mess. That is on you and it is on her. The only thing keeping me from telling Hyram about your supply is my love for Meckin. Oh don't be shocked. It's offensive. I know everything that goes on in Digtown even if it brings you comfort to think I don't. But if I tell Hyram about it, Meckin dies, and though we are no longer together, I still love him more than anyone else in this world."

Barodane laid a hand on her arm. "Please, Imralta. If you don't sell, Hyram will kill you too. He may have wanted my supply before, but now I think he could care less. He wants Digtown itself. He can do what he wants with it, and being this close to Unturrus—"

"Please. Please." She jerked her arm from his grasp. "Please yourself." Acid laced each word. "Did you see Madame Gratha in the parlor below? No? That's because she mourns Danuuk. We listened to the men who slit his throat brag about it in the street last night. And what's left of the Redhand brothers you saw on your way in here. I suppose their death is a luckier thing for you since you won't see their loved ones weep."

Words wouldn't come. At least, none that mattered.

"And Tyne." Imralta flicked a hand in disgust. "Have you seen Tyne?"

A shock ripped through him. "What?"

"It's a simple question, Kord." Imralta spoke slowly. "Have you seen Tyne? Have you seen the face of the mother who lost her child because you would not sell? You can imagine it, can't you? Her face at the news of Jennim's death?"

Anger swallowed him. Through clenched teeth he said, "It's too late to sell."

"Yes. You made a choice to forsake more money than you've ever had for pride. Now you sit there telling *me* to sell. Selfish *and* a hypocrite."

Fist balled, knuckles white, he stood. Jennim stared up at him from memory and murky drink. His hand flew, slapping a trinket off a nearby table and sending it skittering across the floor. Imralta didn't flinch. She watched him coolly. Though his anger ebbed, his tone maintained a sharp edge. "He made his choice! If I had known..." he looked away. "What do you want from me?"

A woman's voice called from the hall beyond the suite. "Baroness?"

"Easy girls," she shouted back. "Kord simply forgot himself. He's alright now." She lowered her voice. "So long as he does what he must."

A tense moment dragged. Feet shuffled outside the room. Floorboards creaked. Barodane's grimy nails pressed into the skin of his palm. He shot a look at the door, cursed, then sat, shoulder sagging. Jennim dead, Danuuk dead, the Redhand brothers dead, Lyansorca captured, Garlenna missing. With both Meckin and Imralta spurning him, there was nothing left to remain him in town but the dead. And they wanted him to run. To keep his torment alive.

"Here's what I want, Kord. I want you to understand what you've done. I want you to see what you've caused. Because with everyone dying, you may be a coward at heart yet, and I don't want you to leave town. You're going to stay. You're going to fight."

"You think I can defeat a dozen men?" He laughed and saw himself charging across a river to slay King Acramis the Twice-Burned. "You're mad." *Madder than me. And I'm the Mad Prince.*

"When Danath led a slave revolt against the Scothean war juggernaut and won, they called him courageous. A crafty old bitch suggests showing a little teeth and you call her mad? Fate favors the confident, Kord." She sniffled. "I don't know what brought you here, and frankly I don't care at this point. You have the eyes of a man who runs from his problems, so perhaps you *are* a coward. If that's the case, go. But I suspect there's still some honor left in you. Enough to die with dignity, I hope."

With a gentle twang, Imralta flicked the painted black honor plate strapped to his shoulder. "Or is this simply ornamental?" Eyebrow raised, she leaned back, hands folded in her lap. "So which is it? Are you the kind of man who sees the world as a knife waiting in the shadows, or are you the kind who sees it as a whetstone to sharpen himself against?"

Life had stabbed him in the back plenty of times thus far. It had taken his brother, his father, his honor...his soul.

Kord sees the waiting knife. In his mind's eye, he watched Garlenna kneel before him in the stable of the Dregs. She was there for him. And now she was gone. *You are an Ironlight.* That was what she'd said.

"Which kind of man do you see?" he asked.

Imralta's smile dragged into a thin, hard line, devoid of mirth. "I hope I see some kind of god that can save us all, but I know that's not the case. Right now, I'll settle for a man with a sword and the courage to wield it."

She does not see Barodane, because you're not him. She sees you! Kord! Garlenna lied about who you are. You're no Ironlight. You've doomed them all.

Panic swept through him. The room became a trapped breath, heavy and stale. For a moment, a shred of him hoped there was an answer to the voices, something he might say to dispute them as he had before, something that might make him the man Imralta spoke of. A man who could fight and die with honor. But he'd lost his will to fight for anyone else the moment he'd sunk his blade into Acramis's chest. Barodane Ironlight died at King's Crossing, alongside his knights and his thirst for vengeance.

And all his courage died with him.

To run, to be a selfish coward, that was Kord. *That's who I am now.*

"I'm sorry, Baroness." He rose, unable to meet her gaze as he hurried to the door. Two whores waited in the hallway, crossbows aimed at his chest.

"Ladies." Slowly, he drew up his hood.

"Act right next time," one said as he descended the stairs.

He considered giving condolences to Madame Gratha in the parlor, but the voices pulled him out the door. *There's no time. You must flee. We're not ready for you to die yet. Abandon...before it's too late.*

He mounted his horse, then headed in the direction of the Rainy Meadows ruins where his past lay buried.

Chapter Forty-Two

ENTANGLEMENT

The boy sleeps as much as a lion.

Our sessions in the River's depths are not long. Less time than he spent in silence beneath the elm tree. But drowning over and over again like this is an endeavor more exhausting than childbirth.

Bags droop beneath Akyris's eyes as he drags his feet past me on his way to bed. The sun has just come up. I touch my Locus, reach, soothe him through our connection. If he notices, he's too tired to acknowledge it.

For weeks now, we've trained.

He wakes and waits beneath the elm tree, all smiles and giddy fidgeting, as if the prospect of drowning or being annihilated excites him. That last part—the excitement—my heart swells to see. Implacable curiosity. Commitment at any cost. Perhaps this is the very reason fate has chosen him to be the Arrow of Light's demise.

For as long as possible, we train. Results progress at a slither. I accept it, for sometimes that is destiny's way of testing weak resolve. The tether of safety I lend Akyris as he wades alone into the deep waters of the River becomes less necessary after the first week. Since then, little has changed.

I worry we've struck a plateau.

Afterward, he eats. More food in a sitting than he used to eat in a day. When he seeks to stand in the River alone and unaided, it stretches every piece of him beyond his limitations. To keep reality whole and resist being pulled apart by the essence of pure flowing consciousness, all that he is and ever has been is required. Every facet of the jewel that is Akyris.

And in tempering his Locus to greater power, the weakness of what he was starves. Becomes brittle and useless. A husk of his former self, shed.

Such rapid change must feed.

So he eats. From midday until the next morning, he sleeps. Bags under eyes deepening. Sun-soaked, caramel skin leaking away and becoming a pallid, sickly white.

Dying.

My tongue wags back and forth over my lower lip. I must seek silence on the matter. My hands fold into my lap as I settle. I fold inward...find my breath. Magomedes probes at me through the River but I've sealed myself from contact.

I need to see.

What I thought would work isn't going at all to plan. Akyris's training is stalled. We're behind schedule. And he seems to be dying. "Damn." If he dies prematurely, the world is doomed to the same. For a long time, I sit watching, waiting for answers to come to me. I'm blocked, bound up in something...something I'm not seeing. Akyris's path is suddenly unclear. An inkblot spilled over the jeweled eye.

"Damn," I mutter.

I scan the dusky horizon and take in the town proper where people scuttle beneath rows of trees and across the lanes, herding small flocks of pigs or goats. Food carts trundle back home, far less full than they'd been in the morning.

I look into the past...

Twelve years ago, a memory as clear as the present moment. My daughter's lips trembled when I told her what needed to be done. Where she needed to go. How she needed to raise her sons. "I wanted a simple life!" she'd said. A drop of blood in the ocean does little to change the color of the tide.

Nevertheless, I did my best to taint it all. She nearly refused. Nearly disowned me. If I told her what really awaited her sons, she would have. Soon she'll know the fate of one. She'll blame me. After that, I cannot see what happens. I am blind. A handful of forking futures lie ahead. None are thrilling to behold.

Like a wildfire, only the winds of fate will determine who faces destruction.

I rise feeling weary. The training isn't overly taxing for me—that's the easy part. The lies. Withholding truth from loved ones in order to sustain the light...that erodes me most fiercely.

Love is not meant to be betrayed. It is like a dog that we train. Treat it with care and it gives in return all that it has until its dying breath. But raise it with a malevolent hand and it is an untrustworthy, dangerous beast. Already, I have felt its bite. Love is a bitch.

More of her teeth will soon find their mark.

Before I head inside, I consider reaching out to Magomedes. I sense she may only have more problems for me. I go for Darkhorn instead. I may be in a mood for self-abuse. Of the two, he's also the better problem solver. I've no time to waste on my pride. Speedy resolution is required. I must decide, act, reflect, decide again. Indecision is the death of my Path.

I explain the situation to the shaman, including Akyris's training sickness.

Darkhorn requests intimate access to me. In order to see what might be the matter, he must pass my Locus's guard. Normally, I would never grant such a thing. I may not like Darkhorn, but I trust him. As if carefully plucking a lash from my eye, he reaches through me, a dense, unyielding energy. A log sliding through water. The probing is abrasive, like the touch of icy fingers at one's naked side, or a callused hand running over the softest part of one's skin.

After a while, he stops and looses a grumble one might call musing.

Suddenly, like a striking cobra, he seizes something in me. I gasp, blazing pain writhing in the grasp of his powerful Locus. I'm a hare in the fox's mouth now.

Darkhorn squeezes harder. I muster my Locus for an attack, but I've already allowed him past my defenses. Shuddering panic scatters concentration. My consciousness dims beneath the pressure of his Locus clamping around mine like an iron vice.

I've failed. Been betrayed. Terror spurs me to wild action. Feeble strikes fall harmlessly against him, waves breaking against stony shores. The Death Shaman has turned against us. Was this the opening he waited for? To pave a smoother path for the Arrow of Light?

I fall deeper into the Abyssal Sea until naught but a speck of light remains...

Darkhorn lets go. Light spreads through my mind's eye as panic and pain fade into memory. My Locus snaps back into my possession. I hone it into a lethal spear of light. "Kurgish bastard! What—"

His voice is calm, curious. "You did not see it?"

"See what?" I hesitate.

"It is too close to you. It resides in your shadow, Locastrii. An entanglement. Look."

I see nothing but manage to relax. "There's nothing there."

"Here. I will show you."

The world condenses into a deafening rush of light, shadow, and color as we plunge through the River. Time blinks. We come to an ear-numbing halt, which trails into a persistent ringing. Heartbeats pass as my surroundings resolve. The sharp ring subsides...

Darkhorn towers beside me. The top of his face from the nose up is tattooed black but for a moon of golden flesh offset around one eye. Massive ebhor horns adorn an open-faced iron helmet, curling down and thrusting out along his jawline. A robe tapers to his feet and flaps in the open air as we hover over a muddy road that cuts through a dilapidated town. Row upon row of a thousand eyes, flames, and hands are embroidered in gold thread onto his hooded robe.

Beneath us, people gather around a barrel. There's a knife jammed into the lid, pinning a slip of parchment. A juggernaut of a woman wearing an eye-patch moves toward the barrel. Hobbling behind her on an inn's landing is a sickly man with the black-enameled pauldron of a shadowguard. An older man with a drinker's belly has a shoulder wedged under the former soldier's armpit.

The crowd parts to admit the big woman through. She moves with an heir of power out of place, as though her body is made of buttered steel, smooth and unbreakable. She pries the lid open. A face stares upward, dead and afraid and drowned in red wine. The tips of the young man's fingers are all but obliterated. Signs of a futile escape.

"Your daughter's boy," Darkhorn points. His finger shifts from the barrel to the sickly shadowguard. "And Prince Barodane."

"Shit." I thought there would be more time before Jennim's death. Having it in the middle of training when Akyris himself is faltering...

Disastrous.

"I can't tell her yet."

"You must." Darkhorn steps in front of me. "This is the entanglement blocking Akyris's progress. Tyne's pain is there with him. Both can feel it, and until it's dealt with, the boy's evolution will stall. You have no choice. You have to tell her."

"If I do that, it'll ruin everything." I suck my teeth. "You think she'll let me keep training the one son when she knows I withheld her other son's death from her. The son I made her give up!"

Guilt pushes from stomach to throat. It's all I can do not to vomit. It had to be done. Knowing we would all die if I didn't is the excuse I leaned into hardest in order to ensure I completed my task. Now, having done it, I'm disgusted with myself.

Truly, I deserve my fate.

Darkhorn looks down at the scene unfolding below. Barodane replaces the lid. He looks terrible. Anything but princely.

"Even we must face our demons if we wish to keep the light. The time is now, Locastrii, as it always is. You *must* tell Tyne. Fate will decide her reaction."

"Fate," I give a mirthless grunt. "Her reaction? She'll take Akyris and disappear. If I'm lucky, she won't try killing me first."

"If she tries, so be it. The Arrow of Light must be stopped at any cost. Even your daughter."

"Easy for you to say."

"No, Locastrii, it isn't." He fixes her with hard eyes. "Do you think our power came to us free? Do you think I've ceased to long for home in my mountain temples watching the children of my children, and their children, wrestling and laughing in the dirt? I miss them. I wish to tell them stories of the Kurgs from before, when we alone were sacred guardians of Unturrus. But I am here with you instead, telling you to perform one of the most vile acts you'll ever have to. If I could take the burden from you, I would, for it might bring me one step closer to rest, to the next horizon where peace awaits. Where the world goes on and the Arrow of Light speeds toward us no more. If I could have that..." Wistfully, he looks at the muddy street a dozen feet below. "...I would never enter the River again. I would live on in humble ignorance, experiencing life as it is. I had a name once, you know."

A tear falls from the eye encircled by a moon of golden flesh. I hear him. The truth, so simple and human for one so powerful. But I too long for such a future. Because he's one of the few Awakened who can travel the River, I cannot see Darkhorn's future. But I need no special powers to see the pain etched into the face of the man standing before me. For him to have the tranquility we both long for, I must do the inconceivable. No matter how hard. Millions like my friend depend on it.

I quiver. I must tell Tyne her son is dead. One does not imagine delivering such news to their child, especially when they are its cause.

"I'll tell her." The words tumble from my mouth around an impotent-feeling tongue. I reassure him. "I *will* tell her."

Darkhorn nods.

We hurtle back through time, away from the entanglement. Darkhorn returns to his place in the River to stand sentry against the other beings who threaten to enter. A lonely and dangerous job. There is no other I trust to do it more.

The Death Shaman is anything but weak.

When I enter the cottage, I'm forced to steady myself against the door's frame. What I've just seen and what I see before me collide in my chest. Tyne holds Akyris in her lap on the ground. Sweat beads the boy's brow, makes dark rings at the armpits of his tunic.

My breaths shorten. My age has never felt so ancient. I feel like a decrepit husk.

It takes less than a second to decide to go back on my word to Darkhorn. I will not tell my daughter about Jennim. Not now. If I can make it work, not ever. Of course Tyne will hate me, but if I'm lucky I'll be dead by the time she finds out. Until then, there are things I can try with Akyris. Things that might push him past the entanglement.

As I consider betraying my promise to Darkhorn, I see clearly my daughter's feelings on the matter of her son's training. A sharp stare cuts straight through me. Her trust in me is shaken.

"What are you doing to him?" she says.

I'm sorry, my daughter. "I told you," I cough, swallow. "The training is not easy."

She glances at Akyris cradled in her lap, dead asleep. "It doesn't seem to be going well. Look at him. I'd say it seems to be going quite poorly."

"Perhaps." I look away. Inhale deep. "Perhaps he could use a couple days of rest. A break might do him well."

"Mother." Tyne purses her lips to calm the rage working to the surface before continuing. More patience than me. More patience by far. "From what little you've told me, I understand this is important. But I'm scared. If you hurt my boy, I swear..."

I scratch my head, stammer, trail off into silence.

"You are hurting him, aren't you?" She sniffles, pulls Akyris tighter to her breast. "You are. I can tell just by looking at him."

My words are wooden. "Tyne, the training is not easy."

"You said that." She flicks a contemptuous hand. "It doesn't matter what I say. You'll do it anyway, won't you? Like you've always done. Something important, lives at stake, and on and on. Meanwhile, my life means nothing."

"That's not true," I say. "You're an important part of—"

"Nothing!" Tyne spits the words, upper lip curling into a snarl. "If I was important I'd not be the one—no." She stares upward. "You know what, I'm done with it. Truly, I am. If anything worse happens to my son, I'm taking him and we're leaving."

I sigh. "You know I'll find you."

"No." Eyes partly closed, she shakes her head, convinced of her plan. "You won't. I have my own ways. You think you know everything but you don't."

"Tyne, listen." I pump the air with a palm. "Let's slow down. Akyris will be alright. He's stronger than we both realize. I'm going to give him a break for a few days." This is my only path forward. I'm out of options, and telling her about Jennim clearly won't work in anyone's favor. "Once he's better, we'll resume training."

Suspicion mars her expression, but before she responds, I add, "And only do it half so often. The rest of the time, he'll go out and be a boy again. Just like you want. A healthy, normal young boy."

Tyne takes a deep breath, releases a punctuated exhale. Finally, she nods, then kisses Akyris's brow. "Fine. Once his training is over though, I want you gone. I want him to live a normal life. I may not know exactly what you're doing with him or what your plans are, but he'll get a chance at a normal life when you're done."

Oh my daughter. My poor daughter. How disappointed you'll be in me.

CHAPTER FORTY-THREE

THE TRIAL OF QUELLING

T he Trial of Quelling rose from the center of the bailey grounds, a murmuring anthill, a sea of color and activity, each face, each sigil, each movement begging for individual attention but receiving none.

Ishoa let the chaotic din wash over her. She'd seen Quellings before. The affair was always tense, but she'd never stood within the low wooden walls of the arena. Never had she needed to risk her life and honor before the critical eyes of an entire city.

The future of Namarr rests on what happens to me today.

She wiped a thin layer of sweat from her brow onto her warskirt then looked down the row of Claimants. Lips whetted perpetually dry lips. The shaking bean pole that was Yurm swallowed a throat full of courage. Stupefied with awe, Unalor Bog and Sweet Ges swept the crowd, mouths hanging open. In contrast to the others, Dragga Omenfaen was still as steel and serious as a sword's edge.

For a moment, there was a gap in the line. A pervasive absence that shouldn't be. A shout of injustice. The echo of a missing Claimant. *It isn't right. Lodaris should be here.* A girl from Twilight Cape stepped back into place. Ishoa blinked and looked away.

Leashed to a stake in the earth, Rakeema's chain jostled as she jammed her whiskered mouth into Ishoa's hand. The ice tiger's chest heaved, panting. *She smells them.*

"It's okay, girl," Ishoa soothed. She caught a whiff of the white wolverine's pungent odor and wrinkled her nose. *I smell them too.*

A score of Joffus Kon's holdguard ringed the low wall, spears at the ready to stab or steer the beasts away from the crowd. Every inch of visible space but the glowing gray sky was filled with spectators from the city of Jarik. Burgeoning holds, not yet large enough to afford the tithe, rubbed greedy elbows with their superiors, striking what deals they could that might bring them a step closer to having a coveted vote in Anjuhkar's court.

In the centuries before Scothea invaded, only those with Anjuhk blood could witness the Trials. Since those days, Belara Frost had opened the Quelling to the public. This small bending of customs had a dual purpose. It deteriorated the alienation of Anjuhkar from other Namorites, and it undermined the potential for Revocation.

Nevertheless, Revocation was in the air.

Syphion Muul was visibly incensed by the mixed crowd. Ishoa watched the man's porcine face as he pointed out non-Anjuhks to the Warnocks, forehead grooved with displeasure. *For someone who hates status so much, he sure seems to love it when it suits his politics.* Every few seconds, he glowered in the direction of the duchess, whose seat was highest amongst the grandstands. Wolst, Hast, and Othwii flanked her.

Arick Quinn took the center of the arena. "Claimants! You have faced the coursing waters of the Blue River and found your footing. You have summited the Ice King's frigid slopes and snared beauty from danger. And now you must look inward to know if you have the courage of a true Anjuhk."

His voice reached for every ear. "In one hand you carry a tool to quell violence. In the other you harbor the steel to mete it out. Your choice is your measure. That is the way of Anjuhks!" The crowd roared approval. Overcome with solemnity, Arick bowed his head.

"Enough pomp and prattle," shouted Syphion Muul. "We grow old."

Some laughed openly at the interruption. Mostly Warnocks and Narls. A good deal more cast about in shock. The intent of the outburst was not lost on Ishoa. *He makes a mockery of grandmother's observance of ritual.* Power was a game of attention, Ishoa had learned. It seemed a gamble for Syphion to act so publicly and risk his reputation, and yet, it was also the quickest route to the most ears. With the smallest of barbs, Syphion forced the holds to question their allegiance.

They could throw in with an Anjuhkar that wallows in its former glory in Namarr's shadow.

Or they could fall in line with stronger ideologies that would see the Anjuhkar of old restored.

But Belara Frost knew the game well. It took only a moment and an equally subtle brush stroke to recapture the confidence of leadership. "Manage yourself, Master Syphion...if you are able." Nonchalant, she chewed at a nail, her tone chiding.

Paint him as rash, a zealot. Dangerous to ally with.

A scowl flickered across Syphion's boot-heel brow as he stiffened. Ishoa hated the man's clenched face and piggish eyes, hated the way it condemned all that it fell upon.

Arick lifted his arms toward the row of Claimants. "May the ancestors be with you."

One of Joffus Kon's trappers drew open the door of an empty iron cage at one end of the arena, slotted it into place directly over the entrance like a guillotine's blade. Then he tossed a haunch of rotting snow bison meat inside. Another furrier held a rope attached to a triggering mechanism. Once a white wolverine climbed into the cage, the door would crash down.

Panels of wall were being removed at the other end of the arena. A woman wearing the livery of Ghastiin leapt onto the top of a cage as it rolled onto the Quelling grounds. The walls were quickly replaced. The woman's boots clanged against the tightly packed bars. *Shod with iron.* It didn't take Ishoa long to see why. The white wolverine inside the cage lunged at the furrier, red mouthed and snarling. The scrape of claw on metal felt as though it vibrated through Ishoa's bones.

Hushed quiet descended.

Dressed in chain, trousers, and warskirt, Unalor took the center of the ring, gripping a flute in both hands. A shield was slung across his back. A sword sheathed at one hip. Sweat dappled his sparse mustache and matted his oily black mane. A cluster of pimples dotted his chin. In a series of rapid glances, he regarded the white wolverine across the way, chest pumping with panic.

"Come now, Unalor!" The lord of Shadowheart stood among Joffus Kon's trappers ringing the arena. It was tradition for the family of the active Claimant to leave their place in the stands and offer support up close. Fang, Megalor's black and gray fox, wore a chain collar and shrunk away at the sight of the white wolverine. "For Shadowheart!" called the ink-pot of a man.

They slid the white wolverine's cage door upward just as Unalor brought flute to sweat-ridden lips. The first note was a piercing one. Ishoa cringed. Despite her dislike of him, she feared for the boy.

The wolverine snarled and raced toward the Claimant. The whites of Unalor's eyes were traced in stark terror. Somehow, he managed to find the next note on his flute. Then the next. The wolverine slowed, padded backward. Seeing the effects of maintaining the tune, Unalor summoned some courage and stared down the beast. It hissed and retreated to the arena's wall, then shirked along, glancing furtively at Unalor commanding the arena's center.

Catching the scent of the carcass nearby, the wolverine hustled to the cage to feast. The furrier with the rope tripped the latch. The door plummeted. A deafening clang. Unalor sighed, shaky palms finding shaky knees. *He looks ready to pass out.*

Instead, walking on rubbery legs to a cacophony of cheers he rejoined the line of Claimants. Megalor leveled a harsh congratulatory slap at his brother's back. They locked hands in upturned fists, and Megalor dragged him over the arena wall. The treekin pummeled him with praise.

Gestryn Narl went next.

Rancid Ges. Ishoa's heart quickened with the memory of his hollow voice on the wind. *I wish you'd tried it. Ugly, craven, foul-breathed slug.*

The wolverine padded toward him, shoulder bulk swaying in quiet determination. The notes from Ugly Ges's flute pattered the air weakly, earthworm lips slobbering over his instrument. With the wolverine showing no signs of slowing, he back stepped. A screech—from flute and then boy. Bitter Ges stumbled, dropped onto his backside in the muddy snow. Arms flailing out to his sides, doughy paunch jiggling fiercely, he floundered to standing again.

The white wolverine charged.

Sour Ges gave consideration to his blade for all of a heartbeat before he fled. Hand dropping to the ground for balance and boots scuffing the turf in his wake, he darted for the open cage with the carcass. "Close it!" He leapt through. The furrier flicked the latch with a curse, leaving the large boy inside and his dignity back in the arena.

A squeal of joy shot to Ishoa's throat, slowed there, pressed her cheeks into a painfully full smile.

Craven Ges it is.

They corralled the white wolverine just as Golthius Narl thundered into the arena. He wore the ugliest piece of jewelry Ishoa had ever seen. A gold chain with a fist-sized slavering mouth. He was lathered in sweat and enraged like a bull. *Or some kind of ape.* His shoulders rotated inward, and the backs of his hands swung straight forward when he walked, and it was a rather apish grunt he made as he took his son by the ear and dragged him from the safety of the cage. "Step out of the damned arena if you wish to quit, fool!" Wincing, Sweet Ges stumbled after his father, pinkish blots from the bison carcass covering his clothes.

If it had come to blades, perhaps I could have taken the coward after all.

The next to go was Yurm the Worm. It was clear from the amused looks of the spectators that they predicted a repeat of Sweet Ges's poor performance. Standing at the center of the Quelling grounds, Yurm Kon looked every inch his moniker. Tent-pole thin, his body failed to fill in around his frame enough to keep the chain armor from swaying with every step. Despite being the weakest Claimant physically, Yurm the Worm appeared confident. Chin held high over distended throat apple, he gave a quick bow to his father.

The cage opened.

Spidery fingers danced the length of the flute. The white wolverine crept tentatively along the wall. Ishoa's ears twitched, seeming to strain to hear better of their own accord as a chill spread from between her shoulder blades.

The amused and dismissive expressions in the crowd disappeared. Joffus Kon, however, retained his knowing grin. The faces of onlookers ranged from happily baffled to outright astonishment.

The wolverine made its way around the ring as far from Yurm Kon as it could without wasting a moment to look at him. Fear of the melodious sound kept it facing forward with its head down all the way to the carcass. The furrier operating the cage door held up a hand in apology as it crashed closed. The beast within ate in silence as if worried Yurm might hear it gnawing at its meal and steal it.

Yurm continued to play. Eyes closed, expression serene, fingers dancing, goading sonorous beauty into the space from hollowed wood. Complexity and meaning birthed from a hunk of simple nothing. This was his weapon of choice. Rich and penetrating thrusts. Humming and sighing feints.

The killing blow, a rolling ethereal note...quieter and quieter, until Ishoa strained to hear its parting kiss.

Then silence.

A clipped inhale. Faces glistened with fresh tears. Red and puffy eyes were fixed on the youth. No one dared to clap or cheer. It was Yurm's space now.

Ishoa swallowed hard. A sob worked its way up the back of her throat. *He's a master.*

Quiet followed Yurm back to the line of Claimants as if sound itself feared challenge him after the impressive display. Bedecked in pristine wolf fur and gold chain, Joffus shouted congratulations to his boy.

The shocked silence persisted over the arena until Belara Frost cleared her throat. "That's a mighty gift your son has, Lord Kon."

Joffus bowed deeply, sunlight shining off gleaming pate.

Belara Frost waved the next Claimant forward.

A half dozen more finished the Trial of Quelling without major issue. A stout, hard eyed girl with bobbed hair from Twilight Cape had to stab her wolverine to death, though it made a mess of her shield and clawed her sword hand in the process. From then on, blood and forearm-length splinters littered the grounds.

A rich merchant's son from Jarik won by default when his wolverine attempted to climb from the arena. It was halfway over by the time the Kon's holdguard killed it.

A chubby boy played the flute twice as well as anyone else, though respectively less than half so well as Yurm the Worm. When the cage door shut, the boy raised a fist in triumph, polished wood instrument sparkling under the midday sun.

Then, it was Dragga Omenfaen's turn.

He held no flute. Wind lifted the curls of his dark mop and pushed aside his orange cape to reveal finely wrought plate. Flames and embers were etched into the burnished steel. Stirrma's anvil capped warhammer filled his hands.

Ishoa knew what came next.

The cage door opened...

Dragga charged. Nature met ingenuity in a shower of sparks as the wolverine's first swipe left deep rents in his leg armor. With a guttural scream, he swung his hammer. The wolverine's body bowed around the anvil head. Ribs cracked as it gave a sickening wheeze and then rolled across the turf. Dragga strode purposely over to the whining, thrashing beast, and brought his weapon overhead. His once beautiful face was haunted with wrath and pain.

Ishoa looked away before the final blow fell, but heard the sickening crunch of the hapless beast's end all the same. She preferred the animals quelled by music rather than violence.

No one cheered.

Without a word, Dragga left the arena. *He's taken Stirrma's hammer, and now he takes her hate as well.*

Ishoa ran fingers along the shaved scalp over one ear. Her insides clenched around the thought of failing the Trial of Quelling. Namarr hung in the balance and one friend already lay dead from her missteps on the Ice King. She fidgeted with her gloves. *Stirrma's death was not in vain. I will honor her sacrifice.*

In her mind's eye, the warhammer whistled in a deadly arc. Stirrma's warcry peeled back the layers of memory...

Memories that swallowed. Memories that strangled. Memories with blighted fur, blackened claws. Troll mouths drooling and lowing. A bestial face staring down at her, slitted pupils within frosty irises...dragging her down, down into the abyss...

Awareness perforated her dark recollections. In her periphery, Yurm Kon's elbow nudged her side. "Princess," he whispered.

A stately throat clearing.

Ishoa blinked and looked up. Her grandmother stared across the way at her. The entire crowd watched. "Ishoa Ironlight." The duchess emphasized her name. "You are next."

I am?

She inhaled sharply, nodded, then threw a look at Rakeema. Like the rest of the crowd, the anjuhtarg stared at her expectantly, tail swaying and keeping time with the passing seconds like a clock from Valat.

Yes, of course.

Hands slapping onto the lip of the wall, she hauled herself over. Thankfully, her toe didn't catch on the way and cause her to tumble through the mud. Laughter would have rained like flaming arrows.

It would have been the end of my bid for the Crown. Revocation would pass the court of Anjuhkar. The fracturing of Namarr would follow. Then Scothean invasion. War and conflict for decades...because of one little slip up. That's all it will take.

Insecurities sang at the back of her mind.

I'm too young.

Woefully naive.

Unworthy of the Ironlight name.

She chewed the inside of her cheek, ripped the flute from her belt as she sped to the arena's center. The center of scorn and praise. The center of chaos and hope.

The future depended on the balance of her feet, the harmony of her instrument, the command she projected to onlooking beasts.

The world grew brighter. Steam rimmed the mouths of the crowd—the only way she knew they cheered. The blood pulsing in her ears and the sharp ring that accompanied it, diffused all sound. Her entire body felt weightless, made of wind. She was light and flexible, swift and powerful.

She turned toward the cage, heartbeat racing at a painfully sharp tempo.

The crowd fell out of mind. The Claimants too.

The cage door rattled open.

The flute was colder than expected against her lips. She played. Worse than Yurm the Worm. Better than Unalor Bog.

The white wolverine moved slow at first, casting wary glances at the crowd hedging it in on all sides. It spotted Ishoa, lips curling back, grime-smeared teeth promising death. Hackles rippled skyward as its head lowered between shoulders.

Then it shambled straight for Ishoa.

She imagined roots stretching through her feet, roots of steel. *Two spear lengths—not a second sooner.* The voice in her head was her own, but the words were Wolst's. Instinct begged her to run, to flee like the craven Sweet Ges.

She straightened, then swiveled around to face the charge. For an instant, her hand twitched toward her sword hilt. If she dropped the tune, there was no going back.

She steeled herself as the beast closed, and kept her lips fixed on the instrument.

The wolverine angled past. Relief burst the tension in her shoulders, and she had to fight back a smile to carry her tune. For a moment, it seemed as though the beast might go straight into the cage.

Instead, it dropped down in front of it and panted. A long minute passed. Then another. Ishoa flowed smoothly into a new song. The sweat on her brow became cool. The sound of the crowd returned. Her panic and adrenaline fell to a low simmer as time stretched long.

Still, the wolverine refused to go in.

Hot tears lined her eyes as she continued to play. *Take the damn carcass!* She started shuffling toward it. A sour taste entered her mouth. If it didn't go in, she'd be forced to kill it.

Faces in the crowd vied for her attention. Three got it. Smug and self-satisfied, the Warnocks and their zealot watched her with hungry expectation.

As if they knew...

She glanced at the wolverine. Like everyone else, it watched her, seemingly content to let her play the flute indefinitely. The furriers were supposed to starve the beasts, and yet this one didn't seem interested in the carcass at all.

Someone fed it.

Anger swelled as Ishoa glanced at the Scarborn leaders. The truth screamed back at her.

She jerked the flute from her lips and whipped it away, sent it skittering across the snow in the direction of her saboteurs. Sword leapt from scabbard. She charged, screaming, "Namarr!"

Caught off guard, the lounging wolverine squirmed to all fours, then stumbled backward into the cage with a low growl of warning. The door slammed close just as Ishoa came within a spear's length. The beast raked the iron bars with a perfunctory swipe.

Now panting, Ishoa let her sword tip drift to the dirt. A hushed silence followed. Someone laughed. Her head jerked toward the sound. Then more laughter. Internally, Ishoa wilted. *So that's it then. I am unworthy.*

A cacophony of claps and cheers joined with the laughter, then drowned it out. Whistling, clamoring, celebrating.

The sound of victory.

She looked to the grand dais. Belara Frost grinned over steepled hands. Othwii bowed her direction. Wolst had lost all composure. Broadswords filling fists, he clashed them together in the air overhead, laughing and hollering louder than any.

I did it.

Ishoa blinked, turned in a circle. She raised her sword, and as she did she locked eyes with Lodecka Warnock and mouthed the words, "For Lodaris." All the way back to the line of Claimants, she savored the flatness in the Scarborn bitch's stare. The twitch at the corner of her mutilated mouth. It was even more pleasing to her than the praise heaped on her by strangers as she left the arena.

"Not a soft princess!"

"She's got a knack with words!"

"The fury of an Ironlight that's for sure!"

Blood returned to Ishoa's wooden legs as she went up and over the wall to rejoin the others.

A gasp moved in a wave from one end of the arena to the other. Ishoa cast about, searching for the source. Faces turned to a disruption in the crowd at one end of the wall. "What's happening?" Ishoa said. No one answered.

They didn't need to.

A pale but determined Lodaris Warnock clambered into the arena. Ishoa surged forward, slamming into the wall with her chest and startling Rakeema at her side. From the look of desperation on the face of the Sister of the Rose chasing him, Ishoa had no doubt her friend had yet to fully recover.

"Lodaris!" Ishoa's shout eddied into the garbled crowd noise and was swept away. Relief fluttered through her breast. *He's here!* She covered her smile with both hands.

Wolst had made good on his promise. The charging snow bison of the Frost's was stitched across Lodaris's chest. The blue tabard covered a shirt of mail and extended to the knees of his gray trousers. An ashen cloak trailed him as he rushed to belt sword and scabbard around his hips.

"Lodaris Warnock, what is it you think you're doing?" The duchess glanced at his parents. "I was under the impression you were healing from difficulties stemming from an unfortunate sleeping arrangement."

Lodecka had turned away as soon as she'd seen her son's attire. Ularis ran his tongue along the back teeth of his open mouth. Face bunched in abject disgust, Syphion Muul folded his arms over his stained shirt and brought them to rest on his potbelly.

The duchess looked to the flustered Sister of the Rose next, eyebrow raised in question. The sister stopped short of climbing into the arena to retrieve her escaped patient. Before she managed to respond to the duchess, Lodaris knelt, head bowed. "Your Highness, I beg you to let me claim my honor and my voice as an Anjuhk." He wobbled, nearly pitched sidelong to the turf. Ishoa's breath caught.

The duchess regarded the young Scarborn, then searched the faces of the crowd. Ishoa assumed it was to check the people's stance on the matter. "You don't look well. If in your state of recovery you cannot even kneel—"

"The boy knows what he's about," said Syphion. The man sensed the right moments to strike. *I'll give him that.* Any indecision by Belara was treated like a wounded fawn limping across the path of an ice tiger. "Would you deny him his honor—his voice—because he is a Scarborn? A Warnock?" He cocked his head. "Both perhaps?"

The duchess sighed in mock exasperation. "If you could hold your tongue for but a moment, you would know my judgment on the matter."

"Aye, Duchess," Syphion said. "We live and breathe to wait upon your judgments."

Wolst bristled. "Enough of that now, Muul."

Syphion leaned forward, folding arms atop the wooden barrier. Belara flashed him an icy glare. *He approaches the limit.*

In what seemed to Ishoa an attempt to cut the tension, Ularis spoke, "Our boy is strong. He has our blood. He'll have no problem. All Scarborn know the way of fighting through pain."

The duchess hesitated. Faces in the crowd turned to the ears of their peers, a sea of unreadable smiles, frowns, and indecipherable whispers. Ripples of power shifting. *But in which direction?*

Ishoa had done her part. She'd completed the Trials, proved her worth, shown she had kotarg, the old honor. She was Anjuhk strong. And yet the energy of the crowd seemed to be sliding from Grandmother's grasp and into Syphion's.

Belara Frost nodded curtly. "So be it." The suddenness of her capitulation only seemed to validate Ishoa's worry. *A small win for Syphion.* "Take your place, Lodaris Warnock." She smiled. "And may the ancestors be with you."

Chapter Forty-Four

THE PENDULUM SWINGS

W ith the Anjuhk cradled under one arm, Thephos slogged onward. Ever onward.

Once the initial high faded, the hidden swaths of godsthorn did not twist Thephos's mind again. Even as they crossed the ground where Olthr and Radea had been killed, what he thought to be reality settled into his bones, a deep cold.

Unturrus's supernatural warmth returned, a veil of heat protecting Thephos from biting winds. That meant the shivers and chattering teeth spawned from within.

I'm dying. From the inside out. From mind to body.

What remained of Thephos of Carthane was sliding inexorably into the Maw Eternal. Almost, he felt the dark waters of the Abyssal Sea lapping at his ankles.

Red, wet snow passed underfoot.

A piece of one of the dead Ascendants went with them. A dangling ribbon of flesh frozen to the Anjuhks foot. Thephos watched it as they journeyed, waiting for it to fall off. But the fleshy scrap clung as the foot lifted and descended, powder erupting around it.

Death clings to you here. I came to be free of a life soaked in it, but like a tick it has only burrowed deeper.

From then on, Thephos was careful to keep his eyes on the horizon instead of the ground.

He ground his teeth like his father used to. As soon as he saw the similarity, he forced his jaw to relax. But fury took hold of him, warmed him like a campfire on a winter's night.

"You came here to kill," the Madness cackled in his mind's eye. *No, I'm not him.* Thephos pushed it down, and let the icy sensation at the center of his being return.

"I love you," said the Anjuhk.

Thephos frowned.

"Hoska, I love you, I promise," she whimpered. "Please just...stop hurting me." She begged. "Please. Let me go."

Thephos stared ahead.

MICHAEL MICHEL

Onward. Ever onward.

They slunk through a break in the trees slower than a criminal walking to the gallows. Speed had no point anymore. No use for the already dead. It seemed wrong to sit in one place and wait for doom though.

So they went. Always upward. Never looking back.

Demons live behind you. In the past.

He kept his eyes ahead.

He assumed Unturrus had some horrible punishment for those who tried to deviate from its course. It wanted them to go upward. That he knew. They all knew. The whisper had summoned them, begged them, tugged at the hollow place inside each. Called them up Unturrus.

So he went.

What else can I do?

He'd been trained to never disobey a command. And so by forces unseen he was dragged up the Mountain of Power. A marionette. Feet dancing over it, a massive grave.

Impossibly, night never came. Just as darkness was about to set in, it retreated. Waxing sunlight. Time working in reverse. For a moment, he attempted to use logic to explain the phenomenon away, saying it wasn't really happening, that it was a trick of the mind because he'd never seen such a thing in real life. Only here. But he shied from the debate, satisfied to let it be what it was. He wasn't a smart man, and his own nattering would serve little to change the mysteries of Unturrus.

Do we even travel upward at all? If he discovered they'd been going downward since the Cusp, it wouldn't have surprised him.

What did surprise him was being spared by both Hemgowwa the Ever-Grasping, and the Madness. He recalled Syn Backlegarm's words at the Numbers. *More suffering leads to more Awakened, more fear leads to more death.*

He glanced at the Anjuhk. Her face was obscured by gales of snow despite being right beside him. She'd been almost peaceful in her insanity as she sang. Thephos had simply sat in the snow beside the godsthorn bushes. More than anything, he had been curious as to whether the violence wrought on his friends was real or simply an effect of the drug coursing through him. There had been fear and sorrow too, but those emotions were distant. Death was all but assured for Ascendants, and he supposed he'd made peace with it where Olthr and Radea had not. They'd tried to escape it, control it, manipulate what might happen. The fear, the sadness, the overwhelming horror...Thephos accepted it. Had been accepting it for many years. In this, the dead Ascendants had failed. It didn't seem to matter if one were afraid, only if they let it lead them.

Thephos shook his head. *I came here to die, yet I'm doing what Radea and Olthr did at the end. There is no strategy for survival, no bargain or clever justification. So why do I seek false hope?*

The answer never came. But what did was a surprise. He straightened his hunched posture, chest lifting with pride as he realized he'd never really experienced hope. Before Unturrus, he retreated from it at every opportunity. Any sensation in his body that indicated he cared, any thought telling him of love for his brothers or himself, any fantasy of hope, he denied, disengaged, crushed. That was his way—no—the only way of dealing with the horrible truths of the world. Truths like a devil father, a dead brother, and an inevitable doom.

For once hope didn't feel like a burden.

He paused, bringing the Anjuhk to a halt beside him. He searched her scarred face as he recalled her bargaining with whoever Hoska was: a promise of love to avert abuse. A lie.

Hope is foolish. An escape from terror, nothing more.

In a flash that drowned out all other sight, the old devil greeted him in his mind's eye. *Why would a pathetic worm like you hope for anything?* The man raged. *You're worthless! Less than nothing. I'd kill you, but I'm already dead.*

Thephos stumbled backward from the vision, falling onto his backside in knee-high snows. He clutched his chest as his heart raced. *He spoke directly to me...as if he were still alive...*

The Anjuhk plopped down beside Thephos. Flakes pinwheeled into her vacant stare. She watched Thephos for a moment, unblinking, a fractal of snow resting on the lens of one eye as she surveyed the surrounding whiteout.

"Momma?" she said. "Momma, where are we?"

Wary, Thephos stood. He searched for the old devil, but the illusion was gone. He lifted the Anjuhk from the snow by the elbow. "Somewhere safe," he lied.

They traversed slick rock hidden beneath heavy drifts, then clambered up a near vertical slope. With what meager strength he had, Thephos hauled the broad woman over a stony ledge, spittle flying from his lips. She keeled over with a heavy flop, and together they turned on hand and knees to find the earth leveled out into a flat plane.

A glacial flow angled up and away into a wreathe of mist to their left. The path to the right was a more gradual slope, dotted on either side by solitary pines.

Easy choice.

Through slurries of wind, Thephos caught sight of colorful bursts beneath the distant trees. He wasn't sure what distance was safe, so steered them clear of the godsthorn as if their blossoms were the glowing eyes of hungry predators in the night.

"Momma!" the Anjuhk cried. "The C'Dathuns will get us!"

"You're okay." Playing along or lying were the only sane things to do anymore. "They won't get us." In the face of unimaginable horrors, lying held endless value. It made the path they walked easier, calmer. Regardless of the violent ends that lurked.

Still, he felt guilty for it. "I'm Thephos." Maybe it won't feel so bad if there's something real between us to make up for it. "What's your name?"

"Lethwii," she said. He wondered if the name was actually hers, her mother's, or the name of someone else she knew.

The pair of stumbling shadows worked their way through dense banks of snow hiding tangles of brush. For the second time that day, night descended.

The halo of clouds surrounding Unturrus was beneath them now, and it was there that the sun fled. Just as darkness threw a pall of haze over the path ahead, the gloom retreated once more, the sun moving suddenly back up into the sky.

Then it fell, faster than before. Far faster.

It rose again, came to rest directly above them in mere seconds.

Mouth agape, Thephos stared. He caught Lethwii in his periphery, gazing at her own feet...

The snow!

It was gone. Not even a wet stain marked its going.

Finally thawed, the frozen scrap of Radea or Olthr, slid from Lethwii's foot to the hard packed earth. "It's warmer."

Thephos nodded and bid her move forward. The path led into a saddle of earth, a stone's throw from wing to wing, filled with tumbled stone. On their way down into the shallow depression, night fell.

On their way back out, day rose. By minutes it shifted. Thephos refused to look, eyes fixed forward, a feeble attempt to block out the broken nature of reality. Death was one thing, madness another. He searched for an explanation, for godsthorn near at hand, but Unturrus needed no such thing. It had its own laws.

The Pendulum of Time, Olthr had called it. Rarer than any demon.

It swung back and forth, faster and faster, blade inching closer to the thin thread tethering Thephos to sanity. Time was the foundation for experiences, the order all things lived by, and without it Thephos was cast headlong into chaos. Panic threatened to pull him apart. It throttled him until he choked on it. He stumbled, pitched forward onto the dusty earth.

Lying on his side, he gasped, huffing, disoriented. He watched Lethwii's feet, her shadow extending and then retracting, a flickering spoke of shadow.

Is she there? Am I here? Where is here or there?

His senses fell outward, spilled like guts, like tongues from dead mouths, trickled away like blood and snowmelt, faded like the past or a dead man's future.

The former pig farmer became a worm, writhing on the ground, unable to rise. With each labored breath, he blew gouts of dust toward Lethwii's feet.

He was exhausted, he realized, not physically. Unturrus had taken care of that. But mentally, he could bare no more. The break was coming, a loop of rope cinched around his awareness. A tighter and tighter knot. Numbness crept from his toes into his legs, the rising dark water of the Abyssal Sea, wrapping him in its everlasting embrace.

He let go.

And it was comforting to surrender the struggle of trying to grasp the inexplicable.

He released into it, plunged beneath the surface, let himself be swallowed by the current.

Warmth suffused him at his belly, his narrow chest, his hatchet face.

Are you mad yet? asked the whisper.

Unsure, he rose and sat back on his knees. Took a sweet, painless breath. The sun came and went in a guttering rush. Staring at his own pulsating shadow hunched over before him, Thephos slid slowly inward.

The pain in his gut became solid. Dense and smooth. His awareness gripped it. He relaxed his focus into the feeling of that ball.

Balance connected him, kept him centered and aligned.

He closed his eyes. Stood.

"Go to sleep," sang Lethwii. "Bend and drop, almost there, go to sleep."

"Those aren't the words, Lethwii." He had to keep moving. *Onward, ever onward.* "Come."

He didn't know why he needed her to be with him. He didn't in truth. To have another person's skin touching his in the chaos would be comforting, he supposed. That was reason enough.

When she didn't take his hand, he opened his eyes and seized her arm. The ground flashed. All around, the landscape's many twists, turns, nooks, and crannies, splashed his eyes with flickering shadows. Bursts of flashing ink.

"Still, isn't it sweet music, Momma? Such sweet music."

Sweet music...

Wrath consumed him. *No, it isn't sweet music.* He wanted to be done with Unturrus and its horrors. It crossed his mind to leave Lethwii. Whoever she'd been had died back at the falls where the Madness killed the crabber. This creature was insane now. Useless. Thephos's body ached from pulling her along. *She's a burden.* Already he'd given her more care than he had his own brothers. The guilt of that weighed heavy. To make it worse, he knew her name now, an intimate thing. *Lethwii...*

He looked at her, saw the eyes of one already dead, and it scooped the last remnants of humanity from him. Despair rushed in, a foul and heavy carcass laid over his shoulders. *It would be more painful to continue with her. Who would ever know? She'll die soon anyway.*

See? a voice whispered. *You came here to kill.* Thephos balked at the violating tone. Rage sang into his bones, a river of flame. Jaw clenched so hard a tooth creaked, he quickened his pace, dragging Lethwii.

"Ouch, Momma! You're hurting me! Please...let me go!"

Thephos noticed his fingers were white with pressure where he held her arm. She jerked back. The anger retreated as quickly as night and day. "I'm sorry." He loosened his grip. Every part of him was chaos, disparate feelings rifling through him like seasons and seconds.

Lethwii's expression changed. The winking shadows etched hatred into the lines of her scarred face. "No, you're not, you fucking bastard. You're an evil man, you know? No. Not even a man at all. My mother was right. I should have married Kroon instead. A criminal he is, but at least he only hurts other men."

She jerked her arm from Thephos's grasp.

"I—I'm sorry." He took a step toward her, palms upturned, supplicating. "It's okay."

"Come, hit me again. Try to kill me this time. Death would be a better future than one where I'm forced to be with you a second longer." Life glimmered in Lethwii's eyes, tears pooling at the corners. As if embarrassed, she covered her mouth with both hands and fled up the trail.

Thephos made to follow, but the disorienting shifts in light caused him to miss an upthrust root. His toe caught. He crashed to the rock-strewn earth. His chin cracked down hard, jarring his teeth. Stone jabbed his palms, his knees. He could feel the blood leaking from a half dozen lacerations as he rolled onto his back and sat up.

Lethwii was gone.

In pain and profoundly alone, he crawled to the stump where the upthrust root originated. He took a seat and stared out at the tops of clouds below, stretching from Unturrus to some distant place. Maybe Carthane. Maybe some other place he'd never know. "Nowhere to be. Nowhere to go."

No one left...just me.

Patiently, he watched night and day dance, molding one into the other until he saw a place between where reality could not touch. His breath told him time passed. That life moved. He sat and it was okay to just sit forever. Every time it wasn't okay, he took another breath and righted himself until the world as he'd always seen it was shrugged off and replaced by some other kind of seeing. What seemed eternal and what seemed impermanent vied for each second's consideration, each moment's truth.

Whether or not he slept became inconsequential, eluded him as casually and easily as his understanding of night or day, right or wrong, light or dark. His environment was stripped to the bone of foundations. His circumstances too. What he once considered who he was and who he was not evaporated, allowing him to pass deeper into the Pendulum of Time. For eternity, he stared at it, swinging before him, an endless track of unceasing motion, cutting the veil of what was and what will be with every stroke.

Thephos looked, and where he saw, *he* was. Shadows and the glisten of sweat alternated in his upturned palms. Nothing changed as it changed, nor would it, nor could it. They were his hands.

Mine alone.

Everything he'd ever known tumbled forth to merge with a mosaic of life reflected in the world outside himself. Contentment in the mystery of great things imminently unfolding. Then a wink of light piercing through the unreal ruminations. Thephos's sight returned from the place between.

He discovered his hands resting gently on his thighs. His breath moving ribs and chest in a deep rhythm. The sun fell in the distance. Night settled. A cool breeze tousled his hair. Warmth spread into his legs, then into groin and abdomen.

For the first time, Thephos peered through life's mysterious shroud of suffering and caught a glimpse of a once elusive truth...

Himself.

CHAPTER FORTY-FIVE

SCARBORN METTLE

Ishoa's conclusion came easy. She watched Lodaris huddle into his cloak as if he could find buried warmth there if he only pressed deeper. Everyone could see it.

He's not ready. Not strong enough.

She licked her lips, parchment dry.

"A flute, please," croaked Lodaris.

Yurm gave him his own.

Lodaris bowed his head to his fellow Claimant, then raised the instrument's lip plate to his mouth. His wiped sweat from his brow with a trembling hand. At least the tinge of his skin was no longer blue but ghostly pale.

Nerves threatening, Ishoa swallowed back bile.

A single note screeched forth as Lodaris tested the flute. Worried expressions wove a tapestry of discomfort throughout the crowd. There were some who smiled, clearly relishing the prospect of a Scarborn's failure.

A few jeered with open hostility.

"Scarborn scum!"

"Traitor!"

Lodaris ignored them. He inhaled then restarted. Ishoa didn't think his hands shook any less the second time. *You are stronger. Stronger than you know. May the ancestors be with you, my friend...*

My love.

The cage door slid open. Musical notes filled the air. Nowhere near the beauty of Yurm's performance, but neither were they as pitiful as Unalor's clumsy rendition.

The white wolverine took a tentative step from its iron cell, sending looks of promised violence back at the furriers of Ghastiin who'd imprisoned it. A trio of cautious steps to one side brought the beast flush with the barrier. As all Claimants would hope, the white wolverine avoided the musician at the center of the arena. Sometimes the Trial of Quelling ended in a matter of moments, the beast hustling across the arena and into the safety of a cage with a pungent meal. On rare occasions, like Ishoa's, it took far longer. Before Scothean occupation, the brother of the Ice King had spent three hours quelling a wolverine. In addition to bruised fingertips and blistered lips, the Ice King's brother—Ishoa's twice great uncle—had his calf horribly mauled, earning him the nickname Adnar Tatterleg.

Ishoa chewed the inside of her cheek. *Please.*

A sheen of sweat marred Lodaris's pale brow, gathering into beads and racing from temple to chin. From there, it trembled and fell a moment later onto his instrument.

Ishoa's fingernails dug grooves into the top of the barrier. *Mother and father, if you hear me, please give Lodaris courage and strength. Please let his wolverine be a fearful one.*

Rakeema seemed to sense Ishoa's distress. The anjuhtarg paced back and forth in the narrow space at her side, rearing back and wrestling at her leash. Ishoa continued invoking every ancestor she knew, Stirrma Omenfaen, as well.

The white wolverine snapped at the outstretched hand of one of Enkita Vulkuu's seal hunters who taunted the beast as it slunk past. The holdguard of Twilight Cape laughed.

The wolverine shambled at a sluggish pace. *Come on now! Move damn you!* Sweat drenched the neck of Ishoa's tabard, a ring of blue turned black. She wasn't sure how long Lodaris could play, much less stay upright. *He's strong! He fought off C'Dathun trolls. He can play a flute no matter how exhausted.*

The wolverine was halfway across the arena now.

A cough sent up a wayward squeaking note as Lodaris faltered. The beast whirled toward the errant chord. Its mouth parted, white skin bunching around its snout. Ochre teeth nestled in onyx gums. One paw then the other cutting the distance between it and Lodaris.

Breath escaped Ishoa. Icy hands scuffed her neck.

The wolverine charged. Backing a step, Lodaris reached for his sword but thought better of it. He resumed playing in a desperate attempt to route the beast. Ishoa found her own hand wrap around the cool leather grip of her sword's hilt.

At the last second, the white wolverine feinted away—a false charge. It gave a warning swipe of its massive paw as it flew past.

Rallying cries percolated the throng. Lodaris's courage to stand strong in place, to neither flee nor fight too early, had won the crowd's favor. Ishoa's arms shot overhead as a less than proper squeal of glee escaped her.

Directing a deep-throated growl at the young Scarborn, the wolverine retreated once more to the wooden wall. Bravery and cowardice were the hallmarks of a great Quelling. Between the last Ironlight's charge, Gestyrn Narl's calamity, Yurm Kon's expertise, and Lodaris's courageous stand, the people of Jarik would have no shortage of talking points in the weeks to come.

If Lodaris means to be a knight of the Crown, he'll have at least this accolade to stake his reputation on. Ishoa smiled at the thought of funding his training and further driving a spear through his parents' pride. The tension clenched around her heart and stomach relaxed, was replaced by warmth and pride. The person she loved was neither cruel nor cowardly. *He will be the truest knight Namarr has ever seen.*

Her hand fell from her sword. Lodaris seemed to feed on the energy of the crowd. Standing straighter than before, the notes of his eerie melody smoothed out, became light and ethereal.

He'll be the first Scarborn in history with a vote at court. In her mind's eye, Ishoa watched the mirth of that realization spark in his eyes. *But will it be against Revocation?*

Across the arena, Ularis grinned at his son's success. Lodecka, however, was impossibly still. Flint-hard eyes betrayed no hint of emotion. Even the short blond braids framing her scar-addled face were stiff as a strong breeze. *He's going to prove you wrong. You don't deserve him.*

Ishoa drew her cloak into a bunch at the neck. Another late autumn gust swept through the Trial of Quelling, and with it came a biting cold.

The white wolverine neared the cage and rotting meat therein.

Lodaris's lungs betrayed him. "Kuh!" The sound was like a hot iron through Ishoa's belly. "Kuhugh! Kuh!"

Lodaris wheezed. The white wolverine froze, craned its head toward the show of weakness. Lodaris blew desperately at the flute as he coughed. Each note was shrill, disjointed, a beacon of vulnerability. Eyes bulging around the convulsive hacking, Lodaris fought to clear his throat by sheer force of will. The veins of his pale neck and face swelled. His skin turned a splotchy red.

"Kuh!"

Flecks of blood spattered the flute. The sight of fine red mist in the air brought a collective gasp from the crowd. Sensing wounded prey, the wolverine opted for a fresh kill over a carcass and rushed the ailing boy.

Wheezing and fighting for breath, Lodaris's flute fell from blood-flecked fingers. He retreated. Fumbled for his sword. Drew his blade—too late. With a maw made for breaking elk bone, the wolverine clamped down on Lodaris's leg. It's claws mauled thigh and calf as it dragged him off his feet.

Lodaris screamed. As one, the crowd stiffened and recoiled. Horror cleaved through Ishoa, and her mouth fell open as she tried to understand what was happening.

Ularis's frantic voice pierced the terrified din. "Kill the damn thing, boy!"

But the wolverine's ferocity gave no room for reprieve. The young Scarborn couldn't free his sword.

He's going to die.

Hands working without thought, Ishoa unclasped her anjuhtarg's leash and then pulled herself over the wall. Rakeema followed, landing lightly behind her. The princess unlimbered her shield then drew her sword.

What am I doing? Came the voice of doubt.

Saving a friend, came the answer, immediate and resolute. *Like Lodaris would.*

She strode forward, banging sword against shield. "Sajac!" The killer focus of ice tiger ancestry upon her, Rakeema stalked into position beneath Ishoa's shield arm. Together, they advanced.

"Isha, no!" Wolst shouted.

Darkness dilated her surroundings, throwing the periphery into a shapeless haze. Shouts from her uncle trailed away...became distant. All that existed was Lodaris and whatever she must do to save him.

If he lived, she didn't care if she violated sacred ground. Her friend's life was worth more. Far more.

Snout bloody, the wolverine turned to face the new threat. It would fight to the death for its kill. Ishoa would oblige it. It locked eyes with Rakeema and snarled, blood-pinked drool hanging like a drape from its rabid maw. The distraction gave Lodaris a moment to finally jerk his sword free. Bone pale, wounded and shaking, he managed a sloppy slash across the wolverine's haunches. It keened—scrabbled clear of the next blow.

With a groan, Lodaris keeled over, hooking an arm over wall of the arena to save himself from falling flat on his face. Leg outstretched, breathe labored, he struggled to lift himself upright. His lower leg was in tatters, a half-dozen rents weeping scarlet tears from pale flesh. When he'd entered the arena, he'd already been ashen faced from his recovery from the cold. Now he was as white as a C'Dathun and looked to be on the verge of going into shock. He needed a Sister of the Rose fast.

Ishoa covered the space between them at a sprint. A blur of motion to her left brought her to a dead stop.

Lodecka Warnock landed within the arena. She ignored the white wolverine and made straight for Ishoa. A longsword hissed from the scabbard on her back. "You cannot interfere with my son's sacred Trial, Princess. This is not your fight."

Chest heaving, Ishoa ground her teeth. "Get out of my way."

Over one of Lodecka's shoulders, Ishoa watched the wolverine creep toward Lodaris.

"No," the Scarborn leader said. "Only a Warnock may call mercy. I will not let you steal his honor."

Ishoa shifted her weight from one foot to the other. She cursed.

With a hand against the wall, Lodaris stood on a single leg, the other now utterly useless. The wolverine false charged at Lodaris. The Scarborn swung. But the beast crouched low, dodging it, then lunged a split-second later.

"Get out of my way!" Ishoa screamed.

The wolverine seized his leg again. Lodaris cried out as he dealt the beast a deep wound to the shoulder. It whined, released, lunged again. Gore-slathered teeth sank into his hip. It dragged him screaming to the ground.

"He's going to die!" Ishoa shouted. "Your son!"

Neither Lodecka's leveled sword or gaze faltered. "Then he dies."

Rage and terror compelled Ishoa forward—a dozen feet from Lodecka. "Move, damn you! Move! I command you!"

"You do not command the sacred rites, Princess. Only my husband or I may call for mercy. My son is Scarborn. Scarborn fight to the death." Lodecka swept her gaze over the crowd. "Anyone who interferes dishonors him." Her eyes settled back on Ishoa with predatory calm. "And anyone who dishonors my son will answer to me."

Sudden realization sickened Ishoa. *She wants him to die...*

The snow bison sigil on Lodaris's tabard was soaked through with dark blood now. *Because he chose me. She knows if he lives, he'll vote against Revocation.* Lodecka would sacrifice her own son just to weaken her foes.

Fury pumped through Ishoa's limbs. She took another step. Lodecka arched an eyebrow. A smile nudged the corners of her mouth upward.

Ishoa glanced at Rakeema. Barely bigger than a dog. And Ishoa may as well have held a bouquet of flowers for the all good it would do against Lodecka Warnock. The woman's reputation for violence was paralleled by few.

"Damn you!" Hot tears rolled down Ishoa's cheeks.

The wolverine whipped Lodaris around like a ragdoll. Besides a pair of deep cuts on the Claimant's forearm, the creatures claws were harmlessly scoring his chain shirt.

Footsteps thudded behind Ishoa. An arm of banded steel encircled her. The scent of her uncle's battle leathers and wolf fur pelts swirled through her nostrils. A comfort amid the storm.

"It's over," Wolst said. "Mercy for the boy."

Lodecka leveled her sword at Ishoa and Wolst. "I will not allow it."

"We'll not wait for the damn thing to start eating his corpse! Consider yourself overruled. Mercy for Lodaris Warnock." Wolst whistled at the Kon's holdguard ringing the arena. "Kill it!"

Lodecka remained impassive, her sword steady. "My warning stands, Warmaster. My family's honor is not to be trifled with."

Ishoa noticed the muscles of her uncle's arm tighten like crossbow winches. "Pfah! What honor?" Wolst shot a withering glare at the furriers of Ghastiin who'd entered the arena but had not executed the warmaster's order. "I said kill it!"

Couching spears to hips, they stalked forward. Leaf-blades flickered. Wounds blossomed, staining white fur red. It was a slow, gruesome process as they were careful to avoid Lodaris's unconscious form stretched out under the predator as it guarded its kill.

Lodecka's placid gaze fell to the ground of the arena. "So be it." She sheathed her sword.

Ishoa raced to Lodaris's side as soon as the wolverine was dead. A pair of furriers dragged it away as a throng swarmed the fallen Claimant. When she reached him, Ishoa gasped. Head to toe, Lodaris was slicked with blood, some wounds still burbling with each heartbeat. The Sister of the Rose worked fast to stem the flow of the most threatening.

A canvas gurney appeared.

"Is he dead?" Ishoa shrieked.

The sister was soaked red to the elbows. "Not yet."

Ishoa's mind fell into a bleak fissure. Recollection became difficult. Bodies jostled. A sea of worried eyes. Stomach churning sour worries. Hands consoling, comforting as blocks of ice. The sight of the Sister of the Rose's grim face slashed away her hopes.

They hurried Lodaris to the infirmary.

He saved me...

Yet I could not do the same.

His hand was limp in hers. "You're strong, stronger than you know." She wasn't sure what else to say but knew she must say something.

I love you.

At the entrance to the infirmary, her eyes drifted upward to meet Lodecka Warnock's. Hatred overtook worry in a flash. The Scarborn leader planted a hand across the doorway, barring Ishoa from entry.

She'd been kept from Lodaris once. Never again.

"Move or I'll kill you," Ishoa said.

Lodecka grunted a laugh. "You've more grit than I first assumed."

"You're laughing? Laughing while..." Ishoa looked down at her hands covered in Lodaris's blood. Her voice fell to a whisper. "Look at this."

Suddenly, the past was all she saw. Begging for understanding. Bringing clarity. Lodaris spoke to her in the alley in Jarik, words like arrows pinning the soul. *At least you do not have to see the way you displease them...perhaps they wouldn't give you all their pain...*

Ishoa knew what needed to be said. "No one will ever love you, Lodecka, and you know it."

The muscles around the Scarborn leader's icy blue eyes constricted. She shifted her weight.

That hurt her! "That's why it's okay for you to hit Lodaris. His love could never find a home in you." Lodecka looked around. Inside, the sister's hurried voice directed what sounded like Ularis in helping her. It seemed like Lodecka didn't want others to hear what Ishoa was saying. So she continued. "You're full of fear. Fear that you aren't worthy of love. So you don't even try to be. You just embrace the fear and force everyone to be scared of you. Well I'm not. Not anymore. To me, you're just a failed mother. Too pathetic to fear. And if Lodaris dies…" She tripped over a sob at the back of her throat. "…at least he'll be free of you."

Wind stirred Lodecka's crimson cloak. Ishoa was surprised to find her words were true. She wasn't afraid of the woman anymore. Hate gave no room for anything else.

"You say a lot, like your great grandmother. One day you may learn swords hold more sway than words."

Steel edged Ishoa's voice. "And you may learn I am *nothing* like my grandmother. If I were the ruler of Anjuhkar, you'd already be dead for—"

"Isha!" Wolst swept up behind her, wrapping tree limb arms around her waist and lifting. "Control your fire!"

Carried through the air, she kicked and tried to free herself to no avail.

Lodecka called after her. "You're right, Princess. I don't mind if he dies. And you shouldn't either. After all, he's just a Scarborn."

As if an arrow struck her heart, Ishoa's hand flew to her chest. A moment of shock passed. She fought to rise higher in Wolst's arms. She hacked then spat. Instead of a single meaty gob, the spit was dry, brittle, a half-dozen foamy flecks that fell far short of the mark. "No! He's better. Better than any of you!"

Once they were out of sight of the Scarborn leader, Wolst put her down. She buried herself in his chest, sobs taking over. He held her, patted her too firmly. "It's okay, Isha. He'll be okay."

Dark thoughts arose, prepared for any outcome.

CHAPTER FORTY-SIX

RAINY MEADOWS MASSACRE

W hat a prince he was.

Barodane rode over the burial mounds of innocents slaughtered by his own hand like some proud conqueror. The shame of it was a rotting cloak. Twisting in the saddle, he looked back at Digtown in the distance. Meckin and Garlenna's faces swam through his mind. More than loyal subjects he'd sworn to protect, they were his friends.

Beneath him, the dead were restless.

You are no prince and you have no friends. You are Kord. No one. Nothing.

A lather of sweat from his horse soaked through to his trousers. Barodane's flight from the Gem Loft to the top of the barrow hills had been frantic. He gulped for breath.

Scab, his stallion, swung his head back, seemingly curious. Barodane patted Scab's neck as he took in the Rainy Meadows ruins, a specter on the horizon of his past.

"Shit." He turned the horse in a circle. *Garlenna's still out there. I can't just leave!*

Atop the burial mounds, the voices were overwhelming. A boy stared at him, the life draining from his eyes. Jennim's eyes too, bulging and bloodshot. A flash of misdeeds.

Abandon, Kord. Abandon...before it's too late.

He snapped the reins and steered his horse toward the ruins. Each hoof beat drew him deeper into his shame.

And a future more shameful still. *Why should the people you love matter? Did you care about us? We had children, husbands, wives. We had friends.*

The Rainy Meadows ruins stretched before him like a starving mouth, all fractured teeth and rotting gums. The sight of it stabbed his heart and twisted. Spheres of light rimmed his vision. Nausea gripped his gut. Memories long suppressed threatened to overwhelm him.

Stone foundations overgrown by lichen lay in tumbled heaps. Only a few of the structures left were taller than Barodane while mounted.

They descended into the valley. Scab whinnied as they approached the dead place.

Splintered doors littered cobblestone lanes. Their iron hinges and handles had been stripped over the years and sold to smiths by bandits or those relegated to the slums ringing Digtown. Even after a decade of heavy rainfall, inky scorch marks told a tale of a once-peaceful city, slaughtered and razed.

Barodane pulled the reins and clicked his tongue. Scab's hooves thudded over the turf as they stalked the perimeter of the ruins at a trot. His pulse pounded through his body. All moisture was sapped from his mouth. He searched for five stacked stones unmarred by flame.

Glimpses of the past assailed him. His body remembered the swirling chaos.

Steel carving flesh and bone. Butchered carcasses clogging the lanes. Severed hands, feet, and heads, serenely still, littering the ground. Hungry tongues of flame devoured roofs, cracked timbers, and danced on the smoking backs of those too slow to escape. Scream swallowed scream swallowed scream and became a singular, persistent moan.

Vacant eyed killers sporting the Ironlight fist and chain on their honor plates did Barodane's bidding. They could not murder quick enough to out-pace the horror of their deeds, nor slow enough to heal the wounds cut into their soul.

Green eyes with brown flecks.

The light within fading.

For an eternity, Barodane's hand gripped the blade.

He slammed a fist against his thigh. "Enough!"

The people of Rainy Meadows, like him, ran and died. Faces stamped and darkened with soot but for the whites of their round and fearful eyes. Confused, uncomprehending. They were cut down. "Why!?" they begged.

No answer. They ran and died. Arrived here, in Barodane's mind. *Do not look away, coward!*

Sweat poured down the back of his neck and dampened his armpits. He couldn't seem to keep his lips whetted as his search dragged.

Lane after lane, the voices and images attacked.

Finally, he spotted the stones tucked behind a redoubt of foundation of what had once been a chapel. Barodane dismounted before Scab came to a halt. He ran to the stones, stumbled, then continued on shaky legs.

A short-handled spade jumped from his belt. *Get the gold and go. Get the gold and go. Get the gold...*

Head-sized stones rolled aside in a dull clatter. He dug. The earth was soft, worm-ridden. The spade sunk into it with ease.

Easier than a sword through flesh.

Get the gold and go. Get the gold and go. Get the...

He gasped. Remembered to breathe. He jerked at his cloak where it rode his throat. With only a small pile of dirt to one side and a foot-deep divot before him, he leaned onto the spade panting, then looked up. A chapel...

It struck him, an arrow of nightmares ripping through his heart. Merciless horror descended. *By the Triune God, I buried the chest where I killed him.*

Green eyes with brown flecks. The darksteel blade had sunk in so easy, like a spade through soft mud. His hand wrapped around the handle of the blade. He drank the boy's life, drank it up like sweet wine.

I was grief-stricken. Out of my mind.

He snatched up the spade and frantically began digging again. *I'm sorry.*

We see what you are. A damning chorus. *A coward. A killer.*

He dug to forget where he was. Dug to forget the world. Sweat soaked through everything, became its own layer of clothing. Cold. Damp. Unforgiving.

You were born here, Kord. The true you. The moment your sword touched the boy's heart, you were born. And it was a good thing. You could never have killed Acramis without first killing the boy...without killing the rest of us.

"No," Barodane whined. "It was wrong. All of it was wrong."

At some point his arms started shaking. His insides quivered. A waist-high mound of churned earth piled up quickly beside him. There was no time to rest. What he sought was buried deep. That he'd made absolutely sure of. He continued digging and chanting, a desperate symphony.

Get the gold and go. Get the gold and go. Get...

Vaguely, he was aware of tears falling from his face. The same tears falling from the boy's face. *No.* Blood raced across his smoke colored blade.

No!

Yes, the dead crooned. *That was you. Who else would do such a thing?*

Green eyes with brown flecks.

Help me. Barodane mouthed the words. *Help me...*

Every part of him ached. He dropped deeper into the hole. Like a wagon wheel he rolled forward over himself in rhythmic purpose, methodically sinking spade into clay and mud, flinging it to the side, then cradling the handle and driving forward once more.

He struck something hard.

He tossed the spade beyond the hole's rim then groped through the mud. A cold and roughened metal rung found his hands. With both boots propped to either side of the pit for leverage, he sat back and strained, muscles burning with effort.

Tightly packed dirt and clay shrugged to the sides of the chest as it came free with a jangle.

From under his shirt, Barodane produced a thin necklace bearing a key. This he inserted into the deadlock of the chest after clapping out a palm full of dirt from within. When he triggered the spring inside, the rusted lock released sluggishly.

He cast it aside, lifted the lid.

Get the gold and go...

Two heavy pouches sat within. Thirty gold wheels.

Memories tumbled back to him, filling the gaps where godsthorn and time had eroded it.

Images swirled by, a gale of wind, too fast to fully comprehend. He recalled being dead in the river, saw himself rising from its waters unscathed. Sword in hand he mounted Scab and made for...

Unturrus.

He blinked hard. Blankness followed. Grimacing, he blinked harder, trying to remember, but the interval between King's Crossing and the armorer's shops at Nine Lakes was a void.

He hefted the coin purses as he remembered selling off darksteel plate piece by piece so as not to draw attention. Two warhorses stolen from the area around the battle as well. The armor alone was worth more gold wheels than the combined whoring the Gem Loft could make in a matter of months. He bought a travel chest, cheap clothing and boots, a nicked sword. The once dead horse, Scab, he'd kept.

With a fraction of the small fortune he'd made from selling his past, he hired the hermit to turn his honor plate into that of a shadowguard.

And then he'd come to Digtown.

Where it all started. Where Kord was born.

You came home.

He rose from the pit and tied the coin purses to his belt. Something poked out from beneath the chest, catching the gray sky's glare—a glimmer of metal. A chill rand down his spine. The voices of the dead shrieked displeasure at the sight, then retreated like a tide going out.

Barodane gulped, cast a wary look around, then stepped back down into the pit.

Stop, fool! You have your gold. Abandon...before it's too late.

He traced his hands through the dirt until they groped the cool touch of steel. Clumps of mire and clay rained down as he hefted sword and sheath into the air.

The leather work of the scabbard was imprinted with images of the fist and chain of Ironlight. He rotated it in his hands, brushing away clods of earth. The guard was the clouded gray-black of darksteel. A squat gauntleted fist was affixed to the pommel. He ran a fingertip over the grooves between steel fingers. His hand slid around the worn black-leather grip.

You are no prince. You are Kord! You are nothing!

Closing his eyes, he grit his teeth and pulled.

The blade slithered out, soundlessly holding the Rainy Meadows ruins in its dark promise. The final note of a death knell trailing into nothing.

An eerie void of color clung to its razor-sharp edge. A paradox of light. The metal so black, it reflected gray. So smoky gray, it reflected an ashen black. Dancing and shifting—light and shadow playing under the bright of the sky like a lake under moonlight.

Inscribed in the fuller were the same words stitched into the Slave Banner. Words spoken by his grandfather, Danath. Words that sparked revolution.

One who does not seek to break their chain is already broken by it.

For a moment, Barodane sat in silence. His grandfather's words rang in his ears. Thundered through his chest.

How far I have fallen. My family would be ashamed.

Something inside him shifted.

One who does not seek to break their chain is already broken by it.

He tore the plain sword and scabbard from his hip and cast it into the pit. With his boot, he kicked mounds of dirt atop it. *I cannot keep running from my past.*

The dead wailed. *You must! You must flee! Kord—*

"I am Barodane!"

Echoes filled the Rainy Meadows ruins.

Baro...dane...

Baro...dane...

Baro...

Energy coursed through him, his pulse a drumbeat. A call to war. The past crumbled and left an unfamiliar tingling across his skin in its wake. For as long as he could remember, it felt as though the entire weight of the ruins were pressing down on his shoulders. He'd been like a beast of burden under yoke, gouging the same tracks of earth with the same dull plow.

No longer.

He fastened scabbard to belt. With a slow exhale, he approached the scorched remains of the chapel.

Help me.

Barodane winced.

Help me.

His feet begged to flee, but he stood motionless, jaw clenched. Determined.

The same blade that had stolen the boy's life fourteen years earlier whispered through the air as Barodane lifted it, and fell to a knee before the ruined chapel. The exact place where the execution occurred. The tip of his sword bit into the earth. His forehead bowed forward to kiss the steel fist adorning the pommel.

For an interminable amount of time, he knelt. Thoughts of Meckin, Garlenna, and the danger they faced, pressed into his awareness. He shoved them aside. *This is something I must do!*

Tears streamed down his cheeks. "Never again."

Light dissolved beneath the narrow slit of his eyelids. The pervasive black of night fell. A drizzle dampened his brow, his greasy hair, and his gloves wrapped around sword hilt. As time slithered past, the misting rain grew dense and pummeled the ruins. Water stream down Barodane's elbows, dripped from the tip of his hawkish nose and the cross-guard of his sword.

Laborious exhales warmed his face. His heart burned in his chest like a well-fed furnace.

Night drew him deeper into his vigil for the dead.

Nearby, Scab clomped down a cobbled street. Barodane didn't care. He let the stallion go.

Help me.

Barodane breathed, letting the image of the boy enter his mind without struggle. He let the past play out. At first, he only apologized as the boy died. Over and over, he imagined the blade entering the boy's chest. "I'm sorry," he would say.

Nothing changed. Hours passed.

In the distance, an owl screeched. The rains devolved into curtains of mist once more, soaking him all the way through.

Lips quivering, body shaking, Barodane whispered aloud, "Never again."

Brown eyes with green flecks regarded him from beneath a crown of blood.

"Forgive me."

The memory changed. The boy staggered toward him from the chapel, bleeding and vulnerable. *Help me.* This time Barodane stayed his hand. They stared at each other, he and the boy, fire crackling around them in an infinite loop of destruction. The boy's face changed. First into Barodane's father, Kordin, then into his brother's...

Then his own.

When he saw himself there, naked and alone, he roared with hatred and struck out, beheading the boy.

Help me.

"Die!"

Every part of him wanted to escape, to find his horse and flee again from the unbearable grief raging through him. But hour after hour night held him. For the sake of justice he remained rooted in place. For the sake of the boy who never had a choice, he willed himself into the past. A dozen times and more, he threw himself into the tangled web of guilt and shame and actions most hollow.

Deeds bereft of humanity.

A boy with a cruel smile greeted him. *Help me*

Who are you? Barodane asked.

Kord, the voices whispered, *the boy's name is Kord. You hate him because you are him.*

He sheathed his sword. *No. You're wrong.*

All that he was and ever had been, flowed into an unbreakable braid, a rope that could not burn and snap. Light and dark. Hope and despair. Good and evil. Connecting past to present in a web of shuddering complexity, the possibility of what had been and what could be again.

Words he'd not considered in many years reached forth from the chasm of self-hate, bridging a lifetime of divide between conflicting truths.

I am Barodane Ironlight.

The boy swelled, changed, grew to be a man with dark hair, tan skin, and a long nose. In one hand, he held a thorn roll. In the other a tankard of godsbrew. He wore the honor plate of a shadowguard.

The man was familiar but different. Kord from Digtown.

Barodane recoiled at the sight of the man he'd been for the last fourteen years. Just behind Kord, a greedy inferno consumed the town of Rainy Meadows. Ash fell in lazy sheets across a filthy brow ringed with the imprint of an absent crown. Unsettled eyes stared at Barodane. Eyes without peace. Flame glittered in the specter's darkened irises.

Help me, Kord's voice was half-laugh, terse and mocking.

Darksteel sang forth. Barodane lunged, skewering the vile man's heart. The voices of the dead screamed as one, a haunting, echoing wail. They were ripped from him, their curses and rebukes trailing away into an empty void. In their absence, a mournful quiet budded to life.

Calm like a mountain lake or snowy field drifted over him. Neither pleasant or unpleasant. Simply, there.

In his mind's eye, the boy returned. Green eyes with brown flecks watched Barodane. The boy cocked his head.

"I'm sorry," Barodane said.

As a Namorite and as a descendant of Danath, I promise you.

"Never again."

His eyes snapped open. He stood. Shoulders pinned back, chest thrust forward, he declared. "Never again."

Birds sang across the sky as dawn rays slashed the horizon with pink and orange. Sometime in the night, the rains had stopped, leaving the scent of damp earth and wet stone to fill Barodane's nose. He drew the tip of his darksteel blade from the topsoil then gave the chapel a final nod as he turned to go.

Somewhere in the distance, a horse whinnied. Bringing a hand to his brow to block the morning sun, he searched for Scab.

A second whinny from a second horse—farther away. He froze. The hair on the backs of his arms stiffened.

A third whinny confirmed his fears.

I'm not alone.

Three riders descended the barrow mounds. By their haste alone, Barodane knew them to be enemies. He cursed and slammed sword into scabbard.

Little more than bearded, pinkish blots bobbing over their horse's withers, they would be on him in minutes. Thin dark lines he assumed to be swords slapped their horses' flanks.

No time at all.

He whistled for Scab as he sprinted down the nearest lane. No response. Even with the familiar grip of darksteel in hand, he was out of practice and trusted his skill at arms little and less. Outrunning them was the only option.

Between last night's vigil and the fire at the Dregs the night previous, he hadn't slept. The weight of exhaustion dogged him. Every step sluggish. Every breath ragged. He didn't need a Sister of the Rose to tell him his recovery from the withers wasn't complete. He wondered if the godsthorn had cleared his system.

Against three mounted men...I'm fucked.

With a quick prayer to the Triune God, he turned down another lane. His thumb and middle finger formed a crab claw in his mouth. He whistled.

An answering whinny drew him toward an apple tree near a fountain at the center of town. A part of the tree decayed on the ground while the rest still managed to generate fruit, as if two different time-lines had split it down the middle.

Scab nudged apples along the ground.

Fire filled Barodane's lungs as he sprinted over, sweating and panting. He wished he'd taken time to get the beast properly trained. *He should come running when I call him!*

He threw out his arms, palms slapping against flank and saddle to slow him. Scab started, then continued to munch a not-yet-rotten apple. Barodane swung up, jerked the reins, wheeled and fled.

Hoof beats ricocheted off the ruins of Rainy Meadows. Nearby shouts told him the riders were close. From a distance, he hadn't spied masonry uniforms on them. Hired men. Assassins. Less fearsome than a trained holdguard of Breckenbright.

But in his condition, facing them was a last resort. He wasn't the only shadowguard in the region.

Heat reached into arms and legs, winding his muscles tight. A spasm shot down his inner thigh, causing him to wince. He shimmied in the saddle and hunkered over the horse's withers. Breath came in rapid sips. Scab grunted as he weaved between scorched ruin and tumbled stone.

"Stop!"

He didn't, though he did afford a glance backward. One had gained on him. Another lagged. The third was nowhere to be seen. *An ambush.* The third cutthroat could skirt the ruins with far greater speed than Barodane could navigate the rubble-strewn streets. *He means to head me off, let these others drive me to him.*

An unpaved street of moss and mud and insurgences of fallen stone whipped past. He needed the next road out. Another flew by. He cursed, spurring his steed to the next lane, committed to take it regardless of its condition.

He jerked the reins...and covered no more than a hundred feet before the third rider appeared at the end of the lane. Barodane reined in. No time to think. No time to run.

One choice remained.

He forced air in through his nose then out slowly through his mouth. Wrapping the reins around one hand, he drew his blade with the other. A gentle ring reverberated off the ruined walls. Darksteel flashed under a glowering gray sky.

He surged forward, his sword heaving backward against the sudden rush of inertia. Wind thudded and swirled in his ears. Splayed out and trailing, his cloak snapped like a sail as he charged. Numbness seeped through his torso, everywhere but his arm which throbbed with anticipation.

The two assassins behind shouted ahead to their comrade. The stutter-stomp of hooves told Barodane they'd taken the turn behind him.

Holding little hope already, despair fell leaden across his chest as he watched a fourth rider descend the hill. *Trapped.* He had scant seconds to dispatch the cutthroat at the lane's end before either the two behind him or the fourth ahead were upon him.

Instinct took over.

Fourteen years of misery spilled forth like blood to bathe Rainy Meadows one final time. "Ironlight!" he shouted.

The man at lane's end charged to meet Barodane. In a fast narrowing-rush, his face came into sharp focus. Blond beard, round face, bald and heavy but not for muscle.

Hoof beats, pounding closer. "Ironlight!"

Pulse hammering. "Ironlight! Bastard!"

They closed. A clang followed by a deafening whoosh. The sweeping of Barodane's arm, the shock of it meeting density stiffened him to the shoulder. A red arc leaping into the air.

Scab drew up sharply. Blood cascaded down its shoulder. It staggered wildly about in pain. Barodane was forced to drop his blade and fight to keep hold of the reins.

The other man crashed to the cobbles.

Barodane hushed his bucking horse as it spun. He glimpsed the fallen cutthroat pushing himself backward across the ground and clutching at a wound in his neck. Scrambling and thrashing, he left a viscous stain of dark blood across the cobbles like some immense slug.

A flap of flesh hung from Scab's shoulder. The stallion reared—Barodane lost his grip. He jumped to safety. The landing was awkward, but he managed to keep his feet.

Riders bore down on him from both sides. The tattoo of hooves was thick in the air. *Rakka-ta. Rakka-ta. Rakka-ta.*

He cast about for his sword. Couldn't find it. Made for the dying man's blade instead. "Gulck," the man said. Crimson leaked from his lips onto his beard and ran between his fingers. As Barodane retrieved the sword, the man grabbed his leg. It wasn't darksteel, but it slid through the dying man easy enough.

He ran to the nearest ruin to make a final stand. Where a door had burned away, the fortification was defensible. They'd have to face him one at a time.

From the sound of it, the fourth cutthroat was pushing his steed hard, horse and rider laboring in tandem.

Barodane waited, heart beating faster than any tune he'd ever played on the banha drum. A wave of dizziness rippled between his ears as he shifted from foot to foot. He flourished his sword and stared at the charred entryway. As an afterthought, he drew the dagger from his chest strap. Close quarters were inevitable.

Then for the second time in fourteen years, the specters of Rainy Meadows heard the war cry of its doom.

"For Namarr!"

The two riders who'd pursued Barodane pounded past the entrance of the ruin he waited within...toward the fourth rider.

The clatter of arms, the screech of steel. A curse, followed by a sickening wet crunch.

Barodane dashed from the burned-out structure and into the streets, sword leading.

His heart skipped.

Mace shining, kite shield brought to bear, Garlenna Renwood wheeled her horse to face the remaining assassin. One man had already been introduced to her martial prowess. He lay stretched out on the lane, legs and hands twitching, the inside of his skull littering the ground like a bloomed rose.

She shouted again, striking the air from Barodane. "For Rainy Meadows! For the Fallen!"

From deep in Barodane's chest came a great sigh. An unwinding of the soul. A relief found only in the acknowledgment of honor lost. In justice served through dedication to future rights in the name of wrongs already done.

"For the Fallen!" Barodane's voice cracked.

Garlenna guided her destrier toward the other man's rouncey with her knees. The assassin swung once, twice, both sword strokes falling impotent against her kite shield. Sentinel quiet, she shoved him with it, nearly unhorsing him. "Yield."

In answer, he stabbed at her horse. But Garlenna was viper fast. She turned the blow with her mace, brought it around in an arc and down against his knee. With a clipped scream, the man toppled from the saddle and landed hard on his side. He wheezed, the breath knocked from him. "I yield!" He sucked ragged breaths and whimpered. "Please, by the Sempyrean, I yield, I yield. Spare me. Please."

Garlenna dismounted. The man writhed, hands shaking over brutalized knee. A bit of pinkish bone poked from his trousers. Garlenna slipped her mace through a belt loop. Seemingly in relief, the man cried hysterically and thanked her.

"You may die yet." She left him there.

Dropping her kite shield, she came to Barodane's side and whispered, "Are you hurt, my Prince?"

Barodane looked into her lone eye, saw a tear there. She too wept. She too suffered his past transgressions. They stared at each other until finally she nodded.

"It is...difficult," she said. "I never thought I'd stand this ground again. I very much hoped I wouldn't."

Barodane clapped a hand to her shoulder. "I am so sorry for what I did. And I am sorry for what I've not done since. I won't ask your forgiveness in words. But..." he hesitated, waiting for the voices. They never came. His doubts were his own once more. He sighed, resolute. "I will go with you. I'll earn your forgiveness by action."

She looked skyward and mumbled a prayer to the Sempyrean. A smile overtook him. He saw her. Garlenna Renwood. His prosort.

My friend.

She looked over his shoulder. "What's this?"

She moved past, bent, lifted his darksteel blade from a ditch. She smiled at it then handed it to him hilt first.

"So...you are an Ironlight after all."

CHAPTER FORTY-SEVEN

JUSTICE

P anels of fading sunlight framed Ishoa's booted feet and Rakeema's slumbering form in an orange glow. It should have been warm. Maybe even set her toes to itching.

But all Ishoa felt was a hammering chill.

A cold that chipped away with the seconds. Creeping darkness lapping at her heart. An ill tide, fast-rising.

For hours, she'd listened to the bustle beyond her window. The trundle of carts. The caterwauling furriers leading away white wolverines. The peremptory shouts of crownguard sweeping gossiping spectators from the bailey. The clack of piled lumber as carpenters disassembled the arena.

None worried for Lodaris's life.

None cared.

None loved him like she did.

He didn't deserve it. Lying on her side on the bed, with a hand outstretched, Ishoa clenched a fist. *The Warnocks didn't deserve him.* She considered her own part in his fate. Guilt stilted her breathing. *I don't deserve him.*

Orange halos turned to silver as the hours dripped by. Night fell. Ink spilled into every corner and cranny, swallowing the room but for a window-shaped burst of light centering around Ishoa's fingertips.

The sounds of work in the bailey wandered off, giving way to the occasional bark of laughter as holdguard walked the walls surrounding the Ice Maiden's Keep.

Ishoa envied their mirth.

Happiness was a useless thing. Fear as well. What she feared seemingly came to pass regardless of her preferences. Sadness, while unpleasant, at least reminded her of love. Of what mattered most.

But wrath. Anger. Hate. By far these were the most useful emotions to cultivate. *Like Lodecka.* The Scarborn's words rolled through Ishoa's like a scythed wheel. *After all, he's just a Scarborn.*

Ishoa came to her knees on the bed. Heat sprinted into her arms. She ground her teeth as she rained punches down on an embroidered pillow. She cursed and snarled. A guard stationed outside her door coughed—a reminder. She didn't care.

Lodecka had known what to say to hurt Ishoa. Pain was the wretched woman's life, her blade and shield both. Someone so vile could never feel bad for her actions. She could never have remorse.

There is only one way to deal with such people.

Murder flashed across her mind, settled inside like a cool drink of water at the height of summer. She bit the pillow's corner like an animal. Tore at the seams until they popped. Slapped her own face and welcomed the sting.

Anything to distract from the gnawing horror within.

She looked at her parents, marred faces of shadow and moonlit sheen. *First them. Now Lodaris.*

She slumped forward and buried her face in her furs and sobbed. *I'm doomed. Cursed to be abandoned by anyone who dares love me.* Tears gushed down her cheeks. With them came the rush of past wounds long suppressed. She gripped handfuls of fur, wishing it were her mother's hand or her father's. *Or the warm handle of a dagger.* One she could use to carve more scars into Lodecka Warnock's hideous face.

Cold worked its way into her bones, but it was grief that had her shaking. Sleep was a ghost, haunting her. Untouchable.

Dawn was an hour from breaking when Wolst stepped furtively into her room. "Isha...are you awake?"

"Yes," a hoarse whisper, so raw and ragged it surprised her.

He eased down onto the beside her. "You're cold. Here—"

He grabbed a fur and slid it up around her shoulders.

Her heart beat galloped. She couldn't move. Frozen, afraid. Trapped like a caged wolverine. She forced a stuttering breath. She'd seen the wounds, the blood, the pale, blotchy flesh.

The truth settled in her bones long before her uncle spoke it aloud.

"I'm sorry, Isha. He's gone."

For a crystalline moment, the news changed nothing. Deep in her gut, she'd already known. Then fire spread over her skin as her body caught up with her mind.

Spasms racked her torso, made it a shuddering mess. Her fingertips tingled. She gasped, moaned, sagged around pitiful cries and wept. Wolst placed a broad hand on her ankle.

Hollow words found their way to the surface. "At least he's not suffering anymore."

A part of her wished Lodaris could return from death to kill his parents. Ishoa would have to do it for him.

"Try to rest." Wolst's expression was downcast, his voice low. "Stay strong, Isha."

With a creak of bed and leather, he wiped at a sniffle and then left her to grieve.

Why? Why is this happening to me? First her parents abandoned her to a lonely life, and now her best friend had done the same. *I should be more practiced at death by now.*

Why was the loss so hard? *After all, he's just a Scarborn...*

She punched her pillow as if she could beat Lodecka Warnock's words from her mind.

No. He was more than that.

He was my friend.

Ishoa sat at counsel like a whipped dog, waiting for another twist of fate's knife. But she'd grown tired of waiting. *Lodaris is gone. My lies can't protect him anymore.*

So she admitted a truth sure to rouse her family.

"Peace with the Scarborn is impossible." Discordant tension swept the room like a battle cry. "They plotted to have me killed atop the Ice King."

She gave an account of what had transpired. All but Wolst listened calmly. The warmaster seethed, face contorted into a wrathful mask, neck tendons jolting with murderous intent. When she finished, he heaved to his feet. "Hast!" Veins writhed around thick knuckles as he pressed fists into the horn table. "I want every knight and half our holdguard at my heels within the hour!"

"Easy, nephew." The duchess unfolded from her chair and stood, a corpse come to life. "Easy." Silks darker than a storm bear's slate fur hid her aging form. Fissures more numerous than glaciers in the eastern fjord's lined her face. Candlelight shimmered along the Kon's gift of dragon skin over one shoulder. With the death of Lodaris so fresh, Ishoa couldn't help but consider how much time was left to her great-grandmother. *A year? Two?* She recalled Ularis's words. *The long game is ours...*

How long though?

The duchess paced the chamber. "They will be dealt with *after* the Trials are complete. Not a moment before."

Othwii pulled at the hummingbird broach about his neck, loosening his collar. Wolst stared at the horn table wearing a pensive frown, ox-broad chest swelling. Arick stared placidly. *Like Mother.* Shame draped Ishoa's shoulders.

If my parents were alive, none of this would have happened.

"We stand on the cliff's edge. Any strong gust—any tremor underfoot—may plummet us into chaos." Belara plucked a curl of white hair from her silk dress and flicked it away. "There are still a number of holds outside our gate that Syphion

Muul may have corrupted. If we go to arrest them now, who knows what violence might erupt. Personally, I prefer more predictable scenarios than pitched battle, so why don't we keep the bloodbaths well away from Jarik. For now."

Ishoa didn't care where the bloodbath happened so long as it did. *My friend is dead. The only person who understood me...gone.* "Where then?" She released clenched fists, folded them atop the table. "When?"

The duchess shot Ishoa a smile. Rapid blinking followed a frown. "I'm surprised you're so quick to dole out justice when you were so slow to report the events that brought you to it. We should have known about the assassination attempt the moment it happened."

Ishoa's will to care about right or wrong was fleeting. The loss of Lodaris was still too dizzyingly fresh. The Scarborn leaders had carted their son's body off to the Fringes for rites as soon as he died, a snub Ishoa had little doubt was directed at her. Ishoa clung to the rage it birthed in her breast.

Now she coveted the Warnock's lives like a wolverine does a carcass.

"Lodaris stopped Sweet Ges." Ishoa felt her upper-lip curl back. "And now he's dead. The Warnocks..." Her voice shook. "They will pay."

Clearing his throat, Othwii stood. "I would speak."

"And you will do so freely." Belara's next words were a punctuated reminder to Ishoa. "This counsel lives and dies by the trust it gives its members to speak the truth."

"Thank you, Highness." Othwii stooped forward, an ancient bird shielding its nest. "Ishoa, we know you grieve. Everyone here has lost someone they loved."

Yesterday though?

Othwii words were measured and soft as silk. "In your love and your grief, you've made mistakes. But even mistakes made in the right can be a detriment. As you and I have discussed, doing good does not always mean serving the *greater* good. This is the lesson you must still learn. And here it is before you. A chance at prudence when a lack of it could lead to ruin."

Wolst had taken a seat. The purple flush splotching his cheeks told her he'd not yet calmed. But it was the punch in his voice that told her he didn't wish to. "Mistakes, aye! Pleasing ones though. Almost worth it to see the damned look on Lodecka's face when you lambasted the Scaborn scum. A couple more feet and you would have spit right in her ass-ugly face."

Scarborn scum.

The insult caused Ishoa to flinch. The image of Lodaris walking the streets of Jarik to contemptuous jeers and hurled hate flashed across her mind. *That's why Lodaris is dead. He wanted to be more than what bigotry made of him.* She shook her head. Wolst was her champion above any. He meant well. *My friend's death is Lodecka's fault.*

"Spitting at Lodecka and threatening her was brash." Animosity stirred with Arick's rebuke. "Celebrating foolishness is the first step in ensuring it is repeated."

Wolst cracked his neck, then his knuckles, a series of resounding wet pops. "Oh?"

"You are right, Arick," said Belara curtly. "Celebration of foolishness begets more of it."

Ishoa's chin slid to her chest. The backs of her hands rested on her thighs, palms upturned. Limp in defeat. *We're going to let them get away with it?*

"But you're also wrong," Belara said. Ishoa snapped to attention. The duchess gave Ishoa a shallow bow, white curls held in place by a series of gem-encrusted hairpins. "Your success at the Quelling showed everyone that, whatever you lack in prudence, you make up for in strength. You charged a white wolverine and sent it scampering into its cage with your ferocity. Further, you threw tradition aside in favor of doing what's right. You stood toe-to-toe with the most feared woman in Anjuhkar—second only to me. And despite only a few in this room witnessing it, you spat at her feet and threatened her."

A frown deepened on Ishoa's brow as her grandmother's smile broadened. "Better you bare your teeth than expose your belly. Better to be predator than prey. My days in this world dwindle, a countdown of sorts for our enemies. So I take at least some solace in them knowing they also tick off the days leading up to Ishoa Ironlight's rise to power. A furious thing indeed. Sadly, having survived every Ironlight but you, Isha, I cannot deny that being bold and reckless is the very nature of your bloodline." A hooked finger came to the duchess's lips, a simple gesture suppressing complex heartache. Her husband. Her son. Her grandchildren. Deaths like a pendulum, cutting deeper at each remembrance. "I would not let you follow in their footsteps to an early grave, if possible. Even with your wild-hearted lineage, you can engender great change. But first we need to ensure that by the time you're of age there remains a crown to occupy."

"Aye, no doubt," Wolst slapped the table. "She's an Ironlight. So what are we to do about it?"

Belara eased back onto a chair, palm rubbing her brow. "A pity Lodaris died. If he'd lived, perhaps he would have voted against Revocation. A crushing blow to the movement. Pity we won't see that. With his tragic death, the Scarborn may have lost a vote for Revocation, but they've managed to eliminate our greatest asset in levying official charges against them. That leaves one alternative."

The duchess crossed her arms as she chewed a nail in thought. After a moment, her voice rose, a marker of imminent commands. "The time for subtlety is over. The Warnocks have erred in setting the pace for brashness. We merely seek to out-pace them in it, and in the process we will outmaneuver them."

Spine rigid, Ishoa leaned forward. "We strike at night when they least expect it."

Wolst shook his shaggy mane. "They're not the type to be unprepared for that."

"Indeed. As it stands, play against the Warnocks of any kind invites heavy casualties." The duchess raised her chin and folded her hands in her lap. "The Narls are the weak ones. The boy, Ishoa's intended assassin. Wolst, before the closing ceremonies are over, I want a hundred of your finest dispatched to White Plains to wait in ambush. I find taking them unawares more suitable than a bloodbath on our doorstep, don't you?"

Ishoa imagined Sweet Ges's terrified face as Wolst threw loops of rope around him. A delighted shiver danced between her shoulders.

"Golthius Narl has fifty holdguard and eight knights in his retinue," said Arick in calculating tones. "A hundred isn't nearly enough to ensure a peaceful arrest, Highness."

"True. The very reason I will write Rigga Hine and ask for the same amount in support," said Belara. "The shepherds of White Plains will know the land. And their matriarch is no fan of the bakers of Prav."

"Deephollow Prison," Wolst nodded to himself. "We'll seize him there. The bridge to Prav goes right by it."

"Excellent." The duchess sucked her teeth. "Gestryn Narl and Lodaris Warnock have failed the Trials. Ishoa has succeeded. Revocation will be crushed at court. The Narl boy will confess to his failed assassination. Then Golthius and the Warnocks will be well on their way to the dark side of a prison cell. A well-deserved destiny, don't you think?"

The only thing Lodecka deserves is a blade straight through her hollow heart. Ularis and Syphion too. Laying blame at their feet gave Ishoa room to breathe. It shifted focus from the emptiness in the pit of her stomach. Gave her a purpose to latch onto, something to keep her from being swallowed by the abyss of loss.

Belara exhaled loudly. "The path is finally set, Isha. The crown will be yours."

But at what cost? I betrayed my friend. Told him I loved him. Let him doom himself by fighting for me. All the while I used him and lied to him, and he refused to do the same. Despite wanting his parents' love and approval, he did what was right. He saved me. He was my better. She thought of her parents, how disappointed they would be. *Maybe I'm the one who should be dead.*

No matter what retribution her grandmother planned, no matter what justice fell upon the Warnocks and Syphion and the Narls, it would never bring Lodaris back.

A bitter taste filled Ishoa's mouth, and tears gathered in her eyes as they ended the meeting with Danath's words.

"Shackles only hold those who allow it.

"One who does not seek to break their chain is already broken by it.

"Here and now.

"Free your swords! Free your souls!

"My Sons and Daughters of Namarr, you cannot die but once. Let us live, boldly and without fear!"

No one lived those words better than Lodaris.

Chapter Forty-Eight

POWERS UNKNOWN

Without saying it, there is a certain way a person moves that tells you they despise you. A certain silence. A certain crispness to their economy of motion.

Tyne snaps linens as she folds them. She shuts doors with excessive force. The resounding bang seems a defamation of my character. She trims the words of every sentence as if they are a gift held back from the undeserving.

She's not wrong to treat me so. Acceptance, however, makes it no easier to bear.

For two full days, Akyris slept. When he finally rose in the late morning on the third day, his faculties had yet to join him before he was stumbling out the door without a word to wait for me under the elm.

With a sigh, I hobbled out to meet him. If I had to guess, the boy had no clue how long he'd rested. At the end of the first night, when he laid in bed thrashing, I nearly manipulated his dreams. But we walked more tentative ground now. To mettle over much was to taint his training and possibly invite disaster. When I sent him the dream of the Mad Prince, he was the boy, Akyris, a worldly creature capable of no greater deed than selfishness. He could barely see what was slapping him across the brow. That wasn't the true Akyris. Not the one I now work to awaken.

This one sees.

I thought Tyne would be his greatest obstacle to our training. Despite preparing her with what little information I could without jeopardizing the path of the future, I knew he would struggle. But never does what we worry about most end up being the most difficult thing to overcome.

It's what we don't see.

I left myself out of the equation. Tyne is my daughter, and in the fashion of all parents who've ever lived, my fear of disappointing her could ruin everything. So I delay sharing Jennim's death. When someone refuses to make eye contact with me, sharing terrible news with them, of which I am the proctor, seems like the last thing I should do.

So, I will wait and do what I can with Akyris in spite of the entanglement. In time, Tyne will settle. When that happens, I'll tell her about Jennim.

I ease down onto the stump beneath the elm tree. "How do you feel?"

He blinks, bovine slow, then swallows. "Better than yesterday. Ready to return."

He thinks it yesterday. I let it slide. No point in worrying him when Tyne is worried enough for the both of them.

Light pours from the jewel slung round my neck. Akyris's face glows gray. I close my eyes, probe forward...

A rush of sound and feeling—the self being filled and then poured out.

I carry Akyris's consciousness through the River. He's lighter now. Far lighter. An unexpected but pleasant shift. Rest did him well. A cloying density smacks into us: the Veil. A littoral zone of burbling creation separating the River's surface from its depths. As we pierce though it, I decide to experiment. I release Akyris.

His Locus wobbles. Threatens to shatter under the Veil's strain.

He continues forward, considerably slower. I lag back some so he doesn't lose the energy signature of my Locus, his guiding beacon through the tumult.

I remember he's just recovered, that I promised Tyne we'd go easy. I extend a tether and aid him. Breaking my promise to Darkhorn was bad enough.

We arrive. The interplay of all that is, ebbs and flows. Clouds of shadow and light. Vibrant hues crackled and dance about us, here hanging dense and heavy as a mountain, there a fine mist dispersed with nothing more than a simple wave of conscious intent through it.

We begin.

He's stronger somehow. He stands alone in the River three times longer than he ever has before the shadowy absence of the Abyssal Sea takes him.

We finish the session and return to our vessels. I tell him of the salient parts of my conversation with his mother. He doesn't take the news well. Training every other day upsets him. I sense him biting back debate. Barely.

After another day of rest, we go back.

Longer he denies the darkness from swallowing him. Power radiates from the space he occupies. The River's coursing energies bow around his consciousness. Although his Locus isn't yet expansive, save for Tahmyrus, the core of it is denser than any I've seen.

There is hope.

Between training days, instead of being a normal boy as Tyne wanted, and as I promised, Akyris forgoes the world of most twelve-year-olds. The trouble that normally follows wild packs of emotionally unstable teenage children roam on without him. Posturing for the attention of girls his age. Vying for acceptance among the other young males through acts of stupidity. Akyris refuses it all.

Sima comes up the lane. I greet her with a smile and make small talk. She's looking for Akyris. "I haven't seen him in weeks," she says. I send her inside to fetch him. Moments later she walks past me and back down the lane, wearing a baffled expression. Tears well at the corner of her eyes as she goes. I know what she's experiencing.

One of the hardest things for a loved one to cope with is seeing the changes in those they care about most. Even when it is for the better, it can feel like a loss. Like they've drifted further from the ground on which the relation was built. A choice by one and not the other. By no fault of Sima's own, Akyris has changed. Fate has taken hold and diverted their paths before the girl was ready.

Such is the way of life sometimes.

Sima could not control Akyris nor halt his change. Just as I can not control Tyne's reaction to the news I've yet to share. To control another is to amplify one's own pain and maybe lose a loved one all the faster. Relationships teach as much to those willing to listen.

Only and ever does control rest in the hands of those who've released it.

Instead of being a boy, Akyris studies. His days off revolve around my book in his hands. He walks around the cottage turning pages and rarely acknowledging Tyne. Frustrated, she demands his attention, then shoots me dirty looks when she gets indifferent responses, as if to say, "This is your fault." If I'm not in line of sight, I hear a sigh loud enough for her to be satisfied with the idea I might have heard it, which I usually do.

In silence, I accept her condemnation. Training continues in spite of it. By the end of the ninth day since his rest, Akyris stands in the River's depths alone for an entire afternoon.

Thrilled with his own progress, he begs to skip the next rest day as we step inside the cottage. "I'm strong enough now. Please, I'll be fine. I can do this."

Tight-mouthed, Tyne watches me sidelong. She acts like she's not part of the conversation, but her presence looms. I sense the storm I'll face if I cave to Akyris's demands. It's a storm I'd rather avoid.

"Even the best need rest," I say. "Myself included. Our breaks are for me as much as they are for you."

Akyris's dark-rimmed eyes narrow around me in a sullen glare. He glances at his mom, then back at me. "Sure you do."

In a sugary voice, Tyne asks Akyris if he will help her in the gardens. The boy's no fool. He knows it's her keeping him from training daily. He gives her a wooden response, then sits on the floor with his book. Pages nearly rip as he slaps at them to find his place. For this, I know I'll soon be blamed.

"Well then," Tyne says dramatically. I seek my own place on the porch in hopes of avoiding her baleful looks. An exasperated sigh chases me out the door.

From dawn until dusk the next day, Akyris stands in the River alone. His Locus pulses with power. At this point, I have little doubt he could stand as long as he pleases.

My peers, however, find little comfort in the facts.

"What happened?" Darkhorn's tone is a mix of hope and concern.

"I let him rest."

A mild reverberation accompanies the shaman's musing. "You've not told her then?"

"You must tell her." Magomedes is harsh, harsher than Darkhorn ever was.

"And here I thought my parents died a hundred years ago." I snap. "Listen to me. He just needed rest. His progress is stunning. He's achieved mastery over his Locus faster than any of us."

"Must you always be such an insolent child?" Magomedes clears her throat, proceeds in an icy tone. "Do your duty, Locastrii."

Now I truly feel like my parents are back from the dead, scolding me into a corner and dressing me in shame.

"Look, you fools! He's doing it!"

"You know it won't last." Darkhorn sounds every bit as tired as he recently indicated. "The entanglement will return. And the next time it does could be dangerous."

Another day in which Akyris stands alone in the River passes. I'm reminded of when Tyne was a baby, how one day she started standing, and then I blinked and found her climbing. In the realm of things both new and difficult, the tiniest step in evolving skill appears as a monumental leap.

With Akyris's consciousness tethered to my own, and both tethered to our mortal vessels beneath the elm, we begin our return from the River. A toddler who no longer topples at the first chance misstep, Akyris's barrels through the Veil. His Locus fixates on his body, a beacon calling his incorporeal energies.

I let him drift away from me. Our essence remains connected by the scantest of threads. In theory, he should need my help to regain the right trajectory. With effort, Akyris pushes his way back to my side. Transitions through the Veil, be they to the past, present, future, or the depths of the River, span only seconds. But to one yet fully trained, it is arduous enough to seem far longer.

Akyris battles furiously to keep pace with me. I slow, laughing to myself and watching him do things he couldn't have fathomed a couple of month ago. My peers have to be wrong. Maybe this is the reason the Path chose him. Maybe...Akyris is different.

Stronger.

Better.

Like the Arrow of Light.

I can't bring myself to believe as my peers do. Akyris is not slowing. In fact, he's sprinting. Now that he can travel through the Veil unaided, he's ready to learn how to wield the jeweled eye.

"I want to congratulate you, my grandson. You're now the youngest person in history to stand alone in the River of conscious reality."

"I am?"

"You bet your wistful little eyes you are. You've worked hard at this. To be honest, I thought you'd have struggled more."

I've manifested our forms so we can share the moment face-to-face. Luminous mists ride amorphous blots of jet in a wave that breaks around us. A rainbow of color corkscrews at an angle to one side and then disappearing into gray void in the distance.

"It wasn't easy," Akyris says. "At first it hurt so bad...but I just kept allowing it. I focused on being calm, on how easy it *could* be in the future if I let it happen in the present. I figured if this place is the foundation of creation, well then it's the foundation of me too."

I nod, reveling too much in his words to form my own. I snap my fingers repeatedly, a form of applause.

Akyris beams. "There's no difference between me and the River. No barrier. No *me* to drown. At least not anymore. When I let myself become one with the River, it's effortless to stand in it."

Love. Pulsating in my breast. As an Awakened, as a grandmother, as an agent of light determined to hold back the dark, I experience hope where only the idea of it once lived.

And yet, there is more work to do if he is to defeat the Arrow. More work if he is to keep the prophet from plunging the world into the Abyssal Sea and unmaking reality.

I mask my dourness with a flourish of arms. "For all your hard work, I celebrate you." I motion with my staff ahead of us. "And for all your hard work, I present you with another challenge. Such is the burden of power."

Where I indicate, waves of light and matter bow outward and then curl back into themselves, like a rolling halo formed in a washbasin around a stream of running water. Mist, absence, color, all condense into an eddying border, vapors of creation spiraling to form a cylindrical tunnel. Its center draws spirals forever away into a pinprick of blackness.

"This," I nod at the spinning avenue. "Is the way humans see life." I throw my arms wide, calling out with my Locus. A hundred more cylindrical avenues appear all around us, a honeycomb of roiling energy coalescing around nodes of midnight.

"And this is how one who wields the jeweled eye sees. How you will learn to see. Now, listen carefully to what is required, for like all things in life, this too is a paradox. What you've recently mastered of standing in the River is vital to your success. You are one with the River now—no barriers, no difference. And to be one with it, as you said, makes standing in it effortless. That you've learned this is an extraordinary thing, and of absolute necessity for what you'll do next."

Akyris nods, brow relaxed despite his focus.

"And now you must release that lesson. To see with the jeweled eye, you must *exist* as a paradox. You must remove any barrier that keeps the River from flowing through you. And you must also simultaneously create barriers against the River in order to manipulate it."

The nodding stops. A line splits his brow as he looks at a handful of the tunnels, seething color, light, and shadow. "So I allow the River in, just as I've done, but then once I do, I have to choose what aspects of it to block?"

"Exactly! Otherwise, you won't be able to direct your Locus. We've developed your Locus's strength to a degree—you can think of it like a shield. Now, you will learn to hone it like a spear." I clear my throat. "Remember, Akyris, you must only allow the River's currents that *you* choose to flow through you. Deny all others." I turn in a circle, gesturing at the honeycomb of pathways spreading out in every direction with my staff. "Otherwise, you may not like where you end up."

A bead of light emanates from the end of a swirling tunnel overhead. Akyris calls to the memory of the hut he grew up in. When Tyne first arrived, they didn't have much. She had stayed in a single room on the other side of town, more chicken coup than hut. Four walls and barely enough room to lay down without tucking her legs.

Akyris was born there. Spent the first years of life there.

Sunlight spilled into the cracks of the hut's roof, splicing the inside with light. In the winter, wind moaned through the loose slats. On chill nights, Tyne was forced to welcome in the goats from the pen next door for warmth.

Faintly, I feel the boy's memories. Lying in Tyne's cradling arms. Playing with a beetle on the dirt floor. Sweet memories. Comforting. Vivid.

For Akyris, a solid first attempt at seeing with the jeweled eye.

Casting coils of consciousness, he pulls the light to him as I've shown him to do. The memory creeps forward from the seething tunnel on waves of undulating light and sound.

The past joins with his present, creates a link, fusing with his Locus. Akyris allows it in. The light grows brighter and color ripples along the haloed edges until it's a blinding affair. The images steady then resolve into a clear picture.

I've an urge to clap. But he needs the full might of his Locus to continue, and I don't wish to be a distraction. Yet it's difficult to hold back. I'm thrilled. For him. For me. For the world.

I figured it would take a half-dozen failures to even establish a link to a memory. Even an easy one that Akyris himself has lived. My guess, however, fell far short of the mark. On his first try, he's already observing the past. Someday soon he'll be looking into the memories of others throughout time and space. If he shows himself to have Darkhorn or Tahmyrus's level of power...

I shake my head, suppressing the thought. Too much to hope for.

I'm dizzy with anticipation. My grandson could be the most powerful of us all. But that doesn't mean what he does is without danger. For the sake of safety, my full attention is required. I flare my consciousness in a way Akyris won't notice and send it scouting the depths for threats.

The momentary distraction is all it takes.

I fail to see a second nimbus of light creeping toward him from a swirling avenue below. It bends up and around, a cobra rising from a basket. This one was not called intentionally.

He sees the new pathway, an eyebrow arched in curiosity.

My instruction is peremptory. "Ignore it."

It pulses brighter. Panes of light dangle before him like a lamprey, begging him to follow where he shouldn't. "It's calling me," he whispers in awe.

He doesn't realize it is himself who called it.

The tunnel overhead recedes, the childhood memory rapidly dimming. The beetle, the hut and my lovely Tyne, begin dissipating back into the ether.

"Deny it." My voice is stone. A thread of light from the trespassing memory winds forth to alight on Akyris's cheek. "Deny it, I said!"

Akyris ignores me.

His Locus shifts to the new memory that is not his own. The image looms like a mouth threatening to swallow him.

A rain swept town ringed by low foothills. A sea of ruins spread across the valley floor on one side of an earthen barrier. A barrows...Rainy Meadows.

More threads of light snake forth to hook into him. They suddenly tense like the chains of a drawbridge being closed.

"Akyris, stop! Stop now!"

The pathway of his childhood memory evaporates. The beetle and Tyne disappear. The tunnel winks closed.

I curse. I prime my Locus to sever his connection to the memory Darkhorn showed me of Jennim submerged in death.

A powerful force hurls me backward. I hold fast to my Locus to keep from being thrown from the River. My sight is momentarily marred, a smudged looking glass.

Recovering from the energetic blast, I cast about for the invading force, Locus poised in defense, sharper than darksteel and with the might of a typhoon. I pour myself against whatever keeps me from severing the connection to…

Shocked, I realize what the force is. Where the power stems from… Akyris.

"Akyris!" My consciousness ripples across the vapors of creation. "Deny it!" I use my Locus to slash at the connection between Akyris and the memory of Jennim.

His Locus repels mine like a finger flicking away a spider. He's placed a barrier between us. This isn't a malicious thing he's done. Simply put, his attention is being swept away by a current of impulse from the shadows of his unconscious mind.

A thing both known and unknown. His Locus entangled with my own.

Having caught me off guard, the shock of his initial attack ebbs, allowing me to assess his strength. The last thing Akyris sees is Barodane's herculean prosort casting aside the lid of the barrel.

I scythe, severing the scintillating hooks connecting him to the memory. In a concussion of light and force, I sunder the barrier protecting his Locus to nothingness with a whip of twisting vapor. He falls into darkness, and it's all I can do to catch him. A blue and white braid snares him before he plummets into the Abyssal Sea.

His eyes glow a soft white. I reach into his battered Locus, soothe him back to consciousness. My attack was an overcorrection that left him stunned. Thankfully only that.

Hours pass before he blinks. "What…what happened?"

How do I explain?

I run fingers through his hair. Do I explain?

"The entanglement will not disappear on its own." Darkhorn's voice greets me in somber tones. "If you don't address this, he'll continue being called to Rainy Meadows."

An explanation *is* needed. Just not to Akyris. Not yet. I kick myself for being such a fool. A coward really. The fear of hurting Tyne nearly cost her another son. The one I didn't force her to give up.

And it almost cost humanity its only hope.

"You're right," I say.

"We can't wait any longer." Magomedes joins the conversation. I realize they've been watching me, waiting to see when I'll do the deed. I feel guilty. I've let them down. Foolishly, I thought there was another way.

"My apologies…to both of you. Tonight. When the boy is asleep. I'll do it tonight." I stare down at Akyris as he comes to. "Now leave me be."

CHAPTER FORTY-NINE

THE REVOCATION OF SYPHION MUUL

T he day had finally come, and it couldn't have been a more bitter one.

Today, I gain both vote and voice in the court of Anjuhkar.

Morning light filtered through open windows arrayed along the vaulted ceiling of the High Hall. A length of gold chain sparkled where it clasped the white wolverine pelt around Ishoa's shoulders.

Her chin dipped as she touched it. *Lodaris should be wearing his own pelt at my side.*

The loss of her best friend and first love came in waves.

Some were gray and frigid and sucked the joy from her in a freezing rush.

Some left her flesh itching for relief from the barely checked anger screaming for the surface.

And sometimes, the waves were numb. Coal-stained hatred. These didn't pass through her so much as she passed through them, a hungry blade, eager to cut injustice from the world.

Lodaris should be here. And Lodecka should be in a shallow grave.

"Chin up, Highness," whispered Arick at her side. "You cannot let them see you sad."

Her gaze roamed her cousin's angular features. Taut skin, eyes of frigid blue, a half-dozen stark white braids descending to mid-back. "If only I had your sunny disposition," she said with disdain.

Of the score of knights arrayed along the dais, a handful stifled laughter. From Arick Quinn, it drew nothing at all. A rock may have had more reaction. He bowed to her, then returned to his place in the crowd.

Emptied of tables and benches, the holds of successful Claimants filled into the front half of the High Hall first. The Warnocks and Narls would filter in after at the back with holds that had only observed the Trials, like the Baels.

From the midst of furriers bedecked in fine leather and chain, Yurm the Worm strolled toward Ishoa on ungainly limbs, pitiful button chin held high. The dancing wolf of Ghastiin was worked into a fist-sized silver medallion around his thin neck as well as the pommel of his sword.

Arm in arm with Lady Hilkka, Dragga approached the dais. They wore black from head to heel, the only splash of color a ring of fiery jewels on Hilkka's dress wrought into embers. A similar pendant pinned Dragga's white wolverine fur to one shoulder. Stirrma's darksteel warhammer hung ominously across his back.

Ishoa nodded to Dragga, a sign of mutual respect born through understanding each other's grief. *Lodaris and Stirrma should be here.* She choked back tears and chewed the inside of her cheek until she tasted coppery blood.

She looked to her uncle for comfort but found him less than calming. Smoothing a gray beard as long as his torso, Wolst surveyed the assembly. Despite the celebratory occasion, there was a tightness around his eyes.

He watches the crowd for threats. And sees them everywhere, no doubt.

More Claimants joined Ishoa in a line before the dais as more holds filed in. Hundreds could fill the High Hall, but the majority of each hold's retinue would remain with their encampments on the slopes outside the Gate of the Bear. Except for the Frosts, only a score of attendants were allowed for each. And these were careful to avoid the blue carpet spread out down the center of the High Hall. Sacred ground the Claimants would walk down once the ceremony was complete.

A two-handed mace rested on a shoulder of Golthius Narl's apish frame as he led his holdguard and Sweet Ges to their place at the back of the High Hall. When Gestryn caught Ishoa looking at him, he leered, looking ever more stupid and ugly.

Ishoa's skin crawled. She pointed at the place she stood on the dais, pushed out her lower lip, then dragged a finger from one eye down her cheek miming a tear falling. The boy's expression twisted with rage. He turned away, abashed.

Bedecked in earthen hues and steel, knights of Shadowheart flanked Megalor Bog as he approached Ishoa. He stopped, a sneer permanently pasted to his face. At his side, Unalor grinned like an idiot. Of the two, Ishoa couldn't decide who she disliked more. Megalor was harsh, abusive to his anjuhtarg, and smelled like he looked. Sour. Unalor on the other hand was a buffoon of the lowest order. If he were to rule, he would undoubtedly cause problems for the people of Shadowheart. Megalor, at least, seemed capable. Dark dealings under dark canopies, the other holds said of the treekin. Watching their wary lord now, Ishoa thought there to be no shortage of credence to the sentiment.

The thin mustache on Unalor's upper lip was beaded with sweat. He shifted foot to foot and stared at Ishoa.

"Tell her," Megalor elbowed his brother in the rib.

"Eh." Unalor swallowed. "My condolences. Lodaris was a true—what was it?"

"Champion," hissed Megalor. He shook his head then pushed his brother aside. "My dolt of a brother wishes to convey that he's sorry for your loss."

"My thanks."

"Would you honor my brother by letting him stand at your side?"

Ishoa frowned, first at Megalor, then at Unalor. She flashed a fake smile. "If he keeps quiet, I suppose."

"He will." Megalor propelled him into place by the collar.

At the rear of the treekin retinue, a looming figure caused the blood to drain from Ishoa. A head taller than any other, he bore no traditional markings of a holdguard nor a knight. No brown, no green, no mirrored oak tree. From head to toe, the man was wrapped in tight-fitting obsidian robes. He moved with the seamless, silent grace of a predatory cat. The looming shadow turned faceless attention on Ishoa. For a heart-stopping moment, he watched her. Then Megalor strode away and the figure followed after. A long wooden haft with an ax on either end adorned his back and reflected Ishoa's obscured face back to her.

A finger jabbed her shoulder. Unalor's corkscrew grin. "The Fly sticks to Megalor like shit. That's why we call him the Fly." He jerked a thumb at the shadowy figure looming behind Shadowheart's lord. "Don't worry, Princess. Everyone stares at the Fly. My brother isn't the most trusting man—though don't tell him I said that, for he's not a kind one either. When he's nervous, he doesn't go anywhere without the Fly."

"I've never seen him before? Why wasn't he at the feast? Or the Trials?" Ishoa wasn't the only one enamored with the man. Throughout the High Hall, dozens of others were pointing at the Fly, whispers eddying around his presence.

"He was watching over the camp then." Unalor chuckled. "Back home, we tell stories about him to scare children into doing what they're supposed to. We say, 'the Fly sees everything. If you're bad, he'll jump from the shadows and take your parents' heads.' That's what we say."

I'll do my best to avoid Shadowheart. If their lords were any indicator, it seemed cruelty was a common practice there. "Wouldn't it be better to scare children with a fictional creature? Once they discover he's just a normal man and not some nightmare out of myth, won't they lose their fear?"

"Normal man." Unalor grew deadly serious. "He's anything but. He's the truest nightmare that ever walked..." He trailed off, glanced back, and then locked eyes with his own toes.

Ishoa looked back, curious as to what had spooked Unalor. Her uncle Wolst had taken up a position among the line of knights along the dais. It seemed a single handshake from the Beast of Anjuhkar had been enough to cow Unalor for life.

The raek helm wrested from the neck of the infamous Bloodhorn nested in the crook of Wolst's arm. Twin broadswords rode the hips of a steel-studded warskirt. A shirt of chain descended from a gouged and pitted breastplate and a storm bear pelt was draped over his shoulders to one side. On his other, an honor plate emblazoned with the chain and fist of Namarr. Thin coils of copper, silver, gold, and platinum wire were attached from one end of the pauldron to the other showing he'd achieved the highest attainable rank.

Of all the things Ishoa thought less of Unalor for, fearing Wolst wasn't one of them. *I'm lucky he loves me.*

Wolst's gaze settled on Megalor Bog's bodyguard. *I'd pay a bag of gold wheels to know what Uncle thinks of the man. Unalor said his older brother only brings the Fly along when he's nervous.*

Shouts in Fjordsong echoed throughout the High Hall. Enkita Vulkuu strode toward the dais, careful to avoid treading on the blue carpet. The gentler ladies and lords and young holdguard shrank back from the dozen angry seal hunters of Twilight Cape in tow. Even for Anjuhks, they cut an unsettling image with their jaws and lower lips tattooed jet black and their necklaces of rattling C'Dathun teeth.

A shiver rode up Ishoa's spine as flashes of a troll's long nose and apish mouth drooled into her face...

The High Hall darkened. Teeth carried the promise of a feast she would attend but never see. Clawed hands wrapped around her throat, squeezing away all air...all but the stink of them...

With a gasp and sharp inhale, Ishoa fled her memories. She shook her head. *Against the odds, I survived. Just like Enkita did on Unturrus.*

The Lady of Twilight Cape stopped at the dais. Othwii had once told Ishoa there was a one in fifty chance of becoming an Awakened for anyone ascending Unturrus, which meant a forty-nine in fifty chance of being killed in some horrible fashion. For Anjuhks though, mathematicians claimed the averages didn't just double, they quadrupled. Unfavorably so. Yet, there Enkita Vulkuu stood. Former pirate turned Lady of Twilight Cape. Guardian of the Eastern Fjords.

And she was very angry.

With both hands, she drove the butt of her spear into the flagstones and barked in Fjordsong. One of the hunters in her retinue translated. "Enkita is too mad to speak Common."

"I see that," said Wolst.

"She wishes to know why her sacred right to bring anjuhtargs in the High Hall has now been denied twice."

Wolst gave a curt bow in her direction. He spoke in a practiced cadence. "I understand your frustration, Lady Vulkuu. They are beautiful beasts. I personally would love to see them up close *after* the ceremony."

"Ugly man. Pretty words." Enkita waved the hunter attempting to interpret to silence. "But not your own."

Wolst's glacial frame relaxed. "Aye. I'll speak plainly then. There are many firsts in the Trials this year, Enkita. Some for the better."

A deafening groan caused Ishoa to whirl. Crownguard heaved the massive High Hall door closed. The last to enter were the Warnocks and their weaponless Scarborn. They intermixed with the cattlemen of Baen's Handle who wore helmets with downward curving horns and leather cuirasses under their checkered brown and white tabards. Most carried spears or mauls on their person. All wore swords at their hips.

Worry plucked at Ishoa's gut. She looked at the Fly, a sentinel shadow in Bog retinue, then looked to her uncle for comfort.

Wolst narrowed his eyes as he watched the Baels and Warnocks mingle. "Some for the worse." Bulbous fingers thrummed the pommel of a broadsword. He shifted his attention back to Enkita. "Our seneschal has informed us all anjuhtargs must be banned in order to accommodate the numbers."

"Not fair." Enkita looked Othwii up and down. "What big bird know of storm bears?"

"A great deal, Lady Vulkuu." Othwii moved from his place beside the duchal throne to the edge of the raised dais. He crouched low. "And more about numbers and logistic."

"We apologize, Lady Vulkuu." Wolst swept out a spade-wide hand. "You may notice you're not the only one without an anjuhtarg."

Heads turned.

Standing slightly apart from the Scarborn, Syphion Muul stood with a foot on the blue carpet, soiling it. Despite being anything but a soldier, the flat-faced man wrapped hands around sword hilts on each hip, potbelly thrust out like some commander.

Ishoa tasted bile. He was alive and breathing while both Lodaris and the daughter he'd starved weren't. *His presence dishonors the entire ceremony.*

Ishoa was not the only one to see it.

After hawking a mighty gob onto the flagstones, Enkita hooked a thumb over her shoulder at Syphion. "But Scarborn get pet? You need chain barking dog outside."

The hunters of Twilight Cape laughed and clapped their diminutive leader's back.

Wolst bowed with a flourish. "If only I could, Lady Vulkuu."

As Enkita led her hold back to their place, she leaned in and whispered in Ishoa's ear. "That's how you spit like hunter. You spit weak, like princess."

Ishoa was dumbfounded. She jerked back and found a yellow grin splitting Enkita's black and pale face. *A joke?* Ishoa gave a tentative smile in return. But the joy of being insulted by one of her heroes didn't last long.

A chill spread between her shoulder blades. Flesh along the back of her neck tightened, tiny hairs stiffening. Slowly, she turned.

The flint-cut visage of Lodecka Warnock watched her, scarred chin angled upward. Their eyes met, lingered in the dance of hateful stares an eternal moment before the indifferent Scarborn leader shifted her attention to the dais.

Blood covered Ishoa's tongue from a small wound she'd chewed on the inside of her cheek. Remembering to breathe, she shrugged at the heavy pelt on her shoulders. In her dreams the night before, she had torn out Lodecka's throat with her bare teeth.

Like a white wolverine might.

A hush fell across the High Hall as the duchess raised a hand for attention. She'd donned her best for the closing ceremony. Gleaming smile included. A pearl necklace bound the deep blue and pure white of her silk dress together in quality unsurpassed. But it was the gift from Joffus Kon that stole the eye most. The ashen-colored dragon skin was pinned beneath a slender ceremonial honor plate that shimmered when it caught the light. Everything about Belara smacked of elegance. Even her white curls seemed tighter and brighter.

"Greetings, Anjuhks. Greetings, Claimants."

Belara paused for an exhaustive stretch of time as she inspected the line of those wearing white wolverine pelts at the foot of the dais. Ishoa had seen her grandmother use the tactic before. Silence pulled people into deeper attention.

And attention was the heart of control.

"Wolst, is this the twentieth of these Trials I've presided over since Unification? Oh...the twenty-first then. I hope you'll all forgive me. The years of waiting between make it difficult to keep track." The purposefully self-deprecating statement drew a few chuckles from the crowd. "Nevertheless, it is a privilege to see such courageous young Anjuhks before me once more. Anjuhks..." At this she paused to look them over one by one.

"I hope all of you hear that word. Anjuhks." Belara straightened. As to how a frail old woman could loom so large, Ishoa had no clue. "It binds you now to honor it wherever you go and in whatever you do. It is a part of you, mind, heart, and soul. Never to be parted from you but by death alone."

Belara dipped her chin, expression somber. "Before we go any further, there are those who *must* be honored. Our holds have paid for the Trials with gold. Some with a life. Let us now honor those Claimants who paid the ultimate price. Let us share the names of the young souls who have been taken somewhere better than here. Stirrma Omenfaen..."

Eyes closed, the crowd hung their heads in silence as Belara honored those who'd died during the Trials in the last decade. After each name was spoken, all executed the Namorite salute. The thud-clang of fists to pauldrons or bare shoulders reverberated through the stony hall.

Ishoa followed suit. Hand numb, she waited for one name in particular, each time fearing it would be the next. Fearing she would lose control. Fearing to feel the truth of it...

Lodaris dead. Lodecka alive. My parents gone, leaving me to rule alone. The world is not just.

Anger took hold. To siphon the pain, she imagined driving a blade into one of Lodecka's placid eyes. Heat spilled through Ishoa's chest, warm and comforting.

Finally, Belara said his name. The last. "Lodaris Warnock."

With every shred of will, Ishoa held back tears. *I will not cry. I will not let her see me weak.*

"Claimants, you've proved yourselves worthy of bearing the mantle of Anjuhkar's highborn." Belara took a tiny pail of proffered water from Othwii. It was collected from the glacial flows surrounding the Ice King as well as the Blue River. Wolst moved a step lower on the dais, arm outstretched to support the duchess. "Please kneel so that I may give you the blessing of those who have come before you."

A stern voice froze the room. "Do not kneel."

All eyes turned to Syphion Muul. "True Anjuhks do *not* kneel."

Belara showed no surprise. Only her ever-present grin. Her response was a threat measured by grace. "Master Syphion, while I—*we*—are so grateful for your presence during this ceremony, a first for you I'm told, it is essential that you remain silent during this time. An absolute rule. Without contradiction."

The rest of the High Hall didn't show half the aplomb of their ruler. Many were visibly shaken by the interruption, all open mouthed and wide-eyed. A few, like Wolst, wore a mask of simmering rage. Seeming to sense this, Belara laid a hand on the arm of her bristling warmaster.

Syphion stepped onto the blue carpet running the length of the hall, seizing the center of the room and every scrap of attention. His paunch tested the limits of a stained roughspun tunic tucked into a thick belt. The dark pit in his bushy gray beard spit forth words soaked with contempt. "You mislead this new generation, Frost, just as you've done for sixty years. We continue to serve as little more than dogs to the Collective. We watch the best of our goods fall into their laps for only a fraction of the return. Meanwhile you grow rich in subservience and proclaim it as necessity for the greater good."

Ishoa's hackles rose. *You're the one misleading people! We maintain the Unification of Namarr to keep Scothea at bay.* A third invasion was the most serious risk to all their freedoms. Not some stupid shift in the tax on goods.

The knights on the dais shifted their weight. Claimants glanced at one another, uncertainty rippling down the line.

"I hear you, Master Syphion. I think we've all heard your rantings a dozen times, for you know not how to live without the sound of your own voice." Belara ingratiated herself to him in tone only. "But let me try to understand. Let us all try to understand. But let us do so when it comes at no cost to the young champions standing before us."

"A facade! I've watched your Trial of Crossing, your Trial of Summit, your Trial of Quelling. Ghostly motions for a dead people who have lost their heart. What made them strong." The whites of Syphion Muul's eyes were wild. Those of a whipped horse. "The only trial we should be having here is yours, Belara Frost!"

Wolst's raek helm was on his head in a heartbeat. Pot lid hands fell to broadswords at either hip. The duchess motioned, commanding restraint. Claimants shrank back. They were exposed and sought the location of their holds. Though none dared act on the fearful impulse.

Ishoa shuffled toward the dais where the knights of Jarik were thickest.

"Words hard to recover from, Muul." Belara dropped the "Master" from his name along with the smile from her face. "My ability to understand you wanes, though I worry that you no longer wish for understanding at all. Such is your fervor. When you came here, I thought you might in truth be a more reasonable man than I'd heard. Before we meet a person we must sometimes wade through so many second-hand accounts. Many of which are ill-conceived. I might even say you have been espousing a similar kind of thing about me. Clearly, you do so now."

Syphion's face bunched. He emitted an angry whine. "These are no stories, Frost. I speak the truth, and everyone shall hear it. Anjuhks! Look at your Ice Maiden. She gathers rare riches to her such as the dragon skin you now see while the rest of us suffer and feed the pockets of Peladonians and the Lah-Tsarene. We serve a shadow crown that will soon rest upon the head of a naive child."

An onslaught of stares fell on Ishoa. She thrust out her chin in defiance, refusing to give the man's words value.

"Anjuhkar can do better," he said. "It can stand on its own."

Belara touched the dragon skin, then shot a stunned look at Joffus Kon. He turned away coldly. Yurm the Worm gulped then stared at his feet.

They knew. Joffus knew it would be used against her. Tingles preceded a wave of nausea and the room darkened. The tempo of Ishoa's heartbeat galloped.

Her grandmother's eyes narrowed. "You are intractable, it seems. If you wish to trade truths like arrow volleys, we shall have it out here and now. You'll find few who bend a bow as well as I." Belara left all sweetness far behind. "I'll remind you all that words are no crime in Namarr. I may be the only one old enough to recall how different that was when Ice Kings ruled. Absolutely and without mercy. My own father was a fairer leader than most, but at times of pettiness, he threw a fanatic or two like yourself in the dungeons to rot. Of course, those who spoke their mind as you do now fared far worse under Scothean occupation. Far worse. But if your words now aim to incite rebellion, Syphion Muul..." She sucked her teeth. "Treason is still punishable by death."

Lodecka Warnock placed a hand on Syphion's shoulder, seemingly in restraint rather than support. Just behind the Scarborn, Ollo Bael's eyes were darting around the room as if he counted something. Then the Lord of Baen's Handle leaned back to whisper into the ear of one of his cattlemen. A second later the holdguard raced out the door of the High Hall. The crownguard who gave the man exit looked to Wolst. He jutted his chin, indicating he should follow the cattleman.

Syphion scoffed. "Anjuhkar has tasted the boot long enough."

The flesh of Ishoa's arms puckered. Despite the thick pelt draped around her shoulders, she was suddenly chilled.

The room was so deadly quiet, Ularis Warnock could be heard whispering in a rush, "Not now, Syphion. Not here. The plan—" The fanatic jerked his shoulder free from Lodecka's restraining hand.

"Listen to them, Syphion." Belara's voice was filled with deadly warning. "You've already lost your daughter by your mad impulse. How many more must die for your foolish cause?"

Spittle flew from his mouth and onto the ceremonial carpet. "You seek to break me with sentiment?" He pounded his chest. "Cowardice! Do not lay the cost of innocent life at my doorstep. You are on trial, I say!

"We joined one slave's rebellion only to become slaves ourselves. We grow tired...the backs of our knees worn from the boot heel dug into them by those who think themselves our betters." He turned in a circle, meeting the eyes of onlookers. "We are not slaves. I say we are Anjuhks. We need no masters!"

He beckoned to the Scarborn. "You would continue under this censure? You would let them silence you? Tell you your worth—your class?" He jabbed a finger at the other holds. "Belara Frost makes us a nation of slaves to Namarr. Will you go on this way, as servile dogs, or would you fight and die for an Anjuhkar that reflects its true people? Only some of you have scars on your flesh, but *all* of you bear the scars of a spirit long abused. I say, no more!"

"Muul," Wolst said. "I'm warning you."

"I'll say what needs to be heard."

Wolst bellowed. "And face the consequences!"

"I am not cowed by tyrannical threats. I will say all that I have to say and more, Warmaster." Syphion's index finger stabbed at the ceiling. "And *more*!"

The final word echoed.

Lodecka gestured. Her Scarborn moved into position beside cattlemen.

Ishoa was jerked backward by the white wolverine pelt and into the waiting arms of a knight of Jarik. Wolst stepped past. Other Claimants joined to their families on hastened feet.

"Crownguard," Wolst said. "Arrest Syphion Muul for sedition and inciting rebellion."

Lodecka Warnock stepped before the fanatic and yanked a sword free from a scabbard at his hip. "He finishes what he has to say." Spectators backpedaled as she leveled the blade at anyone deemed too close.

Crownguard stopped short of striking distance, wary, spears and shields locked at the ready. The other holds cleared space for the conflict.

"Master Muul and Lady Warnock act alone in my eyes," said the duchess as she waved off a knight of Jarik seeking to move her to safety. "Let it be known. No others must fall with them."

"Namarr...Namarr...I tire of it!" Syphion spat then strode to a cattleman of Baen's Handle and snatched his spear.

"What are you doing?" Ularis hissed.

Ignoring his patron, Syphion Muul swept the room with a wild gaze. "Look at your leader, Anjuhks. An ancient hag who plays jester for the Collective of dogs exploiting her people. Whatever ice once pumped through her veins is but vapor now. She seeks to calm me to peace because she knows she will never let Anjuhkar be anything more than a cog. It will never rise to the glory it once held." His challenging stare settled on Belara. She looked sad, almost hurt by Syphion's words. Exhausted to the point of surrender. "Unless she is gone."

Panic trembled through Ishoa's legs. Her grandmother's confidence had always shielded her from the reality of those political enemies who meant their family harm. Vulnerability tingled across her skin.

Syphion spat in Belara's direction. "Curse you, Frost. Curse the yoke you offer us. Curse those who will not fight for a *free* Anjuhkar." The spear tip was angled toward the flagstones. Sunlight glinted off its iron tip. "And curse any who would not die for it."

He twisted his body, spear tip lifting as he drew back to throw.

The room gasped.

Ishoa cringed and closed her eyes.

Air whooshed at Ishoa's side, stirring her hair. She flinched, eyes snapping open just in time to see a spear haft sprout from Syphion Muul's chest. The iron tip erupted from his back in a cloud of bloody mist. The madman gaped, staring at

Wolst as the warmaster's throwing arm lowered. Syphion's piggish face bunched into a grimace. He coughed up blood as his own spear clattered to the ground. "Anjuhkar..." he gurgled. Wild eyes rolled back in death as he toppled face first to the flagstones with a sickening thud.

"Scarborn!" Lodecka Warnock raised her sword. "Kill these dogs!"

Swords leapt from scabbards. Shields and spears clanged into defensive positions. Shoulders squared alongside old allies to face new enemies. Tongues danced over nervous lips.

The ancient song of death began.

CHAPTER FIFTY

THE DREGS

T he injured man whimpered around a shattered knee.

"Constable Lairton," Garlenna said matter-of-factly.

Barodane surveyed the ruins. What needed to be done was unpleasant. But necessary. "Do you have children?" The words ached in his throat.

Garlenna shifted her weight and watched the ground.

"A boy," Lairton said.

Barodane crouched beside the constable. Drew his dagger. The tip rustled against Lairton's coarse mutton chop as he traced them. Lairton went rigid. His eyes rounded.

"Orphans are quite common in Digtown." Barodane brought the dagger point to rest lightly inside the man's ear. "If you had a girl, a pretty one, she'd be taken in by the Baroness. Ugly ones too but they're more likely to be scrubbing seed from the floorboards. A boy though...

"It'll be the slums for him. Fighting off disease and death. Selling himself in whatever way he can to whoever will take him—if his hands aren't quick enough that is. And if they are, it will only take one wrong move with the wrong mark before he ends up face-down in the mud with his throat slashed. It'll be a month before your boy's carcass starts to stink and some disgruntled stranger digs him a shallow grave by the latrines."

The knife wavered in his hand. Jennim as a child, red-headed and gap-toothed flickered in his mind's eye. The boy played at the foot of Tyne's bed, repeatedly pressing the tip of a wooden sword into the heel of Barodane's boot and frowning at it as if wondering why it hadn't gone through.

Teeth gritted, Barodane shook free of the memory. "If you're lucky, perhaps your boss Hyram will put your boy in a wine barrel for your failure and save someone from having to clean up his corpse." Lairton whimpered. Barodane pressed the knife deeper. *This one is real. This one will go through.* Blood, stark against the constable's paling skin, ran in bright rivulets down his cheek.

"Buh—ahem—Kord." Worry laced Garlenna's tone.

He eased the pressure but continued staring into Lairton's frightened eyes. "Whatever we ask, you answer truthfully. If something seems like a lie, you will die and your son will suffer. Nod if you know I speak truth."

Cautious not to be cut by the dagger, Lairton gave a slow nod. Barodane withdrew the dagger from his ear. "Good. Are any more of Hyram's men en route to these ruins?"

"No."

"Who are we?" Garlenna asked.

"I—uh," Lairton blinked at them dumbly. "I don't understand."

Barodane looked back at Garlenna. In silence they exchanged a question: *do you believe that?* There were few people in the history of Barodane's life he could communicate with by a look alone. Garlenna, was one of them. The other was Meckin.

Garlenna shrugged. "Do you remember what was said during the fight?"

Lairton's brow furrowed. He dragged teeth over his lower lip. "I don't know."

Barodane sighed and moved the dagger toward the constable's ear.

"I swear! I've got no idea. I only heard shouting when Kord charged Emurs and then you..." He pointed at Garlenna. "...shouted something. I—I can't remember. Something about falling!"

"Enough." Barodane spotted blood on his hand and smeared it on the cobbles. "Where is Lyansorca?"

"Who?"

Barodane exhaled loudly.

"The whore! Yes, yes, I know who you meant. I just forgot for a second. Ah—" Lairton winced, hands shaking over his knee. A shard of pink poked through the leg of his trousers. "This thing's killing me. You ruined my fuckin' knee!"

"Where is Lyansorca?" Barodane's voice was fury.

Like a cornered animal, Lairton breathed in rapid snorts, gathering his wits through the pain. "I'll...I'll take you to her."

Shouts of pain echoed through the ruins as they got Lairton slung over one of the horses.

"We need to make haste," Barodane said as they mounted. "I worry for Meckin and the Gem Loft."

"This isn't worth it. We should leave Digtown," Garlenna whispered. "Now. While we still can."

Twisting in the saddle, Barodane shot her a look that brooked no further debate. He wasn't leaving. The hint of a smile plastered her cheek. "As you command."

They wound through the countryside, picking their way over stone strewn hills and mud-soaked ravines, Lairton giving directions as they went. A couple miles later, Garlenna drew her horse alongside Barodane's, first making sure they were out of earshot of the bound constable before speaking. "I know where he's taking us. I picked up a trail some days back and found their camp. At least ten men and a bea hound. We just killed two, and I took one outside the Gem Loft. That makes two against seven. At best."

"Poor odds." Barodane shrugged. "Not the worst I've faced though."

Garlenna frowned. "I don't intend to die in a suicide charge, thank you."

"You wanted your prince back, didn't you? I come with a certain style."

"Let's not confuse stupidity with style." She gave his thigh a condescending pat. "Since you're not to be swayed, we'll need to be realistic. Hyram probably has men in town waiting for us." Her head tilted side to side. "It's possible his numbers have grown too. If he's sending men after you, my guess is he thinks he has a handle on the situation."

Barodane snorted. "He's got more than a handle on it." A pit opened in his gut. He looked from Garlenna to the trail ahead. "I make jokes, but the truth is I'm barely holding it together. I'm physically weak. But mentally...I feel broken."

"Don't say that. For your own sake." She paused. "You are an Ironlight."

"You don't understand." He shook his head. "We lived the same experience, but I..." He wished there was a way he could show her what it was like in his head. *Help me.* "Sometimes I...hear things." Their horses huffed. Far behind, Lairton groaned through his gag. "I am not well."

Garlenna fixed him with her azure eye and spoke even lower. "You mean to tell me giving up prince-hood to live out your days as a drug dealer in the filthiest amoral town in all of Namarr came from a rational place?"

A laugh shook him. He coughed. Laughed some more.

"Barodane, you chose to be unwell. You chose to live here at the place closest to the pain. It may not seem like it, but that takes courage. I'd be more worried if you had no issue with what we did. I'd rather serve a man who regrets such horrors in war than one who feels no remorse." She squared her shoulders, faced forward in the saddle. "But you've honored the dead long enough. Fourteen years. By the gods that's a long vigil. Of course it's going to take time for you to feel different, to get better. And you're not yet free of the godsthorn in your system. But you will be soon."

He wanted to convince her he wasn't worth it. That he was too far gone to be saved. That his renewed efforts weren't born of friendship or care. Not for her, Meckin, or Imralta.

But that's exactly what they were.

Help me. Tension ran along his jaw. He swallowed a lump in his throat, then muttered, "Never again."

He snapped the reins.

"It would be better if we had a bow."

"Who would shoot it?" Barodane scoffed. "You have one eye and I'm shaky enough to churn butter. And neither of us were good shots to begin with."

"True," Garlenna jerked the gag from Lairton's mouth. "How many men?"

"Including myself and the ones you killed." Lairton worked his tongue around the inside of his mouth. "Thirteen."

"Unlucky number," Barodane said. "Good thing it's nine now."

Garlenna raised an eyebrow. "Anything else we should be worried about?"

Still slung over a horse and helplessly trussed, the constable hesitated. "No."

Casually, Garlenna clamped a broad hand around the man's mouth. Eyelids stretching back as far as they could go, Lairton watched her jam a dagger into his already ruined knee. Her palm muffled his screams as he bucked and arched.

She held him there until he fell to silent trembling. "Lie again and it's your eye. Do you want to look like me?" She pressed the knife against the skin beneath her eye patch. But Lairton had already fainted.

Barodane raised a questioning eyebrow.

"The bear hound," she said in explanation.

Once Lairton came to, they asked him again what they should worry about. After admitting to lying about the bear hound, he swore there was nothing else. They bound him, gagged him with a strip of cloth cut from Barodane's mud and blood-soaked cloak, then left him with the horses in the shade of a pair of oaks.

The element of surprise was on their side. If they caught Hyram's men unaware, their scant odds improved. Even more if the group was split.

They made their way through the undergrowth and found the camp abandoned. Thin tendrils of smoke still coiled into the shadowed canopy. "This is recent." She nudged coals with her boot.

"This can only mean they've found my supply." Barodane cursed. "Lyansorca must have told them. They're heading to the Dregs." He recalled Hyram's offer on the Gem Loft. *It will be an offer no more than thirty-six hours.* "It's an all-out assault. A warning to the entire town. He's taking the Dregs. The Gem Loft too."

Realization hit Barodane like a thunderbolt. "He's taking Digtown for his own."

Garlenna nodded. "All he needs to do is have outriders like the ones we encountered in the ruins kill anyone trying to flee town. He's already bought the constable." She crossed her arms, mace vertical to the sky. "If he means to establish himself here he'll probably put Eustus in charge, a buffer for his crimes...use Digtown as

MICHEL

a distribution point for godsthorn. So close to the Prince's Highway and Unturrus, he'll be able to set up a network across the entire west of Namarr."

Barodane rubbed his face. "We have to go." *Meckin.* "Now."

Lairton came to, sweaty and mumbling, as they arrived back at the horses. They mounted and made for Digtown, riding as fast as they could with Lairton weighing down the rouncey. Garlenna had to help maneuver it, which made the going slower than desired.

All the while, Barodane thought of Meckin and Imralta. Of Lyansorca and Vey. The stable girl and a dozen other familiar faces from the Dregs. He thought of them having their skulls or hands crushed by masons. He saw their dead faces, staring up from wine barrels.

Hot anger moved from his chest to his hands, a spreading fire. He gripped the reins, palms tingling from the friction.

I will save them even if it means my life.

Help me.

Barodane bore down over Scab's mane. Garlenna beckoned him to slow, but he ignored her and cajoled his stallion to a break-neck pace.

Ahead, the barrow hills curved up and away into a spitting sky.

Garlenna and the rouncey bearing Lairton lagged. Through the howl of wind in Barodane's ears, he barely heard his prosort shouting for him to stop.

Only once he crested the barrows did he listen to her. Scab's hoofs left long gouges in the mud as he came to a stop. Digtown lay below. Rusted. Knotted. Soaked through. A cruelty to the eyes.

Breathing deep but controlled, Garlenna drew her horse alongside Barodane's. "Hasty to die alone are you?"

"We're out of time. He slows us."

The rouncey's side was splashed with Lairton's blood. "He'll die soon without help," she said.

The wind moaned into the silence.

"He's made his choice," Barodane said. "A poor one."

Garlenna swept out a hand, indicating the barrow hills. "Haven't we all. We stand upon ours, and yet we live. Perhaps sparing his life may afford some much-needed good in the eyes of the Sempyrean."

Barodane was no follower of the Sempyrean, but he adhered to unimist ideologies once. Doing good even when difficult was a core principle. One he'd not observed for too long a time. Given he was attempting to right the wrongs of his past, Garlenna's suggestion landed hard.

He met her single eye. "I've ignored your advice for far too long. Never again." He dug heels into Scab's flanks. "I know where we can drop him if we're quick about it."

They shot down the hill. This time Barodane maintained a pace that the rouncey could keep up with. At the sound of their fast approach, the little girl in the stable opened the door to admit them. Digging into his belt pouch, Barodane withdrew a silver wheel and flipped it to her. She snatched it deftly from the air as they came to a stop inside the stable.

The girl followed them in.

"Watch the constable," Barodane said. "He's not to be trusted. Don't let him leave until we return."

"Here," Garlenna held out a dagger to the girl, but she shook her head and then slid a blade of her own from a boot.

"Good." Garlenna nodded. "If he gives you trouble, strongly encourage him to be silent."

Lairton struggled against his bonds and emitted a pained whine. Absent any affect, the stable girl stabbed him in the calf.

Eyes rimmed in wild terror, Lairton screamed into his gag and stared at the girl.

Garlenna raised an eyebrow at Barodane. He smiled. Digtown was no place for sentiments of the heart, like mercy or compassion; it was built on violence he himself had engendered. And so it grew along familiar pathways as a weed might. The kind of place where a child might stab a lawman for little more than silver. "Not quite that strongly," Barodane said. "You may find him calmer to watch over if you treat his wound. Keep him bound when you do though. Gagged too."

"Ready?" Garlenna asked.

"Not really, but that's never stopped me before," Barodane wheeled Scab to the entrance. "I keep wondering if this is all a dream. Like maybe you're not real. Like it's all just a long godsthorn trip I'm never coming back from."

Leading her horse forward, Garlenna blinked at the sky. Swollen clouds holding back rain like a breath in anticipation of the bloodshed to come.

Barodane followed her outside. "After Acramis...there are gaps in my memory. It's like I died...like I've been trapped in a nightmare ever since."

Garlenna's tone aimed to soothe. "If you live to see the day's end, we can worry about the past. For now I need you to be a nightmare to Hyram and his masons."

Barodane swallowed a stony lump.

Then they dug heels to flanks.

They took back alleys until they were close to the Dregs then stashed their horses a couple blocks distant. The masons may have posted lookouts.

Garlenna, they decided, was the far better sneak. She worked her way around the front entrance and then returned, shaking her head.

The back way it is then.

The possibility of a silent assault was washed away by the presence of a single guard at the rear entrance where Meckin had knocked out Jennim. The man's sword was drawn, ready. High alert. To make matters more difficult, thirty paces of open space surrounded him in any direction. Whatever they did, there would be more than enough time for him to see them coming and then retreat into Meckin's kitchen to alert his companions. Luckily, this door didn't have a lock the cutthroat could flip once inside. Barodane gave thanks to Meckin for simply rolling a pair of barrels into place at night's end, followed by his own sleeping cot beside it.

Barodane nodded to his prosort. Her mace whispered into her hand: four flanged rows terminating in sharp corners, one for each of the four gods of light. *We'll need their blessing today, that's for sure.* She swung it in a pair of quick circles to loosen her wrist, black iron ball counter weaving figure eights through the air.

Gentle and quiet, she laid her kite shield against the back of the building they hid behind to free her second hand for her dagger.

They waited for the sentry to look away.

They stepped out, running heel to toe in a half crouch as far as possible without being seen. They got farther than Barodane expected before the guard's head jerked their direction.

"Shit!" he yelped. He twisted, fumbling for the back door's handle. Garlenna bounded past Barodane and flung her dagger. The guard was forced to dodge. Its pommel pelted a shoulder—little harm done.

But Garlenna needed only a moment's distraction, an extra second holding him in place. The guard gave up the door and braced for a fight. "Attack! Here! Atta—!"

The first swing of Garlenna's mace sailed over the man's head, flanged tips stripping a patch of old gray wood from the wall. The guard mustered a stab of his own. But Garlenna sidestepped and bludgeoned his throat flat with a backhand swing. He gaped, tongue fat in his mouth as her next blow uncapped his skull, making his crown a viscous slurry spattering the wall.

Huffing, throat burning, Barodane wasted no time and barreled into the door. Inside, there was a flurry of frantic sound: chairs sliding, feet pounding, steel scraping free of scabbards.

"I'll swing around," Garlenna said. "Take them from the rear."

Barodane nodded, started a countdown from five in hopes of timing his attack just before Garlenna's. If she struck while their attention was on him, she'd wreak havoc in short order.

He hustled through the kitchen without resistance, passing Meckin's sleeping cot on his way to the taproom door. He kicked it open. Flung himself backward.

A crossbow bolt thudded into the frame at eye-level. He dove behind the bar, expecting a second bolt. Instead of a twang and rush of air, he was greeted by a clatter—the crossbow dropping. Barodane popped up to find the man drawing steel instead.

He scanned the taproom. Half the floorboards were torn up, revealing empty earth below where his godsthorn supply had been. A cutthroat with a sword descended the stairs. Scorch marks covered the second story hall where flame had eaten away parts of the roof.

Another cutthroat appeared at the end of the bar.

Barodane faced them, darksteel blade gripped in both hands overhead.

Then, he saw *him*...

Barodane's skin went instantly numb. Air rushed into his lungs with a gasp. At the back of the taproom near the fireplace sat Meckin. Blood dripped from the limp fingertips of one hand, forming a crimson puddle on the floor. Vacant eyes were fixed on the ceiling, no longer seeing. Stretched out on the table beside him, one hand was a pulpy mass. His throat was slashed to tatters. Done passionately rather than professionally.

Cold fury clutched Barodane's stomach. And with it, the voices returned.

See—

The first man's sword fell against Barodane's own with a distant ring. His arms moved as if possessed. A dormant fire blazed to life within. The last time he'd felt this wrath, a king had died. Thought dwindled to a point—death. The world dimmed, became narrow, a singular avenue. Shadows filled his periphery. Only the voices and his blade existed. One path forward...

His sword tip split a man's throat. A jet of crimson spewed onto the floor. Shaking hands failed to stem the bloody torrent.

What—

He flowed forward. Met the next. A corpse sat in the corner. He thought he might know it.

Blades met low. Darksteel slid upward, severed a thumb. A cry of pain, nauseatingly familiar. Pleasant to Barodane's ears. The cutthroat switched sword hands. Futile.

You are?

His enemy lunged feebly, as if by moving slow enough he could kill Barodane. The Mad Prince knocked the fool's blade aside, laughed, twisted around and chopped the cutthroat's hand off.

Barodane spat his hate. "I'll take every piece of you!" From behind, alien warmth sprayed across the back of his neck. A thud followed. Tremors in his feet.

Mad Prince...

He saw the boy. *Help me.*

Draining of color, the cutthroat dropped his sword and tried to cover his spurting wrist-stump. But what was done could not be undone. Life's great tragedy speared Barodane.

Faces of the dead surged forth from memory. He saw them dying all over again. Familiar faces from his nightmares. Death hid in every crease, every blotch of pained flesh. Jennim's face tinged blue. *Please, Kord,* he'd said. Then he had died too. The faces all blurred together. Jennim's, the boy's, Meckin's, the handless cutthroat's.

They became his own. Dying in a bank of snow somewhere out of time. The ghosts of memory.

"I am death!" Barodane struck out—decapitated the shocked man. His body banged off the bar then spun to the ground.

Panting, ears ringing, Barodane fell to his knees. His gaze found Meckin. Faster he heaved, numbness creeping up the sides of his head and into his face. An ache started in his chest. Faster still, the breaths came. Too fast. Uncatchable. His vision dimmed.

A heavy hand fell onto his false honor plate. He whirled, blade rising with him to claim another head. But a second hand clamped his wrist as he came face to face with Garlenna. Her mouth moved. The sound was muffled as if heard under water. As if he were Jennim in the final moments inside the wine barrel before that final darkness came.

A pitched keening filled his ears.

What's happening to me?

"Breathe!" Garlenna shook him, swatted his chest. "Breathe!"

A clipped inhale...then another. Light and color crept back into his vision. His senses returned gradually as if he were coming down from ascending on godsthorn. "Meckin."

The room swam.

Garlenna held onto him as he gagged and dry-heaved. "I'm sorry, Barodane. He's gone. But we must mourn him later if we're to avenge him now."

"I just..." Barodane slammed a fist onto the bar. He looked at Meckin, grit his teeth, then looked away. "Damn it!"

"Come," she said.

They moved through the taproom. He saw the source of the warm wetness on his neck as they stepped over the battered-in skull of the crossbowmen. Another dead man lay beside the entrance, a gaping stab wound pumping blood from his neck. Garlenna had worked quickly, it seemed.

"One of the masons spotted me," Garlenna said. "Rode off before I could catch him."

Sensation was slow to return to Barodane's legs. He paused to catch his breath against the door frame. "Heading for the Gem Loft no doubt."

"They'll know we're coming. I'll need my shield."
This time, there would be no hope of surprise.

CHAPTER FIFTY-ONE

THE ANCIENT SONG

The Scarborn camp was alert. Ready. They always were. Huun Korpa made sure of it.

Ollo Bael's man sucked ragged breaths. "It's happening, Captain." The horned helm marking him as a cattleman from Baen's Handle had fallen off in his flight from the High Hall.

The crownguard who'd chased him was forced to kneel by a pair of Scarborn. Blood leaked from a wound on the man's brow and dripped from his chin. A braided red bead split the face of the charging bison stitched onto the front of his blue tabard.

"We wait for the signal," Huun Korpa said.

"Damn Muul!" the cattleman bent at the waist, palms on kneecaps, chest heaving. "Bastard couldn't wa—"

"Shut your trap." The Scarborn captain listened for shouts of alarm along the wall walks but heard nothing. "Master Syphion is a great man. I'll not have his name besmirched by the likes of you."

"Captain Korpa?" one of his men said.

He knew what they were asking. "I'll do it." When he spoke, it burned. Like always. Bloodhorn's fang had made bloody curtains of his throat long ago, and despite a Sister of the Rose's best efforts, it had never been the same. The puffiness of his lips still felt alien against his tongue as he licked them. Thinly, he tasted copper where his skin was split from the dry cold.

"Fucking traitors." The crownguard's eyelids fluttered as the loss of blood caused him to pitch to one side.

The man that Huun Korpa had once been lay dead on the bloodied battlefields of the past. After the Great Betrayal and years of recovery, only a Scarborn captain remained. The puckered scars covering his skin were reminders to his men that respect was hard earned. To be a survivor, to hold power, one needed internal strength. Flesh was nothing. Indomitable will—everything.

Scars made strong.

With great difficulty, Huun came to stand before the prisoner. Anyone could see that physically the captain was less capable than any new recruit. Pain shot through his mismatched hips like a mother's caressing hand. Needles stabbed at his bent spine like an old, familiar friend. Shining, papery skin clung to him. Death's failed attempt. Each point of suffering was a medal of honor. They served as reminders of why he was captain.

Captain Korpa stood over the kneeling crownguard.

"Not traitors," he rasped. "True Anjuhks."

Before the crownguard could reply, Huun slid his dagger around the captive's neck. He placed a palm on the matted hair of his crown as the man died then saluted. "Rest easy, soldier." The snow turned red at his feet.

A window on the east side of the High Hall shattered. The signal. Huun Korpa breathed in deep. A sweet scent.

There was a reason they'd taken every precaution to be closest to the Gate of the Bear. There was a reason every Scarborn waited silently in their tents in full battle dress.

"Let 'em know," he said.

A soldier dipped an arrow in a brazier then loosed it in a high arc. For weeks, cattlemen and furriers had trickled into Jarik, mixing with the citizens in preparation. Within minutes, those secret forces would attack the Gate of the Tiger as well as aid in fighting the encampments still loyal to the duchess.

Where it concerned their enemies, the Warnocks were nothing if not thorough in their planning for all possibilities. One of many values Huun Korpa shared with his masters.

Now shouts of alarm rose along the battlements. Ripples of warning traveled to the other holds spread out below their camp.

"Scarborn! We go to destiny now!" Captain Korpa's death-rattle bark covered the slopes. "Time to wet your blades! Time to show these soft-born trash the temper of Scarborn steel!"

Dressed in crimson tabards, black leather, and chain, the majority of the Scarborn mercenaries rushed from their tents and up the hill to take the Gate of the Bear in a silent charge. The rest, a score or so, dragged bulwarks into place along the road. These were the true heroes, the ones who would fight to the death to fend off any rear attack to ensure the gate came down.

Once inside, they would bar the other holds without. If Belara's crownguard managed to close the gate in time mattered little; it wouldn't stand long against the Awakened.

To the robed figure standing near, Huun Korpa said, "You're up, Cauldron. Quickly now." He hoped the ghost was worth the dishonor he brought them.

With a stump where a hand should be, Cauldron pushed back his hood, then stripped off his cloak until he was naked to the waist. Scars in the shapes of arrows angled over hairless, pale flesh that culminated at the ghost's sternum. The wounds were meant to represent the five gods of the Sempyrean, and the grizzliest of them descended from his throat. He didn't have nearly so many scars as Huun, but it made the captain shudder in an unmanly way to know these had been self-inflicted for religious purposes. Anjuhk conversions to the Sempyrean were rare. Becoming a ghost was far rarer still. That hadn't stopped the Warnocks from getting one though. And now they would use it.

Huun Korpa spat. Awakened were unnatural devils. Better dead than alive. Except when they served a purpose.

Misty vapor emanated from Cauldron's eyes. Coils of eerie luminous smoke rolled up his arms in waves. Snow melted in the air around his clean-shaven skull, turned it into an aura of light rain. His self-inflicted scars began to seep—half liquid, half gas. Where the corrosive substance dripped from his scars, the ground melted, not just the snow but the earth itself. Fire spit to life at the edges of the holes it left.

Huun Korpa laughed, more crow's caw than human sound. "To the Gate of the Bear then."

Syphion Muul's call to war echoed in Ishoa's ears.

"Kill these dogs!" Lodecka Warnock shouted.

Three men died in the first seconds of confusion, quick thrusts by spear and sword, as most took a moment to assess loyalties. Eyes searched faces for confirmation of allies and enemies.

Lodecka Warnock snatched a spear from a cattleman and hurled it at the dais as if it were drawn on a rope. The duchess only had time to gasp as death sped toward her.

It struck. The hummingbird brooch on Othwii's robes shattered as he stepped before Belara. Momentum carried the seneschal stumbling to the back wall. Belara screamed and scrambled after her servant. When she hauled him upright vacant eyes bent Ishoa's soul. Her mentor died as loyally as he'd lived.

She screamed and drew her own blade.

Arick Quinn snared order from the chaos and confusion. "Protect the princess! Protect the duchess!" Blue tabards moved in a wave to the dais. The knights of Jarik encircled Ishoa.

"Kill all Frosts!" commanded Ularis. "Seize Ishoa Ironlight!"

At mention of her name, Ishoa's mouth went dry. Spears punched through blue-garbed chests to either side of her. Mouths agape, men stared into their own wounds. Hands clawed at nothing in the air before them as they died.

Hands that had waved at Ishoa in the halls of the Sister Keep. Hands that had tousled the furry head of her beloved Rakeema as they past. Hands that had saluted her. Hands bearing weapons in her defense even if it meant their death.

"Frosts to me!" Wolst bellowed.

"Shadowheart!" The nasal voice of Megalor Bog.

The din of shouts and clatter of arms drowned out all other commands too indistinct. Knights of Jarik hurled spears into the tumult. Darksteel shook in Ishoa's hand. She was forced to grip it with the other so she didn't drop it.

Through the gaps in the line of knights before her, she saw the smiths of Summerforge flanked by Scarborn and the Bakers of Prav. From the hips of the Bael's holdguard, every Scarborn had drawn steel. Led by Lodecka, they attacked with deadly efficiency. The knights of Summerforge wore darksteel but it seemed to matter little. Lodecka found their weak points. She stabbed a knight through the throat, sending him to his knees in a fountain of blood, then slashed another at the armpit in an upward swing, spinning him to the ground with a screech. Golthius Narl beat in the skull of a Summerforge dame with his two-handed ball mace so brutally he had to wipe her brains from his face.

To Ishoa's left, a dozen crownguard retreated to the counsel chamber in a ring around the duchess, vastly reducing their numbers in the High Hall. One of them shouted, beckoning Ishoa to follow, but her legs refused to move. She was rooted in place, trembling and hollow. A drum beating between her ears.

Wolst turned to her. The countenance of one about to give instruction flickered by, but then his attention was stolen by a new threat...

The furriers of Ghastiin and another smaller hold had been standing shoulder to shoulder in a defensive line with Wolst's crownguard. Now they turned on their allies, blades sending scarlet ribbons arcing through the air along with shouts of surprise, shouts of the dying, shouts from Joffus Kon's treacherous mouth as he directed his soldiers to cut off Ishoa's escape.

"Where are the rest of our crownguard?" Wolst parried the stab of a Ghastiin spearman, then punched a broadsword into the man's belly up to the hilt. "Keep ranks, damn it!"

The Ghastiin contingent charged at Ishoa. Concussive impact, the clash of steel. The backs of the knights encircling Ishoa bowled back into her. Curses. Grunts. A growl and a gurgle. Metal hewing bone.

A gloved hand reached for Ishoa. She jerked back, stumbled, fell onto her backside. The wind knocked from her, she gasped and struggled to rise, found herself beyond the line of allies.

Amid the furriers of Ghastiin.

One spotted her and leveled his spear. She glanced at the sword shaking in her hands. Tried to breathe. To will blood into her arms enough to move it. The furrier grinned—took a step.

Enkita Vulkuu leapt between them, crouching low. The Awakened hissed and padded forward slowly. The hunters of Twilight Cape filled in behind, surrounding Ishoa. Enkita gave a curt whistle and the hunters drove hard into the men of Ghastiin. Haunting war cries intoned in Fjordsong, warbled from their throats, deep and guttural.

"Princess!" a knight of Jarik wrapped an arm around her, guiding her along the outskirts of the fighting.

"Hold that damn door!" roared Ollo Bael.

Ishoa blinked, looked back.

Horn-helmed cattlemen rushed to obey their lord. But the men of Shadowheart were there to meet them, a whirl of patchwork cloth, hand axes, and cruel smiles. Megalor motioned frantically at his holdguard to win the door.

The two holds clashed.

The men of Baen's Handle bludgeoned forward against the Shadowheart contingent, mauls stoving, spears skewering. The forest dwellers were disorganized at best. Fear seemed to sweep through them like wildfire. When their initial onslaught stalled, they fell back. Wolst had once told Ishoa the greatest of all enemies in battle was not the foe swinging a blade but the friend dropping theirs.

Fear overwhelmed the treekin like a tidal wave...

And broke upon a single hooded figure. He strode from their ranks to meet the surging cattlemen.

The Fly.

His double-ended ax whipped in dizzying fast arcs, reversed direction unexpectedly, flashed out at unpredictable angles. A whirlwind of steel relieving heads from shoulders, hands from wrists, souls from mortal flesh. Lethal grace in motion. It was as if he saw all opponents at once. Every twist of his torso, every pivot on the balls of his feet, every pendulum's swing of his weapon stole life and life again.

Swift was his death dealing. A rhythm. A dance. A sacred ritual.

The cattlemen balked. Those nearest the Fly backpedaled, weapons outstretched in horror as their comrades pushed them forward. Blood pooled at the feet of Megalor's bodyguard, adding slick footing to the cattlemen's troubles. Into threshing death they went. Their doom a guarantee.

The door belonged to the Fly and the Fly alone.

Pouring in behind their champion, the men of Shadowheart opened the door and flooded from the High Hall. A few smaller holds made a mad dash with them.

Once Megalor and Unalor were through, the Fly turned on his heels and followed, leaving the rest of them to their fate.

They've abandoned us.

Ishoa scanned the High Hall, realizing the peril of those who remained. With the treekin gone and the Kon's betrayal, they were woefully outmatched.

Dragga Omenfaen saw it too. With his mother in tow, he and a pair of Summerforge knights carved a path of escape through the Scarborn and Narls. One of the knights had lost his helmet and bled from a partially severed ear. The knight and Dragga swung sword and hammer savagely at their foes, desperate to escape. Sweet Ges lunged. The wounded knight slapped his blade to the floor and then slashed open his side. Dragga swung Stirrma's warhammer in tight spirals, cracking open the face of a Scarborn mercenary and then crushing the shoulder of another. Seeing the might and determination of the young Anjuhk, his opponents gave him an ever-widening berth as he led what remained of his decimated hold from the High Hall.

Ishoa hauled on the honor plate of the knight herding her into a corner. "My uncle needs to retreat!" He ignored her, then pulled her up onto the dais. She wrestled at his wrists and dug in her heels. "They'll die if they don't!"

The knight cursed and released her, forced to face the battle.

Wolst stood at the head of the forces of Jarik as they joined with Enkita Vulkuu and the half-dozen of her hunters remaining on the dais.

The battered furriers fell back, affording a narrow gap between the opposing groups. Jarik's forces held the high ground but were vastly outnumbered.

Heartbeats passed. Blood-soaked, heaving, whimpering, heartbeats. A symphony of unruly breaths that wouldn't stay where they were needed. The dying begged for life and died while those still living waited for their turn at a similar fate.

Lodecka Warnock stepped to the fore of a now-unified force. Ollo Bael, Ularis, and Golthius Narl flanked her. She stared at Wolst and sniffled as if cold nipped at her nose from a chilly morning stroll.

Wolst flourished his broadswords, droplets of blood flinging in a spiral. Neither spoke. The time for words was gone.

Only killing and dying remained.

In silence, the carnage was rejoined. The Scarborn and a half-dozen other holds charged, clambering onto the dais like a swarm of ants, their ferocity bowing the defenders' line.

Booted feet pounded into her chest. Steel slid through her ears. Flashing crimson and sunlit iron drowned her eyes. The mercenaries fought as though fire danced at their backs, driving them forward like wild beasts.

For a horrifying second, Ishoa thought they would be slaughtered outright.

Then a great roar rattled off the stone walls. Prickles rose along Ishoa's nape. Enkita Vulkuu suddenly towered over the battle, a head taller than any man. Veins bulging on her forehead. Neck tendons writhing like snakes. Gray vapor filled her eyes, becoming tracers overhead. Her clothing stretched, seams popping. Torn fabric drifted to the flagstones in fluttering swaths like autumn leaves. The black paint on the lower half of her face split as her figure expanded. Muscles swelled, thickened. Fingernails elongated into black claws. Teeth warped into fangs. Her hair turned to slate fur and spread to cover every inch of skin.

Bile gushed to the back of Ishao's throat as she watched. Like dried paint, the woman's skin cracked then flaked off. The Awakened landed onto all fours, transformed into a titanic storm bear.

Shouts of dismay rippled through the Revocation force's ranks.

The Awakened roared, muzzle drawn back around blackened gums, then bowled forward, her hunters filling the breach she left in the enemy ranks. Their spears flicked outward with deadly precision, skewering any who sought to flank their leader. Enkita swung a monstrous paw, snapped a Scarborn woman's spine. She whirled, snatched an arm in her maw. She jerked the whimpering mercenary to the ground then flattened his head like a rotted melon. Dagger-long claws and fangs left a trail of slashed and shattered limbs in her wake.

Spattered with gore, Wolst spotted Ishoa and her knight escort. "Take her to the counsel chamber!" He rounded, brushed aside the ax of an onrushing dame and sliced through her temple to the nose.

A burly Scarborn with a mane of blond hair rammed through the line.

"Shit!" the knight guarding Ishoa struck out at the downed man.

The Scarborn rolled, came to a knee and lashed out with a greatsword, chopping through the knight of Jarik's shin.

The knight's blade clattered to the floor from a stricken grip. Gaining his feet, the hulking mercenary swung from the hip up into the injured knight's face and sent his limp body into Ishoa before she could react.

She fell back hard, the knight's dead weight accelerating her to the stone floor. Her blade dropped from numb fingers and skittered across the floor. She grabbed at the dead man's shoulders atop her legs, but his furs grew slicker by the second from the blood pumping from what was left of his face. Her hands slipped. Once. Twice. She managed to yank her legs free.

The Scarborn strode after her as she scrambled backward. He showed no emotion at all, as though killing her were nothing more than slaughtering a cow.

Her back and head banged against stone—the wall behind her. Nowhere else to go.

The Scarborn's greatsword rose overhead.

She thought of her parents. She thought of Lodaris's kiss...his warm breath. She thought of Wolst's meaty hand slapping his belly after a loving jest.

I miss Rakeema.

The greatsword poised for the killing stroke.

She'll be lonely without me.

Ishoa lingered on her anjuhtarg in her final moment. A simple desire. A desperate comfort. She wanted nothing more than the soft feel of her ice tiger's fur under hand. For a sunlit morning, looking out on fresh fields of snow and winter blossoms.

CHAPTER FIFTY-TWO

DARK WATERS

T he Pendulum of Time no longer cut. It held steady. The sun sat upon the western horizon, anchoring reality in the way Thephos knew as normal.

He rose from the stump and its many insights and followed in the direction Lethwii had fled.

The trail opened into a shallow gorge with sheer crags on either side. Blankets of grass and lichen greeted his foot with a softness he'd forgotten existed. When the skin knew only torment, it numbed to pleasure, became like an animal's protective shell. For as long as he could remember, Thephos had dismissed good feelings based on their lack of familiarity.

Until now.

He sighed, toes nibbling the plush earth. *I must be dead or mad to be enjoying a moment after what I've been through.*

Sensations like these were meant for princes, not pig farmers. He picked up the pace, letting pleasure rest where it lay and started calling out for Lethwii. The lack of echo where there should be one brought a halt to any more shouting. Nature acting in opposition to itself made his skin crawl. Worse than the demons. The lack of stability in something he'd known and found solace in his entire life gave him the sense that the universe conspired against him.

In silence, he made his way through the gorge, which wound up and around in a never-ending curve to the left, as if he climbed the spire of some castle.

Onward, ever onward.

Panes of daylight reached across the sky as the sun sank.

Night spread. Shadows clinging beneath the overhangs of cliffs. A bandit springing from the boughs of lonely firs to cover everything. Thephos had never been so happy for the sun to set. There was security in the familiar. Enough at least to sleep within the tumultuous root system of a towering oak.

When he woke, a thin blanket of fog crept over the ground. A damp chill came with it, causing Thephos's soiled smock to cling to his slender frame.

He looked to the sky. The Sempyrium claimed their gods lived there, working in holy union to hold life together with their boons of fire, water, earth, wind, absence.

Like his father, Thephos held little stock in the yammering of priests whose hands probed pockets as smoothly as their words probed ears.

Yet, Unturrus had done something to him. Sitting in observation of the Pendulum of Time, he'd glimpsed...something. Demons and devils he'd always understood. The world was rife with them, given over completely to Nacronus and the Maw Eternal.

But the gods of light—the way he saw them had changed. Unturrus let him glimpse what life was, though the memory of it dissolved as quick as sand when he tried to grasp it. Slippery as a wriggling trout in greased hands.

Though he didn't believe in the gods as the Sempyrium ordained, he sensed the existence of power. Something of an equal and incomprehensible magnitude.

Before Unturrus, a door slammed closed any time light shone through its cracks. Suffering was a drunk's hand wrapped around a tankard of godsbrew, and it was the only life he knew.

But now the door was left open and Thephos did not fearfully anticipate its closing. He watched it, waiting to see what lay on the other side.

The sun climbed and so did Thephos. He navigated between a fall of windswept boulders wearing crowns of yellow grass. Their stalks were stiff under hand. Arms trembling, he pulled himself over them. Wildflowers greeted him in jagged rows along a meandering goat trail. Where the goats were or ever had been, he didn't wish to know. Wind pressed his filthy smock tight against his knees as he made his way.

Before he died, he hoped to gain a high peak. Perhaps one overlooking all of Namarr. Maybe he would just watch again. He liked the idea of knowing he would be above anyone else in the world for a short time. It made him feel unique. Different. Special.

Wind rustled a bush to his right. A tan, smooth mound peeked out from under a dense cluster of vibrant blooms. Thephos let his momentum lag. He swallowed hard. With a hand over his brow, he peered at the shadowy place beneath the foliage and then stepped from the trail to inspect it.

The wind snapped at the fabric of his smock. He drew into himself, arms wrapping around his torso for warmth. At a dozen paces, he realized what the mound was: a skull. A surge of energy set his pulse to thudding in his ears. He crept closer. At first glance, he thought it to be human but quickly dismissed the idea when he considered its size. The skull was larger around than Thephos's chest. Its jaws reached forward as if the bone had been stretched. What it had eaten though...

It looks predatory. Yellowish canines longer and thicker than his fingers overlapped rows of flat teeth. Warily, Thephos took another step. A part of him wanted to flee. On Unturrus, nothing good came of curiosities satisfied or impulse explored.

But something stronger drew him to the skull. It burned not to touch it. Delay clawed at his skin. Caution was a rotted carcass filling his belly. He licked dry lips. Its horrible beauty seized him—compelled him to touch the skull. *I need it.* To resist the urge would be an unforgivable betrayal.

A babble of sound arose. Like water boiling at the back of his mind. Storm clouds formed overhead, alien fast. A terrified scream and ecstatic moan thrummed through Thephos. His feet vibrated. He felt himself smiling as he snapped off the bush's limbs where they'd grown into the monstrous skull. He thrashed and grunted as he wrestled away woody tethers holding his prize in place. A broken branch lashed his hand, scoring a cut that filled with a streak of red. He didn't care. He dug at the bush like a rabid dog, teeth clenched, gums aching.

His palms slithered into its eye sockets. Pleasure, warm and tingly, rippled outward from his belly as he dragged it into daylight. In the muddy imprint where the skull was imprisoned, worms writhed and beetles scampered in protest. They too had found a home in it.

A pair of curving horns atop the skull were tangled in a web of thin vines. Tongue darting around his mouth, Thephos rushed over and jerked them to tatters. His heart boomed, a thunder clap of yearning. Slowly, he circled back around, gaze fixed on the waist-high skull. In his bones, he ached to know the creature.

Lightning flashed in the distance, and it began to rain.

He came to stand before the skull. Empty eyes sockets bored into him. The babble at the back of his mind grew louder, hidden words taking shape just beneath the surface—

A bolt slashed the sky. Then a half-dozen more in rapid succession, leaving tracers of blue on either horizon, as if the gods themselves sought to embrace Unturrus. Slick with rainfall, the skull and its bovine horns gleamed. Thephos saw his gleeful reflection in its forehead. Smoke and embers and azure fire swirled at his peripheries. He smiled...felt it twist into a mask of unbridled rage and unsatiated hate.

Lightning flashed, drowning the world in blue-white stains. Peals of thunder rocked the craggy peaks all around, booming echoes ricocheting between curtains of stone. The voice at the back of his mind was neither his, nor his father's, nor anyone he knew. All the same, it greeted him with a sigh from the babbling river of his mind. Like an old friend.

Thephos...you came here to kill.

His cheek twitched. He shrugged a shoulder, twisted his neck to one side, and shrugged the other shoulder. All was silence, but the creak of his clenching teeth.

Thephos...I don't hate you.

The alien voice beckoned with velvet tones, drawing him in. Clawed hands the size of wagon wheels wrapped gently around his shoulders. Ebony talons reached down his forearms. In the skull's reflection, he could almost make out the creature standing behind him. Indigo flame cloaked in onyx. Thephos felt himself sliding into a deep chasm. A warm, safe place.

His eyelids fluttered.

I don't hate you, Thephos. Come. Be with me. I will make you free.

Memories slammed into him, drawn out by the creature. His younger brother, barely ten, placed a caring hand on Thephos's wrist. Their father had just screamed Thephos into a corner—told him he was nothing—that he hated him. Better to be hated by the old devil than loved. But then his little brother, a brave and foolish boy, had placed a hand on Thephos's wrist. "I don't hate you," he'd said. Thephos had nodded, but what he'd really wanted to do was curse the boy and cuff him and call him a dumb little bastard for caring, for helping, for trying to make Thephos feel better. *Too dangerous*, Thephos wanted to scream.

But he hadn't. Instead, he had buried him a month later under the willow tree. *Thephos...be free with me.*

Indigo lightning branched across the horizon. Thunder rattled the air. His hair stood. The creature rubbed his shoulders...in the reflection, a blue flame spit to life where Thephos's heart should be...

He jerked away with a gasp and fell to all fours with his back to the monstrous remains. He glanced back, found the skull watching, empty eye sockets following him as he dug his fingers into the earth and crawled. Flinging clods of dirt in his wake, he scrambled to his feet and bolted up the trail.

Laughter rang at the back of his mind.

Dripping wet, Thephos rested his back against an upthrust slab of granite and shook. The monster's laughter scraped at the base of his skull. His flight from it had been desperate. Yet, now that it was gone, he felt wrong. Like a piece of him had wanted it. He rose and continued, eager to put more distance between himself and the entity.

The storm left a blanket of drab clouds behind. Mud squelched between his toes, cool and silk-smooth. The trail widened and became a series of blind switchbacks.

As he rounded the next bend, he came face to face with Lethwii. Where once her smock had been a pristine white, now it was shredded at the hems. Holes were worn at the shoulders and knees. The wear and tear was far worse than his own, as if she'd been wandering Unturrus for months instead of days or weeks. Her face too was gaunter. Dark pits surrounded her eyes and grime marred her pale Anjuhk skin.

"I found it," she raved, "I found the Hall of Heroes. I found the Hall of Heroes!"

There was no way to prepare for words such as those. A mix of elation, doubt, and confusion swirled through Thephos, dead leaves caught in an Autumn gust. Then he remembered Lethwii was mad.

Thephos grabbed her by the shoulders and searched for sanity. Before, her eyes had been as flat and cold as tundra. Now, they sprang about, failing to be still for more than a second. She twirled out of his grasp, then snatched the sleeve of his smock. "Come! You'll see."

Will it be a hole in the ground? Or a wasp's nest? Maybe she pulls me toward the cliff's edge where she'll step out into empty air.

The crags to either side fell away as they ran, Anjuhk towing pig farmer. The curtains of stone to either side of the path dwindled away until there was nothing but clear skies and distant horizons stretching in every direction save one.

The peak of Unturrus. Ahead of them, a triangular tomb of granite towered. The top of it was hooked like the point of the Madness's sickle.

Thephos stopped. The sleeve of his smock tore as they both jerked to a halt. The Anjuhk pivoted to face him. "There's the entrance!" She released his sleeve and twirled in circles like a dancer, arms upraised, brimming with levity. "There it is! There it is! I told you we were almost there." With every spin, she pointed quickly at a dark speck at the base of Unturrus's looming peak.

Can it truly be the entrance to the Hall of Heroes?

"You did tell me, didn't you?" His eyes narrowed. "Lethwii, why didn't you go in yourself?"

He held his breath and waited for a response.

Laughing, she flopped to the ground. "Because." Her voice changed, taking on a familiar harsh whining. Shivers slithered down Thephos's spine as she said, "I *can't*, Theffy."

Breath quickening with panic, Thephos took a wary step back as if a mother bear flanked by cubs stalked toward him. He glanced at the Hall of Heroes. It had never been his goal to reach it, but now that it was in his sights he wanted nothing more. For the first time in as long as he could remember, he feared death. Lethwii sat between the Hall of Heroes and himself.

"What's wrong, Theffy? This ol' cunt boring you?" Seated on the rock-riddled ground, she propped herself up onto her elbows and thrust up with her pelvis, humping the air.

"You're not Lethwii." Thephos sidestepped toward the entrance to the Hall of Heroes. It was still a few stone throws distant. Impossibly far. He wouldn't get more than a foot. He looked the doppleganger in the eyes. "When did you take her?"

The thing that was once Lethwii laughed. She placed a hand on her face, the other on her chest. Bunching her own flesh into fists like cloth, it tore away the skin.

Out of the lifeless woman's shell, the Madness rose.

Here, on the flat plane outside the Hall of Heroes, his imposing figure was an obelisk of doom. He chuckled. "I am barred from the Hall of Heroes. Obviously. I'm a fuckin' demon. Though for many of the little sheepies like yourself who wander up the hill, I can be somewhat of a hero. That Kanian crabber for instance. He may have convinced himself he didn't know what his heart desired, but I knew he wanted a quick death he didn't see coming, so I gave it to him." The Madness cleared his throat. "Well. That's mostly what he wanted."

"How...how did you know he was a crabber? How do you know so much about us?"

The Madness's black lips trembled with fury. "I just told you I can see your heart's true desires, you fucking dolt. You think I can't spot a crabber? Or smell one for that matter? The man smelled fishier than a dolphin's dickhole." The "ole" sound was dragged out as if it pleased the demon to say it.

Thephos's legs shook. For the first time, he'd found a way to see life differently, and in a moment it would be taken from him. Such joys were fleeting, he supposed, so he inhaled sharply and waited for death. He thought of the stump where he'd glimpsed the true nature of things. At least he'd seen that before the end. His father never did, of that he was certain.

The Madness studied Thephos. "What?" He looked toward the Hall of Heroes. When his pale face turned back, a fat tear glimmered on the fleshy pit under one of the demon's eyes.

Why hasn't he killed me?

In his mind's eye, Syn Backlegarm watched him from the crowd. He told Thephos he had bet five gold wheels on him to return with powers. *Syn treated me as a friend when I hadn't expected it. Maybe this is the same.* "Are you here to help me? Are you a friend?"

The demon's lips curled around soot-dark gums. His teeth looked deadly sharp as he smiled. Holding out a clawed hand, his sickle appeared, its handle filling a pale palm. He scratched the top of his chalk white skull with the blade's tip. Where it touched, a tendril of smoke arose. "You know how many little sheepies like yourself I've slaughtered and shorn over the centuries? Eh, do ya? Enough to fill Nine Lakes with their blood." Holding up the fingers of one hand, he tapped each in turn with the point of his sickle. "Idiots, priests, shamans, thieves, fools, gossips, clods, cretins, cowards, ignoramuses, heroes, warriors, halfwits, morons, rapists, murderers, leches, cheaters, gamblers, pirates, raiders, weaklings, dullards, sisters, brothers, lords, ladies, imbeciles, dolts, assassins, addicts, slaves, whores, knights, bean counters, gluttons, farmers and..." he spat into the snow, a black gob that sizzled where it struck. "Thespians."

Thephos raised an eyebrow.

"Fake people offend me." The Madness smiled, as if remembering his point. "And not one of those sheepies—out of the countless thousands of sheepies—not one ever thought I was their friend. Truly, your father must have been a devil for you to be asking if a demon is your pal."

"My father *was* a devil."

Wind moaned across the mountain. They stared at each other a long time. Thephos shifted his weight and looked away, expecting the killing blow to come at any moment.

"Well, I'm sorry Theffy, but I don't think our friendship is going to last. You wouldn't want to partake in what I think is fun." Black veins bulged in the Madness's eyes, his smile broader than a shovel's head. He raised his sickle menacingly and giggled. "That is unless you wanna kill him?"

"Kill who?"

"Your dad, you stupid eggplant!"

"But...he's dead."

"I know that asshole!" The Madness screamed

Thephos flinched back, eyes reflexively closing. He still expected the sickle's descent at any moment.

The Madness spoke in mocking tones, "Oh yeah, he's dead. Guess we can't. Stupid fuckin' eggplant...just open your eyes and look at me!"

Thephos obeyed. Gasped as if punched in the sternum.

Before him stood his father. From the smoothness of the old devil's cheeks and the lack of wrinkles around the eyes, Thephos guessed he was a decade younger than he'd been when he died.

"It can't be," Thephos whispered. Terror flooded him. "It can't be."

"You said that, Theffy. What kind of pathetic worm are you?" The Madness, who was his father, snickered into a human fist. "I do a pretty good impression, don't I? Better than the rest of those shitty thespians."

Thephos seethed. "Stop this."

"I don't answer to weaklings." His father's voice. "Fucking kill me, boy, or shut your worthless trap."

The old devil tossed the Madness's massive onyx sickle to the dirt at Thephos's feet. The old bastard sneered and crossed his arms in dismissive confidence, waiting in the way of those issuing challenges they knew would never be met.

Rage boiled in Thephos's chest. The muscles in his arms and torso burned with tension. *I've always wanted this.* He grabbed the sickle. His muscles were alive with dark intent and a sudden strength. Power weaved through his belly, stretched down and rooted in his feet. The sickle was light and deadly in his hands. A smile tugged at the corners of his mouth. *Wanted nothing more.*

His father glared.

A few steps separated them.

You came here to kill, the voice said. It wasn't the Madness that spoke—someone else.

Righteous words thundered in his ears. The ring of a hammer striking a coffin's nail. The command of a wrathful god. Power coursed through him from heel to crown. Thephos stepped forward to strike down the evil bastard. *He's a devil. Nothing more.*

He took another step.

"Oh goody! Sorry—ahem—I mean..." The Madness shifted back into his father's voice. "Cowardly fucking boy. Put that sickle down unless you've got the fire in you to use it!"

He was close enough that the scent of godsbrew wafted into Thephos's face and brought with it the past. He faltered.

As he cast the first shaking shovelful of dirt, his brother's swollen face watched the sky. Thephos couldn't have done the deed faster. The shovel ached in his hands. Like the sickle that filled them now, it thirsted for his father's life. It had only seemed a fantasy then, to wish the devil dead. As the last bits of dirt topped the grave, Thephos had regretted not killing the man. If he had, his brother would have lived.

"It should have been me who killed you!" Like the shovel had, the sickle trembled in Thephos's fists. Tears poured down his cheeks and fell from quivering lips. "I should have crushed your skull with a shovel and fed you to the fucking pigs!" A pair of angry strides brought him closer. He wrung the sickle's handle. Close now. So close.

All he had to do was swing.

The old devil shouted back. Spittle landed on Thephos's shoulder. "You best aim well. Cause if you don't, you'll be rottin' beside your brother!"

From the river of his mind, a voice babbled, stoking rage even as it soothed it. *Thephos...you came here to kill.*

With a sharp intake of breath, he raised the sickle. The char-black blade glinted in the light of the fleeing sun. A fire burned within, rage and hate unbridled, and only wrath could see it calmed.

"Die devil!" Thephos wept.

His father's eyes rounded in fear. He cringed in the shadow of the hanging sickle. Thephos saw how afraid he was. Saw how fear motivated the man's every action. The sickle froze overhead.

Wrath demanded a price. To pay it was to claim it. More than revenge, Thephos needed to live in a world different than his father's own.

He hefted the sickle again, but again he could not bring himself to swing it. "I hate you." His body convulsed around the words. The tension, the power, the strength in his muscles dripped from him like a wrung washrag. The sickle grew leaden in his hands. Tears stung his cheeks.

He lowered the weapon.

I came here for me.

The sickle clattered to the ground at his father's feet. "I'll have no more to do with you." The white-hot fury ebbed, the hatred and retribution leeching from his soul.

His father reverted to the Madness in a wink of shadow, to the sound of tearing fabric.

"Oh, some friend you are," the Madness huffed. "No fun. No fun at all."

The Madness, the sickle, and Thephos's desire to kill disappeared in an instant, their going marked by tendrils of twisting darkness.

Thephos fell to his knees and wept.

Without hesitation, Thephos passed through the narrow tunnel entrance into the Hall of Heroes.

Within, there was an oppressive sense of spaciousness, as if he stepped out into the night sky. He worked his way down over the rim of a great bowl, feet passing over thousands of tiny, smooth pebbles. Water sloshed up around his ankles. The light of the cave mouth was above and behind him, casting a shimmering glow onto the water's surface and unknowable distance beyond.

All was pitch black.

Onward, ever onward. Thephos waded into the water until it compressed his thighs. He lowered a hand he couldn't see, touched the water's warm surface and held it there. Nothing disturbed the waters but him. A flat, perfectly level plane.

Which way?

A source of indigo light pulsed to life in the distance then disappeared as quickly as it came. Thephos's heart nearly jumped from his chest. *Here* it seemed to say. Before he knew what he was doing, his legs carried him toward the flash.

The hem of his smock dragged through the water behind him like a lily pad. Coolness swirled around his legs, followed a second later by warmth. The change in the endless dark pool's temperature sent tremors of unease into his gut.

Something splashed nearby.

Thephos went rigid. His heartbeat was in his fingertips and toes, ready to flee. He racked his brain to remember anything Olthr or Radea had said about demons that lived in the Hall of Heroes. He sipped air. Let it out slow. When he heard no further sound he continued onward.

Ever onward. Into the womb and the softly lapping dark.

Water rose to his groin, forcing his genitals to cling tight to his pelvis. Brow knit together, he stopped, unsure if he still went in the direction of the indigo flash. He turned back to the point of light at the cave's entrance.

Another splash. Waves pattered gently against his side. He stepped back from the source of the sound. Behind him, something brushed his leg, smooth and rubbery like a wet boot heel. He stifled a scream as he stumbled a step. Something large twisted abruptly under the water's surface, nearly pushing him off balance. Another something brushed its enormous bulk against his hip, then swam away.

Sharks.

Thephos imagined beady black eyes and rows of jagged teeth hovering near his calves. Panic threatened to steal his breath.

Behind him, one breached the surface. Thephos whirled, water heaving outward from around his rib cage. Light from the Hall's entrance ripple the length of its dorsal fin. His knees went weak. His shoulders ached with the strain of keeping as much of himself out of the water as he could for as long as he could. Another dorsal fin cut the surface like a knife, then joined the other fin to circle him.

Sweat broke across his brow. He found his breath, a rapid rhythm echoing off the cavern walls.

I've come so far.

The old devil's face came to him in a rush.

You're a pathetic worm! A worm dangling on a hook for bigger, meaner, hungrier fish.

"I've faced demons. I've buried a brother. I've ascended Unturrus and faced countless horrors. What have you done but beat children. I am Thephos of Carthane. It's you who is nothing."

In his mind's eye, his father cowered then disappeared.

And I'll continue onward until Unturrus stops me.

Mustering every ounce of willpower, Thephos forced his foot to move. Fins circled closer. His second step was tentative, off-balanced, and caused him to almost fall face first into the surf. Instead, he turned his momentum into a quick third and fourth step. One shark swam round behind and bumped the back of his legs with a bowed snout. He loosed a whimper. Heard it echoed back to him. Summoning courage, he grit his teeth and strode forward more purposefully, each step outstripping the last in distance. He winced as he hurtled forward, expecting a hundred teeth to snare his leg or tear into a hip. Any next step could be the one that called the demons to feast.

"Take me if you wish!" he shouted. His challenge rang throughout the cavernous bowl of rock. To his right, a shark broke the surface, primordial maw of jagged teeth bearing down on him. Just before the killing bite, it drove back beneath the surface, tail fin threshing the water as it turned, dousing Thephos's exposed chest and head.

Indigo light flashed in the distance. Excitement peeled away the fear.

He strode forward. Dorsal fins lagged, then eventually drifted out of sight. Faint burbles fell farther and farther behind.

By the time he stopped, he was sucking in ragged breaths. The water eclipsed his chest now, hampering his ability to draw in enough air. He turned back, found the entrance to the Hall of Heroes, a speck on a horizon of abject blackness. Raising a dripping pinky finger, he closed an eye and then blotted it out. There was no going back.

There never was.

He caught the pulse of indigo light in his periphery. A pleasant warmth wriggled in his stomach. He swam forward, feet barely touching. Light and direction disappeared. Time too dissolved into the darkness.

He floated off of his feet and started kicking. Fatigue set in quickly. At first a tightness in the area where his shoulders attached to his neck, then a burning sensation creeping down his mid-back. His arms churned ineptly at the water. Breath flew from a spittle rimmed mouth as he propelled himself toward the indigo beacon's last sighting. But he was a poor swimmer, and it wasn't long before his frail body met its limit.

He pushed beyond it, farther than he imagined himself capable.

Nevertheless, when his arms were finally numb from effort, he sank. Darkness swallowed him, a moment's reprieve for his muscles, before he felt a tight ache lacing his chest...

He kicked to the surface, gasping for air then sank again into the abyss. Another painful rest was followed by another round of fighting back to the surface for air. A greedy breath broke the monotonous ring of death in his ears, but it was nowhere near enough to live.

He heard his father say, *you have no fire in you, Theffy,* and it pushed him down again.

Lungs screaming, blood rushing through his veins in a desperate scramble for air, he felt his face go slack. Numbness slithered into him from every direction. Death circled closer, the hungriest shark...

A brilliant light the color of an azure sky just before nightfall spread outward from a single sphere overhead. Pure scintillating energy. Richer and deeper than the iciest of blue eyes.

It blossomed, grew, pouring itself into a different shape he struggled to believe. Then it descended.

The Mother.

The water was suddenly gone. All darkness too. Thephos did not gasp with a need for breath; it returned with a blissful calm. He stared into the Mother's dazzling form. Azure wings marbled through with onyx and storm cloud gray, beating and sending a gale of wind whooshing around the vast hollowed-out chamber.

Thephos gaped. Warmth and vibration goaded him to open. All at once, his stomach and heart were empty and full. Tears rolled down his cheeks. *Beautiful...gods...beautiful.*

The Mother's light drowned out all seeing, all further thought and feeling. Every shadow, past and present, was stripped away by light in its purest form. He felt himself melting, folding inward into nowhere and nothing.

What was Thephos of Carthane was no more.

CHAPTER FIFTY-THREE

HUNGRY DOGS

Ishoa was jarred from her dying thoughts by a sickening scrape. Blood sprayed against the wall to one side.

Severed strands of the Scarborn's severed hair jumped into the air above either shoulder. Fury leaked from his face, and his skin went tallow and slack. The tip of the greatsword tumbled from his hands as he turned—blood fountained from a deep cut in the nape of his neck.

That was when Ishoa saw Wolst. He shoved the Scarborn face-first to the floor. "You're alive." Beads of ruby blood glistened in his beard. He jammed his broadsword into the scabbard, then hauled Ishoa to her feet. "To your grandmother's quarters. You'll be safe there until this is over."

She caught sight of her sword near Wolst's feet. He grabbed it, handed it to her, and then propelled her toward the counsel chamber. "Go!"

All alone, her legs shaking like sacks of jelly, she entered and then rounded the horn table within. The iron handle gave a subtle click as she opened the door at the back of the counsel chamber.

She flinched, stumbled back—closed the door to a finger's breadth. A pale woman's head was tilted back onto its crown on the floor. Dead eyes stared at Ishoa. Ruptured flesh reached up at jagged angles around a gaping wound between her breasts. Ribbons of red decorated the walls. Blood trickled down the steps that led up to Belara's quarters.

Steel clanged and echoed down the corridor, jarring Ishoa. Grunt. Curse. The stomp of boots. A pair of Scarborn hurried past then jostled up the stairs.

How? No Scarborn left the High Hall...

She thought of her uncle's frustration in the High Hall. *Where are the rest of the crownguard?* Wolst's words moaned through her like an icy wind. Panic slapped her heart like a rod striking a horse's flank. *I'm trapped.* Her hand was chafed and raw from gripping her sword so tight. Now it shook as she crept to the door leading back into the High Hall.

She waited. Any moment either Scarborn or Wolst and his men would burst through the door. Violent cries greeted her from the other side. Men and women...killing and dying. Her chest heaved. She forced herself to take a slow breath.

The door jerked open. Her sword leaped overhead, poised in both fists for a mighty downward slash. Arick Quinn's grim face floated before her, sporting a shallow cut under his chin.

"Arick!" She lowered her weapon.

"We've lost." He snatched her by the wrist and dragged her along behind him to a tapestry in one corner of the counsel room. "Hurry."

"What about Wolst?" She tried to wrench free of his iron grip.

Arick ripped the tapestry aside, pushed at a trapdoor embedded in the stone wall at chest height, then yanked her toward it.

"What about, Uncle?"

Arick hesitated. "He'll be fine."

When she dug in her heels in protest, he slapped her, grabbed her by the back of the neck, and forced her head first into the passageway. Her cheek stung. Tears welled. "Go." He shoved her farther in, causing her to sprawl onto her face in the dark. "Right now."

Hot tears raced to her chin. She wanted to boot him in the face as he crawled in behind her. "We have to help Un—"

"You're the only hope Namarr has left." His imploring tones resonated in the narrow passage. "You must survive, Princess."

She beat at the cold stones, pounded them with all the futility and impotent fury she could muster until her hand hurt. What more could she do? Arick was right. If she left, maybe there was still a path to vengeance.

Hinges creaked closed behind. Darkness descended.

Ishoa cursed then started to crawl. Thought fell away, her full faculties required to navigate blind. After a dozen feet the passageway dropped away. The first time it did so, she cried out at the sudden disappearance of the ground before her.

"Keep going. It's there." Arick's methodical breathing dogged her in the narrow enclosure. "Feel for it."

She reached down, brushed fingertips against the floor where it continued. Propping herself up with both arms, she dragged her legs into the space. Her knees landed hard against the stone. Pain stabbed up her leg and into her hips.

Relentless, Arick beckoned her to keep crawling.

The smell of horse, straw, and manure filled her nose, faint at first but growing stronger each passing moment. Aricks's hand shoved her backside. "Keep going."

She clenched her jaw.

The screaming and clangoring of battle receded with every crease of stone they crept over. With some separation from impending death and the possibility of survival ahead, the urge to escape lent Ishoa frantic energy. The fighting, the fear, and the violence was falling behind. Before long Arick no longer needed to prod her forward.

Ahead, thin bars of light appeared in the shape of a door just large enough to squeeze through.

An exit into daylight. Ishoa pushed at it to no avail.

"There's a latch to your left," Arick whispered.

Ishoa felt along the seam of the trapdoor, found the latch and flipped it. She pushed...

A heart-stopping screech. Light jabbed her eyes.

She blinked hard then squinted.

Horses flicked their manes and greeted the highborn pair with startled whinnies. With no choice but to fall forward into the loft, Ishoa did so. She landed hard on her shoulder. A poorly driven nail jabbed into the flesh under her white wolverine pelt. She stifled a cry, grabbed at the puncture wound as she lied there, stars illuminating the edges of her vision.

"Are you hurt?" Arick was beside her, the barest hint of compassion in his tone.

Hurt? She saw gore smattering Wolst. Saw the dead crownguard on the stairs. Saw the knight of Jarik's face pumping blood atop her. Saw her grandmother wailing over Othwii among shards of a shattered hummingbird brooch. *Othwii's dead...* The realization struck like a hurled spear. Tears pooled at the corners of her eyes.

"It's nothing." She sniffled and flew to her feet.

Arick stripped the white wolverine pelt roughly from her shoulders and threw it to the floor. "A beacon for our enemies."

Ishoa nodded. They hustled down rickety steps to the barn floor, blades drawn. Arick took the lead. In silence, they swept past rows of horse stalls. Arick paused to snatch a filthy cloak draped over a rail. "Put this on. Keep the hood up."

The stable door was partially open. Splotches of blood marred the snow beyond. Shouts filled the air. "The fighting is widespread then," Ishoa said.

Arick gripped her bicep. "We take horses and flee. We'll return with the Crown's army." When he squared to look at her, sadness rode the lines of his face. "You're the last Ironlight. You cannot be taken by them."

"We have to get Rakeema."

Arick shook his head.

Ishoa spoke with finality. "I'm getting Rakeema."

"You're not. We're going." His grip tightened, a harsh promise. "Even if I must take you unconscious."

"You'll have to," she hissed. "I'm not leaving her behind."

A reedy voice froze them. "Highborn."

Arick whirled toward the partially open stable-door and fell into a defensive posture, sword point whipping to attention.

A pair of Scarborn approached, weapons swaying like vipers. One carried a short spear and sword. The other flourished hatchets.

Arick swung an arm backward, shoving Ishoa into the deeper shadows of the barn. She reeled, then landed in a pile of straw.

Arick darted forward as if to charge but ducked behind the stable door at the last second as one of the mercenaries threw the spear. It sank into the hard-packed floor and quivered.

Before they were inside, Arick jerked the door closed. A hatchet bit into the wood near his head and sent a chip fluttering to the floor.

Ishoa climbed from the hay to retrieve her blade.

"Take a horse and go!" Arick's sword flicked out, met steel out of sight as the Scarborn worked to pull the door open. Intermittent grunts and the swish of blades filled the stable. Horses stamped and screamed.

The Scarborn managed to slide the barn door open wide enough for both of them to come through, but Arick slashed forward, shutting it once more to narrow their window of attack.

"I cannot hold them! You must go!"

Ishoa cursed. The mane of the nearest horse filled her hands as she mounted it.

Daylight spread over the straw-covered floor as the stable door banged open. Dust swirled at Arick's feet. He charged to his left, leveling a series of tight cuts that forced his opponents back out into the snowy, bloodstained courtyard.

Ishoa led her mount out of the stall.

The Scarborn were pressing their advantage, circling Arick to split his attention. The hatchet man deflected one of Arick's attacks and the swordsmen struck out low, slipping past her cousin's guard to clip his calf. Arick grunted.

Ishoa hurtled from the barn into daylight. She slashed at the man nearest her as she flew by, but he ducked it with ease. She glanced back just in time to see Arick stumble on his bad leg. She held her breath as he started to fall. The Scarborn jumped forth to capitalize, but Arick flowed with his forward momentum and dropped a level. A hatchet blow aimed at his head cut air as he rolled and came up on one knee. He twisted around and thrust his blade into the swordsman's gut. The skewered Scarborn shrieked and keeled over, writhing in the snow.

Hope rippled through Ishoa.

Though short lived it was.

A roar ranked Ishoa's attention forward. She pulled her horse's mane, halting it. "Ancestor's give mercy."

Smoke threw an oily haze over the bloodshed raging across the bailey grounds. The snow had turned a pale gray from falling ash. The sky was choked with it. Any direction she looked, chaos bled through the senses. Screams and roaring flames drowned her ears. Hate and violence consumed her eyes. She could taste it all. Bitter at the back of her throat. Acrid in her nostrils.

A distant and impossible sight stole her breath. The Gate of the Bear was gone. A pile of twisted steel and smoldering ruin lay in the gap where it once stood—had stood for generations. To either side, smoke trailed from cracks in Jarik's stone walls. In places, the decimated fortification glowed bright orange, looking hotter than a freshly forged blade.

But that didn't stop the flood of people fleeing for their lives. Servants and the occasional holdguard who'd lost their lord trickled through the coolest parts of the breach.

To the west, cattlemen battled against Frost crownguard atop the battlements around the Gate of the Tiger. To the east, thirty Scarborn swarmed up the ramp leading to the High Hall.

Pockets of crownguard were cut down by superior numbers at every turn. There were more Scarborn, more cattlemen, more furriers than she thought possible. Hundreds more than the retinues camped outside the walls had. Most wore tabards donned over tunics and trousers as if it were a hasty afterthought. As if...

Treachery! They planted soldiers in the city!

Still, it shouldn't have been enough to overrun Jarik almost uncontested. She wheeled her horse in a circle. *Where are the rest of our crownguard?* Between the barracks and those on active duty, there should have been over a thousand men defending the Ice Maiden's Keep.

Far more than this.

"We've lost." Lead filled her as she realized everyone she loved was likely dead. Othwii, Wolst, Grandmother, Arick. All of them gone.

She slapped her horse's flanks. Dread chased her to the Sister Keep. *Rakeema is all I have left.*

A cattleman saw her, tried to grab her as she rode past, but she slashed his forearm. As she neared the barracks, the pockets of fighting intensified, as did the smoke. A lone hunter of Twilight Cape skewered a Scarborn through the heart. Servants unable to make the destroyed Gate of the Bear were being rounded up by men wearing the dancing wolf of Ghastiin, their spears leveled as they yanked hoods from the women's heads. *They're looking for me.*

She sped onward. A pair of cattlemen bludgeoned an aging Frost courier to death with mauls. Though she shut her eyes, she couldn't block out the sound of the old man's last, garbled plea for mercy.

Shifting in her seat, she steered between friend and foe alike, the entrance to the Sister Keep growing closer by the second. Voices called to her. Hands reached to take her. A thrown spear fell short of her horse's chest, and it leapt over the weapon lodged in the earth. Brow furrowed, Ishoa slapped the horse's flanks again. "Faster!"

The barracks lay ahead.

As did the answer to her question of the absent Frost forces. Flames wrapped around the building like the fingers of a closing hand. Furriers and Scarborn battled at the entrances, herding the crownguard back inside into choking death.

Stools burst from windows as Frost soldiers attempted to climb to safety, but these were slaughtered mid-escape by groups of Scarborn patrolling the long building.

Something bulled into Ishoa. Her horse spun, its reins jerked to the side by unseen hands. A snarling face rose—acrid breath—Ishoa stabbed at it as she fought for balance. She slid from the horse's back, then leapt off at an angle.

Without a backward look, she raced toward the barracks and flung her back to the smoking wall. The heat enveloped her, made her damp with sweat as she cast about for her assailant. No one came. She ran, fumbling to keep on her hood.

At the corner of the barracks, she peeked out. Three crownguard managed to win free of the inferno. Blue and white tabards ablaze, cheeks smeared with soot, they squeezed through an opening they'd sundered with axes. Scarborn mercenaries rushed them. The Frost men fought savagely, affording time for their brethren to crawl out and join the fray.

Ishoa's heart sank as she located the source of the fire and the source of the destroyed gate. Vaporous white light poured from the pale, shirtless Awakened's eyes. An oblong metal instrument was strapped to the stump of a missing hand. An unnatural gaseous liquid wept from patchwork scars covering his torso. Ran in rivulets from the stump of his severed hand into the waiting instrument.

With a step forward, the Awakened flung the contents in an arc. Fire exploded across the men who'd fought free of the barracks. Flesh melted off them like the tallow of a candle. Screams rose as did the sizzle of fat and crackle of bone. The Awakened strolled alongside the barracks, casually flinging molten death against its walls. Where he went, smoke and fire followed.

Jarik's forces were no more...

Ishoa waited for a group of furriers to run past before sprinting from the killing grounds of the barracks, head bowed low. The obscurity of smoke, she hoped, would help shield her on her way to rescue Rakeema.

Madness swirled around her. Smoke thickened by the second, until it became a blinding fog. Ishoa coughed. It stung her nostrils and made her eyes water. A silhouette stumbled toward her. She raised her blade—the man fell to his knees, a gash across his belly. He reached out. "A drink." Then he pitched onto his face.

A woman on a horse pounded past, pursued by a soldier from an unknown hold brandishing an ax.

Fight or flee. Kill or die. That was all.

A chained storm bear stood on its hind legs and roared, muzzle mere feet from Ishoa's face. She stumbled back, scurried clear of it, then ran to the Sister Keep.

Familiar stone greeted her hands. She picked along the wall to find the entrance as she rounded a drum-tower.

Soldiers. She shrank back then leaned out. A handful of cornered treekin faced Golthius Narl with a knight of Prav to either side of him and a dozen holdguard behind. "Surrender or die," the fat lord said.

The men of Shadowheart cursed as they dropped their weapons. A second later they screamed as they were cut down. The lord of Prav's double chin shook with laughter. "Cowards."

Ishoa balled the fabric of her fetid cloak in a painfully tight fist. It was too much to hope that the Golthius's son was dead. She did so anyway.

Once the bakers of Prav left, Ishoa crept into the Sister Keep.

The key slipped from numb fingers and pinged when it struck the ground. She picked it up, jammed it into the lock, and turned. Inside, Rakeema stared at her wide-eyed a startled moment then continued pacing back and forth beneath the window. Between growls, she made an odd chattering sound Ishoa knew to be worry. "It's okay, girl."

Ishoa went to her anjuhtarg. The horrifying scene beyond the window stopped her cold. Ash and snow rained. Where the smoke was thin, the bailey grounds were dotted by dark blossoms of crimson. Above the dense pall, the fighting had become more organized. Pitched battles at vital points.

With Rakeema at her side, Ishoa turned to leave. "Come."

She froze.

A brown vested cattleman with a maul entered her room. Two Scarborn with spears flanked him.

"I told you I saw her," said one of the Scarborn.

A growl rolled through Rakeema's throat. Arms quaking, mouth trembling, Ishoa drew her sword. She glanced at the portrait of her parents. *I'll see you soon enough.*

She took glacier breaths. Slow and cool. As Wolst taught her.

"Sajac!"

Rakeema flew into position beneath her naked shield arm. The men shuffled slowly inside. Rakeema's tail swished. Emerald predatory eyes fixed around the man to Ishoa's weak side. Wolst's voice told her to turn her hips to face the majority of her enemies. *Trust your anjuhtarg, Isha. Let her guard you where you're blind.*

"Alright men, altogether now," said a Scarborn. "Keep your heads cool—even if she cuts ya. Lodecka wants her alive."

They spread out.

The cattleman on her flank took a probing step, evoking a hiss from Rakeema followed by a warning swipe. No bigger than a large dog, the cat's claws were still deadly sharp. The man's tongue darted from under his horned half-helm to wet dry lips.

Although it went against Wolst's teachings, Ishoa backed up. She tried to pull Rakeema back with her, but the ice tiger had the battle fever upon her. A good master could cut through their anjuhtarg's instinct. Rakeema was too young though, too impulsive and untrained.

"Kill that fucking cat," the Scarborn said.

Ishoa held up a hand. "Wait!" She lowered her sword. "If I surrender, will you spare my anjuhtarg?"

"Doesn't matter what I say. That cat ain't giving you up without a fight." He gestured at Rakeema with his spear. "Kill it."

Not her too. Hands strangling the hilt, Ishoa raised her sword.

The cattleman hefted his maul. Rakeema hunkered low, ready to dodge or strike. Ishoa would never know which...

A colossal shadow filled the doorway. Body facing forward, the Scarborn leader craned his head around as a sword point exploded from his chest. His spear clattered to the floor as he gazed down in astonishment at the blood-greased steel protruding from his heart.

Wolst cast the man aside like a discarded doll.

Mouth agape, the cattleman and remaining Scarborn turned to the new threat.

The Beast of Anjuhkar was among them.

Rakeema lunged for the cattleman's throat, but Wolst was somehow quicker. Before the ice tiger struck, the warmaster blasted the man in the middle of his downswing with a booted heel. The force of the blow jerked the cattleman out from under his helmet. He flew backward into the wall, head cracking against it with a spurt of scarlet.

Rakeema leapt into empty space and landed gently.

"Sajac!" Ishoa called. This time, the ice tiger listened and bounded to her master's side.

The remaining Scarborn attempted to spear Wolst from behind. But the Beast of Anjuhkar moved with uncanny speed, a bull with the quickness of an ice tiger. The mercenary stabbed naught but air.

The warmaster's gaze deadlocked onto his opponent. The Scarborn gave a pitiful warcry and lunged. Wolst ducked the first stab, hewing the shaft in two as he did. The second thrust came as a splintered haft. Wolst batted the sundered weapon away as he weaved around a third strike and punched his other blade through the man's forehead with a muted crunch. Gore drained from the Scarborn's nose as he dangled limply on Wolst's broadsword.

Bile rose in Ishoa's throat, but she held it back.

Wolst yanked his sword free. "Isha, grab your cat and follow me." He crossed the room to the cattleman struggling to reorient from his collision with the wall. Wolst whipped his arm in an arc, perfunctorily splitting the man's neck. Blood shot across the storm bear rug...

My rug...

"Now!" Wolst cut through the shock settling into Ishoa's bones. Hand shaking, she sheathed her sword. Rakeema would be difficult to manage, so she grabbed a blanket from her bed to enfold the ice tiger. The anjuhtarg struggled, but Ishoa was determined to protect her at all costs. Once in the blanket with her paws bound, it was easier than expected.

Booted footfalls accompanied the jostle of chain in the stairwell. Wolst moved to the door. "Behind me now. Whatever happens, keep your feet moving. Don't stop for anything. Not even me. We make for the Gate of the Tiger. Do you hear?"

She nodded...hesitated. "I—I love you."

"Aye." Wolst sniffled and pointed a sword at the painting of her parents. "They'd be damn proud of you, Isha. Like I am."

The clatter of weapons and pounding of boots drew closer.

Wolst whirled his broadswords and spat. "Let's show these bastards it's right to fear the *Barn* of Anjuhkar." Somehow, in the madness of it all, Ishoa laughed. A clip of painful mirth.

Just as the first Scarborn crested the stairs, Ishoa stepped in behind Wolst, keeping as close as possible without tripping his feet. She cradled Rakeema tight to her chest.

"Come then!" Wolst bellowed. "Have a dance!"

His shoulders jerked forward and back, body pivoting around a powerful core. Steel clashed. Flesh shrieked. Wood splintered. Hot blood splashed and jumped, painting the stairwell and making footing slick. Gargling screams and hoarse curses echoed in the tight passage. With each downward step, a body fell before Wolst and Ishoa stepped over them. Faces, young and old—all unknown—stared up at her and died at her feet.

Shouts rose above the din of violence. The Scarborn beckoned for reinforcements against the furious tide bearing down on them. "The Warmaster! Here—the Beast of Anjuhkar is here!"

"Bring them all!" Wolst roared in answer. "Come! Stand in the fire!"

A man screamed. A man died. Wolst hewed and stabbed and sent them all into the endless dark.

Rakeema writhed in Ishoa's arms. She stumbled, reached out and caught the belt of her uncle's warskirt. Wolst grunted, body jolting underhand. Crimson beads raced down his exposed calf and smeared at the top of his boot.

No...

Horror lodged in Ishoa's throat.

Rakeema fought to free herself and loosed a claw. The young anjuhtarg raked Ishoa's arm. Panes of red sprang from the deep scratch. Ishoa bit her lip against the searing agony and wrestled the ice tiger's claw back into the swaddling.

Whatever happens, keep your feet moving forward. Don't stop for anything. Ishoa grit her teeth and stepped methodically forward. She kicked the hand of a dying man as he tried to grab her ankle

Wolst jolted—another stab winning through his defenses. Ignoring the wound, he surged forward with a growl. "A sting!" He hacked, skewered, slashed, stroke after deadly stroke in a fluid, unstoppable rhythm. "Into the fire with you!" Blood poured down his blade, soaking his fists red.

But more jolts came. More grunts of pain. Scarborn spears were finding their way past Wolst's guard with regularity. Ishoa felt him slowing, sensed the strength draining from him. Blood streaked down his legs. His boots made a squelching sound.

They're killing him.

Then it was over and they stepped out onto even ground as the last of the Scarborn spun to the floor without the top of his head. Wolst sucked ragged breaths as he flopped a shoulder against the wall. "Stay...behind me...Isha." His eyes lolled lazily. "Make for...the gate."

"I don't want to leave you." Her voice quavered.

A Scarborn sprinted toward them. "No choice!" With effort, Wolst heaved off the wall. "I'll stay with you as long as I can." He feinted, leaned to one side—ax whistling past to spark against stone—then he ran the man through.

Ishoa hurried along the wall behind her uncle to an intersecting corridor where a Scarborn woman with red braids stumbled into them. Wolst bashed in her face with the pommel of a sword and a pitcher sized fist.

They sprinted down the corridor, then slowed.

Wolst cursed.

Ularis Warnock filed into the hall behind a half-dozen Scarborn. Their escape was blocked. Ishoa's stomach churned. She glanced at Wolst then at Rakeema who'd calmed some.

"Follow me, Isha! Don't stop!"

Seeing that the Beast of Anjuhkar rushed headlong toward them, the Scarborn frantically took up position, spears couched between hips and hands. Two crossbows drew a bead. Wolst bounded ahead. "Don't stop!"

With Rakeema locked in her arms, Ishoa sprinted for the exit leading out to the bailey. Her uncle would reach them before her. A crossbow twanged, its bolt striking the wall to one side. A fragment ricocheted, cutting her cheek.

"Not her, fool!" hissed Ularis. "The Beast!"

"Scarborn tinder!" Wolst closed with them. "Into the fire!"

He bulled into their left flank with reckless abandon. Ishoa angled to that side, skirting the wall. Wolst's dull broadswords rang against shield, chain, and spear as he wrought havoc in their ranks. Single-handedly, he corralled them to one side of the hall. Such was the ferocity of the Beast of Anjuhkar.

Whatever happens, keep your feet moving forward. Don't stop for anything.

Ishoa sprinted into the gap just as the second crossbow found its mark. A bolt sprouted from her uncle's chest as she ran by. She cried out then a hand snatched her by the hood of her cloak. She choked and was nearly jerked her off her feet. She rounded, found Ularis Warnock's scarred face. A lewd smile hooked his mouth. "Princess, you—"

Wolst burst through the line of Scarborn and leapt toward their leader, a spear buried in his back. "Tinder!"

He laid out, broadsword humming through the air.

Ishoa felt a warm spray across her face. Ularis's hand fell to the floor. His smile melted into open-mouthed shock as he stared at the spurting stump where his hand should be. He screamed.

Whatever happens, keep your feet moving forward.

Ishoa ran. The last she saw of her uncle Wolst was a smile full of blood. His grunts of death trailed her out the door and into the sunlit chaos beyond.

Tears streamed down her cheeks. *Wolst, Othwii, grandmother, Arick... Lodaris.* Numbness hollowed out her limbs.

She was destined to die as she'd lived.

Utterly alone.

She drew up her hood and hurried toward the Gate of the Tiger. The defenders were hard pressed and wouldn't hold long. By the time Ishoa reached them, the Scarborn would possess the gate. Then her uncle's last hope for her escape would be gone.

She walked toward it anyway.

She stayed in motion to stay ahead of her emotions. Everything in her wanted to collapse into the snow, to lie there until capture. They would execute her...but maybe that wasn't such a bad thing. Grandmother, Wolst, Arick, Othwii, Lodaris...everyone who mattered was dead. Her parents too waited for her.

Low back burning from lugging Rakeema, she shambled onward. The anjuhtarg panted in the blanket. She'd given up squirming minutes ago.

Most of the fighting appeared to have migrated to the last holdouts at the ramp and the Gate of the Tiger. Her chances of passing through undetected were scant.

Do I even want to live? came the question.

It doesn't matter, because you won't, came the answer.

As she neared the Gate of the Tiger, a familiar face assaulted her vision. She stopped. Lodecka Warnock directed Scarborn forces from the back of a horse.

Ishoa altered course. The scabbard holding her darksteel blade hung heavy at her hip. A comfort. A final chance to right at least one grievous wrong.

She deserves to die.

The Scarborn matriarch stared impassively in the direction of the gate. Mercenaries swathed in black leather and bearing the scarlet droplets of the Fringes rushed to their leader's side, one after another. Lodecka nodded or gave a brief command to send them on their way. A trio of mercenaries guarded her. Ishoa doubted they'd be wary of a young girl, but they also wouldn't ignore her. If given a chance, Lodecka would recognize her instantly.

Ishoa chewed her lip. Escape was a dwindling dream, barely better than her chance of slaying Lodecka. But survival was nothing without someone to survive for.

The gutted barracks still blazed. Tongues of fire pulled down sections of its blackened skeleton. Trampled, muddy grass formed a halo around the charred structure. The roof had collapsed. Hundreds of corpses had been left to smolder.

Ishoa's lips pressed into a hard line. Such sights made the choice far easier. She unsheathed her sword. Rakeema tensed. "Sorry girl. Shhhh."

Ishoa's heart hammered for vengeance. Rakeema could feel it. Of that she was sure.

Fifty strides off, Lodecka flicked the reins of her horse. It sprang into a measured trot, guards close behind.

Ishoa made to run after, but a hand clamped around her mouth from behind. A dagger lay sharp against her throat. "You're coming with me, Princess." Ishoa cursed and struggled, but the hand around her mouth was iron tight. The dagger cut into her neck, drawing blood. Then it slid down, poised at the nape of Rakeema's neck. "Or I kill your anjuhtarg first."

CHAPTER FIFTY-FOUR

MUD AND STEEL

T hin sheets of rain swept the streets of Digtown, turning them into a slurry. The normal stream of activity on the main thoroughfare had waned to a hurried trickle.

The people of Digtown know the smell of violence.

Denizens of the slums sauntered across their path, shirtless and grimy. A handful of common folk shot wary looks their way. It was enough to tell Barodane what waited for them at road's end.

No need to rush.

They lacked the element of surprise and faced superior numbers. It would do little but kill them faster to rush headlong into an ambush. So they proceeded with caution, surveying the stoops, alleys, eaves, and windows of every building they passed.

The cooper nodded to the man he thought to be Kord but avoided eye contact with Garlenna. Their horse's hooves slapped at the mud to the beat of a slow drum.

A bucket hung over the town well, clinking and creaking in the wind, twisting gently on a rope. Barodane recalled a jail on fire...a sign reading "Crown Justice," plummeting to the ground. Fourteen years ago, the Mad Prince had come to burn a town and kill its people.

Now he went to stop the same.

How fate's knife does twist.

In the distance, a row of figures waited in the street. Their intentions were no mystery.

The wooden icon of the Sempyrean jabbed at an overcast sky from where it perched atop the chapel. Four arrows representing Srah, Maletha, Ozoi, and Payon reached upward while a fifth pointed down. The last belonged to Nacronus, the Taker of Light, Scion of the Abyssal Sea, Lord of the Eternal Maw. By day's end, more than a few souls would meet the dark god's cold embrace.

The sun peeked from behind a bank of rainclouds, then disappeared as quick as it came. Wisps of shadow from cloud cover wormed across the mud and the rain was more air than water.

Two hundred strides from the Gem Loft, they brought their horses to a stop.

Arrayed in a line were four mounted men and a spare horse, as well as a footman with a bear hound at his heels. Hyram was the only one in plate armor. Besides Eustus and the footman, the rest bore the bronze honor plates of Breckenbright holdguard. Gray cloaks descended over their horse's flanks. Hammers and small round shields filled their hands.

The towering Eustus wore homespun trousers, boiled leather, and a dark cloak pinned around his lanky frame. Drab but for the polished steel blade Barodane knew rested in the scabbard at his hip.

Barodane took their measure. Garlenna's stallion flicked its mane. Leather creaked as the mason with long braids shifted in the saddle. Digtown residents watched from their windows. Those far drunker than the rest stood at the edge of the street, staring from under brooding brows.

"So..." Squeezed into a silk dress of forest green, Imralta stood in the stoop of the Gem Loft, arms crossed, chin held high. "They're here now. Are you going to—"

"Be silent, whore," Hyram said.

Imralta's upper lip curled back, icy rage flashing across her face. After a moment of staring death into Hyram's back, she locked eyes with Barodane, then tipped her crown at a pale-faced Lyansorca sitting in front of Eustus in the saddle.

The urge to blame burned in Barodane's chest. Lyansorca had led the masons to his supply and caused Meckin's murder. But it cooled once he remembered it was his own fault for acting too late. When he noticed how much she'd been through, not a scrap of blame remained.

Shoulders sagging, the whore turned spy looked exhausted. Dark circles clung beneath her eyes. Dozens of fingertip-shaped bruises ran the lengths of her arms where men had held her fast to brutally use her. Her tattered shift sloughed off one shoulder, revealing bite marks and red lines along her neck, likely from strangulation.

The abuse Lyansorca had gone through was no one's fault but Barodane's. The deaths of Jennim and Meckin too. And more might die still because of his pride. Lyansorca. Imralta. Garlenna...

Never again.

Lyansorca watched Barodane intently as he ushered his mount across the muddy chasm of violent possibilities. Garlenna followed. The bear hound barked, bullish shoulders convulsing. It's master, a holdguard with a blond bowl-cut silenced it with a single, harsh command.

At a hundred strides, Hyram Olabran's voice made them stop. "Kord." He hiked a thumb over his shoulder at Lyansorca. "I have to say thank you for this little gift. She kept my men occupied for a generous amount of time. So...I've thought about it and decided I'm willing to take her off your hands. Consider it your final gesture of goodwill for the trouble you've caused. In exchange, you and your haggard woman friend there may leave town."

"Haggard?" said Garlenna under her breath.

Hyram leaned over his horse's withers, one side of his face angled toward them as if sharing a secret. "How does that sound?"

"That," declared Imralta, "sounds like a man misunderstanding a situation."

Hyram's nostrils flared. Malice tinged every word as he glanced sidelong back at the stoop. "I thought I told you to shut your mouth."

"You did. And I didn't." Imralta casually strolled down the landing's steps to the muddy street. Her legs were shaky, but Barodane admired her courage. "She's a whore—not a slave. No matter what happens with Kord, you will pay her for whatever she *chooses* to do for you and your men. And then you'll pay me fifty percent of that plus a gold wheel for damaging her."

Hyram laughed. "Greedy old bitch, aren't you? Do you still think this a negotiation?" He snapped his fingers. "Let me be more clear."

Eustus sniffled then cast Lyansroca from the saddle. She landed hard on her head and left arm, crying out in pain as lower body toppled over upper. Barodane flinched.

From within the Gem Loft, a woman shouted, "Fuckers!" Imralta held up a hand, beckoning restraint to those unseen within.

Lyansorca lied whimpering and rocking side to side on her back. Eustus dismounted and stood over her, his dull expression unchanging. Barodane hated the way the man's too-small head sat upon a too-long neck.

Longsword leapt from scabbard at the assassin's hip.

Cradling her arm, Lyansorca emitted a stuttering cry. "It's—br—broken."

Hyram sighed. "Field dressings for the lady, Eustus. We're on a tight schedule, and I've already wasted all my time listening to queen whore ramble on about choices, or slaves, or the morality of whoring, or some such nonsense."

"Stop!" shouted Barodane. "Don't hurt her."

A single line creased Hyram's thick brow. "I'm sorry, Kord, but why are you still here? I said thank you for the gift. I said you could leave. I found your supply, I killed your men, and now I own everything that made you worth a moment of my time. Our deal is done. You're free to take your beast-woman and go." He gestured toward their weapons. "Well, after you lay down your arms of course. We'll be keeping those. From the look of blood spattering your clothes, you've clearly killed some of my men, which means I'll need more weapons to arm the new ones I'll be hiring."

"I challenge you," said Barodane.

Hyram slapped a thigh. "Still such a funny man! Of course I refuse. A truly silly idea. Eustus...if you please."

The rangy assassin snatched a wad of brown curls and hoisted Lyansorca upright to her knees. He laid the edge of his sword against her neck. She went rigid and released a stilted cry. Specks of spit flung from her lips onto the blade. "Please," she begged. "Please…"

"Kord, are you going to make me kill your gift or are you going to lay down your arms like I asked?"

"Go, Kord," said Imralta.

"I can't," he replied.

Imralta fumed. "I will handle it. Just go."

"I've had my share of party guests who don't know when it's time to leave, but really Kord, how many women's heads must I give you before you understand?" Hyram blew Garlenna a kiss. "I know it's just you now. Though it was clever to make me think there were more. Alas, the Sempyrean favors me with superior numbers."

Garlenna spoke low, "Perhaps we should—"

"I'm not leaving," Barodane said in a rush.

"I was going to say charge."

Barodane rolled a shoulder but failed to loosen the tightness there. "If we do, she's dead."

"If we don't, she's dead."

Barodane cursed. *Never again.* He gripped the leather handle of his blade.

Eustus raised his sword, then lowered it, practicing the arc of execution. "Don't move now," he told Lyansorca in nasally monotone. "It'll get messy if you do."

"Go!" shouted Imralta. "Please!"

Blood cascaded through Barodane's ears. His heart beat in his gut.

Eyes closed, Lyansorca chanted, "Please, please, please…"

Help me.

"They killed Meckin," Barodane said.

Imralta stiffened. "What?" her voice was a heavy whisper.

"Last chance." Hyram scratched his nose.

Imralta's jaw trembled. Her hands rose, forming white-knuckled claws.

Hyram looked back, saw the Baroness's rage and laughed.

"Girls!" Imralta screamed. She pointed at the Breckenbright lordling, her mouth shaking with fury. "Kill these bastards!"

The second story windows of the Gem Loft slid open. Crossbows clattered forth onto the sills, held by an array of arms: slender and youthful, heavy with fat, leathery with age, lean muscled…

Their trigger fingers worked as good as any man's.

Hyram's laughter died. His smile dropped.

The first bolt pinned Eustus's hand against his thigh. He stared at it—a moment of horrified awe—then he screamed.

Winches clicked. *Twang!* A half dozen more bolts sped toward their targets in rapid succession. Masons cursed, jerked their horse's reins, wheeled away. Bolts gave a brief, punctuated whistle, then thudded into the mud or sank into upraised shields.

Garlenna spurred forth, mace flourishing. Darksteel drawn, Barodane charged after.

"To me!" shouted Hyram. He drew his sword.

Lyansorca looked back at her wounded assailant, then clambered to her feet. Grimacing, Eustus followed after, blade whipping through the air behind the fleeing whore. The sound of slicing meat filled Barodane's ears. Lyansorca stumbled and fell against the steps of the Gem Loft in a splash of blood. One arm, half-severed, flopped uselessly against the landing at her side.

The bear hound's chest jolted with savage barks. It leapt back from a bolt that punched into the ground an inch from its paw. A second bolt slammed into Eustus's chest, dropping him backward into the mud with a squelch. He keeled over, eyes vacant.

The mason with the blond bowl-cut hid behind his horse, turned it broadside for cover. A bolt zipped into the horse's flank and sent it whirling, bucking, and screaming. A hoof caught the mason in the shoulder and hurled him onto his ass. The bear hound snapped at the horse, trying to corral it to keep its master from harm.

Imralta grabbed the stunned Lyansorca by her tattered shirt and hauled her inside. Blood spurted across the stoop in their wake.

Garlenna closed with Hyram. A bolt hummed overhead, close enough that it nearly struck them both. Hyram came in fast and hard, aiming at her horse. She wheeled her mount with her legs and took the blow on her kite-shield. Splinters flitted through the air like the feathers of a slaughtered hen. From the corner of her eye, Garlenna saw Hyram's blade sweep overhead to deal a deadly cut to her unarmored back as she came around. Garlenna twisted her knees, accelerating the horse's movement, and swung her mace in a backhand arc violent enough to crush a cinder block. With a cry of dismay, Hyram blocked the blow then retreated.

On his way to aid Garlenna against Hyram, Barodane took a charge in the flank from one of the holdguard. The mason's half-helm sat low on his forehead, giving him shadowed pools for eyes. His shoulders were large but soft looking. Muscle gone to fat with age. Streaks of white in the veteran holdguard's dark beard confirmed better days gone by. Their horses collided at the withers and their mounts sped round in a circle. Scab bit a chunk from the other stallion's cheek as their riders pushed and jockeyed for space to strike.

The veteran leaned back and leveled a blow at Scab. Despite a lack of practice, Barodane was quicker than his opponent and caught the hammer with the edge of his sword. Raindrops jumped on impact. Smoke and shadow rippled the length of Barodane's blade.

"For the masonry!" cried the other holdguard from behind. "For Breckenbright!"

Barodane punched the veteran. The impact sent a sharp twinge up his wrist and he spun to face his incoming opponent, clean shaven and younger than the first. Tawny braids flowed behind the mason as his hammer clanged against Barodane's sword.

At the edge of awareness, Barodane heard someone shout, "Gnasher! Heeti!"

Garlenna drove Hyram back. Frustration etched the highborn's face. Beads of milky sweat lined his temples as he hewed at her, neck tendons straining. The prosort absorbed his strikes with stout shield and flicks of her mace. It wouldn't be long before he tired himself out enough for her to—

Clawed feet scrabbled around behind her. A deep growl followed. She opened her guard, swung in a wide arc to drive Hyram back, then wheeled—too slow.

Before she could raise her weapon, the bear hound leapt. A well-trained beast. It snared her arm in its crushing jaws. One side of its mouth clamped around her leather gauntleted wrist, applying bone-crushing force, while the rest of its teeth sank into her unarmored forearm. The grueling pressure sucked the air from her lungs and she was nearly jerked from the saddle.

Her shoulder popped, suffused with a sudden, tingling heat as she bore the bear hound's weight. Through sheer strength alone, she kept her seat.

Seeking to capitalize, Hyram struck out, his face a mask of grinning hate. Garlenna heaved her shield and sent the cut skittering off the banded rim. The bear hound growled and writhed its body like a trout. White spots crowded her vision. The bear hound tore at her arm, sending lacerating agony shotting into her shoulder.

Spotting Garlenna's predicament with the dog in his periphery, Barodane launched a furious attack at the veteran mason. With the advantage of speed, he came straight forward, each stab and slash, fast and tight. The veteran blocked the first few, then surprised Barodane by ducking a cut and at the same time jerking the reins. His horse reared. Shod hooves lashed out, deadening Barodane's thigh where it struck.

The holdguard with braids lunged into striking range, missed, then steered clear. Unlike those Barodane had encountered at the Dreg's, these men were disciplined professionals. Patiently they circled the injured prince, awaiting the right opportunity...

Meanwhile, Garlenna dropped her mace. The dog stared at her, eyes vacant but for one purpose: to hold on and bear her down.

She obliged.

She swung a leg over her destrier's neck. The bear hound dragged her to the ground and immediately sank into its haunches to yank at her. Where it wasn't already numb, her arm burned from the unrelenting pressure and tearing damage.

A short ways off, Hyram struggled to close with her. The bear hound was not the only well-trained animal around. Affording a glance back, Garlenna saw her destrier execute a series of spins, rear hooves punching out at Hyram and his mount. The highborn cursed, wheeled, and disappeared.

Garlenna snagged the folds along the back of the bear hound's head. With a fistful of flesh and fur, she dragged it toward her while jamming her wounded forearm deeper into the dog's maw. Feeling the pinch at the hinge point of its jaw, the bear hound released, then snapped onto her gauntleted hand with a scrape of teeth on metal. The armor bowed under the dog's crushing bite strength, but the skin of her forearm was finally safe.

With a barrier of steel between the hound's teeth and her flesh, she could resist. She worked her way to her feet then sat back into a squat. The bear hound churned backward in the mud, but the prosort had her footing now. A dagger hissed from her boot. She slashed the bear hound's shoulder. It yelped and scurried away, sending wary looks back at her as it ran past Barodane and the two holdguard circling him.

Sweat soaked the Mad Prince's clothing and rain dripped down his nose amid puffs of hot breath.

Chest heaving, lip split, the bearded veteran hacked then spit a pinkish gob. "Throw down your weapon."

"Fuck that." Braids whipping in the wind, the younger mason lurched toward Barodane. "Kill him!"

The one-time prince deflected the holdguard's hammer and backhanded him. The mason's half-helm sprang off his head, blood sprouting from a gash along his brow.

The young holdguard fought to recover, cheeks slathered red from the wound as Barodane wheeled Scab around to face the veteran.

"That sword," the veteran said. He pushed back his half-helm to reveal beady blue eyes. "That sword..."

"This sword!" Barodane surged forth, hacking at the man's face. His blade whistled. High—low—low again. The veteran huffed with effort as he met Barodane's attack with his small shield. He swung a sloppy counterstrike and missed, overextending himself.

Barodane felt the familiar parting of flesh in the added weight to the sword's handle as darksteel ripped uncontested down the man's side. The bearded veteran shrieked, his wound a memory of sickly pressure against Barodane's palm.

The mason dropped the reins and fled down the street, slouched in the saddle.

Barodane spun about in time to watch a hammer pass within an inch of his nose. The mason came at him, blood filling his twisted smile. "Now I'm pissed."

Hammer and sword rang. When they disengaged a moment later, Barodane led Scab into the man's blood-blind eye. The mason tried blinking away the mess on his face, but when that didn't work, he wiped it, smearing it around and making it worse. With a cry of frustration, Braids lashed out blindly. Barodane slipped the onslaught with ease and parried. His blade slid into the man's side and scraped a rib halfway in.

The mason whimpered as Barodane yanked his sword free. The force of the motion dragged the man from his saddle, down into mud and death below.

Braids splayed out. Body twitching.

Horse hooves pounded close—

Barodane twisted around. Hyram almost upon him. He deflected the first blow and it sent shock rattling up his arm. The highborn had the famed strength of an Olabran alright.

"Kord!" he shouted. Swords met, jarring Barodane's teeth. He cursed, pulled Scab's reins, and backed up hoping to create some much needed space. But Hyram was an equal horseman. Barodane gave him that. The bull-necked man cleaved at the former prince's defenses with mighty two-handed strokes as he steered his warhorse with his thighs.

He hammered at Barodane, spittle flying from thick lips. "Your muddy fucking kingdom. Your fucking godsthorn. Your fucking Gem Loft and your whores. It's going to be mine!" Hyram stood in the stirrups, sword poised to deliver a vicious downward blow.

Barodane caught it, outstretched arm forced slowly back until the crossguard of his own sword was an inch from his face. Scab stumbled sideways as Barodane was nearly bent over backward. He was a strong push from tumbling out of the saddle.

"Your head too!" Hyram Olabran twisted away instead, winding up for the killing blow. "Mine!"

Garlenna rode by at a gallop, mace whipping out as she passed the incensed Hyram. The strike caught him in the side, crippling the armor inward. His face bulged as the air went out of him in a wheezing gush. Veins marbled blotchy flesh. He looked ready to vomit. His sword arm lifted slightly...then the hilt slipped from his grasp. He loosed a harrowing yowl and reached for his crushed side.

Barodane drew up alongside the man. The young lord of Breckenbright gawked, face purpling, fat lips quivering. "The only thing you'll have is my blade in your chest. This is for Jennim and Meckin...and everyone else who's had to suffer you."

Hyram watched with bloodshot eyes, his upper body folded protectively over his side. White spit formed at the corners of his mouth. Barodane jammed his sword into the man at the collarbone. Darksteel scraped as it punched through inferior armor. Glistening blood quickly filled the rent.

Hyram grabbed feebly for the blade. Barodane withdrew it, and the man toppled.

Garlenna trotted over. "No one calls me haggard." One arm was cradled in her lap holding the reins, and a dark wetness soaked it to the elbow. "But I am a beast of a woman."

"Thanks," Barodane said. Any feeling of victory faded when he surveyed the bloodied street. The veteran had vanished, as had the bear hound. The horse that had taken the bolt in its flank lay in the mud breathing heavily. The stoop of the Gem Loft was drenched in scarlet. "Lyansorca," he snapped the reins.

"Wait." Garlenna grabbed his arm. "There was another." She craned her head, listening to something. "The bear hound's master."

Cries of alarm issued from the Gem Loft. A man's inchoate shouting. Then a series of barks.

They rode up to the Gem Loft entrance, dismounted, and hurried inside.

Madame Gratha pointed up the stairs. Weapons drawn, they ascended. A man's harsh voice filtered through the whorehouse. Behind them, Madame Gratha huffed and motioned for them to go faster with an upward sweep of palms.

At the top of the staircase, a woman lay face down, red tangles of hair spilling across the floorboards. A crossbow lay within arm's reach. Down the hall, two women stood outside the open door to Imralta's room. One pointed a crossbow within while the other held a rusty knife. An errant bolt was embedded in the door frame.

"I walk free or Gnasher eats Queen Whore!"

The woman with the rusty knife screamed, "You ain't leaving this room alive!"

"You'll change your tune when I take her first finger. You've got between now and twenty seconds to get out of the room and get me a horse saddled. Here, let me show you—"

A scream—Imralta's.

Not wanting to startle the whores and get shot, Barodane announced himself when the scream subsided. The crossbow woman whirled about quicker than a jousting quintain, but managed not to shoot. She withdrew a step, allowing prince and prosort entry.

Imralta clutched a bloodied hand to her bosom. Dark stains spread over her green dress. The man with the bowl-cut gripped the back of her neck and held a knife to her throat. Standing guard in front of master and captive, the broad-chested bear hound, Gnasher, growled at a pair of whores brandishing daggers.

"Pick it up," said the houndmaster. Sobbing, Imralta bent to retrieve her blood-soaked finger from the floor. "Gnasher."

The bear hound whirled.

"Sit. Now toss it."

With a pale grimace, Imralta complied. Gnasher hopped, caught the finger, and choked it down greedily.

The mason laughed. "Good boy. You'll eat well if these whores don't get my fucking horse. Oh—" He peeked over Imratlta's shoulder and noticed Barodane and Garlenna had slid into the room. He shifted from foot to foot, hunkering behind the mutilated madame. Despite holding the stump where her finger once was, Imratla stood as straight as ever.

"Where's Hyram?" The tough tone the mason had taken with the whores vanished.

"Dead," said Barodane. "The others too."

The man let out an exasperated breath. His voice wavered. "I figured that since you're here and they aren't. But that doesn't matter now. Gnasher and I are leaving. Everyone get out. You included, or Queen Whore never grips cock again." To emphasize his point, he grabbed her bloody hand and brought it up to the knife at her throat.

"Drop the weapon now and you live." Garlenna's tone demanded concession. Certain. Clear. She was still every bit the commander of bygone days. "Harm her again and die. The choice is yours." The room tightened around her words. "You have twenty seconds."

"Why should I believe a couple of drug dealers giving words of promise? Fuck you. I'll give Gnasher your skull as a piss pot if you don't leave."

Garlenna gathered her cloak around her wounded wrist as she stepped forward. "You have no other option. After what you've done, these whores aren't letting you leave here alive."

"Fucking bastard killed Ruby!"

"She tried to shoot me," the mason yelled back. "Your one eye blinds you, woman. Here's what I see. Gnasher is gonna attack anyone who fucks with me. And until my way out is secure, I keep practicing my whittling skills on Queen Whore's cock hand."

"You have ten seconds! Put down your weapon," Garlenna said. "There's no place to go. If you surrender, I'll ensure you live. You've no other option. All you can do is—"

"Lies," he said. "I'm giving *you* five seconds to leave." Gnasher's crocodilian head sank between its shoulders. A paw padded forward.

"Last chance." Garlenna stared at the bear hound and adjusted the collar of her cloak. "You have three—"

"Heeti!"

Gnasher lunged. Instead of retreating, Garlenna stepped at the bear hound, removing her cloak and casting it into the animal's face in one fluid motion.

With both hands, Imralta grabbed the mason's wrist and hauled downward, angling her body out of the way as she did. For her trouble, she received a shallow cut from chest to shoulder during the fall. Whores closed in on either side of the houndmaster, knives jabbing the air.

Garlenna brought her mace down on the bear hound's hindquarters as it thrashed to win free of her cloak. Her next blow sundered a floorboard as the dog slipped clear of the makeshift net and whirled about, its rear leg hobbled.

Barodane skirted the dog, stepped past a whore, and squared up with the mason.

The houndmaster flipped his knife into a reverse grip and unslung a hammer from his belt loop. "Come on then." He feinted with the knife, came around with the hammer. Barodane stepped back—countered. The mason deflected Barodane's thrust, then brought his hammer in an upward arc. Darksteel snaked out and licked the man's hand.

"Gah!"

The houndmaster grit his teeth and drove at Barodane. Knife sparked against sword, hammer following with a clang. A narrow gap of vulnerability opened in the mason's defenses. Room enough for Barodane's blade to spit his heart. The mason made a face like he was about to sneeze, tongue fat in his mouth, eyes and nose scrunched.

Blood flowed from the mason's mouth and over his chin. He hung rigid a moment then dropped straight forward like felled timber.

Meanwhile, Gnasher barked and scampered forth, drool trailing, jaws snapping. Garlenna swung—missed. The dog ducked and retreated a step. A sneaky whore at the bear hound's flank stomped the floor. It snapped at the sound.

Garlenna's opening.

A resounding crack accompanied the blow she dealt it on the skull from behind. The bear hound wobbled but spun back around, blinking and snarling as it jumped.

Garlenna swatted it from the air with her mace. A tooth bounced off the floorboards as the dog crashed into a corner. If bear hound lore was true, once its master had been slain Gnasher would never cease attacking.

Only death could stop it. She understood the sentiment better than most.

She followed the dog to the ground, dagger drawn.

A few furious moments later, Garlenna sat astride the dead bear hound caked in sweat, her arm burning from the deadly struggle. She chucked her knife across the room and then sat back against the wall. "Assholes..." she said through heaving breaths. "Made me...kill a dog."

"That they did." Barodane reached down a hand to help her up, but she refused. Too tired to rise. "For what it's worth, I think the horses all lived. Even the one with the bloodied flank looked okay when we rode past."

Garlenna nodded, chin drooping to her chest, lank hair covering her eye. She called to a nearby whore. "Is Lyansorca okay?"

The girl shook her head.

CHAPTER FIFTY-FIVE

THE JEWELED EYE

Akyris woke with a start. Something banged against the wall of the cottage. He sat bolt upright. Heart pounding, ears buzzing with the sudden demand of alertness, he froze and listened intently. His knife wasn't far. He waited—two aching seconds.

No screams.

He inhaled deep...exhaled...inhaled. Calm washed over him. Slow, as if moving moved underwater, he grabbed the knife from his cot.

Crickets saturated the night with their chirping. Through it he heard the strain of a pleading voice.

Grandmother?

He craned his head in the direction of the sound. Just outside. Heavy sobs. His mother wailed. He flinched. He'd never seen or heard her shed a single tear.

Something horrible has happened.

Against his better judgment, Akyris crept quietly from his room to the front door. A cool breeze swam through its partial opening. He placed his ear at the gap.

His mother's weeping brimmed with fury and agony that pounded at his guts and boiled his heart. Even in the lulls of silence, there was no relief. They were quiet valleys where violent suffering brewed. The bottoms of climbing heaves of emotion. Like a bow being pulled to strain before it's fired.

"Come here," said Locastrii.

Cloth slid over cloth. There came a thud as one of the women flopped against the outside of the cottage. "Don't touch me!"

Icy fingers of fear gripped Akyris's spine. *Mother hates her.*

To Akyris, their relationship always seemed a distant thing. There were glimmers of care for one another, but overall he sensed pressure in their dynamic.

"I'm sorry, Tyne. Just know that...I am *so* sorry."

Mismatched footsteps tromped through the dirt. Stamp—clomp. Stamp—clomp. Grandmother came into view a second later as she made her way to the front porch. Moonlight cast a silver glaze over her face, mired by heavy wrinkles.

Ridden with shame. The bags under her eyes were swollen, red-rimmed, and raw. It was clear she'd rubbed away her own share of tears.

Akyris flinched as mother flew up behind Locastrii, finger skewering her with blame. From nostril to lip, snot glistened in a viscous strand. Her hair was tangled. Her eyes wild. "I want you gone! I don't care if there are a thousand bandits on the Prince's Highway—you leave tonight."

Grandmother turned, eyes traveling the length of a finger leveled mere inches from her nose.

Mother spoke the last in a deadly whisper. "You won't have him too."

Locastrii took her hand. Mother tried to jerk it free but was drawn into an embrace instead. Once there, she gave up the fight and sobbed into Grandmother's shoulder.

"I'll go," Locastrii said. "I'll go."

What happened? It felt like Akyris should be angry about whatever his grandmother had done, but the last thing he wanted was for her to leave. He licked his lip in a way similar to Locastrii.

His mother wailed. She looked exhausted and brittle. Locastrii rocked her from foot to foot where they stood in the dirt lane. When it seemed safe enough to reveal himself, Akyris pushed open the door.

"Mom, are you okay? What's happening?"

Mother shoved herself out of Locastrii's embrace. She turned to Akyris, her face stretched into a mask of horror. Frowning, he stepped back. *Am I the cause?*

She waved him over, arms outstretched, tears welling under moonlight. She hugged him so tight it hurt his neck. With a shrug of discomfort, he pushed back to look her in the eyes. "Tell me what's happening. Did I do—"

Shaking her head, she submerged him in her arms once more. "Nothing you did, love." In a chilly tone, she added, "But your grandmother is no longer welcome here. She's leaving. Immediately."

When he searched Locastrii's eyes, he was certain he'd see defiance there. A rebuke of his mother's words. Anything to tell him she wasn't guilty of whatever Mother blamed her for.

A bottomless sadness lined her face. A quivering lip and downcast gaze admitted her guilt. She cleared her throat, lips puckering as she chewed on her words. Words that clogged her. Words she couldn't dislodge.

Finally, she nodded, and hobbled toward the cottage. "I'll gather my things."

Mother straightened, shoulder blades pinned back. Her words lashed the old woman as she went. "Faster would be better...if you can manage."

Locastrii labored up the steps, the butt of her staff clattering against each board.

"I'm going with her," Akyris said.

"No, you are not!"

Akyris struggled from his mother's grasp. "I don't know what's going on between you two...and I don't care."

In retrospect, he thought the words "don't care" wounded his mother most. Or maybe it was the sentiment of sides taken before there was understanding. Whichever it was, he never finished the thought. His mother emitted a single gasp as if stabbed through the heart and then fled out of sight down the lane.

"Oh, Akyris...Akyris, my boy. Little do you know how much salt you've just added to a very open wound." Behind him, Locastrii sucked in a breath and leaned against the open doorway. "It's not your fault though. She'll forgive you in time. You're just a boy—her boy. But me..." She shrugged then sighed. "Your mother hates me. Rightly so."

"Is it because you lied to her?" The accidental hurt he'd caused his mother filled him with tingling shame. His voice cracked. "Like you lie to me."

Her head jerked his direction.

"I'm no boy. You said it yourself. I'm the youngest person in history to stand in the River alone. I'm sick of being kept in the dark. Now tell me what you did to—"

"You *are* a boy!" Locastrii's eyes were as hard as stone. "A little bird squawking after the truth. Look at you now. *Demanding* it. Pha! Trust me when I tell you that you do not wish to meet such monsters. There are truths in this world that'll eat you alive, boy, and if you think you deserve to know them because you did one impressive thing, it only proves you to be a feckless, impulsive brat. You think life owes you something because you have no father?" Grandmother drew back at her own words and grimaced at the moon, half hidden behind a bank of clouds.

Akyris's shoulders sagged. "It's not fair."

Locastrii's voice fell low, her tone urgent. "I'm sorry. You have no father, but you have something far better. You have a mother enough to replace a sea of such cowardly men. This is what I mean, boy. This is exactly why you're not ready for the truth. You've got to let go of these childish delusions. Fair? Drivel and rot! But who you are right now is being created. Moment by moment. Step by painstaking step. The path of an Awakened lies ahead of you, but you'll never have it if you keep fighting for what's already behind you. Ideas like "fair" and what you think you deserve will only hold you back. They'll drag you into emptiness. Damn it, Akyris, you can be an Awakened! It's time to let go of the story you were born into. You're not unworthy. You're not unloved. You're not unlucky. You are lucky! The power you hold within..." She slapped her thigh. "Damned lucky!"

"And your mother." A tear trembled on her wrinkle puckered chin. "The sacrifices she's made..." Locastrii paused, head dipping, tongue darting across her lower lip.

Akyris managed a calm whisper, "What sacrifices?"

"Forget it." She waved a hand dismissively. "You're not ready. Still just a bird with hollow bones. You were never meant to know."

With a curse, Akyris turned away to go find his mother, but hesitated. He squeezed his eyes shut and took a breath. *I see more than you think.*

He let the River course through him...

Gentle ripples, meandering and warm, threaded him from toe to crown. Sima. The elm tree. His connection to mother and grandmother. All of them tugged at the center of his being. Colder and more distant strands intertwined with the pleasant ones to form a braid of everything present. The absence of a father. Sima's stinging palm. His many failures in the River... All of it flowed into him. A thousand experiences, finding their home. A thousand bits of life leaving a groove as they passed beyond the borders of his vessel. A thousand eyes blinking in concert. Past, present, future. Unification observed. Every facet of himself. Every angle of his life. He saw it now. The web that formed him worked in concert with all others.

The jeweled eye opened...

He saw their webs too. Mother. Grandmother. Sima. They chose what they must—what they could. Right or wrong, it made no difference.

The memory of the dream where he'd flown came to him. So real. The screams of dying horses. The shambling voar dragging steel rods. The terrifying speed of the striking raek. The fountain of blood from Acramis's chest. The Mad Prince rising from the river's surf—alive.

Another source of energy snaked toward him from somewhere unknown. This time, Akyris denied it. He drew his Locus into a cocoon. The probing energy source dissipated against his defenses.

"You see that I'm ready." He turned on his heels, eyes fluttering open. Locastrii studied him. "Yet you keep secrets from me? How can I be Awakened if you believe me too weak to bear them?"

"Because." She bundled her shawl tight at the throat. "It could destroy you."

An image of a man swathed in shadow holding a sword flashed across his mind. He inhaled sharply and looked down. Two and a half feet of steel, smoke, and ash jutted from his chest.

The jeweled eye closed. He tried to bring it back but couldn't.

He loosed a frustrated growl. As soon as his guard was down, the River had lashed him with its mystery. His momentary confusion and fear had caused him to lose control and expose himself to attack. Glancing at Locastrii, he noted the wry smile twisting a corner of her mouth. *It was her. She tests me.*

Akyris tapped into his Locus, barring further assault. "If I'm to choose my Path, I deserve to know where it leads, and where it ends. Let me be destroyed. Let me drown. Let me die. But don't lie to me. Not anymore." He raised his chin. "I know something important is happening...and I know it was you who sent me the dream about the Mad Prince. If you really believe in me as much as you claim, you'll tell me why. Right now."

"Maybe your bones aren't so hollow." Though she looked weary, a smug laugh escaped her. "You're right. I apologize for keeping you in the dark. I apologize for many things this night. A night of many regrets. You have shown restraint. You've kept focus and strength in the face of unknown turmoil. I'd say you've earned the truth." Easing herself down onto the lip of the porch, she patted the spot beside her. "Have a seat."

They sat in the moonlit dark, letting the chirrups of crickets and frogs wash over them. In the distance, an owl gave a warning call to something crossing into its territory.

Without turning, Locastrii said, "Your brother is dead."

"What?" Akyris frowned. "I—I don't have a brother."

"You did, actually." Her tone was matter-of-fact. "And now he's dead. Drowned in a barrel of wine northwest of here."

"But I don't—"

"Listen. You didn't have a grandmother a few months ago either, did you? Now is not the time to be thick. I'm telling you the truth just like you wanted. Question it on your own time."

Tension dragged his chin to his chest, lips parted. *The sacrifice she has made.* The words suddenly made sense. "Oh."

My brother...is dead. Mother's son.

Locastrii placed a hand on Akyris's back. "His name was Jennim. He fell into troubled times and was forced into a difficult situation by dangerous people."

Akyris's face screwed up, palms held skyward on his thighs. "But why—why wasn't he with us?"

"That was my fault." Locastrii gazed into the distance. The direction her daughter had gone. "After your mother had Jennim, pieces of her future kept coming to me without my calling. What's known as an entanglement."

"That's what I saw!" Akyris jumped from the porch. "In the River's depths, that was an entanglement, wasn't it?" A sick feeling entered his stomach as fragments of memory collided with what he now knew of his brother's death. Chills prickled the hair on his arms. *I nearly witnessed it happening...*

Locastrii nodded. "Thankfully, I stopped you from seeing it fully. It would have haunted you for the rest of your life. Just like Tyne's future haunted me. I saw what needed to be done and told her as much."

There was a long silence. When it appeared Locastrii would speak no more, Akyris asked, "What did you tell her to do?"

"Live in a misery-soaked town for a handful of years. Move to Breckenbright and give Jennim up to an orphanage. Never see him again. You know, normal parental advice."

The pain of her transgressions poured into a laugh. It was not shared.

"How could you do that?" Akyris sneered.

"Wrong question." Locastrii wagged a finger. "Why would your mother do it?"

He watched her like a deer spotting a wolf as he considered her words. *There's only one explanation as to why someone would give up their child.* "You threatened her. Or Jennim. Just like you threatened Sima! You said you'd kill her. You're..." he gulped, wondering if he was safe. "Evil."

With both hands wrapped around her staff, Locastrii slammed the butt of it into the dirt. "Evil!" A loose fold of skin beneath her chin wobbled. "I'll show you evil."

Gray light poured from her eyes as if a white-hot blade was quenched by cold water in her skull. More tendrils wound upward from her shoulders. The jewel hanging round her neck flickered then glowed in steady brilliance.

Akyris shielded his eyes thinking she meant to kill him. He retreated into his Locus and made ready.

But no attack came.

A flash of light. Then an emptiness of being. He yelped as his Locus was seized, his consciousness dragged from his body into darkness. At first he thought his grandmother *had* killed him. But the familiar rush of incorporeal weight pressing in on all sides told him they traveled through the Veil. Locastrii's voice echoed in his mind. "I will show you *why* your mother listened to me. Why you train. Why you will listen to me."

They ripped through the Veil separating the River's surface and its depths, faster than ever before. So fast that Akyris worried Locastrii might lose him. But her grip was stronger than the roots of an oak tree and they went faster still.

Normally reaching the River's depths took less than what felt like a couple of minutes. This time they plunged for far longer. Spinning, winding, energy inverting and folding like they were mere wisps of roiling smoke, or waves being swallowed back into the sea.

Disorientation.

A blurring of what was Akyris and what was everything else.

Borderless nothingness leeching at him...

The edges of his being disintegrating.

She's so powerful.

Just as he thought himself lost, they were birthed into a different reality. Blinding light stabbed his eyes. He fell forward onto...something...

Something and nothing. It felt like the River's depths, and yet it wasn't. They hovered fifteen feet in the air above the earth and it shifted beneath him.

He heard the seething mass before he registered what it was.

A sea of people. He stood above it, feet planted on a solid and invisible plane. The smell of the gathered crowd nearly knocked Akyris back to his knees. Beside him, Grandmother watched placidly with the slightest tension to her jaw. "You wanted to know why, Akyris? This is why. You think being a fatherless boy in a small town is the worst thing in the world? Look before you at a fatherless nation. I forced my daughter to abandon one child and that makes me evil." She scoffed, voice trembling with rage. "What if it stops a hundred thousand children from being abandoned when their parents march off to war? A million more from certain death! You want to know the truth? What evil truly looks like? Look with your own damn eyes!" She swept out her arms.

They were in a narrow canyon. Layers of ruddy, tan, and pastel green rock hemmed them in on either side. At roughly fifty feet, the sheer walls leveled out onto even ground. A score of caves pitted the canyon walls, smooth-lipped entrances filled to brimming with onlookers. Many of those huddled and teeming within appeared to be starving, skin sucked tightly to the bone underneath. Shoeless, shirtless, and sporting naught but loin cloths, Akyris saw every fibrous shred of them. Every sinew and striation.

Humanity and dignity withering away.

But for every hundred of the impoverished, a noble shuffled among them. Akyris found it odd that they didn't require a special space or adhere to any kind of separation by status. The wealthy stood shoulder-to-shoulder with the starved and sickly. Most of the rich wore masks depicting a hissing viper in beaten brass and silk scarves covering their heads.

Akyris frowned and squinted. The gathered throng looked subtly different than Namorites. Their cheek bones were higher, like his own. Their eyes slightly narrower. Most were caramel-skinned like a Kanian, but some were pale. There were no redheads and scant blondes. Something about these people was familiar. Like he should know who they were. He glanced upward. Waves of heat shimmered across the drooping sun. Dusk. A hot one.

Not autumn in Namarr.

A glint of steel caught his eye. Posted at either end of the seething mass of humans were scores of soldiers. Like the rich, they too wore face coverings. These in the form of slitted great helms. Axes were couched atop their shoulders, crescent blades facing the sky. Despite the heat, they wore heavy plate and the white and gold tabards of...

Scothea.

A melodious voice melted the noise of the canyon. Wormed over it like a warm wind. "Life is suffering."

Akyris's attention snapped to the mouth of the canyon. A path rose at an incline for hundreds of feet until it came to a choke-point nearly at ground level. The only space where people didn't occupy for as far as Akyris could see was in a concentric circle around a lone boy sitting cross-legged in the dust. Soldiers stood guard in shining ranks behind him atop the canyon walls. Their shadows stretched over the crowd.

The boy's voice pattered gently through the gorge, a comforting chime.

"We all know this. And still we cling to our suffering. We seek it at every turn. Beg it to give us what is deserved. This is the same thinking of those in power. Of those who make you starve. They are not the most skilled, the most capable, the most deserving of their riches or their station. They are not the most anything." The boy's index finger shot upward. "Except the most greedy."

At this, many in the crowd laughed.

The boy smiled then blinked—peacefully slow. "To lust. To desire. To covet what is not yours. To be jealous of those who are not you. To wish to be anywhere other than where you are...that's what it is to lead a normal life. But you do not wish this normal life, do you? You wish for one without such pain. Without suffering."

Most nodded in vehement agreement.

"Then you cannot be like the rich who slowly kill you. Who eat you with their greed. If you are to have true bliss, you must deny the very same things they covet. You must forfeit even the idea of them. If you don't, you will carry your suffering like a carcass on your back into the Final Song. For those who are rich among us, you know better than any the taint of guilt and bitter evil that grows inside you when you possess the means of life denied to so many others."

Those few wearing lavish clothing and viper masks nodded knowingly as the boy continued. "All of you, rich and poor alike, those who bear the blade and those who fall beneath it, you are like hungry mesa wolves with their legs in a trap. If you are to be free, you must gnaw away that which burdens you. Even when it cripples you to do so! Your freedom is worth more!"

Akyris's mouth fell open. He recognized the shirtless boy. Knew him all too well. *It's just a coincidence. Nothing more.*

"For those who wish to be free today—approach. Whatever you choose to release, consider it a blessing given unto yourself, for you have chosen it. You have chosen to unburden your soul. You have chosen true freedom and you will sing the Final Song!"

The throng seethed forward, eager and silent. Soldiers managed the crowd as they gathered before the concentric circle of emptiness, and then trickled past the boy. Most fell to their knees when they were nearest to him and profusely kissed the dirt, rising moments later with dust-caked lips and tear-streaked cheeks.

The rich cascaded riches, relieving themselves of bags of gold, rings, and assorted jewels. The majority of the crowd could have lived off a single donated trinket for years, but none dared touch them. The boy didn't even look at the heaps of wealth.

Instead, he stared with a countenance of pure calm into the faces of the nobles or poor folk laying down their burdens. Under his captivating stare, they wept, unable to match the boy's intensity for more than a moment, then strode away, arms outstretched, face lifted, as if released from prison. Some screamed in ecstasy.

Other items fell into the rising piles: charcoal stylus, bones of a loved one, clothing. To Akyris's horror, a few parents thrust their children into the circle, most younger than the boy at its center. They plopped to the dusty earth, stone-faced as their parents left them.

"This is why I train you, Akyris. I need you. The world needs you. His name is Siddaia. His followers call him the Arrow of Light. As you see, his power and influence grow quickly. He's the most dangerous Awakened alive, and his very existence puts reality itself on course with annihilation." Locastrii inhaled slowly. "We must stop him at any cost. More specifically, *you* must stop him."

"Why me?"

I'm just a boy...

Wind whipped through the canyon, kicking up ruddy dust into the faces of the crowd. Grandmother and grandson hovered a hundred strides from the Arrow of Light.

Akyris searched Siddaia's eyes, irises so dark he thought them black. It was the only difference he could find. Everything else was exactly the same.

"Why..." Akyris swallowed a hard lump in his throat. "Why does he look just like me?"

"Don't you see, Akyris?" Locastrii turned to him. "He is you."

Suddenly, Siddaia perked up. The prophet sniffed the air, a gentle crease in his strong brow. A mirror to Akyris's own.

The Arrow of Light's face drifted upward—then locked on Akyris. Dark eyes met green. Akyris brought fingertips to the side of his face and stroked a cheek as he stared. *It can't be.*

The briefest flutter of recognition crossed Siddaia's expression.

"We've lingered too long." Locastrii grabbed Akyris's shoulder. The Arrow of Light stood as he continued staring at Akyris. "We must go."

Before they plummeted into the Veil, Akyris thought he saw Siddaia nod at him. Then his consciousness was whisked away, back to a reality he once thought of as his and his alone.

CHAPTER FIFTY-SIX

SACRED REMAINS

Lyansorca looked made of porcelain, lying there unmoving on a cot. If not for the weak rise and fall of her chest, Barodane would have thought her a corpse being prepared for final rest. Everything about her was as he remembered. Everything except her right arm of course. Wrapped in thick bandages soaked through with blood, it terminated just below the elbow. The room stank of cotton, sweat, and an herbal aroma he couldn't pinpoint.

Clutching a damp cloth in a golden hand, Madame Gratha dabbed the prostrate woman's brow. She squinted at Garlenna's mauled arm and gestured with the cloth. "Go and see Qippa, dear. Ask for honeyroot."

Garlenna shook her head. "I wish to stay beside her a while first."

Madame Gratha brushed a strand of Lyansorca's hair from her cheek. "Let's not let our goodness make us fools now. A dog's bite can be quite nasty. It would be a shame to have two armless women roaming about." Gratha tapped the sagging skin beneath her own empty eye socket. "Two eyeless ones are plenty enough, I think. Now go. I'll not hear another word."

Barodane patted his prosort's shoulder. She turned to go but paused in the doorway. "It's not often I meet another woman who has lost an eye. Usually it is I on the receiving end of inquiry, so I feel compelled to ask. How?"

Madame Gratha's frail fingers brushed Lyansorca's pallid arm. "Taken by a man of course. Same as any woman."

A grunt. Then the creak of floorboards as Garlenna left in search of honeyroot.

Alone with the Kurg, Barodane kissed the tips of his fingers before placing them on Lyansorca's lips. He untied one of the pouches from his belt, hefted it, handed Madame Gratha the small fortune of thirty gold wheels. "Half for her when she wakes. Tell her to start her own whorehouse somewhere. Or never work again. Whatever she wants. I don't care. Just make sure she knows I'm sorry. The rest is for you and the other—"

"No," said Madame Gratha.

"Please," he said. "You deserve all that and more. For the work you've done. For saving her and—"

"Oh, I am taking my share. But you do not give gold when you are sorry. You simply don't." The back of her hand slapped into the palm of the other as she said the last. "What you do is you never let yourself forget. Not with gold. Not with drink. Not with godsthorn. Tyne's boy. Meckin. Lyansorca...you don't get to wipe their misfortune away for the sake of your own guilt. Not with a simple payoff."

"I understand," Barodane nodded. "All too well. I promise—"

"Words." Madame Gratha flicked a hand. "Empty ones. You have felt nothing. You have seen falsely. You have done horrible wrong, and many have suffered for it. For too long you've done this. I think it's time you set aside hollow promises."

She stepped close. A wrinkled thumb rose to his forehead.

"Uh..." He watched it with a frown but did not move. Her manner was strange but not dangerous.

"I will ensure you never forget." A wink of light flashed in the Kurg's empty eye socket.

Barodane gasped, seized by forces unseen.

Waves of warmth spread from her leathery touch. Reached down into his throat and chest. His eyes fluttered as he fought to keep them open. Her other hand alighted on his chest. Euphoric ripples radiated from her palm, lulling him into numb surrender. A pleasant tingle filled his belly as if he'd drunk fine spirits.

Impossibly heavy eyelids slid shut.

A whisper...

Faint. Distant. "Barodane Ironlight." Madame Gratha's voice.

Panic surged, a whole troubled sea of it. Rendered impotent a moment later by the tranquil power of the Kurg. The insides of his eyelids glowed red-orange from some external source of dazzling light. He forced open a narrow slit at the bottom of his vision and glimpsed an age-spotted hand wreathed in coils of soft white light. Coils that reached into his heart. Madame Gratha's voice echoed somewhere inside his mind, a buttery reverberation. "You fight me, Barodane Ironlight..."

He jolted as if stabbed. An all too real image of an armored man bearing a blade stood before him.

"Let yourself be," she crooned.

Barodane felt his mouth move. Words came unbidden to his lips. *Help me.* Void of emotion, the hallucinated man thrust a darksteel sword into Barodane's chest. Excruciating pain wracked his entire body.

Tongues of flame jumped along the blade's length and molten fire dripped in sizzling fat gobs from its edges. Smoke pooled around the wound, boiling blood hissing as it fountained from his cloven heart.

Barodane stared into the face of his killer—his own. A face from the past. Not Kord but the grandson of Danath Ironlight.

His vision dimmed. Shadows lurked at his peripheries, waiting hungrily. He felt their hunger. Their desire to consume him. They undulated and moaned, a crackling vortex of suffering malice. Sickness flooded him, made jellied sacks of his limbs.

A luminous ray shot from his heart where the blade had impaled him, and as it did the intense pain in his chest started to dissipate. A wall of light emanated from the wound, growing brighter as it spread. And inch by crawling inch, the sword disintegrated in its wake.

Coruscating brightness swam up the specter's arms. He stared into the face of his former self as it became a formless, haunting white...until only dark pits for eyes remained. Voices cried out from the encircling, hungry darkness. Where the light touched the rippling shadows were peeled back. Smoking. Burning.

And then they were gone.

With a final deafening roar, light consumed it all.

Reality slammed into Barodane's senses.

His eyes snapped open. Madame Gratha, the Awakened, stood before him smiling coyly. The room seemed brighter, more defined. He felt taller too; his shoulders broader. The tightness pinching the base of his skull was gone, as was the vice clenching his heart.

A weight had been lifted from the very center of him. "I'm..."

"As you should be now. You will honor those who've suffered by your hand with better deeds. Not with your gold, nor your misery, but with every scrap of life you have left to you." She waved him from the room. "Now go. And best to avoid the Baroness. She's not pleased."

Once Garlenna's wounds were treated, they retrieved their horses and then started down the main street. Foot traffic was sparse. Mostly beggars from the slums. In the hours following a violent struggle, not to mention weeks of Hyram Olabran's outriders harassing drovers in the surrounding countryside, the people of Digtown seemed hesitant to return to business as usual.

Not all was bleak though.

At the stable, Barodane had given the little girl half of his remaining gold wheels. When he'd presented them, her mouth fell open. Wordlessly, she'd launched herself at Barodane and wrapped him in a hug. Despite her meager stature, he was both surprised and unsurprised to find she was strong enough to squeeze the breath from him.

Better deeds can sometimes be gold, Madame Gratha.

Side by side, prosort and prince rode down the street. Some of those in the crowd stared openly at them. "We'd best hurry." Garlenna shifted in the saddle. "They're starting to wonder."

He drew up the hood of his cloak. "I suppose a fight against the masonry in broad daylight wasn't so good for our anonymity."

"It worked out better for us than the masons," she said. "Nevertheless in a day's ride we'll need to change our appearance."

They picked up the pace.

A growing sense of unease crawled through Barodane's bowels as they neared the Dregs. He blinked away the image of Meckin, dead and staring at the ceiling. He cursed under his breath, drawing a frown from Garlenna, but she left it at that.

Flanked by a pair of whores at the stoop of the Dregs was the Baroness Imralta. Her skin had a noticeably paler tinge than usual. Fastened tight at the throat, and everywhere else, she wore a midnight blue dress trimmed with gold lace. She clutched her bandaged hand before her like a priest of the Sempyrium holding an icon of the gods.

They came to a halt.

Imralta watched Barodane. Wind stirred her hair. Slowly, her face swiveled to the edge of town then back to him. She sucked air through her teeth. "I ask one final thing, Kord." She indicated the alley adjacent the Dregs. "I ask that you leave town that way. The least you could do is ride by Meckin on your way out. We'll lay him to rest tomorrow. Best you aren't there. But you'll want to say farewell, I imagine. He's the one in the cart...alone. I personally made sure he was separated from those other scum."

Barodane pursed his lips. Nodded.

Imralta walked slowly down the landing steps. With her bandaged hand she made to pat Scab's mane but drew it back at the last second as if she'd forgotten her dismemberment.

"Remember this," she said in icy tones. "We will handle your mess. We will handle the Crown Justice when they come from Breckenbright looking for their lost lord. We, the ladies of the Gem Loft, will handle the shit handed to us by men. Just like we've always done. But do us a fucking favor and remember...without us, you'd have died." She threw a withering stare at Garlenna. "Don't give us your pity or your tears. Save it for the dead. Save it for Meckin, who you should *never* have survived."

"You're right." Barodane stared down the alley. Dread pricked his shoulders at the thought of seeing his friend's body again. "At least on that we can agree." He looked at the Baroness. "My stables are yours now. The horses might fetch a nice price. The armor too—"

"A death sentence," she said. "We'll be lucky to get rid of them for bronze wheels to a butcher if we want to avoid suspicion from the Crown Justice. The arms and armor we'll bury at the Rainy Meadows ruins."

Ah. The best place. Barodane cleared his throat. "You'll find two more of Hyram's men there as well."

"So many dead." Imralta sniffled. "Meckin…"

Barodane leaned in the saddle to place a hand on her shoulder in attempted comfort. "I loved him too."

Jaw set, she wrenched away, then strode back into the Dregs with a strangled cry. Her erect posture collapsed around quiet sobs as she disappeared within.

Inside it was dark, but Barodane managed to spot Vey on hands and knees cleaning. Water sluiced across red-streaked floorboards and lapped against cotton rags that were piled and stained with gore.

So young. Too young to be witness to such.

One of Imralta's whores pulled a chair into place in front of the entrance to let others know the inn was closed. He suspected it might also be a way for the woman to protect her grieving Madame. Calm and a sense of rightness warmed Barodane at the sight of such loyalty. *Meckin was loyal. To the death, he was loyal.*

Barodane's grip tightened on the reins. *Never again.*

Garlenna shifted in the saddle behind him. She'd saved him too. And not for the first time. She bowed her head at the retreating Imralta. "Strong woman."

They passed the stable where Garlenna had struck him then rounded the building. The wall was splashed with dried blood where they'd overtaken Hyram's cutthroat at the rear entrance. Not much farther along were the handcarts. One was stacked precariously high with the dead. The other held only Meckin. Crimson splotches seeped through his linen wrappings. Rope bound feet and shoulders, securing the cloth.

Barodane stopped. He waited, half expecting the voices of the dead to return and heap shame and blame over his already heavy heart. None came. Whatever Madame Gratha had done to him in the parlor had banished them for good. His hatred and shame were entombed in the past.

And with that came relief. Relief to simply feel his pain rather than bury it beneath a mountain of wrath.

A drizzle swept toward them from the barrow hills. As if Digtown knew no other way to say farewell. Clouds crept in from the east, pushed by a gentle wind that stirred Scab's mane. Minutes passed in quiet vigil for the man who had been there for Barodane during his darkest days. Sobs climbed up his throat.

Meckin, you were a hard man but a good man—a good friend. My brother to the last.

In the yawning silence, a desiccated leaf skittered over a patch of stones. Nothing lasts that wasn't meant to. There was sacredness in that.

Garlenna drew her mace and thrust it at the sky. "Honor, Meckin!" Her battle commander's voice rang. "A true Namorite!"

Tears jumped to Barodane's eyes. He stared at the innkeeper's linen-swaddled body as Garlenna's words echoed in his bones.

Never again.

"Come," Barodane finally said with a sniffle. "This place belongs to the dead."

Sunlight pierced the cloud cover as they ascended the barrow hills. They cut east toward Martyr's Isle. Another old friend lived there—Nserthes the Sophophant. But it was miles away yet, and Breckenbright rested between them, a looming nest of potential enemies. They would have to pass close by it or triple their journey's length.

Sunlight poured over the hillside. It was the brightest day Barodane had seen in fourteen years. He closed his eyes, letting its sudden warmth pull him forward, a guide out of darkness. It burned the cold and rain from his bones. Burned away the past. Burned the strange man by the name of Kord to ash and memory.

It burned it all away until there was nothing left.

Only he remained...

Barodane Ironlight. The Crown Prince of Namarr.

EPILOGUE 1

Holdguard flanked the doorway, bedecked in bronze pauldrons and gray cloaks. Warhammers longer than a man is tall stood upright in their fists. Roddic Olabran's boots rang sharply against the stone halls of Breckenbright. The holdguard moved hastily to admit him into the chapel's infirmary. Crisscrossing hammers framed by laurels were wrought in gold above the door. Lord Roddic kissed his fingertips, then touched the sigil of his hold as he passed beneath.

Inside the low-ceilinged room, a holdguard and a woman from the Sisterhood of the Rose hovered over the prostrate body of a dying man with a salt and pepper beard. One of Roddic's own. Blood saturated the bed. The linens. The sister's apron.

"He was brought in on a cart this morning, my lord," said the holdguard. "From what the merchant who helped him said, he'd been riding a couple days before his horse gave out from under him."

"Will he die?" Roddic asked.

The Sister of the Rose, a young woman, wrung her hands. Roddic knew almost instantly he would not believe whatever she said next. Certainty was necessary for his trust. Self-doubt sowed disrespect. "It is in the hands of nature now. I have done what I can. But there is a chance—"

"What chance?" The speaker's voice was high in pitch and cruel in tone. "He's a dead man."

"So you're here." Roddic turned to find his knight-captain, Sir Alber Gwinn, leaning against the wall, warhammer cradled across his chest. "Report."

"Please, my lord." The sister's begging tone sickened Roddic. "If I am allowed a moment alone with the man, there is a prayer—"

Roddic waved a hand. "You may go."

"But, my lord." Her eyes darted sidelong at the dying man. "A Sister of the Rose cannot leave their patient until..."

Roddic leveled a placid stare at her. "Oh, please continue. Educate me on the edicts of the Sisterhood in my own hold. You realize I sit at the Collective Table with the High Mother Tanghelka? Shall I tell her of your impudence?"

The sister swallowed then shook her head. With a rustle of robes, she scurried into the hall beyond, escorted by the holdguard.

Besides the dying man, only Roddic and Sir Alber Gwinn remained.

"Shouldn't be long now," the squat knight-captain said.

"And this was one of the men with Hyram?"

Sir Alber nodded. "The lone survivor, my lord."

"So it's true then." Roddic drew a breath forcefully through his nose. "Hyram was a fool but—ah well—I thought even he could deal with a mission so meager as Digtown."

Alber laughed. "You should have sent me, like I told you."

Anger flared in the lord of Breckenbright. "Save your insolence, Warpig. My son is dead. It may not look it, but it pains me. I'll not have you wax righteous. I want the men who did this hunted down. Before the new moon. That's how you'll prove your worth."

"Not men..." The bearded mason's voice was a weak rasp. "A man...and a woman."

Roddic threw an arched eyebrow at the wounded mason. "He speaks." Beady blue eyes drank the ceiling, and his face was whiter than eggshell. Both Sir Alber and Roddic leaned over the man as he stammered. "A...big woman."

"Interesting. Gwinn, I want these criminals found. Notify the local chainman and—"

"...that sword," the veteran wheezed—coughed wetly.

Roddic paused. "Sword? What sword?"

The mason's eyelids fluttered. "Dark...steel."

Alber Gwinn scoffed. "Dying makes fools of all men. He sees what he wants. Makes 'em feel better if they get killed by something special."

"...that sword," the man gasped. "Like...smoke."

Roddic squinted. "Very interesting. Gwinn, I have a better idea. Notify every mason and chainman in western Namarr." He turned. "And send for our friends in Valat. I want these criminals kneeling at my feet yesterday. Alive. I will grant enough gold wheels for early retirement to whomever brings them to me."

"Consider it done, my lord." The Warpig snarled a gob of phlegm into his mouth and then spit it onto the stone floor.

Roddic recoiled. "You are disgusting." As soon as he said it, he noted the truth of his words. *Gods, he even looks a swine.* The stout knight-captain's face was pinched around a thick porcine nose. Greasy hair fell in loose tangles around a chin where sparse and spindly black beard hairs clung. Shadowed, deep-set eyes regarded Roddic Olabran. *I'll not suffer insubordination on the day of my son's death.* "And an insolent one at that. Pray to the Sempyrean I do not come to my good senses and have you flogged." Roddic thrust out his chin, tone dangerous and low. "And mark my words, I certainly will do so the day you stop being useful. Do not fail me."

Fear, especially of other men, was a stranger to Sir Alber. Anger, however, was an erstwhile friend. This was the very man Roddic needed to carry out the more unsavory side of his business endeavors.

Sir Alber darkened with a flush. A shade from being a purple-skinned hog. Tone tighter than a coiled snake, the knight-captain said, "If you were not highborn—" He bit back the final words. "I understand your threat, my lord."

A sour taste cloyed at the back of Roddic's throat. While it sickened him to employ such trash, necessity begged his discomfort on the matter. He sighed. "You are certain you've no Kurgish blood in you?"

"My mother may have been a whore..." The Warpig shrugged. "...but she wasn't vermin." He wheezed a laugh at his own joke.

Roddic joined in with a tight-lipped chuckle before recalling the death of his son. He cut the levity short. "Hyram's funeral will take place in one week's time."

"But we don't have his body yet. We'll need to retrieve—"

"There's no time for that." Roddic had almost forgotten the dying man on the bed under his nose until he heard the rattle of death. A sigh gave forth. The man's body slumped.

Roddic continued. "Hyram's gone. His body is of little import. I want all focus on finding whoever killed him. It will be said that he died on a hunting trip. Fallen over a waterfall or some such thing where it would make sense for his body to be missing."

Sir Alber shifted the warhammer into the crook of one elbow then scratched vigorously at his wiry beard. "What do we say about this one?"

"Did he have holdings?" Roddic watched flakes of dry skin drift to the floor.

"A farm to the east. Another of Hyram's men owned a piece of a tavern in Central Square."

Through a window over the bed, the city of Breckenbright spread out in a cacophony of commerce. Gulls wheeled above the streets and screamed. Chisels and hammers and trundling carts. The pulse that beat Roddic's heart. "Gold comes and goes. Good businesses can last generations. Buy out their families and add the holdings as reward for whomever brings me my son's killer."

"You're too generous, my lord."

Steel rang in the Hammer's tone. "Is it?" Sir Alber was scum, through and through. But Roddic had learned long ago the man wielding power in one hand must hold filth in the other. For the masonry to maintain its strength, it had to sometimes do shameful things. The Warpig was an avatar of such necessary shame. A protector, not only by hammer and vengeful spirit but as an ethical catch-all too. So that Roddic might feel clean, Sir Alber Gwinn acted as his filthy hand.

"You confuse generosity for caution then. Consider...my son Hyram was a trained knight. Digtown's constable and two of our finest holdguard were with him. Plus a bear hound and a handful of other hired killers." Roddic waved a hand, lip curled. "That unnerving character that Hyram pulled from the dungeons was there as well—the tall one. All of them are now dead." To emphasize his point, Roddic lifted the dead mason's arm and let it flop back down. "If you think there's nothing suspicious here, I name you fool. Dangerous endeavors demand just rewards. Now go, and take your scrutiny of my plans with you. And send me my son."

Prone to rage or nonchalance with little reason as to the why of which, Alber Gwinn shrugged. "Which one?"

"Merric."

The knight-captain of Breckenbright stopped at the door and looked back at the dead body. "And what of the sister and the holdguard who helped?"

"Find out if what they know is compromising. Then have them watched." Roddic narrowed his eyes. "No further action without my consent."

A contemptuous laugh trailed the Warpig out.

Roddic Olabran mused aloud. "A man and a...big woman." Wetness spread around the veteran's crotch. The lord of Breckenbright turned up his nose. "Bearing darksteel? Very interesting indeed."

He dragged his fingers over the dead man's eyes, shutting them forever. There was a great deal to do and little time for sentiment.

EPILOGUE 11

- UNTURRUS -

"I hear you like to wear masks." The Madness's long, black tongue wormed over his lips. "I'm a bit of an expert on parading around wearing the faces of others myself. Wanna see?"

The Wordfox cowered behind a snowcapped stump. "Please," he whined. "Leave me in peace."

"Pieces you mean!" The Madness snarled. "Get the fuck out from behind that stump before I thresh you like a stalk of wheat."

Torn at one shoulder, the Wordfox's smock accentuated his skeletal frame as he hesitantly unfolded from hiding. Twigs were matted into his mushroom cap of smoky gray hair and tufts of the same swirled around an exposed nipple no larger than a doll's button eye. Starved flesh lay taut over every indent and crevice of bone.

The Wordfox gulped. "You're going to kill me."

The demon pouted. "You look sad about it. Aren't you a poet? I thought your type loves sad shit."

"My type...loves sad shit?"

The Madness cocked his head. "I swear I just said that same thing. Living on a mountain for centuries makes me mighty sensitive to echoes." He shrugged dramatically. "Hearing them puts me in a rather murderous mood."

Legs flush together, the poet's hands rose pleadingly from his sides, arms trembling. "I'm sorry. It—it won't happen again."

"I know that. But you poets don't get it. Too fucking morose. We thespians understand. Death is pleasant as pecan pie...when its done right." A smile twitched at the corner of the Madness's mouth. "When it's done to those who deserve it."

A crease split the Wordfox's brow.

Wind stirred the spindly hairs clutching the back of the demon's bulbous white skull. "You're thicker than you think so I'll show you since you're as close to a thespian as I'm like to get for a while anyway. They're a self-involved bunch, unlikely to risk their skin for a chance at power."

The Madness snapped taloned fingers.

The Wordfox hissed, eyes wild with hate, his hands forming claws.

The Duke of Peladonia, Onai Saud, watched the poet quizzically. "What's the matter? Afraid to perform for me again?"

The poet bent slowly at the waist and took up a branch. White foam gathered at the corner of his mouth. "I'm not the one who should be afraid."

Onai Saud raised an eyebrow. "Oh my. Another original masterpiece from the great rhyme lord himself. Let's see if you recall my choice words for you..." He bowed, straightened, then began. "You should consider changing your name to the Wordkit, for your poetry has no teeth with which to bite into the fabric of meaningful topics already woven by braver souls. Rather than live in the shadows of your betters, why don't you cast your own."

The harsh words beat the Wordfox's face slack. His eyes became shark-like and hungry. His upper lip curled back into a snarl as he listened, bony hands wringing the branch as if it were a chicken's neck.

"Come back to me in a decade and we'll see if you've grown incisors enough to play before my court again." Duke Saud eyed the club in the poet's hands—scoffed. "Your actions are as impotent as your words it seems. If you mean to kill me, try using something that'll do the trick, Wordkit."

In a puff of smoke, the sickle appeared in the air between them, hovered there a second, and then thudded to the ground at the Wordfox's feet.

The weapon seemed to contract when the Ascendant lifted it. A moment later, the gleaming point sank into Onai Saud's face with a heavy, wet impact.

In all the ways one could use the sickle to stab or slice, the Wordfox's creativity was boundless. By the end of it, Duke Saud was a viscous ruin at the heaving poet's feet. Gore-soaked and grinning, he dropped the sickle.

A gravelly laugh echoed across the powdered slopes of Unturrus. The poet turned in a circle, huffing, and searching for the source of the sound.

"Where words fail, murder gets the job done right," the Madness said. "And what better way to kill a man than to do it from his own shadow. Give the Duke a sweet head-splitting for me!"

Shadow erupted from Onai Saud's corpse, an oily layer of it sticking to the tip of the Wordfox's finger. He waggled it but it clung. He felt the digit grow cold as he leapt back from the encroaching onyx cloud. His heel snagged on a stone and he keeled over backward with a stilted shriek.

Tendrils of darkness pooled overhead then descended.

The Wordfox screamed—choked as it swept into his throat. He gagged on the cold, dark substance. When his ears went numb, he knew it entered him there too.

Tingling sensation retreated. Numbness spread, claiming him from crown to anus, right through the core of him. Hoarse cries of fear softened to whimpers, became like a woman's early stages of orgasm. Shadows continued to fill him, and with it, so did the pleasure. He smiled, wondering if this was his reward. An ecstatic gift earned by bloody deeds.

Finally, the world acknolwedges my greatness! His grin broadened.

Heat built in his lungs—kept building. His smile faded as a fire burned throughout his chest. The excruciating sensation shot up his spine and blazed in his limbs. The acrid smell of roasting meat made him gag, then he arched his back, throat and pelvis suddenly bared to the sky. He strained to look down—caught sight of his shaking arm. Charred skin belched forth embers where it split along his wrist. Shadows seemed to leak from his eyes, his palms, his feet.

Darkness oozed from every pore and split.

Then, as quick as it came, it was gone. He wilted, shuddering, steaming, limp.

For hours he lay there twitching until finally he sat up and stared at a hand. Shadow wreathed it like a spider's webbing. He tried to flick it off but failed; it only dissipated a brief moment before coalescing once more, and when it did, orgiastic power surged into his bones.

He stumbled down the mountain, moaning with both pain and pleasure. Drunken godhood pumped through his veins. Horrible burn wounds covered him, but already they were healing.

Something incredible was coming to life inside him now and it seemed eager to keep him safe.

Night began to settle as he descended Unturrus. A greedy kind of joy kissed his heart at the sight of darkness pooling beneath the trees.

The shadow of a looming evergreen crossed his path. He paused a moment, watching it with a budding awareness...as if it held a secret he should already know.

The Wordfox scoffed, dismissing the thought, then stepped onto the tree's shadow—

He plummeted.

For a full two seconds, he tumbled through empty space, flailing and thinking it was a body of water he hadn't seen. *Fool!* He could breathe and felt no wetness. Yet he floated as if in water, like some jelly bobbing calmly in the sea.

He swept a hand in an arc. Coolness wrapped his fingers. Above him, he could just make out the looming evergreen through a filter of hazy murk. He swam upward through emptiness—stopped when his eyes were level with the ground.

A gasp came unbidden...as awe followed understanding. He was inside the tree's shadow.

What did the demon say? No better way to kill a man than to do it from his own shadow.

He twisted experimentally in the floating void, sweeping his arms like he might while swimming. Laughing, he moved from one shadow to the next unimpeded.

Down Unturrus he careened, treading air and hurtling forward faster than a galloping horse, gliding like a shark through murky shoals of shadow, a rushing sound reverberating in his ears. Onward he sped, entranced by the freedom and power he felt.

I was never meant to be a poet. I'm an Awakened!

More eager now, the Wordfox weaved through his subterranean realm, seamlessly rising from its depths before sinking again, his control over his newfound shadow-realm absolute.

In the distance, a watchtower perched above the earth. The poet chuckled at the lone crownguard holding a spear, its tip glinting in the sun's final rays of light. The muscles of his face ached from the exultant smile he wore at the idea of testing his new powers.

In the span of heartbeats, he dove into the watchtower's shadow, then shot up its length unhindered by its height. Darkness spit him out directly behind the unaware crownguard. A freshly lit torch flickered on either end of the wooden railing, casting watery orange light onto the dagger blade tucked into the unsuspecting man's belt.

A cackle-wheeze laugh came unbidden. The crownguard rounded with a curse, the whites of his eyes flashing surprise, and then thrust his spear at the Wordfox's heart. An instant too late...

The poet let the crownguard's own shadow swallow him. He dropped into an endless well of dark then slipped under the man who was swiveling to either side in search of an enemy no longer there.

The Wordfox chuckled and moved, stepping out from underneath the watchtower's handrail. The panting crownguard stabbed at the darkness at his feet where the Wordfox vanished a split second later. Unseen, the poet wrapped spidery fingers around the dagger hilt in the man's belt. In one fluid motion, he jerked it free and pushed the man from behind before receding into the inky river where his power lay.

The crownguard stumbled, palms slapping against the watchtower's lip to keep from toppling out and over. The Wordfox wouldn't mind seeing that. The man regained his balance, then spun about, spear gripped in white-knuckled hands.

For a long while, the crownguard waited, heartbeat visible in the veins at his neck. His gaze darted about, knowing his enemy could attack him from any direction. Once, he stared directly at the place where the Wordfox waited. But his eyes moved on quickly, seeing nothing. "He can't see me!" the Wordfox crowed aloud with joy. The crownguard seemed to hear nothing, either.

In the shadows, the Wordfox could fly. In the shadows, he was invisible. Strength he'd never felt before, he now possessed. He could do as he wished to whomever he wished. He could rob the Dawn Tower in Alistar. He could stand in the court of Malzacor's Imperial family. Better yet...

A wolf's grin stretched from cheek to cheek at the thought of splitting Onai Saud's owlish face in two. The idea felt like a juicy secret only he could know. Its sweetness caused him to sputter. *I could kill him—take everything he loves. Maybe his children first. A dagger in their vile hearts. Maybe their bellies first to drag out the suffering.*

The choices of his vengeance were limitless.

He gave praise to Unturrus and thanked the Madness for his boon. *I shall write a poem to honor you!*

No thing to fear, the Madness.
No ill to bear, my sadness.
I'll wear their gifts and travel my rifts, as given to me with gladness.
No thing to fear of madness.

A tear threatened as he considered his life leading up to that fateful moment with Unturrus's famed executioner, but his ruminations were cut short when the crownguard overcame his own fear and lunged for the far wall of the tower's platform. The Wordfox watched without concern. He could kill the man anytime he wished.

The man groped along a row of hooks and retrieved a black bell. Frantically, he shook it, sending up a high-pitched clangor. Miles in either direction, there came an answering alarm of the same pitch. More bells from the other watchtowers. Shouts erupted from below the curtain wall.

"Ruptured!"

"A Ruptured has descended!"

"Dominarri! Get the Dominarri!"

The Wordfox growled in rage. He considered killing the crownguard, but a honeyed voice rose from somewhere out of sight to utter an urgent warning. *The Dominarri come. You must flee.*

Within his abyssal haven, the poet spun to confront whoever spoke, dagger gripped firmly in his fist. "Who's there?" Power coursed through him. He was invincible. "I'll kill you."

I'm your friend. The voice was light, gentle, coaxing. More shouts drifted from the Eastshadow settlement. *Now you must flee. They're coming. I would not see you harmed.*

Despite wishing to test his powers, the Wordfox didn't want to find out what gifts Unturrus had given the mysterious order that hunted alleged Ruptured. He'd heard enough stories of the Dominarri from the drunk priest. Besides, he had other more pressing business to attend to.

He traveled along the watchtower's angled frame, walking as a man where he needed to when the shadows did not align and reentering them where he could.

At the curtain wall, he slid the fifteen feet to the top, then froze. A group of armed men rushed past leading a cowled figure—a Dominarri. "I'm an Awakened. They should be greeting me as a brother, not some enemy," he growled. *Like the voice.*

The group stopped, allowing the Dominarri to hunt. The cowled woman cocked her head, listening. Cold fear babbled to life within, sweat matting the Wordfox's dense hair as he waited. Seemingly satisfied, the robed woman motioned for the group to move on.

The Wordfox sighed.

Once inside the settlement at Eastshadow, and with night all but upon them, he moved with ease down the lanes. Near a place called The Numbers, a tall bald man bedecked in ridiculous clothing stood outside the black and white pavilion speaking with a handful of crownguard. When the Wordfox made to slip past, the tall man swept the darkness with narrowed eyes and whispered a warning. The eyes of the man beside him kindled with a sudden glow. White light poured into the space around him as five orbs of humming energy whirred to life in a concentric circle around The Numbers.

The Wordfox retreated behind a pile of grain sacks to watch.

With each passing second, the orbs grew brighter...brighter. Painfully bright.

The Wordfox hissed, recoiling as the darkness around him was peeled back. It touched his toe, scalding it. He fled, light nipping at his back as he made a mental note to avoid the Dominarri at all costs from then on.

For the rest of the night, he was careful, playing both hunter and hunted.

It took until the gloom before dawn to find what he sought.

He slipped inside the shamans' tent and found them sleeping. The female from the mountain enclaves stretched across her sleeping cot, her ram's head helm nestled on a hook on the tent's center pole. The poet had never cut a throat before but knew if he sawed fast and hard enough, there was no coming back for her.

The most unpleasant part was her muffled gurgling into his palm. Disgusting. A few moments later, her vacant eyes stared upward, blood pumping from the lacerations in her throat onto the cot. It was all the Wordfox could do to keep his heaving breaths quiet as he shifted his attention to the shaman from the forest enclaves. A black rectangle tattooed around one eye offered a perfect target to sink his dagger.

"An eye for an eye," the Wordfox whispered to himself in excitement. He held the blade poised over the man's face. Both eyes fluttered open. The Wordfox yelped and stabbed. A flurry of cloth and grunts and arms followed. He kept stabbing—stabbed anything that moved. He thought he felt the dagger stick into something a dozen times or more. Flashes of exposed neck, head, and blocking hands.

"Ruptured!" the shaman from the plains bellowed as he leapt from bed holding a stone chaswa. The Wordfox melted into the dark, leaving his victim moaning on the bed with a score of wounds and a feeble chance at surviving them.

The Wordfox moved under the remaining Kurg, a naked stump of sinews and muscle hunkered around his chaswa. The Wordfox breached from darkness, slashing the shaman's calf. The Kurg fell to one knee with a gasp. "Ruptured!" he yelled, weaker this time. He swung.

The Wordfox saw it coming and had already disappeared, materializing a moment later to hew the arm holding the chaswa at the wrist. Blood spurted from the gash. To his credit, the plains shaman remained standing, his chin tilted upward in proud defeat.

"My mask," The Wordfox said. "Where is it?"

The Kurg's eyes darted, betraying the mask's location in the corner of the room. There it sat, broken in two. Discarded like some trivial toy.

A rush set the Wordfox's heart to hammering. "I told you, you'll die for that."

The Kurg lunged stupidly, all but ramming his own chest onto the blade in the Wordfox's hand. "Fool," the poet hissed. The shaman's lids bobbed, heavy with death as he slumped to the floor.

The Wordfox retrieved his mask. Where his hand held it, shadow snaked forward to weave between the cracked parts, binding the two pieces together once again. *A gift for you...friend.* The velvet voice.

"My thanks," the Wordfox said aloud, then exited the tent through a slash in the back.

Dawn was coming. Light, his newfound enemy, would return to steal his power from him. He looked up. A hawk swooped low overhead, its shadow trailing across the ground...

He stepped into it and flew.

ABOUT THE AUTHOR

Michael Michel lives in Bend Oregon with the love of his life and their two children. When he isn't obsessively writing, editing, or doing publishing work, he can be found exercising, coaching leaders in the corporate world, and dancing his butt off at amazing festivals like Burning Man. His favorite shows are Dark, The Wire, and Norsemen. He loves nature and deep conversations with—anyone really—and few things bring him more joy than a couple of hours playing table tennis.

REVIEWS: If you enjoyed this book and feel it should be spread far and wide, please leave a review on Goodreads, Amazon, or wherever else you feel called to share. I would greatly appreciate it!

SOCIAL MEDIA:
Goodreads - https://www.goodreads.com/book/show/63945821-the-price-of-power

Instagram - @michaelmichelauthor

Website – https://michaelmichelauthor.com/

Twitter - @michael_michel

ACKNOWLEDGMENTS

When a book has been written over the course of twenty-three years, the number of people in need of acknowledgment is endless. I've never been a quitter though, so I'll do my best to name them all.

The first thanks must go to the lawnmower. Thank you for being there when the idea sparked to life. Such spaces of boredom are necessary for any imagination, and you facilitated it well.

A special thanks to those who directly influenced the course of my work. Jason Letts, you're lightning meets lasers when it comes to editing. To my beta readers: Kris M., Kyle C., Rachel S., Kris H., Danielle C., Kelila J., Beth G., Amanda S., Nick D., Kurt C., Clayton C.. Your time and unguarded opinion were crucial to shaping this book. JDL Rosell, Garrett Marco, Jerry Oltion, Sage Liskey and James Aaron, you were huge supports with some key decisions and you provided a lot of vital information. To the rest of those in the indie-publishing community, your combined knowledge is so helpful to those looking to take the leap as I did. Never stop.

To my partner, Jess. This book owes you its life. Draft after draft, you goaded this baby into existence like a master doula. You deserve to be canonized for putting up with my writing obsession and listening to me disentangle my cat's cradle of a plot.

To my daughter, Ella. You inspire me to be a better version of myself every single day. If there's someone I feel understands the sheer awe-filled madness of being a writer, it's you.

To Jordan, you rock. Plain and simple.

To my friends who never let me get away with anything. You know who you are. Our dissection of films, books, and television over the years ensured that the worst parts of this manuscript will stay in the shadows where they belong.

To my dad for showing me the joy that hard work can bring. "Greatness is on the other side of hard." This was well-needed wisdom at just the right time.

To my mom for writing down all my crazy stories about 28,000,000-pound, nine-foot-tall monsters and then keeping them around to laugh at decades later (you're the best kind of pack rat, and your love never ceases).

To my whole family for making humor a transcendent value for a little kid with a desire to entertain others. This book couldn't exist without you. *I* couldn't exist without you.

And to the fantasy fans across the world who have lived at a time or in a home where they never felt comfortable being themselves. For those who have been ashamed to love absurd worlds, or feared to claim their truest passions, I wrote this book with unconditional love just for you. I hope that loves finds you between these pages.

I hope you carry it forward to someone else.

Printed in Great Britain
by Amazon

36662670R00283